RUSSIAN
FAIRY TALES

Translated by Norbert Guterman
from the collections of Aleksandr Afanas'ev

Illustrations by Alexander Alexeieff

Folkloristic commentary by Roman Jakobson

RUSSIAN
FAIRY TALES

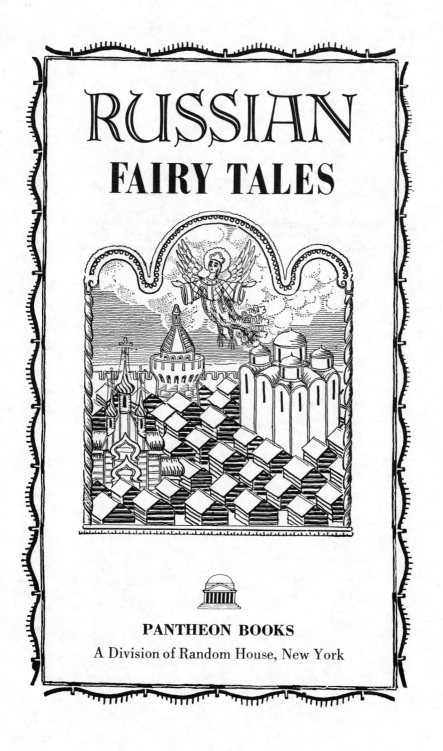

PANTHEON BOOKS

A Division of Random House, New York

CONTENTS

THE WONDROUS WONDER,
THE MARVELOUS MARVEL

ONCE THERE WAS a wealthy merchant who traded in rare and precious goods, traveling with his wares every year to foreign lands. One day he fitted out a ship, made ready for his voyage, and said to his wife: "Tell me, my joy, what shall I bring you as a gift from foreign lands?" The merchant's wife answered: "In your house I have all I want and enough of everything! But if you want to gladden my heart, buy me a wondrous wonder, a marvelous marvel." "Very well. If I find one, I shall buy it."

The merchant traveled beyond thrice nine lands, to the

13

thrice tenth kingdom, sailed into a great and wealthy port, sold all of his cargo, bought a new one, and loaded his ship. Then he walked through the city and thought: "Where shall I find a wondrous wonder, a marvelous marvel?" He met an old man, who asked him: "What are you pondering about, what makes you so sad, my good young man?" "How can I help being sad?" answered the merchant. "I am looking for a wondrous wonder, a marvelous marvel to buy for my wife, but I do not know where to find one." "Eh, you should have told me that in the first place! Come with me. I have a wondrous wonder, a marvelous marvel, and since you must have it, I will sell it to you."

The old man led the merchant to his house and said: "Do you see that goose walking in my yard?" "I do." "Now see what's going to happen to it. Hey, goose, come here!" And the goose came into the room. The old man took a roasting pan and again spoke to the goose: "Hey, goose, lie down in the roasting pan." And the goose lay down in the roasting pan. The old man put it in the oven, roasted the goose, took it out, and set it on the table. "Now, merchant," said the old man, "let us sit down and eat. Only do not throw the bones under the table; instead, gather them all into one pile." So they sat at the table and between them ate the whole goose. Then the old man took the picked bones, wrapped them in the tablecloth, threw them on the floor, and said: "Hey, goose! Get up, shake your wings, and go out into the yard!" The goose got up, shook its wings, and went into the yard as though it had never been in the oven! "Indeed, my host, yours is a wondrous wonder, a marvelous marvel," said the merchant, and began to bargain with him for the goose, which he finally bought for a high price. Then he took the goose with him aboard ship and sailed back to his native land.

He returned home, greeted his wife, gave her the goose, and told her that with this bird she could have a roast every day without spending a penny—"Just roast it, and it will come to life again!" Next day the merchant went to his stall in the bazaar and in his absence his wife's lover came to see her. She welcomed him with great joy, and offered to prepare a roast

14

goose for him. She leaned out of the window and called: "Goose, come here!" And the goose came into the room. "Goose, lie down in the roasting pan!" But the goose refused. The merchant's wife grew angry and struck it with the roasting pan. As she did so, one end of the pan stuck to the goose and the other to her. It stuck so fast that she could not in any way pull herself loose from it. "Oh, sweetheart," cried the merchant's wife, "wrench me loose from this roasting pan! That accursed goose must be bewitched!" The lover grasped the merchant's wife with his two hands to wrench her loose from the roasting pan, but he himself stuck to her.

The goose ran out into the yard, then into the street, and dragged them both to the bazaar. The clerks saw their plight and rushed forward to separate them, but whoever touched them stuck to them. A crowd gathered to look at this wonder, and the merchant too came out of his stall. He saw that something was wrong. Who were all these new friends of his wife's? "Confess everything," he said, "otherwise you will stay stuck together like this forever." There was no way out of it, so the merchant's wife confessed her guilt. Then the merchant pulled them apart, soundly thrashed the lover, took his wife home and gave her a good hiding too, repeating with each blow: "Here is your wondrous wonder, your marvelous marvel!"

THE FOX PHYSICIAN

ONCE UPON A TIME there was an old man who lived with his old wife. The husband planted a head of cabbage in the cellar and the wife planted one in an ash bin. The old woman's cabbage withered away completely, but the old man's grew and grew till it reached the floor above the cellar. Then the old man took an ax and cut a hole right over the cabbage. Again the cabbage grew and grew until it reached the ceiling; again the old man took an ax and cut a hole right above the cabbage. Again the cabbage grew and grew until it reached the sky. How could the old man look at the top of his cabbage now? He climbed and climbed up the stalk until he reached the sky, cut a hole in the sky, and climbed out there. He looked about him. Millstones were standing all around; whenever they gave a turn, a cake and a slice of bread with sour cream and butter appeared, and on top of these a pot of gruel. The old man ate and drank his fill and lay down to sleep.

When he had slept enough, he climbed down to the ground and said: "Old woman, old woman! What a good life one leads in heaven! There are millstones there; each time they turn, one finds a cake, a slice of bread with sour cream and butter, and on top a pot of gruel." "How can I get there, old man?" "Sit in the bag, old woman; I will carry you there." The old woman thought for a while, then seated herself in the bag. The old man took the bag in his teeth and began to climb to heaven. He climbed and climbed—he climbed for a long time. The old woman grew weary, and asked: "Is it still far, old man?" "It's still far, old woman." Again he climbed and climbed, and climbed and climbed. "Is it still far, old man?" "Still half way to go!" And again he climbed and climbed, and climbed and climbed. The old woman asked a third time: "Is it still far, old man?" He was about to say "Not far," when the bag dropped out of his teeth. The old woman fell to the ground and was smashed to bits. The old man climbed down the stalk and picked up the bag, but in it there were only bones, and even they were broken into little pieces.

The old man set out for home, weeping bitterly. On his way he met a fox, and she asked him: "Why are you weeping, old man?" "How can I help weeping? My old woman has been smashed to pieces." "Be quiet, I will heal her." The old man threw himself at the fox's feet: "Heal her, I will give you anything you ask in return." "Well, heat up a bath, put out a bag of oatmeal, and a crock of butter, and put the old woman beside it, and stand behind the door, but don't look in."

The old man heated a bath, brought what was called for, and stood behind the door. The fox entered the bathhouse,

16

latched the door, and began to wash the old woman's bones. Actually she did not wash them so much as lick them clean. From behind the door the old man called: "How is the old woman?" "She is stirring!" answered the fox. She finished eating the old woman, gathered the bones together, piled them up in a corner, and began to prepare a hasty pudding. The old man waited and waited, and finally called: "How is the old woman?" "She is sitting up," answered the fox, and spooned up the rest of the pudding. When she had finished eating she said: "Old man, open the door wide." He opened it and the fox leaped out of the bathhouse and ran home. The old man entered the bathhouse and looked around. All he found of his old wife were her bones under the bench, and even they were licked clean; the oatmeal and the butter were gone. The old man remained alone in his misery.

THE DEATH OF THE COCK

A HEN AND A COCK were walking in the priest's barnyard. Suddenly the cock began to choke on a bean. The hen was sorry for him, so she went to the river to ask for some water. The river answered: "Go to the lime tree and ask for a leaf; then I will give you some water."

The hen went to the lime tree. "Lime tree, lime tree, give me a leaf; I will take it to the river and the river will give me water; I will take the water to the cock, who is choking on a bean—he cannot breathe and he cannot sneeze, he is lying like one dead!" The lime tree answered: "Go to the dairymaid and ask for some thread; then I will give you a leaf."

The hen went to the dairymaid. "Dairymaid, dairymaid, give me some thread; I will take it to the lime tree, and it will give me a leaf; I will take the leaf to the river, and the river will give me water; I will take the water to the cock, who is choking on a bean—he cannot breathe and he cannot sneeze, he is lying like one dead!" The dairymaid answered: "Go to the cow and ask for some milk; then I will give you the thread."

The hen went to the cow: "Cow, cow, give me some milk; I will take it to the dairymaid, who will give me some thread; I will take the thread to the lime tree, and it will give me a leaf; I will take the leaf to the river, and the river will give me water; I will take the water to the cock, who is choking on a bean—he cannot breathe and he cannot sneeze, he is lying like one dead!" The cow answered: "Go to the mowers and ask them for some hay; then I will give you the milk."

The hen went to the mowers: "Mowers, mowers, give me some hay; I will take it to the cow, who will give me some milk; I will take the milk to the dairymaid, who will give me some thread; I will take the thread to the lime tree, and it will give me a leaf; I will take the leaf to the river, and the river will give me water; I will take the water to the cock, who is choking on a bean—he cannot breathe and he cannot sneeze, he is lying like one dead!" The mowers answered: "Go to the smiths, bid them forge a scythe. Then we will give you the hay."

The hen went to the smiths: "Smiths, smiths, forge me a scythe; I will take it to the mowers, who will give me some hay; I will take the hay to the cow, who will give me some milk; I will take the milk to the dairymaid, who will give me some thread; I will take the thread to the lime tree, and it will give me a leaf; I will take the leaf to the river, and the river will give me water; I will take the water to the cock, who is choking on a bean—he cannot breathe and he cannot sneeze, he is lying like one dead!" The smiths answered: "Go to the Laians* and ask them for some coal. Then we will forge you a scythe."

The hen went to the Laians: "Laians, Laians, give me some coal; I will take it to the smiths, who will forge me a scythe; I

*Inhabitants of the village of Laia—near the river Laia, a confluent of the northern Dvina—who extracted coal for the smithies in the port of Archangel.

will take the scythe to the mowers, who will give me some hay; I will take the hay to the cow, who will give me some milk; I will take the milk to the dairymaid, who will give me some thread; I will take the thread to the lime tree, and it will give me a leaf; I will take the leaf to the river and the river will give me water; I will take the water to the cock who is choking on a bean—he cannot breathe and he cannot sneeze, he is lying like one dead!"

The Laians gave her some coal. The hen took the coal to the smiths and the smiths forged her a scythe. She took the scythe to the mowers and the mowers mowed some hay for her. She took the hay to the cow and the cow gave her some milk. She took the milk to the dairymaid and the dairymaid gave her some thread. She took the thread to the lime tree and the lime tree gave her a leaf. She took the leaf to the river and the river gave her some water. She took the water to the cock. But he was lying there quite still, neither panting nor breathing. He had choked to death on a bean!

MISERY

IN A CERTAIN VILLAGE there lived two peasants, blood brothers; one was poor and the other rich. The rich one went to live in the town, built himself a big house, and joined the merchants' guild. But the poor one often had not even a piece of bread in his house, and his little children sometimes wept and begged for something to eat. From morning till night this peasant struggled like a fish against ice, but he never could earn anything. One day he said to his wife: "I will go to the town and ask my brother for help." He came to the rich man and said: "Ah, my own brother, help me a little in my misery; my wife and children are without bread, they go hungry for days on end." "Work in my house this week, then I will help you." What could the poor man do? He set to work, swept the yard, curried the horses, carried water, and chopped wood. At the end of the week the rich brother gave him one loaf of bread. "This is for your work!" he said. "Thank you even for that," said the poor brother; he bowed low before the rich man and was about to go home. "Wait a minute! Come to visit me tomorrow and bring your wife with you. Tomorrow is my name day." "Eh, little brother, I don't belong here, you know it well. Your other guests will be merchants in boots and fur coats, and I wear plain linden bark shoes and a wretched gray caftan." "Never mind. Come; there will be a place for you." "Very well then, brother, I will come."

The poor man returned home, gave the loaf of bread to his wife, and said: "Listen, wife, we are invited to a feast tomorrow." "To a feast? Who has invited us?" "My brother. Tomorrow is his name day." "Very well, then, we'll go." Next morning they rose and went to the town; they came to their rich brother's house, congratulated him, and sat down on a bench. Many prominent guests were already seated at the table. The host served them all abundantly, but he forgot even to think about his poor brother and sister-in-law, and did not offer them anything; they just sat and watched the others eating and drinking. The dinner was over, the guests began to rise from table, and to thank the host and hostess. The poor man too rose from his bench and bowed to the ground before his brother. The guests went home, drunken and merry; they were noisy and sang songs.

The poor man, however, went home with an empty stomach. He said to his wife: "Let us sing a song too." "Eh, you blockhead! The others are singing because they ate savory dishes and drank their fill. What gives you the idea of singing?" "Well, after all, I have been at my brother's feast; I am ashamed to walk without singing. If I sing, everyone will think that I too had a good time." "Well, sing if you must, but I won't." The peasant began singing a song and heard two voices. He stopped and asked his wife: "Was it you who accompanied me in a thin voice?" "What is the matter with you? I wouldn't think of singing a note!" "Then who was it?" "I don't know," said the woman, "but sing again, I will listen." He sang again, and although he alone sang, two voices could be heard. He stopped and said: "Is it you, Misery, who are singing with me?" Misery answered: "Aye, master, I am singing with you." "Well, Misery, let us walk together." "We shall, master. I will never desert you now."

The peasant came home, and Misery asked him to go to the

tavern with him. The peasant answered: "I have no money." "Oh, little peasant! What do you need money for? I see you have a sheepskin, but of what use is it? Summer will be here soon, you will not wear it anyhow. Let us go to the tavern and sell the sheepskin." The peasant and Misery went to the tavern and drank away the sheepskin. On the following day Misery began to moan that his head ached from drinking, and he again called upon his master to drink some wine. "I have no money," said the peasant. "What do we need money for? Take your sledge and cart—those will do." There was nothing to be done, the peasant could not rid himself of Misery; he took his sledge and cart, dragged them to the tavern, and drank them away with his companion. The following morning Misery moaned even more and called upon his master to go drinking again; the peasant drank away his harrow and plow. Before a month had gone by, he had squandered everything; he had even pawned his hut to a neighbor and taken the money to the tavern. But Misery again pressed him: "Come, let us go to the tavern." "No, Misery, do as you like, there is nothing more to sell." "Why, has not your wife two dresses? Leave her one, and the second we will drink away." The peasant took one dress, drank it away, and thought: "Now I am cleaned out! I have neither house nor home, nothing is left to me or my wife!"

Next morning Misery awoke, saw that the peasant had nothing left to be taken away, and said: "Master!" "What is it, Misery?" "Listen to me. Go to your neighbor and ask him for his cart and oxen." The peasant went to his neighbor and said: "Give me a cart and a pair of oxen for a short time; I will work a week to pay you for the hire of them." "What do you need them for?" "To go to the woods for some logs." "Very well, take them; but don't overload the cart." "Of course I won't, my benefactor!" He brought the pair of oxen, sat with Misery on the cart, and drove into the open field. "Master," said Misery, "do you know the big stone in this field?" "Of course I know it." "Then go straight to it." They came to the stone, stopped, and climbed down from the cart. Misery ordered the peasant to lift the stone. The peasant lifted it with Misery's help; under it they saw a ditch filled to the brim with gold.

"Well, why do you stare?" said Misery. "Hurry up and get it into the cart."

The peasant set to work and filled the cart with gold. He took everything out of the ditch, down to the last ruble; when he saw that nothing was left, he said: "Have a look, Misery, is there any money left?" Misery leaned over the ditch. "Where?" he said. "I cannot see anything." "But it's shining there in the corner." "No, I don't see it." "Crawl into the ditch, then you will see it." Misery crawled into the ditch; he no sooner had got in than the peasant covered him with the stone. "That way it will be better," said the peasant, "for if I take you with me, miserable Misery, you will drink away all this fortune, even though it will take a long time." The peasant came home, stored the money in his cellar, took the oxen back to his neighbor, and began to consider how to establish himself in society. He bought wood, built himself a large wooden house, and lived twice as richly as his brother.

After some time, a long time or a short time, he went to the town to invite his brother and sister-in-law to his name day feast. "What an idea!" his rich brother said to him. "You have nothing to eat, yet you are celebrating your name day." "True, at one time I had nothing to eat, but now, thank God, I am no worse off then you. Come and you will see." "Very well then, I will come." The next day the rich brother and his wife came to the name day feast; and lo and behold, the once wretched man had a large wooden house, new and lofty, such as not every merchant has! The peasant gave them a royal feast, fed them with all kinds of viands, and set various meads and wines before them. The rich brother asked him: "Tell me, please, how did you become so wealthy?" The peasant told him truthfully how miserable Misery had attached himself to him, how he had led him to drink away all his possessions, down to the last thread, till nothing was left but the soul in his body, how Misery had shown him the treasure in the open field, how he had then taken the treasure and got rid of Misery.

The rich man was envious. He thought to himself: "I will go to the open field, lift the stone, and let Misery out—let him ruin my brother completely, so that he will not dare to boast of his riches to me." He sent his wife home, and rushed to the field; he drove to the big stone, turned it to one side, and stooped to see what was beneath it. Before he could bend his head all the way down, Misery jumped out and sat on his neck. "Ah," he shrieked, "you wanted to starve me to death in there, but I'll never leave you now." "Listen, Misery," said the merchant, "in truth it was not I who imprisoned you beneath that stone." "Who then did it, if not you?" "It was my brother who imprisoned you, and I came for the express purpose of freeing you." "No, you are lying! You cheated me once, but you won't cheat me again!" Misery sat securely on the rich man's neck; the rich man carried him home, and his fortune began to dwindle away. From early morning Misery applied himself to his task; every day he called upon the merchant to drink, and much of his wealth went to the tavern keeper. "This is no way to live," thought the merchant. "It seems to me that I have sufficiently amused Misery. It is high time I separated from him —but how?"

He thought and thought and finally had an idea. He went out into his broad courtyard, cleft two oaken spikes, took a new wheel, and drove a spike into the hollow shaft that went through the hub of the wheel. He came to Misery. "Why, Misery, do you always lie on your side?" "What else shall I do?" "What else? Come into the courtyard and play hide-and-seek with me." Misery was delighted with this idea. They went into the yard. First the merchant hid; Misery found him at once, and now it was Misery's turn to hide. "Well," he said, "you won't find me so soon. I can get into any hole, no matter how small!" "You're bragging," said the merchant. "You can't even get into that wheel, let alone a hole." "I can't get into that wheel? Just wait and see how I shall hide." Misery crawled into the hollow shaft; the merchant drove another oaken spike into the other end of the hollow shaft, picked up the wheel, and cast it together with Misery into the river. Misery drowned, and the merchant lived again as of old.

THE CASTLE OF THE FLY

A FLY BUILT a castle, a tall and mighty castle. There came to the castle the Crawling Louse. "Who, who's in the castle? Who, who's in your house?" said the Crawling Louse. "I, I, the Languishing Fly. And who art thou?" "I'm the Crawling Louse."

Then came to the castle the Leaping Flea. "Who, who's in the castle?" said the Leaping Flea. "I, I, the Languishing Fly, and I, the Crawling Louse. And who art thou?" "I'm the Leaping Flea."

Then came to the castle the Mischievous Mosquito. "Who, who's in the castle?" said the Mischievous Mosquito. "I, I, the Languishing Fly, and I, the Crawling Louse, and I, the Leaping Flea. And who art thou?" "I'm the Mischievous Mosquito."

Then came to the castle the Murmuring Mouse. "Who, who's in the castle?" said the Murmuring Mouse. "I, I, the Languishing Fly, and I, the Crawling Louse, and I, the Leaping Flea, and I, the Mischievous Mosquito. And who art thou?" "I'm the Murmuring Mouse."

Then came to the castle the Wriggly Lizard. "Who, who's in the castle?" said the Wriggly Lizard. "I, I the Languishing Fly, and I, the Crawling Louse, and I, the Leaping Flea, and I, the Mischievous Mosquito, and I, the Murmuring Mouse. And who art thou?" "I'm the Wriggly Lizard."

Then came to the castle Patricia Fox. "Who, who's in the castle?" said Patricia Fox. "I, I, the Languishing Fly, and I, the Crawling Louse, and I, the Leaping Flea, and I, the Mischievous Mosquito, and I, the Murmuring Mouse, and I, the Wriggly Lizard. And who art thou?" "I'm Patricia Fox."

Then came to the castle Highjump the Hare. "Who, who's in the castle?" said Highjump the Hare. "I, I, the Languishing Fly, and I, the Crawling Louse, and I, the Leaping Flea, and I, the Mischievous Mosquito, and I, the Murmuring Mouse, and I, the Wriggly Lizard, and I, Patricia Fox. And who art thou?" "I'm Highjump the Hare."

Then came to the castle Wolf Graytail. "Who, who's in the castle?" said Wolf Graytail. "I, I, the Languishing Fly, and I, the Crawling Louse, and I, the Leaping Flea, and I, the Mischievous Mosquito, and I, the Murmuring Mouse, and I, the Wriggly Lizard, and I, Patricia Fox, and I, Highjump the Hare. And who art thou?" "I'm Wolf Graytail."

Then came to the castle Bear Thicklegs. "Who, who's in the castle?" said Bear Thicklegs. "I, I, the Languishing Fly, and I, the Crawling Louse, and I, the Leaping Flea, and I, the Mischievous Mosquito, and I, the Murmuring Mouse, and I, the Wriggly Lizard, and I, Patricia Fox, and I, Highjump the Hare, and I, Wolf Graytail. And who art thou?"

"I'm Rumbling Thunder! I'll tumble you under! I'm Bear Thicklegs!" And he laid his thick paw on the castle, and smashed it!

THE TURNIP

GRANDFATHER PLANTED a turnip. The time came to pick it. He took hold of it and pulled and pulled, but he couldn't pull it out. Grandfather called grandmother; grandmother pulled grandfather, and grandfather pulled the turnip. They pulled and pulled, but they couldn't pull it out. Then their granddaughter came; she pulled grandma, grandma pulled grandpa, grandpa pulled the turnip; they pulled and they pulled, but they couldn't pull it out. Then the puppy came; he pulled the granddaughter, she pulled grandma, grandma pulled grandpa, grandpa pulled the turnip; they pulled and they pulled, but they couldn't pull it out. Then a beetle came; the beetle pulled the puppy, the puppy pulled the granddaughter, she pulled grandma, grandma pulled grandpa, grandpa pulled the turnip; they pulled and they pulled, but they couldn't pull it out. Then came a second beetle.

The second beetle pulled the first beetle, the first beetle pulled
the puppy, the puppy pulled the granddaughter, she pulled
grandma, grandma pulled grandpa, grandpa pulled the turnip;
they pulled and they pulled, but they couldn't pull it out. (Repeated for a third beetle, and a fourth.) Then the fifth beetle
came. He pulled the fourth beetle, the fourth beetle pulled the
third, the third pulled the second, the second pulled the first,
the first beetle pulled the puppy, the puppy pulled the granddaughter, she pulled grandma, grandma pulled grandpa,
grandpa pulled the turnip; they pulled and they pulled, and
they pulled out the turnip.

THE HEN

IN grandmother's yard
   Lived a speckled hen.
   She laid an egg one day;
The egg rolled down
From shelf to shelf
And in the end it found itself
In a little keg of aspen wood
Away in a corner under a bench.
A mouse ran by too near the keg,
Wiggled his tail, and broke the egg!

At this great catastrophe
An old cripple began to cry,
An ugly crone let out a sigh,
A startled chicken rose to fly;
The gateposts shrieked,
All doors creaked,
The swilltub leaked;
The priest's daughter,

Carrying water,
Broke her buckets.

All in a dither
She came to her mother
And said:

> "Mother, mother, have you heard the news?
> In grandmother's yard
> Lived a speckled hen.
> She laid an egg today;
> The egg rolled down
> From shelf to shelf
> And in the end it found itself
> In a little keg of aspen wood
> Away in a corner under a bench.
> A mouse ran by too near the keg,
> Wiggled his tail, and broke the egg!

> "At this great catastrophe
> An old cripple began to cry,
> An ugly crone let out a sigh,
> A startled chicken rose to fly;
> The gateposts shrieked,
> All doors creaked,
> The swilltub leaked;
> And I, your daughter,
> Carrying water,
> Broke my buckets."

The wife of the priest
Dropped her yeast
And her precious dough fell to the floor.
She headed straight
Through the churchyard gate
And said:

> "Husband, husband, have you heard the news?
> In grandmother's yard

Lives a speckled hen.
She laid an egg today;
The egg rolled down
From shelf to shelf
And in the end it found itself
In a little keg of aspen wood
Away in a corner under a bench.
A mouse ran by too near the keg,
Wiggled his tail, and broke the egg!

"At this great catastrophe:
An old cripple began to cry,
An ugly crone let out a sigh,
A startled chicken rose to fly;
The gateposts shrieked,
All doors creaked,
The swilltub leaked;
Our dear daughter,
Carrying water,
Broke her buckets;
And I, your wife,
Dropped my dough to the floor."

The holy father with a terrible look
Tore the pages out of his book
And scattered them on the floor.

RIDDLES

NEAR A HIGHWAY a peasant was sowing a field. Just then
the tsar rode by, stopped near the peasant, and said:
"Godspeed, little peasant!" "Thank you, my good
man!" (He did not know that he was speaking to the tsar.) "Do
you earn much profit from this field?" "If the harvest is good,

I may make eighty rubles." "What do you do with this money?" "Twenty rubles go for taxes, twenty go for debts, twenty I give in loans, and twenty I throw out of the window." "Explain to me, brother, what debts you must pay, to whom you loan money, and why you throw money out the window." "Supporting my father is paying a debt; feeding my son is lending money; feeding my daughter is throwing it out of the window." "You speak the truth," said the tsar. He gave the peasant a handful of silver coins, disclosed that he was the tsar, and forbade the man to tell these things to anyone outside of his presence: "No matter who asks you, do not answer!"

The tsar came to his capital and summoned his boyars and generals. "Solve this riddle," he said to them. "On my way I saw a peasant who was sowing a field. I asked him what profit he earned from it and what he did with his money. He answered that if the harvest was good he got eighty rubles, and that he paid out twenty rubles in taxes, twenty for debts, twenty as loans, and twenty he threw out of the window. To him who solves this riddle I will give great rewards and great honors." The boyars and generals thought and thought but could not solve the riddle. But one boyar hit upon the idea of going to the peasant with whom the tsar had spoken. He gave the peasant a whole pile of silver rubles and asked him: "Tell me the answer to the tsar's riddle." The peasant cast a glance at the money, took it, and explained everything to the boyar, who returned to the tsar and repeated the solution of the riddle.

The tsar realized that the peasant had not abided by the imperial command, and ordered that he be brought to court. The peasant appeared before the tsar and at once admitted that he had told everything to the boyar. "Well, brother, for such an offense I must order you put to death, and you have only yourself to thank for it." "Your Majesty, I am not guilty of any offense, because I told everything to the boyar in your presence." As he said this, the peasant drew from his pocket a silver ruble with the tsar's likeness on it, and showed it to the tsar. "You speak the truth," said the tsar. "This is my person." And he generously rewarded the peasant and sent him home.

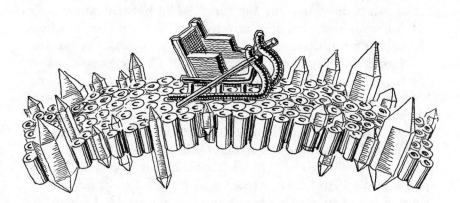

THE ENCHANTED RING

I N A CERTAIN LAND, in a certain big village, there lived a
peasant who was neither poor nor rich. He had a son,
and bequeathed to him three hundred rubles, saying:
"Here, my son. I give you my blessing, with three hundred
rubles when you come of age." The son grew up, came to the
age of reason, and said to his mother: "I remember that my
deceased father gave me his blessing with three hundred
rubles; now give me at least one hundred of them."

She gave him a hundred rubles, and he took to the road.
He met a peasant leading a flap-eared dog. He said: "Peasant,
sell me that dog." The peasant said: "Give me a hundred rubles
for it." He gave his hundred rubles for the dog, led him home,
and gave him food and drink. Then he asked his mother for
another hundred rubles. The mother gave him another hundred rubles, and he took to the road. Again he met a peasant,
this time a fellow leading a cat with a golden tail. He said:
"Peasant, sell me that cat." The peasant answered: "Buy him!"

31

"And what do you want for him?" The peasant answered: "If you want him, give me a hundred rubles." And he gave him the cat for a hundred rubles. The young man took the cat, led her home, and gave her drink and food. Then he again asked his mother for a hundred rubles. The mother said to him: "My beloved child, what do you spend the money on? Your purchases are useless." "Eh, mother, do not worry about the money; somehow it will come back to us." She gave him the third hundred, and he again took to the road.

So far, so good. Then, in a certain land, in a certain city, a princess died, and on her hand was a golden ring; our youth wanted badly to get this ring from her finger. He bribed the sentries to let him come near the princess' bier; he came very close to her, took the ring off her finger, and went home to his mother. No one had stopped him.

He lived at home for some time, a long time or a short time; then he went out on the porch and moved the ring from one hand to the other. Three hundred strong men and a hundred and seventy knights jumped out of the ring and said: "What work do you order us to do?" "This is what I order you to do. First, knock down my old hut and on the same spot build a stone house, and let my mother know nothing about it." They did this task in one night. His mother arose, and asked, surprised: "Whose house is this?" Her son answered: "Mother, be not surprised, but pray to God. This house is ours." And so they lived in it for some time, a long time or a short time, until the youth came to manhood and wanted to take him a wife.

In a certain kingdom in a certain land a certain king had a daughter, and our young man wanted to marry her. He said to his mother: "In such and such a kingdom, such and such a king has a beautiful daughter. Woo her for me, mother." The mother answered him: "My beloved child, how can such as we get a princess?" He answered her: "Mother, my good parent! Pray to the Savior, drink kvass, and go to bed. The morning is wiser than the evening." The good youth himself went on the porch, moved the ring from one hand to the other, and three hundred strong men and a hundred and seventy knights jumped out and asked him: "What do you order us to do?" "Find for me things so precious that the king does not have them, and bring them to me on golden trays; I must give presents to the king and his daughter." They straightway brought him such things, and he sent his mother to the king to make the match for him.

The mother came to the king and he said with surprise: "Old woman, where did you get these things?" The princess came out, looked at them, and said: "Well, old woman, tell your son to build in one night in the king's sacred meadow a new palace more splendid than my father's own, and to hang a crystal bridge from one palace to the other, and to cover the crystal bridge with all kinds of embroidered rugs. If he does all this I will marry him. If he does not, there will be no pardon for him, and he must lay his rash head on the block!"

The old woman went home in tears and said to her son: "My beloved child, I told you not to seek the princess in marriage. Now she has ordered me to tell you that if you want to marry her, you must build a new palace in the sacred meadow in one night, and it must be more splendid than her father's own, and a crystal bridge must lead from one palace to the other, and this crystal bridge must be covered with all kinds of embroidered rugs; and if you fail to do these things you must lay your rash head on the block! Now what are you going to do, my child?" He answered: "Mother, my parent! Have no misgivings, pray to the Savior, drink kvass, and go to bed. The morning is wiser than the evening."

Our youth himself went on the porch, moved the ring from one hand to the other, and three hundred strong men and a hundred and seventy knights jumped out and asked: "What do you order us to do?" He said to them: "My dear friends, try in one night to build for me a new palace in the king's sacred meadow, and let it be more splendid than the king's own, and let a crystal bridge hang between one palace and the other, and let this bridge be covered with all kinds of embroidered rugs." In one night the strong men and knights built everything they were commanded to build. In the morning the king rose, looked at his sacred meadow through a spyglass, marveled at the new palace more splendid than his own, and sent a messenger to tell the good youth that he could come to woo the princess and that the princess had agreed to marry him. So the match was made, the wedding was celebrated, and a great feast was held.

They lived together for some time, a long time or a short time, and then the princess asked her husband: "Please tell me how you accomplished such a thing in one night? From now on we shall think together." She flattered him, exhorted him, and served him all kinds of liquors. She made him dead drunk, and he told her what she wanted to know: "I did it with this ring!" She took the ring from the drunken man, moved it from one hand to the other, and three hundred strong men and a hundred and seventy knights jumped out and asked her: "What do you command us to do?" "This I command. Take that drunkard and throw him on my father's meadow, and carry me with the whole palace beyond thrice nine and three lands, beyond the tenth kingdom, to such and such a king." In one night they carried her to where she bade them.

In the morning the king arose, looked through the spyglass at his sacred meadow, and there was no palace and no crystal bridge; only one man was lying there. The king sent forth messengers, saying: "Find out what man is lying there." The messengers went there, came back, and said to the king: "Your son-in-law is lying there alone!" "Go and bring him to me." They brought him and the king asked: "What did you do with the princess and the palace?" He answered: "Your Majesty, I do not know; it is as though I lost her while I was asleep." The king said: "I give you three months' time to discover where the princess is—else I will put you to death." And he put the good youth into a strong dungeon.

Then the cat said to the flap-eared dog: "Imagine it! Our master is in prison. The princess deceived him, took the ring off his finger, and went away beyond thrice nine lands, beyond the tenth kingdom. We must get the ring; let us run together!" They ran; whenever they had to cross a lake or a river, the cat sat on the neck of the flat-eared dog, and the dog carried her to the other side. After some time, a long time or a short time, they ran beyond thrice nine lands, beyond the tenth kingdom. The cat said to the dog: "If someone from the king's kitchen

sends for wood, do you run at once. I will go to the pantry, to the housekeeper; whatever she wants, I will serve."

They began to live in the king's palace. The housekeeper said to the king: "In my pantry there is a cat with a golden tail; whatever I want, she serves!" The cook said: "And I have a flap-eared dog; when I send the boy for wood, he rushes out and gets it." The king answered: "Bring the flap-eared dog to my bedroom." And the princess said: "And to me bring the cat with the golden tail." The dog and cat were brought, and stayed in the palace night and day. But whenever she went to sleep, the princess put the ring in her mouth. One night a mouse ran across the princess' chamber and the cat snatched him by the neck. The mouse said: "Do not harm me, cat! I know what you have come for; you have come for the ring, and I will get it for you." The cat let him go; he jumped on the bed, straight on the princess, stuck his tail into her mouth and wiggled it; the princess spat and spat out the ring. The cat snatched it and cried to the flap-eared dog: "Hurry!"

They jumped out of the window and ran. They ran over land and swam across lakes and rivers; they arrived in their kingdom and went straight to the prison. The cat climbed in; her master saw her and began to stroke her. The cat sang songs and put the ring on his hand; the master was overjoyed and moved it from one hand to the other, and three hundred strong men and a hundred and seventy knights jumped out and said: "What do you order us to do?" He said: "To ease my grief, I want magnificent music played for a whole day." The music began to play. And the king sent a messenger to him to ask whether he had considered the matter. The messenger went and became absorbed in listening to the music; the king sent another messenger, and he too became absorbed in listening; the king sent a third one, and he too became absorbed in listening. Then the king himself went to his son-in-law, and the king too was bewitched by the music. As soon as the music stopped, the king began to question his son-in-law, who answered: "Your Majesty, free me for one night, and in a trice I will get your daughter."

He went on the porch and moved the ring from one hand to

the other. Three hundred strong men and a hundred and seventy knights jumped out and asked him: "What do you order us to do?" "Bring back the princess, with the entire palace, and let everything be in the old place and done in one night." The princess arose in the morning, saw that she was in the old place, and became frightened because she did not know what would happen to her. Her husband came to the king. "Your Majesty," he asked, "what punishment shall we give the princess?" "My dear son-in-law, let us exhort her with words, and then do you two live together and prosper!"

FOMA AND EREMA,
THE TWO BROTHERS

OH, Foma and Erema, two brothers they were
Alike in body, alike in mind.
Alike their noses, their eyes, their hair—
Oh, two such brothers you'll seldom find.
One day the two went to church to pray,
One in a pew, the other at the altar.
Erema took hymnal, Foma took psalter;
Erema recited and Foma prayed
And this was heard by priests who stayed
On hilltops, learnéd priests devout
Who came to church and kicked them out,
One out the window and one out the door,
And they hastened away for evermore.
They went to the woods where later they met
And there they decided gray rabbits to get,
Gray rabbits, fast runners, to hunt and to kill,
But none could they find in hollow or hill.
Instead they went to the river banks steep,

To river banks steep where waters ran deep.
Two ducks a-swimming they saw down below,
One duck was white, the other like snow.
Erema took stick, and Foma grasped knife,
Each was longing to take a duck's life.
But Foma threw far, Erema too near,
And the ducks swam away, swam away from there.
The brothers then thought to catch some fish,
To catch some fish was now their wish.
Oh, Erema sat in a deep-bottomed boat,
But the boat had no floor and would not float.
And Foma did sit him down in a barge
That had no bottom but was very large.
Three years they sank but could not drown;
Three devils in vain tried to pull them down.
The brothers now wished their bodies to feed,
To feed their bodies was now their need.
They made up their minds to plow their fields
To take whatever the good earth yields.
To market went Foma, Erema to fair,
A foal and a colt the brothers bought there.
Erema's colt refused to work,
And Foma's foal his tasks did shirk.
The brothers then slew their horses, they say,
And ran from the fields, oh, quickly away!

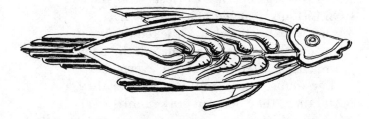

THE JUST REWARD

THE KING OF A CERTAIN COUNTRY lost his ring while on a drive through his capital. He at once placed a notice in the newspapers, promising that whoever might find and return the ring would receive a large reward in money. A simple private was lucky enough to find it. "What shall I do?" thought the soldier. "If I report my find at regimental headquarters, the whole affair will be referred to my superiors, each in his turn, from the sergeant to the company commander, from the company commander to the battalion commander, from the battalion commander to the colonel, and from the colonel to the brigadier general—there will never be an end to it. I would rather go straight to the king."

He came to the palace. The officer on guard asked him: "What do you want here?" "I have found the king's ring," said the soldier. "Very well, brother! I will announce you, but only on condition that I get half the reward that the king gives you." The soldier thought to himself: "For once in my life I have had a piece of luck, and now I have to share it!" However, he answered the officer on guard: "Very well, I agree. Only give me a note stating that half the reward is for you and half for me."

The officer gave him the note and announced him to the king. The king praised the soldier for having found the ring. "Thank you, brave soldier!" he said. "I shall give you two thousand rubles as a reward." "No, Your Royal Majesty! That is not a soldier's reward. A soldier's reward is two hundred lashes." "What a fool you are!" said the king, and ordered that the sticks be brought in.

The soldier began to undress, unbuttoned his tunic, and the note dropped on the floor. "What paper is that?" asked the king. "Your Majesty, that is a note stating that only half the reward is for me, and that the other half must go to the officer on guard." The king laughed, called the officer on guard, and ordered that he be given a hundred lashes. The order was carried out, and when it was time to count the last ten lashes, the soldier drew near to the king and said: "Your Majesty, since he is so greedy, I will give the other half of the reward to him too." "How kind you are!" said the king, and ordered that the officer on guard be given the second hundred lashes. After this reward the officer could hardly crawl home. As for the soldier, the king gave him an honorable discharge from the service and presented him with three thousand rubles.

SALT

IN A CERTAIN CITY there lived a merchant who had three sons: the first was Fyodor, the second Vasily, and the third Ivan the Fool. This merchant lived richly; he sailed in his ships to foreign lands and traded in all kinds of goods. Once he loaded two ships with precious merchandise and sent them beyond the sea with his two elder sons. Ivan, his youngest son, always went to inns and alehouses, and for that reason his father did not trust him with any business; but when Ivan learned that his brothers had been sent beyond the sea, he straightway went to his father and begged him to be allowed to show himself in foreign lands, see people, and earn money by his wits. For a long time the merchant refused, saying: "You'll spend everything on drink and come home without your head!" However, when he saw that his son persisted in his prayers, he gave him a ship with the very cheapest cargo—beams, boards, and planks.

Ivan made ready for the voyage, lifted anchor, and soon overtook his brothers. They sailed together on the blue sea for one day, two days, three days; but on the fourth strong winds arose and blew Ivan's ship to a remote and unknown island. "Very well, boys," cried Ivan to his crew, "make for shore!" And they reached the shore. Ivan stepped out on the island, told his crew to wait for him, and started walking along a path. He walked and walked until he reached a very high mountain. And he saw that in this mountain there was neither sand nor stone but pure Russian salt. He returned to the shore and ordered his sailors to throw all the beams and planks into the water and to load the ship with salt. As soon as this was done, Ivan lifted anchor and sailed away.

After some time, a long time or a short time, and after they had sailed some distance, a great distance or a short one, the ship approached a large and wealthy city, sailed into its harbor, and cast anchor. Ivan, the merchant's son, went into the city to make obeisance to the king of the country and to obtain permission to trade freely, and he took a bundle of his merchandise, Russian salt, to show to the king. His arrival was immediately reported to the sovereign, who summoned him and said: "Speak! What is your business, what do you want?" "Just this, Your Majesty! Permit me to trade freely in your city!" "And what goods do you sell?" "Russian salt, Your Majesty." The king had never heard of salt; in his kingdom the people ate without salt. He wondered what this new and unknown merchandise might be. "Come," he said, "show it to me." Ivan, the merchant's son, opened his kerchief; the king glanced at the contents and thought to himself: "This is only white sand!" And he said to Ivan with a smile: "Brother, this can be had here without money!"

Ivan left the palace feeling very downcast. Then it occurred to him to go to the king's kitchen and see how the cooks prepared meals there and what kind of salt they used. He went into the kitchen, asked to be allowed to rest for a while, sat on a chair, and watched. The cooks ran back and forth: one was busy boiling, another roasting, another pouring, and still another crushing lice on a ladle. Ivan, the merchant's son, saw

41

that they were not the least bit concerned with salting the food. He waited till a moment came when everyone else was out of the kitchen; then he seized the chance to pour the proper amount of salt into all the stews and sauces. The time came to serve the dinner, and the first dish was brought in. The king ate of it, and found it savory as never before. The second dish was served, and he liked it even better.

Then the king summoned his cooks and said to them: "I have been king for many years, but never before have you cooked me such savory dishes. How did you do it?" The cooks answered: "Your Majesty, we cooked as of old and did not add anything new. But the merchant who came to ask permission to trade freely is sitting in the kitchen. Perhaps he has added something." "Summon him to my presence!" Ivan, the merchant's son, was brought before the king to be questioned. He fell on his knees and asked forgiveness. "Your Majesty, I confess my guilt. I have seasoned all the dishes and sauces with Russian salt. Such is the custom in my country." "And for how much do you sell this salt?" Ivan realized that his business was in a fair way and answered: "It is not very dear— for two measures of salt, one measure of silver and one of gold." The king agreed to this price and bought the whole cargo.

Ivan filled his ship with silver and gold and sat down to wait for a favorable wind. Now the king of that land had a daughter, a beautiful princess. She wanted to see the Russian ship and asked her father's permission to go down to the port. The king gave her permission. So she took her nurses, governesses, and maidservants with her and drove forth to see the Russian ship. Ivan, the merchant's son, showed her every part and told her its name—the sails, the rigging, the bow, and the stern—and then he led her into the cabin. He ordered his crew to cut away the anchor, hoist the sails, and put out to sea; and since they had a good tail wind, they were soon a good distance from the city. The princess came up on deck, saw only the sea around her, and began to weep. Ivan, the merchant's son, spoke to her, comforted her, and urged her to dry her tears; and since he was handsome, she soon smiled and ceased grieving.

For some time, a long time or a short time, Ivan sailed on the sea with the princess. Then his elder brothers overtook him, learned of his audacity and good fortune, and greatly envied him. They came on board his ship, seized him by his arms, and threw him into the sea; then they cast lots between them and divided the booty: the eldest brother took the princess, and the second brother took the ship full of silver and gold.

Now it happened that when they flung Ivan from the ship he saw one of the boards that he himself had thrown into the sea. He clutched this board and for a long time drifted on it above the depths of the sea. Finally he was carried to an unknown island. He went ashore and walked along the beach. He met a giant with an enormous mustache, on which hung his mittens, which he was drying thus after the rain. "What do you want here?" asked the giant. Ivan told him everything that had happened. "If you so desire, I will carry you home. Tomorrow your eldest brother is to marry the princess. Sit on my back." He took Ivan up in his hands, seated him on his back, and ran across the sea. Ivan's cap dropped off. "Ah me," he said, "I've lost my cap!" "Never mind, brother," said the giant, "your cap is far away now, five hundred versts behind us." He brought Ivan to his native land, put him on the ground, and said: "Now promise that you will not boast to anyone about having ridden on my back; if you do boast, I shall crush you." Ivan, the merchant's son, promised not to boast, thanked the giant, and set out on the homeward journey.

When he arrived, everyone was already at the wedding table, preparing to go to church. As soon as the beautiful princess saw him, she jumped from her seat and threw herself on his neck. "This is my bridegroom," she said, "and not he who sits here by my side." "What is this?" asked the father. Ivan told him everything—how he had traded in salt, how he had carried off the princess, and how his elder brothers had pushed him into the sea. The father was very angry at his elder sons, drove them out of the house, and married Ivan to the princess.

Now a gay feast began. The guests got drunk and began to boast, some about their strength, some about their wealth, and some about the beauty of their young wives. And Ivan sat and sat and then drunkenly boasted: "What are your boasts worth? I have something real to boast about. I rode horseback on a giant across the entire sea!" The moment he said these words, the giant appeared at the gate. "Ah, Ivan, son of the merchant," he said, "I told you not to boast about me. Now what have you done?" "Forgive me," Ivan implored him, "it was not I who boasted, but my drunkenness!" "Come, show me. What do you mean by drunkenness?"

Ivan gave orders that a hundred gallon barrel of wine and a hundred gallon barrel of beer be brought. The giant drank the wine and the beer, got drunk, and began to break up and ruin everything in his path; he knocked down trees and bushes and tore big houses asunder. Then he fell down and slept three days and nights without awakening. When he awoke, he was shown all the damage he had done. The giant was terribly surprised and said: "Well, Ivan, son of the merchant, now I know what drunkenness is. Henceforth you may boast about me all you like."

THE GOLDEN SLIPPER

AN OLD MAN and his old wife had two daughters. Once the old man went to town and bought a fish for the elder sister and a fish for the younger sister. The elder sister ate her fish, but the younger one went to the well and said: "Little mother fish, what shall I do with you?" "Do not eat me," said the fish, "but put me into the water; I will be useful to you." The maiden dropped the fish into the well and went home.

Now the old woman had a great dislike for her younger daughter. She dressed the elder sister in her best clothes, made ready to take her to mass, and gave the younger one two measures of rye, ordering her to husk it before their return from church.

The young girl went to fetch water; she sat on the edge of the well and wept. The fish swam to the surface and asked her: "Why do you weep, lovely maiden?" "How can I help weeping?" answered the maiden. "My mother has dressed my sister in her best clothes and gone with her to mass, but she left me home and ordered me to husk two measures of rye before her return from church." The fish said: "Weep not; dress and go to church; the rye will be husked." The maiden dressed and went to mass. Her mother did not recognize her. Toward the end of the mass, the girl went home. Very soon her mother too came home also and said: "Well, you ninny, did you husk the rye?" "I did," the daughter answered. "What a beauty we saw at mass!" her mother went on. "The priest neither chanted nor read, but looked at her all the time—and just look at you, you ninny, see how you're dressed!" "I wasn't there, but I know all about it," answered the maiden. "How could you know?" asked her mother.

The next day the mother dressed her elder daughter in her best clothes, went with her to mass, and left three measures of barley for the younger one, saying: "While I pray to God, you husk the barley." So she went to mass, and her younger daughter went to fetch water at the well. She sat down at the edge and wept. The fish swam to the surface and asked: "Why do you weep, lovely maiden?" "How can I help weeping," the maiden answered. "My mother has dressed my sister in her best clothes and taken her to mass, but she left me at home and ordered me to husk three measures of barley before she returns from church." The fish said: "Weep not. Dress and go to church after her. The barley will be husked."

The maiden dressed, went to church, and began to pray to God. The priest neither chanted nor read, but looked at her all the time. That day the king's son was attending mass; our beautiful maiden pleased him tremendously and he wanted to know whose daughter she was. So he took some pitch and threw it under her golden slipper. The slipper remained when the girl went home. "I will marry her whose slipper this is," said the young prince. Soon the old woman too came home. "What a beauty was there!" she said. "The priest neither chanted nor read, but all the time looked at her—and just look at you, what a tatterdemalion you are!"

In the meantime the prince was traveling from one district to another, seeking the maiden who had lost her slipper, but he could not find anyone whom it fitted. He came to the old woman and said: "Call your young daughter hither; I want to see whether the slipper fits her." "My daughter will dirty the slipper," answered the old woman. The maiden came and the king's son tried the slipper on her: it fitted. He married her and they lived happily and prospered.

I drank beer at their wedding; it ran down my lips, but never went into my mouth. I was given a flowing robe to wear, but a raven flew over me and cawed: "Flowing robe! Flowing robe!" I thought he was crying: "Throw the robe!" So I threw it away. I asked for a cap but received a slap. I was given red slippers, but the raven flew over me and cawed: "Red slippers! Red slippers!" I thought he was crying: "Robbed slippers!" So I threw them away.

EMELYA THE SIMPLETON

ONCE THERE WERE three brothers of whom two were wise and the third a simpleton. The wise brothers went to buy merchandise in the towns and told the simpleton: "Now mind, simpleton! Obey our wives and respect them as you would your own mother. We shall buy you red boots, a red caftan, and a red shirt in return." The simpleton said: "Very well, I will respect them." Having thus instructed the simpleton, the brothers went to the towns and the simpleton lay down on the stove and stayed there. His sisters-in-law said to him: "What are you doing, simpleton? Your brothers told you to respect us and promised to bring you gifts in return,

46

but you are lying on the stove and doing no work at all; at least go and fetch water."

The simpleton took the pails and went to fetch water. He drew water, and a pike got into one of the pails. The simpleton said: "Thanks be to God! Now I shall cook this pike, I shall eat my fill, and I will not give any to my sisters-in-law, for I am angry at them." The pike said to him with the voice of a man: "Simpleton, do not eat me; put me back into the water, and you will be happy!" The simpleton asked: "What happiness will you give me?" "This happiness I'll give: whatever you say will come to pass. For instance, say now: 'By the pike's command, by my own request, go, pails, go home by yourselves, and stand in your accustomed place.'"

As soon as the simpleton said this, the pails straightway went home and stood in their place. The sisters-in-law beheld this and marveled. "He is not a simpleton at all," they said. "He is so clever that his pails have come home by themselves and stand in their place!" Then the simpleton came home and lay down on the stove. Again his sisters-in-law said to him: "Why do you lie on the stove, simpleton? We have no wood. Go and fetch wood!" The simpleton took two axes, sat in the sled, but did not harness the horses to it. "By the pike's command, by my own request," he said, "roll, sled, into the woods!"

The sled rolled speedily forward as though someone were driving it with a horse. The simpleton had to drive through the town, and without a horse he ran over so many people that it was a disaster. Everyone cried: "Stop him, catch him!" But they could not catch him. The simpleton entered the woods, got off his sled, sat down on a tree trunk, and said: "Let one ax cut from the root, let the other ax chop wood!" And the wood was chopped and loaded on the sled. The simpleton said: "Now, ax, go and cut a stick for me, so that I will have something to lift the load with." The ax cut a stick for him; the stick came and lay on the sled. The simpleton sat in the sled and drove homeward. He passed through the town, but there the people had assembled to wait for him; they caught him and began to belabor him. The simpleton said: "By the pike's command, by my own request, go, stick, and take care of this mob!"

The stick jumped up and set about hitting and thrashing to left and to right, till it had beaten up a great multitude of people, who fell to the ground like sheaves of grain. Thus the simpleton got rid of them and came home, stacked up the wood, and sat on the stove.

Now the inhabitants of the town went to the king with a petition against him. "He should be seized," they said. "He must be lured by a stratagem, and best of all would be to promise him a red shirt, a red caftan, and red boots." The king's messengers came to the simpleton. "Go to the king," they said, "he will give you red boots, a red caftan, and a red shirt." The simpleton said: "By the pike's command, by my own request, stove, go to the king!" He sat on the stove, and the stove went. The simpleton arrived at the king's. The king wanted to put him to death, but his daughter conceived a great liking for the simpleton and began to beg her father to let her marry him. Her father grew angry, wedded them, and had them both put in a barrel. Then he had the barrel covered with pitch and thrown into the sea.

For a long time the barrel sailed on the water. Finally the simpleton's wife asked him: "Make that we be thrown out on the shore." The simpleton said: "By the pike's command, by my own request, let this barrel be thrown on the shore and broken to pieces." They climbed out of the barrel, and now the simpleton's wife asked him to build some kind of hut. The simpleton said: "By the pike's command, by my own request, let a marble palace be built, and let this palace be right opposite the king's palace!" All this was accomplished at once; next morning the king saw the new palace and sent someone to find out who was living in it. As soon as he heard that his daughter was living there, he demanded that she and her husband appear before him. They came; the king forgave them, and they began to live happily together and to prosper.

THE THREE KINGDOMS

O NCE UPON A TIME there lived an old man with his old
wife. They had three sons—Egorushko the Nimble,
Mishka the Bandy-legged, and Ivashko Lie-on-the-
Stove. Their father and mother wanted to marry them off. They
sent their eldest son to find a bride for himself. He walked and
walked for a long time; wherever he looked at the girls, he
could not choose a bride for himself, because none was to his
liking.

Then he met a three-headed dragon on the road and was
frightened. The dragon said to him: "Where are you going, my
good fellow?" Egorushko answered: "I have set out to get
married, but I cannot find a bride." The dragon said: "Come
with me; I will lead you. We shall see whether you can get a
bride." They walked and walked, until they came to a big
stone. The dragon said: "Turn up the stone; there you will get
what you wish." Egorushko tried to turn it up, but could not
move it. The dragon said to him: "There is no bride for you!"
Egorushko returned home and told his father and mother what
had happened.

Again the father and mother pondered over what they should
do, and then sent their middle son, Mishka the Bandy-legged,
to find a bride. The same thing happened to him. The old man
and his old wife thought and thought and wondered what to
do; for if they sent Ivashko Lie-on-the-Stove, he surely would
not accomplish anything!

However, Ivashko Lie-on-the-Stove began to beg for a chance
to have a look at the dragon. His father and mother at first
would not let him go, but later they consented. Ivashko too
walked and walked, and met the three-headed dragon. The
dragon asked him: "Whither are you going, my good fellow?"
Ivashko answered: "My brothers wanted to get married but
could not find a bride; now it is my turn." "Come with me,
then; I will show you whether you can get a bride." And so the
dragon went along with Ivashko and they came to the same

stone, and the dragon told him to turn up the stone from its place. Ivashko took hold of it, and the stone rolled off. There was a hole in the ground, and near it some thongs were fixed. The dragon said: "Ivashko, sit on the thongs; I will lower you, then you will come to three kingdoms, and in each of them you will see a maiden."

Ivashko was lowered, and started on his way. He walked and walked, until he came to the copper kingdom. He entered it and saw a beautiful maiden. She said: "Welcome, rare guest! Come in and sit down where you see a smooth place, and tell me whence you come and whither you are going." "Ah, fair maiden," said Ivashko, "you have not given me food nor drink, yet you ask me questions." The maiden placed all sorts of food and drink on the table; Ivashko ate and drank and told her that he was seeking a bride for himself. "And if I find favor with you," he said, "please be my wife." "No, my good man," said the maiden. "Travel on still farther. Then you will come to the silver kingdom; there lives a maiden even more beautiful than I." And she gave him a silver ring. The gallant youth thanked the maiden for her hospitality, said farewell to her, and went on.

He walked and walked and came to the silver kingdom. He entered it and saw a maiden even more beautiful than the first. He asked a blessing and made obeisance: "I salute you, fair maiden!" She answered: "Welcome, strange youth! Sit down and boast about who you are, and whence and for what business you have come here." "Ah, fair maiden," said Ivashko, "you have not given me food nor drink, yet you are asking me questions." The maiden set the table and brought all kinds of food and drink; Ivashko ate and drank as much as he wanted, then told her that he had set out to find a bride and asked her to be his wife. She said to him: "Go on still farther; beyond there is a golden kingdom, and in it lives a maiden even more beautiful than I." And she gave him a golden ring. Ivashko said farewell to her and went on.

He walked and walked, and came to the golden kingdom. He entered it and saw a maiden more beautiful than the others. So he asked a blessing and saluted the maiden, as is becoming.

The maiden began to ask him whence he came and whither he was going. "Ah, fair maiden," said he, "you have not given me food nor drink, yet you ask me questions." So she put all kinds of food and drink on the table, the best imaginable. Ivashko Lie-on-the-Stove treated himself amply to everything, and began to tell his story: "I am on my way to find a bride. If you wish to be my wife, come with me." The maiden consented, and gave him a golden ball. They set out together. They walked and walked, and came to the silver kingdom; there they took the maiden with them; and again they walked and walked, and came to the copper kingdom; there, too, they took the maiden. Then all of them went to the hole from which they had to climb out, and they found the thongs hanging there. And the elder brothers were already standing by the hole, about to climb into it to find Ivashko.

Now Ivashko seated the maiden from the copper kingdom on the thongs and shook them; the brothers pulled and lifted out the maiden, and lowered the thongs again. Then Ivashko seated the maiden from the silver kingdom, and the brothers pulled her out, and sent down the thongs. Finally he seated the maiden from the golden kingdom, and the brothers pulled her out too, and dropped back the thongs. Ivashko now seated himself on them; his brothers pulled him too, pulled and pulled, but when they saw that it was Ivashko, they thought: "If we pull him out he might refuse to give us a maiden." And they cut the thongs, and Ivashko fell down. Well, there was nothing he could do; he wept and wept, and then went on. He walked and walked, and this is what he saw. On a tree trunk sat an old man as big as an inch, with a beard a cubit long. Ivashko told him everything that had happened to him, and how. The old man instructed him to go farther. "You will come to a little house," he said, "and in the house there lies a man so tall that he stretches from corner to corner, and you must ask him how to get to Russia."

So Ivashko walked and walked, and came to the little house; he entered it and said: "Mighty giant, do not kill me. Tell me how to get to Russia." "Fie, fie!" said the giant. "No one asked these Russian bones to come here; they have come by themselves. Well, go beyond thirty lakes. There a little house stands on a chicken leg, and in the house lives Baba Yaga. She has an eagle, and he will take you out."

The good youth walked and walked, and came to the little house. He entered it, and Baba Yaga cried: "Fie, fie, fie! Russian bones, why have you come here?" Then Ivashko said: "Little grandmother, I came by order of the mighty giant to ask for your powerful eagle, that he might take me up to Russia." "Go to the garden," said Baba Yaga. "At the gate there stands a sentry. Take the keys from him and go beyond seven doors. As you open the last door, the eagle will flutter his wings, and if you are not frightened by him, sit on him and fly. Only take some meat with you, and each time he looks back, give him a piece." Ivashko did as Baba Yaga told him. He sat on the eagle and off they flew. They flew and flew; the eagle looked back, and Ivashko gave him a piece of meat. They flew and flew, and he gave meat to the eagle often; and now he had given the eagle all the meat he had, and there was still a long distance to fly. The eagle looked back, and there was no meat; so the eagle plucked a piece of flesh from Ivashko's shoulder, ate it, and dragged him out through the same hole to Russia. When Ivashko got down off the eagle, the eagle spat out the piece of flesh and told him to put it back into his shoulder. Ivashko did so, and his shoulder healed. He came home, took the maiden of the golden kingdom from his brothers, and they began to live happily together and are still living. I was at their wedding and drank beer. The beer ran along my mustache but did not go into my mouth.

THE PIKE
WITH THE LONG TEETH

THE NIGHT BEFORE St. John's a pike was born in the
Sheksna River, a pike with teeth so long that God preserve us from any such! Shad, perch, flounder—all assembled to stare and marvel at this wonder. At the time of the
birth, the water in the Sheksna became agitated, a ferryboat
sailing across it almost sank, and some lovely maidens who
were taking a walk on the riverbank scattered. Such a long-
toothed pike was he! And he began to grow not by the day, but
by the hour; with every day that passed, an inch was added
to his size. And the pike with the long teeth began to roam
about the Sheksna catching shad and perch. He would sight a
shad from afar, snatch him with his teeth, and the shad was
as good as gone; only his bones crackled between the pike's
long teeth. Such was the marvelous happening in the Sheksna.

Now what could the shad and perch do? They were very
sad: if things went on like this, the pike would eat them all,
wipe them out. So all the small fry gathered together and debated about how to get rid of that ravenous pike with the long
teeth. To the meeting also came Perch Perchson, who held
forth in a loud voice: "Stop pondering, racking your wits, and
cudgeling your brains. Listen to what I have to say. All of us
in the Sheksna are now sorely tried. The pike with the long
teeth gives us no rest: he gobbles up all kinds of fish. There's
no life for us any more in the Sheksna! Let us move to smaller
rivers, to the Sizma, the Konoma, and the Slavenka. There no
one will bother us, and we'll live happily and beget children."
So all the shad, flounder, and perch left the Sheksna for the
smaller rivers, for the Sizma, the Konoma, and the Slavenka.
On the way, as they swam, a cunning fisherman caught many
of them on his line. He cooked a savory fish soup, and, it
appears, ate it on a fast day. From that time on, almost no small
fry has been found in the Sheksna. A fisherman can cast his

line into the water and pull out nothing; once in a while he gets a little sterlet—nothing else. And that is the whole story of the ravenous pike with the long teeth. That rascal caused a lot of trouble in the Sheksna, but later he came to a bad end himself. When there was no small fry left, he went after worms and got caught on a hook. The fisherman made a fish soup out of him, ate it, and praised it highly, for the flesh of the pike was quite succulent. I was there and ate the soup with him; it ran down my mustache but never got into my mouth.

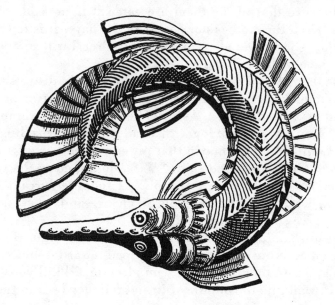

THE BAD WIFE

THERE WAS ONCE a bad wife who made life impossible for her husband and disobeyed him in everything. If he told her to rise early, she slept for three days; if he told her to sleep, she did not sleep at all. If her husband asked her to make pancakes, she said: "You don't deserve pancakes, you scoundrel!" If her husband said, "Don't make pancakes, wife, since I don't deserve them," she made an enormous panful, two whole gallons of pancakes, and said: "Now eat, scoundrel, and be sure that all of them are eaten!" If he said, "Wife, do not wash the clothes nor go out to cut hay—it is too much for you," she answered: "No, you scoundrel, I will go and you shall come with me."

One day, after a quarrel with her, he went in distress to the woods to pick berries, found a currant bush, and saw a bottomless pit in the middle of it. As he looked at it, he thought to himself: "Why do I go on living with a bad wife and struggling with her? Could I not put her in that pit and teach her a lesson?" He went back home and said: "Wife, do not go to the woods for berries." "I shall go, you fool!" "I found a currant bush, don't pick it!" "I shall go and pick it clean—and, what is more, I won't give you any currants!"

The husband went out and his wife followed him. He came to the currant bush and his wife jumped toward it and yelled: "Don't go into that bush, you scoundrel, or I'll kill you!" She herself went into the middle of it, and fell plop!—into the bottomless pit.

The husband went home happily and lived there in peace for three days; on the fourth day he went to see how his wife was getting along. He took a long towrope, let it down into the pit, and dragged out a little imp. He was frightened and was about to drop him back into the pit, when the imp began to shriek and then said imploringly: "Peasant, do not put me back, let me out into the world. A bad wife has come into our pit—she torments, bites, and pinches all of us, we are sick to

56

death of her. If you let me out, I will do you a good turn!"
So the peasant let him go free in holy Russia. The imp said:
"Well, peasant, let us go to the town of Vologda; I will make
people sick and you shall cure them."

Now the imp set to work on merchants' wives and daughters;
he would enter into them and they would go mad and fall ill.
Our peasant would go to the house of the sick woman; the imp
would leave, a blessing would come on the house; everyone
thought that the peasant was a doctor, gave him money, and
fed him pies. The peasant thus amassed an uncountable sum
of money. Then the imp said to him: "You now have plenty,
peasant. Are you satisfied? Next I shall enter a boyar's daughter, and mind you do not come to cure her, else I shall eat
you."

The boyar sent for the peasant, the famous "doctor." He
came to the boyar's beautiful house and told him to have all
the townspeople and all the carriages and coachmen gather in
the street in front of the house; he gave orders that all the
coachmen should crack their whips and cry aloud: "The bad
wife has come, the bad wife has come!" Then he went into the
sick maiden's room. When he came in, the imp was enraged at
him and said: "Why have you come here, Russian man?
Now I will eat you!" He said: "What do you mean? I have not
come to drive you out, but to warn you that the bad wife is
here!" The imp jumped on the window sill, stared fixedly, and
listened intently. He heard all the crowd in the street cry in
one voice: "The bad wife has come!" "Peasant," said the imp,
"where shall I hide?" "Return to the pit; she won't go there
again!" The imp went there and joined the bad wife. The boyar
rewarded the peasant by giving him half his possessions and
his daughter in marriage; but the bad wife to this day sits in the
pit in nether darkness.

THE MISER

T HERE WAS ONCE a wealthy merchant named Marka, and never was anyone so stingy as he! One day he went for a walk; on his way he saw an old beggar asking for alms: "For Christ's sake, pious men, give me something!" Marka the Wealthy passed him by. But a poor peasant who followed him felt pity for the beggar and gave him a kopek. The rich man felt ashamed, stopped, and said to the peasant: "Listen, fellow countryman, lend me a kopek. I want to give something to the beggar, but I have no small coins." The peasant gave him a kopek and asked: "When shall I come to collect my loan?" "Come tomorrow." The next day the poor man went to the rich man for his kopek. He entered the broad courtyard. "Is Marka the Wealthy at home?" "He is. What do you want?" asked Marka. "I have come for my kopek." "Ah brother, come some other time, I have no small coins now." The poor man bowed low and said: "I will come tomorrow." The following day he came and again was told: "I have no small coins, but if you have change for a hundred rubles, you can get your kopek. If not, come in two weeks." Two weeks later, the poor man again went to the rich man. When Marka the Wealthy saw him through the window, he said to his wife: "Listen, wife, I will undress completely and lie under the icons; and you cover me with a shroud and sit down and lament me as though I were dead. When the peasant comes for his loan, tell him that I died today."

The wife did as her husband ordered her; she sat down and shed burning tears. The peasant came into the room, and she asked: "What is it?" "I have come to collect my loan from Marka the Wealthy," answered the poor man. "Ah, little peasant, Marka the Wealthy wished you a long life; he has just died!" "May he go to the kingdom of heaven! Permit me, hostess, to do something for him for my kopek—at least I can wash his sinful body." Saying this, he snatched a kettle of boiling water and poured it over Marka the Wealthy. Marka could barely stand it; he gritted his teeth and jerked his feet. "I don't care whether you jerk. Give me back my kopek!" said the poor man. He washed the body and prepared it for burial. "Now, hostess, buy a coffin and have it taken to the church; I will read the psalter over him." Marka the Wealthy was put in a coffin and taken to the church, and the peasant began to read the psalter over him.

Dark night came. Suddenly a window opened and thieves broke into the church; the peasant hid behind the altar. The thieves began to share the spoils among them. They shared everything; only a golden saber remained, and each one wanted it for himself and refused to yield it to the others. The poor man suddenly jumped out and cried: "Why do you quarrel? Whoever cuts off the dead man's head shall have the saber!" At this Marka the Wealthy jumped up, beside himself with fear. The thieves were frightened, threw away their money, and took to their heels. "Now, little peasant," said Marka, "let us share the money." They shared it evenly; both of them got a great deal. "And how about my kopek?" said the poor man. "Eh, brother! You can see for yourself, I have no small coins!" And so Marka the Wealthy never returned the kopek.

THE NOBLEMAN
AND THE PEASANT

ONE DAY A NOBLEMAN went to market and bought a canary for fifty rubles. A peasant happened to see this, and when he came home he told his wife: "Imagine, today I was at the market and I saw the *barin* buying a small bird for fifty rubles. I will take my gander to him, perhaps he will buy that." "Take it." The peasant brought his gander to the nobleman. "*Barin*, buy this gander." "How much is it?" asked the nobleman. "A hundred rubles!" "You idiot!" "Since you were willing to pay fifty rubles for a small bird, a hundred is cheap for this one!" The nobleman flew into a rage, beat the peasant, and took his gander for nothing. "Very well," said the peasant, "you will remember this gander."

He returned home, disguised himself as a mason, took a saw and ax, and went by the nobleman's house, crying: "Who wants a warm vestibule built?" The nobleman heard him, called him in, and asked: "How will you do it?" "It's very simple. Near here are warm trees; a vestibule built of those warm trees does not have to be heated in winter." "Ah, brother," said the nobleman, "show me those trees at once." "With pleasure."

Both of them went to the woods. There the peasant cut an enormous pine tree and began to slice it into two halves; he cut the tree lengthwise and began to drive in a wedge. The nobleman watched him for a while and then foolishly thrust his hand into the cut. No sooner had he done this than the peasant pulled out the wedge and the nobleman's hand was firmly caught. Then the peasant took a leather strap and began to thrash the nobleman, repeating: "Don't beat a peasant, don't take his gander! Don't beat a peasant, don't take his gander!" He thrashed to his heart's delight and said: "Well, *barin*, I have beaten you once, and I will beat you again unless you return my gander and add a hundred rubles into the bargain." Having said this he left, and the nobleman stayed in the woods till nightfall. In the end his family became worried, but much time went by before they found him and freed him from the vise.

The nobleman fell ill, he lay on his bed and moaned. The peasant picked herbs and flowers, stuck them all over himself, disguised himself as a doctor, and once again went near the nobleman's courtyard, crying: "Does someone need curing?" The nobleman heard him, called him in, and said: "Who are you?" "I am a doctor, I can cure every illness." "Ah, brother, please cure me." "Certainly. Have a bath heated." Straightway a bath was heated. "Now come to be cured," said the peasant to the nobleman. "Only don't take anyone with us to the bathroom—watch out for the evil eye!" They went to the bathroom

60

and the nobleman undressed. "Well, sir," asked the doctor, "can you bear it if in this heat I apply ointment to you?" "No, I can't," said the nobleman. "What shall we do then? Do you want to be tied?" "Please tie me." The peasant tied him with a rope, took a whip, and began to drub and pommel him, repeating: "Don't beat a peasant, don't take his gander! Don't beat a peasant, don't take his gander!" When he was about to leave, he said: "Now, *barin,* I have beaten you twice; I shall beat you a third time unless you return the gander and two hundred rubles into the bargain." The nobleman got out of his bath more dead than alive, decided not to wait for a third time, and sent the peasant the gander and two hundred rubles.

THE GOAT COMES BACK

BILLY GOAT, billy goat, where have you been?
I was grazing horses.
And where are the horses?
Nikolka led them away.

And where is Nikolka?
> *He went to the larder.*

And where is the larder?
> *It was flooded with water.*

And where is the water?
> *The oxen drank it.*

And where are the oxen?
> *They went to the mountain.*

And where is the mountain?
> *The worms gnawed it away.*

And where are the worms?
> *The geese ate them all.*

And where are the geese?
> *They went to the junipers.*

And where are the junipers?
> *The maids broke them.*

And where are the maids?
> *They all got married.*

And where are their husbands?
> *They all died.*

IVANUSHKO

THE LITTLE FOOL

ONCE UPON A TIME there lived an old man and his old wife. They had three sons: the two older ones were clever, but the third was called Ivanushko the Little Fool. The clever brothers grazed sheep in the field, but the fool did nothing at all; the whole day long he sat on the stove, catching flies. One day the old woman prepared some rye dumplings and said to the fool: "Here are some dumplings, take them to your brothers for their dinner." She filled a pot with the dumplings, and he took it and lumbered off to find his brothers. It was a sunny day; when Ivanushko came out on the road, he saw his shadow at his side and thought: "Who is this man? He walks by my side and does not leave me for an instant; surely he wants some dumplings." He began to throw dumplings at his shadow, and one after another threw them all away, but the shadow still kept walking at his side. "What an insatiable glutton," said the fool angrily and hurled his pot at the shadow—and the shards flew in all directions.

He came empty-handed to his brothers. They asked him: "Why have you come here, fool?" "I have brought your dinner." "Where is it? Give it to us at once." "Well you see, brothers, a stranger followed me all the way here, and he ate it all up." "What stranger?" "Here he is! Even now he is standing by my side." The brothers began to swear at him and thrash him; having thrashed him, they told him to tend the sheep, and themselves went home to have their dinner in the village.

The little fool set about tending the sheep; seeing that they scattered all over the field, he decided to gather them together and tear out their eyes. He herded them in a little spot, plucked out the eyes of every one of them, made them huddle together in a heap, and sat there as happy as a lark; he thought that he had done something worth while. The brothers ate their dinner and returned to the field. "You fool, what kind of mess have you made here? Why is the flock blinded?" "What do they need their eyes for, brothers? When you went away, they scattered everywhere, so I thought it would be a good idea to catch them, gather them together, and pluck out their eyes. It was a lot of work and it made me quite tired." "Just wait, we'll show you what it means to be tired," said the brothers, and began to belabor him with their fists; the fool was well rewarded for his trouble.

Some time passed, not much, not little. One day the old parents sent Ivanushko the Little Fool to town to buy provisions for the holidays. Ivanushko bought many things—a table and spoons and cups and salt. He loaded a whole cart with objects of every description. He started to drive home, but his horse, it seems, was not quite strong enough for this heavy load and walked rather slowly. Ivanushko thought to himself: "After all, the table has four legs, just like the horse; why shouldn't it run home by itself?" So he put the table out on the road. He drove on, a long distance or a short distance, and the ravens circled over him cawing and cawing. "The little sisters must be hungry, else why would they cry like that?" thought the fool, and put out dishes with victuals to treat the ravens. "Eat, little sisters, you're welcome," he said. And he rattled on slowly.

Ivanushko drove through a wood of young trees; along the road was a row of burned-down trunks. "Ah," he thought, "the poor boys have no caps, they'll catch a cold that way." So he put his earthen pots and crocks on them. Then Ivanushko came to a river. He set about watering his horse, but it refused to drink. "Probably he doesn't want water without salt," he thought, and began to salt the river. He poured out a whole bag of salt, and the horse still refused to drink. "Why don't you drink, you old carcass—have I poured out a whole bag of salt for nothing?" he said, and he struck the horse with a log right on its head and killed it on the spot. Now all Ivanushko had left was a bag of spoons, which he slung over his shoulder. He walked, and the spoons behind him kept rattling—tra-ta-ta-tam, tra-ta-ta-tam, tra-ta-ta-tam! He thought that the spoons were saying: "Ivanushko's a fool!" So he threw them down and trampled upon them, repeating: "That'll teach you to call me a fool! Don't you dare taunt me, you wicked things!"

He returned home and said: "I bought everything we need, little brothers." "Thanks, little fool, but where are your purchases?" "The table is coming, but apparently it is late. Our little sisters, the ravens, are eating from the dishes. The pots and crocks I put on the boys' heads in the woods. I used the salt to season the horse's water, and the spoons taunted me, so I dropped them on my way." "Hurry, fool, go gather everything you have scattered on the road." Ivanushko went to the woods, removed the pots from the burned trunks, knocked out their bottoms, and strung a dozen of them, small and big, on a rope. When he brought them home, his brothers thrashed him, went to town themselves to make their purchases, and left him at home. He listened and heard the beer in the tub brewing and brewing. "Beer, stop brewing, don't tease the fool!" said Ivanushko. But the beer did not heed him; so he let it all out of the tub, sat in the trough, and drove around the room singing little songs to himself.

When the brothers returned, they were terribly angry. They seized Ivanushko, sewed him up in a sack, and dragged him to the river. They set the sack down on the shore and went to find a hole in the ice. Just then a nobleman happened to drive by in a carriage drawn by three gray horses, and Ivanushko began to shout: "I've been appointed governor, to rule and to judge, but I know neither how to rule nor how to judge." "Wait, you fool," said the nobleman, "I know how to rule and to judge. Creep out of that sack!" Ivanushko crept out, sewed up the nobleman, sat in his carriage, and drove out of sight. The brothers came, dropped the sack under the ice, and the water made a sound like "gray-gray-gray." "He must be trying to catch a fish," said the brothers, and set out for home. As though from nowhere, Ivanushko appeared before them driving a troika and bragging: "See the horses I caught? There's still one gray horse left, a real jewel!" The brothers became envious and said to the fool: "Sew us up in the sack and drop us quickly into the hole. We'll get the gray." Ivanushko the Little Fool dropped them in the hole and drove home to drink beer to honor the memory of his dead brothers. Ivanushko had a well; in this well was a bell; and that's all I have to tell.

THE CRANE
AND THE HERON

THERE ONCE WAS an owl, a merry bird was she. She flew
and flew, perched on a tree, wiggled her tail, rolled
her eyes, and took wing again. She flew and flew,
perched on a tree, wiggled her tail and rolled her eyes. . . .
But that's the flourish, just for fun; the real tale has not
begun!

Once upon a time a crane and a heron lived in a bog; they
had little huts, one at each end of it. The crane grew weary of
living alone and decided to marry: "I will go woo the heron!"
The crane set out—flap, flap!—and he flapped over the bog
for seven versts. Finally he arrived and asked: "Is the heron
at home?" "She is." "Heron, be my wife." "No, crane, I will
not be your wife; your legs are too long, your clothes are too
short, your flying is poor, and you cannot support me. Go
away, you spindleshanks!"

The crane returned home with a long face. Later the heron
changed her mind and thought to herself: "Why should I live
alone? It would be better to marry the crane!" She came to
him and said: "Crane, take me to wife." "No, heron, I don't
need you. I don't want to get married and I don't take you to
wife. Get out!"

The heron wept for shame and went home. The crane
changed his mind and thought to himself: "I was wrong not to
marry the heron; it is wearisome to live alone. I will go now
and take her to wife." He came and said: "Heron, I have decided to marry you; be my wife." "No, crane, I won't be your
wife!"

So the crane went home. Then the heron changed her mind
and thought: "Why did I refuse him? What good is it to live
alone? I'd rather marry the crane!" So she came to propose,
and this time the crane refused. And to this very day they go
to each other to propose, but never get married.

66

ALIOSHA POPOVICH

IN THE HEAVENS a bright new moon was born, and on earth, in the house of Leonti, the old priest of the cathedral, a son, a mighty hero. He was named Aliosha Popovich, a fine name. He was given meat and drink, and in one day he grew as much as other babes in a week; in one week he was as others at the end of a year. Soon he began to walk in the streets and to play with other little children. If he grasped someone by the arm, the arm came off; if he grasped someone by the leg, the leg came off; terrible were his games. If he took a man by the body, he pulled off his belly. Then Aliosha came of age and asked his father and mother to give him their blessing and their permission to try his luck in the field of battle. His father answered: "Aliosha Popovich, you are going into the field of battle; there are mightier men than you on this earth; therefore, take Maryshko Paranov's son as your faithful servant." So the brave knights mounted their good steeds; and as they rode off into the great world, a pillar of dust smoked behind them, and they were gone.

Soon the brave knights came to the realm of Prince Vladimir. Aliosha Popovich went straight to the prince's white stone palace, crossed himself as is prescribed, and bowed, as he had been taught, to all four sides, and to Prince Vladimir in addition. Prince Vladimir welcomed them, bade them sit down at the oaken table, and gave them meat and drink before he questioned them. They ate marvelous gingerbreads, washing them down with heady wines. Then Prince Vladimir asked them: "Who are you, brave youths? Are you bold and mighty heroes, or chance travelers, untrustworthy persons? I know neither your names nor your fathers' names." Aliosha Popovich answered: "I am the son of Leonti, the old priest of the cathedral, and my name is Aliosha Popovich; here by my side is my servant, Maryshko Paranov's son." When he had eaten and drunk his fill, Aliosha Popovich went to the brick stove to rest, for it was after midday, but Maryshko Paranov's son remained seated at the table.

At that time Tugarin Zmeevich, Son of the Dragon, a mighty champion, invaded and scourged Prince Vladimir's kingdom. Tugarin Zmeevich came to Prince Vladimir's white stone palace; with one stride of his left leg he crossed the threshold; with one stride of his right leg he reached the oaken table; he ate and drank and embraced the princess. He made mock of Prince Vladimir; he put one loaf of bread in one cheek, and another in the other cheek, and then he put a whole swan on his tongue, pushed it in with a pancake, and swallowed everything in one gulp.

Aliosha, who was lying on the brick stove, spoke these words to Tugarin Zmeevich: "My father, the old priest Leonti, once had a big cow, a gluttonous cow that went from brewery to brewery and drank whole barrels of beer and their dregs. Then this big cow, this gluttonous cow, went to a lake and drank all the water from it, and suddenly she burst—and so may you, Tugarin Zmeevich, burst at this table!" Tugarin became enraged at Aliosha Popovich and hurled a steel knife at him, but Aliosha Popovich was quick and dodged behind an oaken pillar. Then Aliosha spoke these words: "Thanks, Tugarin Zmeevich, mighty champion, for giving me thy steel knife, with it I will cut open thy white breast, dim thy bright eyes, and behold thy fiery heart."

As Aliosha said these words, Maryshko Paranov's son jumped from behind the oaken table onto his nimble feet, grabbed Tugarin by the neck, pulled him from the table, and hurled him against the white wall. The glass windows were shattered in splinters. Aliosha Popovich spoke up from the brick stove: "O you, Maryshko Paranov's son, faithful and devoted servant!" Maryshko Paranov's son answered: "Give me the steel knife, Aliosha Popovich; I will cut open Tugarin's white breast, dim his bright eyes, and behold his fiery heart." Aliosha answered from the brick stove: "O Maryshko Paranov's son, do not befoul this white stone palace. Let him go into the open field; there we shall meet him tomorrow and give him battle."

Next day Maryshko Paranov's son rose at the very break of dawn and led the spirited horses out to drink water at the swift-flowing stream. Tugarin, the dragon's son, flew through the air and challenged Aliosha Popovich to come to the open field. And Maryshko Paranov's son came to Aliosha Popovich saying: "God be thy judge, Aliosha Popovich, that thou gavest me not the steel knife; I would have cut open this knave's white breast, I would have dimmed his bright eyes and beheld his fiery heart. Now what will you take from this Tugarin? He is flying through the air." Aliosha spoke these words: "If I do not triumph, heaven is betrayed."

Aliosha brought forth his good steed, saddled him with a Circassian saddle, tightened it with twelve silken girths, not for beauty's sake, but for strength, and went to the open field. He rode all around it and beheld Tugarin Zmeevich flying through the air. And Aliosha Popovich made this prayer: "Holy Mother of God, send me a black cloud, and send a pelting rain from the black cloud to wet Tugarin's paper wings!" Aliosha's prayer reached heaven; a threatening black cloud rolled over the sky, from it God made a heavy pelting rain to fall, and Tugarin's paper wings wilted; he fell to the damp earth and rode into the open field.

Like two mountains rolling together, so did Tugarin and Aliosha meet. They clashed with their maces; the maces broke at the handles. They clashed with their spears; the spears twisted on their staves. They swung their sabers; the sabers broke. Aliosha fell from his saddle like a sheaf of oats, and Tugarin Zmeevich began to smite him, but Aliosha was quick and dodged under the horse's belly. Then he crawled out from under the horse's belly on the other side and struck Tugarin with his knife under the right breast, and threw him down from his good steed, and began to shout at him: "Thanks, Tugarin Zmeevich, for thy steel knife; I will cut open thy white breast, I will dim thy bright eyes, I will behold thy fiery heart."

And Aliosha cut off Tugarin's rash head, and carried it to Prince Vladimir. He rode and he played with the head, tossing it high in the air and catching it on the tip of his spear. Look-

70

ing from afar, Vladimir took fright. "Behold Tugarin carrying Aliosha's rash head!" he said. "Now in sooth he will enslave our Christian kingdom!" Maryshko Paranov's son answered: "Grieve not, Vladimir, our little red sun, our prince of the capital city of Kiev! If the foul Tugarin rides on the ground and flies not through the air, he will lose his rash head by my steel spear. Be not distressed, Prince Vladimir. When the time comes, I shall fight him."

Then Maryshko Paranov's son looked into the spyglass and recognized Aliosha Popovich. "I know him by his mighty gait and his heroic posture," he said. "It is Aliosha turning his steed sharply, tossing the head high and catching it on the tip of his spear. It is not the foul Tugarin riding yonder, but Aliosha Popovich, the son of Leonti, the old priest of the cathedral. And on his spear he carries the head of the foul Tugarin Zmeevich."

THE FOX CONFESSOR

LISTEN TO THIS amazing story. A fox was coming from
distant deserts and saw a cock perched on a tall tree.
She spoke to him kindly: "O chanticleer, my beloved
child! You are sitting on a tall tree and thinking thoughts
that are evil and accursed. You cocks keep many wives: some
of you have as many as ten of them, some twenty, some thirty,
with time their number reaches even forty! Whenever you
chance to meet, you fight over your wives and concubines.
Come down to the ground, my beloved child, and do penance.
I myself have been in distant deserts, I have not eaten nor
drunk and have suffered many hardships; and all the time I
longed to hear your confession, my beloved child." "O holy
mother fox, I have not fasted and I have not prayed; come some
other time." "O my beloved child, you have not fasted and
you have not prayed, but come down to the ground none the
less. Repent, else you will die in sin." "O holy mother fox,

your mouth is as honey, your words are kind, your tongue is sweet! 'Judge not, that ye be not judged'; what we have sown, that we shall reap. You want to bring me to repentance by force—not to save me, but to devour my body." "O chanticleer, my beloved child, why do you say such words? Have you read the parable of the publican and the Pharisee, in which the publican is saved, and the Pharisee perishes because of his pride? My beloved child, unless you repent you shall perish on your tall tree. Come down lower, then you will be closer to repentance; you will be pardoned and absolved and admitted to the kingdom of heaven."

The cock recognized the mortal sin in his soul; he was moved to tears and began to descend from branch to branch, from twig to twig and from stem to stem; he came down to the ground and sat in front of the fox. The fox, cunning beast that she was, jumped, gripped the cock in her sharp claws, glared at him with ferocious eyes, and gritted her sharp teeth, ready to devour him alive, the impious bird.

Quoth chanticleer to the fox: "O holy mother fox, your mouth is as honey, your words are kind, your tongue is sweet! But will you save me if you devour my body?" "I do not want your body nor your colored garment. I want to pay you back an old favor. Do you remember? Once as I was going to a peasant's house to eat a little chick, you, idle fool that you are, perched on a high roost, and wailed and shouted in an enormous voice. You began to stamp your feet and flap your wings; then the hens began to gabble, the geese began to cackle, the dogs began to bark, the stallions to neigh, and the cows to moo. Everyone on the place was aroused; the women came running with broomsticks and the men with axes. They wanted to kill me, all on account of that little chick—and yet an owl has been staying with them from generation to generation and always eats their chicks. No, you idle fool, you shall not escape alive!"

Quoth the cock: "O holy mother fox, your mouth is as honey, your words are kind, your tongue is sweet! Yesterday I was asked by the Trunchinsk metropolitan to be a deacon; I was praised before the whole choir and congregation as a handsome youth, respectable, eager for learning, and with a beautiful voice! Could I not persuade you by my entreaty, mother fox, to become at least my wafer woman? We shall profit greatly; we shall be given sweet cakes, great roasts, butter, eggs and cheeses."

The fox was moved by the cock's plea, and her hold on him weakened. The cock tore himself loose, flew up to the tall tree, and wailed and shouted in an enormous voice: "My dear Mrs. Wafer Baker, welcome! Is not the profit great, are not the wafers sweet? Have you not rubbed off your hump carrying the roasts? Wouldn't you gladly get to the nuts, little rascal? But have you enough teeth?"

The fox went into the woods, with a very long face, and lamented bitterly: "I have been all over the world, and nowhere have I seen anything so disgraceful. Since when are cocks deacons, and foxes wafer bakers?" So glory and power to the Lord for all time to come, and this is the end of our tale.

THE BEAR

ONCE THERE LIVED an old man and his old wife and they had no children. The old woman said to her husband: "Old man, go get some wood." He went and met a bear, who said: "Old man, let us fight." The old man took his ax and cut off one of the bear's paws. He returned home and said to his wife: "Old woman, cook the bear's paw." She removed the skin, placed it under her, and began to pluck out the fur while the paw was cooking on the stove. The bear roared and roared, then thought the matter over, and made himself a paw of lime tree wood. He hobbled on his wooden paw to the old man's house and sang:

74

Creak, my paw,
Creak, limewood!
The water sleeps,
And the earth sleeps,
The townsmen sleep,
The villagers sleep;
Only one woman is awake,
Sitting on my skin,
Spinning my fur,
Cooking my flesh!

The old man and his wife were terrified. He hid on the shelf and covered himself with a trough, and she hid on the stove and covered herself with some black shirts. The bear entered the room. From fear the old man groaned under the trough, and the old woman coughed under the black shirts. The bear found them and ate them.

THE SPIDER

IN DAYS OF YORE, in very, very olden times, one lovely spring, one hot summer, a great plague spread over the world: mosquitoes and midges in great swarms began to bite people and drink their blood. Then a spider came, a brave knight, and he began to twist his legs and weave his webs in the paths of the mosquitoes and the midges. A dirty fly fell into the spider's web, and the spider began to beat her, torment her, strangle her. The fly implored the spider: "Little father spider, do not beat me, do not kill me; I would leave behind many orphans who would fly into all the yards and annoy the dogs." The spider let her go. She flew away buzzing and announced to all the mosquitoes and midges: "Hey, you mosquitoes and midges, hide under the aspen tree root; a spider has come who

75

twists his legs and weaves his webs in the paths of mosquitoes and midges; he'll catch you all."

They flew away, hid under the aspen tree root, and lay as though dead. The spider called together a cricket, a beetle, and a wood bug: "You, cricket, sit on a cabbage and smoke a pipe of tobacco; you, beetle, beat a drum; and you, wood bug, go to the aspen tree root, and spread the news that I, the valiant spider, the brave knight, am no longer alive. Say that I was sent to Kazan, that in Kazan my head was cut off on the block and the block was cleft asunder." The cricket sat on a cabbage and smoked a pipe of tobacco; the beetle beat a drum, and the wood bug went to the aspen tree root, and said: "Why do you hide, why do you lie as though dead? The valiant spider, the brave knight, is no longer alive; he was sent to Kazan, and in Kazan his head was cut off on the block and the block was cleft asunder." They cheered and rejoiced, made the sign of the cross, flew away, and all fell into the spider's webs. He said: "You're nice little things! You should visit me more often, drink beer and wine, and treat yourselves fine!"

BABA YAGA
AND THE BRAVE YOUTH

ONCE UPON A TIME there lived a cat, a sparrow, and a brave youth. The cat and the sparrow went to the forest to chop wood and said to the brave youth: "You keep the house, but mind you: if Baba Yaga comes and counts the spoons, do not say a word, keep quiet!" "Very well," said the brave youth. The cat and the sparrow went away, and the brave youth sat on the stove behind the chimney. Suddenly Baba Yaga came in, took the spoons, and began to count them: "This is the cat's spoon, this is the sparrow's spoon, and this is the brave youth's spoon." The brave youth could not restrain himself and cried: "Baba Yaga, don't touch my spoon!" Baba Yaga seized the brave youth, sat on the mortar, and flew off; she drove the mortar, spurring it with the pestle and sweeping away her tracks with her broom. The brave youth shouted: "Cat, run! Sparrow, fly!" They heard him and rushed to his help. The cat began to scratch Baba Yaga and the sparrow to peck at her; thus they rescued the brave youth.

The next day the cat and the sparrow again prepared to go to the forest to chop wood, and told the brave youth: "Mind you, if Baba Yaga comes, do not say anything; today we are going far away." As soon as the brave youth had sat down on the stove behind the chimney, Baba Yaga came again, and again began to count the spoons: "This is the cat's spoon, this is the sparrow's spoon, and this is the brave youth's spoon." The brave youth could not restrain himself and shouted: "Baba Yaga, don't touch my spoon!" Baba Yaga seized the brave youth and dragged him along with her. The brave youth shouted: "Cat, run! Sparrow, fly!" They heard him and rushed to his help. The cat began to scratch and the sparrow to peck at Baba Yaga. Thus they rescued the brave youth. Then they all went home.

The third day the cat and the sparrow prepared once more to go to the forest and chop wood, and they said to the brave youth: "Mind you, if Baba Yaga comes, be silent; today we are going even farther." The cat and the sparrow left, and the brave youth sat on the stove behind the chimney. Suddenly Baba Yaga again took the spoons and began to count them: "This is the cat's spoon, this is the sparrow's spoon, this is the brave youth's spoon." The brave youth did not say a word. Baba Yaga counted again: "This is the cat's spoon, this is the sparrow's spoon, and this is the brave youth's spoon." The brave youth did not say a word. Baba Yaga counted a third time: "This is the cat's spoon, this is the sparrow's spoon, and this is the brave youth's spoon." The brave youth could not restrain himself any longer and cried loudly: "Don't touch my spoon!" Baba Yaga seized the brave youth and dragged him along with her. He cried: "Cat, run! Sparrow, fly!" But his brothers did not hear him. Baba Yaga took him home, put him in the wooden shed by the stove, made a fire in the stove, and said to her eldest daughter: "I am going to Russia. Meanwhile, roast this brave youth for my dinner." "Very well," said the daughter.

The stove grew hot and the girl told the brave youth to come out of the shed. He came out. "Lie down on the roasting pan," said the girl. He lay down, held up one of his feet so that it touched the ceiling, and put the other on the floor. The girl said: "Not that way, not that way!" The brave youth said: "How then? Show me." The girl lay down on the roasting pan. The brave youth quickly seized an oven fork, pushed the pan with Baba Yaga's daughter on it into the oven, and went back into the shed to wait for Baba Yaga. Suddenly she ran in and said: "Now I am going to feast and regale myself on the brave youth's bones!" The brave youth answered her: "Feast and regale yourself on your own daughter's bones!" Baba Yaga was startled and looked into the oven. She found her daughter all roasted, and roared: "Aha, you cheat, just wait, you won't get away!" She ordered her second daughter to roast the brave youth and went away.

Her second daughter made a fire in the stove and told the brave youth to come out. He came out, lay on the pan, put one foot on the ceiling and the other on the floor. The girl said: "Not that way, not that way!" "Show me how." The girl lay on the pan. The brave youth shoved her into the oven, went back to the shed, and sat there. Suddenly he heard Baba Yaga crying: "Now I am going to feast and regale myself on the brave youth's bones!" He answered: "Feast and regale yourself on your own daughter's bones!" Baba Yaga flew into a rage: "Eh," she said, "just wait, you won't get away!"

She ordered her youngest daughter to roast him, but to no avail; the brave youth shoved her into the oven too. Baba Yaga flew into an even greater rage: "Now," she said, "this time I swear you won't get away!" She made a fire in the stove and cried: "Come out, brave youth, lie on the pan!" He lay down, touched the ceiling with one foot, the floor with the other, and thus could not be got into the oven. Baba Yaga said: "Not that way, not that way!" And the brave youth still pretended that he did not know how. "I don't know how," he said. "Show me." Baba Yaga at once curled up and lay on the pan. The brave youth quickly shoved her into the oven, ran home, and said to his brothers: "That's what I did with Baba Yaga!"

PRINCE IVAN
AND PRINCESS MARTHA

FOR MANY YEARS a certain tsar had kept under lock and key a little peasant all made of copper, with iron hands and a steel head—a cunning man, a wizard of a man! Prince Ivan, the tsar's son who was still a little boy, walked by the prison. The old man called him and began to beg: "Prince Ivan, please give me a drink!" Prince Ivan did not know anything yet, he was very little, so he drew some water and gave it to him; with the help of the water the old man vanished from the prison. This was reported to the tsar, who ordered Prince Ivan to be driven from the kingdom. The tsar's word was law. Prince Ivan was banished and he left home not knowing where to go.

He walked for a long time; at last he arrived in another kingdom, presented himself to the king, and asked to be taken into his service. The king accepted him and appointed him stableboy. But all he did in the stable was sleep; he did not tend the horses, and the stable master beat him more than once. Prince Ivan bore all this patiently. Meanwhile another king had asked for the hand of this king's daughter, was rebuffed, and declared war. The king departed with his troops, and Princess Martha, his daughter, was left to rule the kingdom. Even before this she had noticed that Prince Ivan was not of lowly origin; now she appointed him governor of one of her provinces.

Prince Ivan left for his province and governed it. One day he went hunting; he had no sooner left the town than the peasant all made of copper, with iron hands and a steel head, appeared from nowhere. "Good day, Prince Ivan!" he said. Prince Ivan returned his greeting. The old man said: "Come, pay me a visit." They walked together. The old man led him into a rich house and called to his little daughter: "Hey, give us food and drink and a half-gallon cup of wine!" They began to eat; suddenly the daughter brought in a half-gallon cup of wine and presented it to Prince Ivan. He refused, saying: "I cannot drink all that!" The old man told him to try. The young prince took the cup and suddenly felt great strength in him; in one draught he drank all the wine. Then the old man asked him to go for a walk with him; they came to a stone that weighed about twenty thousand pounds. The old man said: "Lift that stone, Prince Ivan!" He thought: "I surely cannot lift that stone, but I will try." He picked it up, tossed it easily, and said to himself: "Whence comes all this new strength? Probably the old man has given it to me with the wine."

They walked some time, then returned home. The old man

told his second daughter to bring a gallon of wine. Prince Ivan boldly took the cup and drank it in one draught. Then again they went for a walk and came to a stone that weighed forty thousand pounds. The old man said to Prince Ivan: "Try to toss this stone." Prince Ivan snatched it at once, tossed it, and thought to himself: "What strength there is in me!" Again they returned home, and the old man told his youngest daughter to bring a gallon and a half of green wine. Prince Ivan drank that, too, in one draught, went again to walk with the old man, and this time easily tossed a stone that weighed sixty thousand pounds. Then the old man gave him a self-serving tablecloth and said: "Now, Prince Ivan, you have such strength that no horse will carry you! Have the porch of your house made over, else it will not support you; you also need other chairs, and more rafters under the floor. God speed you!"

All the people laughed when they saw the governor returning from the hunt on foot and leading his horse by the bridle. He came home, had supports put under the floors, had his chairs made over, dismissed all his cooks and chambermaids, and lived alone like a hermit. Everyone wondered how he could live without eating: no one cooked for him, for he was fed by his self-serving tablecloth. He ceased visiting anyone, because none of the chairs in other people's houses could support his weight.

The king returned from his campaign, learned that Prince Ivan was governor of a province, ordered that he be replaced, and again made him a stableboy. There was nothing Prince Ivan could do about it, and he began once more to live as a stableboy. One day the groom ordered him to do something and struck him; Prince Ivan could not restrain himself; he struck back and knocked off the groom's head. This affair reached the ears of the king; Prince Ivan was brought before him. "Why did you kill the groom?" asked the king. "He struck me first; I hit back, not very hard, but somehow his head fell off." The other stableboys said the same thing—that the groom had hit first and that Prince Ivan had not hit him back hard. No punishment was meted out to Prince Ivan; but he was sent from the stables to the army and began to live as a soldier.

A short time afterward a little man no bigger than a nail, with a beard a cubit long, came to the king and handed him a letter from the Water King with three black seals on it. The letter ran as follows: "If the king does not put his daughter, Princess Martha, on such and such an island on such and such a day to be given in marriage to the Water King's son, he will kill all the people and burn the whole kingdom, and a three-headed dragon will come for Princess Martha." The king read this letter, and wrote a letter to the Water King saying that he would give him his daughter; he politely escorted the little old man to the door of the palace, then summoned his senators and councilors to hold council as to how they might defend his daughter against the three-headed dragon. If he failed to send her to the island, the Water King would devastate the whole kingdom. A call was issued: "Will someone volunteer to rescue Princess Martha from the dragon?" To him the king would give her in marriage. A boastful nobleman responded to the call, took a company of soldiers, and brought Princess Martha to the island; he left her in a hut, and he himself waited for the dragon outside.

Meanwhile Prince Ivan learned that Princess Martha had been taken to the Water King, so he too armed himself and went to the island. He came into the hut and found Princess Martha weeping. "Don't weep, princess," he said to her. "God is merciful." He lay on a bench, put his head on Princess Martha's knees, and fell asleep. Suddenly the dragon appeared and water rushed in after him to a height of three yards. When the water began to rise, the boastful nobleman who was stationed there with his soldiers ordered: "March to the woods!" All the soldiers hid in the woods. The dragon came out and made straight for the hut. Princess Martha saw the dragon coming for her and awakened Prince Ivan. He jumped down from the bench, in one stroke cut off all the three heads of the dragon, and left. The nobleman took Princess Martha home to the king, her father.

After a short time, the little old man no bigger than a nail, with a beard a cubit long, again came out of the water and brought a letter from the Water King with six black seals on it, summoning the king to put his daughter on the same island, to be taken by a six-headed dragon; if the king refused to surrender her, the Water King threatened to flood the whole kingdom. The king wrote in answer that he agreed to surrender Princess Martha. The little old man left. The king issued a call, and messengers were sent everywhere: could not a man be found to rescue the princess from the dragon? The

same nobleman presented himself again, saying: "Your Majesty, I will rescue her; only give me a company of soldiers." "Don't you need more than a company? This time it is a dragon with six heads." "No, a company is enough, I don't need more."

The party gathered and they took Princess Martha away. When Prince Ivan learned that the princess was again in danger, remembering the kindness that she had done him by appointing him governor, he went to the island; again he found Princess Martha in the hut, and entered. She was waiting for him and rejoiced to see him. He lay down and fell asleep. Suddenly the six-headed dragon began to emerge, and six yards of water rushed in. This time the nobleman and his soldiers had posted themselves in the woods immediately. The dragon entered the hut, and Princess Martha awakened Prince Ivan. The dragon and Prince Ivan came to blows, and fought and fought; Prince Ivan cut off one head of the dragon, a second, a third, and finally all six heads, and cast them into the water, and went away as though nothing had happened. The nobleman and his soldiers came out of the woods, and went home and reported to the king that God had helped them to rescue Princess Martha. And it seems that this same nobleman threatened the princess in some manner, for she did not dare to say that it was not he who had rescued her. The nobleman began to insist upon marrying her, but Princess Martha told him to wait. "Let me recover from my fear," she said. "I was terribly frightened!"

Suddenly once more the same little old man no bigger than a nail, with a beard a cubit long, emerged from the water and brought a letter with nine black seals, demanding that the king straightway send Princess Martha to such and such an island on such and such a day, to be carried off by a nine-headed dragon, and threatening, if he did not send her, to flood the whole kingdom. Again the king wrote in answer that he agreed, and began to seek a man who could rescue the princess from the nine-headed dragon. The same nobleman again presented himself and left with a company of soldiers and Princess Martha. Prince Ivan heard about it, armed himself and went to the island too, and Princess Martha was waiting for him. She was overjoyed to see him and began to question him as to his place of birth, his father's name, and his own name. He did not answer, but lay down and fell asleep. The nine-headed dragon began to emerge, and brought with him a flood of water nine yards high. Again the nobleman ordered the soldiers to march to the woods, and they hid there. Princess Martha began to rouse Prince Ivan, but could not awaken him. The dragon was nearing the threshold. She wept, but still could not awaken Prince Ivan. The dragon began to crawl close, ready to snatch Prince Ivan, but still he slept. Princess Martha had a penknife, and with it she cut Prince Ivan's cheek. He awoke, jumped up, and began to shout insults at the dragon. Now the dragon began to have the upper hand in the fight. Out of nowhere appeared the little peasant all made of copper, with iron hands and a steel head, and he gripped the dragon; the two together cut off all his heads, cast them into the water, and left. The nobleman was happier than ever, came rushing out of the woods, went home to his kingdom, and began to press the king to celebrate the wedding. Princess Martha refused. "Wait a little while, let me recover," she said. "I was terribly frightened."

Again the little man no bigger than a nail, with a beard a cubit long, brought a letter. The Water King demanded the dragon's slayer. The nobleman did not feel like going to the Water King, but there was nothing that he could do. He was ordered to go there. A ship was rigged out and they set sail (Prince Ivan was now serving in the fleet, and somehow happened to be on this ship). They were sailing along briskly when a ship came toward them. It flew like a bird and from it came cries as it rushed by: "The culprit! The culprit!" They sailed on a little farther and met another ship, and again cries came from it: "The culprit! The culprit!" Prince Ivan pointed at the nobleman; he was thrashed and thrashed until he was half dead. The ship went by. Now they came to the Water King. He ordered that a bath of iron or steel be heated red hot and the culprit put in it. The nobleman was terrified, his heart went into his boots—little father death was coming! But one man on the ship had become attached to Prince Ivan and served him faithfully, realizing that he was not of lowly birth. Prince Ivan sent him, saying: "Do you go and sit in that bath." He went at once, and, wonder of wonders, nothing happened to him; he came back unharmed. Again the culprit was sent for, this time to be brought before the Water King himself. The Water King abused him roundly, thrashed him, and had him driven out. Then they all went home.

Upon his return the nobleman began to boast even louder than before. He did not leave the king's side for a moment, so impatient was he to have the wedding celebrated. The king agreed, and a day was set for the nuptials. Now the nobleman was very proud—so proud, no one dared to touch him or come near him! But the princess said to her father: "Father, command all the soldiers to assemble; I want to look at them." Straightway the soldiers were assembled. Princess Martha reviewed them all. When she came to Prince Ivan, she glanced at his cheek and saw the scar she had made when she cut him with her penknife. She took him by the hand and led him to her father. "Here is the man who rescued me from the dragon, father," she said. "I did not know who he was, but now I recognize him by the scar on his cheek. The nobleman just sat in the woods with his soldiers." All the soldiers were asked whether they had sat in the woods while the dragon was slain, and they answered: "That is the truth, Your Royal Majesty!" The nobleman was half dead from shame. He was disgraced and banished; but Prince Ivan married Princess Martha, and they began to live and chew bread together.

THE CAT, THE COCK,
AND THE FOX

ONCE THERE WAS an old man who had a cat and a cock. The old man went to work in the woods; the cat brought him some food and the cock was left to watch the house. Just then a fox came to the house.

> Cock-a-doodle-doo, little cock,
> Golden crest!
> Look out the window
> And I'll give you a pea.

Thus sang the fox as he sat under the window. The cock opened the window and poked out his head to see who was singing. The fox snatched the cock in his claws and carried him off to eat him for dinner. The cock cried out: "The fox is carrying me away, he is carrying the cock beyond dark forests, into distant lands, into foreign countries, beyond thrice nine lands, into the thirtieth kingdom and the thrice tenth empire! Cat Cotonaevich, rescue me!" In the field the cat heard the cock's voice, rushed after him, overtook the fox, rescued the cock, and brought him home. "Now mind, Petya," said the cat to the cock, "don't look out of the window again, don't trust the fox; he'll eat you up, bones and all!"

Once again the old man went to work in the woods and the cat went to bring him food. Before leaving, the old man told the cock to watch the house and not to look out of the window. But the fox was wily, he wanted very badly to eat the cock; so he came to the hut and began to sing:

> Cock-a-doodle-doo, little cock,
> Golden crest!
> Look out the window
> And I'll give you a pea—
> I'll give you seeds too.

The cock walked about the room and did not answer. Once again the fox sang his song and cast a pea in through the window. The cock ate the pea and said: "No, fox, you cannot fool me! You want to eat me, bones and all." "Don't say such things, Petya. I have no idea of eating you. I just wanted you to pay me a visit, to see my house and take a walk around my estate." And he sang again:

> Cock-a-doodle-doo, little cock,
> Golden crest!
> I gave you a pea,
> I'll give you seeds too.

The cock looked out of the window and at once the fox snatched him in his claws. The cock cried in a shrill voice: "The fox is carrying me off, carrying the cock beyond dark woods, beyond thick forests, along steep banks, up high mountains! He wants to eat me, bones and all!" In the field the cat heard him, rushed after him, rescued him, and brought him home. "Did I not tell you not to open the window, not to poke out your head, or the fox would eat you, bones and all? Listen now, heed my words! Tomorrow we shall be even farther away."

Again the old man went to work and again the cat went to bring him his food. The fox stole under the window and began to sing the same song; he sang it three times, but the cock remained silent. The fox said: "What's the matter, has Petya become dumb?" "No, fox, you cannot fool me, I won't look out of the window." The fox cast a pea and several wheat grains in at the window and again sang:

> Cock-a-doodle-doo, little cock,
> Golden crest,
> Butter head,
> Look out the window!
> I have a big mansion:
> In every corner
> There's a measure of wheat;
> Eat your fill!

Then he added: "And, Petya, you should also see my collection of curios! Don't believe the cat; if I wanted to eat you, I would have done so long ago. The truth is, I like you, I want to show you the world, to develop your mind, to teach you how to live. Now show yourself, Petya! I'll go behind a corner," and he concealed himself closer to the wall. The cock jumped up on a bench and looked through the window from a distance; he wanted to see whether the fox was still there. Then he poked his head out of the window, and at once the fox snatched him and darted off. The cock sang the same tune as before, but the cat did not hear him. The fox carried the cock away and ate him up behind a fir grove, leaving only his tail feathers for the wind to scatter. The old man and the cat came home and discovered that the cock was gone. They were deeply distressed and said to each other: "This is what comes of not heeding warnings!"

BALDAK BORISIEVICH

IN THE FAMOUS CITY of Kiev, in Tsar Vladimir's castle, dukes and boyars and mighty champions assembled for a solemn feast. Tsar Vladimir spoke these words: "Hail, boys! Gather together, sit down around one table." They gathered around one table, ate and drank half their fill, and Tsar Vladimir spoke: "Who would render me a great service? Who would go beyond thrice nine lands, to the thrice tenth kingdom, to the Turkish sultan, and take his steed with the golden mane, kill his talking cat, and spit in the sultan's own face?" The brave knight Ilya Muromets, son of Ivan, offered to go. Tsar Vladimir had a beloved daughter, and she said these words: "My father, Tsar Vladimir, although Ilya Muromets is boasting loud, he will not perform this task. Disband the solemn feast, father; go to all the taverns in your town and seek the young Baldak, son of Boris, seven years of age."

And the tsar heeded his daughter, and went to seek the young Baldak Borisievich, and found him in a tavern sleeping under a bench. The tsar pushed him with the toe of his boot and Baldak jumped up from his sleep, as though nothing had happened. "Hail, Tsar Vladimir, what do you want of me?" Whereupon Tsar Vladimir answered: "I invite you to the solemn feast." "I am not worthy to go to the solemn feast; I get drunk in taverns and wallow on the floor." Tsar Vladimir spoke these words to him: "If I invite you to the feast, you must come; we have great need of you." And young Baldak Borisievich bade the tsar return from the tavern to the royal castle, and said that he himself would soon follow.

Baldak remained alone in the tavern, drank enough green wine to chase away his drunkenness, and went without delay to the castle of Tsar Vladimir. He crossed himself as was prescribed, bowed low as he had been taught, bowed to all sides, and in addition to the Tsar himself. "Hail, Tsar Vladimir," he said. "Why have you bidden me to this feast?" Tsar Vladimir answered him: "Young Baldak Borisievich, render me a

90

great service. Go beyond thrice nine lands, to the thrice tenth kingdom, to the Turkish sultan. Take from him his steed with the golden mane, kill his talking cat, and spit in the sultan's own face. Take as many troops as you need, take as much gold as you please!" And young Baldak Borisievich answered: "As you have commanded, Tsar Vladimir! For my troops give me only twenty-nine youths. I myself will be the thirtieth."

Speedily a tale is spun, with less speed a deed is done. Young Baldak Borisievich set out on his way to the Turkish sultan and managed to arrive just at midnight. He entered the sultan's courtyard, took the steed with the golden mane from the stables, seized the talking cat and tore him in twain, and spat in the sultan's own face. And the sultan also had a favorite garden, which extended for three versts; all kinds of tree were planted in this garden, all kinds of flower grew in it. Young Baldak Borisievich ordered his companions, the twenty-nine youths, to cut down the entire garden; he himself fetched fire and with this fire razed everything to the ground. Where the garden had been he pitched thirty thin white canvas tents.

Early in the morning the Turkish sultan awoke; his first glance went to his favorite garden, and as soon as he looked he saw that all the trees had been cut down and burned, and that thirty white canvas tents stood where the garden had been. "Who has thus trespassed upon my garden?" he thought. "An emperor, a king, or a very mighty champion?" The sultan cried in a loud voice for his favorite Turkish pasha, called him before him, and spoke these words: "My kingdom fares ill! I have been expecting a Russian villain, young Baldak Borisievich, and now I am invaded—by whom? An emperor, a king, or a mighty champion? I do not know, nor do I know how to find out."

As he took counsel, the eldest daughter of the Turkish sultan appeared and said to her father: "What are you holding council about, and what is it that you cannot find out? O Father, Turkish sultan! Give me your blessing and order that twenty-nine maidens, the most beautiful in the whole kingdom, be chosen! I myself will be the thirtieth. We will go to spend the night in those canvas tents and will find the culprit for you." And her father consented and she went to the tents with twenty-nine maidens, the most beautiful in the kingdom. Young Baldak Borisievich came out to meet her, took her by her white hands, and cried in his loud voice: "Eh you youths, my companions! Take the lovely maidens by their hands, lead them to your tents, and do what you know how to do." They slept together one night. Next morning the sultan's eldest daughter returned to him and said: "My beloved father, order the thirty youths from the white canvas tents to come to your house; I myself will point out the culprit."

Straightway the Turkish sultan sent his favorite pasha to the tents to summon to him young Baldak Borisievich with all his companions. The thirty youths came out of their tents: they were all of one face, like blood brothers, hair for hair, voice for voice! And they spoke these words to the envoy: "Go back, we shall soon follow you." Young Baldak Borisievich asked his boys: "Is there not some sign on me? Examine me carefully." And they found that his legs were smeared with gold up to the knees, and his arms with silver up to the elbows. "She is cunning, but I understand her stratagem," said Baldak, and put the same signs on all his companions: their legs were now gold up to the knees and their arms silver up to the elbows. He ordered them to put on gloves. "Let no one," he commanded, "take them off without my order when we arrive in the sultan's house."

Now they arrived at the sultan's house. The eldest daughter came forth and pointed out young Baldak Borisievich as the culprit. Baldak said to her: "How do you recognize me—by what proof?" The sultan's eldest daughter answered: "Remove your boots from your legs, and your gloves from your hands: there I have put my signs. Your legs are gold up to the knees, your arms silver up to the elbows." "Have we not many such youths?" said young Baldak Borisievich, and gave an order to his boys: "Let everyone remove a boot from one leg, and a glove from one hand!" The same signs that he had were found on everyone—the chambers were illumined by the brightness of the silver and gold. And the Turkish sultan was merciful and kind, and did not believe his daughter. "You lie," he said.

92

"I need one culprit, and now, according to you, there are thirty culprits!" And the Turkish sultan commanded: "Get out, all of you!"

Thereupon he became even more distressed and aggrieved, and again began to think and to take counsel with his favorite pasha about how to discover the culprit. To their meeting came the sultan's second daughter and said to him: "Father, give me twenty-nine maidens; I myself will be the thirtieth. I will go to the white canvas tents, spend one night there, and discover the culprit for you." No sooner said than done. Next morning the Turkish sultan sent his favorite pasha to summon young Baldak Borisievich and his companions to his palace. As before, Baldak answered: "Go back, we shall soon follow you." As soon as the pasha left, young Baldak cried in his loud voice: "Come out of the tents, all of you, my companions, you twenty-nine youths! See whether there is a sign on me. Straightway they all came out of the tents and found golden hair on his head. Young Baldak Borisievich said: "She is cunning, but I understand her stratagem." He put golden hair on all the youths, just as had been done to him, and ordered them to cover their rash heads with caps. "Let no one," he warned, "remove them without my order when we are in the Turkish sultan's palace."

As soon as young Baldak Borisievich and his companions entered the sultan's palace, the sultan said to his second daughter: "My beloved daughter, show me the culprit." And she knew with certainty who it was, because she had spent the night with him; she walked straight to young Baldak and said: "Here is the culprit." To this young Baldak Borisievich answered: "How do you recognize me—by what proof?" "Remove your cap from your head: there I have made a sign— golden hair." "Have we not many such youths?" answered Baldak, and ordered all his boys to throw down their caps. Their golden hair appeared, and the chambers were illumined! The sultan grew angry at his second daughter: "You do not speak the truth! I need one culprit, and according to you all of them are culprits!" And he commanded her: "Leave my palace!"

Now the Turkish sultan was even more distressed and aggrieved than before. But his third and youngest daughter came forth, chided her two elder sisters, and begged her father: "My beloved father, order me to choose twenty-nine maidens, the loveliest in the kingdom. I myself will be the thirtieth, and will find the culprit." The sultan acceded to the request of his youngest daughter, and she went to the same tents to spend the night. Baldak Borisievich jumped out of his tent, took the sultan's daughter by her white hands, and led her to his tent. And to his youths he cried in a loud voice: "My boys, take the lovely maidens by the hands and lead them to your tents." The maidens spent the night there and next morning went home. The sultan sent his favorite pasha for the good youths. The envoy went to the white canvas tents and summoned young Baldak and his companions to the Turkish sultan himself. "Go back, we shall soon follow you," was the reply. Young Baldak Borisievich spoke to his companions: "Well, boys, see whether there is a sign on me." They looked and searched all over him, but could not find any sign. "Ah brothers, it looks as if I am lost now," said Baldak, and asked them to render him a last service. He gave them each a sharp saber and told them to conceal the weapons under their clothes. "And when I give the signal," he bade them, "cut in all directions!"

As soon as they came before the Turkish sultan, the youngest daughter came forth and pointed at young Baldak. "Here is the culprit!" she said. "He has a golden star under his heel." And a golden star was found under his heel just as she had said. The sultan sent all of the twenty-nine youths out of his palace, and held only the culprit, young Baldak, son of Boris, and cried to him in a loud, shrill voice: "I will take you, put you on the palm of one hand, and clap with the other. There will be nothing left of you but a moist spot." Young Baldak answered him: "O Turkish sultan! Emperors, kings, and mighty heroes fear you, but I, a seven-year-old boy, do not fear you. I took your steed with the golden mane, I killed your talking cat, spat in your own face, and cut and burned your favorite garden!" The sultan fell into an even greater rage than before and ordered his servants to set up in the square two oaken pillars with a maplewood crossbeam, and to prepare three nooses on this crossbeam—the first of silk, the second of hemp, and the third of bast. And he proclaimed through the whole town that all the people, big and little, should assemble on the square to see how the Russian culprit would be put to death.

The Turkish sultan himself got into a light carriage and took with him his favorite pasha and his youngest daughter, who had discovered the culprit. Young Baldak was tied and chained and placed at their feet, and all of them drove straight to the oaken pillars. On the way young Baldak spoke thus: "I will propose riddles, and you, Turkish sultan, shall guess them. A horse runs fast. Why does his tail drag?" "What a blockhead you are," answered the sultan. "Every horse is born with a tail." They drove a little farther, and Baldak spoke again: "The front wheels are moved by the horse, but why the devil do the back wheels roll?" "What a blockhead! In sight of death he has lost his mind and is all confused! The master made the four wheels, so four wheels roll." They arrived at the square and got out of the carriage. They took the culprit, untied him and unchained him, and led him to the gallows.

Young Baldak Borisievich made the sign of the cross, bowed low to all sides, and spoke in a loud voice: "O Turkish sultan, do not give the order that I be hanged, order me to speak." "Speak! What is it?" "I have a gift from my father, a blessing from my mother: a playing horn. Order me to play it for the last time." Young Baldak played a gay tune, and everyone's mind was clouded; people became absorbed in looking at him and listening to him, and forgot why they had come; the sultan's tongue could not move. The twenty-nine youths heard the horn, came from the back rows, and began to cut down all the people with their sharp sabers. Young Baldak played until his companions had cut down all the crowd and reached the gallows.

Then young Baldak, son of Boris, ceased playing and said these last words to the Turkish sultan: "Aren't you the blockhead rather than I? Turn around, look behind you. My geese are pecking your wheat!" The Turkish sultan turned around and saw that all his people were slain and lying on the ground, and that at the gallows only three were left—himself, his

9 5

daughter, and his favorite pasha. Young Baldak ordered his youths to hang the sultan with the silken noose, his favorite pasha with the hempen noose, and his youngest daughter with the noose of bast. With this they had finished their enterprise, and departed for the famous city of Kiev, to return to Tsar Vladimir himself.

KNOW NOT

I N A CERTAIN VILLAGE, not far, not near, not high and not low, there lived an old man and his three sons, Grishka and Mishka and the third, Vaniushka. Vaniushka was neither clever nor wise, but sharp as a needle! Work he did not, but all of the time he lay on the stove; he wore his sides off lying there, and said to his brothers: "Eh, you old fools, open the door! I want to go forth, I know not where." And he began to importune his father and mother: "Give me my share, I renounce my claim on what is left to my brothers." The old man yielded to his entreaty and gave him three hundred rubles. Vaniushka took the money, bowed to his parents, hurried out of the village, arrived in the capital, and began to roam about the city, frequenting inns, regaling himself, and gathering all the drunkards about him. The drunkards asked him: "What is your name?" He said: "Truly brothers, I know not. When the priest baptized me and gave me my name, I was young and stupid." For that reason he was nicknamed "Know Not."

Know Not spent all his money in revels with the drunkards and began to wonder, poor wretch that he was, how he would live and avoid utter misery. He went to some cattle dealers and offered to hire himself to them. "What do you want for wages?" they asked. Know Not thought to himself that bread stays put, but money rolls away, and answered: "I don't want wages in money. Only let me eat my fill and drink till I'm drunk. I won't ask you for anything, nor will you ask me for anything." The cattle dealers agreed to this readily, for a worker who wanted no money was much to their liking; straightway they signed the bond, making it formal and legal. Know Not was delighted with his free bread and wine. He began to live a gay life: every day he got drunk and lay in a stupor; as soon as he woke he fell upon the wine again, and passed hours with the bottle, never working. When ordered to work he would say: "Be gone! Why do you bother me? Did we not agree that you should let me eat my fill and drink till I was drunk, that I would not ask anything of you, nor you of me?" When his term was up, the cattle dealers were glad to get rid of him. "We have lost our bread and wine," they said, "and will be lucky if he does not sue us in court!"

From the cattle dealers Know Not went to the tsar's gardeners and hired himself out as a watchman. The gardeners quickly made an agreement with him on the same basis as the cattle dealers—not to pay anything for his work, but to give him his fill of food and drink. Know Not was supposed to watch the gardens, but he caroused by night and by day, and was never sober. One night all the gardeners happened to be out, and Know Not decided to replant the apple trees, the grapevines, and the shrubs.

The tsar had three daughters; the two elder ones were resting, but the youngest sat among the flowers and did not sleep all night. She saw Know Not ruin the gardens, displaying his strength, tearing out old trees by their roots and flinging them over the fence. Next morning the gardeners came to work and began to shout and swear: "What kind of fool are you? You cannot watch anything! Who did it?" "I know not!" They seized him like a thief and brought him before the tsar. Know Not found himself in the tsar's palace, crossed himself as is prescribed, saluted as he had been taught, came close, bowed low, stood erect and spoke out boldly: "Your Majesty! Your gardens were not laid out in good order; it is no calamity that the trees were uprooted and flung over the fence! Give me permission to repair everything, I will do whatever is necessary!"

The tsar gave him permission, and the next night Know Not set about putting the gardens in order; a tree that twenty men could not lift, he would pick up with one hand. By morning all the gardens were ready, laid out in order. The tsar called Know Not before him, poured him a cup of wine, and Know Not took the cup in his right hand, and drank it down in one gulp. After that, he took out three apples and presented them to the princesses: to the eldest daughter he gave an overripe one, to the second a ripe one, and to the youngest a green one. The tsar saw this and realized that his princesses were of age, that the eldest should long since have been married, that the second one's time had come, and that even the youngest had not long to wait. On that very day he gathered together his dukes and boyars and wise councilors; they began to ponder how to marry off the three princesses. At last they thought of a plan: they printed official edicts and sent them with messengers to all the sovereign nations, announcing that their tsar desired to give his daughters in marriage, and that suitors from every country should come to his court.

And so emperors' sons and kings' sons and mighty champions gathered together in the tsar's court, and the tsar gave them a great feast; all the suitors ate their fill and drank their fill and sat there drunken and gay. The tsar ordered his daughters to dress in many-colored garments, come out of their private apartments, and choose their future husbands, each according to her heart's desire. The princesses dressed in many-colored garments, came forth to look at the suitors, stood near them, and curtsied politely. These maidens were stately of form and agile of mind; their eyes were as bright as the falcon's, their brows as black as the sable's. They poured cups of green wine and passed along the rows to choose their bridegrooms. The eldest daughter gave her cup to an emperor's son, the middle one gave hers to a king's son, but the youngest one carried her cup up and down the rows, then put it on the table and said to her father: "My father, my sovereign, there is no groom for me here." "Ah, my beloved daughter, most valiant knights are here. Is there nevertheless none to your liking?" After the feast, the guests departed.

Again the tsar assembled the sons of dukes, boyars, and wealthy merchants, and ordered his youngest daughter to dress in a many-colored garment and choose a bridegroom. She dressed, came forth, poured a cup of green wine, walked and walked along the rows, put the cup on the table, curtsied before her father, and said: "My father, my sovereign, there is no groom to my liking here!" Her father answered: "Ah, my fussy daughter, from among what men will you choose a groom? Since you are so minded, I will now gather together burghers and peasants, simpletons and drunkards, buffoons, stage dancers and singers; from among them you shall choose your husband, whether you like it or not!"

The tsar sent his edict to all the towns, villages, and hamlets; at his court there assembled a great multitude of burghers and peasants, fools and drunkards, buffoons, stage dancers and singers, among whom was also Know Not. The princess dressed in a many-colored garment, came forth to the palace entrance, and beheld the lowly crowd. She saw Know Not. In stature he was taller than everyone else; he was stouter of body too, and his curls fell over his shoulders like pure gold. She came close to him, curtsied low, gave him the loving cup, and said these words: "Drink, my betrothed, you will perform every task!" Know Not received the cup in his right hand, drank it down in one gulp, took the princess by her white hands, kissed her on her sweet lips, and together they went to the tsar himself. The tsar then ordered all his sons-in-law to celebrate their weddings; they celebrated their weddings and feasted at their feasts, and soon the princesses began to live happily with their husbands.

Absorbed in these weddings, the tsar forgot to recall his messengers, who had continued on their way, summoning suitors from still other foreign lands. When the messengers reached the Saracen kingdom, they issued a call in the market places and at the fairs, and announced the tsar's edict. And so three brothers gathered together—valiant warriors, mighty champions, who had traveled in many lands and conquered many kingdoms. First the youngest brother set out on his way, followed by a vast army. He approached the tsar's capital and learned that the princesses were already married. He grew wrathful and sent a threatening letter to the tsar, saying: "I came from the Saracen kingdom with peaceful intentions, to woo your daughters; for that purpose I have traveled through many lands and provinces. Now I find that you have given your daughters in marriage, and failed to recall your messengers; therefore pay me for the damage and expenses I have suffered. If you do not, I shall burn the whole city, slay all the people, and put you yourself, despite your great age, to a cruel death!"

Then the tsar said: "My beloved sons-in-law, what shall we do?" The emperor's son and the king's son answered: "We do not fear this threat, we shall ourselves battle the champion! Assemble a host of troops, father, and the mounted guard as well." Thereupon a considerable army assembled; the emperor's son commanded the infantry regiments, the king's son the mounted regiments. Both went out to the open field, beheld the valiant warrior, the mighty champion, took fright, and fled to their country estates, beyond thick forests and swampy marshes, so that nobody could find a trace of them. Their regiments were left leaderless, helpless, and fearful of judgment day. Know Not lay on the stove, and his heroic heart boiled with rage. He said to his wife: "My beloved wife, let us go to the country; any time now the city may be burned, the people slain, and your own father taken captive; we are not responsible for this affair, we are guiltless of this disaster." "No," answered the tsar's daughter, "I would rather die than leave my father and mother." She said farewell to Know Not and went to her father on the balcony. The tsar stood on the balcony watching the field of battle through a spyglass.

Know Not dressed as a peasant, donned a cap, a caftan, and mittens, went out of the city unseen and unknown, came to a high hill, and shouted a heroic shout and whistled a warlike whistle. At his call, there galloped from the open field a good steed bearing a full suit of armor; from his mouth a flame streamed, from his ears rolled curls of smoke, from his nostrils sparks flew; the steed's tail was three cubits long and his mane reached to his hoofs. Know Not the Simpleton came closer and put on the horse saddlecloths, blankets, and a Circassian saddle; he tightened the twelve saddle girths and laid the thirteenth over the chest. The girths were of white silk, the buckles of red gold, and the clamps of steel, not for beauty's sake, but for heroic strength; for silk does not tear, steel does not bend, and red gold does not rust in the ground. He himself donned all the warlike accouterments—iron mail, a steel shield, a long spear, a battle mace, and a sharp sword. He mounted his good steed and lashed him on his slender flanks, cutting his flesh to the white bone. The steed flew into a passion and raised himself from the damp earth—higher than the tall-standing trees, only lower than the moving clouds he began to leap, and each leap measured a verst. From beneath his mighty hoofs enormous clumps of earth were dug up, underground springs gushed into the air, the water in the lakes surged forth and mixed with the yellow sand, and the trees in the forests shook and bent to the ground.

Know Not shouted a mighty shout, whistled a warlike whistle, and the wild beasts on chains began to roar, the nightingales in the gardens began to sing, and the snakes and adders began to hiss. Such was Know Not's ride. He rode past the tsar's palace, past the front entrance, and cried: "Hail, great sovereign, with all your royal retinue!" He jumped over the white stone walls and the corner towers, into the open field where stood the host of troops and the mounted guards, and cried: "Hail, men, where are your leaders?" And in the open field he beheld the valiant warrior, the mighty champion, galloping on his good steed, taking wing like an eagle, casting terror into the host of troops. Know Not shouted in a shrill voice like a loud trumpet, and the two warriors rode toward each other, raising their iron maces that weighed each two thousand pounds.

When they came together, the shock of mail on mail was like a mountain avalanche; their maces clashed and broke, only the staffs remained in their hands. Once more they jumped far apart in the open field, wheeled their good steeds around, and rode again to meet in one place; they thrust their spears together and the spears bent to the handles and could not pierce the mail. But now the Saracen champion wavered in his saddle. Once more they rode apart in the open field, and when they met for the third time, they struck each other with their sharp swords, and Know Not knocked the Saracen knight out of the saddle onto the damp earth; in the foe's eyes the light grew dim, from his mouth and nose blood began to flow. Know Not jumped from his steed, pressed the hero to the damp earth, drew from his pocket an enormous dagger, a steel knife that weighed sixty pounds, cut open the colored garment of the Saracen knight, bared his white breast, searched for his fiery heart, shed his hot blood, and destroyed his heroic strength. Then he cut off the rash head, lifted it on his spear, and cried in a mighty voice: "Oh my beloved friends! Come out, sons-in-law, come out of the thickets, and take command of your armies, they are all safe and sound!"

Then Know Not turned his good steed around; like the bright falcon the horse flew, and did not touch the ground. He soon approached the city. The tsar and his retinue and Know Not's own wife all ran down from the balcony to meet him. But Know Not covered his face—"Let no one recognize me!" The tsar spoke to him thus: "Brave young knight! Of what birth are you, of what father and mother, and who has sent you to aid us from what cities? I know not what gifts to give you, I wot not what rewards. Welcome to our palace!" The good knight answered: "I shall not eat your bread, nor do I heed your words!" He rode beyond the city into the green thicket, unsaddled his horse, and let him go free; he removed his steel armor, his iron coat of mail, put his accouterments away in their hiding place for the time being, and went home. When he came to his dwelling, he donned his old clothes and lay down to sleep on the stove.

His young wife rushed to him and said: "Ah Know Not, my husband dear! You know nothing, for you have heard nothing. From the thicket a young warrior rode forth, he cried in a shrill voice, so that all the citizens were frightened. He jumped over these white stone walls and the corner towers, into the open field where stood a host of troops and the mounted guard, and they had hardly time to make room for him. He blew into a loud trumpet; the Saracen knight heard it and turned his steed about. They rode toward each other and clashed together like storm clouds; their maces met and broke, only the staffs remained in their hands. They clashed for the second time, they thrust their spears together and the spears bent to their handles; they clashed for the third time, fought with swords, and the Saracen knight fell on the damp earth, and the young warrior jumped from the saddle, onto his mighty chest, cut open his white body, searched for his fiery heart and cut his rash head off his shoulders, lifted it on his long spear, and rode into the open field." "Ah you, foolish woman! You don't know the ways of men nor the ways of beasts in the dark forest. There are no such heroes in the white world!"

Meanwhile the tsar's sons-in-law came forth from the woods and the thickets, met in the open field, assembled their host of troops and their mounted guard, and led them into the city. There the bells tolled, the regiments beat their drums, played their trumpets, and sang their songs. Overjoyed, the tsar quickly opened the gates for them, let the host of troops and the mounted guard into the city, treated the soldiers to wine in all the taverns and inns, and gave a great feast for all the good folk. For six whole weeks they feasted; everyone drank and ate his fill, everyone in the city was drunken and gay. Only Know Not, the tsar's youngest son-in-law, did not enjoy this celebration; no one knew of his part in the affair nor of the great burden he had borne. So he said to his wife: "My beloved wife, unloved by her father, go and ask the tsar for a cup of green wine with a piece of ham for me to eat."

The princess went to her father's throne, came near to him, curtsied low, looked straight at him, and spoke out boldly: "My father, my sovereign, I beg your favor. Give my husband and your son-in-law, Know Not the Simpleton, a cup of new wine to drink and a piece of ham to eat." The tsar answered: "Water does not flow under a resting stone! Your husband and our son-in-law, when we were in distress, fled to the country;

he was a laughingstock to all; and now when we are victorious he has returned and lies on the stove. If only, my beloved daughter, you had married a knight who could have ridden into battle to defeat the enemy host! Then we would have been pleased and you would not have been offended! But since things are as they are, you must be satisfied with the remnants when the feast is over." The tsar's daughter replied: "It is not given to all, as it is to your elder sons-in-law, to hide in the dark woods at the hour of battle, and to rush back to the feast, to drink and be gay when the battle is over! Is it fitting that my husband and I should lick the plates after them?"

The feast was not yet over when a speedy messenger arrived in the Saracen kingdom. Straightway he came to the other two mighty champions, and announced the disaster. "A young warrior rode forth," he said, "and slew your brother, whose body lies on the field; his hot blood was shed, and all his host of troops and his mounted guard were taken captive." The brother champions became angry, speedily mounted their steeds, donned their steel armor and their coats of iron mail and took up their warlike arms—their steel swords, battle maces, sharp sabers, and long spears—and set out on their way. Ahead of them they sent a messenger to the tsar, bearing the following letter: "Surrender the knight who shed our brother's blood. If you refuse, we shall cut down all your troops with the sword, set your capital city on fire, take your people captive, and give you over to a cruel death, despite your great age." The messenger arrived in the tsar's palace and handed this letter to the tsar, who took it, unsealed it, and read it—and then his nimble legs collapsed under him, his white hands trembled, and his bright eyes could not see, for burning tears flowed from them.

The tsar took thought, sent couriers out in all directions to summon his councilors, generals, and highest officers, and questioned everyone, humble and great, about the hero who had conquered the Saracen knight. No one knew who he was; the higher ranks referred the question to the middle ranks, the middle ranks referred it to the lower ranks, and from the lower ranks there was no answer. So the tsar sent the messenger back without an answer. The Saracen champions approached and began to lay waste cities and villages and to set them on fire. Know Not lay on the stove, his fiery heart boiling with rage, and spoke thus to his wife: "My beloved wife, unloved by her father, come to the country with me, life here has become uncomfortable." The tsar's daughter answered: "I will not go to the country, I would rather die here." Know Not came down from the stove and said, sighing heavily: "Farewell, my beloved wife. If your father is killed, you will not remain alive either."

He dressed in peasant clothes, put a cap on his head, took a stick in his hand, and went out and looked around, trying not to be seen. The tsar noticed him from the balcony. "What is the matter with this simpleton?" he said. "He wants to run away, but he does not realize that if anything happens every member of our family will be ferreted out!" The elder sons-in-law stood beside him, thinking how they might show their valor. "Father, our sovereign, assemble a host of troops and the mounted guard. We shall help you in your need."

The tsar set about assembling an army and organizing regiments. His sons-in-law summoned their own troops and marched to the field of battle. The Saracen champions rushed on these forward regiments, smote them terribly with swords, and trampled twice as many with their steeds; blood flowed in rivers, the moans of the wounded resounded. Know Not heard them, rushed to their help, came to a high hill, and shouted a hero's shout and whistled a mighty whistle. At his call the good steed came running from the open field; as he ran he stumbled. "Ah, you carcass for wolves, you bag of weeds," cried Know Not, "why do you stumble? Do you smell misfortune?" The good steed answered: "There will be blood on both the horse and the master!" Know Not put on his horse a bridle, saddle-cloths, blankets, and a German saddle. He tightened the twelve saddlegirths, and put the thirteenth on the horse's chest. All the girths were of white Persian silk, the buckles of red Arabian gold, the clasps of steel from far-off lands, not for the sake of beauty, but for heroic strength; for silk does not tear, steel does not bend, and red gold does not rust. He accoutered his steed,

then began to accouter himself: he donned the knight's garment and the steel armor, took the steel shield and the battle mace in his hand, hooked the long, strong spear to his legs, the sharp saber to his waist, and the steel sword behind him.

Then he mounted his good steed, put his nimble feet into the German stirrups, took a silken riding crop and lashed his steed on his slender flanks, cutting his skin. The steed flew into a passion, rose from the damp earth higher than the standing trees, lower only than the moving clouds. He jumped from mountain to mountain, straddling rivers and lakes with his legs, sweeping deep marshes with his tail. From his mouth a flame streamed, from his nostrils sparks flew, from his ears curling smoke rolled out, beneath his hoofs enormous clumps of earth were dug up and underground springs gushed forth. Know Not shouted a mighty shout, whistled a mighty whistle, and the water in the lakes surged forth, mixing with the yellow sand; old oaks shook, bending their tops to the ground. In the open field, the Saracen knight sat on his horse, firm as a heap of hay. His steed flew like a falcon without touching the damp earth, and the knight himself boasted that he would swallow Know Not whole.

When the two knights met, Know Not's horse said: "Well, master, bend your head over my mane, perhaps you will be saved." Know Not had no sooner lowered his head than the Saracen hero swung his sword, wounded Know Not's left arm, and cut off his horse's left ear; at the same time Know Not thrust his spear into the Saracen knight's chest below the neck and turned him over like a sheaf of corn. The Saracen fell on the damp earth, lay there and wallowed in his hot blood. Soon the host of troops moved up, the mounted guard galloped forth, and Know Not rode on his good steed to the tsar's palace and shouted in a loud voice: "My good people, do not let me die in vain, stop my hot blood from flowing!" All the tsar's retinue rushed from the balcony, and the princess, Know Not's wife, was the first to reach him. With her own handkerchief she bandaged his left arm. But she failed to recognize her husband, for he was wiping the sweat from his brow, thus hiding his face.

Know Not rode to his hut, left his horse without tying him, entered the hall, fell on the floor, and covered his face with his hand. The tsar knew nothing; he stood on the balcony and watched his sons-in-law finishing the battle. But Know Not's wife approached the hut and beheld the hero's steed with full accouterment at the entrance, and the hero himself lying in the hall. She hurried home and told her father everything. Straightway the tsar went to the hut with his retinue, opened the door, fell on his knees, and spoke kind words: "Tell us, good knight, of what family and tribe are you? What is your name, what is your father's name?" Know Not answered: "Ah, my God-given father and sovereign—do you not recognize me? You have always called me a simpleton." Then all recognized him and paid him homage as a mighty hero. And the elder sons-in-law, as soon as they heard of this triumph, packed up their belongings and went with their wives to their own homes. Know Not soon recovered from his wounds, drank green wine, and made a great feast for all. And after the tsar's death he ascended the throne and his life was long and happy.

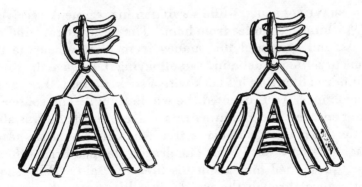

THE MAGIC SHIRT

A BRAVE SOLDLIER, while serving in his regiment, received a hundred rubles from home. The sergeant got wind of it and borrowed this money from him. When the time came to settle the debt, instead of paying it, he gave the soldier a hundred blows on his back with a stick, saying: "I never saw your money. You invented the whole thing!" The soldier became enraged and ran away into a deep forest; he was about to lie down to rest under a tree when he saw a six-headed dragon flying toward him. The dragon stopped beside the soldier, questioned him about his life, and said: "Why should you trudge through the woods like this? Instead, come and serve me for three years." "With pleasure," said the soldier. "Sit on me, then," said the dragon. The soldier began to load all his belongings on the dragon. "Eh, veteran, why are you taking all this trash with you?" "How can you ask that, dragon? A soldier gets flogged for losing even a button, and now you want me to drop all my belongings!"

The dragon brought the soldier to his palace and charged him as follows: "Sit by the kettle for three years, keep the fire going, and cook my kasha!" The dragon himself went to travel in the world during all that time. The soldier's work was not hard: he put wood under the kettle and sat beside it drinking vodka and eating tasty snacks—and the dragon's vodka was not like ours, all watered down, but quite strong! After three years the dragon came flying home. "Well, veteran, is the kasha ready?" "It must be, for all these three years my fire did not go out once." The dragon ate the whole kettleful in one meal, praised the soldier for his faithful service, and hired him for the next three years.

These years passed too, and the dragon ate his kasha again and left the soldier for still another three years. For two years our soldier cooked the kasha, and toward the end of the third began to think, "Here I am living with the dragon for the ninth year, cooking his kasha all the time, and I don't even know what it tastes like. I must try it." He raised the lid and found his sergeant sitting in the kettle. "Ah, my friend," thought the soldier, "now I'm going to give you a good time; I'll pay you back the blows you gave me." And he began to drag in wood and put it under the kettle, as much as he could, and made such a fire that he cooked not only the flesh but even the bones of the sergeant to a pulp. The dragon returned, ate the kasha, and praised the soldier: "Well, veteran, the kasha was good before, but this time it was even better. Choose whatever you like as your reward." The soldier looked around and chose for himself a mighty horse and a shirt of thick cloth. This shirt was not an ordinary shirt, but a magic one: he who put it on became a mighty champion.

The soldier then went to a king, helped him in a difficult war, and married his beautiful daughter. But the princess disliked being married to a common soldier. So she intrigued with a neighboring prince, and in order to find out whence came the soldier's mighty strength, she coaxed and flattered him. Having discovered what she wanted, she seized the opportunity when her husband was asleep to remove his shirt and give it to the prince. The prince put on the magic shirt, took a sword, cut the soldier into little pieces, put them in a hempen bag, and said to the stableboys: "Take this bag, tie it to some battered jade, and drive her into the open field!" The stableboys went to carry out this order, but meantime the soldier's mighty steed had turned himself into a battered jade and put himself in the stableboys' path. They took him, tied the bag to him, and drove him into the open field. The mighty steed darted off faster than a bird, came to the dragon's castle, stopped there, and for three nights and three days neighed without ceasing.

The dragon was sound asleep, but he was finally awakened by the horse's loud neighing and stamping, and came out of his palace. He looked into the bag and groaned aloud! He took the pieces, put them together, washed them with the water of death—and the soldier's body was joined together. He sprinkled it with the water of life, and the soldier came to. "Fie," he said, "I have slept a long time!" "You would have slept very long indeed without your good horse!" answered the dragon, and taught the soldier the difficult science of assuming different shapes. The soldier turned into a dove, flew to the prince with whom his faithless wife now lived, and sat on the sill of the kitchen window. The young cook saw him. "Ah," she said, "what a pretty little dove!" She opened the window and let him into the kitchen. The dove struck the floor and became a goodly youth. "Do me a service, lovely maiden," he said, "and I will marry you." "What shall I do for you?" "Get from the prince his shirt of thick cloth." "But he never takes it off, except when he bathes in the sea."

The soldier found out at what time the prince bathed, went out on the road, and turned into a flower. Soon the prince and the princess came to the beach, followed by the cook carrying clean linen. The prince noticed the flower and admired it, but the princess guessed at once what it was: "Ah, that accursed soldier must have turned himself into this!" She picked the flower and began to crumple it and pluck the petals, but the flower turned into a little fly and without being noticed hid in the cook's bosom. As soon as the prince undressed and went into the water, the fly flew out and turned into a bright falcon. The falcon snatched the shirt and carried it away, then turned

112

into a goodly youth and put it on. Then the soldier took a sword, put his treacherous wife and her lover to death, and married the lovely young cook.

THE THREE PENNIES

A WEALTHY MERCHANT hired an unknown man to work for him. The man worked for a year, then asked the merchant to settle his account. The merchant gave him the wages he had earned, but the worker took only one penny for his work, went to the river, and threw the penny into the water. "If I have served faithfully and truly," he said, "my penny will not sink." The penny sank. Again he went to work for the same merchant. He worked for a year and the merchant again gave him his due, but the worker took only one penny, went to the same place, and threw the penny into the water. The penny sank. So he went to work for the merchant for a third time; he worked for a year, and the merchant gave him more money than before as a reward for his zealous service. But the worker again took only one penny, went to the river, and threw it into the water—and lo and behold, all three pennies rose to the surface! He took them and went along the road to his own village.

Suddenly he met a merchant who was going to mass; he gave the merchant a penny and asked him to put a candle before the icons on his behalf. The merchant went to the church, took money from his pocket for candles, and accidentally dropped the worker's penny on the floor. Suddenly a fire arose from this penny. The people in the church were surprised and asked who had dropped the penny. The merchant said: "I dropped it, but it is not mine: a worker gave it to me to buy a candle for him." Each of the worshipers took a candle and lit it from this penny. Meanwhile the worker continued on his way.

113

He met another merchant who was going to the fair; he drew a penny from his pocket and gave it to the merchant, saying: "Buy some merchandise for me at the fair." The merchant took the penny, bought the merchandise he wanted for himself, and wondered what he should buy for the worker's penny. Just then he happened to meet a boy who wanted to sell a cat and asked for it no more and no less than one penny. The merchant could find no other suitable merchandise, so he bought the cat.

This merchant sailed with his ships to trade in another kingdom. Now, that kingdom was overrun with countless rats. The merchant's ships stopped at the port and every now and then the cat ran away from the ships and ate the rats. The king was told about this, and asked the merchant: "Is this beast expensive?" The merchant said: "It is not my beast; a certain young man asked me to buy it." Then he added in a calculating tone: "That cat is worth three ships." The king gave the merchant three ships and took the cat. The merchant returned, and the worker went to the market, found him, and asked: "Did you buy any merchandise for my penny?" The merchant answered: "There's no use denying it, I bought three ships." The worker took the three ships and sailed on the sea.

After some time, a short time or a long time, he came to an island. An oak stood on this island; he climbed up on the oak and heard the devil below boasting to his comrades that the next day he would steal the king's daughter in broad daylight. His comrades said to him: "If you do not get her, we shall whip you with iron rods!" After this conversation they left. The worker climbed down the oak and went to the king's palace. He drew the last penny from his pocket and lit it. The devil also ran to the palace, but could not steal the king's daughter. He returned to his brothers, who began to lash him with iron rods; they lashed and lashed him, and then threw him down into a nameless place. But the worker married the king's daughter and prospered the rest of his days.

THE PRINCESS
WHO WANTED TO SOLVE RIDDLES

ONCE THERE WAS an old man who had three sons, of whom the third was called Ivan the Simpleton. At that time there was a certain tsar—for this was long ago—who had a daughter. She said to her father: "Permit me to solve riddles, father. If I solve a man's riddles, let his head be cut off; but him whose riddle I cannot solve, I will marry." Immediately they sent forth a call. Many men presented themselves and all of them were put to death, for the princess was able to solve their riddles. Ivan the Simpleton said to his father: "Give me your blessing, father! I want to go to the tsar's court and propound riddles." "What an absurd idea, you fool! Better men than you have been put to death!" "If you give me your blessing, I will go; if you do not, I will go anyway!" So the father gave him his blessing. Ivan the Simpleton set out. On his way he saw a field of grain, and in the field a horse. He drove the horse away with his whip to prevent him from trampling the grain, and said: "Here I have a riddle!" He went on farther, saw a snake, pierced it with his spear, and thought: "Here is another riddle!"

He came to the tsar's palace, was received by the princess, and was told to propound his riddles. He said: "On my way here, I saw a good thing, and in this good thing a good thing, and I took a good thing and drove out the good thing from the good thing; and the good thing ran away from the good thing out of the good thing." The princess rushed to look for this riddle in her book, but it was not there. She did not know how to solve it, so she said to her father: "Father, I have a headache today, my ideas are all confused, I will solve this riddle tomorrow." So the audience was postponed till the next day. Ivan the Simpleton was given a room and he sat there smoking his pipe. The princess chose a faithful chambermaid, and sent her to Ivan. "Go," she said, "ask him the answer to this riddle, promise him gold and silver, as much as he wants."

The chambermaid knocked at his door. Ivan the Simpleton opened it; the maid entered and asked the answer to the riddle, promising him mountains of gold and silver. Ivan the Simpleton answered: "What do I need money for! I have plenty of my own. Let the princess stand all night in my room without sleeping, then I will tell her the answer to my riddle." The chambermaid told the princess this answer; she accepted, and stood all night in Ivan's room without sleeping. In the morning Ivan the Simpleton told her that the answer to his riddle was that he had driven a horse out of the grain. So the princess was able to solve the riddle before the tsar and his court.

Then Ivan the Simpleton proposed another riddle: "On my way here I saw an evil thing, so I struck it with an evil thing, and the evil thing died from the evil thing." Again the princess looked in her book, but could not solve the riddle, and asked for a postponement till the next morning. At night she sent her chambermaid to get the answer from Ivan the Simpleton. "Promise him money," she said. "What do I need money for!" said Ivan. "I have plenty of my own. Let the princess stand all night in my room without sleeping, then I will tell her the answer." The princess agreed, did not sleep during the night, and was thus able to solve the riddle before the tsar and his court.

Ivan the Simpleton did not put his third riddle to the princess, but instead asked that all the senators be gathered together. In their presence he propounded a riddle about how the princess had been unable to solve the other riddles and had sent her chambermaid to bribe him with money. The princess could not solve this riddle either; again she questioned him, promising to give him silver and gold, as much as he wanted, and to send him home in a coach-and-four. But her efforts were in vain. Again she stood up all night without sleeping; and when Ivan the Simpleton told her what the riddle was about, she still could not tell the solution to the court, for then everyone would find out how she had obtained the answers to his first two riddles. She had to declare: "I cannot solve this riddle." So Ivan the Simpleton and the princess were married; they had a fine wedding and a gay feast and lived happily ever after.

A SOLDIER'S RIDDLE

TWO SOLDIERS on a trip stopped to rest in an old woman's house. They asked for some food and drink, but the old woman said: "What shall I offer you? I have nothing, my boys." Yet in her oven she had a boiled cock in a pot under the roasting pan. The soldiers guessed this; one of them—who was a roguish fellow—went out into the yard, upset a cart full of sheaves of grain, returned to the house, and said: "Little grandmother, go out, the cattle are eating your grain." The old woman went out and the soldiers peered into the oven, took the cock out of the pot, put an old shoe in the pot instead, and hid the cock in their bag. The old woman came back and said: "My dear boys, didn't you set the cattle loose? Why do you cause mischief like that? Don't do that again, please." The soldiers sat in silence awhile, then asked again: "Please, little grandmother, give us something to eat." "Take some kvass and bread, my boys; that will do."

Then the old woman wanted to crow because she had cheated them and proposed a riddle to them: "Well, my boys, you've traveled a lot, you've seen the world. Now tell me—is Mr. Cock Cockson still living in Ovenia, at Potburg near Pantown?" "No, little grandmother." "Who, then, is living there?" "Mr. Shoe Shoeson." "And what has happened to Mr. Cock Cockson?" "He moved to Bagville, little grandmother." After that the soldiers left. The old woman's son returned from the field and asked her for some food. She said: "Imagine, my son, some soldiers came by here and asked me for something to eat. But

117

instead of giving it to them I posed them a riddle about the cock that I have in the oven, and they couldn't solve it." "And what riddle did you pose them, mother?" "This one—'Is Mr. Cock Cockson still living in Ovenia, at Potburg near Pantown?' They did not solve it. They said: 'No, little grandmother.' 'But where is he?' I asked them. 'He has moved to Bagville,' they said. They never guessed, the sons of bitches, what I had in my pot." She looked into the oven, but the cock had flown away; she dragged out only an old shoe. "Ah, my little son, those accursed fellows robbed me after all." "You should have known better, mother; a soldier knows the world, he cannot be cheated!"

THE DEAD BODY

A POOR OLD PEASANT lived with his wife. They had three sons: two were clever, but the third was Ivan the Fool. Sometimes the elder brothers went hunting and the fool followed them; the two clever brothers caught wild beasts and game birds, but the fool caught rats and mice, magpies and crows. Once the brothers sowed peas in the garden and told Ivan the Fool to guard the plants against crows. Their old mother had to go to the garden; as soon as she came there, Ivan the Fool noticed her and said to himself: "Just wait, I'll catch that thief; he'll remember me!" He stole up to the old woman quietly, raised his stick, and gave her such a blow on the head that she fell asleep forever without so much as a gasp.

The fool's father and brothers began to chide, reproach, and abuse him. But he sat on the stove, dug in the soot, and said: "Why the devil did she try to steal? You yourselves put me there to watch." "You fool," said the brothers, "you've made your bed, now lie on it; get down from the stove and dispose of the body." The fool muttered: "I'll do it as well as anyone."

He took the old woman, dressed her in her Sunday best, put her in the back of a carriage, placed an embroidery frame in her hands, and drove through the village.

He met an official driving toward him. "Get over to the side, peasant!" The fool answered: "Get over to the side yourself. I'm carrying the king's embroiderer." "Run over that scoundrel," said the official to his coachman, and as soon as their horses passed each other, the wheels of the two carriages caught, and the fool and the old woman were hurled out to a distance. "Gentlemen, boyars," cried the fool to all the people, "they've killed my mother, the king's embroiderer!" The official saw that the old woman was dead, got frightened, and began to implore the fool: "Take anything you want, little peasant, only don't gather a crowd." The fool did not want to make too much of a fuss, and said: "Give me three hundred rubles and arrange with the priest to bury the dead woman." This ended the matter; the fool took the money, turned back, came home to his father and brothers, and they all began to live happily together.

THE FROG PRINCESS

LONG AGO, in ancient times, there was a king who had three sons, all of them grown. The king said: "My children, let each of you make a bow for himself and shoot an arrow. She who brings back your arrow will be your bride; he whose arrow is not brought back will not marry." The eldest son shot his arrow, and a prince's daughter brought it back to him. The middle son shot his arrow, and a general's daughter brought it back to him. But little Prince Ivan's arrow was brought back from the marsh by a frog who held it between her teeth. His brothers were joyous and happy, but Prince Ivan became thoughtful and wept: "How will I live with a frog?

After all, this is a life task, not like wading across a river or walking across a field!" He wept and wept, but there was no way out of it, so he took the frog to wife. All three sons and their brides were wed in accordance with the customs of their country; the frog was held on a dish.

They began living together. One day the king asked that all three brides make him gifts, so that he could see which of them was the most skillful. Prince Ivan again became thoughtful and wept: "What can my frog make? Everyone will laugh at me!" The frog only hopped about on the floor and croaked. When Prince Ivan fell asleep, she went out into the street, cast off her skin, turned into a lovely maiden, and cried: "Nurses, nurses! Make something!" The nurses at once brought a finely woven shirt. She took it, folded it, placed it beside Prince Ivan, and again turned herself into a frog, as though she had never been anything else! Prince Ivan awoke, was overjoyed with the shirt, and brought it to the king. The king received it, examined it, and said: "Well, this is indeed a shirt to wear on holidays!" Then the second brother brought a shirt. The king said: "This one is good only to wear to the bath!" And of the shirt the eldest brother brought he said: "This one is fit to be worn only in a lowly peasant hut!" The king's sons left, and the two elder ones decided between themselves: "We were wrong to make fun of Prince Ivan's wife; she is not a frog, but a cunning witch!"

The king again issued a command to his daughters-in-law—this time that they should bake bread, and show it to him, so that he might see which of them baked best. Before the first contest, the brides of the two elder sons had made fun of the frog; but now they sent a chambermaid to spy on her and see how she would go about baking her loaf. The frog was aware of this, so she mixed her dough, rolled it, hollowed out the oven from above, and poured her dough right there. The chambermaid saw this and ran to tell her mistresses, who forthwith did the same. But the cunning frog had deceived them; the moment the chambermaid left, she dug the dough out of the oven, cleaned and plastered up everything as though nothing had happened, then went on the porch, got out of her frog's skin, and cried: "Nurses, nurses! Bake me such a loaf of bread as my dear father ate only on Sundays and holidays!" The nurses brought the bread at once. She took it, placed it beside the sleeping Prince Ivan, and turned into a frog again. Prince Ivan awoke, took the bread, and went with it to his father. Just then the king was examining the loaves of bread brought by his elder sons. Their wives had dropped the dough into the oven just as the frog had, and all they had pulled out was formless lumps. First the king took the eldest son's loaf, looked at it, and sent it back to the kitchen; then he took the second son's loaf and sent it back too. Then came Prince Ivan's turn: he presented his loaf. The father received it, examined it, and said: "Now this bread is good enough for a holiday! It is not slack-baked, like that of my elder daughters-in-law!"

After that the king decided to hold a ball in order to see which of his daughters-in-law danced best. All the guests and the daughters-in-law assembled, and also the sons, except Prince Ivan, who became thoughtful: how could he go to a ball with a frog? And our Prince Ivan began to sob. The frog said to him: "Weep not, Prince Ivan! Go to the ball. I will join you in an hour." Prince Ivan was somewhat heartened when he heard the frog's words; he left for the ball, and the frog cast off her skin, and dressed herself in marvelous raiment. She came to the ball; Prince Ivan was overjoyed, and all the guests clapped their hands when they beheld her: what a beauty! The guests began to eat and drink; the princess would pick a bone and put it in her sleeve; she would drink of a cup and pour the last drops into her other sleeve. The wives of the elder brothers saw what she did, and they too put the bones in their sleeves, and whenever they drank of a cup, poured the last drops into their other sleeves. The time came for dancing; the tsar called upon his elder daughters-in-law, but they deferred to the frog. She straightway took Prince Ivan's arm and came forward to dance. She danced and danced, and whirled and whirled, a marvel to behold! She waved her right hand, and lakes and woods appeared; she waved her left hand, and various birds began to fly about. Everyone was amazed. She finished dancing, and all that she had created vanished. Then the other daughters-in-law came forward to dance. They wanted to do as the frog had done: they waved their right hands, and the bones flew straight at the guests; and from their left sleeves water spattered, that too on the guests. The king was displeased by this and cried: "Enough, enough!" The daughters-in-law stopped dancing.

The ball was over. Prince Ivan went home first, found his wife's skin somewhere, took it and burned it. She arrived, looked for the skin, but it was gone, burned. She lay down to sleep with Prince Ivan, but before daybreak she said to him: "If you had waited a little, I would have been yours; now only God knows when we will be together again. Farewell! Seek me beyond the thrice ninth land, in the thrice tenth kingdom!" And the princess vanished.

A year went by, and Prince Ivan longed for his wife. In the second year, he made ready for his journey, obtained his father's and mother's blessing, and left. He walked a long time and suddenly he saw a little hut standing with its front to the woods and its back to him. He said: "Little hut, little hut, stand the old way, as thy mother stood thee, with thy back to the woods and thy front to me!" The hut turned around. He entered. An old woman was sitting there, who said: "Fie, fie! Of a Russian bone not a sound was heard, not a glimpse was seen, and now a Russian bone has come to my house of its own free will. Whither goest thou, Prince Ivan?" "First of all, old woman, give me to eat and to drink, then ask me questions." The old woman gave him to eat and to drink and put him to bed. Prince Ivan said to her: "Little grandmother, I have set out to find Elena the Fair." "Oh, my child, how long you have been away! At the beginning she often remembered thee, but now she no longer remembers thee, and has not come to see me for a long time. Go now to my middle sister, she knows more than I do."

In the morning Prince Ivan set out, came to a hut, and said: "Little hut, little hut, stand the old way, as thy mother stood thee, with thy back to the woods and thy front to me." The hut turned around. He entered, and saw an old woman sitting there, who said: "Fie, fie! Of a Russian bone not a sound was heard, not a glimpse was seen, and now a Russian bone has come to my house of its own free will. Whither goest thou, Prince Ivan?" "To get Elena the Fair, little grandmother." "Oh, Prince Ivan," said the old woman, "thou hast been long a-coming! She has begun to forget thee, she is marrying someone else; the wedding will take place soon! She is now living with my eldest sister. Go there, but be careful. When thou approachest their house, they will sense it; Elena will turn into a spindle, and her dress will turn into gold thread. My sister will wind the gold thread; when she has wound it around the spindle, and put it into a box and locked the box, thou must find the key, open the box, break the spindle, throw the top of it in back of thee, and the bottom of it in front of thee. Then she will appear before thee."

Prince Ivan went, came to the third old woman's house, and entered. The old woman was winding gold thread; she wound it around the spindle and put it in a box, locked the box, and put the key somewhere. He took the key, opened the box, took out the spindle, broke it just as he had been told, cast the top in back of him and the bottom in front of him. Suddenly Elena the Fair stood before him and greeted him: "Oh, you have been a long time coming, Prince Ivan! I almost married someone else." And she told him that the other bridegroom was expected soon. Elena the Fair took a magic carpet from the old woman, sat on it with Prince Ivan, and they took off and flew like birds. The other bridegroom suddenly arrived and learned that they had left. He too was cunning! He began to pursue them, and chased and chased them, and came within ten yards of overtaking them: but on their carpet they flew into Russia, and for some reason he could not get into Russia, so he turned back. The happy bride and groom came home; everyone rejoiced, and soon Ivan and Elena began to live and prosper, for the glory of all the people.

THE SPEEDY MESSENGER

IN A CERTAIN LAND, in a certain kingdom, there were certain impassable swamps. A circuitous road went around them; it took three years to travel fast on this road, and if one traveled slowly, even five were not enough! Near the road lived a poor old man who had three sons: the first was named Ivan, the second Vasily, and the third was little Semyon. The old man determined to clear the swamps, to lay a straight road for travelers on foot and travelers on horseback, and to build white hazelwood bridges over the streams, so that a man on foot could pass through the swamps in three weeks and a rider on horseback in three days. He set to work together with his sons, and after not a little time everything was finished just as he had planned it: sturdy were the white hazel bridges and cleared was the fine straight road.

The poor man returned to his hut and said to Ivan, his firstborn: "Go, my beloved son, sit under the first bridge and listen to what folk say about us—whether it will be good or evil." Obedient to his father's command, Ivan hid himself under the bridge.

Two venerable hermits walked over the bridge and said to each other: "To him who laid this bridge and cleared the road, whatever he asks of the Lord, the Lord will give it to him!" As soon as Ivan heard these words, he came out from under the hazelwood bridge, and said: "This bridge I laid with my father and brothers." "And what do you wish of the Lord?" the holy men asked him. "That the Lord make me rich for the rest of my life!" "Very well, go to the open field. In the open field there is an old oak. Under that oak is a deep vault, and in that vault are gold and silver and precious stones galore. Take a shovel and dig—the Lord will make you rich for life!" Ivan went to the open field, dug up much gold and silver and many precious stones under the oak, and took them home. "Well, little son," the poor man asked him, "have you seen anyone walking or driving over the bridge? And what do people say

124

about us?" Ivan told his father that he had seen two venerable men and that they had rewarded him for life.

The next day the poor man sent Vasily, his middle son, to the bridge. Vasily sat under the hazel logs and listened. Two venerable men walked over the bridge, came to the spot above his hiding place, and said: "He who laid this bridge, whatever he asks of the Lord, the Lord will give it to him." As soon as Vasily heard these words, he came out and said: "This bridge I laid with my father and brothers." "And what do you ask of the Lord?" "That the Lord give me bread for the rest of my life!" "Very well, go home, stake out a piece of fresh land, and sow it; the Lord will give you bread for all your life!" Vasily came home, told his father all that had happened, marked out a piece of fresh land, and sowed it with grain.

The third day the poor man sent his youngest son to the bridge. Little Semyon sat under the logs and listened. Two venerable men walked over the bridge, came to the spot above his hiding place, and said: "He who laid this bridge, whatever he asks of the Lord, the Lord will give it to him." Little Semyon heard these words, came out, and said: "This bridge I laid with my father and brothers." "And what do you ask of the Lord?" "I ask of him a favor—to serve as a soldier to the great sovereign!" "Ask for something else. A soldier's service is hard; if you become a soldier, you will fall captive to the Sea King, and many tears will you shed!" "Eh, you are venerable hermits and you know very well he who does not weep in this world will weep in the next!" "Well, since you will serve the king, we give you our blessing!" said the venerable old men. They put their hands on little Semyon and turned him into a fleet-footed stag.

The stag ran to his father's house. From the window his father and brothers saw him, jumped out of the hut, and wanted to catch him. The stag turned back. He came running to the two venerable old men, and they turned him into a hare. The hare darted back to the house; the father and brothers saw him, jumped out of the hut, and wanted to catch him, but he turned back again. He came running to the two venerable old men, who turned him into a little bird with a golden head.

125

The bird flew to the house and sat on the window sill. The father and brothers saw him and jumped up to catch him, but he took wing and flew back. The bird came flying to the two venerable old men, who turned him into a human again and said: "Now, little Semyon, you can go into the king's service. If you ever need to run somewhere in a hurry, you can turn into a stag, a hare, and a bird with a golden head. We have taught you how."

Little Semyon went home and asked his father's permission to go into the king's service. "Why should you go?" answered the poor man. "You are still young and foolish." "No, father, let me go; it is God's will." The poor man gave permission, and little Semyon made his bundle, said farewell to his father and brothers, and set out on his way.

After some time, a long time or a short time, he came to the king's court, went straight to the king himself, and said: "Your Majesty, do not punish me, let me speak." "Speak, little Semyon." "Your Majesty, take me into your service." "Impossible! You are small and foolish; how could you serve?" "Although I am small and stupid, I will serve no worse than the others; God will help me." The king consented, took him as a soldier, and ordered him to stay near his person. Some time passed, and suddenly a certain king declared a terrible war against our king. He began to prepare himself to take the field; at the appointed hour his whole army assembled. Little Semyon asked permission to go to war; the king could not refuse him, so took him with him and set out to the field of battle.

For a long, long time the king marched with his troops. He left many, many lands behind him, and soon was close to the enemy—in about three days he would have to give battle. At that moment the king realized that he had neither his battle mace nor his sharp sword with him. He had forgotten them in his palace; he had nothing to defend himself with, to defeat the enemy forces with. He issued a call to all his troops: would someone undertake to go to the palace in a hurry and bring him his battle mace and sharp sword? To him who would do this service he promised his daughter, Princess Maria, in marriage, half his kingdom as a dowry, and the other half after his death.

Volunteers presented themselves; some said that they could do the errand in three years; others, in two years; still others, in one year. But little Semyon said to the sovereign: "Your Majesty, I can go to the palace and bring the battle mace and the sharp sword in three days." The king was delighted, took him by the hand, kissed him on the mouth, and at once wrote a letter to Princess Maria telling her to trust this messenger and to give him the sword and the mace. Little Semyon took the letter from the king and set out on his way.

Having traveled about one verst, he turned into a fleet-footed stag and darted off like an arrow from a bow. He ran and ran until he got tired and turned from a stag into a hare; then he raced ahead at a hare's pace. He ran and ran until all his legs were weary and then turned from a hare into a little bird with a golden head; he flew even faster, flew and flew, and in a day and a half reached the kingdom where Princess Maria was. He turned back into a human, entered the palace, and gave the princess the letter. Princess Maria took it, unsealed it, read it, and said: "But how could you run across so many lands so speedily?" "This is how!" answered the messenger; he turned into a fleet-footed stag, ran once or twice across the princess' chamber, approached the princess, and put his head on her knees. She took her scissors and cut a tuft of fur from his head. The stag turned into a hare, the hare capered a little in the chamber and jumped on the princess' knees. She cut a tuft of fur from him then too. The hare turned into a little bird with a golden head, the bird flew about the room a little and perched on the princess' hand. Princess Maria cut a golden feather from his head, and wrapped all these—the stag's fur, the hare's fur, and the golden feather—into a handkerchief and hid them on her person. The bird with the golden head then turned back into a messenger.

The princess gave him meat and drink, helped him to get ready for his journey, and gave him the battle mace and the sharp sword; then they said good-by to each other, kissed heartily in farewell, and little Semyon went back to the king. Again he ran as a fleet-footed stag, bounded as a slant-eyed hare, flew as a little bird, and by the end of the third day saw the king's camp near by. At about three hundred paces from the army he lay down on the beach near a bayberry bush, to rest from his journey; he put the battle mace and the sharp sword by his side. From great weariness he fell asleep soon, and soundly. Just then a general happened to pass by the bayberry bush, saw the messenger, straightway pushed him into the sea, took the battle mace and the sharp sword, brought them to the king, and said: "Your Majesty, here are your battle mace and sharp sword, I fetched them myself—and that braggart, little Semyon, will surely take three years!" The king thanked the general, began to fight with the enemy, and in a short time won a brilliant victory over him.

As for little Semyon, we have seen that he fell into the sea. That very moment the Sea King seized him and carried him to the deepest depth. He lived with this king for a whole year, grew bored and sad, and wept bitterly. The Sea King came to him and said: "Well, little Semyon, are you bored here?" "I am bored, Your Majesty!" "Would you fain go to the Russian world?" "I would, if such is your royal favor." The Sea King carried him out exactly at midnight, left him on the shore, and himself returned to the sea. Little Semyon prayed to God: "Lord, give me some sun!" Just before the rising of the red sun the Sea King came, again snatched him and carried him to the depths of the sea.

Little Semyon lived there for another whole year. He became bored, and wept very bitterly. The Sea King asked him: "What is the matter, are you bored?" "I am bored," said little Semyon. "Would you fain go to the Russian world?" "I would, Your Majesty." The Sea King took him out to the shore at midnight, and himself returned to the sea. Little Semyon prayed to God with tears in his eyes: "My Lord, give me some sun!" Day had just begun to break when the Sea King came and snatched him and carried him once more to the depths of the sea. Little Semyon lived in the sea for a third year, became bored, and wept bitterly, inconsolably. "What is the matter, Semyon, are you bored?" the Sea King asked him. "Would you fain go to the Russian world?" "I would, Your Majesty." The Sea King cast him out on the shore, and himself returned to the sea.

Semyon, the little youth, prayed to God with tears in his eyes: "My Lord, give me some sun!" Suddenly the sun shone with his bright rays, and now the Sea King no longer could take him into captivity.

Little Semyon set out for his kingdom. He turned first into a stag, then into a hare, and then into a little bird with a golden head. After a short time he found himself near the king's palace. And while all this had been happening, the king had come back from the war and betrothed his daughter, Princess Maria, to the deceitful general. Little Semyon entered the chamber in which the bridegroom and the promised bride were sitting at table. Princess Maria saw him and said to the king: "Sovereign, my father! Do not punish me, let me speak." "Speak, my dear daughter! What do you wish?" "Sovereign, my father! My bridegroom is not the one who is sitting at the table, but the one who has just come! Now show us, little Semyon, how at that time you ran speedily for the battle mace and the sharp sword." Little Semyon turned into a fleet-footed stag, ran once or twice across the chamber, and stopped near the princess. Princess Maria took from her kerchief the bit of fur she had cut from the stag, showed the king the spot at which she had clipped it, and said: "Look, father! Here are my proofs." The stag turned into a hare; the hare capered in the chamber and leapt to the princess' knee. Princess Maria took the bit of hare's fur from her kerchief. The hare turned into a little bird with a golden head; the bird flew a little in the chamber and perched on the princess' hand. Princess Maria untied the third knot in her kerchief and showed the golden feather. Then the king learned the real truth, ordered the general to be put to death, married Princess Maria to little Semyon, and made him his heir.

VASILISA
THE PRIEST'S DAUGHTER

IN A CERTAIN LAND, in a certain kingdom, there was a priest named Vasily who had a daughter named Vasilisa Vasilyevna. She wore man's clothes, rode horseback, was a good shot with the rifle, and did everything in a quite unmaidenly way, so that only very few people knew that she was a girl; most people thought that she was a man and called her Vasily Vasilyevich, all the more so because Vasilisa Vasilyevna was very fond of vodka, and this, as is well known, is entirely unbecoming to a maiden. One day, King Barkhat (for that was the name of the king of that country) went to hunt game, and he met Vasilisa Vasilyevna. She was riding horseback in man's clothes and was also hunting. When he saw her, King Barkhat asked his servants: "Who is that young man?" One servant answered him: "Your Majesty, that is not a man, but a girl; I know for a certainty that she is the daughter of the priest Vasily and that her name is Vasilisa Vasilyevna."

As soon as the king returned home he wrote a letter to the priest Vasily asking him to permit his son Vasily Vasilyevich to come to visit him and eat at the king's table. Meanwhile he himself went to the little old back yard witch and began to question her as to how he could find out whether Vasily Vasilyevich was really a girl. The little old witch said to him: "On the right side of your chamber hang up an embroidery frame, and on the left side a gun; if she is really Vasilisa Vasilyevna, she will first notice the embroidery frame; if she is Vasily Vasilyevich, she will notice the gun." King Barkhat followed the little old witch's advice and ordered his servants to hang up an embroidery frame and a gun in his chamber.

As soon as the king's letter reached Father Vasily and he showed it to his daughter, she went to the stable, saddled a gray horse with a gray mane, and went straight to King Barkhat's palace. The king received her; she politely said her prayers, made the sign of the cross as is prescribed, bowed low to all four

131

sides, graciously greeted King Barkhat, and entered the palace with him. They sat together at table and began to drink heady drinks and eat rich viands. After dinner, Vasilisa Vasilyevna walked with King Barkhat through the palace chambers; as soon as she saw the embroidery frame she began to reproach King Barkhat: "What kind of junk do you have here, King Barkhat? In my father's house there is no trace of such womanish fiddle-faddle, but in King Barkhat's palace woman-ish fiddle-faddle hangs in the chambers!" Then she politely said farewell to King Barkhat and rode home. The king had not found out whether she was really a girl.

And so two days later—no more—King Barkhat again sent a letter to the priest Vasily, asking him to send his son Vasily Vasilyevich to the palace. As soon as Vasilisa Vasilyevna heard about this, she went to the stable, saddled a gray horse with a gray mane, and rode straight to King Barkhat's palace. The king received her. She graciously greeted him, politely said her prayers to God, made the sign of the cross as is prescribed, and bowed low to all four sides. King Barkhat had been advised by the little old back yard witch to order kasha cooked for supper and to have it stuffed with pearls. The little old witch had told him that if the youth was really Vasilisa Vasilyevna he would put the pearls in a pile, and if he was Vasily Va-silyevich he would throw them under the table.

Supper time came. The king sat at table and placed Vasilisa Vasilyevna on his right hand, and they began to drink heady drinks and eat rich viands. Kasha was served after all the other dishes, and as soon as Vasilisa Vasilyevna took a spoonful of it and discovered a pearl, she flung it under the table together with the kasha and began to reproach King Barkhat. "What kind of trash do they put in your kasha?" she said. "In my father's house there is no trace of such womanish fiddle-faddle, yet in King Barkhat's house womanish fiddle-faddle is put in the food!" Then she politely said farewell to King Barkhat and rode home. Again the king had not found out whether she was really a girl, although he badly wanted to know.

Two days later, upon the advice of the little old witch, King Barkhat ordered that his bath be heated; she had told him that

132

if the youth really was Vasilisa Vasilyevna he would refuse to go to the bath with him. So the bath was heated.

Again King Barkhat wrote a letter to the priest Vasily, telling him to send his son Vasily Vasilyevich to the palace for a visit. As soon as Vasilisa Vasilyevna heard about it, she went to the stable, saddled her gray horse with the gray mane, and galloped straight to King Barkhat's palace. The king went out to receive her on the front porch. She greeted him civilly and entered the palace on a velvet rug; having come in, she politely said her prayers to God, made the sign of the cross as is prescribed, and bowed very low to all four sides. Then she sat at table with King Barkhat, and began to drink heady drinks and eat rich viands.

After dinner the king said: "Would it not please you, Vasily Vasilyevich, to come with me to the bath?" "Certainly, Your Majesty," Vasilisa Vasilyevna answered, "I have not had a bath for a long time and should like very much to steam myself." So they went together to the bathhouse. While King Barkhat undressed in the anteroom, she took her bath and left. So the king did not catch her in the bath either. Having left the bathhouse, Vasilisa Vasilyevna wrote a note to the king and ordered the servants to hand it to him when he came out. And this note ran: "Ah, King Barkhat, raven that you are, you could not surprise the falcon in the garden! For I am not Vasily Vasilyevich, but Vasilisa Vasilyevna." And so King Barkhat got nothing for all his trouble; for Vasilisa Vasilyevna was a clever girl, and very pretty too!

THE WISE MAIDEN
AND THE SEVEN ROBBERS

ONCE UPON A TIME there was a peasant who had two sons. The younger one traveled, the elder stayed at home. Before the father died he bequeathed all that he had to his elder son, and left nothing to the younger one, thinking that a brother would surely not wrong a brother. The elder son buried his father and kept all of the inheritance. The second son returned and wept bitterly on finding his father dead. His brother said to him: "Our father left everything to me alone." Yet this brother had no children, while the younger brother had a son of his own and an adopted daughter.

And so the elder brother took all of the inheritance, grew rich, and began to trade in precious goods, while the younger brother was poor, chopped wood, and carted it to market. His neighbors, pitying his poverty, took up a collection for him and offered him money to enable him at least to set himself up as a retail merchant. The poor man was afraid and said to them: "No, my good neighbors, I won't take your money; for should I suffer losses in trade, who will pay my debt to you?" Then two of his neighbors determined to give him money by a stratagem. One day when the poor man went to get wood, one of these neighbors contrived to meet him by taking a detour and said: "I had just left the house for a distant voyage, when someone who owed me three hundred rubles met me on the way and paid me. Now I don't know where to put the money. I don't want to return home, so please take it, keep it for me, or rather trade with it. I won't be back for a long time; you can pay me later, little by little."

The poor man took the money, brought it home, and was afraid that he might lose it or that his wife might find it and spend it instead of his own money. He thought and thought, and finally hid it in a wooden tub full of ashes. While he was away, traders who bought ashes and paid for them in goods came to his house; his wife exchanged the tub of ashes for some goods. When the husband returned and saw that the tub was gone he asked his wife: "Where are the ashes?" His wife answered: "I sold them to the traders." He was frightened and very unhappy, but kept silent nonetheless. His wife saw that he was sad; she began to press him to tell her what misfortune had befallen him and why he was so distressed. He confessed that some money that did not belong to him was hidden in the ashes. His wife grew angry, shouted, and wept. "Why didn't you trust me?" she said. "I would have hidden the money in a better place!"

Again the peasant went for wood to sell at the market so that he might buy bread. Another of his neighbors overtook him, told him the same thing as the first, and gave him five hundred rubles to keep for him. The poor man refused to take them, but the neighbor forced the money into his hands and rode away. The money was in bills; our poor man thought and thought about where to put it and finally stuck it under the lining of his cap. He came to the forest, hung his cap on a pine tree, and began to chop wood. As ill luck would have it, a raven snatched his cap with the money in it and flew away. The peasant was sad but resigned himself to his fate. He lived as before, traded in wood and other cheap things, and somehow struggled along. The neighbors waited for some time and then realized that the poor man's lot had not improved. They asked him: "Are you unsuccessful in your trade, brother? Or are you afraid that you will lose our money? If so, better give it back to us." The poor man wept and told them how he had lost the money. His neighbors did not believe him and brought the matter to court. "How shall I decide this case?" thought the judge. "This peasant is a peaceful man, but penniless; he has nothing that can be taken from him, and if I send him to prison his family will die of starvation!"

The judge was sitting by the window sunk in meditation when he was distracted by some boys playing in the street. One of the boys, an alert little fellow, said: "I will be the burgomaster; you come to me with your cases and I will judge them." He sat on a stone; another boy approached him, bowed to him, and said: "I loaned money to this peasant, and he has not paid me back; I have come to Your Honor to complain about him." "Did you borrow money from him?" the burgomaster asked the defendant. "I did." "Then why don't you pay it back?" "I have nothing to pay it with, little father." "Listen, plaintiff! Since the defendant does not deny having borrowed money from you, and since he cannot pay, extend the term of the debt for five or six years; by that time he may come into money and if so he will repay the debt with interest. Do you agree?" The two boys bowed to the burgomaster and said: "Thank you, little father, we agree." The judge heard all this, was overjoyed, and said: "This boy has enlightened me! I will tell my plaintiffs to give the poor man an extension of time." Upon his advice, the rich neighbors agreed to wait for two or three years, in the hope that by then the peasant would have bettered his lot.

The poor man again went to the forest for wood and chopped half a cartful, and then night came. He remained in the woods, intending to return home in the morning with a full cart. He wondered where he would spend the night. The forest was deserted, and teeming with wild beasts; if he lay beside his horse, they might devour him. He went deeper into the thicket and climbed into a big pine tree. At night seven robbers came there and said: "Open, open, little gate!" At once a little gate leading underground opened; the robbers carried in their loot, and when all was hidden, said: "Close, close, little gate!" The gate closed, and the robbers left to get more loot. The peasant saw all this. When everything around him was quiet, he climbed down from the tree, thinking, "Let me try—maybe the gate will open for me too." He had no sooner said, "Open, open, little gate," than it opened. He entered the cave and saw piles of gold, silver, and all sorts of other valuable objects lying around. The poor man rejoiced, and at daybreak began to drag away the bags of money; he threw away his wood, loaded his cart with silver and gold, and hastened home.

His wife went out to meet him. "Oh, little husband, I nearly died of grief, worrying about you! I thought that a tree had crushed you or that wild beasts had devoured you." But the peasant said happily: "Cheer up, my wife! God gave me luck. I found a treasure; help me to carry these bags." After the bags were carried in, he went to his rich brother, told him about everything, and invited him to accompany him on another trip to the cave. The brother agreed; they went together to the woods, found the pine tree, and cried: "Open, open, little gate!" And the little gate opened. They set about dragging out bags of money; the poor brother filled his cart and was satisfied, but the rich brother could not tear himself away. "Well, little brother," he said, "you go home, I shall soon follow you." "Very well! But don't forget to say: 'Close, close, little gate!'" "I won't." The poor man left, but the rich man could not get enough of the treasure; it was impossible to take everything at once, and to leave it was a pity. Night overtook him in the same place. The robbers arrived, found him in the cave, and cut off his head. They removed their bags from the cart, put the slain man in it, lashed the horse, and set it loose. The horse ran out of the woods and brought him home. The robber chieftain chided the robber who had killed the rich brother. "Why did you kill him prematurely? You should have asked him first where he lived, for much of our goods is missing and probably he stole it! How can we find it now?" The chieftain's assistant said: "Let the man who killed him look for him!"

Shortly afterward, the murderer began to scout for the gold. He came to the poor man's little store; he bought a thing or two, noticed that the storekeeper was dejected, and asked him: "Why are you so sad?" He answered: "I had an elder brother, but misfortune came; someone killed him. The day before yesterday his horse brought him home with his head cut off, and he was buried today." The robber saw that he was on the right track and, pretending to be very sorry, began to investigate.. Upon learning that the slain man had left a widow, he asked: "Has his widow at least a roof over her head?" "Oh, yes, she has a big house." "Where? Show it to me." The peasant showed him his brother's house; the robber took some red paint and marked the door. "What are you doing that for?" the peasant asked him. He answered: "I want to help the widow, and I have made that sign in order to find her house more easily." "Eh, brother, my sister-in-law needs no help; thank God, she has enough of everything." "And where do you live?" "Here is my hut!" The robber made the same sign on his door too. "And what is that for?" "I like you very much," said the robber. "The next time I come here, I will stop at your house to spend the night; believe me, brother, you will profit by it." The robber returned to his band, related all that had happened, and they decided to rob and kill everyone in the houses of the two brothers and recover their gold.

Meanwhile the poor man came home and said: "I have just made the acquaintance of a young fellow who smeared my door with paint and said that he would stop in my house to spend the night whenever he was in this village. He is so kind-hearted! How sorry he was for my brother, how he wanted to help my sister-in-law!" His wife and son listened in silence, but his adopted daughter said to him: "My father, didn't you make a mistake? Perhaps the same robbers who killed my uncle have now discovered that their gold is missing and are trying to find us. Now they may come and rob us, and you won't escape death." The peasant was frightened. "That is quite possible! After all, I never saw the man before. What a misfortune! What shall we do?" His daughter said: "Take some paint and smear the same signs on all the doors in the neighborhood." The peasant did this. When the robbers came they could not find anything; they went back and thrashed their scout for not having made the signs properly. Finally they decided that they had been outwitted by a clever person, and after a while prepared seven barrels; they put a robber in each of them, except one that they filled with oil.

The former scout took these barrels straight to the poor brother's house; he arrived at sunset and asked whether he could stay overnight. The poor brother welcomed him as a friend. The daughter went to the yard and began to inspect the barrels; she opened one, and found oil; she tried to open another, but could not; she put her ear to it and heard someone stirring and breathing inside. "Ah," she thought, "that's an evil ruse!" She came into the house and said: "Father, we must treat our guest; I will make a fire in the stove and prepare something for supper." "Very well," the poor man said. The daughter made a fire in the stove and while cooking supper, she boiled water and poured it into the barrels, thus scalding the six robbers to death. Her father and his guest ate supper, and the daughter sat in the back room waiting to see what would happen next. When the hosts went to bed, the guest went out into the yard and whistled. No one answered; he approached the barrels, and steam came out of them. The robber guessed what had happened, harnessed his horses, and left with the barrels.

The daughter closed the door, went to rouse her family, and told them what she had done. Her father said: "Well, little daughter, you have saved our lives, now be my son's lawful wife." There was a gay feast and a wedding. The young bride kept telling her father that he should sell his old house and buy a new one, for she was very much afraid of the robbers, who might return sooner or later. And her fears came true. After some time, the same robber who had come with the barrels disguised himself as an officer, came to the peasant's house, and asked whether he could spend the night. He was admitted. No one guessed anything, but the young bride recognized him and said: "Father, this is the same robber who came before." "No, my daughter, it is not." She did not answer; but when bedtime came, she put a sharp ax beside her and stayed awake all night watching. In the middle of the night the pretended officer rose, took his saber, and was about to cut off her husband's head. She did not lose her presence of mind, but swung her ax and cut off his right hand; then she swung again and cut off his head. Her father now realized that his daughter was really very wise; he followed her advice, sold his old house, and bought himself a hostelry. He moved to his new residence and began to prosper and increase his trade.

His neighbors, the same who had given him money and later sued him in court, stopped at his hostelry. "Hey, how do you happen to be here?" "This is my house, I bought it recently." "It's a magnificent house! Apparently you are in money. Why don't you pay your debts?" The host bowed and said: "Thank God! The Lord has been good to me, I found a treasure, and I am ready to pay you even threefold." "Very well, brother. Let us now celebrate the housewarming!" "You are welcome." So they had a good time.

And near the house there was a beautiful garden. "May we look at your garden?" "With pleasure, gentlemen—I will accompany you." They walked and walked in the garden and in a remote corner found a tubful of ashes. When the host saw it he gasped: "Gentlemen, this is the same tub that my wife sold." "Let us see whether the money is not in the ashes." They shook the tub and found the money. Then the neighbors believed that the peasant had told them the truth. "Let us examine the trees in the woods," they said. "The raven who snatched the cap must have built a nest in it." They walked and walked, saw a nest, pulled it down with hooks, and there was the cap! They threw out the nest and found the money. The host paid his debt to his neighbors and began to live in prosperity and happiness.

THE MAYORESS

ONCE THERE WAS an ambitious woman. When her husband came home from the village council she asked him: "What did the council deliberate about?" "We did not deliberate about anything; we gathered to elect a new mayor." "And whom did you elect?" "For the time being, no one." "Elect me, then," said the woman. And so the husband went to the council (his wife was a bad one and he wanted to teach her a lesson) and reported this to the elders; they immediately elected her mayoress. So she began to rule and judge; she drank wine with the peasants, and took bribes.

The time came for collecting the poll tax. The mayoress was unable to collect it on time. A Cossack came and asked for the mayor, but the woman upon hearing that he had arrived ran home to hide. "Where shall I hide?" she asked her husband. "Dear little husband, tie me up in a bag and put me over there with the bags of grain!" There were about five bags of spring seed in the room. The peasant tied up the mayoress and put her among the bags. The Cossack came and he said: "Oho, the mayor has hidden himself!" And he began to lash the bag with his whip. The woman roared at the top of her lungs: "Oh, little father, I don't want to be mayoress, I don't want to be mayoress!" The Cossack gave her a good thrashing and left, and thereafter the woman no longer wanted to be mayoress, and obeyed her husband.

I N A CERTAIN LAND, in a certain kingdom, there lived an old man and his old wife. They had three sons, of whom the third was called Ivan the Simpleton. The first two sons were married, but Ivan the Simpleton was a bachelor. The first two were busy: they managed the house, plowed, and sowed, but the third did nothing at all. One day the old father and his daughters-in-law sent Ivan to finish plowing a few rods of land. The young boy came to the field, harnessed his horse, drove once or twice over the field with his plow, and saw countless swarms of mosquitoes and midges. He grabbed a whip, lashed one side of his horse, and killed a host of these bugs; he lashed the other side of his horse and killed forty gadflies. He thought to himself: "Here with one stroke I have killed forty mighty knights and a countless host of lesser warriors!" He gathered them all together, put them in a pile, and covered them with horse dung; he did not continue plowing, but unharnessed his horse and drove home. Upon his return he said to his sisters-in-law and his mother: "Give me a piece of thick cloth and a saddle, and you, father, give me the rusty saber that hangs on the wall. I am not a real peasant, I have no land!"

His family laughed at him, and to mock him gave him a cracked clod instead of a saddle; our fellow attached girths to it and laid it across a wretched mare. Instead of a piece of thick cloth, his mother gave him a ragged old dress of hers; he took this, sharpened his father's saber, made ready for his journey, and left. He came to a crossroads, and since he knew how to write a little, he wrote on the guidepost: "Let the mighty Ilya Muromets and Fyodor Lyzhnikov come to such and such a kingdom to see the strong and mighty hero who in one stroke killed forty mighty knights and an unnumbered host of lesser warriors, and covered them all with a stone."

Soon after him, Ilya Muromets came to the same crossroads and read the inscription on the post. "Ha!" he said. "A strong and mighty hero has passed by here; it is not meet to disobey him." He rode on and overtook Vaniukha, and while he was still at a distance, doffed his cap and saluted him: "Good day, strong and mighty hero!" Vaniukha did not doff his cap, and said: "Good day, Iliukha!" They rode together. After a short time Fyodor Lyzhnikov came to the same post, read the inscription, and decided that he too should heed the summons—after all, Ilya Muromets had heeded it! So he rode in the same direction; while he was still at a distance he doffed his cap and said: "Good day, strong and mighty hero!" But Vaniukha did not doff his cap, and said: "Good day, Fediunka!"

All three of them rode together; they came to a certain kingdom, and stopped in the royal meadows. The heroes pitched their tents, and Vaniukha spread his old dress; the two heroes tied their steeds with silken ropes, but Vaniukha broke a twig from a tree, twisted it, and tied his mare with it. And so they settled themselves. From his castle the king saw that strangers were foraging in his meadows and at once sent one of his familiars to find out who they were. He came to the meadows, approached Ilya Muromets, and asked him what manner of men they were and why they thus trampled the king's meadows without permission. Ilya Muromets answered: "It is not for me to answer! Ask our chief, the strong and mighty hero."

The envoy approached Vaniukha, who began to shout at him before he could utter a word: "Get away while you still can, and tell the king that in his meadows there is a strong and mighty hero who in one stroke killed forty mighty knights and an unnumbered host of lesser warriors and covered them with a stone—and that Ilya Muromets and Fyodor Lyzhnikov are with him, and that he demands the king's daughter in marriage!" The envoy conveyed this message to the king. The king consulted the annals: Ilya Muromets and Fyodor Lyzhnikov were mentioned there, but the third one, who in one stroke had killed forty knights, was not. Then the king ordered his army to gather, seize the three knights, and bring them before him. But this was no easy task! When Vaniukha saw the army approaching he cried: "Ilyukha, drive away this rabble!" And he himself lay down, stretched out, and watched the scene like an owl.

143

At his command Ilya Muromets jumped on his steed, galloped forward, and did not so much smite with his hands as trample with his steed; he knocked down the whole army, leaving only a few messengers to inform the king of what had happened. Upon hearing the news of the disaster, the king assembled even greater forces and sent them to seize the three knights. Ivan the Simpleton cried: "Fediunka, drive away this scum!" Fyodor jumped on his steed and knocked them all down, leaving only a few messengers.

What could the king do? He was in sore straits; the three knights had defeated his army. He began to cudgel his brains, and recalled that in his kingdom there lived a strong hero, Dobrynya. He sent him a letter, asking him to come to the royal meadows and conquer the three knights. Dobrynya came; the king received him on his third-story balcony, and Dobrynya on horseback was level with the king on the balcony—so mighty was he! He saluted the king and they spoke together. Then he went to the king's meadows. Ilya Muromets and Fyodor Lyzhnikov saw Dobrynya riding toward them, became frightened, jumped on their steeds, and made away. But Vaniukha had no time to run away, for while he got his mare ready, Dobrynya approached him and began to laugh at the sight of this vaunted hero—he was so short and so thin! Dobrynya bent his head down level with Vaniukha's face and stared at him in amusement. Vaniukha did not lose his presence of mind; he drew out his saber and cut off Dobrynya's head.

The king saw this and was frightened. "Oh," he said, "the knight has slain Dobrynya. Now we are indeed in trouble! Go quickly, call the hero to my palace." Such a brilliant delegation came to fetch Vaniukha that, Lord save us, the very best carriages and people of the highest rank were there. They seated him in a coach and brought him before the king. The king received him hospitably and gave him his daughter in marriage; they celebrated their wedding, and are still alive to this very day and chewing bread.

I was at their wedding and drank mead; it ran down my mustache but did not go into my mouth. I asked for a cap,

144

and received a slap; I was given a robe, and on my way home a titmouse flew over me cackling: "Flowing robe!" I thought she was saying, "Throw away the robe," and threw it away. This is not the tale, but a flourish, for fun. The tale itself has not begun!

FATHER NICHOLAS
AND THE THIEF

IN A CERTAIN TOWN there lived a thief who caused much sorrow. One day he happened to rob a wealthy man; the theft was discovered and men were sent in pursuit of the thief. He ran for a long time through the woods, but in front of these woods there was an open steppe that extended for at least ten versts. When the thief reached the edge of the woods, he stopped and wondered what to do next. If he ran over the steppe, he would be caught at once, for there everything could be seen from a distance of two versts; and he heard his pursuers coming closer. Then he began to pray: "Lord, forgive my sinful soul; hide me, Father Nicholas, and I will set a ten kopek candle before your image."

Suddenly out of nowhere an aged man appeared and asked the thief: "What did you just say?" The thief answered: "I said: 'Father Nicholas, hide me in this wilderness.' And I promised to put a candle before his image." And he confessed his sin to the old man, who said: "Creep into this piece of carrion." For a piece of carrion was lying nearby. The thief had no other choice than to creep into the carrion, for he did not want to be caught. He crept in, and that very minute the old man became invisible. He was Father Nicholas himself.

Now the pursuers came nearer; the men rode out on the steppe, rode for half a verst, and, seeing nothing, turned back.

Meanwhile the thief lay in the carrion, hardly able to breathe, so foul was the smell. When his pursuers left, he crept out and saw the same old man standing near by, gathering wax. The thief approached him and thanked him for his rescue. Then the old man asked again: "What did you promise Father Nicholas when you sought refuge?" The thief answered: "I promised to buy him a ten kopek candle." "Well, just as you were stifled lying in that carrion, so Father Nicholas would be stifled by your candle." And the old man admonished him: "Never pray to the Lord and his saints to help you in evil deeds; for the Lord does not bless evil deeds. Now heed my words, and tell others never to pray to God for help in evil deeds!" Having said this, he vanished from sight.

BURENUSHKA,
THE LITTLE RED COW

IN A CERTAIN KINGDOM, in a certain land, there lived a king and a queen, and they had an only daughter, Princess Maria. When the queen died, the king took another wife, Yagishna. Yagishna gave birth to two daughters: one had two eyes, and the other three eyes. The stepmother disliked Princess Maria, and ordered her to take Burenushka, the little red cow, to pasture, and gave her a crust of dry bread for her dinner. The princess went to the open field, bowed to Burenushka's right leg, ate and drank her fill, and dressed in fine attire; all day long, dressed like a lady, she tended Burenushka. At the end of the day, she again bowed to the little cow's right leg, removed her fine attire, went home carrying back her crust of bread, and put it on the table. "How does the slut keep alive?" wondered Yagishna. The next day she gave Princess Maria the same crust, and sent her elder daughter with her, saying: "Give

146

an eye to what Princess Maria feeds herself with." They came to the open field and Princess Maria said: "Little sister, let me pick the lice from your head." She began to pick them, at the same time saying: "Sleep, sleep, little sister! Sleep, sleep, my dear! Sleep, sleep, little eye! Sleep, sleep, other eye!" The sister fell asleep, and Princess Maria rose up, went to Burenushka, bowed to her right leg, ate and drank her fill, dressed herself in fine attire, and all day long walked around like a lady. Night came; Princess Maria removed her fine attire and said: "Get up, little sister, get up, my dear, let us go home." "Ah," said the sister unhappily, "I have slept through the day, and have not seen anything; now my mother will scold me." They came home; the mother asked her: "What did Princess Maria eat, what did she drink?" "I have not seen anything." Yagishna scolded her; next morning she got up and sent her three-eyed daughter, saying: "Go and see what that slut eats and drinks." The girls came to the open field where Burenushka grazed, and Princess Maria said: "Little sister, let me pick the lice from your head." "Pick them, little sister! Pick them, my dear!" Princess Maria began to pick, saying at the same time: "Sleep, sleep, little sister! Sleep, sleep, my dear! Sleep, sleep, little eye! Sleep, sleep, other eye!" She forgot about the third eye, and the third eye looked and looked at what Princess Maria was doing. She ran to Burenushka, bowed to her right leg, ate and drank her fill, dressed in fine attire. When the sun began to set, she again bowed to Burenushka, removed her fine attire, and went to rouse the three-eyed one: "Get up, little sister! Get up, my dear! Let us go home!" Princess Maria came home and put her dry crust on the table. The mother questioned her daughter: "What does she eat and drink?" The three-eyed one told everything. Yagishna said to her husband: "Slaughter Burenushka, old man!" And the old man slaughtered the cow. Princess Maria begged him: "Please, my dear, give me at least a bit of the entrails!" The old man threw her a bit of the entrails. She took it, placed it on a gatepost, and a bush with sweet berries grew up on it, and all kinds of little birds perched there and sang songs of kings and of peasants. Prince Ivan heard about Princess Maria, came to her stepmother, put a dish on

147

the table, and said: "Whichever maiden picks a dishful of berries for me, her I will take for my wife." Yagishna sent her elder daughter to pick berries; the birds did not even let her come near, she had to guard her eyes lest the birds peck them out. Yagishna sent her other daughter, and they did not let her come close either. At last she sent Princess Maria. Princess Maria took the dish and went to pick the berries; and as she picked them, the little birds placed twice and thrice as many on the dish as she herself could pick. She returned, placed the berries on the table, and bowed to the prince. There was a gay feast and a wedding; Prince Ivan took Princess Maria away, and they began to live happily and prospered.

After some time, a long time or a short time, Princess Maria gave birth to a son. She wanted to visit her father, and went to his house with her husband. Her stepmother turned her into a goose and disguised her elder daughter as Prince Ivan's wife. Prince Ivan returned home. The old tutor of the child got up early in the morning, washed himself very clean, took the baby in his arms, and went to an open field, stopping near a little bush. Geese came flying, gray geese came. "My geese, gray geese! Where have you seen the baby's mother?" "In the next flock." The next flock came. "My geese, gray geese! Where have you seen the baby's mother?" The baby's mother jumped to the ground, tore off her goose skin, took the baby in her arms, and nursed him at her breast, crying: "I will nurse him today, I will nurse him tomorrow, but the day after I will fly beyond the forests dark, beyond the mountains high!" The old man went home. The little fellow slept till next morning without awakening, and the false wife railed at the old man for having gone to the open field and for having starved her son. Next morning again he got up very early, washed himself very clean, and went with the child to the open field; and Prince Ivan got up, followed the old man unseen, and hid in the bush. Geese came flying, gray geese came. The old man called to them: "My geese, gray geese! Where have you seen the baby's mother?" "In the next flock." The next flock came. "My geese, gray geese! Where have you seen the baby's mother?" The baby's mother jumped to the ground, tore off her goose skin, threw it

behind the bush, nursed the baby at her breast, and said farewell to him: "Tomorrow I will fly beyond the forests dark, beyond the mountains high!" She gave the baby to the old man and said: "Why is there a smell of burning?" She turned to put her goose skin on, and realized that it was gone: Prince Ivan had burned it. He grasped Princess Maria; she turned into a frog, then into a lizard, and into one kind of loathsome insect after another, and at last into a spindle. Prince Ivan broke the

spindle in two, threw the top back of him and the bottom in front of him, and a beautiful young woman stood before him. They went home together. Yagishna's daughter yelled and shouted: "The wrecker is coming, the killer is coming!" Prince Ivan gathered the dukes and boyars together and asked them: "With which wife do you advise me to live?" They said: "With the first." "Well, gentlemen, whichever wife is the first to climb the gate, with her will I live." Yagishna's daughter at once climbed to the top of the gate, but Princess Maria only clutched it and did not climb up. Then Prince Ivan took his gun and shot the false wife, and began to live with Princess Maria as of old, and they prospered.

THE JESTER

IN A CERTAIN VILLAGE there lived a jester. A priest decided to visit him and said to his wife: "I think I will go to the jester, perhaps he will play some clever trick to amuse me." He made ready and went; he found the jester walking around his yard tending his farm. "May God help you, jester!" "Welcome, father, whither is God taking you?" "To you, my dearest one; won't you play a trick to amuse me?" "With pleasure, father; only I left the trick with seven other jesters, so dress me up warmly and give me your horse that I may go and fetch it." The priest gave him his horse, sheepskin, and cap, and the jester drove away. He came to the priest's wife and said: "Little mother, the priest has bought twelve thousand pounds of fish; he sent me to you on his horse, he wants three hundred rubles." The priest's wife straightway gave him three hundred rubles; the jester took them and drove back. He came home, put the sheepskin coat and the cap in the sledge, set the horse free in the enclosure, and hid himself. The priest waited and waited, finally lost patience, and returned to his wife. She asked: "Where is the fish?" "What fish?" "What do you mean? The jester was here to get the money; he said that you had bought twelve thousand pounds of fish, and I gave him three hundred rubles." Thus the priest learned what kind of trick the jester had played on him!

The next day he again went to the jester. The jester expected him; he had disguised himself as a woman and was sitting by the window spinning. Suddenly the priest appeared. "May God help you!" "You are welcome!" "Is the jester home?" "No, father." "But where is he?" "Yesterday he played a trick on you, and since then he has not been home." "What a rascal! He will probably come home tomorrow." On the third day the priest came again, and the jester still was not at home. The priest thought: "Why should I come here for nothing? This girl is probably his sister; I will take her to my house and make her work off my money." He asked her: "Who are you? A relation of the jester's?" She said: "I am his sister." "The jester took three hundred rubles from me; so come, my little dove, work them off." "Well, if I must go, I will." She made ready, went with the priest, and lived in his house for a long time.

The priest had several young daughters to marry. One day the matchmakers came to him: a rich merchant wanted to marry his son to one of the priest's daughters. But the priest's daughters were not to the merchant's liking, and instead he asked the priest's cook, the jester's pretended sister, to marry his son. There was a gay feast and a wedding, everything was done in the proper way. That evening the pretended bride said to her husband: "Drop me out of the window on a sheet, I want to get some fresh air; when I shake the sheet, pull me back." The husband dropped her into the garden; the supposed wife tied a she-goat to the sheet, shook it, and the bridegroom pulled it back. When he dragged it into the room, he found a she-goat instead of his wife. He began to shout: "Oh, evil people have bewitched my wife!" Everyone rushed to his room and began to exorcise the she-goat; the women began to conjure her, trying to turn her into a woman again, and in the end tormented her so much that she died.

Meanwhile the jester came home, changed his clothing, and went to the priest, who welcomed him and invited him to stay and dine with him. The jester ate and drank, talked about one thing and another, and then asked: "Father, where is my sister? Did you not take her into your home?" "I did," answered the priest, "but I married her to a rich merchant." "What do you mean? Without my permission? Does the law permit that? I'll sue you in court!" The priest began to argue with him, begging him not to sue. The jester obtained three hundred rubles from him. Then he said: "Now, father, take me to my brother-in-law, show me how they are living." The priest did not want to start a new argument, so he went with him.

They came to the merchant, who received them hospitably. The jester sat there for a long time, but his sister did not appear. Finally he said: "Kinsman, where is my sister? I have not seen her for a long time." The others began to get restless. He asked again; they told him that evil people had bewitched his sister and changed her into a she-goat. "Show me the goat, then!" said the jester. They said: "She died." "No! No she-goat died—you killed my sister. How could she change into a goat? I will go to court about this." They began to beg him: "Please don't go to court, we'll pay you whatever you ask." "Give me three hundred rubles, then I won't sue you." They counted out the money, the jester took it and left, made a coffin somewhere, put the money in it, and drove home.

On his way he met the seven other jesters. They asked him: "What are you carrying, jester?" "Money." "And where did you get it?" "It's very simple! I sold a dead man, and now I am carrying his coffin full of money." The jesters without saying a word went home, slew their wives, made coffins, put the coffins on carts, and drove into town, calling: "Dead people, dead people! Who wants to buy dead people!" When the Cossacks heard this, they immediately galloped over to them and began to lash them with whips. They lashed them for a long time, saying: "That will teach you to sell dead people!" Then they drove them out of the town. The seven jesters had a narrow escape; they buried their dead and went to the first jester's house to revenge themselves for the trick he had played on them. He was expecting them and had prepared everything in advance.

They came, entered his house, wished him good day, and sat down on a bench. Now, there was a she-goat running about in the jester's house; she ran and ran and suddenly dropped a silver ruble. The jesters saw it and asked: "How did the she-goat drop a silver ruble?" "She always drops silver coins!" They began to press him to sell the goat; he stubbornly refused, arguing that he wanted her himself. But the other jesters insisted and finally he agreed to sell the goat for three hundred rubles. The jesters gave him the money and took the goat away with them; they put her in a room, spread rugs on the floor, and waited for the morning, thinking, "She'll drop a tubful of coins for us!" Instead she only befouled the rugs.

Again the jesters went to take vengeance on our jester. He knew that they would come and said to his wife: "Now woman, mind you. I am going to fasten a bladder full of blood under your arm. When the jesters come to thrash me, I shall ask you to serve dinner. The first time I ask you, don't heed me; the second time I ask you, still don't heed me; the third time I ask you, still don't heed me. I will snatch a knife and thrust it into the bladder, the blood will flow, and you will fall, pretending that you are dead. Then I will take a whiplash and lash you once; you will stir. I will lash you a second time, and you will turn over; I will lash you a third time, and you will jump up and set the table." The jesters arrived. "Well, brother," they said, "you have been cheating us long enough. This time we are going to kill you." "Too bad! Kill me if you must, but let us have dinner together for the last time. Eh, woman, serve the dinner!" She did not move; he ordered her a second time and still she did not move; he ordered her a third time and still she did not move. The jester took a knife and slashed her in the side; blood flowed from her in streams, she fell to the floor, and the jesters became frightened. "What have you done, you dog? Now you'll get us involved in this!" "Quiet, boys! I have a special whiplash with which to cure her."

He got the whiplash, lashed once, and his wife stirred; he lashed a second time and she turned over; he lashed a third time and she jumped up and began to set the table. The jesters said: "Sell us that whiplash!" "Buy it." "How much do you want for it?" "Three hundred rubles." The jesters counted out the money, took the whiplash, and went to town with it. They saw a rich man's funeral and cried: "Stop, stop!" The procession stopped. "We shall bring the dead man back to life." They lashed the dead man once, but he did not stir; they lashed him a second time, with the same result; they lashed him a third, fourth, and fifth time—still the dead man refused to stir. Then the good fellows were seized and given lashes in their turn; and the people who lashed them with whips kept saying: "That's for you doctors! That's for you doctors!" This time they were lashed till they were half dead. They somehow managed to trudge home, and when they had recovered they said: "Well, boys, the jester has made fools of us long enough; let us kill him once and for all."

They made ready and went; they found the jester at home, seized him, and dragged him to the river to drown him. He begged them: "Please let me at least say farewell to my wife and family. Bring them here!" They agreed, and went to get his family, after tying him in a sack and leaving him near the ice hole. They had no sooner left than a soldier drove by with a pair of bay horses. The jester coughed in his sack. The soldier stopped, got off his sledge, and asked: "Ah, jester, why have you crept into this sack?" "Well, I eloped with so and so [he named the girl], and her father began to look for us; we hid in sacks, and had ourselves tied up and set down in different places in order to mislead our pursuers." The soldier was a widower and he said: "Brother, let me get into that sack." The jester obstinately refused, but the soldier pressed him and finally persuaded him. The jester got out, tied the soldier in the sack, took his horses, and drove away. The soldier sat and sat in the sack and finally fell asleep.

The seven jesters returned without our jester's family, took the sack, and cast it into the water; the sack went down to the bottom and the water made a gurgling noise that sounded like "gray-glack-gray-glack." The jesters ran home, sat down to rest, and our jester drove by their windows with a pair of horses fine enough to take your breath away! "Stop!" shouted the seven jesters. He stopped. "How did you get out of the water?" "Ah, you fools! Didn't you hear me saying as I went down: 'Grays and blacks, grays and blacks'? I was fishing for horses. There are plenty of them, and what horses! What I have harnessed here is just trash, because they were near the shore, but a little farther out there are black horses—real prizes!" The jesters believed him and begged: "Brother, drop us into the water— we too want to get some horses!" "With pleasure!" He tied them all in sacks and dropped them into the water, one after the other. When he had dropped them all, he just waved his hand and said: "Now drive out on your black horses!"

IN ONE VILLAGE there lived two brothers, Danilo and
Gavrilo. Danilo was rich and Gavrilo poor. One cow was
Gavrilo's only possession, and Danilo envied him even
that. One day Danilo went to town to buy something, and upon
his return came to his brother and told him: "Brother, why do
you keep a cow? I was in town today and saw that cows can be
had very cheap, at five or six rubles a head, but hides are selling
at twenty rubles." Gavrilo believed him, slaughtered his cow,
ate the meat, and at market time went to town to sell his cow-
hide. A tanner saw him and asked: "Is that hide for sale, my
good man?" "It is." "How much do you want for it?" "Twenty-
five rubles." "Are you out of your mind? I'll give you two
rubles and a half." Gavrilo refused to sell the hide at this price
and dragged it around with him all day, but no one offered
him any more. Finally, he dragged the hide to the bazaar. A
merchant saw him and asked: "Is that hide for sale?" "It is."
"What is your price?" "Twenty-five rubles." "Are you mad?
Who ever heard of such an expensive hide? I'll give you two
and a half." Gavrilo thought and thought, and finally said:
"So be it, Mr. Merchant, I will accept your price. But give me
at least a glass of vodka." "Very well, we won't quarrel about a
drink." The merchant gave him two rubles and a half, drew a
handkerchief out of his pocket, and said: "Now go to that stone
house over there, give the hostess this handkerchief, and tell
her from me to give you a full glass of wine."

Gavrilo took the handkerchief, went to the house, and the
hostess asked him: "What do you want?" Gavrilo said: "Thus
and so, Madam! I sold your husband a hide for two rubles and
a half, and a full glass of wine in addition; he sent me here to
give you this handkerchief and ask you to serve me the wine."
The hostess immediately poured a glass, but not quite a full
one, and offered it to Gavrilo; he drank it and stood there.
The hostess asked him: "Why are you still standing there?"
Gavrilo answered: "Our agreement was for a full glass of

wine." At that time the merchant's wife had her lover in the house; he heard Gavrilo's words and said: "Pour him some more, sweetheart!" She poured him half a glass; Gavrilo drank it and still stood there. Again the hostess asked him: "What are you waiting for now?" Gavrilo answered: "Our agreement was for a full glass, and you gave me half a glass." The lover told her to serve him for the third time; then the merchant's wife took the wine decanter, put the glass in Gavrilo's hand, and poured so much wine that it overflowed the rim. Gavrilo had no sooner drunk his wine than the merchant knocked at the door. The wife did not know where to hide her lover and began to cry: "Where shall I put you?" The lover ran back and forth in the room, and Gavrilo after him, crying: "And where shall I go?" The woman opened the trapdoor and pushed them both in.

The merchant came in, bringing guests with him. When they had drunk some liquor they began to sing songs, and Gavrilo, sitting in the pit, said to his companion: "Do what you will, but this is my father's favorite song, and I shall sing it too." "For heaven's sake, please, don't sing! Here are a hundred rubles for you, only keep quiet." Gavrilo took the money and kept quiet. After a short time the merry band above them began another song. Gavrilo again said to his companion: "Do what you will, but this time I must join them: that is my mother's favorite song!" "Please, don't sing! Here are two hundred rubles for you." This suited Gavrilo: he now had three hundred rubles; he put the money in his pocket and kept quiet. Soon the guests began a third song. Gavrilo said: "This time give me four hundred rubles, else I'll sing." The lover begged him not to, and said that he had no more money. The merchant's wife heard them wrangling in the cellar, opened the trapdoor, and whispered: "What is the matter?" Her lover asked her for five hundred rubles; she quickly returned with the money, and Gavrilo took it and kept quiet.

After a while he noticed a pillow and a barrel of tar in the pit; he ordered his companion to undress. After the lover had undressed, Gavrilo smeared him with tar, then cut open the pillow, and ordered him to roll in the feathers. After the man

157

had rolled himself in the feathers, Gavrilo opened the trap-door, sat himself astride his companion, and rode out, crying: "The ninth devil is leaving this house!" The guests became frightened and rushed home, thinking that devils had come. After all of them were gone, the merchant's wife said to her husband: "I told you that strange things were going on here." The merchant foolishly believed her and sold his house for a song.

Gavrilo came home and sent his eldest son to ask Danilo to come to him and help him count his money. But Danilo laughed in his nephew's face. "What is there to count?" he said. "Can't your father count two and a half rubles?" "Oh no, uncle, father has brought home lots of money!" Then Danilo's wife said: "Go there, at least to make fun of him." Danilo heeded his wife and went to his brother's. When Gavrilo poured out the pile of money before him, Danilo was surprised and asked: "Brother, where did you get so much money?" "What do you mean, where? I slaughtered my cow, and sold its hide in town for twenty-five rubles; for this money I bought five cows, slaughtered them, and sold their hides at the same price; and so on." Upon hearing that his brother had made a fortune so easily, Danilo went home, slaughtered all his cattle, and began to wait for market day; and since it was summer, the flesh of the slaughtered animals rotted. When he brought his hides to town, no one wanted to give him more than two and a half rubles for each. He was forced to sell them at a loss, and began to live more miserably than Gavrilo had ever lived. But Gavrilo became a sharp merchant and amassed a large fortune.

THE CROSS IS PLEDGED
AS SECURITY

IN A CERTAIN TOWN there lived two merchants at the very edge of the river. One was Russian, the other Tartar; both were extremely wealthy. Now it came to pass that the Russian merchant went bankrupt as a result of some unfortunate dealings, and nothing was left of his wealth: all his possessions were seized. He was now in bad straits, and as poor as a churchmouse. He went to his friend the Tartar and asked him to lend him some money. The Tartar said: "Who will be your guarantor?" "Whom shall I name? I have no one left. But wait a minute—let the life-giving cross on the church be your security." "Very well, my friend," said the Tartar, "I will trust your cross; what you believe in is good enough for me." And he gave the Russian merchant fifty thousand rubles. The Russian took the money, said farewell to the Tartar, and again set out to trade in foreign lands.

At the end of two years he had earned one hundred and fifty thousand rubles with the original fifty thousand. He happened to be sailing with his goods on the Danube, from one town to another; suddenly a storm came up and the ship seemed about to founder. The merchant then recalled that he had borrowed money against the security of the life-giving cross, and had not paid his debt; he decided that this was the reason for the storm. He had no sooner come to this conclusion than the storm began to subside. The merchant took a barrel, counted out fifty thousand rubles, wrote a note to the Tartar, put it in the barrel with the money, and threw the barrel into the water, thinking, "Since I gave the cross as security, the cross will deliver the money to its rightful owner."

The barrel sank to the bottom at once, and everyone thought that the money would be lost. But instead, what happened? The Tartar had a Russian cook. One day she went to fetch water at the river. She saw a barrel floating; she waded into the river and tried to grasp it, but every time she came close to it, it moved away; when she waded from the barrel to the bank, it followed her. She struggled with it for some time, then went home and told her master about it. At first he did not believe her, but then decided to go to the river and see this barrel for himself. He came, and saw that the barrel was really floating near the bank. He undressed, went into the water, and no sooner had he begun to wade than the barrel drifted to him by itself; the Tartar took it home, opened it, and found the money and the note. He read the note, which ran thus: "My dear friend, I am returning to you the fifty thousand rubles that I borrowed from you against the security of the life-giving cross."

The Tartar read the note and was amazed at the power of the life-giving cross. He counted the money: the whole sum was there. Meanwhile the Russian merchant, having traded for about five years, had earned a handsome little fortune. He returned to his own town, and thinking that his barrel had been lost, decided that his first duty was to settle his debt to the Tartar; so he came to him and offered him the money. Then the Tartar told the merchant everything that had happened, and how he had found the barrel with the money and the note in the river. He showed the Russian the note and asked: "Is this really in your hand?" The Russian merchant answered: "It is." Everyone was amazed at the miracle, and the Tartar said: "So you see, brother, you don't owe me any money; take it back." The Russian merchant offered a thanksgiving service to God. The next day the Tartar had himself and his family baptized. The Russian merchant was his godfather, and the cook his godmother. After that both merchants lived long and happily; they reached a ripe old age and died in peace.

THE DAYDREAMER

A POOR PEASANT walking in a field saw a hare under a bush and was overjoyed. He said: "Now I'm in luck! I will catch this hare, kill him with a whip, and sell him for twelve kopeks. For that money I will buy a sow, and she will bring me twelve piglets; the piglets will grow up and each bring twelve piglets; I will slaughter them all, and have a barnful of meat. I will sell the meat, and with the money will set up housekeeping and get married. My wife will bear me two sons, Vaska and Vanka. The children will plow the field, and I will sit by the window and give orders. "Hey, you boys!" I will cry. "Vaska and Vanka! Don't overwork your laborers; apparently you yourselves have never known poverty!" And the peasant shouted these words so loudly that the hare was startled and ran away, and his house with all his riches and his wife, and his children were lost.

THE TAMING OF THE SHREW

MARTYNKO WAS LONELY. He decided to get married and went to propose to the priest's daughter, Ustinia. The priest told him: "Eh, Martynko, I would gladly give her to you, but how will you live with her? She is so capricious!" Martynko answered him: "Father, I am alone; with her there will be two of us, but there will be no one to be angry at and no one to quarrel with." The priest agreed to give Ustinia to Martynko, and they were married. Martynko took his wife to his house. She asked: "When you get angry, what do you do?" He said: "When I am angry, I get drunk on water!" Then

161

he asked Ustinia: "And you, Ustinia, what do you do when you get angry?" "When I am angry, I sit on the stove with my face to the corner and put the front of my headband to the back." Next morning our Martynko took his piebald horse to plow for the spring sowing. Ustinia made curd cakes and brought them to her husband, crying: "Peasant, come and eat!" He pretended not to hear and went on plowing. Ustinia grew angry, went home, ate her cakes, and sat on the stove, turning her face to the corner. When Martynko came home, he drank two jugs of water, took a lamb and tore it asunder, started to climb up to his wife on the stove, fell down, rolled on the floor as far as the door, and began to snore. His wife quietly got down from the stove, did not dare open the door, got wood through the window, made a fire in the stove, and cooked dinner for Martynko. He awoke, she served him his dinner, and asked him to take her to visit her father. Martynko harnessed his piebald mare to the sledge—although it was spring—and they set out. On the way their mare refused to pull, so Martynko cut off her head and harnessed his Ustinia to the sledge. He drove to his father-in-law's house; the priest's wife and her daughters saw that Ustinia was dragging Martynko. They rushed out to meet the two; some of them pulled the shafts and some the ropes, to help Ustinia; and the priest thanked Martynko for having given a lesson to all shrews. They came to the priest's house; Ustinia asked her family to keep water out of sight and to serve only wine and beer, saying that when Martynko drank water, he was terribly angry. The next day a cook left a pail of water in the entrance hall. Martynko drank some water, became as foolish as a drunken man, and ordered Ustinia to harness herself to the sledge; she trembled, and begged her father to give them his chestnut horse. The priest made them a gift of a horse; Martynko and Ustinia drove home, and to this day they are still living and chewing bread. And Ustinia is a most obedient wife.

QUARRELSOME DEMYAN

ONCE THERE WAS a peasant who liked to pick a fight; he invited another peasant to his house, told his wife to set the table, and asked his guest to sit down. The guest said politely: "You shouldn't have gone to so much trouble, Demyan Ilyich." Demyan Ilyich slapped him in the face and said: "Always obey the master when you're in someone else's house." The guest sat down, the host offered him food, and he ate. The host began to cut numberless slices of bread. The guest said: "Why do you cut so much bread, Demyan Ilyich?" Demyan Ilyich gave him another slap in the face, saying: "Don't give advice in someone else's house. Do what the host tells you." The guest became unhappy, and when offered food did not eat it, thus disobeying Demyan, who kept beating him and saying: "In someone else's house, obey the master!"

At that moment another fellow, shabbily dressed, but lively and robust, opened the gate, and without being invited, rode into the yard. Demyan went out on the porch and saluted him: "Welcome, welcome!" For he wanted to thrash this guest, too! The fellow was not backward. He removed his hat and said: "Forgive me, Demyan Ilyich, for having come without first asking permission." "Never mind, you are welcome, please come in!" The fellow came in. The host bade him sit down at table and ordered his wife to serve the dishes and bring bread. The fellow ate and ate, without contradicting his host. No matter how Demyan tried to provoke this guest, he could not find a pretext for striking him. Finally he resorted to tricks; he brought out his very best clothes and said to the stranger: "Take off what you are wearing, put this on." He thought to himself: "He will refuse out of politeness, and then I will thrash him." But the fellow did not refuse; he put on the clothes that his host gave him. Demyan offered him this and that; still the fellow did not quarrel. Demyan brought out a good horse, saddled it with his best saddle, put a good bridle on it, and said to his guest, "Take my horse, yours is a poor

163

jade"—thinking to himself that the man would surely refuse. But the fellow mounted the horse. Demyan told him to ride forth; he silently urged on the horse, went out of the yard, and said: "Farewell, Demyan! The devil didn't send me, I came here of my own accord." And he was never heard of again. Demyan followed him with his eyes, clapped his hands, and said: "Well, at last I've found my equal! Not he, but I was fooled—I wanted to thrash him, and instead I lost my horse." And his horse with its trappings was worth perhaps as much as a hundred and fifty rubles.

THE MAGIC BOX

AN OLD COUPLE had a son. When he grew up, his father did not know what trade to teach him, but finally decided to apprentice him to a master who made all kinds of objects. He went to town and agreed with the master that the boy should be his apprentice for three years and come home only once during that time. Then he brought his son to the master. The young fellow lived with him for one year, then for another. Soon he learned how to make precious things and surpassed his master. Once he made a clock worth about five hundred rubles, and sent it to his father. "Perhaps he can sell it," he said, "and ease his misery." But the father would not even think of selling it. He could not feast his eyes enough on that clock, because his son had made it. Finally the day came for the young fellow's visit to his parents. His master was a magician and said: "Go! I give you three hours and three minutes; if you fail to return on time, you will die." The son thought: "How will I travel so many versts to my father?" Answering his thoughts, the master said: "Take this carriage; as soon as you sit down in it, blink your eyes."

Our fellow did this, and no sooner did he blink his eyes than

164

he found himself at his father's house. He stepped down from the carriage and came into the room, but no one was there. His father and mother, seeing a carriage drive up to their house, had been frightened and hid themselves in the cupboard near the stove. It took their son a long time to persuade them to come out. They greeted one another. The mother wept, for they had not seen each other in a long time. The son gave them the presents he had brought for them. While they exchanged blessings and conversed, time passed by. Three hours passed; only three minutes remained—now only two—now only one! An evil spirit whispered to the young man: "Hurry up, else your master will take you to task!" The young man was worried, said farewell to his parents, and left. Soon he arrived at his master's house, and an evil spirit tormented his master because the apprentice was late. The young man apologized to his master, fell at his feet, and said: "Forgive me for being late, I'll never do it again!" The master only chided him and truly forgave him.

Our young man resumed his former life and began to make all sorts of things better than anyone else. The master thought: "If the young man leaves me, he will take all my trade away, for he is now better than his master!" So he commanded him: "Worker! Go to the underground kingdom and bring me a little box that stands on the king's throne!" So together they made a long ladder by sewing one thong to another, and attached a little bell at each seam. The master lowered his apprentice into a ravine and told him to pull one thong as soon as he got the box; this would set the bells to ringing and the master would hear him. The young man went down into the earth, saw a house, and entered it. A score of peasants rose from their seats, bowed to him, and in one voice said: "Welcome, Prince Ivan!" The young man was surprised: what an honor! He entered another room that was full of women; they too stood up, bowed to him, and said: "Welcome, Prince Ivan!" All these people had been sent there by the master. Then the young man went into a third room; there he saw a throne, and on the throne a box; he took the box, went from the house, and all the people followed after him.

166

They came to the thong ladder, shook it, tied a man to it, and the master pulled it. The apprentice intended to tie himself to the ladder, with the box, when all the others had been raised up. The master pulled out half the people. Suddenly one of his workers came running to tell him that an accident had happened in his shop. The master ordered his worker to pull everyone out from underground except the peasant's son, and left the spot. So all the people were pulled out by the thongs and only our young man was left. He walked and walked in the underground kingdom and at last happened to shake the box. Thereupon a dozen strong fellows appeared and asked: "What is Prince Ivan's desire?" "Pull me up to the surface!" The men seized him and lifted him out. He did not go to his master, but to his father. Meanwhile the master remembered the box, ran to the ravine, and shook and shook the ladder—but his apprentice was gone. The master thought: "Apparently he has gone off somewhere! I must send someone for him."

After some time the peasant's son chose a fertile spot, tossed the box from hand to hand, and suddenly twenty-four strong fellows appeared: "What is your desire, Prince Ivan?" "Build a kingdom on this spot and let it be better than all other kingdoms." In no time the kingdom was there! Our young man established himself there, married, and began to live gloriously.

In his kingdom there was a little fellow, quite insignificant, whose mother often came to Prince Ivan begging for alms. Her son said to her: "Mother, steal the little box from our king." One day Prince Ivan was not at home; his wife gave the old woman alms and left the room. The old woman snatched the box, put it in a bag, and brought it to her son. He tossed the box from hand to hand and the same strong fellows jumped out. He ordered them to cast Prince Ivan into a deep ditch, where only cattle carcasses were thrown, and disposed of his wife and parents—he made them lackeys or banished them somewhere. He himself became king.

And so the peasant's son sat in the ditch a whole day, then a second, then a third. How could he get out? He saw a huge bird dragging a carcass. Just then a dead animal was thrown into the ditch, so he tied himself to it. The bird swooped down, snatched the carcass, carried it out, and perched on a pine tree. Prince Ivan dangled there, for he could not untie himself. A huntsman appeared, took aim, and shot. The bird took wing and flew away, dropping the dead cow from its claws. The cow fell and Prince Ivan fell with it. He untied himself and walked down the road, wondering how to recover his kingdom. He felt in his pocket—there was the key of the box! He tossed it, and two strong men jumped out. "What is your desire, Prince Ivan?" "You see, brothers, I am in trouble!" "We know it, and it is lucky that we two remained with the key." "Couldn't you bring me the box, brothers?" Prince Ivan had no sooner said this than the two men brought him the box. When he beheld it he took heart, ordered the beggar woman and her son to be put to death, and became king as before.

BUKHTAN BUKHTANOVICH

IN A CERTAIN KINGDOM in a certain land there lived one Bukhtan Bukhtanovich, who had a stove built on pillars in the middle of a field. He lay on the stove in cockroach milk up to his elbows. A fox came to him and said: "Bukhtan Bukhtanovich, would you like me to marry you to the tsar's daughter?" "What's that you're saying, little fox?" "Do you have any money?" "I have one five kopek piece." "Hand it over!" The fox took the coin, exchanged it for smaller coins— kopeks, pennies, and halfpennies, went to the tsar, and said: "Tsar, give me a quart measure to measure Bukhtan Bukhtanovich's money." The tsar said: "Take one!" The fox took it home, stuck one kopek behind the hoop around the measure, brought it back to the tsar, and said: "Tsar, a quart measure is not big enough; give me a peck measure to measure Bukhtan Bukhtanovich's money." "Take one!" The fox took it home, stuck a kopek behind the hoop of the measure, and brought it back to the tsar. "Tsar, a peck measure is not big enough; give me a bushel measure." "Take one!" The fox took it home,

168

stuck what remained of his coins behind the hoop, and brought it back to the tsar. He said: "Have you measured all his money, little fox?" The fox answered: "All of it. Now, tsar, I have come for a good purpose: give your daughter in marriage to Bukhtan Bukhtanovich." "Very well; show me the suitor."

The fox ran home. "Bukhtan Bukhtanovich, have you any clothes? Put them on." He dressed and, accompanied by the fox, went to the tsar. They walked along the market place and had to cross on a board over a muddy ditch. The fox gave Bukhtan a push and he fell into the mud. The fox ran to him. "What is the matter with you, Bukhtan Bukhtanovich?" Saying this, the fox smeared him with mud all over. "Wait here, Bukhtan Bukhtanovich, I shall run to the tsar." The fox came to the tsar and said: "Tsar, I was walking with Bukhtan Bukhtanovich on a board over a ditch—it was a wretched little board; we were not careful enough and somehow fell into the mud. Bukhtan Bukhtanovich is all dirty and unfit to come to town; have you some clothes you could lend him?" "Here, take these." The fox took the clothes and came to Bukhtan Bukhtanovich. "Here, change your clothes, Bukhtan, and let us go."

They came to the tsar, and at the tsar's palace the table was already set. Bukhtan did not look at anything except himself: he had never seen such clothes in his life. The tsar winked to the fox: "Little fox, why does this Bukhtan Bukhtanovich look only at himself?" "Tsar, I think he is ashamed to be wearing such clothes; never in his life has he worn such mean garments. Tsar, give him the garment that you yourself wear on Easter Sunday." And to Bukhtan the fox whispered: "Don't look at yourself!"

Bukhtan Bukhtanovich stared at a chair—it was a gilded one. The tsar again whispered to the fox: "Little fox, why does Bukhtan Bukhtanovich look only at that chair?" "Tsar, in his house such chairs stand only in the bathhouse." The tsar flung the chair out of the room. The fox whispered to Bukhtan: "Do not look at one thing; look here a bit and there a bit."

They began to talk about the purpose of their visit, the match. And then they celebrated the wedding—does a wedding take long in a tsar's palace? There no beer need be brewed, no wine distilled—everything is ready. Three ships were loaded for Bukhtan Bukhtanovich and they traveled homeward. Bukhtan Bukhtanovich and his wife were on one of the ships, and the fox ran along the shore. Bukhtan saw his stove and cried: "Little fox, little fox, there is my stove." "Be quiet, Bukhtan Bukhtanovich, that stove is a disgrace."

Bukhtan Bukhtanovich sailed on, and the fox ran ahead of him on the shore. He came to a hill and climbed it. On the hill stood a huge stone house, and around it was an enormous kingdom. The fox went into the house and at first saw no one; then he ran into a chamber, and there in the best bed lay Dragon, Son of the Dragon, stretching himself. Raven, Son of the Raven, was perched on the chimney, and Cat, Son of the Cat, sat on a throne. The fox said: "Why are you sitting here? The tsar is coming with fire and the tsarina with lightning, they will scorch and burn you." "Little fox, whither shall we go?" "Cat, Son of the Cat, go into the barrel." And the fox sealed him up in the barrel. "Raven, Son of the Raven, go into the mortar!" And the fox sealed him up in the mortar; then he wrapped Dragon, Son of the Dragon, in straw and took him out into the street.

The ships arrived. The fox ordered all the beasts to be thrown into the water; the Cossacks threw them in at once. Bukhtan Bukhtanovich moved all his possessions into that house; there he lived happily and prospered, ruled and governed, and there he ended his life.

THE FOX AND THE WOODCOCK

A FOX WAS RUNNING in the woods; she saw a woodcock on a tree and said to him: "Terenti, Terenti, I've been to town!" "Bu-bu-bu, bu-bu-bu, if you've been, you've been!" "Terenti, Terenti, I learned about a new law!" "Bu-bu-bu, bu-bu-bu, if you've learned, you've learned!" "A law forbidding you woodcocks to perch on trees, and ordering you always to walk in the green meadows!" "Bu-bu-bu, bu-bu-bu, to walk is to walk!" "Terenti, who is coming over there?" asked the fox, hearing the trampling of horses' feet and the barking of dogs. "A peasant." "Who is running after him?" "A colt." "And how does he hold his tail?" "It's twisted to one side." "Now farewell, Terenti, I have urgent business at home!"

THE FOX AND THE CRANE

THE FOX AND THE CRANE used to be good friends, they even stood godparents for the same child. The fox wanted to treat the crane to dinner and invited him to her house: "Come to see me, gossip! Come, my dear, you'll see how nicely I'll entertain you!" So the crane came to her house. Meantime the fox had cooked gruel and spread it over a dish. She served it and urged her guest: "Eat, my darling, I cooked it myself." The crane pecked with his bill, knocked and knocked at the dish, but nothing got into his mouth, while the fox lapped and lapped the gruel until she had eaten it all. After the gruel was gone, the fox said: "I'm sorry, dear friend, but that's all I have to offer you." "Thank you, my friend, for what you have given me. You must come to visit me soon."

The next day the fox came to the crane's house. The crane

171

had made a soup and put it in a pitcher with a narrow neck. She placed it on the table and said: "Eat, my friend, that's all I have to offer you." The fox began to trot around the pitcher, she approached it from one side, then from another, she licked it and smelled it, but all to no avail. Her snout could not get into the pitcher. Meanwhile the crane sucked and sucked until he had drunk all the soup. "I am sorry, my friend, that's all I have to offer you." The fox was greatly vexed; for she had thought she would eat for a whole week, and now she had to go home with a long face and an empty stomach. It was tit for tat; and from that moment on the friendship between the fox and the crane was over.

THE TWO RIVERS

FOR A LONG TIME the Volga River and the Vazuza River disputed as to which of them was the cleverer, stronger, and deserving of the greater honors. They argued and argued and neither would give in to the other. Finally they decided to settle the matter in this way. "Let us lie down to sleep," they said, "and whichever of us wakes up and reaches the Khvalinsky Sea first will be considered the cleverer, stronger, and deserving of the greater honors."

The Volga lay down to sleep and so did the Vazuza. In the middle of the night the Vazuza rose quietly, ran away from the Volga, chose a short, straight road to the sea, and started flowing. The Volga, upon awakening, flowed neither too slowly nor too fast, but just as a river should flow. At Zubtsov she overtook the Vazuza with such force that the Vazuza was frightened by her younger sister, and begged her, the Volga, to take her, the Vazuza, in her arms and carry her to the sea. Nevertheless, it is still the Vazuza that wakes first in the spring and rouses the Volga from her long winter sleep.

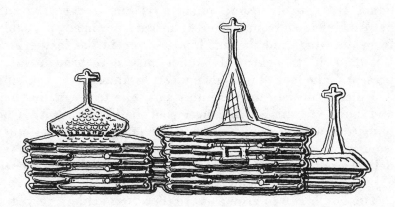

NODEY,
THE PRIEST'S GRANDSON

IN A CERTAIN KINGDOM, in a certain land, there lived a widowed priest and his daughter. He took very good care of the girl, and whenever he went to see someone in his parish he always brought her presents; his parishioners knew that our priest had a daughter and that she expected presents. One day he went to a village of his parish about twelve versts away, to give someone communion, and was received very hospitably. He forgot to ask for a present for his daughter, and set out for home. As he was riding on the road, he beheld a human head burning—in fact, it was almost all burned, only ashes remained. At first he passed it by, but then he changed his mind. "Here is a human head burning," he thought. "I will take it, put the ashes in my pocket, bring them home, and place them in the cellar."

He picked up the ashes, mounted his horse again, and rode home. His daughter came out to meet him in the yard and helped him down from his horse; he had a headache, probably from the wind, and she put him to sleep in the featherbed. But then she thought: "My father must have brought me a present." She looked into his pocket; meanwhile the ashes he had picked up had turned into a box. She took out this box and said: "Oh, this is a fine box; what shall I do with it?" She touched it with her tongue and became pregnant. What other women bear after long weeks, she bore in hours; her time for delivery came, and she gave birth to a boy. He was christened at once and named Nodey, the priest's grandson.

The boy began to grow; what other boys achieve in years, he achieved in hours; at six weeks he went out into the street to play ball with the other boys. When he hit a ball, it flew, one heard it buzz through the air, but one did not see it. If he struck someone in the leg, the leg came off; if he struck someone in the arm, the arm came off; and when he struck someone in the head, the poor fellow's head came off. The fathers of these children came to the priest and said to him: "Father, please do not allow your grandson to go into the street to play with the other children; he has done a great deal of damage." One would complain that his boy had lost his head, another that his child had lost an arm. "Please, Father," they said, "keep him in the house."

So the priest kept Nodey at home until summer came; by then he had grown quite big, and said: "Dear grandfather, what work shall we do now?" The priest was overjoyed and said to his daughter: "My beloved daughter, God be thanked for having given us an heir; he is a godsend, he is so strong. Now what shall we undertake? Let us work." And he said to his grandson: "Come, grandson, let us clear some marshy ground." "Let us go, grandfather."

So they went to the marshes and chose a place; the grandfather began to cut a pine tree, and Nodey said: "Grandfather, don't you work, but give me your blessing." "Well," said the grandfather, "may God bless you." And the boy set to work with such vigor that the woods began to tremble; he gave one

174

blow with his ax, and the tree flew down. Before noon he had cleared about four acres of marshy ground. The grandfather said: "Now we have to chop the wood and burn it." He answered: "Grandfather, let us simply pile it up."

After three days the former wilderness had become farmland. With the help of his grandfather Nodey sowed oats, and the oats throve beautifully, as never before. Now a bear began to haunt that field of oats. The priest went to inspect the new field and found that much of the grain had been eaten. He returned home, and his grandson asked him: "Well, grandfather, how is our field?" "Very fine, little grandson, only some wild horse has begun to frequent it—he has an enormous appetite and has done much damage." "Do you mean to say, grandfather, that after all the work I did, a good-for-nothing like that has done so much damage? I'll go catch him. Find me some hemp, as much as you can."

He sat down, wove a hempen bridle, and having eaten his dinner, went to the woods. When he saw the field, he was amazed at the sight. "My God," he said, "what mischief this horse has done! it's frightful!" And he sat down on a tree stump in the field. As he sat thus, the bear came out of the woods, went straight into the oat field, and began to trample the plants. Our brave youth was surprised. "What a strange creature!" he said. "I never saw such a horse. And how he spoils the oats!" Meanwhile the bear came close to him; he was not frightened by the man on the tree stump, but took him to be part of it. When he came quite close, Nodey jumped down and—one, two, three—caught the bear by the ears, hugged him tight, and pressed him to the ground. The bear thought to himself: "What's this?" He tried to get up; but Nodey would not let him; he put the hempen bridle on him, and led him home. And while he was leading him, whenever the bear caught on a tree, the tree was uprooted.

Well, Nodey brought him home, tied him to a pillar in the middle of the yard, and went into the house. "Lord, what a horse that was, grandfather! How tired I am from dragging him home!" The priest looked out into the yard and gasped. "Look, my daughter," he said, "what your little son, my grand-

175

son, has done!" And for a long time they gazed in admiration. Nodey said: "Don't stare, but tell me what we will do with this horse, what work we will give it, for it is very strong." "Use it to bring wood," said the grandfather.

So Nodey took the bear, harnessed him to a cart, and began to use him to carry wood. In three days he had carted off the whole village. The villagers did not venture to go out, for the entire village had disappeared. They came to the priest and said to him: "Put him wherever you will, but he must not stay here; what kind of behavior is this? In three days he has taken the whole village away. We cannot go out for fear of him."

"Ah, my daughter," said the priest, "what are we to do? I am sorry for your son, my grandson, but we must send him away; let him go wherever you will." And he called his grandson to him and said: "Well, my beloved grandson, the villagers have come with a request that we send you away; I am sorry for you, but you must go." "Eh, my beloved grandfather, you should have told me that long ago, and I would have gone without delay. My beloved mother, bake a loaf of bread for me!" His mother baked a loaf of bread for him and put it in his knapsack.

He rose very early and washed himself clean. Then he put his knapsack on his back and asked for a blessing: "My beloved mother and my dear grandfather, give me your blessing for my journey." He said his prayers and set out; he came to the open field, and instead of taking a road or a path, went through thick forests and deep swamps and walked for seven days, with his mouth open and his tongue hanging out. And he came to the thrice ninth land, to the thrice tenth kingdom, and found himself in an open field, near a steep mountain, and saw there Gorynya, the mighty hero, who kicked mountains about like balls.

Nodey, the priest's grandson, went to him and said: "God be with you, Gorynya, mighty hero! What immense strength is in you, that you can kick mountains about like balls!" Gorynya answered him: "Eh, brave youth, do not admire my strength! It is said that beyond thrice nine lands, in the thrice tenth kingdom, there is a certain Nodey, a priest's grandson, who is much stronger than I. He brought a bear from the woods and on this bear loaded his entire village. His bones will not be carried by a raven, he will not be borne by a good young steed!" And Nodey answered him: "Ah, brother Gorynya, mighty hero! The raven did not carry his bones, but he himself is here." Gorynya said: "Ah, brother, so you are Nodey, the priest's grandson! Take me with you as your younger brother!" Nodey took him, and they traveled to many far lands and conquered many mighty knights and captured many cities; then they both got married, and they and their brides prospered.

THE POOR WRETCH

ONCE THERE WAS A PEASANT named Nesterka who had six children but no land; he had nothing with which to support himself and his family, and he was afraid to steal. One day he harnessed his cart, took his children, and went out into the world. On the road he looked back and saw, lying in the dirt, a little old man who had no feet. This little old man begged him: "Please, take me with you!" "How can I, little father?" said Nesterka. "I have six children and my horse is a wretched nag." Again the footless man said: "Please take me!" Nesterka took the poor wretch, seated him in the cart, and drove on. The poor wretch said to him: "Let us cast lots to see which of us is to be the elder brother." They cast lots and it fell to the poor wretch to be the elder brother.

They came to a village. The poor wretch said: "Now go and ask if we can spend the night in that house." Nesterka began to beg for shelter. An old woman came out of the house and answered him: "We have no place for you. Even without you, we are crowded." Nesterka returned to the cripple and said: "They won't let us in there." But the cripple sent him back again, telling him to insist. Nesterka went and obtained permission to spend the night; he drove into the yard, carried his children into the house, and carried in the cripple also. The mistress of the house ordered him to put the children under the bench and the footless man on the shelf above the stove. He did as the woman bade him. "Where is your husband?" the cripple asked the hostess. "He has gone out stealing and has taken my two sons with him," she said.

After a while the husband returned. He brought twelve carts laden with silver into the yard, put the horses in the stable, and came into the house. He saw the poor people and began to shout at his wife: "What kind of people have you let in?" "They are beggars who have no place to spend the night." "It was quite unnecessary to let them in here! They could have spent the night in the street." Then the husband, the wife, and their two sons sat down to supper but did not invite the poor people to share. The cripple drew half a holy wafer from his bag, ate of it himself, and gave a bit of it to Nesterka and his children; all ate their fill.

The host was amazed. "How can this be?" he said. "The four of us have eaten a whole loaf of bread and we are still hungry, and the eight of you have been sated with half a wafer!"

When their hosts fell asleep, the cripple sent Nesterka out into the yard to see what was going on there. Nesterka went out and found that all the horses were eating oats. The cripple sent him out again, saying: "Go and have another look." He went out and saw that all the horses had their yokes on. The cripple sent Nesterka for the third time; he went out again and saw that all the horses were harnessed. He returned to the house and said: "All the horses are harnessed." "Well," said the cripple, "now carry out your children and myself, and we'll leave."

They sat on their cart and left the yard, and the robber's twelve horses followed them with the carts. They drove and drove; then the cripple ordered Nesterka to return to the house where they had spent the night and bring him his mittens. "I forgot them on the shelf," he explained. Nesterka went back, but there was no house. It was as though the building had dropped down through the earth: only the mittens remained by the chimney. He took the mittens, returned to the cripple, and told him that the whole house had fallen through the ground. "That is the Lord's punishment for stealing! Take these twelve carts for yourself, with everything in them," said the cripple, and vanished from sight. Nesterka returned home, found the carts laden with silver, and began to prosper.

His wife said to him: "Why do you keep your horses idle? Take them to serve as carriers." He made ready and went to the town. On the way he met a maiden whom he had never seen before. "These horses are not yours," she said. "That's true," said Nesterka, "since you have recognized them, take them, and God be with you." The maiden took the twelve horses and the peasant returned home. The next day the same maiden came to his window and said: "Here, take your horses; I was only joking, yet you gave them to me." Nesterka took the horses, and lo and behold, the carts were laden with even more silver and gold than before!

THE FIDDLER IN HELL

ONCE THERE WAS A PEASANT who had three sons. He lived richly, gathered two potfuls of money, and buried one pot in the threshing barn and the other under the gate. This peasant died without having told anyone about his money. One day there was a holiday in the village; a fiddler was walking about leisurely, when suddenly he fell through the ground and found himself in hell, at the very spot where the rich peasant was being tormented. "Good day, my friend," said the fiddler. The peasant answered: "You have fallen into the wrong place; this is hell, and I am in hell." "But, uncle, why were you sent here?" "Because of my money. I had a great deal of it, but I never gave to the poor, and buried two pots of it in the ground. Now I will be tormented, struck with sticks, and lacerated with claws." "What shall I do? I might be tormented too." "Sit on the stove behind the chimney, do not eat for three years: thus you will be saved."

The fiddler hid behind the chimney; the devils came and began to beat the rich peasant, saying all the time: "That's for you, rich man! You hoarded a great deal of money, and you did not know how to hide it; you buried it in such a place that we have a hard time guarding it. There is constant coming and going through the gate, the horses crush our heads with their hoofs, and in the threshing barn we are thrashed with flails."

As soon as the devils left, the peasant said to the fiddler: "If you ever get out of here, tell my children to take the money—one pot is buried under the gate and the other in the threshing barn—and tell them to give it to the poor." Again a whole band of devils came rushing in and asked the rich peasant: "Why is there a Russian smell here?" The peasant said: "You have just been to Russia and you have the Russian smell in your nostrils." "Impossible!" They began to search, found the fiddler, and cried: "Ha, ha, ha! A fiddler is here!" They dragged him down from the stove and forced him to play the fiddle. He played for three years but it seemed to him like three days; he got tired and said: "How strange! Sometimes I played and tore all my strings in one evening, and now I've played for three days, and not one string has broken, blessed be the Lord!" He had no sooner said these words than all his strings snapped. "Well, brothers," he said, "you can see for yourselves, my strings have broken, I have nothing to play on." "Just wait," said one devil, "I have two sets of strings and I'll bring them to you." He ran away and came back with some strings; the fiddler took them, tightened them, and again said, "Blessed be the Lord," when the two sets of strings snapped. "No, brothers," he said, "I cannot use your strings; I have some of my own at home; if you let me go, I'll bring them here." The devils refused to let him go. "You won't come back," they said. "If you don't trust me, send one of your number to escort me." So the devils chose one of their company to go with the fiddler.

He came to the village and heard a wedding being celebrated in the last house. "Let's go to that wedding!" "Let's!" They went into the house. Everyone recognized the fiddler and asked him: "Where have you been for three years?" "I was in the other world." They regaled themselves, then the devil said to the fiddler: "We must go now." The fiddler said: "Wait a little while; let me play my fiddle and amuse the young couple." They stayed there until the cocks began to crow; then the devil vanished, and the fiddler said to the rich peasant's sons: "Your father orders you to take his money: one pot is buried under the gate, and another in the threshing barn; and he said that you should give it all to the poor." The sons dug up the two pots and began to distribute money to the poor; but the more they gave, the more there was in the pots.

They put the pots on a crossroads; whoever passed by took out of them as many coins as his hand could clutch, and still the money in them did not decrease. A petition was sent to the tsar, saying that in a certain town there was a winding road about fifty versts long and that a straight road would reduce this distance to about five versts; and the tsar gave orders that a straight bridge be built. A bridge five versts long was erected and this used up all the money contained in the two pots. At that time a maiden gave birth to a son and abandoned him; this boy did not eat or drink for three years, and an angel of God always accompanied him. The boy came to the bridge and said: "Ah, what a wonderful bridge! May God give the kingdom of heaven to him whose money built it!" The Lord heard that prayer and ordered his angels to release the rich peasant from the darkness of hell.

THE OLD WOMAN
WHO RAN AWAY

AN OLD MAN AND HIS WIFE sat on the stove. The old woman looked at the field through the window and said: "If we had a little son Ivanushko and a little daughter Alionushka, our son would have plowed the field and sowed grain, the grain would have grown, and our daughter would have mowed it; I would have grown malt, brewed beer, and invited all my kin, but I would not have invited your kin!" "No, invite mine, but not yours!" said the old man. "No, no, I will invite my own folk, not yours!" The old man jumped up and began to drag his wife by her braid; he dragged and dragged her and finally pushed her off the stove.

Then the old man went to get wood and the old woman made ready to run away; she baked bread and pies, put them in a big bag, and went to say farewell to a neighbor. Somehow the old man got wind of it, returned home, took out of the bag everything his wife had prepared for her trip, put the bread and the pies in the larder, and himself sat in the bag. The old woman came home, placed the bag on her shoulders, and set out on her journey.

After walking for five or six versts, she stopped and said: "It would be nice to sit on a tree stump now and eat a cake." The old man cried from the bag: "I can see everything, I can hear everything!" "Ah, the accursed devil, he might catch me!" thought the old woman, and went on. Again she walked for about six versts, and said: "It would be nice to sit on a tree stump now and eat a cake." "I can see everything, I can hear everything!" cried the old man. Again she hurried on; she walked many versts, and not having eaten or drunk anything, she got so tired that her strength failed her. "Come what may, I will stop here," thought the old woman. "I will have a little rest and a bite."

Then she discovered that her husband was in the bag. She begged him: "Little father, forgive me, I will never try to run away again!"

The old man forgave her, and they went home together.

ANECDOTES

A WOMAN CAME TO AN INN and asked about her husband: "Was not my drunkard here?" "He was." "Ah, the scoundrel, the knave! How much did he drink?" "Five kopeks' worth." "Well, give me ten kopeks' worth!"

ONCE A TURNIP SAID: "I taste very good with honey." "Go along, you boaster," replied the honey, "I taste good without you."

THE SINGING TREE
AND THE TALKING BIRD

ONCE THERE WAS a very curious king who eavesdropped at the windows of his subjects. A certain merchant had three daughters, and one day the king heard these maidens conversing with their father. One said: "I wish I were married to the king's caterer!" The second daughter said: "If only the king's body servant would take me for his wife!" And the third daughter said: "And I should like to be married to the king himself; I would bear him two sons and one daughter."

Some time later the king fulfilled their wishes: he married the eldest daughter to his caterer, the second daughter to his body servant, and the youngest he took to wife himself. He lived happily with his wife, and she became pregnant; when her time came she began to have labor pains. The king wanted to send for the midwife of the city, but the king's sisters-in-law said: "Why send for a midwife? We ourselves can do what is necessary." When the queen gave birth to a son, these midwives told the king that his wife had given birth to a puppy, put the newborn boy in a box, and dropped it in the pond in the king's garden. The king became enraged at his wife and wanted to have her shot; but visiting kings dissuaded him from this, arguing that a first offense should be forgiven. So the king forgave her, postponing punishment against a second time.

A year later the queen again became pregnant and bore a son; this time her sisters told the king that she had given birth to a kitten. The king became even more enraged and wanted to put his wife to death, but he was again dissuaded after many entreaties, and postponed punishment against a third time. The sisters put the second baby likewise into a box and dropped it into the pond. Then the queen became pregnant for the third time, and bore a beautiful daughter; the sisters reported to the king that his wife had given birth to God knows what. The king became more enraged than before, had gallows erected, and wanted to hang his wife; but some kings who had come from other countries to visit him, said to him: "Rather, build a chapel next to the church, and put your wife in it; whoever goes to mass is to spit in her face." The king followed this advice; and people not only spat in the queen's face but hurled at her whatever they had in their hands, loaves of bread or cakes. As for the babies brought into the world by the queen and dropped by her midwives into the pond, the king's gardener took them into his house and brought them up.

These children of the king grew not by the year, but by the month—not by the day, but by the hour. The princes became handsome youths such as no mind can imagine nor pen describe; and the princess was such a beauty that she took one's breath away! And they came of age and asked the gardener to allow them to build a house outside the town. The gardener gave them his permission, they built a fine big house, and began to live happily. The brothers loved to catch hares; one day they went hunting, and the sister remained at home alone. A little old woman came to the house and said to the maiden: "Your house is comfortable and beautiful, but you lack three things." The princess asked her: "What do we lack? It seems to me we have everything." The aged woman said: "This is what you lack—the talking bird, the singing tree, and the water of life."

The brothers returned from the hunt and the sister went out to meet them and said: "My brothers, we have everything except three things." The brothers asked her: "What do we not have, little sister?" She said: "We do not have the talking bird, the singing tree, nor the water of life." The elder brother began to beg her: "Little sister, give me your blessing, I will go forth to get these marvels. And if I die or am killed, this is how you will know it: I will thrust this penknife into the wall; when blood begins to drip from the knife, it will be a sign that I am dead."

He left, and having walked for a long time, he came to a wood. A little old man sat on a tree, and the prince asked him: "How can I get the talking bird, the singing tree, and the water of life?" The man gave him a little spool and said: "Follow this spool wherever it rolls." The spool began to roll and the prince followed it; it rolled up to a high mountain and vanished from sight. The prince started to climb up the mountain, reached a point halfway to the top, and then suddenly vanished too. At his house blood at once dripped from his penknife, and the sister said to the younger brother that their elder brother had surely died. The younger brother said to her: "Now I will go, little sister, to get the talking bird, the singing tree, and the water of life." She gave him her blessing and he left; after having walked for a long time, he came to a wood. A little old man sat on a tree, and the prince asked him: "Little grandfather, how can I get the talking bird, the singing tree, and the water of life?" The little old man said: "Here is a spool for you. Follow it wherever it rolls." The old man threw the spool, it began to roll, and the prince followed it; it rolled up to a high mountain and vanished from sight; the prince started climbing the mountain, reached the halfway point, and suddenly vanished too.

The sister waited for him, many many years, and still he did not come back. Then she said: "My second brother too must

186

have died." And she went herself to get the talking bird, the singing tree, and the water of life. She walked for some time, a short time or a long time, and came to a wood. On the tree there sat a little old man, and she asked him: "Little grand-father, how can I get the talking bird, the singing tree, and the water of life?" The little old man answered: "You cannot get them! Cleverer persons than you have tried, but they all per-ished." The maiden still begged him: "Please tell me." And the little old man said to her: "Here is a spool; follow it." After some time, a short time or a long time, this spool rolled up to a high mountain; the maiden began to climb it, and she heard voices shouting at her: "Whither are you going? We shall kill you! We shall devour you!" But she kept on climbing and climbing; she came to the top of the mountain, and there sat the talking bird.

The maiden took this bird and asked it: "Tell me where I can get the singing tree and the water of life?" The bird said: "Go over there." She came to the singing tree; in this tree all kinds of birds were singing. She broke a branch off it and went on farther; she came to the water of life, drew a little pitcher of it, to take it home. She began to climb down the mountain and sprinkled it with the water of life; suddenly her brothers jumped up and said: "Ah, little sister, we have been asleep a long time." "Yes, brothers, were it not for me you would have slept here forever." And she added: "I have got the talking bird, the singing tree, and the water of life." The brothers were overjoyed. They went home and planted the singing tree in their garden; it spread out over the whole garden and birds sang on it in various voices.

One day the brothers went hunting and happened to meet the king. He liked these hunters and asked them to come to see him. They said: "We shall ask our sister's permission; if she grants it, we shall certainly come." They returned from the hunt, the sister met them, and attended them joyfully. Her brothers said to her: "Give us permission, little sister, to visit the king; he graciously asked us to come." The princess gave them permission, and they went to visit the king. The king received them cordially and invited them to feast with him;

they spoke to the king and asked him to visit them in turn. After some time, the king came to them and they received him most hospitably, and showed him the singing tree and the talking bird. The king was amazed and said: "I am a king, and yet I do not have these things." Then the sister and the brothers said to him: "But we are your children." The king learned the whole truth, was overjoyed, and stayed with them forever; he freed the queen from the chapel, and they lived together for many years in great happiness.

THE RAM
WHO LOST HALF HIS SKIN

A CERTAIN NOBLEMAN had many head of cattle. One day he killed and skinned five sheep, because he wanted to have a coat made of the skins. He sent for a tailor and said to him: "Now sew up a sheepskin for me." The tailor measured him and found that he needed half a skin more. "You don't

have enough skins," he said. "I need some more for the lapels." "That's easy," answered the nobleman, and ordered his lackey to remove half the skin of one ram. The lackey carried out the order. The ram became angry at the nobleman, called the goat, and said to him: "Let's run away from this wicked man; we can live in the woods, eat grass, drink water, and be happy." And so they did. They went to the forest, built a cabin for the nights, and lived happily eating grass.

Many other beasts also disliked living with the nobleman, and a cow, a pig, a cock, and a gander also left his farm. While it was warm, these creatures lived in the open, but when icy winter came, they sought a refuge from the cold. They walked and walked through the woods, found the ram's cabin, and begged him to let them in. "Please, give us shelter," they said. "We are very cold." But the ram and the goat refused. Then the cow came up to the door and said: "Let us in, else I will knock down your cabin!" The ram saw that he had no choice and admitted the cow. The pig came up. "Let me in," he said, "else I will dig up all the ground around your house, make a tunnel to the door, and freeze you out!" There was nothing they could do, so they admitted the pig. A moment later, the gander said: "Let me in or I'll peck a hole in the wall, and the cold wind will come in." And the cock said: "Let me in, or I'll befoul your whole roof." What could they do? They admitted the birds too and all of them began to live together.

After some time, a long time or a short time, robbers passed by the cabin and heard cries and noises coming from inside. They came close, listened, could not guess who was there, and sent one of their companions to find out. "Go in," they said, "else we shall put a rope around your neck and throw you into the water." There was nothing the fellow could do, so he opened the door. The moment he set foot in the cabin, he was attacked from all sides and was forced to turn back. "Well, brothers," he said, "do what you will, but I won't go back in there for anything in the world. In all my life I have never been so frightened. The moment I stepped in, a woman began to thrash me with an oven fork; her daughter fell upon me in her turn; then a cobbler thrust an awl into my back; then a tailor cut me with his scissors; then a soldier armed with spurs jumped at me in such fury that his hair stood on end; he shouted in a terrible voice. And the biggest of them all began to mutter threateningly. I was scared out of my wits." "Not so good," said the robbers. "Let's move out of this—they might come after us." And they left.

And so the beasts went on living together. One day wolves came to their cabin and by the smell knew who was there. They said to one of their band: "Go in, be the first of us." He had no sooner opened the door than all the beasts in the cabin began to thrash him and he barely escaped with his life. The wolves did not know what to do. A hedgehog was with them, and he said: "Just wait, let me try; I think I can do better." For he knew that the ram had lost one side of his skin. So he waddled in and pricked the ram; the ram gave a tremendous jump over all his companions and ran away. All of them followed him and took to their heels. Then the wolves moved into the cabin and stayed there.

THE FOX AS MIDWIFE

A WOLF AND A FOX lived together in true friendship. They had a little keg of honey. The fox liked sweets; she lay with her crony the wolf in their little house and stealthily rapped the floor with her tail. "Friend fox," said the wolf, "there's a knocking at the door." "Ah, it's someone coming to ask me to help deliver a child," murmured the fox. "Well, go then," said the wolf. The fox went out of the house, straight to the honey keg, licked her fill of it, and returned. "What has God given?" asked the wolf. "A first child," said the fox.

Another time, the fox again lay quietly rapping her tail. "Friend, I hear a knocking," said the wolf. "It's probably someone who needs a midwife." "Well, go then." The fox again went to the honey keg and licked her fill of it, so that only a little remained at the bottom. "What has God given?" asked the wolf. "A second child." Then the fox cheated the wolf still a third time, and finished all the honey. "What has God given?" asked the wolf. "A last child."

After some time, a long time or a short time, the fox pretended to be ill and asked her friend the wolf to bring her some honey. He went to the keg and found that not even a drop was left. "Friend, friend," cried the wolf, "the honey is all eaten up!" "What do you mean?" asked the fox angrily. "Who could have eaten it except you?" The wolf swore that it was not he. "Very well, then," said the fox, "let us lie in the sun; whoever sweats out the honey is the culprit." They lay down in the sun. The fox did not sleep but the gray wolf snored with his whole snout. After a while, the fox got hold of some honey and quickly smeared the wolf with it. "Friend, friend," she said, nudging the wolf, "what's this? Who has eaten the honey?" The wolf had no choice but to admit his guilt.

There's a tale for you, and a crock of butter for me.

THE FOX, THE HARE,
AND THE COCK

ONCE UPON A TIME there lived a fox and a hare. The fox had a hut made of ice, and the hare a hut made of lime tree bark. The radiant spring came and the fox's hut melted, while the hare's stood as before. The fox asked the hare to let her in to warm herself and then drove him out. The hare walked along the road weeping, and met some dogs. "Bow-bow-bow, why are you weeping, little hare?" The hare said: "Let me alone, dogs! How can I help weeping? I had a hut made of lime tree bark and the fox had a hut made of ice; she begged me to let her into my hut, then drove me out." "Don't weep, hare!" said the dogs. "We shall drive her out." "No you won't."

"Yes we shall!" They came to the hut and barked: "Bow-bow-bow! Go away, fox!" But the fox replied from the stove: "As I jump out, as I leap out, only tufts will fly all around!" The dogs took fright and ran away.

Again the hare walked down the road weeping. He met a bear. "Why are you weeping, hare?" And the hare said: "Let me alone, bear! How can I help weeping? I had a hut made of lime tree bark, and the fox had a hut made of ice; she begged me to let her into my hut, then drove me out." "Don't weep, hare, I'll drive her out." "No you won't! The dogs tried it and could not, and you will do no better." "I shall!" So they both went to drive out the fox. "Go away, fox!" growled the bear. The fox replied from the stove: "As I jump out, as I leap out, only tufts will fly all around!" The bear took fright and ran away.

Again the hare walked down the road weeping, and met a bull. "Why are you weeping, hare?" "Let me alone, bull! How can I help weeping? I had a hut made of lime tree bark, and the fox had a hut made of ice; she begged me to let her into my hut, then drove me out." "Let us go there, I will drive her out!" "No, bull, you won't! The dogs tried it and couldn't; the bear tried it and couldn't; and you will do no better." "I shall!" They went to the hut. "Go away, fox!" roared the bull. But the fox replied from the stove: "As I jump out, as I leap out, only tufts will fly all around!" The bull took fright and ran away.

Again the hare walked down the road weeping, and met a cock carrying a sickle. "Cock-a-doodle-doo! Why are you weeping, hare?" "Let me alone, cock! How can I help weeping? I had a hut made of lime tree bark, and the fox had a hut made of ice; she begged me to let her into my hut, then drove me out." "Let us go there, I will drive her out." "No you won't! The dogs tried it and couldn't; the bear tried it and couldn't; the bull tried it and couldn't; and you will do no better." "Yes I shall!" They came to the hut: "Cock-a-doodle-doo!" crowed the cock. "I have a sickle on my shoulders, I am going to cut the fox to pieces! Get out, fox!" The fox heard the cock, took fright, and said: "I am getting dressed!" The cock called again: "Cock-a-doodle-doo! I have a sickle on my shoulders, I am going to cut the fox to pieces! Get out, fox!" The fox said: "I am putting on my fur!" The cock shrilled for the third time: "Cock-a-doodle-doo! I have a sickle on my shoulders, I am going to cut the fox to pieces! Get out, fox!" The fox ran out; the cock cut her with his sickle, and began to live with the hare and to prosper.

There's a tale for you, and a crock of butter for me.

BABA YAGA

A CERTAIN PEASANT and his wife had a daughter. The wife died; the husband married another woman, and had a daughter with her also. His wife conceived a dislike for her stepdaughter and the orphan had a hard time. Our peasant thought and thought, and finally took his daughter to the woods. As he drove in the woods, he beheld a little hut standing on chicken legs. The peasant said: "Little hut, little hut, stand with your back to the woods, and your front to me!" The hut turned around. The peasant entered it and found Baba Yaga: her head was in front, her right leg was in one corner, and her left leg in the other corner. "I smell a Russian smell!" said Yaga. The peasant bowed to her and said: "Baba Yaga the Bony-legged One, I have brought you my daughter to be your servant." "Very well, serve me, serve me!" said Yaga to the girl. "I will reward you for it." The father said farewell and returned home.

Baba Yaga gave the girl a basketful of yarn to spin, told her to make a fire in the stove, and to prepare everything for dinner. Then she went out. The girl busied herself at the stove and wept bitterly. The mice ran out and said to her: "Maiden, maiden, why are you weeping? Give us some gruel: we shall return your kindness." She gave them some gruel. "And now," they said, "stretch one thread on each spindle." Baba Yaga came back. "Well," she said, "have you prepared everything?"

194

The girl had everything ready. "And now wash me in the bath!" said her mistress. She praised the maiden and gave her several beautiful dresses.

Again Yaga went out, having set even more difficult tasks for her servant. Again the girl wept. The mice ran out. "Lovely maiden," they said, "why are you weeping? Give us some gruel: we shall return your kindness." She gave them gruel, and again they told her what to do and how. Baba Yaga upon her return again praised the maiden and gave her even more beautiful dresses.

One day the stepmother sent her husband to see whether his daughter was still alive. The peasant drove into the woods; when he came to the house on chicken legs, he saw that his daughter had become very prosperous. Yaga was not at home, so he took the maiden with him. As they approached their village, the peasant's dog began to bark: "Bow! wow! wow! A young lady is coming, a young lady is coming!" The stepmother ran out and struck the dog with a rolling pin. "You're lying!" she said. "You should bark, 'Bones are rattling in the basket!' " But the dog kept barking the same thing as before. The peasant and his daughter arrived. The stepmother began to press her husband to take her daughter to Baba Yaga. He took her.

Baba Yaga set a task for her and went out. The girl was beside herself with spite, and wept. The mice ran out: "Maiden, maiden," they said, "why are you weeping?" But she did not even let them speak; she struck them with a rolling pin and scolded them roundly and did not do her work. Yaga came back and became angry. Another time the same thing happened. Then Yaga broke her in pieces and put her bones in a basket.

Now the stepmother sent her husband for his daughter. The father went and brought back only her bones. As he approached his village, his dog barked on the porch: "Bow! wow! wow! Bones are rattling in the basket!" The stepmother came running out with a rolling pin: "You're lying!" she said. "You should bark, 'A young lady is coming!' " The husband arrived; and then the wife moaned and groaned.

There's a tale for you, and a crock of butter for me.

THE RAM, THE CAT,
AND THE TWELVE WOLVES

AN OLD COUPLE had a cat and a ram. The old woman prepared cream to make butter with, and the cat stole some of it. "Old man," said the old woman, "there's mischief in our cellar!" "You must see," said the old man, "whether some stranger is not playing tricks on us." The old woman went to the cellar and saw the cat pushing the lid of the pot aside with his paw and lapping some cream; she drove him out of the cellar and went back into the house, but the cat had preceded her and hidden on the stove in a corner. "Husband," said the old woman, "we did not believe that our own cat was the offender, but it is he indeed; let us kill him." Hearing these words, the cat jumped from the stove, rushed to the ram in the stall, and said: "Brother ram, I am to be killed tomorrow, and you are to be slaughtered."

The two animals decided to run away from their owner that night. "But how shall I do it?" the ram asked. "I should be glad to take flight with you, but my shed is locked." "Never mind!" said the cat. He climbed up the door, removed the string from the nail with his paw, and set the ram free. And so they went wandering along the roads. They found a wolf's head, took it up, and continued walking; then they saw a little fire in the woods at some distance, and went straight to the fire.

They came up and found twelve wolves warming themselves around the fire. "God be with you, wolves!" "Welcome, cat and ram!" "Brother," said the ram to the cat, "what do we have for supper?" "We have twelve wolves' heads. Go and choose the fattest." The ram went into the bushes, raised high the wolf's head they had found on the road, and asked: "This one, brother cat?" "No, choose a better one!" The ram raised the head once more and asked: "How about this one?" The wolves took such fright that they would gladly have run away, but they did not dare do so without first asking permission. Four

196

wolves came to the cat and the ram, begging: "Please, let us go get some wood for you!" And these four left. The remaining eight wolves became even more fearful than before, thinking, "Since they could eat twelve, they will be able to eat eight even more easily!" Four more wolves asked permission to go for water. The cat let them go. "You may go, but come back soon," he said.

The last four wolves went to get the others, saying: "Why haven't they come back?" The cat let them go, ordering them even more sternly to come back soon; but he and the ram were really happy that the wolves had gone.

The wolves gathered together and went farther into the woods. They met the bear, Mikhailo Ivanovich. "Have you heard, Mikhailo Ivanovich, of a cat and a ram who ate twelve wolves?" "No, my boys, I haven't heard of them." "But we have seen this cat and ram ourselves." "I too should like to see how brave they are!" "Eh, Mikhailo Ivanovich, the cat is awfully quick-tempered, there is no way of winning his favor; at any moment he may jump on you and tear you to pieces. We are nimble with dogs and hares, but the cat is a different matter. It would be better to invite them for dinner." They sent for the fox and said to her: "Go and invite the cat and the ram." The fox began to excuse herself: "It's true I am nimble, but I am not good at dodging—they might eat me." "Go!" There was nothing to be done, so the fox ran to invite the cat and the ram. She came back and said: "They promised to come. Ah, Mikhailo Ivanovich, how fierce that cat is! I found him sitting on a tree stump and breaking it with his paws: he was sharpening his knives against us! And he rolled his eyes in the most terrifying manner!" The bear was scared, put one wolf on a high tree stump to be the lookout, gave him a piece of rag, and said: "When you see the cat and the ram, wave the rag, and we'll all go out to meet them." They began to cook dinner; four wolves dragged up four cows, and the bear appointed a marmot as cook.

The cat and the ram were on the way to pay their visit, when they saw the lookout and suspected foul play. The cat said: "I will crawl quietly in the grass and sit close by the tree stump

197

facing the wolf; and you, brother ram, take a run and hit him with your head as you pass him at full speed." The ram began to run and hit the wolf with all his strength and threw him down, while the cat jumped at his snout and clawed it and scratched it till it bled. When the bear and the wolves saw this, they began to talk among themselves: "Now you see what the cat and the ram can do! They managed to throw Evstifeyko the wolf from a high tree stump and maul him: how can we hold our ground against them? Apparently they do not give a fig for our preparations; they have come here not to enjoy a treat but to hurt us. Ah, brothers, wouldn't we do better to hide?"

All the wolves scattered in the woods, the bear climbed into a pine tree, the marmot crawled into a hole, and the fox hid under a log. The cat and the ram fell upon the prepared feast. As the cat ate he kept mewing: "Not much, not much!"

Then he happened to look back, saw the marmot's tail sticking from the hole, took fright, and jumped into the pine tree. The bear was frightened by the cat, flung himself down from the pine tree, and rushed forward, almost crushing the fox under the log. The bear ran away and so did the fox. "So you hurt yourself?" said the fox to the bear. "No, mate. If I had not jumped off the tree, the cat would have eaten me long ago!"

THE FOX
AND THE WOODPECKER

THERE WAS ONCE a woodpecker who built her nest in an oak tree, laid three eggs, and hatched three young. A fox took to visiting their tree; she rapped the mossy oak with her long tail and said: "Woodpecker, climb down the oak! I need oak wood for my tools." "Eh, little fox," answered the woodpecker, "you wouldn't let me hatch even one little child!" "Eh, woodpecker, throw him down, I will teach him the blacksmith's trade." The woodpecker threw down one young one, and the fox ran from bush to bush, from tree to tree, and ate up the young woodpecker.

Again she went to the woodpecker and rapped the mossy oak with her long tail and said: "Woodpecker, climb down the oak, I need oak wood for my tools!" "Eh, little fox," answered the woodpecker, "you wouldn't let me hatch even one little child!" "Eh, woodpecker, throw him down, I will teach him the cobbler's trade." The woodpecker threw down another young one, and the fox ran from bush to bush, from tree to tree, and ate up the young woodpecker.

Again she went to the woodpecker and rapped the mossy oak with her long tail and said: "Woodpecker, climb down the oak. I need oak wood for my tools!" "Eh, little fox," answered the woodpecker, "you wouldn't let me hatch even one little child!" "Eh, woodpecker, throw him down, I will teach him the tailor's trade." The woodpecker threw down the last young one, and the fox ran from bush to bush, from tree to tree, and ate up the last young woodpecker.

THE SNOTTY GOAT

IN A CERTAIN KINGDOM, in a certain land, there lived a merchant who had three daughters. He built himself a new house and sent his eldest daughter to spend the night there. In the morning he asked her what she had seen in her dream. She had dreamed that she would marry a merchant's son. On the second night the merchant sent his second daughter, and she dreamed that she would marry a nobleman. The third night it was the youngest daughter's turn, and she—poor little thing—dreamed that she would marry a goat.

Her father was frightened and forbade his youngest daughter to go out even on the porch. But one day she disobeyed and did go out, and a goat seized her on his tall horns and carried her away beyond the steep mountains. He brought her to his house and put her to sleep on the shelf above the stove; snot ran down his nose, slobber ran down from his mouth, and the unfortunate girl never stopped wiping him with a handkerchief, for she was not a bit squeamish. The goat was pleased— he combed his beard in his pleasure.

Next morning our beauty arose and saw that the yard was inclosed with a picket fence, and that there was a maiden's head on every picket; only one picket was empty. The poor girl rejoiced at having escaped death. Then the servants began to hurry her, saying: "Madam, this is no time to sleep—this is the time to bestir yourself, sweep the rooms, and carry the garbage out into the street."

She went to the porch and saw geese flying. "Ah, geese, my gray geese, do you not come from my land, do you not bring me news of my own little father?" And the geese answered her: "We do come from your land, and we have brought you news: there is a betrothal in your house, your elder sister is being married to a merchant's son." The goat on his shelf heard everything and said to his servants: "Hey you, my faithful servants, bring out the splendid garments, harness the black steeds; let them jump thrice and go where I desire to be."

The poor girl dressed herself richly and got into the carriage; the steeds brought her to her father's house in a trice. The guests were being welcomed on the porch and in the house a magnificent feast was set out. Meanwhile the goat turned into a handsome youth and walked into the yard playing his gusla. One could hardly avoid inviting a gusla player to sit down at one's table. He came in and began to sing: "Wife of the goat, wife of the snot-nose! Wife of the goat, wife of the snot-nose!" The unhappy girl slapped him on one cheek, slapped him on the other, jumped into her carriage, and was gone.

She returned home and found the goat lying on the shelf. Snot ran down his nose, slobber ran down from his mouth. The poor girl wiped him with a handkerchief without ceasing; she was not a bit squeamish. Next morning the servants roused her: "Madam, this is no time to sleep—this is the time to rise, sweep the rooms, and carry the garbage out into the street." She rose, set the rooms in order, and went to the porch; and she saw geese flying. "Ah, geese, my gray geese, do you not come from my land, do you not bring me news of my own little father?" And the geese answered her: "We do come from your land, and we have brought you news: there is a betrothal in your house, your second sister is being married to a wealthy nobleman." Again the poor girl drove to her father's house; on the porch the guests were being welcomed, in the house a magnificent feast was set out. Meanwhile the goat turned into a handsome youth and walked into the yard playing his gusla. He came in and began to sing: "Wife of the goat, wife of the snot-nose! Wife of the goat, wife of the snot-nose!" The unhappy girl slapped him on one cheek, slapped him on the other, jumped into her carriage, and was gone.

She returned home and found the goat lying on the shelf. Snot ran down his nose, slobber ran down from his mouth. Another night passed; in the morning the poor girl rose and went to the porch; again geese were flying. "Ah, geese, my gray geese, do you not come from my land, do you not bring me news of my own little father?" And the geese answered her: "We do come from your land, and we have brought you news: your father is giving a dinner." She drove to her father's house; the guests were being welcomed on the porch and in the house a magnificent feast was set out. In the yard the gusla player was walking about and strumming on his gusla. He was asked to come in and again began to sing: "Wife of the goat, wife of the snot-nose!"

The poor girl slapped him on one cheek, slapped him on the other, and drove home in a trice. She looked on the shelf and found only a goatskin: the gusla player had not yet had time to turn into a goat. She flung the goatskin into the stove—and the merchant's youngest daughter found herself married not to a goat but to a handsome youth, and they began to live happily and prosperously.

RIGHT AND WRONG

ONCE THERE WERE two peasants, both of them very poor. One lived by means of all kinds of lies and deceit, he swindled and stole. But the other followed the path of truth and honest labor. These two peasants had a dispute over the manner of living that each had chosen. One said: "It is better to live by wrong." And the other said: "You cannot live by wrong all your life, it is better to live by right." They quarreled and quarreled, but neither could convince the other. They went out to the road and agreed to ask the first three people whom they should meet to settle their dispute. So they walked and walked and finally saw a serf plowing a field. They approached him and said: "God speed you, friend! Please settle our quarrel: how is it better to live in the world— by right or by wrong?" "Brothers, you cannot live long by right; it is easier to live by wrong. Take my case, for instance. Our masters constantly take our days away, and we have no

202

time to work for ourselves; but if you pretend that you cannot come because you are ill, you can manage to go get some wood for yourself, if not during the day—since it is forbidden—at least by night." "Do you hear? I am right!" said the wicked peasant to the righteous one.

Again they walked along the road, waiting to see what the next person whom they should meet would say. They walked and walked, and at last saw a merchant in a carriage driving a pair of horses. They approached him and said: "Please stop a moment. If Your Grace does not take it amiss, we should like to ask you something. Settle our quarrel: how is it better to live in the world—by right or by wrong?" "No, my boys, it is hard to live by right, it is easier to live by wrong. We are cheated, and we must cheat others too." "Do you hear? I am right!" said the wicked peasant again to the righteous one.

So they walked farther along the road, waiting to see what the third person would tell them. They walked and walked till they saw a clerk driving toward them. They approached him and said: "Stop a moment, settle our quarrel: how is it better to live in the world, by right or by wrong?" "What a question to ask! By wrong, of course! What right is there nowadays? For doing right you are sent to Siberia, accused of scheming." "Do you hear?" said the wicked peasant to the righteous one. "Everyone says it is better to live by wrong." "No, one must live in God's way, as God has commanded us; come what may, I will not live by wrong," the righteous man answered the other.

Again they walked on the road together. They walked and walked. The wicked man managed to get along everywhere; he got all the food he needed, he even got cakes; but the righteous man was fed only when he worked for his keep. And the wicked man continually made fun of him. Once the righteous man begged the wicked one for a piece of bread: "Please give me a piece of bread." "And what will you give me in return?" asked the wicked one. "Take whatever you wish, whatever I have," said the righteous man. "Shall I gouge out one of your eyes?" "Go ahead, gouge it out," said the righteous man. And so the wicked man gouged out an eye of the righteous one and gave him a bit of bread. The righteous man did not protest; he took the bread, ate it, and again they walked along the road.

They walked and walked, and again the righteous man began to beg the wicked one for a piece of bread. Again the wicked one began to make fun of him: "Let me gouge out your other eye, then I'll give you a piece." "Ah, brother, have pity on me! If you do that, I shall be blind," the righteous man implored him. "No, it's because you are righteous and I live by wrong," the wicked man told him. There was nothing to be done, so the righteous man said to the wicked one: "Well, gouge out my other eye, if you do not fear to commit such a sin." The wicked one gouged out his other eye, gave him a little bread, and left him on the road, saying: "You cannot expect me to guide you!"

What should he do now? The blind man ate his little piece of bread and went on slowly, groping with his stick. He walked till he got off the road and did not know where to go. Then he prayed to God: "Lord, do not forsake thy sinful servant!" He prayed and prayed. Then he heard a voice saying: "Go to the right. On the right you will find a wood. When you come to the wood, grope for the path. When you find the path, walk along it. Somewhere along the path you will come to a spring. When you come to the spring, wash yourself with the water from it, drink it, and wet your eyes with it; then you will recover your sight. Then go upstream along the spring, and you will see a big oak. When you find the oak, go to it and climb up into it. There await the night; and when night comes, listen to what the evil spirits say under this oak—for there they gather together to discuss their affairs."

He somehow managed to reach the wood. When he reached the wood, he stumbled and plodded through it, and somehow managed to find the path; he walked along this path, till he reached the spring. He washed himself with water from the spring, drank some water, and wetted his eyes; and he saw God's world, for he had recovered his sight. And when he recovered his sight he walked upstream along the spring; he walked and walked and at last saw a big oak, under which the ground was trampled flat. He climbed up into this oak, and awaited the night. Then devils came from all directions and assembled under the oak. They came and came, and each began to tell where he had been. One of them said: "I was with such and such a princess; I have been tormenting her for ten years.

They have tried to drive me out of her in every possible way, but in vain; only he can drive me out who goes to such and such a wealthy merchant and gets from him the image of the Smolensk Mother of God that is nailed to his gate."

Next morning, when all the devils had dispersed, our righteous man climbed down from the oak. He went to search for the merchant the devil had named. He searched and searched for him, till at last he found him. Then he asked the merchant whether he could work for him: "I will work for you a whole year, and all I want for wages is the image of the Mother of God on your gate." The merchant consented and hired him as a laborer.

And so he worked for the merchant with all his strength for a whole year round. Having thus worked, he asked for the image. However, the merchant said: "Well, brother, I am satisfied with your work, but I do not wish to lose that image; take money instead." "No, I do not need money; give me the image as we agreed." "No, I will not give you the image. Work for me another year, then I will give it to you."

So it came to pass that our righteous peasant worked for another year; he did not rest by night or day, he worked all the time, so diligent was he. Having thus worked, he again asked for the image of the Mother of God on the gate. The merchant again was loath to give him the image and release him, and said: "No, I would rather reward you with money—unless you want to work for another year, then I will give you the image."

There was nothing the peasant could do, so he began to work for a third year. He worked even harder than before; everyone marveled at him, he was such a hard worker. Having thus worked a third year, he asked for the image. The merchant now had no choice but to take the image from the gate and give it to him. "Well, take the image," he said, "and God speed you." He gave him food and drink and rewarded him with a small sum of money.

And so it came to pass that he took the image of the Smolensk Mother of God and hung it on himself; then he went to the king of that country, to cure the princess who was tormented by a devil. He walked and walked till he came to the palace. He said to the king: "I can cure your princess." And so he was admitted to the king's private chambers and shown the suffering princess. He asked for water and water was given him. He made the sign of the cross and bowed three times to the ground, and prayed to God; having prayed, he removed the image of the Mother of God from his body, and with a prayer on his lips immersed it in the water three times, and then put it on the princess; having put it on her he told her to wash in the same water. And when she put the image on her and washed in that water, suddenly her disease, that is, the evil spirit, flew out of her; and when he flew out, she was as whole as before. Seeing this, all the company rejoiced mightily and did not know how to reward the righteous peasant: they offered him land, a hereditary estate, and a large pension. But he would not accept anything. Then the princess said to the king: "I want to marry this man." "Very well," said the king. And so they wedded, and our peasant began to wear royal garments, live in royal apartments, and eat and drink just like the rest of the king's family. He lived like this for a long while and became accustomed to their manners and way of life.

And having become accustomed to them, he said: "Let me go to my native village; there I have my old mother, who is very poor." "Very well," said the princess, that is to say, his wife, "let us go together." So he and the princess went together. Their horses, clothes, trappings, carriage, everything, were royal. They drove and drove and finally approached the peasant's native village. On the road they happened to meet the wicked man who had quarreled with him as to whether it is better to live by wrong or by right. As the carriage approached this fellow, the righteous man said, "Good day, brother," and called him by his name. The man was amazed that the magnificent nobleman in the carriage, whom he had never seen, should know him.

"Do you recall," the stranger said, "that we once had a dispute as to whether it is better to live by wrong or by right, and you gouged out my eyes? I am that same man!" The other was afraid and did not know what to do. But the righteous man said to him: "No, do not be afraid, I am not angry at you, I wish you the same good fortune. Go to such and such a wood"—and he proceeded to instruct him just as he himself had been instructed by God. "In that wood you will see a path. Go along that path. You will reach a spring; drink water from it, and wash; and after you have washed, go upstream along the spring, and you will see a big oak. Climb up on it, and sit there all night. Under it evil spirits gather. Listen and you will hear your fate."

The wicked man followed these instructions to the letter. He found the wood and the path. He went along the path and came to the spring, drank of it, and washed. Having washed, he went upstream and saw the big oak and the ground all trampled flat under it. He climbed up into the oak and awaited the night, and then he heard evil spirits coming from all directions to gather there. When they had gathered they heard him breathing in the oak, and, having heard him, they tore him to shreds. And so this affair was concluded: the righteous man became the king's son-in-law and the iniquitous one was put to death by the devils.

THE POTTER

ONCE A POTTER was driving along the road with his pots and fell asleep as he went. Tsar Ivan the Terrible overtook him. "There are people on the road who want to pass," the tsar said. The potter looked behind him. "Thank you humbly," he said. "So you've been slumbering?" "I've been slumbering, great king! Fear not him who sings songs, but him who takes a nap!" "You're a bold one, potter! I love such as you. Coachman, drive more slowly! And you, potter, tell me, how long have you been engaged in this trade?" "From my youth, and now I am middle-aged." "Do you support your children?" "I do, Your Majesty, and yet I do not plow, I do not reap, I do not mow, and the cold does not freeze me." "True, potter, and yet the world is not without evil." "Yes, Your Majesty, there are three evils in the world." "And what are these three evils, my little potter?" "The first evil is a bad neighbor; the second evil is a bad wife; and the third evil is a bad mind." "And now tell me, which of these evils is the worst?" "From a bad neighbor I can go away; from a bad wife I can also go away if she agrees to stay with the children; but from one's own bad mind one cannot go away, it is always with one." "Yes, that is true, potter, you are a smart fellow. Listen: you stick to me, and I'll stick to you. Geese will come from

Russia: pluck their feathers, and leave them in the proper condition!" "I will leave them in the proper condition, and I will pluck them clean." "Well, potter, stop for a while, I want to see your pottery."

The potter stopped and displayed his merchandise. The tsar looked at it and chose three earthen dishes. "Will you make me some more of these?" "How many does Your Majesty want?" "I need about a dozen cartfuls." "How much time can you give me?" "A month." "I can deliver them in two weeks. I'll stick by you, and you stick by me." "Thanks, potter." "And you, king, where will you be when I bring this merchandise to town?" "I will be staying in the merchant's house." The tsar arrived in town and gave orders that everyone use only earthenware at all receptions, and that no silver, lead, copper or wooden dishes be set on the table.

The potter finished the tsar's order and brought his merchandise to town. A certain boyar came to buy earthenware from him and said to him: "God be with you, potter." "I am your humble servant." "Sell me all your merchandise." "No, I cannot, I made it for a special order." "Don't worry about that. Take this money. You cannot be held to your promise if you did not receive an advance payment for your work. Well, how much do you want?" "Fill each of my vessels with money." "My dear little potter, don't try to make a fool of me; that is too much." "Very well then, for each vessel filled, you will get two. Do you agree?" They agreed— "You stick to me, and I'll stick to you." They began to fill the pots and empty them, to pour in and pour out. They ran out of money, and there was still a great deal of merchandise. The boyar went home to get more money. Again they poured and poured, and there still was a great deal of merchandise left, and no money. "What shall we do, my little potter?" the boyar asked. "You were too greedy and now you haven't enough money to pay! I will take your plight into consideration, but in the meantime, do you know what I shall make you do? Pull me to that house: then I will give you both the merchandise and all the money."

The boyar hesitated for a long time. He was sorry about his money, and also about his dignity; but there was nothing to be done, so he finally agreed. The horse was unharnessed, the peasant sat in the cart, and the boyar began to pull him; the potter sang a song, and the boyar dragged and dragged. "Where shall I pull you?" he asked. "To that house over there." The potter sang merrily, and when he was close to the house he raised his voice high. The tsar heard him, ran out on the porch, and recognized the potter. "Ha, welcome, potter!" "Thank you, Your Majesty." "What are you driving on?" "On a bad mind, Your Majesty." "Well, you are a smart fellow, potter, you have managed to sell your goods. Boyar, take off your boyar's garment and your boots, and you, potter, take off your caftan and your shoes of bast. You put them on, boyar, and you, potter, put on this boyar's garments. He knew how to sell his goods! The potter did not work long, but he earned a great deal—and you did not know how to guard your boyar's rank. Well, potter, did the geese come from Russia?" "They did." "Did you pluck their feathers, and leave them in the proper condition?" "No, Your Majesty, I plucked him clean, all of him."

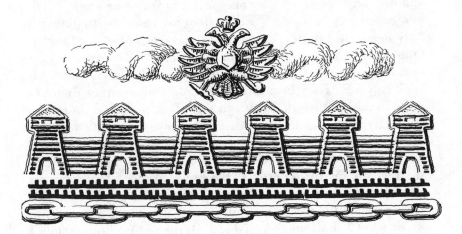

THE SELF-PLAYING GUSLA

IN A CERTAIN KINGDOM, in a certain land, there lived a peasant who had a son. The peasant's name was Alexei and the son's Vanka. When summer came Alexei plowed his land and planted turnips; and the turnips throve so well and grew so big and succulent that it was a marvel to behold them. The peasant was glad; he went to his field every morning, rejoiced in his turnips, and gave thanks to God. One day he noticed that someone was stealing his turnips and began to watch the field; he watched and watched, but saw no one. Then he sent Vanka to the field, saying: "Go watch the turnips."

Vanka came to the field and saw a boy digging up the turnips and filling two enormous bags with them; he slung them over his back and began to drag them along with great difficulty—his legs bent under him, his back creaked! The boy dragged and dragged the bags till his strength failed him; then he threw the bags on the ground and suddenly saw Vanka standing before him. "Do me a favor, my good man," said the boy. "Help me carry these bags home; grandfather will reward you for it." When Vanka saw the boy, he stood as if petrified, staring at him with wide eyes. Then he came to and said: "All right, I'll help you!" He slung the two bags of turnips over his shoulders and carried them after the boy, who skipped ahead, saying: "Grandfather sends me for turnips every day. If you bring them to him, he will give you much silver and gold. But don't take it. Ask for the self-playing gusla instead."

After a while they came to the boy's house; in the corner there sat a gray-haired man with horns. Vanka bowed to him. The old man gave him a lump of gold for his trouble; Vanka's eyes began to gleam, but the boy whispered to him: "Don't take it." Vanka said: "I don't want gold. Give me the self-playing gusla, and all the turnips will be yours." When he mentioned the self-playing gusla, the old man's eyes popped out an inch, his mouth opened to his ears, and the horns on his forehead began to jump. Vanka was seized by fear, but the boy said: "Give it to him, grandfather." "You want a great deal! But so be it: take the gusla, and in return give me whatever is dearest to you in your own home." Vanka thought to himself: "Our little house barely sticks out of the ground; surely there is nothing precious in it." But aloud he said: "I agree." And he took the self-playing gusla and went home. When he arrived he found his father dead on the threshold. He wept and mourned for him, buried him, and went forth to seek his fortune.

He came to a large city, the capital of a great king. In front of the king's palace was a meadow in which pigs were grazing. Vanka went to the swineherd, bought some pigs from him, and began to tend them. Whenever he strummed the self-playing gusla, his whole herd began to dance. One day when the king was away, his daughter sat by the window and saw Vanka sitting on a tree stump and strumming his gusla while his pigs danced before him. The princess sent her maid to ask this swineherd to sell her at least one of the dancing pigs. Vanka said: "Let her come herself!" The princess came and said: "Swineherd, sell me one of your pigs." "My pigs are not for sale, they are sacred." "And what is their sacred price?" "Well, princess, if you wish to have one of my pigs, show me your white body up to your knees." The princess thought and thought, looked all around her to make sure that no one was looking, and raised her dress up to her knees, revealing a little birthmark on her right leg. Vanka gave her a pig; the princess ordered it to be led to her palace, called the musicians, and made them play. She wanted to see how the pig would dance to their music, but it only hid in the corners, howling and grunting.

The king returned and decided to give his daughter in marriage. He summoned all the boyars and lords and merchants and peasants; kings and princes and people of all kinds came from foreign lands and gathered in his palace. The king said: "He who guesses what mark there is on my daughter, to him I shall give her in marriage." None of them could guess; and no matter how they tried, they could not find out where the mark was. Finally Vanka stepped forth and said that the princess had a little birthmark on her right leg. "You have guessed right," said the king. He married Vanka to his daughter and gave a great feast for all the people. Vanka was now the king's son-in-law and began to live a carefree life.

MARCO THE RICH
AND VASILY THE LUCKLESS

IN A CERTAIN KINGDOM, in a certain land, there once lived a very wealthy merchant. He had an only daughter, Anastasya the Fair, who was only five years of age. The merchant's name was Marco, and his surname was "the Rich." He could not endure beggars; whenever they came begging at his window, he ordered his servants to drive them away and loose the dogs upon them.

One day two old gray-haired men came begging to his window. Marco saw them and ordered the dogs to be let loose upon them. Anastasya the Fair heard of it and began to implore her father: "My dear father, for my sake at least let them take shelter in the cattle shed!" The father consented and ordered the beggars to be led to the cattle shed.

When everyone in the house was asleep, Anastasya rose up and went to the cattle shed; she climbed up to the loft and watched the beggars. When it became time for matins, the candle beneath the icon lighted by itself; the old men rose up, took priestly vestments out of their bags, put them on, and began the service of matins. An angel of God came flying and said: "In such and such a village, a son is born to such and such a peasant; by what name shall he be called, and what shall be his fortune?" One of the old men said: "I give him the name of Vasily and the surname of "the Luckless," and I hereby present him with all the wealth of Marco the Rich, under whose roof we are now spending the night." Anastasya

213

heard all this. At daybreak, the old men made ready to go and left the cattle shed. Anastasya went to her father and told him everything that she had seen and heard there.

The father wondered whether the prophecy would come true and decided to see whether a babe had really been born in the village; he had his carriage harnessed, went straight to the priest of the village, and asked him: "Was a babe born in your village on such and such a day?" "Yes," said the priest, "a babe was born to our poorest peasant; I christened him Vasily and surnamed him 'the Luckless,' but I have not yet baptized him because no one wants to stand as godfather to the poor man's child." Marco offered to stand as godfather, asked the priest's wife to be godmother, and bade them prepare a rich repast; the little boy was brought to the church and baptized, and everyone feasted to his heart's content.

The next day Marco the Rich summoned the poor peasant to him, spoke kindly to him, and said: "Friend, you are a poor man, you won't be able to bring up your son; give him to me, I will help him to rise in the world, and I will give you a thousand rubles for your own maintenance." The poor man thought and thought and finally consented. Marco gave him the promised money, took the child, wrapped him in fox furs, put him in his carriage, and drove away. It was winter. Having driven several versts, Marco bade his coachman stop, handed him the godchild, and said: "Take him by the legs and hurl him into the ravine." The coachman did as he was ordered and hurled the child into a deep ravine. And Marco said: "Now, Vasily, take possession of my wealth!"

Two days later some merchants chanced to travel by the same road; they were carrying twelve thousand rubles that they owed to Marco the Rich. When they came near the ravine they heard the wailing of a child. They stopped, listened, and sent a servant to see who it could be. The servant went down into the ravine and beheld a green meadow; in the meadow a child sat, playing with flowers and whimpering. The servant told all this to his master, who went to the ravine himself, took the child, wrapped him in a fur coat, returned to his carriage, and drove on. The merchants came to Marco the Rich, who asked

214

them where they had found the child. They told him, and he guessed at once that it was Vasily the Luckless, his own god-child; he took the boy in his arms, held him for a while, and gave him to his daughter, saying: "Take him, my daughter, and nurse him."

Then he plied the merchants with all kinds of drink and asked them to let him keep the child. The merchants at first refused, but when Marco told them that he would cancel their debt, they consented and left. Anastasya was so overjoyed that she immediately found a cradle, hung curtains around it, and began to tend the boy, not leaving him by night or by day. One day went by, then another; on the third day Marco came home late, when Anastasya was asleep, took the child, put him into a little barrel, tarred it, and threw it into the water of the port.

The barrel sailed and sailed, till finally it floated up to a monastery. A monk happened to be fetching water. He heard the wailing of a child; he looked about him and saw the barrel. He immediately took a boat, caught up the barrel, broke it open, and found the child. He brought the babe to his abbot. The abbot named the child Vasily and surnamed him "the Luckless." Vasily the Luckless lived in the monastery for six-teen years and learned how to read and write. The abbot loved him and made him his sacristan.

It came to pass that Marco the Rich was traveling to a for-eign kingdom to collect debts owed to him and on his way stopped at the monastery. He was received as befits a rich man. The abbot ordered the sacristan to go to the church; he went, lighted the candles, and read and sang. Marco the Rich asked the abbot: "Has this young man been with you long?" The abbot told him how the boy had been found in a barrel, and when. Marco reckoned the time and realized that the sacristan was his godchild. He said to the abbot: "If I had an intelligent young man like your sacristan, I would appoint him chief clerk and put him in charge of all my treasure; could you not give him to me?" For a long time the abbot made excuses. Finally Marco offered him twenty-five thousand rubles for his monas-tery. The abbot consulted the brothers, and after long delibera-tion they consented to part with Vasily the Luckless.

Marco sent Vasily home and gave him a letter to his wife, which ran as follows: "Wife, when you receive this letter, take its bearer immediately to our soap works, and when you pass near the great boiling cauldron, push him in. Do not fail to do this; if you fail, I shall punish you severely, for this youth has evil designs on me." Vasily took the letter and went on his way. He met an old man who said: "Whither are you going, Vasily the Luckless?" Vasily said: "To the house of Marco the Rich, with a letter to his wife." "Show me this letter." Vasily took it out and gave it to the old man, who broke the seal and asked Vasily to read it. Vasily read it and burst into tears. "What have I done to this man," he said, "that he should send me to my death?" The old man said: "Do not grieve, God will not forsake you." Then he breathed on the letter and the seal resumed its former shape. "Go now," said the old man, "and give the letter to the wife of Marco the Rich."

Vasily came to the house of Marco the Rich and gave the letter to his wife. She read it, pondered deeply, then called her daughter Anastasya and read Marco's letter to her. This is what the letter now said: "Wife, one day after you receive this letter, marry Anastasya to the bearer. Do this without fail, otherwise you shall answer to me." In rich people's houses, beer does not have to be brewed nor wine distilled—everything is ready for a gay feast and a wedding. Vasily was dressed in rich garments, shown to Anastasya, and she found him to her liking. So they were wedded.

One day the wife of Marco the Rich was told that her husband had arrived in port, and accompanied by her son-in-law and daughter she went to meet him. Marco looked at his son-in-law, fell into a rage, and said to his wife: "How dared you to wed our daughter to him?" "By your command," answered his wife. Marco asked to see his letter, read it, and found that it was written in his hand.

Marco lived with his son-in-law for one month, a second, and a third. One day he summoned the young man before him and said to him: "Take this letter beyond thrice nine lands, to the thrice tenth kingdom, to my friend, King Dragon; collect from him rent for twelve years for a palace he built on my land, and find out what has happened to twelve of my ships that have not been seen these three years. Set out on your way tomorrow morning." Vasily took the letter, went to his wife, and told her what Marco had commanded him to do. Anastasya wept bitterly but dared not ask her father to change his mind.

Early next morning Vasily prayed to God, took some biscuits in his knapsack, and set out. He walked on the road for a long time or a short time, a long way or a short; in any case, at one point he heard a voice at the side of the road saying: "Vasily the Luckless, whither are you going?" He looked around him on all sides and said: "Who is calling me?" "I, the oak, am asking you whither you are going." "I am going to King Dragon to collect rent for twelve years." The oak said: "If you arrive in time, remember to ask how much longer the oak must stand after standing for three hundred years."

Vasily listened carefully and continued on his journey. He came to a river and sat in the ferryboat. The old ferryman asked him: "Whither are you going, my friend?" Vasily told him what he had told the oak. And the ferryman requested him to ask the king how much longer he would have to ferry, for he had now been ferrying thirty years. "I shall ask him," said Vasily. He went on, reached the sea; a whale lay stretched out across the sea and people were walking and driving over her. When Vasily stepped on the whale, she said: "Vasily the Luckless, whither are you going?" Vasily told her what he had told the ferryman, and the whale said: "If you arrive in time, remember to ask how much longer I must lie here stretched across the sea, for people on foot and people on horseback have worn down my body to my very ribs."

Vasily promised to ask and went on. He came to a green meadow; in the meadow stood a huge palace. Vasily entered the palace and went from room to room; each was more splendid than the last. He went into the farthest room and found a lovely maiden sitting on the bed and weeping bitterly. When she saw Vasily, she rose up, approached him, and said: "Who are you and how did you happen to come to this accursed place?" Vasily showed her the letter and told her that Marco the Rich had ordered him to collect rent for twelve years from King Dragon. The maiden threw the letter into the stove and said to Vasily: "You have been sent here not to collect rent, but as food for the dragon. But tell me, what roads did you take? Did you see or hear anything on your way here?" Vasily told her about the oak, the ferryman, and the whale. They had no sooner finished talking than the earth and the palace began to tremble; the maiden put Vasily into a chest under the bed and said to him: "Now listen to my conversation with the dragon." And saying this she went out to meet him.

When King Dragon entered the room, he said: "Why is there a Russian smell here?" The maiden said: "How could a Russian smell get here? You have been flying over Russia and the Russian smell is in your nostrils." The dragon said: "I am terribly exhausted. Pick the lice in my head." And he lay down on the bed. The maiden said to him: "King, what a dream I had while you were away! I was going along a road, and an oak cried to me: 'Ask the King how long I must stand here!'" "It will stand," said the King, "until someone comes to it and kicks it with his foot; then it will be uprooted and will fall, and beneath it there is an enormous amount of gold and silver—Marco the Rich does not have as much!"

The maiden went on: "And then I dreamed that I came to a river and the ferryman asked me how long he would have to ferry." "Let him put on the ferryboat the first man who comes to him, and push the boat away from the shore—and this man will ferry forever, and the ferryman will go home." "And then I dreamed that I walked across the sea on a whale, and she asked me how long she would have to lie there." "She shall lie there till she vomits up the twelve ships of Marco the Rich; then she will go down into the water and her body will grow again." When King Dragon had said this he fell sound asleep.

The maiden let Vasily out of the chest and advised him thus: "Do not tell the whale that she must vomit up the twelve ships of Marco the Rich, until you have crossed to the other side. Likewise, when you come to the ferryman, do not tell him what you have heard, until you have crossed. And when you come to the oak, kick it toward the east, and you will discover count-

less riches." Vasily the Luckless thanked the maiden and went away.

He came to the whale and she asked: "Did he say anything about me?" "He did; as soon as I cross I shall tell you." When Vasily had crossed over he said: "Vomit up the twelve ships of Marco the Rich." The whale vomited up the ships and they sailed forth, wholly unscathed; and Vasily the Luckless found himself in water up to his knees. Then he came to the ferryman, who asked: "Did you speak about me to King Dragon?" "I did," said Vasily, "but first ferry me over." When he had crossed over, he said to the ferryman: "Whoever comes to you first, put him on the ferryboat and push it away from the shore; he will ferry forever, and you will go home."

Vasily the Luckless came to the oak, kicked it with his foot, and the oak fell; beneath it he found gold and silver and precious stones without number. Vasily looked back and lo and behold, the twelve ships that had been thrown up by the whale were sailing straight to shore. And the ships were commanded by the same old man whom Vasily had met when he was carrying the letter of Marco the Rich to his wife. The old man said to Vasily: "This, Vasily, is what the Lord has blessed you with." Then he got off his ship and went on his way.

The sailors transported the gold and silver to the ships and then set out with Vasily the Luckless. Marco the Rich was told that his son-in-law was coming with twelve ships and that King Dragon had rewarded him with countless riches.

Marco grew furious that what he desired had not come to pass. He had his carriage harnessed and set out to drive to King Dragon's palace and upbraid him. He came to the ferryman and sat in the ferryboat; the ferryman pushed it away from the shore, and Marco remained to ferry forever. But Vasily the Luckless came home to his wife and mother-in-law, began to live with them and gain wealth, helped the poor, gave food and drink to beggars, and took possession of all the wealth of Marco the Rich.

IVANKO THE BEAR'S SON

IN A CERTAIN VILLAGE there lived a wealthy peasant and his wife. One day the wife went to the forest for mushrooms, lost her way, and stumbled into a bear's den. The bear kept her with him, and after some time, a long time or a short time, she had a son by him. This son was a man down to the waist and a bear below the waist; his mother called him Ivanko the Bearlet. Years went by, and when Ivan grew up he wanted to go away with his mother and live with the peasants in the village; they waited until the bear went to a beehive, made ready, and ran away. They ran and ran and finally came to their own village. The peasant saw his wife and was overjoyed —he had given up hope that she would ever return. Then he beheld her son and asked: "And who is this freak?" His wife told him all that had happened, how she had lived in the bear's den and had a son by him and that this son was human to the waist and a bear from the waist down. "Well, Bearlet," said the peasant, "go to the back yard and slaughter a sheep; we must make dinner for you." "And which one shall I slaughter?" "Whichever one stares at you."

Ivanko the Bearlet took a knife, went out to the yard, and called the sheep; all of them began to stare at him. He forthwith slaughtered them all, skinned them, and went to ask the peasant where he should store the skins and the meat. "What's this?" yelled the peasant. "I told you to slaughter one sheep, and you have slaughtered them all!" "No, father, you told me to slaughter whichever one stared at me; but when I came out into the yard all of them, without exception, began to stare at me." "You certainly are a clever fellow. Take the meat and skins into the barn, and at night guard the door against thieves and dogs." "Very well, I will guard it." It so happened that on that night a storm broke and the rain fell in buckets. Ivanko the Bearlet broke the door off the barn, took it into the bathhouse, and spent the night there. Thieves took advantage of the darkness; they found the barn open and without a guard, so they took whatever they pleased. Next morning the peasant arose, went to see whether everything was in order, and found that nothing was left: what the thieves had not taken, the dogs had eaten up. He looked for the guard, found him in the bathhouse, and began to chide him even more severely than the first time. "But, father, it is not my fault," said Ivanko. "You yourself told me to guard the door, and I did guard it. Here it is; the thieves did not steal it, nor did the dogs eat it up."

"What can I do with this fool?" thought the peasant to himself. "If this goes on for a month or two, he will ruin me completely. I wonder how I can get rid of him." Then he hit upon an idea; the next day he sent Ivanko to the lake and told him to wind ropes of sand. In that lake dwelt many devils, and the peasant hoped that they would drag him into the water. Ivanko the Bearlet went to the lake, sat on the shore, and began to wind ropes of sand. Suddenly a little devil jumped out of the water and asked: "What are you doing here, Bearlet?" "Can't you see? I'm winding ropes; I want to thrash the lake and torment you devils, because you live in our lake but do not pay any rent." "Wait a while, Bearlet, I'll run and tell my grandfather," said the little devil, and—flop!—he jumped into the water.

Five minutes later he was out again and said: "Grandfather said that if you can run faster than I, we'll pay the rent; if not, he told me to drag you down into the lake." "Aren't you a nimble fellow!" said Ivanko. "But you cannot hope to run faster than I. Why, I have a grandson who was born only yesterday, and even he can outrun you. Do you want to race with him?" "What grandson?" "He is lying there behind a bush," said the Bearlet, and cried to a hare, "Hey, hare, do not fail me!" The hare darted off into the open field like mad and in a trice vanished from sight; the devil rushed after him, but it was of no use—he was half a verst behind.

"Now, if you wish," said Ivanko, "race with me. But on one condition—if you lag behind, I will kill you." "O no!" said the devil, and once more flopped into the water.

After a while, he jumped out, carrying his grandfather's iron crutch, and said: "Grandfather said that if you can throw this crutch higher than I can, he will pay the rent." "Well, you throw first!" The devil threw the crutch so high that it was hardly visible; it fell back with a terrible rumble and thrust half its length into the ground. "Now you throw it," said the devil. The Bearlet took the crutch in his hand and could not even move it. "Wait a while," he said, "a cloud is coming near, I shall throw the crutch on it." "O no, that won't do, grandfather needs his crutch!" said the little devil. He snatched the crutch and rushed into the water.

After a while, he jumped out again, saying: "Grandfather said that if you can carry this horse around the lake at least one more time than I can, he will pay the rent; if not, you will have to go into the lake." "Is that supposed to be hard? All right, begin!" answered Ivanko. The devil heaved the horse on to his back and dragged it around the lake; he carried it ten times, till he was exhausted and sweat streamed down his snout. "Well, now it's my turn," said Ivanko.

He mounted the horse and began to ride around the lake; he rode so long that finally the horse collapsed under him. "Well, brother, how was that?" he asked the little devil. "I must admit," said the devil, "that you carried it more times than I, and in what a strange fashion! Between your legs! That way I couldn't have carried it even once! How much rent must we pay?" "Just fill my hat with gold, and work for a year as my laborer—that's all I want." The little devil ran to fetch the gold; Ivanko cut the bottom out of his hat and placed it above a deep pit; the devil kept bringing gold and pouring it into the hat. He worked at this for a whole day and only by evening was the hat filled. Ivanko the Bearlet got a cart, loaded it with gold coins, had the devil drag it home, and said to the peasant: "Now be happy, father! Here is a laborer for you, and gold too."

THE SECRET BALL

THERE WAS ONCE a widowed king who had twelve daughters, one more beautiful than the other. Every night these princesses went away, no one knew whither; and every night each of them wore out a new pair of shoes. The king could not get shoes for them fast enough and he wanted to know where they went every night and what they did there. So he prepared a feast, summoned kings and princes, noblemen, merchants, and simple people from all lands, and said: "Can anyone solve this riddle? He who solves it will receive his favorite princess in marriage and half the kingdom as a dowry." However, no one would undertake to find out where the princesses went at night, except one needy nobleman, who said: "Your Royal Majesty, I will find out." "Very well, find out."

Soon the needy nobleman began to doubt and thought to himself: "What have I done? I have undertaken to solve this riddle, yet I do not know how. If I fail now, the king will put me in prison." He went out of the palace and walked outside the town with a sad face. He met an old woman who asked him: "Why are you so sad, my good man?" He answered: "Grandmother, how can I help being sad? I have undertaken to find out for the king whither his daughters go every night." "Yes, that is a difficult task. But it can be accomplished. Here is an invisible cap; with its help you can find out many things. But mind you: when you go to bed, the princesses will give you a sleeping potion; however, turn your face to the wall, pour the drops into your bed, and do not drink them!" The nobleman thanked the old woman and returned to the palace.

At nightfall he was assigned a room next to the princesses' bedroom. He lay on his bed and made ready to watch. Then one of the princesses brought him sleeping drops in wine and asked him to drink to her health. He could not refuse, took the cup, turned to the wall, and poured it into his bed. On the stroke of midnight the princesses came to see whether he was asleep. The nobleman pretended to be sleeping so soundly that nothing could rouse him, but actually he was listening to every rustle. "Well, little sisters," said one of them, "our guard has fallen asleep; it is time for us to go to the ball." "It is time, high time!"

They dressed in their best garments; the oldest sister pushed her bed to one side and disclosed a passage to the underground kingdom, to the realm of the accursed king. They began to climb down a ladder. The nobleman quietly rose from his bed, donned his invisible cap, and followed them. Accidentally he stepped on the youngest princess' dress. She was frightened and said to her sisters: "Ah, little sisters, someone seems to have stepped on my dress; this is a bad omen." "Don't worry, nothing will happen to us." They went down the ladder and came to a grove where golden flowers grew. The nobleman picked one flower and broke off a twig, and the whole grove rumbled. "Ah, little sisters," said the youngest princess, "do you hear how the grove is rumbling? This bodes no good." "Fear not, it is the music in the accursed king's palace."

They came to the palace and were met by the king and his courtiers. The music began to play and they began to dance; they danced till their shoes were torn to shreds. The king ordered wine to be served to the guests. The nobleman took a goblet from the tray, drank the wine, and put the goblet in his pocket. At last the party was over; the princesses said farewell to their cavaliers, promised to come the next night, returned home, undressed, and went to sleep.

The next morning the king summoned the needy nobleman. "Well," he said, "have you discovered what my daughters do every night?" "I have." "Then where do they go?" "To the underground kingdom, to the accursed king, and there they dance all night." The king summoned his daughters and began to question them: "Where were you last night?" The princesses denied everything. "We did not go anywhere," they said. "Have you not been with the accursed king? This nobleman testifies against you and is ready to offer proof." "Father, he cannot offer proof, for he slept like the dead all night." The needy nobleman drew the golden flower and the goblet from his pocket. "Here," he said, "is the proof." The princesses had no choice but to confess everything to their father; he ordered the passage to the underground kingdom to be walled up, married the needy nobleman to his youngest daughter, and all of them lived happily ever afterward.

THE INDISCREET WIFE

ONCE UPON A TIME there lived an old man and his wife. They built weirs in the river and put a basket in each one. Then they went home. On the way the old woman saw a treasure and immediately began to tell everyone about it. What could the old man do? He decided to play a trick on her, went to the field, caught a hare, then stopped at the river to look at his traps. He found a pike in one of them. He took it out and put the hare in its place; then he carried the pike into the field and laid it among the peas. When he got home he asked his wife to go with him to pick peas.

They made ready and went. On the way the old man said: "There is a rumor that fish are now living in the fields and that the beasts have moved to the river." "What nonsense, old man!" They came to the field. "But the rumor is true!" cried the old man. "Look here, a pike has crawled into our peas."

"Catch him!" The old man took the pike, put it into his basket, and said: "Now let us go to the river and see whether there is anything in our traps." He took out a trap and said: "Now you see? What people are saying is true! Look, a hare has fallen into the trap!" "Hold him tight or he may jump back into the water." The old man took the hare and said: "Now let us go and get our treasure."

They took all the money and drove home. On the way, the old woman saw a bear tearing a cow apart and said: "Hey, old man, look, there is a bear tearing a cow to pieces." "Be quiet, wife! That is the devil thrashing our *barin*." They came home; the old man went to hide the money, and the old woman ran to tell the news to her neighbor. The neighbor told it to the steward, and the steward told it to the *barin*, who called the old man before him and said: "Have you found a treasure?" "Why, no!" "But your wife says you have." "Well, it won't be her first lie." The *barin* sent for the old woman and asked her: "Is it true, old woman, that you have found a treasure?" "We have, little father." "Then why, old man, do you say that you have not?" asked the *barin*. The old man turned to his wife and said: "You foolish woman, why are you lying? Where have we found a treasure?" "What do you mean, where? In the field, of course; it was on the same day that we found a pike swimming in the peas and a hare caught in our fish trap." "Ah, you old hag, did anyone ever see a pike living in a field, and a hare swimming in the water?" "Have you forgotten everything? And at the same time a devil was thrashing our *barin*!" The *barin* boxed her ears: "What are you raving about, fool! When did the devil thrash me?" "But he did, I swear he did!" The *barin* grew angry, ordered rods to be brought in, and had her punished in his presence. The good woman was laid down and lashed; but she kept saying the same things even under the blows. The *barin* spat with disgust and drove the old couple out of his house.

THERE WAS ONCE a merchant who had a son. One day the merchant sent his son to the city to buy merchandise and instructed him: "Mind you, little son, be careful and don't make friends with redheads." The merchant's son set out on his way. It was a cold day; he felt chilly and stopped at an alehouse to warm himself. When he entered he found a redheaded servant pouring out liquor. "Pour me a glass of good liquor," said the merchant's son to him. He drank it and found it very much to his taste. "That's fine liquor," he said, "it's worth a hundred rubles. Pour me another glass." He drank the second glass and it seemed even better. "Well, brother," he said, "this glass is worth two hundred rubles." The man behind the counter was quick-witted: he wrote on the wall the sums mentioned by the merchant's son.

When the time came to pay the bill, the merchant's son said: "How much do I owe you?" "Three hundred rubles." "Are you out of your mind to charge me such a price?" "You set the price yourself, and now you are trying to go back on your word! No, brother, you can't wriggle out of it; unless you pay, I will not let you go." There was nothing to be done. The merchant's son paid three hundred rubles, went on his way, and thought to himself: "I'll remember now not to make friends with redheads! My father spoke the truth, and one should always listen to one's parents."

At that very moment he met a redheaded peasant driving a cart. When the merchant's son saw him, he jumped out of his carriage and lay flat in the snow, trembling with fear. "What's the matter with him?" the peasant wondered. He went over to the merchant's son and tried to raise him to his feet: "Get up, brother!" he said. "Let me alone! One redhead cheated me, you'll cheat me too." "Don't be foolish, brother! There are redheads of all kinds; some are cheats, some are honest. But who cheated you?" "So-and-so, the redheaded man who serves liquor in the neighboring village." "Come back with me, I'll take care of him."

They returned to the alehouse. The peasant cast a glance around him and noticed that a shoulder of mutton was hanging from the main beam; he went to the servant, asked for a glass of vodka, and at the same time tapped him on his shoulder and said: "How about selling me that shoulder?" "I'll sell it for a ruble." The peasant gave him a ruble, then drew a big knife from his pocket and gave it to the merchant's son, saying: "Now, brother, cut off his shoulder, I'll have it with my vodka." "Are you crazy?" said the servant. "I sold you the shoulder of mutton, not my shoulder." "Don't tell me any such stories, you won't cheat me as you cheated this merchant's son. I'm no fool." The servant began to beg and implore him, bowing almost to the ground. "Very well," said the peasant, "I will forgive you if you will return all the money to the merchant's son." The servant returned the three hundred rubles, and that was what the peasant wanted. "You see," he said to the merchant's son. "There are redheads of all kinds—cheats and honest people. Now go in peace."

The merchant's son was glad to go; he got into his carriage, spurred his horses, and said to himself: "Thank God I got away! The redheaded servant is a cheat, but this peasant is an even greater cheat; if I had become friendly with him, he would surely have skinned me alive."

THE MAIDEN TSAR

IN A CERTAIN LAND, in a certain kingdom, there was a merchant whose wife died, leaving him with an only son, Ivan. He put this son in charge of a tutor, and after some time took another wife; and since Ivan, the merchant's son, was now of age and very handsome, his stepmother fell in love with him. One day Ivan went with his tutor to fish in the sea on a small raft; suddenly they saw thirty ships making toward them. On these ships sailed the Maiden Tsar with thirty other maidens, all her foster sisters. When the ships came close to the raft, all thirty of them dropped anchor. Ivan and his tutor were invited aboard the best ship, where the Maiden Tsar and her thirty foster sisters received them; she told Ivan that she loved him passionately and had come from afar to see him. So they were betrothed.

The Maiden Tsar told the merchant's son to return to the same place the following day, said farewell to him, and sailed away. Ivan returned home and went to sleep. The stepmother led the tutor into her room, made him drunk, and began to question him as to what had happened to him and Ivan at sea. The tutor told her everything. Upon hearing his story, she gave him a pin and said: "Tomorrow, when the ships begin to sail toward you, stick this pin into Ivan's tunic." The tutor promised to carry out her order.

Next morning Ivan arose and went fishing. As soon as his tutor beheld the ships sailing in the distance, he stuck the pin into Ivan's tunic. "Ah, I feel so sleepy," said the merchant's son. "Listen, tutor, I will take a nap now, and when the ships come close, please rouse me." "Very well, of course I will rouse you," said the tutor. The ships sailed close to the raft and cast anchor; the Maiden Tsar sent for Ivan, asking him to hasten to her; but he was sound asleep. The servants began to shake him, pinch him, and nudge him. All in vain—they could not awaken him, so they left him.

The Maiden Tsar told the tutor to bring Ivan to the same place on the following day, then ordered her crews to lift anchor and set sail. As soon as the ships sailed away, the tutor pulled out the pin, and Ivan awoke, jumped up, and began to call to the Maiden Tsar to return. But she was far away then and could not hear him. He went home sad and aggrieved. His stepmother took the tutor into her room, made him drunk, questioned him about everything that had happened, and told him to stick the pin through Ivan's tunic again the next day. The next day Ivan again went fishing, again slept all the time, and did not see the Maiden Tsar; she left word that he should come again.

On the third day he again went fishing with his tutor. They came to the old place, and beheld the ships sailing at a distance, and the tutor straightway stuck in his pin, and Ivan fell sound asleep. The ships sailed close and dropped anchor; the Maiden Tsar sent for her betrothed to come aboard her ship. The servants tried in every possible way to rouse him, but no matter what they did, they could not waken him. The Maiden Tsar learned of the stepmother's ruse and the tutor's treason, and wrote to Ivan telling him to cut off the tutor's head, and, if he loved his betrothed, to come and find her beyond thrice nine lands in the thrice tenth kingdom.

The ships had no sooner set sail and put out to sea than the tutor pulled the pin from Ivan's garment; he awoke and began to bemoan his loss of the Maiden Tsar; but she was far away and could not hear him. The tutor gave him her letter; Ivan read it, drew out his sharp saber, and cut off the wicked tutor's head. Then he sailed hurriedly to the shore, went home, said farewell to his father, and set out to find the thrice tenth kingdom.

He journeyed onward, straight ahead, a long time or a short time—for speedily a tale is spun, but with less speed a deed is done—and finally came to a little hut; it stood in the open field, turning on chicken legs. He entered and found Baba Yaga the Bony-legged. "Fie, fie," she said, "the Russian smell was never heard of nor caught sight of here, but now it has come by itself. Are you here of your own free will or by compulsion, my good youth?" "Largely of my own free will, and twice as much by compulsion! Do you know, Baba Yaga, where lies the thrice tenth kingdom?" "No, I do not," she said, and told him to go to her second sister; she might know.

Ivan thanked her and went on farther; he walked and walked, a long distance or a short distance, a long time or a short time, and finally came to a little hut exactly like the first and there too found a Baba Yaga. "Fie, fie," she said, "the Russian smell was never heard of nor caught sight of here, but now it has come by itself. Are you here of your own free will or by compulsion, my good youth?" "Largely of my own free will, and twice as much by compulsion! Do you know, Baba

Yaga, where lies the thrice tenth kingdom?" "No, I do not," she said, and told him to stop at her youngest sister's; she might know. "If she gets angry at you," she added, "and wants to devour you, take three horns from her and ask her permission to blow them; blow the first one softly, the second louder, and the third still louder." Ivan thanked the Baba Yaga and went on farther.

He walked and walked, a long distance or a short distance, a long time or a short time, and finally beheld a little hut standing in the open field and turning upon chicken legs; he entered it and found another Baba Yaga. "Fie, fie, the Russian smell was never heard of nor caught sight of here, and now it has come by itself," she said, and ran to whet her teeth, for she intended to eat her uninvited guest. Ivan begged her to give him three horns: he blew one softly, the second louder, and the third still louder. Suddenly birds of all kinds swarmed about him, among them the firebird. "Sit upon me quickly," said the firebird, "and we shall fly wherever you want; if you don't come with me, the Baba Yaga will devour you." Ivan had no sooner sat himself upon the bird's back than the Baba Yaga rushed in, seized the firebird by the tail, and plucked a large handful of feathers from it.

The firebird flew with Ivan on its back; for a long time it soared in the skies, till finally it came to the broad sea. "Now, Ivan, merchant's son, the thrice tenth land lies beyond this sea. I am not strong enough to carry you to the other shore; get there as best you can." Ivan climbed down from the firebird, thanked it, and walked along the shore.

He walked and walked till he came to a little hut; he entered it, and was met by an old woman who gave him meat and drink and asked him whither he was going and why he was traveling so far. He told her that he was going to the thrice tenth kingdom to find the Maiden Tsar, his betrothed. "Ah," said the old woman, "she no longer loves you; if she gets hold of you, she will tear you to shreds; her love is stored away in a remote place." "Then how can I get it?" "Wait a bit! My daughter lives at the Maiden Tsar's palace and she is coming to visit me today; we may learn something from her." Then the old woman

turned Ivan into a pin and stuck the pin into the wall; at night her daughter flew in. Her mother asked her whether she knew where the Maiden Tsar's love was stored away. "I do not know," said the daughter, and promised to find out from the Maiden Tsar herself. The next day she again visited her mother and told her: "On this side of the ocean there stands an oak; in the oak there is a coffer; in the coffer there is a hare; in the hare there is a duck; in the duck there is an egg; and in the egg lies the Maiden Tsar's love."

Ivan took some bread and set out for the place she had described. He found the oak and removed the coffer from it; then he removed the hare from the coffer; the duck from the hare, and the egg from the duck. He returned with the egg to the old woman. A few days later came the old woman's birthday; she invited the Maiden Tsar with the thirty other maidens, her foster sisters, to her house; she baked the egg, dressed Ivan the merchant's son in splendid raiment, and hid him.

At midday, the Maiden Tsar and the thirty other maidens flew into the house, sat down to table, and began to dine; after dinner the old woman served them each an egg, and to the Maiden Tsar she served the egg that Ivan had found. The Maiden Tsar ate of it and at once conceived a passionate love for Ivan the merchant's son. The old woman brought him out of his hiding place. How much joy there was, how much merriment! The Maiden Tsar left with her betrothed, the merchant's son, for her own kingdom; they married and began to live happily and to prosper.

IVAN THE COW'S SON

IN A CERTAIN KINGDOM, in a certain land, there lived a king with his queen; they had no children, and after they had lived ten years together, the king issued a call to all the kings, all the cities, all the nations, and even to the common people, asking who could cure the queen of her barrenness and make her bear a child. Princes and boyars, wealthy merchants and peasants, gathered in the king's palace; he gave them meat and drink till they were drunk and then began to question them. But no one knew. No one could say how the queen might be made to bear a child—no one, except the son of a peasant. The king gave him a handful of gold coins and told him that in three days he must give the answer.

Well, although the son of the peasant had undertaken to cure the queen, he had not even dreamed of what he should suggest; so he went outside the town and began to ponder deeply. He met an old woman who said: "Tell me, peasant lad,

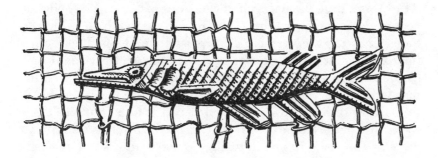

what are you thinking about?" He answered her: "Be quiet, old hag, don't annoy me!" But she ran after him and said: "Tell me your secret thoughts; I am old, I know everything." He thought that perhaps he had been wrong in offending her, that perhaps she really knew something, and said: "Little grandmother, I undertook to tell the king how the queen might be made to bear a child, but I do not know it myself." "Oho! But I know! Go to the king and tell him to have three silken nets prepared. In the sea beneath the king's window there is a pike with golden wings, which always swims in front of the palace. When the king catches the pike and cooks it, and the queen eats of it, she will bear a child."

The young peasant himself then went to fish in the sea. When he cast in the three silken nets, the pike leaped out, tearing all three nets. He cast in the nets for the second time, and again the pike tore them. Then the young peasant took his belt and the silken kerchief from his neck, tied up the nets, and cast them in for the third time. This time he caught the pike with the golden wings; he was overjoyed and brought it to the king. The king ordered the pike to be washed, cleaned, fried, and served to the queen. The cooks washed and cleaned the fish and threw the entrails out of the window. A cow swallowed these entrails. As soon as the cooks had fried the pike, a scullery maid put it on a dish, took it to the queen, and on the way tore off a wing and tasted it. Thus all three of them—the cow, the scullery maid, and the queen—became pregnant on the same day, at the same hour.

Speedily a tale is spun, with much less speed a deed is done. After some time the dairymaid came out of the cattle shed and reported to the king that a cow had given birth to a human babe. The king was very much surprised; and he had no sooner heard this news than he was told that the scullery maid had given birth to a boy exactly like the cow's son. And a few minutes later it was reported to him that the queen had given birth to a son as like the cow's son as one pea is like another. They were all wonderful boys! They grew by the hour as other boys grow by the year; in one hour they were as others in one year; in three hours, they were as others in three years. When they came of age, they sensed in themselves a mighty and heroic strength; they came to their father, the king, and asked his permission to go to the town, to see people, and show themselves to the world. He granted them permission, told them to behave soberly and peaceably, and gave them as much money as they could carry.

And so the good youths set out. One was called Ivan the Prince, the other Ivan the Scullery Maid's Son, and the third Ivan the Cow's Son, and nicknamed also Buria Bogatyr, Champion of Champions. And they walked and walked, but did not buy anything. Then Ivan the Prince saw some glass balls and said to his brothers: "Brothers, let us each buy a ball and throw it upward; whoever throws it highest will be our eldest." The brothers agreed and cast lots as to who should throw first. The lots fell out in favor of Ivan the Prince. He threw high, but Ivan the Scullery Maid's Son threw still higher, and Buria

Bogatyr threw the ball so high that it vanished from sight, and he said: "Henceforth I am your eldest!" Ivan the Prince grew angry. "What do you mean?" he said. "You are the cow's son, yet you want to be our eldest!" Ivan the Cow's Son answered him: "It must be God's will that you should obey me."

They set out on the road and came to the Black Sea; in it the sea serpent was wallowing. Ivan the Prince said: "Brothers, whoever of us subdues this serpent, he will be our eldest." The brothers consented. Ivan the Cow's Son said: "Subdue him, Prince Ivan! If you succeed, you will be our eldest." Prince Ivan began to shout in order to subdue the serpent, but the serpent only grew more ferocious. Then Ivan the Scullery Maid's Son tried to subdue him, but failed also. Then Buria Bogatyr shouted and threw a stick into the water, and the serpent vanished in a trice. He said again: "I am your eldest." Price Ivan grew angry and said: "We do not want to be the inferior brothers!" "Then I shall leave you," said Ivan the Cow's Son, and he returned to his native land. The two brothers went on straight ahead.

When the king learned that Ivan the Cow's Son had returned alone, he ordered him to be imprisoned in a fortress; for three days he was not given any food or drink. The mighty champion knocked with his fist on the stone wall and shouted in a mighty voice: "Ask your king and my foster father why he does not feed me! Your walls and bars are no bars to me. If I want to, I can smash them all with my fist." This was straightway reported to the king. The king came to him and said: "What are you bragging about, Buria Bogatyr?" "My foster father, why do you not feed me, why have you starved me for three days? I have not committed any misdeed." "But what have you done with my sons, your brothers?" Ivan the Cow's Son told him everything that had happened. "My brothers are alive," he said. "They are safe and sound and went straight ahead." The king asked: "Why did you not go with them?" "Because Prince Ivan wants to be the eldest, although the lots fell out making me the eldest." "Very well then, I will send for them." Ivan the Cow's Son said: "No one except myself can overtake them, for they went to the land of the dragons, to the place where dragons with six, nine, and twelve heads come up from the Black Sea." The king begged him to go after them. Ivan the Cow's Son made ready for his journey, took his battle mace and his steel sword, and left.

Speedily a tale is spun, with much less speed a deed is done. Ivan the Cow's Son walked and walked, and finally overtook his brothers near the Black Sea, near the white hazelwood bridge; and by that bridge there stood a post, and on it was written that this was the place where the three dragons always come out of the sea. "Good day, brothers!" he said to his brothers. They were overjoyed to see him and said: "Good day, Ivan the Cow's Son, our eldest brother." And he said: "I see that what is written on the post is not to your taste." He looked around and near the bridge he saw a little hut on chicken legs and with a cock's head, turned with its front to the wood and its back to them. Ivan the Cow's Son cried: "Little hut, little hut, stand with thy back to the wood, and thy front to us!" The little hut turned around; they entered it and found that the table was set with meat and drink in abundance; in the corner stood a bed of timber and on it lay a featherbed of down. Buria Bogatyr said: "You see, brothers, without me you would not have had any of this."

They sat down and dined, then lay down to rest. When they arose, Ivan the Cow's Son said: "Brothers, tonight the six-headed dragon will come out of the sea; let us cast lots as to who shall stand guard." They cast lots and the task fell to Ivan the Scullery Maid's Son. The Cow's Son said to him: "Mind you, a little pitcher will jump out of the sea and begin to dance before you; do not look at it, just spit at it and smash it." When the Scullery Maid's Son came to the sea he fell asleep. But Buria Bogatyr, knowing that his brothers were unreliable, went out himself; he walked on the bridge, tapping from time to time with his stick.

Suddenly a little pitcher jumped up before him and began to dance; the Cow's Son spat upon it and smashed it to smithereens. Then a duck quacked, the earth opened, the sea surged up, and out of the waves crawled Chudo Yudo, a sea monster. It was the six-headed dragon. He whistled and shouted with a mighty hiss, in a truly powerful voice: "Magic steed, horse of my need! Stand before me as leaf before grass!" The steed ran out, the earth shook, whole hayricks flew from under his hoofs, from his ears and nostrils thick smoke rolled. Chudo Yudo mounted the horse and rode toward the white hazelwood bridge. Suddenly his steed stumbled under him. "Why do you stumble, carrion flesh?" the dragon asked. "Do you scent a friend or an enemy?" The good steed answered: "There is an enemy—Ivan the Cow's Son." "You lie, carrion flesh! Even his bones were not brought here by a raven in a bladder, and he himself is certainly not here." "Ah, Chudo Yudo," said Buria Bogatyr, "no raven has brought my bones. I walked here myself." The dragon asked him: "Why have you come? To woo my sisters or daughters?" "No, brother, I came to meet you in the field, not to become your kin. Let us fight!"

Buria Bogatyr swung his battle mace and cut off three of the dragon's heads; he swung again, and cut off the other three. He cut the dragon's trunk in pieces and cast them into the sea, hid the heads under the white hazelwood bridge, tied the horse to the legs of Ivan the Scullery Maid's Son, and put the steel sword by his head; he himself went back to the little hut and lay down to sleep as though nothing had happened. Ivan the Scullery Maid's Son awoke, saw the steed, and was overjoyed; he sat upon him, rode to the little hut, and cried: "Buria Bogatyr, you told me not to look at the pitcher, but I did look, and the Lord gave me this steed." Ivan the Cow's Son answered: "He has given you the steed, but promised us more."

The next night it fell to Prince Ivan's lot to stand guard. Buria Bogatyr told him the same thing about the pitcher. The prince began to walk on the bridge and to tap with his walking stick; the little pitcher jumped out and danced before him; he stared at it and fell sound asleep. But Ivan the Cow's Son, not relying upon his brother, went out himself; he walked on the bridge and tapped with his walking stick; the little pitcher jumped out and danced before him. Ivan the Cow's Son spat upon it and smashed it to smithereens. Suddenly a duck quacked, the earth opened, the sea surged up, and out of the waves crawled Chudo Yudo, a sea monster, and whistled and

239

shouted with a mighty hiss, in a truly powerful voice: "Magic steed, horse of my need, stand before me as leaf before grass!" The steed ran out, the earth shook; from his ears and nostrils rolled pillars of smoke, from his mouth a flame streamed; he stood before the dragon, rooted to the spot. Chudo Yudo the nine-headed dragon sat upon him and rode to the white hazelwood bridge; as he rode upon the bridge, the steed stumbled under him. Chudo Yudo smote him on his great flanks: "Why do you stumble, carrion flesh? Do you scent a friend or an enemy?" "There is our enemy, Ivan the Cow's Son!" "You lie! Even his bones were not brought here by a raven in a bladder, and he himself is certainly not here." "Ah, Chudo Yudo, sea monster," answered Ivan the Cow's Son, "I have been walking here for two years." "Well, Ivan, Cow's Son, have you come to woo my sisters or my daughters?" "I have come to meet you in the field, not to be your kin; let us join in combat."

Ivan the Cow's Son swung his battle mace and cut off three of the dragon's heads as easily as if they had been cabbage heads; he swung again and cut off three more heads; he swung a third time and cut off the rest. He chopped the trunk into pieces and cast them into the Black Sea, hid the heads under the white hazelwood bridge, tied the steed to Prince Ivan's legs, and put the steel sword by his head; he himself went back to the little hut and lay down to sleep as though nothing had happened. Next morning Prince Ivan awoke, saw a steed even better than the first one, was overjoyed, rode on him, and cried: "Eh, Ivan the Cow's Son, you told me not to look at the little pitcher, but God has given me a steed even better than the first one." He answered: "God has given you two steeds, and to me only a promise."

The third night was approaching and Buria Bogatyr, Champion of Champions, made ready to stand guard; he set up a table and lit a candle, thrust a knife into the wall, hung a towel on it, gave his brothers a pack of cards, and said: "Play cards, boys, and do not forget me; when the candle begins to run out, and when blood drips from this towel onto the dish, hasten to the bridge to aid me."

Buria Bogatyr walked on the bridge, tapping with his walk-

240

ing stick; a little pitcher jumped out and danced before him; he spat upon it and smashed it to smithereens. Suddenly a duck quacked, the earth opened, the sea surged up, and out of the waves crawled Chudo Yudo the sea monster; this time it was the twelve-headed dragon. He whistled and shouted with a mighty hiss, in a truly powerful voice: "Magic steed, horse of my need, stand before me as leaf before grass!" The steed ran out, the earth shook; from his ears and nostrils rolled pillars of smoke, from his mouth a fiery flame streamed; he ran to the dragon and stood rooted to the spot. Chudo Yudo sat upon him and rode to the bridge; when the steed stepped upon the bridge he stumbled. "Why do you stumble, carrion flesh? Do you scent an enemy?" the dragon cried. "There is an enemy of ours, Buria Bogatyr, the Cow's Son." "Be quiet; the raven has not brought his bones here in a bladder." "You lie, sea monster, I have been walking here for three years." "Well, Buria Bogatyr, do you want to marry my sisters or my daughters?" "I have come to fight you in the field, not to be your kin; let us join in combat." "Ah, you killed my two brothers, so you think you can defeat me too!" "We shall see what God's will is. Now listen, Chudo Yudo, you have a horse and I am on foot; let us agree that if either of us falls to the ground the other must not strike him."

Buria Bogatyr swung his battle mace and cut off three of the dragon's heads in one stroke; he swung again, and the dragon knocked him down. Cried Ivan the Cow's Son: "Halt, Chudo Yudo! Our agreement was not to strike a man while he lay on the ground." Chudo Yudo let him get up; he rose, and at once three heads flew like so many cabbage heads. They began to struggle bitterly; they fought for several hours, till both grew exhausted; the dragon lost three more heads and our hero's battle mace broke. Buria Bogatyr removed his left boot, flung it into the little hut, and knocked down half of it; but his brothers were asleep and did not hear him. He removed his right boot and flung it also; the little hut flew apart into boards, but still his brothers did not awaken. Buria Bogatyr took a fragment of his mace, hurled it at the stable where their two horses stood, and broke the stable door; the horses galloped onto the bridge and unsaddled the dragon. Our hero was over-joyed, ran up to the dragon, and cut off his remaining three heads. He chopped the dragon's body into pieces, cast them into the Black Sea, and stuck the heads under the white hazel-wood bridge. Then he took the three horses, led them into the stable, and hid under the bridge without wiping the blood off it.

In the morning his two brothers awoke and saw that the hut had crumbled to bits and that the dish was full of blood; they went to the stable and found three horses; they wondered what had happened to their eldest brother. They sought him for three days but did not find him. They said: "They must have killed each other, and their bodies have vanished; let us go home." They had saddled their horses and were making ready to go when Buria Bogatyr awoke and came out from under the bridge. "So you are deserting your companion, brothers?" he said. "I saved you from death, but you were asleep and did not come to my aid." Then they fell on their knees before him and said: "Forgive us, Buria Bogatyr, our eldest brother!" "God will forgive you!" He murmured over the little hut: "Be as thou wert before!" The little hut reappeared just as it was before, full of meat and drink. "Now, brothers," said Ivan the Cow's Son, "dine, for without me you might have starved to death; then we shall set out."

They dined and set out on their way. When they had gone two versts, Buria Bogatyr said: "Brothers, I forgot my riding crop in the little hut. Amble along while I go back to fetch it." He rode to the little hut, climbed down from his steed, and set him free in the sacred meadows, saying: "Go, my good steed, until I call thee!" Then he changed himself into a fly, flew into the little hut, and sat on the stove. After a while, Baba Yaga came in and sat down in the front corner. Her young daughter-in-law came to see her and said: "Ah, mother, Buria Bogatyr —Ivan the Cow's Son—has killed your son, my husband. But I will revenge myself for this insult: I will precede him, send upon him a hot day, and turn myself into a green meadow. In this green meadow I will turn into a well. In this well a silver cup will float. And I will also turn myself into a timber bed. The brothers will want to feed their horses, to rest and drink

242

water; and then they will be blown to bits like poppy seed." Her mother said to her: "That is what those evildoers deserve!"

Then her second daughter-in-law came and said: "Ah, mother, Buria Bogatyr—Ivan the Cow's Son—has killed your son, my husband. But I will revenge myself for this insult: I will precede him and turn into a lovely garden; fruits of every description will hang above the fence, juicy and fragrant! They will want to pick them, each his favorite fruit; and then they will be blown to bits like poppy seed!" Her mother said: "You, too, have thought up a good revenge!"

The third and youngest daughter-in-law came and said: "Ah, mother, Buria Bogatyr—Ivan the Cow's Son—has killed your son, my husband. But I will revenge myself for this insult: I will turn into a little old hut. They will want to spend the night in it, but as soon as they set foot inside they will be blown to bits like poppy seeds." "Well, my beloved daughters-in-law, if you fail to kill them yourselves, I will run in front of them tomorrow, turn into a sow, and swallow them all."

Buria Bogatyr heard these words while sitting on the stove and then flew outside. He struck the earth and turned into a good youth. He whistled and shouted, with a mighty whistle, a powerful cry: "Magic steed, horse of my need, stand before me as leaf before grass!" The steed ran out; the earth shook. Buria Bogatyr sat upon him and rode on; he tied a wisp of bast to a stick, overtook his companions, and said to them: "Here, my brothers, I cannot live without such a riding crop!" "Eh, brother, was it worth while to return for such trash? We could have gone to town and bought a new one." And they rode on over steppes and through valleys; and the day was so hot that they could not bear it, and thirst tormented them. They came upon a green meadow, and in the meadow the grass was lush, and on the grass there was a timber bed. "Brother Buria Bogatyr," the younger two said, "let us feed our horses on this grass and rest ourselves on the timber bed; there is also a well, let us drink of the cool water." Buria Bogatyr said to his brothers: "The well is amidst the steppes and deserts; no one shall take water or drink from it." He jumped down from his

good steed, began to smite and cut the well, and blood spattered out; suddenly the day became misty, the heat subsided, and they were not thirsty. "Now you see, brothers," he said, "how stale this water is; it is like blood."

They rode on farther. After a long time or a short time, they came to a beautiful garden. Prince Ivan said to the eldest brother: "Allow us each to pick an apple." "Eh, brothers, this garden is amidst steppes and deserts; perhaps the apples are old and rotten, and if you eat them a disease may strike you. First let me see." He went into the garden and began to smite and cut; he cut down all the trees, down to the last one. His brothers became angry at him for not doing what they wanted.

They rode along and were overtaken by dark night; soon they came to a hut. "Brother Buria Bogatyr," the younger brothers said, "rain is beginning to fall; let us spend the night in this hut." "Eh, brothers, let us pitch our tents and spend the night in the open field rather than in this hut; it is an old hut, and if we enter, it may fall and crush us; let me go and see." He entered the hut and began to cut it down; blood spattered out, and he said: "You can see for yourselves what kind of hut this is, rotten through and through! Let us ride on farther." The brothers grumbled but did not show their anger. They rode on farther; suddenly the path branched into two. Buria Bogatyr said: "Brothers, let us take the left path." They said: "Take the path you want, we shall not go with you." And so they turned to the right and Buria Bogatyr to the left.

Buria Bogatyr—Ivan the Cow's Son—came to a village; in this village twelve blacksmiths were working. And he cried and whistled, with a mighty whistle, a powerful cry: "Blacksmiths, blacksmiths, all of you come here!" The blacksmiths heard him and twelve of them ran to him: "What do you wish?" "Stretch an iron sheet around the smithy." In a trice they did it. "Forge twelve iron rods, blacksmiths, and heat the tongs red hot. A sow will come to you and say: 'Blacksmiths, blacksmiths, surrender the culprit; if you do not surrender the culprit, I will swallow you all with the smithy.' And you say: 'Ah, mother sow, take this fool from us, he has long been a thorn in our flesh; only thrust your tongue into the smithy, and we will put him on your tongue.' "

Buria Bogatyr had no sooner given them this order than a huge sow came to them and cried in a loud voice: "Blacksmiths, blacksmiths, surrender the culprit!" The blacksmiths answered in one voice: "Mother sow, take this fool from us, he has long been a thorn in our flesh; only thrust your tongue into the smithy: we will put him on your tongue." The sow was simple-minded and gullible, she thrust her tongue in a whole cubit's length. Buria Bogatyr seized it with the red-hot tongs and cried to the blacksmiths: "Take the iron rods, thrash her soundly!" They thrashed her until they bared her ribs. "And now," said

245

Buria Bogatyr, "hold her fast, I will give her a treat." He seized an iron rod and smote her, breaking all her ribs in two. The sow began to implore him: "Buria Bogatyr, let my soul repent!" Buria Bogatyr said: "And why have you swallowed my brothers?" "I will throw them up at once." He seized her by her ears; the sow vomited and the two brothers jumped out with their steeds. Then Buria Bogatyr raised her and with all his strength smashed her against the damp earth: the sow shattered into a myriad of evil spirits. Said Buria Bogatyr to his brothers: "Do you see, you fools, where you have been?" They fell on their knees begging: "Forgive us, Buria Bogatyr, Cow's Son!" "Well, now let us set out on our way. Nothing shall stop us."

They came to a kingdom, to the Indian king, and pitched their tents in his sacred meadows. In the morning the king awoke, looked through his spyglass, saw the tents, and summoned his prime minister, saying: "Go, brother, take a horse from the stable, ride to the sacred meadows, and find out what uncouth people have come there, pitched their tents without my permission, and made fires in my sacred meadows." The prime minister went to the brothers and asked: "What kind of people are you, kings or princes, or mighty champions?" Buria Bogatyr, the Cow's Son, answered: "We are very mighty champions, we have come to woo the king's daughter. Report to your king that he must give his daughter to Prince Ivan in marriage; and if he refuses, let him send an army." The king asked his daughter whether she would marry Prince Ivan. She answered: "No, father, I do not want to marry him; send an army." Straightway the bugles blew, the cymbals clashed, the troops gathered and went to the sacred meadows; and it was such a big host that Prince Ivan and Ivan the Scullery Maid's Son took fright.

At that moment Buria Bogatyr was cooking some gruel for breakfast and stirring it with a ladle; he went out and with one swing of the ladle knocked down half the army; he went back, stirred his gruel, went out, swung again, and knocked down the other half, leaving only a one-eyed man and a blind man. "Tell your king," he said to them, "that he must give his daughter Princess Maria to Prince Ivan in marriage; and if he refuses, let him send another army, and come with it himself." The one-eyed man and the blind man came to their king and said: "Your Majesty, Buria Bogatyr sent us to tell you that you must give your daughter to Prince Ivan in marriage; and he was frightfully angry, and slew all our troops with a ladle." The king entreated his daughter: "My beloved daughter, please marry Prince Ivan." The daughter said: "We have no choice, I must marry him. Have a carriage sent for him."

The king forthwith sent a carriage and stood waiting before the gate. Prince Ivan came with his two brothers; the king received them courteously and kindly, with music and drums, and seated them at oaken tables covered with checkered tablecloths, on which were placed sweet viands and heady drinks. Then Buria Bogatyr whispered to Prince Ivan: "Mind you, Prince Ivan, when the princess asks you for permission to leave for an hour, say to her: 'You may go even for two hours.' " After a while, the princess came to Prince Ivan and said: "Prince Ivan, permit me to go to another room to change my dress." Prince Ivan let her go; she went out of the chambers and Buria Bogatyr followed behind her quietly. The princess struck herself against the porch, turned into a gull, and flew out to sea. Buria Bogatyr struck the ground, turned into a falcon, and flew after her. The princess came to the seashore, struck the ground, turned into a lovely maiden, and said: "Grandfather, grandfather, golden head, silver beard, let me speak to you!" Her grandfather emerged from the blue sea and said: "My little granddaughter, what do you want?" "Prince Ivan is wooing me; I do not wish to marry him, but all our army is slain. Grandfather, give me three hairs from your head; I will show them to Prince Ivan and ask him to guess from what root comes this grass."

The grandfather gave her three hairs; she struck the ground, turned into a gull, and flew home. And Buria Bogatyr struck the ground, turned into the same lovely maiden, and said: "Grandfather, grandfather, come out again, I want to speak to you, I have forgotten to tell you something." The grandfather had no sooner stuck his head out of the water than Buria Bogatyr seized it and tore it off; he struck the ground, turned into an eagle, and came back to the palace ahead of the princess. He called Prince Ivan out to the entrance hall and said: "Prince Ivan, take this head; the princess will show you three hairs and ask you to guess from what root this grass comes; for answer just show her this head."

A little later the princess came to Prince Ivan, showed him the three hairs, and said: "Prince, guess from what root this grass comes; if you guess right, I will marry you, if not, do not hold it amiss if I don't." Prince Ivan took the head from under his coat and struck the table with it, saying: "Here is your root." The princess thought to herself: "They are brave knights!" Then she said: "Please, Prince Ivan, let me change my dress in another room." Prince Ivan let her go; she went on the porch, struck the ground, turned into a gull, and again flew out to sea. Buria Bogatyr took the head from the prince, went into the yard, struck the head against the porch, and said: "Where you were before, be now too." The head flew forth, came to the place ahead of the princess, and grew together with the body.

The princess stopped at the seashore, struck the ground, turned into a lovely maiden, and said: "Grandfather, grandfather, come out and speak to me!" Her grandfather came out saying: "My little granddaughter, what do you want?" "Was not your head in our palace?" "I do not know, granddaughter, I have been sound asleep." "No, grandfather, your head was there." "Apparently it was torn off the last time you came here to speak to me." She struck the ground, turned into a gull, and flew home. She changed her dress, came back to the banquet hall, and sat beside Prince Ivan.

The next day they went to the church to be lawfully wedded; after they returned, Buria Bogatyr led Prince Ivan to his bedroom, showed him three rods, one of iron, one of copper, and one of pewter, and said: "If you want to remain alive, let me lie with the princess in your place." The prince consented. The king led the young couple to their nuptial bed. At that moment Buria Bogatyr took the place of the prince, lay down, and began to snore; the princess put one leg on him, then another, and began to smother him with a pillow. Buria Bogatyr jumped from under her, took the iron rod, and began to beat her. He beat her until he broke the rod; then he took the copper rod and broke it too; then he began to beat her with the pewter rod. The princess began to implore him and swore solemn oaths that she would never again try to do such a thing. Next morning Buria Bogatyr rose, went to Prince Ivan, and said: "Now, brother, go and see how well I have chastised your wife; the three rods I prepared are all broken. Now live happily together, love each other, and do not forget me."

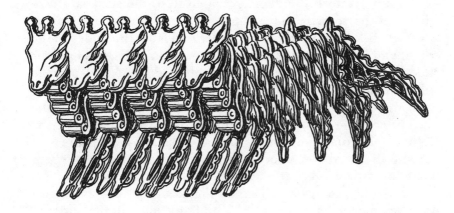

THE WOLF AND THE GOAT

ONCE UPON A TIME there was a goat who built herself a little hut in the woods and lived there with her kids. She often went deep into the forest to look for food; whenever she left the hut the kids locked the little door and stayed inside. When the goat returned she would knock at the door and sing: "My little baby kids, unlock the door and open it! I, the she-goat, have been in the forest; I have eaten soft grass and drunk spring water. Milk flows down in the udder and from

the udder to the hoof and from the hoof into the damp earth."
The kids would at once open the door and let their mother in.
Then she would feed them and go again into the forest, and
the kids would lock the door very tight.

The wolf overheard all this. Once when the goat had gone to
the forest he came to the little hut and cried in his rough voice:
"Hey, little kids, hey, my dear ones, unlock the door and open
it! Your mother is back and has brought you milk aplenty."
But the kids answered: "We hear you, we hear you, but yours
is not our mother's voice! Our mother sings in a soft voice and
sings different words." The wolf went away and hid himself.
Then the goat came and knocked at the door, singing: "My little
baby kids, unlock the door and open it! I, the she-goat, have
been in the forest, I have eaten soft grass and drunk spring
water. Milk flows down in the udder and from the udder to the
hoof and from the hoof into the damp earth." The kids let their
mother in and told her that the wolf had come and tried to
devour them. The goat fed them and when she left again for
the woods gave them strict orders not to let in anyone who
might come to the little hut and beg in a rough voice saying
other words than she said. As soon as the goat was gone the wolf
ran to the little hut, knocked at the door, and began to chant
in a soft voice: "My little baby kids, unlock the door and open
it! I, the she-goat, have been in the forest, I have eaten soft
grass and drunk spring water. Milk flows down in the udder to
the hoof and from the hoof into the damp earth." The kids
opened the door and the wolf ran in and ate them all; only one
little kid escaped by hiding in the stove.

The goat came back, but no matter how sweetly she sang, no
one answered her. She came closer to the door and saw that it
was open; she looked into the room and saw that it was empty;
she looked into the stove and found one kid there.

When the goat learned of her misfortune, she sat down on a
bench, began to weep bitterly, and sang: "Oh, my baby kids,
why did you open the door to the wicked wolf? He has devoured you all, and left me with great grief and sadness in my
soul." The wolf heard this, came into the hut, and said to the
goat: "Ah, neighbor, neighbor, why do you slander me? Would

I do such a thing? Let us go to the forest together and take a walk." "No, neighbor, I have no heart for walking." "Let us go," the wolf insisted.

They went into the forest and found a pit in which some brigands had recently cooked gruel. There was still some fire left in it. The goat said to the wolf: "Neighbor, let us see which of us can jump across the pit." The wolf tried first, and fell into the hot pit; his belly burst from the heat of the fire, and the kids ran out of it and rushed to their mother. From then on they lived happily, acquired wisdom, and eschewed evil.

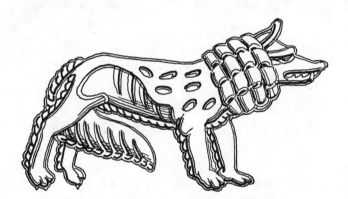

THE WISE LITTLE GIRL

Two brothers were traveling together: one was poor and the other was rich, and each had a horse, the poor one a mare, and the rich one a gelding. They stopped for the night, one beside the other. The poor man's mare bore a foal during the night, and the foal rolled under the rich man's cart. In the morning the rich man roused his poor brother, saying: "Get up, brother. During the night my cart bore a foal." The brother rose and said: "How is it possible for a cart to give birth to a foal? It was my mare who bore the foal!" The rich brother said: "If your mare were his mother, he would have been found lying beside her." To settle their quarrel they went to the authorities. The rich man gave the judges money and the poor man presented his case in words.

Finally word of this affair reached the tsar himself. He summoned both brothers before him and proposed to them four riddles: "What is the strongest and swiftest thing in the world?

What is the fattest thing in the world? What is the softest thing? And what is the loveliest thing?" He gave them three days' time and said: "On the fourth day come back with your answers."

The rich man thought and thought, remembered his godmother, and went to ask her advice. She bade him sit down to table, reated him to food and drink, and then asked: "Why are you so sad, my godson?" "The sovereign has proposed four riddles to me, and given me only three days to solve them." "What are the riddles? Tell me." "Well, godmother, this is the first riddle: 'What is the strongest and swiftest thing in the world?' " "That's not difficult! My husband has a bay mare; nothing in the world is swifter than she is; if you lash her with a whip she will overtake a hare." "The second riddle is: 'What is the fattest thing in the world?' " "We have been feeding a spotted boar for the last two years; he has become so fat that he can barely stand on his legs." "The third riddle is: 'What is the softest thing in the world?' " "That's well known. Eider down —you cannot think of anything softer." "The fourth riddle is: 'What is the loveliest thing in the world?' " "The loveliest thing in the world is my grandson Ivanushka." "Thank you, godmother, you have advised me well. I shall be grateful to you for the rest of my life."

As for the poor brother, he shed bitter tears and went home. He was met by his seven-year-old daughter—she was his only child—who said: "Why are you sighing and shedding tears, father?" "How can I help sighing and shedding tears? The tsar has proposed four riddles to me, and I shall never be able to solve them." "Tell me, what are these riddles?" "Here they are, my little daughter: 'What is the strongest and swiftest thing in the world? What is the fattest thing, what is the softest thing, and what is the loveliest thing?' " "Father, go to the tsar and tell him that the strongest and fastest thing in the world is the wind; the fattest is the earth, for she feeds everything that grows and lives; the softest of all is the hand, for whatever a man may lie on, he puts his hand under his head; and there is nothing lovelier in the world than sleep."

The two brothers, the poor one and the rich one, came to the tsar. The tsar heard their answers to the riddles, and asked the poor man: "Did you solve these riddles yourself, or did someone solve them for you?" The poor man answered: "Your Majesty, I have a seven-year-old daughter, and she gave me the answers." "If your daughter is so wise, here is a silken thread for her; let her weave an embroidered towel for me by tomorrow morning." The peasant took the silken thread and came home sad and grieving. "We are in trouble," he said to his daughter. "The tsar has ordered you to weave a towel from this thread." "Grieve not, father," said the little girl. She broke off a twig from a broom, gave it to her father, and told him: "Go to the tsar and ask him to find a master who can make a loom from this twig; on it I will weave his towel." The peasant did as his daughter told him. The tsar listened to him and gave him a hundred and fifty eggs, saying: "Give these eggs to your daughter; let her hatch one hundred and fifty chicks by tomorrow."

The peasant returned home, even more sad and grieving than the first time. "Ah, my daughter," he said, "you are barely out of one trouble before another is upon you." "Grieve not, father," answered the seven-year-old girl. She baked the eggs for dinner and for supper and sent her father to the king. "Tell him," she said to her father, "that one-day grain is needed to feed the chicks. In one day let a field be plowed and the millet sown, harvested, and threshed; our chickens refuse to peck any other grain." The tsar listened to this and said: "Since your daughter is so wise, let her appear before me tomorrow morning—and I want her to come neither on foot nor on horseback, neither naked nor dressed, neither with a present nor without a gift." "Now," thought the peasant, "even my daughter cannot solve such a difficult riddle; we are lost." "Grieve not," his seven-year-old daughter said to him. "Go to the hunters and buy me a live hare and a live quail." The father bought her a hare and a quail.

Next morning the seven-year-old girl took off her clothes, donned a net, took the quail in her hand, sat upon the hare, and went to the palace. The tsar met her at the gate. She bowed to him, saying, "Here is a little gift for you, Your Majesty," and

254

handed him the quail. The tsar stretched out his hand, but the quail shook her wings and—flap, flap!—was gone. "Very well," said the tsar, "you have done as I ordered you to do. Now tell me—since your father is so poor, what do you live on?" "My father catches fish on the shore, and he never puts bait in the water; and I make fish soup in my skirt." "You are stupid! Fish never live on the shore, fish live in the water." "And you—are you wise? Who ever saw a cart bear foals? Not a cart but a mare bears foals."

The tsar awarded the foal to the poor peasant and took the daughter into his own palace; when she grew up he married her and she became the tsarina.

DANILO THE LUCKLESS

IN THE CITY OF KIEV our Prince Vladimir had many servants and peasants in his household, and he also had a nobleman called Danilo the Luckless. When Sunday came, Prince Vladimir treated everyone to a glass of liquor, but Danilo received only a kick in the backside. On the great holidays, everyone received a gift, but he received nothing at all. On Easter

Eve, just before Easter Day, Prince Vladimir summoned Danilo the Luckless before him, gave him forty times forty sables, and commanded that he fashion for his master a fur coat for the holiday; the sables were not skinned, the buttons were not molded, the loops were not braided; and the prince ordered him to mold the shapes of forest beasts in the buttons, and to embroider the shapes of birds of foreign lands in the loops.

Danilo the Luckless grew discouraged with his task, threw it down, and went to walk beyond the city gates; he walked aimlessly along the road, weeping bitter tears. An old woman stopped him and said: "Hey, Danilo, don't be so silly! Why are you weeping, you luckless wretch?" "Ah, you old hag, all stitched and patched, and eaten by fever, let me alone, I have troubles of my own!" He walked on a little farther, then thought to himself: "Why did I abuse her so?" He went back to her and said: "Little grandmother, little dove, forgive me! This is why I am distressed: Prince Vladimir has given me forty times forty sables and wants a fur coat made of them by tomorrow, with many molded buttons and braided silken loops— there must be golden lions on the buttons, and birds from foreign lands singing sweet songs must be embroidered on the loops. And how can I do all that? I would rather stand in the tavern with a cup of vodka in my hands."

The old woman replied: "Ah, now I am the grandmother, the little dove! Well, go to the blue sea, stand by the old oak. At midnight the blue sea will surge up, and Chudo Yudo, the sea monster without hands, without feet, and with a gray beard, will come to you. Seize him by his beard and thrash him until he asks you: 'Why are you thrashing me, Danilo the Luckless?' And you answer: 'I want the lovely Swan Maiden to stand before me, and through her feathers let her body be seen, and through her body let her bones be seen, and through her bones let it be seen how from bone to bone the marrow flows, like pearls poured from one vessel to another.' " Danilo the Luckless came to the blue sea, stood by the old oak, and at midnight the sea surged up, and Chudo Yudo, the sea monster without hands, without feet, with nothing but a gray beard, came up to

256

him. Danilo seized him by his beard and began to beat him against the damp earth. Chudo Yudo asked him: "Why do you thrash me, Danilo the Luckless?" "This is why: I want the lovely Swan Maiden to stand before me. And through her feathers let her body be seen, and through her body let her bones be seen, and through her bones let it be seen how from bone to bone the marrow flows, like pearls poured from one vessel to another."

After a little while the lovely Swan Maiden came sailing to the shore and said these words: "Danilo the Luckless, are you shirking a great deed or trying to perform one?" "Ah, lovely Swan Maiden! If I am shirking a great deed, then double is my need! Prince Vladimir has ordered me to make him a fur coat for tomorrow; but the sables are not skinned, the buttons are not molded, the loops are not braided!" "Will you take me as your wife? Then everything will be done." He thought to himself: "How can I marry her?" "Well, Danilo, why are you hesitating?" "I will take you!" She shook her wings, nodded her head, and there came forth twelve strong men—masons, carpenters, and bricklayers. In a trice a house was ready. Danilo took her by her right hand, kissed her sweet lips, and led her into the princely chambers; they sat at table, ate, drank, and refreshed themselves, and plighted their troth. "Now, Danilo, lie down and rest. Do not worry, everything will be done."

She put him to bed and went out on the crystal porch. There she shook her wings and nodded her head, saying: "My own father, give me my craftsmen." Twelve youths appeared and asked her: "Lovely Swan Maiden, what do you command us to do?" "Sew me a fur coat. The sables are not skinned, the buttons are not molded, the loops are not braided." They set to work: some prepared the skins and sewed the fur coat, some smelted and molded the buttons, some braided the loops, and in a trice a marvelous fur coat was ready. The lovely Swan Maiden roused Danilo the Luckless: "Awake, my beloved! The fur coat is ready and the church bells are ringing in Prince Vladimir's city of Kiev; it is time for you to rise and attend matins."

Danilo rose, donned the fur coat, and went forth. The Swan

Maiden looked through the window; she stopped him, gave him a silver cane, and told him: "When you leave the church, strike your chest with this cane; the birds will sing merrily and the lions will roar terribly. Take the fur coat off your shoulders and give it forthwith to Prince Vladimir, that he may not forget us. He will invite you to his table and give you a cup of wine; do not drink it to the bottom, for if you do, evil will befall you. And do not boast of me, do not boast that in one night we built a house." Danilo took the cane and set out. The Swan Maiden called him back again, and gave him three eggs, two silver eggs and one golden egg, and said: "Offer the silver ones to the prince and his wife, and the golden one to her with whom you will live all your life."

Danilo the Luckless said farewell to her and went to attend matins. All the people were amazed: "Here is Danilo the Luckless, and he has finished the fur coat for the holiday!" After matins he approached the prince and his wife, congratulated them as is the custom at Easter, and by accident took out the golden egg. Aliosha Popovich, the rake, saw it. The people began to leave the church. Then Danilo the Luckless struck his chest with the silver cane, and the birds began to sing and the lions to roar. All were amazed and looked at Danilo, but Aliosha Popovich disguised himself as a crippled beggar and begged for holy alms. Everyone gave him something, only Danilo the Luckless stood there wondering: "What shall I give him? I have nothing!" And because it was such a great holiday he gave him the golden egg. Aliosha Popovich took the golden egg and donned his usual clothes.

Prince Vladimir invited everyone to his house, and they ate and drank and refreshed themselves and boasted of their exploits. Danilo got drunk and in his drunkenness boasted of his wife. Aliosha Popovich, the rake, began to boast that he knew Danilo's wife. Danilo said: "If you know my wife, let my head be cut off; if you do not, yours shall be cut off!"

Aliosha went he knew not whither; he walked and wept. An old woman stopped him and said: "Why are you crying, Aliosha Popovich?" "Go away, old hag, I have my own troubles." "Very well, but I might have been useful to you." He began to question her: "My dear grandmother, what did you want to tell me?" "Aha, now I am the dear grandmother!" Then he told her: "I boasted that I knew Danilo's wife." "Ah, little father, how could you know her? Not even a little bird has flown where she is. Go to such and such a house, invite her to dine with the prince. She will begin to wash and make ready and will put a little chain on the window. Take this chain and show it to Danilo the Luckless."

Aliosha came to the high-arched window and summoned the lovely Swan Maiden to dine with the prince. She began to wash, to dress and make ready for the feast. Meanwhile Aliosha took away the chain, ran to the palace, and showed it to Danilo the Luckless. "Well, Prince Vladimir," said Danilo the Luckless, "I see that my head must be cut off. Permit me to go home and say farewell to my wife."

He went home and said: "Ah, lovely Swan Maiden, what have I done? I boasted of you in my drunkenness and have forfeited my life." "I know everything, Danilo the Luckless. Go and invite to your house the prince and his wife, and all the citizens. And if the prince excuses himself because of the dust and the mud, if he says that the roads are not good, that the blue sea has surged up and swamps have appeared, say to him: 'Fear not, Prince Vladimir! Across the swamps, across the rivers, there are white hazelwood bridges with oaken planks, and on the bridges are spread purple cloths, and everything is nailed with copper nails. The brave knights' boots will not be covered with dust, the hoofs of their horses will not sink into the mud.'" Danilo the Luckless went to invite his guests, and the lovely Swan Maiden went out on the porch, shook her wings, nodded her head, and made a bridge from her house to the palace of Prince Vladimir. The bridge was all spread with purple cloth and nailed with copper nails; on one side of it flowers bloomed and nightingales sang; on the other side apples ripened and other fruit trees blossomed.

The prince and the princess set out on their way with all the brave warriors. They came to the first river and fine beer flowed in it; near that beer many soldiers fell. They came to the second river and fine mead flowed in it; more than half of the brave troops bowed to that mead and lay down. They came to the third river and fine wine flowed in it; here the officers fell to and drank themselves into a stupor. They came to the fourth river and strong vodka flowed in it; the prince looked back and saw all his generals lying dead drunk on the bank. The prince remained with only three companions—his wife, Aliosha Popovich the rake, and Danilo the Luckless. The guests arrived, entered the high chambers, and there found tables of maplewood, with silken tablecloths and painted chairs. They sat at table and there were many meats of every description, and of foreign wines not bottles, not barrels, but whole rivers flowed. Prince Vladimir and the princess did not eat nor drink but waited only to see the lovely Swan Maiden.

They sat at table for a long time, they waited for her a long time; finally, the moment came to return home. Danilo the Luckless called her once, twice, and thrice—but no, she did not come out to her guests. Aliosha Popovich the rake said: "If my wife did this, I would teach her to obey her husband." The lovely Swan Maiden heard this, came out on the porch, and said these words: "This is how I teach husbands!" And she shook her wings, nodded her head, soared up, and flew away. And the guests remained sitting in the mud: on one side there was the sea, on the other the mountains, on the third were forests, and on the fourth were swamps. Put your pride away, prince—try to ride home on Danilo!

Before they got home to their palace they were smeared with mud from top to toe. Then I wanted to see the prince and princess, but they kicked me out of the yard. I jumped under the gate, and my whole back ached.

IVAN THE PEASANT'S SON
AND THE THUMB-SIZED MAN

IN A CERTAIN KINGDOM, in a certain land, there lived a king;
in his courtyard there was a pillar, and on the pillar three
rings, one of gold, one of silver, and one of copper. One
night the king dreamed that a horse was tied to the golden ring;
every hair on the horse's body was silver, and on his brow was
a glistening moon. In the morning the king arose and sent forth
a call proclaiming that to anyone who could tell him the meaning of this dream and get for him that horse, he would give his
daughter and half his kingdom as a dowry.

In answer to the king's summons a multitude of princes,
boyars, and lords of every description gathered together; they
thought and thought, but not one of them could tell the mean-

ing of the dream and not one of them would undertake to get the horse. At last it was reported to the king that a certain poor old peasant had a son, named Ivan, who could explain his dream and get the horse for him. The king sent for Ivan and asked him: "Can you explain my dream and get that horse?" Ivan answered: "Tell me first what the dream was and what horse you want." The king said: "Last night I dreamed that to the golden ring in my courtyard a horse was tied, and every hair on his body was silver, and on his brow was a glistening moon." "That was not a dream, but a reality," said Ivan. "For last night the twelve-headed dragon came to your kingdom on that horse and wanted to steal your daughter." "And can you get that horse?" "I can," answered Ivan. "But not before I have passed my fifteenth year."

At that time Ivan was only twelve years old. So the king took him into his palace and gave him food and drink till he reached his fifteenth year. When his fifteenth year had passed, he said to the king: "Sire, give me a horse on which to ride to the land of the dragon." The king led him to his stables and showed him all his horses. But Ivan could not find one strong enough to carry his great weight; when he put his mighty hand on a horse, the horse would fall to the ground. Then Ivan said to the king: "Let me go into the open field and seek a horse suited to my strength." The king let him go.

Ivan the peasant's son looked for three years and nowhere could he find a horse. He was returning in tears to the king, when he met an old man who asked him: "Why are you weeping, young fellow?" Ivan answered this question rudely and chased the old man away. The old man said: "Mind you, young fellow, do not speak ill of me!" Ivan walked for a little distance away from the old man and thought to himself: "Why did I offend him? Old people know a great deal." He turned back, caught up with the old man, fell at his feet, and said: "Grandfather, forgive me, I offended you because of my own grief. This is why I am weeping: for three years I have traveled in the open field through many droves of horses, and nowhere can I find a horse strong enough for me." The old man said: "Go to such and such a village. There in the stable of a peasant is a mare. That mare has given birth to a mangy colt. Take this colt and feed him. Soon he will be suited to your strength."

Ivan bowed deeply to the old man and went to that village. He went straight to the peasant's stable, saw the mare with the mangy colt, and put his hands upon him. The colt did not shy away in the least. Ivan took him from the peasant, fed him for some time, went back to the king, and said that he had found a horse for himself. Then he began to make ready to visit the dragon. The king asked him: "How many men do you need, Ivan?" Ivan answered: "What do I need men for? I can get the horse by myself; but you might give me half a dozen men to carry messages back and forth."

The king gave him six men; they made ready and set out. Whether they traveled a long time or a short time, no one knows. But we do know that they came to a river of fire; over the river was a bridge and around it an enormous forest. They pitched a tent in the forest, got out a variety of refreshments, and began to eat, drink, and make merry.

Ivan the peasant's son said to his companions: "Let us each stand guard every night in turn, to see whether anyone crosses this river." But all of Ivan's companions when they kept watch got drunk and did not see anything. Finally, Ivan the peasant's son himself stood guard, and just at midnight he saw a three-headed dragon, who crossed the river and said: "I have no enemy and no slanderer, except perhaps one enemy and one slanderer, Ivan the peasant's son. But the raven has not even brought his bones here in a bladder!"

Ivan the peasant's son sprang out from under the bridge. "You lie!" he said. "I am here." "If you are here, let us join in combat." And the dragon rode on horseback against Ivan, but Ivan advanced on foot, took a swing with his saber, and cut off all three of the dragon's heads, took his horse, and tied him to the tent. The next night Ivan the peasant's son slew the six-headed dragon and on the third night the nine-headed one, and cast them each into the river of fire. When he went to the bridge on the fourth night, the twelve-headed dragon came to him and said angrily: "Who is Ivan the peasant's son? Why did he slay my sons? Let him come out to meet me forthwith!"

264

Ivan the peasant's son stepped forward and said: "First let me go to my tent, then we shall join in combat." "Very well, go." Ivan ran to his companions, and said: "Here, boys, is a bowl. Look into it; when it is filled with blood, come to me." He returned and faced the dragon; and when they rode apart and then clashed, Ivan at the first blow cut off four of the dragon's heads, but himself sank into the earth up to his knees. They clashed a second time, and Ivan cut off three dragon heads, and sank into the earth to his waist. They clashed a third time, and he cut off three more heads, but sank into the earth up to his breast. Finally he cut off one more head, and sank into the earth up to his neck. Then only did his companions remember him; they looked into the bowl and saw that blood was overflowing its brim. They rushed out, cut off the last head of the dragon, and pulled Ivan out of the earth. Ivan the peasant's son took the dragon's horse and led him to the tent.

Night passed and morning came; the brave youths began to eat and drink and make merry. Ivan rose from the merrymaking and said to his companions: "Wait for me." He changed himself into a cat, crossed the bridge over the river of fire, came to the house of the dragons, and made friends with the cats there. In the whole house only the dragon's wife and her three daughters-in-law remained alive. They sat in the chamber and spoke among themselves: "How can we destroy that scoundrel, Ivan the peasant's son?"

The youngest daughter-in-law said: "Wherever Ivan the peasant's son goes, I will bring a famine on the road, and turn myself into an apple tree; when he eats one of my apples he will burst!"

The second daughter-in-law said: "And I will make a thirst on the road, and turn myself into a well; let him try to drink!"

The eldest said: "And I will bring a drowsiness upon him, and turn myself into a bed; when Ivan the peasant's son lies down upon it, he will die at once."

Finally their mother-in-law said: "And I will open my mouth from earth to sky and devour them all."

Ivan the peasant's son heard everything they said, went out

of the chamber, turned into a man, came back to his companions, and said to them: "Well, boys, make ready to go."

They made ready, set out, and at once a terrible hunger came to them; but they had nothing to eat. Suddenly they saw an apple tree; Ivan's companions wanted to pluck some apples, but Ivan forbade them. "This," he said, "is not an apple tree." He began to cut it down; and blood spurted out of its trunk. Soon afterward they were overwhelmed by thirst. Ivan saw a well, forbade his companions to drink from it, and began to hack its stones; blood flowed from the well. Then drowsiness came upon them; a bed stood on the road, but Ivan slashed through it too. At last they came to a mouth opened from earth to sky. What could they do? They thought of jumping over it on the run, but no one could jump it, except Ivan the peasant's son. He was rescued from this predicament by his wonderful horse, every hair of whose body was silver, and whose brow bore a glistening moon.

He came to a river; near the river stood a little hut. There he met a little man as big as a thumb, with a mustache seven versts long, who said to him: "Give me your horse, and if you do not give him to me willingly, I will take him by force." Ivan answered: "Get out of my path, accursed reptile, or I shall crush you under my horse!"

The little man as big as a thumb, with a mustache seven versts long, knocked him to the ground, sat himself on the horse, and rode away. Ivan entered the hut and grieved greatly for his horse. In the hut a footless and handless man was lying on the stove. He said to Ivan: "Listen, brave youth—I know not how to call you by name—why did you try to fight him? I was a greater champion than you, yet he ate off my hands and my feet." "Why?" "Because I ate bread from his table." Ivan asked the man how he could recover his horse. The footless and handless man said to him: "Go to such and such a river, take the ferryboat, ferry for three years, accept money from no one—then you may get your horse back."

Ivan bowed deeply to him, went to the river, took the ferryboat, and for three whole years ferried and took no money for it. Once he ferried three old men across the river; they offered him money, but he refused it. "Tell me, brave youth, why don't you take money?" He answered: "Because of a promise I made." "What promise?" "A perfidious man took my horse, and a good man told me to row the ferry for three years and accept money from no one." The old men said: "If you wish, Ivan, peasant's son, we can help you to get back your horse." "Do help me, my friends!"

These old men were not ordinary people; they were the Freezer, the Glutton, and the Magician. The Magician stepped on the shore, drew the picture of a boat on the sand, and said: "Brothers, do you see this boat?" "We see it." "Sit in it." All four of them sat in the boat. The Magician said: "Now, little light boat, serve me as you have served me before." Suddenly the boat rose in the air and in a trice, like an arrow shot from a bow, brought them to a big, stony mountain. On that mountain stood a house, and in the house lived the little man as big as a thumb, with a mustache seven versts long. The old men sent Ivan to ask for the horse. Ivan asked for it; the little man as big as a thumb, with a mustache seven versts long, said to him: "Steal the king's daughter and bring her to me; then I will return your horse."

Ivan told this to his companions, and they left him at once and went to the king. The king learned what they had come for and ordered his servants to heat a bath red hot— "Let them suffocate there!" He asked his guests to go into the bath; they thanked him and went. The Magician ordered the Freezer to go first. The Freezer went into the bath and cooled it; then they washed and steamed themselves and came before the king. The king ordered a great feast to be served; a vast array of viands was placed on the table. The Glutton ate everything.

At night the three guests made secret preparations, stole the princess, brought her to the little man as big as a thumb, with a mustache seven versts long, and got the horse in exchange. Ivan the peasant's son bowed deeply to the old men, bestrode the horse, and started on his journey back to the king. He rode and rode, stopped in the open field to take a rest, pitched his tent, and lay down. When he awoke, he discovered the princess lying beside him. He was overjoyed and asked: "How did you get here?" The princess said: "I changed into a pin and stuck myself into your collar."

At that moment she again turned into a pin; Ivan the peasant's son stuck her in his collar and rode on. He came to the king, who, upon seeing the marvelous horse, received the brave youth with honor and told him that his daughter had been stolen. Ivan said: "Do not grieve, Sire, I have brought her back." He went into the next room and the pin in his collar turned into a lovely maiden. Ivan took her by the hand and led her to the king. The king was even more overjoyed, took the horse for himself, and gave his daughter to Ivan the peasant's son in marriage. And even now Ivan is living happily with his young wife.

DEATH OF A MISER

THERE WAS ONCE an old miser who had two sons and a great deal of money. When he heard Death coming, he locked himself up in his room, sat on his oaken chest, swallowed his gold coins, chewed up his bills, and thus ended his life. His sons came, laid out the dead body under the holy icons, and invited the sexton to chant the psalms. At midnight a devil in human form suddenly appeared, took the old man on his shoulders, and said: "Hold up the flap of your coat, sexton!" And he shook the dead man, saying: "The money is yours, but the bag is mine." And he vanished, taking the body with him.

THE FOOTLESS CHAMPION
AND THE HANDLESS CHAMPION

ACERTAIN PRINCE decided to get married and had a particular bride in mind, a beautiful princess, but he did not
know how to win her. Kings and princes and brave
champions from many lands had wooed her, but had achieved
nothing. They had only lost their rash heads, which were stuck
on the fence poles around the palace of the proud maiden.
The prince was sad and distressed and wondered who would
help him. Then appeared Ivan the Naked, a poor peasant who
had nothing to eat or drink and whose clothes had long since
fallen from his shoulders. He came to the prince and said:
"You cannot win the maiden by yourself, and if you go to woo
her alone, you will lose your rash head. It would be better if

we went together. I shall save you from danger and arrange the whole match. Only promise to obey me." The prince promised to follow the peasant's advice, and the very next day they set out on their journey.

They arrived in the maiden's kingdom and began to woo her. The princess said: "First, the bridegroom must prove his strength." She invited the prince to a feast and regaled him lavishly; after dinner the guests began to play various games. "Now bring me my gun that I take on the hunt," said the princess to her attendants. The door opened and forty men appeared, carrying not a gun but a cannon. "Well, my intended bridegroom," said the princess, "fire my gun." "Ivan," said the prince, "see whether this gun is any good." Ivan the Naked took the gun out on the porch, gave it a shove with his foot, and it flew far away and fell into the blue sea. "No, Your Majesty," reported Ivan the Naked, "it is a wretched gun, unfit to be fired by a champion like yourself." "What is the meaning of this, princess?" said the prince. "Do you wish to make mock of me? You asked me to fire a gun that my servant hurled into the sea with a single kick."

The princess ordered her bow and arrow to be brought. Again the door opened and forty men carried in the bow and arrow. "My intended bridegroom, see if you can shoot an arrow with my bow." "Eh, Ivan," cried the prince, "see whether this bow is fit for me to shoot with." Ivan the Naked drew the bow and shot the arrow: it flew a hundred versts, hit Marko the Runner, and shot off both his hands. Marko the Runner cried in a mighty voice: "Ah you, Ivan the Naked, you have shot off both my hands; but you will not escape misfortune either." Ivan the Naked took the bow and broke it in twain. "Prince," he said, "it is a wretched bow, unfit to be used by a champion like yourself." "What is the meaning of this, princess?" the prince said. "What kind of bow have you given me? My servant drew it, shot an arrow with it, and it broke in twain at once."

The princess ordered her spirited steed to be brought from the stable. Forty men led the steed and could hardly keep him on his chain halter, so fierce and untamable was he. "Well, my intended bridegroom," said the maiden, "take a ride on my steed. I myself ride him every morning." The prince cried: "Eh, Ivan, see whether this horse is fit for me to ride." Ivan the Naked ran to the horse and began to stroke him; he stroked him for some time, then took his tail, gave it a pull, and tore off his skin. "No," he said, "it is a wretched nag. I barely touched his tail and his whole skin came off." The prince complained: "Eh, princess, you are still making mock of me; instead of giving me a mighty steed you gave me a miserable jade." The princess ceased trying the prince's strength and married him the next day. After the wedding they lay down to sleep; the princess put her hand on the prince's body and he could barely endure it; he began to lose his breath. "Ah," thought the princess, "so that is the kind of champion you are! Very well then, I'll show you!"

One month later the prince made ready to go to his own kingdom with his young wife. They rode one day, two days, three days, then stopped to give their horses a rest. The princess climbed out of the carriage, saw that Ivan the Naked was sound asleep, took an ax, and cut off both his feet. Then she ordered the horses put to her carriage, commanded the prince to stand on the footboard behind, and returned to her kingdom, leaving Ivan in the open field.

One day Marko the Runner passed through that field. He saw Ivan, spoke to him in a friendly fashion, took him on his back, and went with him into a deep dark forest. The champions began to live in the forest. They built themselves a hut, made themselves a little wagon, got a gun, and hunted birds of passage. Marko the Runner dragged the wagon, and Ivan the Naked sat in it, shooting birds. They fed on this game all year round.

After a while they grew weary of their life and decided to steal a maiden from her father and mother. They went to a certain priest and asked him for alms. The priest's daughter came out of the house, bringing them bread. As soon as she was near the wagon, Ivan seized her by her hands, sat her next to himself, and Marko ran with them at full speed. A minute later they were in their hut. "Maiden," they said, "be our sister, cook our dinner and supper, and look after the house." Thus

271

they lived peacefully and quietly and did not complain of their lot.

One day the champions went hunting, stayed away for a whole week, and upon their return could hardly recognize their sister, she had grown so thin. "What has happened to you?" they asked her. She told them that a dragon had flown to her every day and that she had grown thin because of him. "We will catch him," said the champions. Ivan the Naked lay under the bench and Marko the Runner hid behind the door in the entrance hall. About half an hour later, the trees in the forest suddenly began to rustle and the roof of the hut shook: the dragon came, struck the damp earth, turned into a goodly youth, sat at table, and asked for food. Ivan seized him by his feet and Marko fell upon the dragon with all his body and thrashed him terribly. Then they dragged the dragon to an oaken stump, split the stump, stuck his head into the crack, and began to flog him with rods. The dragon implored them: "Let me go, mighty champions! In return, I'll show where to find the water of life and the water of death."

The champions consented. The dragon led them to a lake; Marko was overjoyed and wanted to jump into the water at once, but Ivan held him back. "First we must try it," he said. He took a green twig and threw it into the water; the twig burned at once. Again the champions set upon the dragon; they drubbed him and drubbed him till he was more dead than alive. He led them to another lake; Ivan picked up a rotten trunk and cast it into the water; it sprouted at once and grew green leaves. The champions jumped into the lake, bathed in it, and came ashore with new limbs: Ivan had his feet and Marko his hands. They took the dragon, dragged him to the first lake, and threw him in—and only smoke was left of him.

They returned home. Marko the Runner was old. He brought the priest's daughter back to her father and mother and began to live with them, because the priest had declared that whosoever brought his daughter back would be allowed to live and eat in his house till the end of his days. But Ivan the Naked got himself a mighty steed and went to look for his prince. He rode by an open field and saw the prince tending swine. "Hail,

272

prince!" he said. "Hail!" answered the prince. "And who are you?" "I am Ivan the Naked." "Why do you boast like that? If Ivan the Naked were alive, I would not be a swineherd." "This is the end of your toil," said Ivan. They exchanged clothes. The prince rode ahead on the mighty steed and Ivan the Naked followed him driving the swine. The princess saw him, ran out on the porch, and cried: "Ah, you good-for-nothing! Who told you to drive the pigs home before sunset?" Then she ordered the swineherd to be seized and thrashed in the stable. Ivan the Naked did not wait. He seized the princess by her braid and dragged her around the yard until she repented and solemnly promised to obey her husband in everything. After that the prince and the princess lived in concord for many years, and Ivan the Naked served them.

OLD FAVORS
ARE SOON FORGOTTEN

A WOLF FELL into a trap but somehow managed to wrench himself free and began to run through the forest. Some hunters spied him and began to trail him. The wolf was compelled to run across a road, where a peasant returning from the field with a bag and a flail happened to be walking along. The wolf said to him: "Do me a favor, dear peasant, hide me in your bag; some hunters are on my trail." The peasant consented, hid him in his bag, tied it up, and slung it over his shoulder. He walked on and soon met the hunters. "Haven't you seen a wolf in this neighborhood, peasant?" they asked. "No, I haven't seen anything," answered the peasant. The hunters galloped on and vanished from sight. "Have my pursuers gone?" asked the wolf. "They have." "Well, then, let me out." The peasant untied the bag and let the wolf out into the free world.

The wolf said: "Well, peasant, now I will devour you." "Ah, wolf, wolf," said the peasant, "I saved you from a dire fate, and now you want to devour me!" "Old favors are soon forgotten," replied the wolf. The peasant realized that he was in bad straits, and said: "Well, if so, let us walk on, and if the first person we meet agrees with you that old favors are soon forgotten, I will submit and you can devour me."

So they walked on and met an old mare. The peasant stopped her and said: "Please, little mother mare, settle our dispute. I have rescued the wolf from a dire fate, and now he wants to devour me." And he told her all that had happened. The mare thought and thought and said: "I lived with my master for twelve years, bore him twelve foals, worked for him with all my strength, but when I grew old and could not work any longer, he dragged me into a ravine; I climbed and climbed, until at last I climbed out by dint of much effort, and now I am plodding along I know not whither. Yes, old favors are soon forgotten." "You see, I am right," said the wolf. The peasant was grieved and implored the wolf to wait until they met some-one else.

The wolf consented and soon they met an old dog. The peas-ant asked him the same question. The dog thought and thought and then said: "I served my master for twenty years, guarding his house and his livestock, and when I grew old and could bark no longer, he drove me out of his house, and now I am plodding along I know not whither. Yes, old favors are soon forgotten." "Well, you see, I am right," said the wolf. The peasant be-came even sadder than before and implored the wolf to wait for a third encounter, saying: "Then you may do as you will, since you refuse to remember my favor."

The third beast they met was a fox and the peasant repeated his question to her. The fox began to argue. "But how is it possible," she asked, "that a wolf, such a big beast, should have been able to climb into this small bag?" Both the wolf and the peasant swore that he had, but the fox still refused to believe it and said: "Well, little peasant, let me see how you put him in that bag." The peasant opened the bag and the wolf stuck his head into it. The fox cried: "But did you hide only his head?"

The wolf crawled in with his whole body. "Well, little peasant," the fox went on, "show me how you tied him." The peasant tied the bag. "Well, little peasant, how did you thresh the grain in the field?" The peasant began to thresh the bag with his flail. "And now, little peasant, how did you swing around?" The peasant swung around, struck the fox on her head, and killed her, saying: "Old favors are soon forgotten."

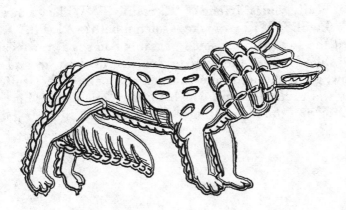

THE SHEEP, THE FOX,
AND THE WOLF

A SHEEP RAN away from a certain peasant's flock. She happened to meet a fox, who asked her: "Where is God taking you, friend?" "Oh, oh, my friend, I was in a peasant's flock, but my life was very hard; whenever the ram did some mischief, I, the sheep, was held responsible. So I made up my mind to go away, I know not whither." "It's the same thing with me," answered the fox. "Whenever my husband caught a chicken, I, the vixen, was always held responsible. Let us run together." After some time they met a wolf. "Good day, friends," he said. "Good day," said the fox. "Are you going far?" he asked. "I don't know where I'm going," the fox said and told him her troubles. The wolf said: "It is the same with me: whenever the she-wolf slaughtered a lamb, I, the wolf, was held responsible. Let us go together."

They went. On the way the wolf said to the sheep: "Hey, sheep, you are wearing my coat!" The fox heard him and said: "Is it really yours, friend?" "Certainly." "Will you swear to it?" "I will." "Will you take a solemn oath?" "I will." At this point the fox saw that some peasants had set a trap near the road. She brought the wolf to the edge of the trap and said: "Now, go in there to take your solemn oath." The wolf foolishly went into the trap, which snapped and caught his snout. The fox and the sheep at once ran away from him for good.

THE BRAVE LABORER

A CERTAIN MILLER had a laborer. He sent this laborer to throw wheat into the hopper, but instead the fellow strewed it on the millstone. The mill began to turn and all the wheat was scattered. When the miller came to the mill and saw the scattered wheat, he drove the laborer away. The laborer set out for his own village, but got lost on the way. He went into some bushes and lay down to sleep. A wolf came; seeing that the laborer was asleep, he came closer and began to sniff him, but the laborer snatched the wolf by his tail, killed him, and skinned him.

The laborer went up a hill and on the hill stood an empty mill; he decided to spend the night in this mill. Three brigands came there; they lit a fire and began to divide their booty. One of them said: "I'll put my share underneath the mill." The second said: "I'll shove mine under the wheel." And the third said: "I'll hide mine in the hopper." But our laborer was lying in the hopper, and fearing that the brigands would kill him, he thought that he should try to frighten them. So he cried: "Hey, you there, go down! And you, strike from the side. And you, hit from there, while I strike from here! Stop them, boys! Get at them, boys!" The brigands took fright, threw down their plunder, and ran away.

The laborer crawled out of the hopper, gathered his booty, went home, and told his father and mother: "Here is everything I earned at the mill. Now let us go to market, buy ourselves a gun, and go hunting." They went to market, bought a gun, and on their way back the laborer said to his father: "Look sharp to see whether we meet a hare, a fox, or perhaps even a marten." The two men dozed as they drove and finally fell asleep. Two wolves came, killed their horse, and devoured it entirely. The father awoke and lashed out with his whip—at his horse, as he thought, but actually he hit the wolf. The wolf got into the horse's collar and began to drag the cart and the father began to drive it. The other wolf tried to seize the laborer from behind. This wolf had a deep scar. The laborer lashed the wolf with his whip and the knot of his whip got stuck in the wolf's scar. The laborer dragged him after his cart, so that one wolf pulled the cart while the other ran behind it. They came home; their dog ran out barking wildly. The wolves took fright; the one made a sharp turn, overturning the cart and spilling the father and son on the ground. The other wolf jumped out of the horse collar and the laborer dropped his whip; the two wolves ran away and the old man and the laborer were left with nothing.

They were well off indeed! Their yard was in the form of a circle. Three birch poles stood in it. The poles were tied by their tops. Three stakes were driven into the ground. Three twigs were wound around the stakes. The sky covered their estate from above and the whole world inclosed it!

DAUGHTER AND STEPDAUGHTER

A WIDOWED PEASANT with a daughter married a widow who also had a daughter; thus they each had a stepchild. The stepmother was envious and nagged the old man constantly, saying: "Take your daughter to the woods, to a mud hut; there she will spin more." What could the peasant do? He did as his wife told him, took his daughter to a mud hut, gave her a steel and flint and a bag of grits, and said: "Here is fire for you, do not let it die out; cook your kasha, sit and spin, and keep the hut locked." Night came. The girl heated the stove and cooked her kasha; from somewhere a little mouse came out and said: "Maiden, maiden, give me a spoonful of kasha." "Oh, little mouse, cheer me in my loneliness, and I will give you more than one spoonful of kasha. I shall let you eat your fill of it." The mouse ate his fill and left.

At night a bear broke into the hut and said: "Now, girl, put out the light and let us play blindman's buff." The mouse ran up the maiden's shoulder and whispered into her ear: "Fear not, maiden. Say to him, 'Very well, let us play.' Then put out the light and crawl under the stove; I shall run about and ring the little bell." So they did. The bear chased the little mouse but could not catch him; he began to roar and hurl logs of wood; he hurled and hurled them but did not hit his mark. He got tired and said: "Ah, little girl, you're an expert player of blindman's buff. To reward you I shall send you a drove of horses and a cartful of goods tomorrow morning."

Next morning the old man's wife said: "Go, old man, visit your daughter, see how much she has spun since yesterday." The old man went and his wife sat and waited for him to bring back his daughter's bones. Suddenly the dog began to bark: "Bow-wow-wow, the daughter is coming, with her father driving a drove of horses and bringing a cartful of goods." "You're lying, dog! Those are her bones rattling and clattering in my husband's basket." The gate creaked, the horses ran into the yard, and the stepmother beheld the father and daughter sit-

278

ting on a cart laden with goods. The woman's eyes gleamed with greed. "That's not very much," she cried. "Now take my daughter to the woods for the night. She will come home driving two droves of horses and bringing two cartfuls of goods."

The peasant took his wife's daughter to the mud hut and provided her also with food and fire. At nightfall she cooked gruel. The mouse came and asked her for some kasha. But she cried: "Oh, you vermin!" And she hurled a spoon at him. The mouse ran away, Natasha gobbled up all the kasha by herself, and, having eaten, put out the light and lay down in a corner. At midnight the bear broke into the mud hut and said: "Hey, where are you, little girl? Let's play blindman's buff." The maiden did not answer, but her teeth rattled from fear. "Ah, so there you are! Here's a little bell. Run, I will try to catch you." She took the little bell, her hand trembled, the bell rang incessantly, and the mouse said: "That wicked maiden will meet her death."

Next morning the wife sent the old man to the woods, saying: "Go now! My daughter will bring back two cartfuls of goods and drive two droves of horses." The peasant went and his wife sat at the gate. The dog barked: "Bow-wow-wow, the wife's daughter is coming, her bones are rattling in the basket, and the old man sits on an empty cart." "You're lying, dog! My daughter is driving herds and bringing full carts." She looked up and there was the old man at the gate. He handed his wife a basket; she opened the basket, saw the bones, began to howl, and grew so angry that from grief and spite she died the next day. But the old man lived happily with his daughter all his life and took into his house a wealthy son-in-law.

THE STUBBORN WIFE

ONCE A PEASANT shaved his beard and said to his wife: "Look how well I have shaved." "But you haven't shaved, you have only clipped your beard!" "You're lying, you wretch, I have shaved." "No, it's clipped." The husband thrashed his wife and insisted: "Say it's shaved, or I'll drown you!" "Do what you will, it's still clipped." He took her to the river to drown her. "Say it's shaved!" "No, it's clipped." He led her into the water up to her neck and shoved her head in. "Say it's shaved!" The wife could no longer speak, but she raised her hand from the water and showed by moving two fingers like a pair of scissors that his beard was clipped.

ANECDOTES

AN OLD MOTHER was admonishing her son not to go bathing in the river: "Now, mind you, you rascal, if you drown, don't dare to come back home!"

ONCE IN WINTERTIME some drivers were driving on the Volga. One horse became restive and jumped off the road; his driver ran after him and was about to hit him with his whip, when the horse fell into a hole and sank with the cart. "Well, you should be thankful you escaped," said the peasant. "I was going to give you a terrible thrashing!"

A YOUNG PEASANT went hunting and his wife walked with him part of the way; after having walked for a verst she began to cry. "Don't cry, wife, I'll soon be back," the peasant said. "But that's not why I'm crying," the wife said. "I'm crying because my feet are ice cold."

ONCE A FOOL was soundly thrashed during the night and the next morning everyone made fun of him. "You should thank God," he said, "that the night was clear; otherwise I would have played a trick on you." "What trick? Tell us!" "I would have hidden myself."

THREE TRAVELERS dined at an inn, then continued on their way. "Well, my friends," said one of them, "it seems to me that we paid a very high price for our dinner!" "Well, although I spent a great deal," said another, "I got my money's worth." "How?" "Didn't you notice? As soon as the host looked away, I snatched a handful of salt from the salt cellar, and crammed it into my mouth."

A PEASANT bought a quart of wine, drank it, and felt no effects. He bought a pint—and still was not drunk. He drank a half-pint and became drunk. Then he began to feel sorry for himself: "Why did I buy the quart and the pint? I should have bought the half-pint to begin with. That would have done the job!"

SNOW WHITE AND THE FOX

ONCE THERE WERE an old man and his wife who had a granddaughter, Snow White. Her little friends wanted to go to the woods for berries and asked her to join them. For a long time the old couple would not consent, but after many entreaties they let her go, telling her on no account to separate from her friends. But walking in the woods and picking berries, shrub after shrub, bush after bush, Snow White did become separated from her friends. They hallooed and hallooed her but Snow White did not hear them. Night fell and her friends went home.

Seeing that she was all alone, Snow White climbed up into a tree and began to weep bitterly, saying to herself: "Ai, ai, Snow White, little dove, grandfather and grandmother had a little granddaughter, Snow White; some girls lured her to the woods, and having lured her there, abandoned her." A bear came by and asked: "Why are you weeping, Snow White?" "How can I help weeping, little father bear? I am grandfather's and grandmother's only granddaughter, Snow White; some girls lured me to the woods, and having lured me there, abandoned me." "Come down, I will carry you home." "No, I am afraid of you, you will devour me."

The bear left her. Again she began to cry, saying: "Ai, ai, Snow White, ai, ai, little dove!" A wolf came by and asked: "Why are you weeping, Snow White?" She answered him as she had answered the bear. "Come down, I will carry you home." "No, I am afraid of you, you will devour me."

The wolf left her and Snow White wept again, saying: "Ai, ai, Snow White, ai, ai, little dove!" A fox came by and asked: "Why are you weeping, Snow White?" "How can I help weeping, little fox? Some girls lured me to the woods, and having lured me, abandoned me." "Come down, I will carry you home."

Snow White came down, sat on the fox's back, and the fox

darted off with her; she ran up to the house and with her tail began to knock at the gate. "Who is there?" they called from within. The fox answered that she had brought home to the old man and old woman their granddaughter, Snow White. "Ah, our beloved, come in, come in, where shall we seat you and what shall we offer you?" They brought out milk, eggs, and cheese curds, and began to feast the fox for her kindness. But the fox asked that a chicken be brought out into the field as a reward. The old couple said farewell to the fox, put a chicken in one bag and a dog in another, and took the bags to the place named by the fox. There they let the chicken out: the fox had no sooner jumped upon it than they let out the dog. Seeing the dog, the fox rushed into the woods and never came back.

FOMA BERENNIKOV

ONCE UPON A TIME there lived an old woman who had a one-eyed son named Foma Berennikov. One day he went to plow his field with his wretched horse. He was suddenly overcome by misery and sat down on a mound of earth, to ease himself; the flies buzzed and buzzed around the dung. He seized a twig, beat the swarm of flies, and began to count how many he had killed. He counted five hundred of them and many of them were still uncounted. Foma decided that they were numberless. He came to his horse and found twelve gadflies sitting on it; he slew them all. Then he returned to his mother and asked her for her solemn blessing: "I have slain countless small fry," he said, "and twelve mighty heroes. Let me go forth, mother, to do great deeds, for plowing the land is not a hero's business but a peasant's." His mother gave him her blessing, praying that he might do great deeds and carry out heroic exploits. He hung his best basket at his girdle, took his blunt scythe off his shoulders, and placed it in the basket.

He traveled along the road in unfamiliar country till he came to a post, and he wrote with chalk on this post—for although he had neither gold nor silver in his pocket, he did happen to have some chalk. He wrote: "Champion Foma Berennikov, who slew twelve mighty heroes at one blow and an unnumbered army in addition, passed this way." Having written this, he went on. Ilya Muromets traveled along the same road, came to the post, beheld the inscription, and said: "Here is the champion's mark; he does not spend gold nor silver, only chalk." And he wrote in silver: "Following Foma Berennikov, Champion Ilya Muromets passed this way." He overtook Foma Berennikov and said (apparently the chalk inscription had impressed him): "Mighty Foma Berennikov, where shall I ride—in front of you or behind you?" "Ride behind me," answered Foma.

Young Aliosha Popovich traveled the same road; he came to the same post and from afar saw an inscription blazing like fire on the post. He read the inscriptions of Foma Berennikov and Ilya Muromets, drew pure gold from his pocket, and wrote: "Following Ilya Muromets, Aliosha Popovich passed this way." He overtook Ilya Muromets and said: "Tell me, Ilya Muromets, shall I ride in front of you or behind you?" "Ask not me but my elder brother, Foma Berennikov." Young Aliosha Popovich rode up to Foma Berennikov. "Brave Foma Berennikov, where shall Aliosha Popovich ride?" "Ride behind us."

They traveled along the road in unfamiliar country till they came to green gardens. Ilya Muromets and Aliosha Popovich pitched their white tents and Foma Berennikov spread his pair of drawers. These gardens belonged to the Prussian king, and the Chinese king, aided by six mighty champions, was at that time waging war on the Prussian king. And the Prussian king sent a letter to Foma Berennikov, saying: "The Chinese king is waging war against me, the Prussian king; will you aid me?" Foma was not strong in the art of reading; he gazed at the letter, shook his head, and said: "Very well."

The Chinese king approached the city. Ilya Muromets and young Aliosha Popovich came to Foma Berennikov and spoke these words: "They are attacking the king, approaching his city; we must defend him. Will you go yourself or send us?" "You shall go, Ilyushka Muromets!" Ilya Muromets slew all the attackers. Then the Chinese king sent forth his six champions and another unnumbered host of troops. Ilya Muromets and Aliosha Popovich came to Foma Berennikov saying: "Tell us, Foma Berennikov, will you go yourself or will you send us?" "You shall go, Aliosha Popovich, my young brother!" Young Aliosha Popovich rode forth and slew the host of troops and the six mighty champions. The Chinese king said: "I have still another champion, whom I have up till now kept for breeding purposes; now I will let him fight too."

So he brought an unnumbered host of troops and with them his secret mighty champion, and the king said to him: "The Russian champion beats us not by force but by cunning; now do everything that the Russian champion does." Ilya Muromets and young Aliosha Popovich came to Foma Berennikov asking: "Will you go yourself or will you send us?" "I shall go myself. Bring me my horse!" The champions' horses were grazing in the open field and Foma's stood near by, eating oats. Ilya Muromets came to Foma's horse and it began to rear and snap! Ilya Muromets grew angry, took Foma's horse by the tail, and flung him across the hedge. Young Aliosha Popovich said to him: "Did not Foma Berennikov see us? He will punish us for this!" "Apparently his strength is not in his horse but in himself," said Ilya Muromets and brought the wretched nag to Foma Berennikov.

Foma bestrode the horse and thought to himself: "Let them kill me! It won't be all at once." He rode forward, bending down to the horse's mane and blinking his eyes. The Chinese champion, remembering the king's instructions, also bent down to his horse's mane and blinked. Foma got off his horse, sat on a stone, and began to sharpen his scythe; the Chinese champion too got off his mighty horse and began to sharpen his sword. He saw that Foma Berennikov was one-eyed and thought: "He has closed one eye; I will be even trickier and close both eyes."

He had no sooner closed his eyes, than Foma Berennikov cut off his head. Foma took the champion's mighty steed, tried to mount it, but could not. So Foma tied the mighty steed to a hundred-year-old oak, climbed up the tree, and leaped upon the steed. As soon as the steed felt a rider on his back he rushed forward, tearing out the oak with its roots; he galloped with all his mighty strength, dragging the enormous oak after him. Foma Berennikov cried: "Help, help!" But the stupid Chinamen did not know the Russian language and from fear took to their heels. The mighty horse trampled them under his hoofs and smote them with the hundred-year-old oak; he slew them all to the last man.

Now the Chinese king wrote a letter to Foma Berennikov, saying: "Never again shall I wage war against you." That promise was just what Foma wanted. Ilya Muromets and young Aliosha Popovich marveled at Foma Berennikov.

Now Foma went to the Prussian king. "What shall I reward you with?" asked the king. "Take as much gold from my treasure as you will, or half of my glorious kingdom, or my beautiful daughter." "Give me the beautiful daughter," Foma replied, "and invite to the wedding my younger brothers, Ilya Muromets and young Aliosha Popovich." And Foma Berennikov married the beautiful princess.

Thus not only mighty men have luck! He who shouts loudest about himself fares best.

THE PEASANT,
THE BEAR, AND THE FOX

APEASANT WAS PLOWING a field. A bear came to him and said: "Peasant, I will break your bones." "No, do not touch me; I am sowing turnips here, and I will take only the roots for myself and give you the tops." "So be it!" said the bear. "But if you cheat me, do not dare to come into my forest for wood." Having said this, he went off into the thickets. Harvest time came; the peasant dug the turnips and the bear came out of the thicket, saying: "Now, peasant, let us share!" "Very well, little bear; I will bring the tops." And the peasant brought him a cartful of leaves and stalks. The bear was satisfied that the division was honest.

The peasant loaded his turnips on a cart and started driving to town to sell them. The bear met him and asked: "Peasant, where are you going?" "I am going to town, little bear, to sell my roots." "Let me taste one of those roots." The peasant gave him a turnip. When the bear ate it he began to roar: "Aha, so you've cheated me, peasant! Your roots are sweet. Do not dare come to me for wood; I will tear you to pieces." The peasant returned from town and was afraid to go to the forest. He burned his shelves and his benches and his tubs, but in the end there was nothing he could do—he had to go to the forest. He drove in quietly; from somewhere a fox came running. "Why do you walk on tiptoe, little peasant?" she asked. "I am afraid of the bear; he is angry at me and has threatened to tear me to pieces." "Don't fear the bear. Chop your wood, and I will make noises like those the hunters make. If the bear asks, 'What is this?' say: 'It is a bear and wolf hunt.' "

The peasant began to cut wood. Suddenly the bear rushed toward him, crying: "Hey, old man, what is this noise?" The peasant said: "It is a bear and wolf hunt." "Oh, little peasant, put me in your sledge, cover me with wood, and tie me with a rope; they will think I am a log." The peasant put him in the

288

sledge, tied him with a rope, and hit him on the head with the butt end of his ax until he was dead. The fox came and said: "Where is the bear?" "He is dead." "Well, little peasant, now you must treat me to something." "Please, little fox, come to my house; I shall indeed treat you."

The peasant drove home and the fox ran ahead of him; when the peasant was close to his house, he whistled to his dogs and set them on the fox. The fox ran to the wood, jumped into a hole to hide, and said: "O little eyes, what did you do while I was running?" "O little fox, we saw to it that you did not stumble." "And you, little ears, what did you do?" "We listened all the time to hear whether the hounds were far behind." "And you, tail, what did you do?" "I," said the tail, "threw myself between your legs to entangle you, so that you would fall and be torn to pieces by the dogs." "Ah, you scoundrel! Let the dogs eat you then." And sticking her tail out of the hole, the fox cried: "Eat the fox's tail, dogs!" The dogs dragged the fox out by the tail and strangled her.

So does it often happen: because of the tail, the head perishes.

GOOD ADVICE

ONCE THERE WAS a wealthy merchant who died leaving a son called Ivan the Luckless. Ivan squandered all his wealth on drink and revelry and then went to look for work. He walked in the market and a very handsome fellow he was. At that time a lovely maiden, the daughter of a merchant, was sitting in her window embroidering a carpet with various silks. When she saw the merchant's son she fell in love with him. "Let me marry him," she said to her mother. At first the old woman would not hear of it but later she talked matters over with her husband. "Perhaps his luck will be improved by his wife's," she said. "For our daughter was born with a veil over her face and a silver spoon in her mouth." So they assented to their daughter's wish and gave her to Ivan in marriage. She bought cotton, embroidered a carpet, and sent her husband to sell it. "Sell this carpet for a hundred rubles," she said. "But if you meet a virtuous man, give it to him in exchange for a piece of good advice."

Ivan met an old man, who began to bargain for the carpet. He agreed to buy it for a hundred rubles, took out the money, and said: "Which do you prefer—money or a piece of good advice?" The merchant's son thought and thought: he had not forgotten what his wife had told him. "Give me your advice," he said. "Do not fear anything before death," said the old man. Then he took the carpet and left. The merchant's son went home and told his wife all that had happened; she thanked him, bought silk, embroidered another carpet, and again sent her husband to sell it. "Sell it for five hundred rubles," she said, "but if you meet a good man, give it to him in exchange for a piece of good advice." The merchant's son went to the market; he met the same old man, who agreed to buy the carpet for five hundred rubles and as he took out the money said: "But if you prefer, I will give you a piece of good advice." "Here is the carpet; give me your good advice." "Keep cool, use your judgment, don't cut off a head," said the old man. Then he took the carpet and left. The merchant's son returned home and told his wife all that had happened, but she did not say a word.

One day the merchant's son's uncles made ready to sail across the sea and trade in foreign lands; the merchant's son somehow managed to rig up a ship, said farewell to his wife, and went with them. They sailed upon the ocean; suddenly a sea monster came out of the water. "Give us a Russian man to judge a dispute," said the monster to the merchants. "I will bring him back." The uncles thought and thought, then came to their nephew and asked him to go into the sea. He recalled the old man's advice—"Do not fear anything before death"—and went into the sea with the monster. There he found the Sea Fate trying to solve the question of which is the most precious—gold, silver, or copper. "If you settle this problem," said the Sea Fate, "I will reward you." "Certainly copper is more valuable than the other metals," said the merchant's son. "For without copper one cannot settle an account; with copper one has kopeks and pennies, with copper one can also make a ruble; you cannot bite that off gold or silver." "You are right," said the Sea Fate. "Go back to your ship." The monster took him back to his ship and he found it loaded to the brim with precious stones.

The uncles had sailed far ahead, but the merchant's son caught up with them and began to quarrel with them as to whose merchandise was better. They said to him: "Nephew, you have only one ship, we have a hundred." They quarreled and quarreled, then the uncles grew angry and went to complain about him to the king. At first the king wanted to have the merchant's son hanged without trial for contradicting his uncles, but later he asked that the merchandise be brought to him for inspection. The uncles brought gold and silken fabrics, and the king was lost in contemplation of them. "Now let me see your merchandise," he finally said to the merchant's son. "Sire, order your windows to be closed; I want to show you my merchandise in the dark." The king ordered the windows to be closed; the merchant's son drew a precious stone from his pocket and it illumined everything. "Your merchandise is better, merchant's son. For that, take all your uncles' ships!"

He took his uncles' ships, traded for exactly twenty years, acquired much goods of every kind, and returned home with enormous, countless riches. He entered his house and beheld his wife lying in bed with two young fellows. His heart boiled with rage and he drew out his sharp saber: "Now I will slay my wife's friends," he thought. But then he recalled the old man's good advice: "Keep cool, use your judgment, don't cut off a head." He roused his wife and she jumped up and began to nudge the young fellows, saying: "My children, your father has come back!" Then the merchant's son learned that in his absence his wife had borne him twins.

ONCE THERE WAS a laborer to whom God had given great
strength. He learned that a dragon was haunting the
king's daughter, and he boasted that he alone could
destroy this terrible beast. The king's men heard his boasts and
they pressed him: "Go, laborer, heal the princess!" If the ale
is drawn it must be drunk; so the laborer went to the king and
said: "I can heal the princess; what will I receive for my trouble?" The king was overjoyed and said: "I will give you the
princess in marriage." The laborer asked for seven oxhides,
iron nuts, iron claws, and an iron hammer. He donned the
seven oxhides and the iron claws, filled his pocket with nuts,
real ones and iron ones, took the big hammer in his hands, and
went to the princess' room.

The dragon flew to the princess. Upon seeing the laborer he
gnashed his teeth and said: "Why have you come here?" "For
the same purpose as you," said the laborer, and remained sitting where he was, cracking nuts. The dragon saw that he could
accomplish nothing by force, so he came over to the laborer
and asked for some nuts; the laborer gave him the iron ones.
The dragon tried to crack them with his teeth and then spat
them out: "Brother, your nuts are no good. Let us play a game
of cards instead." "With pleasure, but for what stakes?" They
agreed that he who lost would get a thrashing. They began to
play and the dragon lost. The laborer took his hammer and
gave the dragon such a thrashing that he was almost stunned.
"Now," said the dragon, "let us play for our skins; whoever
loses will have his skin torn off." The laborer lost; the dragon
tore one oxhide off him. "Let us play another game," the
dragon said. This time the dragon lost; the laborer immediately plunged his iron claws into the dragon's skin and tore it
off. The dragon died on the spot.

When the king heard of this he was overjoyed and married
his daughter to the laborer. But the princess grew tired of living with a simple peasant; she ordered him to be taken to the
woods and slain there. Her servants seized him, led him to the

woods, but pitied him and did not kill him. The laborer wandered through the woods weeping. He met three men who were engaged in a dispute. The moment they came up to him they began to implore him: "Please, good man, settle our dispute. We have found a pair of boots that walk, a flying carpet, and a magic tablecloth. How shall we divide them?" "This way: whoever climbs up that oak first shall have them all." They foolishly consented and rushed to the tree. As soon as they had climbed up the laborer donned the walking boots, sat on the flying carpet, took the magic tablecloth, and said: "I want to be near the king's city."

And in a trice he was there. He pitched a tent, ordered his tablecloth to spread a dinner, and invited the king and his daughter to visit him. They came to him but they did not recognize him. He feasted them, gave them meat and drink, then led the princess to the flying carpet, quietly took the tablecloth, pushed the princess onto the carpet, and ordered it to fly into a dark forest. In the forest the laborer told the princess who he was; she began to caress and cajole him, and succeeded in beguiling him. As soon as he fell asleep, the princess seized the magic tablecloth, sat on the flying carpet, and was gone.

The laborer awoke and saw that the princess, the flying carpet, and the magic tablecloth were gone; only his walking boots remained. He wandered and wandered through the woods; he felt hungry, spied two apple trees, plucked an apple from one of them, and began to eat it. He ate one apple and a horn grew on his head; he ate another apple and another horn grew on his head. He tried the apples of the other tree; at once his horns vanished and he turned into a handsome youth. He filled his pocket with apples from both trees and went to the king's city. He walked by the palace and saw a scullery maid, one of the princess' servants, who was very ugly. "Don't you want an apple, little dove?" She took one and ate it, and turned into such a beauty as no tongue can tell of nor pen describe. The scullery maid went to the princess and the princess gasped. "Buy some for me," she said, "buy them without fail!" The maid went out and bought some; but when the princess ate of them, horns grew on her head.

Next day the laborer came to the princess and told her that he could turn her back into a beauty. She implored him to do so. He told her to go into the bath chamber; there he undressed her and belabored her so severely with iron rods that he was sure that she would remember it for a long time. Then he told her that he was her lawful husband. The princess repented, gave him back his flying carpet and his magic tablecloth, and the laborer gave her some of the good apples to eat. And they began to live happily and to prosper.

THE ARMLESS MAIDEN

IN A CERTAIN KINGDOM, not in our land, there lived a wealthy merchant; he had two children, a son and a daughter. The father and mother died. The brother said to the sister: "Let us leave this town, little sister; I will rent a shop and trade, and find lodgings for you; we will live together." They went to another province. When they came there, the brother inscribed himself in the merchant's guild, and rented a shop of woven cloths. The brother decided to marry and took a sorceress to wife. One day he went to trade in his shop and said to his sister: "Keep order in the house, sister." The wife felt offended because he said this to his sister. To revenge herself she broke all the furniture and when her husband came back she met him and said: "See what a sister you have; she has broken all the furniture in the house." "Too bad, but we can get some new things," said the husband.

The next day when leaving for his shop he said farewell to his wife and his sister and said to his sister: "Please, little sister, see to it that everything in the house is kept as well as possible." The wife bided her time, went to the stables, and cut off the head of her husband's favorite horse with a saber. She awaited him on the porch. "See what a sister you have," she said. "She has cut off the head of your favorite horse." "Ah, let the dogs eat what is theirs," answered the husband.

On the third day the husband again went to his shop, said farewell, and said to his sister: "Please look after my wife, so that she does not hurt herself or the baby, if by chance she gives birth to one." When the wife gave birth to her child, she cut off his head. When her husband came home he found her sitting and lamenting over her baby. "See what a sister you have! No sooner had I given birth to my baby than she cut off his head with a saber." The husband did not say anything; he wept bitter tears and turned away.

Night came. At the stroke of midnight he rose and said: "Little sister, make ready; we are going to mass." She said: "My beloved brother, I do not think it is a holiday today." "Yes, my sister, it is a holiday; let us go." "It is still too early to go, brother," she said. "No," he answered, "young maidens always take a long time to get ready." The sister began to dress; she was very slow and reluctant. Her brother said: "Hurry, sister, get dressed." "Please," she said, "it is still early, brother." "No, little sister, it is not early, it is high time to be gone."

When the sister was ready they sat in a carriage and set out for mass. They drove for a long time or a short time. Finally they came to a wood. The sister said: "What wood is this?" He answered: "This is the hedge around the church." The carriage caught in a bush. The brother said: "Get out, little sister, disentangle the carriage." "Ah, my beloved brother, I cannot do that, I will dirty my dress." "I will buy you a new dress, sister, a better one than this." She got down from the carriage, began to disentangle it, and her brother cut off her arms to the elbows, struck his horse with the whip, and drove away.

The little sister was left alone; she burst into tears and began to walk in the woods. She walked and walked, a long time or a short time; she was all scratched, but could not find a path leading out of the woods. Finally, after several years, she found a path. She came to a market town and stood beneath the window of the wealthiest merchant to beg for alms. This merchant had a son, an only one, who was the apple of his father's eye.

He fell in love with the beggar woman and said: "Dear father and mother, marry me." "To whom shall we marry you?" "To this beggar woman." "Ah, my dear child, do not the merchants of our town have lovely daughters?" "Please marry me to her," he said. "If you do not, I will do something to myself." They were distressed, because he was their only son, their life's treasure. They gathered all the merchants and clerics and asked them to judge the matter: should they marry their son to the beggar woman or not? The priest said: "Such must be his fate, and God gives your son his sanction to marry the beggar woman."

So the son lived with her for a year and then another year. At the end of that time he went to another province, where her brother had his shop. When taking his leave he said: "Dear father and mother, do not abandon my wife; as soon as she gives birth to a child, write to me that very hour." Two or three months after the son left, his wife gave birth to a child; his arms were golden up to the elbows, his sides were studded with stars, there was a bright moon on his forehead and a radiant sun near his heart. The grandparents were overjoyed and at once wrote their beloved son a letter. They dispatched an old man with this note in all haste. Meanwhile the wicked sister-in-law had learned about all this and invited the old messenger into her house: "Come in, little father," she said, "and take a rest." "No, I have no time, I am bringing an urgent message." "Come in, little father, take a rest, have something to eat."

She sat him down to dinner, took his bag, found the letter in it, read it, tore it into little pieces, and wrote another letter instead: "Your wife," it said, "has given birth to a half dog and half bear that she conceived with beasts in the woods." The old messenger came to the merchant's son and handed him the letter; he read it and burst into tears. He wrote in answer, asking that his son be not molested till he returned. "When I come back," he said, "I will see what kind of baby it is." The sorceress again invited the old messenger into her house. "Come in, sit down, take a rest," she said. Again she charmed him with talk, stole the letter he carried, read it, tore it up, and instead ordered that her sister-in-law be driven out the moment the letter was received. The old messenger brought this letter; the father and mother read it and were grieved. "Why does he cause us so much trouble?" they said. "We married him to the girl, and now he does not want his wife!" They pitied not so much the wife as the babe. So they gave their blessing to her and the babe, tied the babe to her breast, and sent her away.

She went, shedding bitter tears. She walked, for a long time or a short time, all in the open field, and there was no wood or village anywhere. She came to a dale and was very thirsty. She looked to the right and saw a well. She wanted to drink from it but was afraid to stoop, lest she drop her baby. Then she fancied that the water came closer. She stooped to drink and her baby fell into the well. She began to walk around the well, weeping, and wondering how to get her child out of the well. An old man came up to her and said: "Why are you weeping, you slave of God?" "How can I help weeping? I stooped over the well to drink water and my baby fell into it." "Bend down and take him out." "No, little father, I cannot; I have no hands, only stumps." "Do as I tell you. Take your baby." She went to the well, stretched out her arms, and God helped, for suddenly she had her hands, all whole. She bent down, pulled her baby out, and began to give thanks to God, bowing to all four sides.

She said her prayers, went on farther, and came to the house where her brother and husband were staying, and asked for shelter. Her husband said: "Brother, let the beggar woman in; beggar women can tell stories and recount real happenings." The wicked sister-in-law said: "We have no room for visitors, we are overcrowded." "Please, brother, let her come; there is nothing I like better than to hear beggar women tell tales." They let her in. She sat on the stove with her baby. Her husband said: "Now, little dove, tell us a tale—any kind of story."

She said: "I do not know any tales or stories, but I can tell the truth. Listen, here is a true happening that I can recount to you." And she began: "In a certain kingdom, not in our land, lived a wealthy merchant; he had two children, a son and a daughter. The father and mother died. The brother said to the sister: 'Let us leave this town, little sister.' And they came to another province. The brother inscribed himself in the merchant's guild and took a shop of woven cloth. He decided to marry and took a sorceress to wife." At this point the sister-in-law muttered: "Why does she bore us with her stories, that hag?" But the husband said: "Go on, go on, little mother, I love such stories more than anything!"

"And so," the beggar woman went on, "the brother went to trade in his shop and said to his sister: 'Keep order in the house, sister.' The wife felt offended because he had said this to his sister and out of spite broke all the furniture." And then she went on to tell how her brother took her to mass and cut off her hands, how she gave birth to a baby, how her sister-in-law lured the old messenger—and again the sister-in-law interrupted her, crying: "What gibberish she is telling!" But the husband said: "Brother, order your wife to keep quiet; it is a wonderful story, is it not?"

She came to the point when her husband wrote to his parents ordering that the baby be left in peace until his return, and the sister-in-law mumbled: "What nonsense!" Then she reached the point when she came to their house as a beggar woman, and the sister-in-law mumbled: "What is this old bitch gibbering about!" And the husband said: "Brother, order her to keep quiet; why does she interrupt all the time?" Finally she came to the point in the story when she was let in and began to tell the truth instead of a story. And then she pointed at them and said: "This is my husband, this is my brother, and this is my sister-in-law."

Then her husband jumped up to her on the stove and said: "Now, my dear, show me the baby. Let me see whether my father and mother wrote me the truth." They took the baby, removed its swaddling clothes—and the whole room was illumined! "So it is true that she did not tell us just a tale; here is my wife, and here is my son—golden up to the elbows—his sides studded with stars, a bright moon on his forehead, and a radiant sun near his heart!"

The brother took the best mare from his stable, tied his wife to its tail, and let it run in the open field. The mare dragged her on the ground until she brought back only her braid; the

298

rest was strewn on the field. Then they harnessed three horses and went home to the young husband's father and mother; they began to live happily and to prosper. I was there and drank mead and wine; it ran down my mustache, but did not go into my mouth.

FROLKA STAY-AT-HOME

THERE WAS ONCE a king who had three daughters, and such beauties they were as no tongue can tell of nor pen describe. Their garden was big and beautiful and they liked to walk there at night. A dragon from the Black Sea took to visiting this garden. One night the king's daughters tarried in the garden, for they could not tear their eyes away from the flowers; suddenly the dragon appeared and carried them off on his fiery wings. The king waited and waited but his daughters did not come back. He sent his maidservants to look for them in the garden, but all in vain; the maidservants could not find the princesses. The next morning the king proclaimed a state of emergency and a great multitude of people gathered. The king said: "Whoever finds my daughters, to him I shall give as much money as he wants."

Three men agreed to undertake this task—a soldier who was

a drunkard, Frolka Stay-at-Home, and Erema; and they set out
to look for the princesses. They walked and walked till they
came to a deep forest. As soon as they entered it they were
overwhelmed by drowsiness. Frolka Stay-at-Home drew a
snuffbox out of his pocket, tapped on it, opened it, shoved a
pinch of tobacco into his nose, and cried: "Eh, brothers, let us
not sleep, let us not rest, let us keep going." So they went on;
they walked and walked and finally came to an enormous
house, and in that house was a five-headed dragon. For a long
time they knocked at the gate, but no one answered. Then
Frolka Stay-at-Home pushed the soldier and Erema away and
said: "Let me try, brothers!" He snuffed up some tobacco and
gave such a knock at the gate that he smashed it.

They entered the yard, sat in a circle, and were about to eat
whatever they had. Then a maiden of great beauty came out
of the house and said: "Little doves, why have you come here?
A very wicked dragon lives here, who will devour you. You are
lucky that he happens to be away." Frolka answered her: "It
is we who shall devour him." He had no sooner said these words
than the dragon came flying and roared: "Who has ruined my
kingdom? Do I have enemies in the world? I have only one
enemy, but his bones won't even be brought here by a raven."
"A raven won't bring me," said Frolka, "but a good horse did."
The dragon upon hearing this said: "Have you come for peaceful purposes or to fight?" "I have not come for peaceful purposes," said Frolka, "but to fight."

They moved apart, faced each other, and clashed, and in
one stroke Frolka cut off all the five heads of the dragon. Then
he put them under a stone and buried the body in the ground.
The maiden was overjoyed and said to the three brave men:
"My little doves, take me with you." "But who are you?" they
asked. She said that she was the king's eldest daughter; Frolka
told her what task he had undertaken, and they were both glad.
The princess invited them into the house, gave them meat and
drink, and begged them to rescue her sisters. Frolka said: "We
were sent for them too!" The princess told them where her
sisters were. "My next sister is even worse off than I was," she
said. "She is living with a seven-headed dragon." "Never

mind," said Frolka, "we shall get the better of him too; it may be somewhat harder to deal with a twelve-headed dragon." They said farewell and went on.

Finally they came to the abode of the second sister. The house where she was locked up was enormous and all around it there was a high iron fence. They approached it and looked for the gate; finally they found it. Frolka banged upon the gate with all his strength and it opened; they entered the yard and, as they had done before, sat down to eat. Suddenly the seven-headed dragon came flying. "I smell Russian breath here," he said. "Bah, it is you, Frolka, who have come here! What for?" "I know what for," answered Frolka. He began to fight with the dragon and in one stroke cut off all seven of his heads, put them under a stone, and buried the body in the ground. Then they entered the house; they passed through one room, a second, and a third, and in the fourth they found the king's second daughter sitting on a sofa. When they told her why and how they had come there, she brightened, offered them food and drink, and begged them to rescue her youngest sister from the twelve-headed dragon. Frolka said: "Of course, that is what we were sent for. But there is fear in my heart. Well, perhaps God will help me! Give us each another cup!"

They drank and left; they walked and walked till they came to a very steep ravine. On the other side of the ravine there stood enormous pillars instead of a gate, and on the pillars were chained two ferocious lions that roared so loudly that only Frolka remained standing on his feet; his two companions fell to the ground from fear. Frolka said to them: "I have seen worse terrors, and even then I was not frightened. Come with me!" And they went on. Suddenly an old man, who looked to be about seventy, came out of the castle; he saw them, came to meet them, and said: "Whither are you going, my friends?" "To this castle," answered Frolka. "Ah, my friends," said the old man, "you are going to an evil place; the twelve-headed dragon lives in this castle. He is not at home now, else he would have devoured you at once." "But he is the very one we have come to see," said Frolka. "If so," said the old man, "come with me, I will help you get to him." The old man went up to the

301

lions and began to stroke them, and Frolka with his companions got through to the courtyard.

They entered the castle; the old man brought them to the room where the princess lived. Upon seeing them she quickly jumped off her bed and began to question them as to who they were and why they had come. They told her. The princess offered them food and drink and began to make ready to go. As they were preparing to leave the house, they suddenly saw the dragon flying at a verst's distance from them. The king's daughter rushed back into the house and Frolka and his companions went out to meet and fight the dragon. At first the dragon attacked them with great force, but Frolka, a clever fellow, managed to defeat him, cut off all of his twelve heads, and cast them into the ravine. Then they returned to the house and in their joy reveled even more than before. Following this feast they set out on their way, stopping only for the other princesses.

Thus they all came back to their native land. The king was overjoyed, opened his royal treasury to them, and said: "Now, my faithful servants, take as much money as you want for a reward." Frolka was generous: he brought his big three-flapped cap, the soldier brought his knapsack, and Erema brought a basket. Frolka began to fill his cap first: he poured and poured, the cap broke, and the silver fell into the mud. Frolka began to pour again; he poured, and the money dropped from the cap! "There is nothing to be done," said Frolka. "Probably all of the royal treasury will fall to me." "And what will be left for us?" asked his companions. "The king has enough money for you too," said Frolka. While there was still money, Erema began to fill his basket, and the soldier his knapsack; having done this, they went home. But Frolka remained near the royal treasury with his cap and to this very day he is still sitting there, pouring out money for himself. When his cap is filled, I shall go on with my story, but now I am too tired.

I N A CERTAIN LAND, not in our kingdom, there lived a king who had a son named Ivan and a daughter named Elena the Fair. A bear with iron fur appeared in this kingdom and began to eat the king's subjects. The bear ate one person after another and the king sat powerless and wondered how he could save his own children. He ordered a high tower to be built, seated Prince Ivan and Elena the Fair on top of it, and provided them with supplies for five years.

The bear ate up all the people, ran into the royal palace, and out of spite began to gnaw a birch broom. "Do not bite me, bear with iron fur," the broom said to him. "Instead, go out into the open; there you will see a tower, and on that tower sit Prince Ivan and Elena the Fair." The bear came to the tower and began to shake it. Prince Ivan took fright and threw him some food; the bear ate it and lay down to sleep.

The bear slept, and Prince Ivan and Elena the Fair ran away as fast as they could. On the road they met a horse. "Horse, horse, save us!" they cried. But no sooner had they mounted the horse than the bear caught up with them. He tore the horse to pieces, took the prince and princess in his jaws, and brought them back to the pillar. They gave him food; he ate it, and again he went to sleep. The bear slept, and Prince Ivan and Elena the Fair ran away as fast as they could. On the way they met some geese. "Geese, geese, save us!" they cried. They sat on the geese and flew off, but the bear awoke, singed the geese with a flame, and brought the prince and the princess back to the pillar. Again they gave him food; he ate it, and again he fell asleep. The bear slept, and Prince Ivan and Elena the Fair ran away as fast as they could. On the road stood a three-year-old bullock. "Bullock, bullock, save us! The bear with iron fur is pursuing us!" "Sit on me," said the bullock. "You, Prince Ivan, sit with your back to my head, and when you see the bear coming, tell me." As soon as the bear caught up with them, the bullock relieved himself and pasted the bear's eyes shut with dung. Three times the bear caught up with them, and three times the bullock pasted his eyes shut. Then the bullock began to cross a river; the bear went into the water after him and drowned.

Ivan and Elena were hungry and the bullock said to them: "Slaughter me and eat my flesh, but gather my bones together and strike them; from them will arise a little fist of a man, as big as an inch, with a beard a cubit long. He will do everything for you that needs to be done." Time went by. They had eaten the bullock and again wanted to eat; they lightly struck the bones and the little fist of a man appeared. They went to the woods; in the woods stood a house and that house was a robbers' lair. Little Fist killed the robbers and their chieftain and put their bodies in a certain room; he told Elena not to go there. But she could not restrain herself, looked in, and fell in love with the chieftain's head.

She asked Prince Ivan to get for her the water of life and the water of death. As soon as she had the water of life and the water of death, she brought the chieftain back to life and plotted with him how to destroy Prince Ivan. First they sent him to get wolf's milk. Prince Ivan went with Little Fist. They found the she-wolf and said to her: "Give us some milk." She asked them to take her wolf cub too, because he was a good-for-nothing. Having taken the milk and the young wolf, they came back to Elena the Fair; they gave her the milk and kept the young wolf for themselves. Since the lovers had not been able to destroy Prince Ivan in this way, they sent him to get bear's milk. Prince Ivan and Little Fist went to get bear's milk. They found the she-bear and said: "Give us some milk." She asked them to take the young bear too, because he was a good-for-nothing. Taking the milk and the young bear, they came back to Elena the Fair; they gave her the milk and kept the young bear. Since the lovers had not been able to destroy Prince Ivan in this way either, they sent him to get lion's milk. Prince Ivan went with Little Fist; they found the lioness and took her milk, and she asked them to take her lion cub too, because he was a good-for-nothing. They returned to Elena the Fair, gave her the milk, and kept the young lion.

The chieftain and Elena the Fair, seeing that Prince Ivan could not be destroyed in this way, sent him to get the eggs of the Firebird. Prince Ivan and Little Fist went to get the eggs. They found the Firebird, but when they tried to take the eggs, she became enraged and swallowed Little Fist; and Prince Ivan went home without the eggs. He came to Elena the Fair and told her that he had been unable to get the eggs and that the Firebird had swallowed Little Fist. Elena the Fair and the chieftain were overjoyed and thought that Prince Ivan would be helpless now, without Little Fist. They ordered him to be killed. Prince Ivan heard this order and asked his sister whether he might bathe before dying.

Elena the Fair ordered the bath to be heated. Prince Ivan went to the bath and Elena the Fair sent someone to tell him to wash faster. Prince Ivan did not obey her; he continued washing himself unhurriedly. Suddenly the young wolf, the young bear, and the young lion ran to him and told him that Little Fist had escaped from the Firebird and would soon come to him. Prince Ivan ordered them to lie down on the threshold, and kept on washing. Elena the Fair again sent someone to tell him to wash faster, and that if he did not finish soon, she would come herself. Prince Ivan still disobeyed her and did not come out of the bath. Elena the Fair waited and waited, became impatient, and with the chieftain went to see what Prince Ivan was doing. When she came to the bath she saw that he was still washing himself and had not obeyed her order; she grew angry and boxed his ear. Suddenly Little Fist appeared, ordered the young wolf, the young bear, and the young lion to tear the chieftain to little pieces, and tied Elena naked to a tree, so that her body might be devoured by mosquitoes and flies. Then he and Prince Ivan set out traveling.

In the distance they beheld a great palace. Little Fist said: "Do you not want to marry, Prince Ivan? In this house lives a champion maiden; she seeks a brave youth who is strong enough to defeat her." They went to her house. Before reaching it, Prince Ivan mounted a horse, Little Fist mounted behind him, and they challenged the champion maiden to combat. They fought and fought; the champion maiden struck Prince

306

Ivan in the chest and he almost fell to the ground, but Little Fist held him. Then Prince Ivan struck the champion maiden with his spear and she fell from her horse at once. When he had knocked her down she said: "Now, Prince Ivan, you may marry me."

Speedily a tale is spun, less speedily a deed is done. Prince Ivan married the champion maiden. "Well, Prince Ivan," Little Fist said to him, "if you don't feel well the first night, come to me; I will help you in your trouble." Prince Ivan went to bed with the champion maiden. Suddenly she put her hand on his chest and he fell ill. He asked her to let him go out; when he got outside he called Little Fist and told him that the champion maiden wanted to strangle him. Little Fist went to the champion maiden and began to belabor her, repeating: "Respect your husband, respect your husband!" From then on they began to live happily and to prosper.

Some time later the champion maiden asked Prince Ivan to untie Elena the Fair and to take her to live in their house. He straightway sent to have her untied and brought to him. Elena the Fair lived in his house for a long time. One day she said to him: "Brother, let me pick the lice from your head." She began to pick his lice and thrust a dead tooth into his head; Prince Ivan began to die. The young lion saw that Prince Ivan was dying and pulled the dead tooth out; the prince began to come back to life and the young lion began to die. The young bear pulled out the tooth; the young lion began to come back to life and the young bear began to die. A fox saw that he was dying; she pulled out the dead tooth. And because she was cleverer than all of them, when she had pulled out the tooth she threw it into a pan and it crumbled to pieces. To punish his sister for this wicked deed Prince Ivan ordered that Elena the Fair be tied to the tail of a mighty horse and that the horse be set loose in the open field.

I was there and drank mead; it ran down my mustache, but did not go into my mouth.

HOW A HUSBAND WEANED
HIS WIFE FROM FAIRY TALES

THERE WAS ONCE an innkeeper whose wife loved fairy tales above all else and accepted as lodgers only those who could tell stories. Of course the husband suffered loss because of this, and he wondered how he could wean his wife away from fairy tales. One night in winter, at a late hour, an old man shivering with cold asked him for shelter. The husband ran out and said: "Can you tell stories? My wife does not allow me to let in anyone who cannot tell stories." The old man saw that he had no choice; he was almost frozen to death. He said: "I can tell stories." "And will you tell them for a long time?" "All night."

So far, so good. They let the old man in. The husband said: "Wife, this peasant has promised to tell stories all night long, but only on condition that you do not argue with him or interrupt him." The old man said: "Yes, there must be no interruptions, or I will not tell any stories." They ate supper and went to bed. Then the old man began: "An owl flew by a garden, sat on a tree trunk, and drank some water. An owl flew into a garden, sat on a tree trunk, and drank some water." He kept on saying again and again: "An owl flew into a garden, sat on a tree trunk, and drank some water." The wife listened and listened and then said: "What kind of story is this? He keeps repeating the same thing over and over!" "Why do you interrupt me? I told you not to argue with me! That was only the beginning; it was going to change later." The husband, upon hearing this—and it was exactly what he wanted to hear —jumped down from his bed and began to belabor his wife: "You were told not to argue, and now you have not let him finish his story!" And he thrashed her and thrashed her, so that she began to hate stories and from that time on forswore listening to them.

THE COCK AND THE HEN

A HEN AND A COCK lived together. One day they went to the woods for nuts. They came to a hazel tree; the cock climbed up the tree to pick nuts, and the hen remained on the ground to gather them up for the winter. Then the cock threw a nut that hit the hen's eye and knocked it out. The hen went away crying. Some boyars drove by and asked: "Little hen, little hen, why are you crying?" "The cock knocked out my eye." "Little cock, little cock, why did you knock out the hen's eye?" "The hazel tree tore my trousers." "Hazel tree, hazel tree, why did you tear the cock's trousers?" "Because the goats ate my bark." "Goats, goats, why did you eat the hazel tree's bark?" "Because the shepherds do not tend us." "Shepherds, shepherds, why don't you tend the goats?" "Because the peasant's wife does not give us pancakes." "Peasant's wife, peasant's wife, why don't you give the shepherds pancakes?" "Because my pig spilled my dough." "Pig, pig, why did you spill the dough?" "Because the wolf carried off my piglet." "Wolf, wolf, why did you carry off the piglet? "I was hungry and God told me to eat."

THE FOX AND THE LOBSTER

A FOX AND A LOBSTER were standing together and talking. The fox said to the lobster: "Let's have a race!" The lobster said: "Why not? Let's!" They began to race. As soon as the fox started, the lobster hung on to his tail. The fox ran to the goal and still the lobster did not detach himself. The fox turned around to see where the lobster was. He shook his tail and the lobster detached himself and said: "I have been waiting here for a long time."

NIKITA THE TANNER

A DRAGON APPEARED near Kiev; he took heavy tribute from the people—a lovely maiden from every house, whom he then devoured. Finally, it was the fate of the tsar's daughter to go to the dragon. He seized her and dragged her to his lair but did not devour her, because she was a beauty. Instead, he took her to wife. Whenever he went out, he boarded up his house to prevent the princess from escaping. The princess had a little dog that had followed her to the dragon's lair. The princess often wrote to her father and mother. She would attach her letter to the dog's neck, and the dog would take it to them and even bring back the answer. One day the tsar and tsarina wrote to their daughter, asking her to find out who in this world was stronger than the dragon. The princess became kindlier toward the dragon and began to question him. For a long time he did not answer, but one day he said inadvertently that a tanner in the city of Kiev was stronger than he.

When the princess heard this, she wrote her father to find Nikita the Tanner in Kiev and to send him to deliver her from captivity. Upon receiving this letter, the tsar went in person to beg Nikita the Tanner to free his land from the wicked dragon and rescue the princess. At that moment Nikita was currying hides and held twelve hides in his hands; when he saw that the tsar in person had come to see him, he began to tremble with fear, his hands shook, and he tore the twelve hides. But no matter how much the tsar and tsarina entreated him, he refused to go forth against the dragon. So they gathered together five thousand little children and sent them to implore him, hoping that their tears would move him to pity. The little children came to Nikita and begged him with tears to go fight the dragon. Nikita himself began to shed tears when he saw theirs. He took twelve thousand pounds of hemp, tarred it with pitch, and wound it around himself so that the dragon could not devour him, then went forth to give him battle.

Nikita came to the dragon's lair but the dragon locked himself in. "Better come out into the open field," said Nikita, "or I will destroy your lair together with you!" And he began to break down the door. The dragon, seeing that he could not avoid trouble, went out to fight in the open field. Nikita fought him for a long time or a short time; in any event, he defeated him. Then the dragon began to implore Nikita: "Do not put me to death, Nikita the Tanner; no one in the world is stronger than you and I. Let us divide all the earth, all the world, into equal parts; you shall live in one half, I in the other." "Very well," said Nikita, "let us draw a boundary line." He made a plow that weighed twelve thousand pounds, harnessed the dragon to it, and the dragon began to plow a boundary from Kiev; he plowed a furrow from Kiev to the Caspian Sea. "Now," said the dragon, "we have divided the whole earth." "We have divided the earth," said Nikita, "now let us divide the sea; else you will say that your water has been taken." The dragon crawled to the middle of the sea; Nikita killed him and drowned him in the sea.

That furrow can be seen to this very day; it is fourteen feet high. Around it the fields are plowed, but the furrow is intact; and those who do not know what it is, call it the rampart. Nikita, having done his heroic deed, would not accept any reward, but returned to currying hides.

THE WOLF

AN OLD MAN and his old wife had five sheep, a colt, and a calf. A wolf came to them and began to sing:

> *There once was a farmer*
> *Who had five sheep,*
> *A colt, and a calf—*
> *Seven beasts in all!*

The old woman said to the old man: "Oh, what a fine song! Give him a sheep!" The old man gave him a sheep. The wolf ate it and came again, singing the same song; and he came singing it until he had eaten the sheep, the colt, the calf, and the old woman. The old man remained alone; again the wolf came to him with the same song. The old man took a poker and began to belabor the wolf. The wolf ran away and never again came near the old man; and the old man remained alone in his wretchedness.

THE TALE
OF THE GOAT SHEDDING
ON ONE SIDE

WOULD YOU LIKE to hear the tale of the weak little goat shedding on one side? Then listen, listen! There was once a peasant who had a little hare. The peasant went to the field and there he saw a goat lying on the grass; one side of her had lost its hair, and the other not. The peasant pitied her, took her home, and put her in the shed. Having supped and rested a little, he went to his kitchen garden, and the hare went after him. Then the goat came from the shed to the house and bolted the door with a hook.

The hare wanted to eat and ran to the door of the house; he pushed with his paw, but the door was locked. "Who is there?" asked the little hare. The goat answered: "I, the weak little goat, shedding on one side. If I come out I'll break all your ribs!" The little hare was grieved, he went out into the road and wept. He met a wolf, who asked him: "Why are you weeping?" "There is someone in our house," the hare said through his tears. "Come with me," said the wolf. "I will drive him out." They came to the door. "Who is there?" asked the wolf. The goat stamped her feet and said: "I, the weak little goat, shedding on one side. If I come out I'll break all your ribs!" They went away from the door. The little hare again began to weep, and went out into the road, and the wolf ran away to the woods.

Then the hare met a cock, who said: "Why are you weeping?" The hare told him, and the cock said: "Come with me, I will drive her out." Near the door, the hare, to frighten the goat, said: "A cock has come with me; he carries a saber on his shoulder, he is coming to kill the goat and cut her head off." They came to the door and the cock asked: "Who is there?" The goat answered as before: "I, the weak little goat, shedding on one side. If I come out I'll break all your ribs!"

Again the hare went into the street, weeping. A busy bee flew to him and said: "Who has hurt you? Why are you crying?" The hare told her and the bee flew to the house. She asked: "Who is there?" and the goat answered as before. The bee grew angry and began to fly around the walls. She buzzed and buzzed till she found a little hole; she crawled through it, stung the goat on her shedding side, and made a swelling there. The goat rushed out of the door as fast as she could and never came back. The little hare ran into the house, ate and drank, and lay down to sleep. When he awakens, the real tale will begin.

THE BOLD KNIGHT, THE APPLES
OF YOUTH, AND THE WATER OF LIFE

A CERTAIN KING grew very old and his eyes began to fail. He heard that beyond the ninth land, in the tenth kingdom, there was a garden with the apples of youth, and in it a well with the water of life; if an aged man ate one of those apples, he would grow young, and if a blind man's eyes were bathed with that water, he would see. That king had three sons. So he sent his eldest forth on horseback to find that garden and bring him the apples and the water, for he wanted to be young again and to see. The prince set out for the distant kingdom; he rode and rode and came to a pillar. On this pillar three roads were marked: if he followed the first, the marker said, his horse would be sated and he himself would be hungry; if he followed the second, it said, he would lose his own life; if he followed the third, it said, his horse would be hungry and he himself sated.

He thought and thought and finally took the road that promised food for himself; and he rode and he rode till he saw a very beautiful house in a field. He approached it, looked all around, opened the gates, did not doff his cap nor bow his head, and galloped into the yard. The owner of the house, a widow who was not very old, called to the young man: "Welcome, dear guest!" She led him in, seated him at the table, prepared all sorts of viands, and brought him large beakers of heady drinks. The young man regaled himself and lay down to sleep on the bench. The woman said to him: "It is not fitting for a knight nor honorable for a gallant man to lie alone! Lie with my daughter, the beautiful Dunia." He was quite pleased with this proposal. Dunia said to him: "Lie closer to me, so that we will be warmer." He moved toward her and fell through the bed. In the cellar into which he fell he was compelled to grind raw rye all day long and he could not climb out. In vain the king waited and waited for his eldest son to come back. Finally he gave up waiting.

314

Then he sent his second son to get the apples and the water. This prince took the same road and suffered the same fate as his elder brother. From long waiting for his sons, the king became very sad.

Now the youngest son began to beg his father's permission to go forth to seek the garden. But his father absolutely refused to let him go and said to him: "A curse is on you, little son! Your older brothers perished on this quest and you, who are still a tender youth, will perish even sooner than they." But the young prince kept imploring his father and promised him that he would bear himself more bravely for the king's sake than any brave knight. His father thought and thought and finally gave the boy his blessing for the journey.

On his way to the widow's house, the young knight passed the same pillar as his older brothers had. He too came to the widow's house, dismounted from his horse, knocked at the gate, and asked whether he could spend the night there. The widow received him kindly just as she had his brothers, and invited him in, saying: "Welcome, unexpected guest!" She bade him sit down to table and placed all kinds of meat and drink before him, enough to stuff himself. He ate his fill, and asked whether he might lie down on the bench. The woman said to him: "It is not fitting for a knight nor honorable for a gallant man to lie alone! Lie with my beautiful Dunia." But he answered: "No, little aunt! A visitor must not do that without first making certain preparations. Why don't you heat up a bath for me? And let your daughter lead me to the bathhouse."

So the widow prepared a very, very hot bath and led him to the bathhouse with the beautiful Dunia. Dunia was just as wicked as her mother; she made him go in first, locked the door to the bath, and stood in the hall. But the bold knight pushed open the door and dragged Dunia with him into the bathroom. He had three rods—one of iron, one of lead, and one of cast iron—and with these rods he began to belabor the young girl. She wept and implored him to stop. But he said: "Tell me, wicked Dunia, what you have done with my brothers!" She said that they were in the cellar grinding raw grain. Then only did he let her go. They came back to the main room, tied one

315

ladder to another, and freed his brothers. He told them to go home; but they were ashamed to appear before their father, because they had lain down with Dunia and had failed in their mission. So they wandered about in the fields and woods.

The knight went on; he rode and rode till he came to a farmhouse. He entered; there sat a pretty young girl weaving towels. He said: "God bless you, pretty maiden!" And she answered: "Thank you! What are you doing, good knight? Are you running away from an adventure or are you trying to find one?" "I am trying to carry out a mission, pretty maiden," said the knight. "I am going beyond the ninth land, to the tenth kingdom, to a certain garden, where I hope to find the apples of youth and the water of life for my aged, blind father." She said to him: "It will be hard, very hard, for you to reach that garden. However, continue on your way; soon you will come to the house of my second sister. Go in to see her; she knows better than I how to find the garden and will tell you what to do."

So he rode and rode till he came to the house of the second sister. He greeted her just as he had the first, and told her who he was and where he was going. She bade him leave his horse with her and ride on her own two-winged horse to the house of her older sister, who would tell him what to do—how to reach the garden and how to get the apples and the water. So he rode and rode till he came to the house of the third sister. She gave him her four-winged horse and told him: "Be careful. In that garden lives our aunt, a terrible witch. When you come to the garden, do not spare my horse. Spur him strongly, so that he clears the wall in one bound; for if he touches the wall, the strings with bells that are tied to it will sing out, the bells will ring, the witch will awaken, and you won't be able to get away from her! She has a horse with six wings; cut the tendons under his wings so that she cannot overtake you."

He did as she bade him. He flew over the wall on his horse, but his horse lightly touched one string with his tail; all the strings sang and the bells rang, but softly. The witch awoke but did not clearly distinguish the voice of the strings and the bells, so she yawned and fell asleep again. And the bold knight galloped away with the apples of youth and the water of life. He stopped at the houses of the sisters, where he changed horses, and darted off to his own kingdom on his own horse. Early next morning the terrible witch discovered that the apples and the water had been stolen from her garden. At once she mounted her six-winged horse, galloped to the house of her first niece, and asked her: "Has someone passed by here?" The niece answered: "A bold knight went by here, but that was long ago." The witch galloped on farther and asked her second and her third niece the same question, and they gave her the same answer. She rode on and almost overtook the bold knight, but he had reached his own land and no longer feared her: there she dared not enter. She only looked at him and in a voice hoarse with spite said: "You are a fine little thief! You have succeeded very well in your mission! You got away from me, but nothing will save you from your own brothers." Having thus foretold his fate, she returned home.

Our bold knight went on his way in his own land, and found his vagabond brothers sleeping in a field. He set his horse loose, did not awaken his brothers, but lay down beside them and fell asleep. The brothers awoke, saw that their brother had returned to his own land, softly took the apples of youth out of his breast pocket, and threw him, still sleeping, over a precipice. He fell for three days, till he reached the dark kingdom where people do everything by firelight. Wherever he went, he found the people sad and weeping. He asked the cause of their sorrow and was told that their king's only daughter, the beautiful princess Paliusha, was to be given the next day to a terrible dragon, who would eat her up. In that kingdom, they explained, a maiden was given to the seven-headed dragon every month; that was the law! And now it was the turn of the king's daughter. When our bold knight heard this, he went straightway to the king, and said to him: "King, I will save your daughter from the dragon, but later you must do for me whatever I ask of you." The king was overjoyed, promised to do anything for him, and to give the princess to him in marriage.

The next day came. The beautiful princess Paliusha was led to a three-walled fortress on the edge of the sea and the knight went with her. He took with him an iron rod that weighed about two hundred pounds. He and the princess waited there for the dragon; they waited and waited, and while they waited they conversed. He told her about his adventures and said that he had the water of life with him. Then the bold knight said to the beautiful princess Paliusha: "Pick the lice out of my head, and should I fall asleep before the dragon comes, waken me with my rod—otherwise you will not arouse me!" And he laid his head in her lap. She began to look for lice in his hair; he fell asleep.

The dragon flew inshore and circled above the princess. She tried to waken the knight by shaking him, but did not hit him with his rod as he had asked her to do, for she did not wish to hurt him. She could not waken him and began to weep; a tear dropped on his face, and he woke up and exclaimed: "Oh, you have burned me with something pleasant!" Meanwhile the dragon had begun to swoop down on them. The knight took up his two-hundred pound rod, swung it, and at one stroke knocked off five of the dragon's heads. He swung back a second time, and knocked off the remaining two. He gathered up all the heads, put them under the wall, and cast the monster's trunk into the sea.

An envious fellow saw all this, stole lightly around the other side of the wall, cut off the knight's head, cast it into the sea, and bade the beautiful princess Paliusha tell her father, the king, that he had saved her. He swore that if she did not say this, he would strangle her. There was nothing to be done; Paliusha wept and wept as they went to her father, the king. The king came out to meet them. She told him that this fellow had saved her. The king was enormously happy and at once set about the preparations for the wedding feast. Guests arrived from foreign lands, kings, tsars, and princes, and all of them drank and amused themselves. The princess alone was sad; she would go into a corner behind the barn and shed burning tears for her bold knight.

It occurred to her to ask her father to send fishermen to catch

318

fish in the sea, and she herself went with them. They cast a net and drew out fish, an enormous quantity! She examined them and said: "No, that is not the fish I want!" They cast another net and dragged out the head and trunk of the bold knight. Paliusha rushed to him, found a phial with the water of life in his breast pocket, placed the head on the body, and wet it with the water from the phial, and he came to life. She told him how she loathed the man who wanted to take her. The knight comforted her and told her to go home; later he would come himself and set things right.

So the knight came to the royal palace and found all the guests drunk, sporting and dancing. He declared that he could sing songs in various modes. The guests were pleased at this idea and asked him to sing. First he sang for them a gay song, full of jests and old saws, and the guests were all charmed and praised him for singing so well; then he sang a song so sad that all the guests burst into tears. The knight asked the king: "Who saved your daughter?" The king pointed out the envious fellow. "Well, king," said the knight, "let us go to the fortress with all your guests. If he can find the dragon's heads there, I will believe that he saved Princess Paliusha." All of them went to the fortress. The fellow pulled and pulled but could not pull out even one head: it was far beyond his strength. But the knight pulled them all out as soon as he tried. Then the princess told the whole truth about who saved her. Every-one realized that the bold knight had saved the king's daughter; and the fellow was tied to the tail of a horse and dragged over a field till he died.

The king wanted to marry the bold knight to his daughter. But the knight said: "No, king, I don't need anything from you. Only take me back to our bright world; I have not yet finished my mission for my father—he is still waiting for me to bring him the water of life, for he is blind." The king did not know how to take the knight up to the bright world; and his daughter did not want to part from him, she wanted to go up with him. She told her father that there was a spoonbilled bird that could take them there, provided she had enough to feed it on the way.

So Paliusha had a whole ox killed and took it with her as a store of food for the spoonbill. She and the knight said farewell to the underground king, seated themselves on the bird's back, and set out for God's bright world. When they gave more food to the bird, it flew upward faster; thus they used up the whole ox to feed it. Now they were perplexed and afraid lest the bird should drop them down again. So Paliusha cut off a piece of her thigh and gave it to the spoonbill; the bird straightway brought them up to this world and said: "Throughout our journey you fed me well, but never in my life did I taste anything sweeter than that last morsel." Paliusha showed the bird her thigh, and the bird moaned and spat out the piece; it was still whole. The knight put it on Paliusha's thigh, wet it with the water of life, and healed the princess.

Then they went home. The father, the king of the land in our own world, met them and was overjoyed to see them. The knight saw that his father had grown younger from having the apples, but that he was still blind. The knight at once anointed his father's eyes with the water of life. The king began to see; he embraced his son, the bold knight, and the princess from the dark kingdom. The knight told how his brothers had taken his apples and thrown him into the nether world. The brothers were so frightened that they jumped into the river. And the knight married the princess Paliusha and gave a most wonderful feast. I dined and drank mead with them, and their cabbage was toothsome. Even now I could eat some!

TWO OUT OF THE SACK

ONCE THERE WAS an old man who lived with his wife. The wife constantly abused her husband; not a day passed on which she did not beat him with a broomstick or oven fork; he had no peace with her at all! He went into the field with some traps and set them. He caught a crane and said to him: "Be like a son to me! I will take you to my home and perhaps she won't scold me so much." The crane answered: "Little father! Come home with me!" So they set out for the crane's house. When they arrived the crane took a sack from the wall and said: "Two out of the sack!" At once two strong fellows climbed out of the sack, set oaken tables, spread silken cloths, and served food and drink of various kinds. The old man beheld delicacies such as he had never seen in his life, and rejoiced greatly. The crane said to him: "Take this sack and bring it to your wife."

The old man took the sack and went home; he went the long way, and stopped to spend the night with his godmother, who had three daughters. They made a supper for him, out of whatever they had on hand. The old man tasted it and said to his godmother: "Your fare is poor!" "It is all we have," answered the godmother. So he said: "Remove your fare!" And he spoke to the sack as the crane had bidden him to: "Two out of the sack!" At once two men jumped out of the sack, set up oaken tables, spread silken cloths, and served food and drink of various kinds.

The godmother and her daughters were amazed and decided to rob the old man of his sack. The godmother said to her daughters: "Go, heat up a bath; perhaps my godson will steam himself a little." As soon as he went to the bath, the godmother commanded her daughters to sew up a sack exactly like the old man's; they sewed it, put it in the place of the old man's, and took his own for themselves. The old man came out of the bath, took the new sack, and cheerfully went home to his wife. While still in the yard he called in a loud voice: "Old woman, old woman, come to meet me and my son the crane!" The old woman cast a quick glance at him and muttered between her teeth: "Just wait, old dog, till I get after you with this oven fork." But the old man kept repeating: "Old woman, come to meet we with my son, the crane!" He entered the hut, hung the sack on a hook, and cried: "Two out of the sack!" No one came out. He cried again: "Two out of the sack!" Again no one came out. The old woman thought he was raving, seized a wet broom, and began to belabor him.

The old man became frightened, wept, and went back into the field. Out of nowhere the crane appeared, saw his misfortune, and said: "Come, little father, come again to my house." So they went. Another sack just like the first one hung on the wall. "Two out of the sack!" said the crane. Two men climbed out of the sack and served a magnificent dinner, just as the other men had done. "Take this sack," the crane said to the old man. He took it and went home; he walked and walked along the road, got hungry, and, as the crane had told him to, said: "Two out of the sack!" Two strong men with big sticks climbed out of the sack and began to thrash him, saying: "Go not to the godmother, steam not in the bath!" They thrashed and thrashed him until he managed to say: "Two into the sack!" The moment he said this the two men went back into the sack.

The old man took the sack and went on; he came to the same godmother, hung his sack on a hook, and said: "Heat a bath for me." She did. He went to the bath, steaming himself a little, but mainly passing the time away. The godmother called her daughters and told them to sit down, for she was hungry. "Two out of the sack!" said she. Two strong men with big sticks climbed out of the sack and began to thrash the godmother, saying: "Return the old man's sack!" They thrashed and thrashed her. Then she said to her eldest daughter: "Go and call my godson from the bath; tell him that the two men have beaten me up!" "I have not steamed myself yet," answered the old man. And they thrashed her with more blows, saying: "Return the old man's sack!" The godmother sent her second daughter, saying: "Hurry, bring my godson back into the room." He answered: "I have not yet washed my

head!" The godmother could not bear it any longer; she ordered her daughter to bring back the stolen sack. Then the old man came out of the bathroom, saw his old sack, and said: "Two into the sack!" The two men with the sticks went back into it.

The old man took both sacks, the punishing one and the kindly one, and went home. While he was still in the yard he called to his wife: "Come, meet me and my son the crane!" She cast a quick glance at him and said: "Just wait till you come into the hut, I'll thrash you!" The old man came into the room and called to his wife: "Sit down!" Then he said: "Two out of the sack!" The two men climbed out of the sack and served food and drink. The old woman ate and drank her fill and praised her husband: "Well, old man, now I won't thrash you!" The old man, having eaten, went into the yard, put the kindly sack into the larder, hung the punishing one on a hook, and walked about in the yard, not so much to walk as to pass the time.

The old woman wanted to drink some more, so she repeated the words she had heard her husband say: "Two out of the sack!" Two men with big sticks climbed out of the sack and began to thrash the old woman; and they thrashed her so hard that she could bear it no longer. She called her husband: "Old man, old man, come into the hut, the two men are beating me up!" But he walked around, laughing and saying: "They'll show you how it's done!" The two men thrashed the old woman even harder, repeating: "Don't thrash your husband! Don't thrash your husband!" At last the old man took pity on her, came in, and said: "Two into the sack!" And the two men disappeared into the sack. From that time on the old man and his wife lived in such peace and friendship that he always boasted of her goodness, and that is the end of the story.

THE MAN
WHO DID NOT KNOW FEAR

IN A CERTAIN KINGDOM there lived a merchant's son, strong and brave, who from his youth had never feared anything; he wanted to know fear and set forth to travel through the world with a laborer. After a long time or a short time, they came to a thick forest and at this moment, as though by design, night fell. "Drive into the forest," said the merchant's son. "Eh, master," said the laborer, "it is fearsome to drive there; it is night, and we may be attacked by beasts or assailed by robbers." "Are you afraid, or what? Do what I order you to do," said the merchant's son.

They drove into the forest and after a while they saw a corpse hanging on a tree. The laborer was even more frightened than before, but the merchant's son remained calm; he removed the corpse from the tree, put it in his carriage, and ordered the laborer to drive on. After an hour or two they came to a big house; in its windows there were lights. "That is fine," said the merchant's son. "We have a shelter for the night." But the laborer objected: "I would rather spend the night in the woods than in this house; we might fall into robbers' hands; they will rob us of everything we have and we may even lose our lives." In fact, robbers did live in that house; but the merchant's son refused to heed the laborer's words, opened the gate himself, and drove into the courtyard. He unharnessed his horses and, taking the laborer with him, walked into the house.

They found the robbers sitting around a big table, all of them richly dressed, with fine sabers at their belts, drinking a variety of drink and eating fish. "Good evening, gentlemen," the merchant's son said to them. "Invite me to your table to eat and drink with you." The robbers looked at him, wondering what kind of man he was, and did not answer. The uninvited guests came to the table. The merchant's son took a piece of fish, ate it, and said: "Well, gentlemen, your fish is no good at all! Eh, laborer, bring that white sturgeon we have in our carriage." The laborer went out and brought the corpse. The merchant's son put the corpse on the table, cut off a piece of it with a knife, smelled it, and cried: "No, that sturgeon is no good either. Laborer, catch some live fish!" And he pointed at the robbers, who in their fright scattered in all directions and hid wherever they could. "Well, you were frightened," said the merchant's son to the laborer. "But what is there to fear? Let us sit down and have our supper." They sat down, ate and drank, but did not stay for the night; they harnessed their horses and continued on their way.

They came to a graveyard. "Stop," said the merchant's son. "We will spend the night here." Again the laborer protested: "It is terrible here, the dead rise up at night." "Ah, what kind of fellow are you?" said the merchant's son. "You are afraid of everything." They stopped and lay down to rest on a grave. The merchant's son fell asleep but the laborer could not sleep. Suddenly a dead man in a white shroud, who seemed of enormous size, rose from that grave; he fell upon the merchant's son and began to strangle him. The merchant's son awoke, knocked the dead man under him, and began in turn to beat and torment him in every possible way. The dead man suffered blow after blow and finally began to beg for grace. "I might let you go," said the merchant's son, "if you promise to bring me within the hour the daughter of such and such a king who lives beyond the thrice ninth land." "I will bring her—only let me go!" said the dead man. The merchant's son let him go, and an hour later a sleeping princess appeared near his carriage, on the same bed in which she ordinarily rested in her royal palace. The merchant's son did not rouse the princess but waited till she awoke by herself; and upon his return home he made her his lawful wife.

The merchant's son traveled a great deal in various lands but never experienced fear; he came home, and this is what happened to him one day. He had a great passion for fishing; he spent entire nights and days on the river. His mother greatly disliked his being away from home for such long stretches of time and she asked the fishermen to frighten him somehow.

The fishermen caught perches and, seizing an opportunity when the merchant's son dozed off in his boat, quietly sailed toward him and put a few perches in his bosom. The perches began to wriggle; the merchant's son awoke, was frightened, and fell into the water, but managed to save himself. Then for the first time he learned what it means to be afraid.

THE MERCHANT'S DAUGHTER
AND THE MAIDSERVANT

THERE WAS ONCE a very wealthy merchant who had a marvelously beautiful daughter. This merchant carried goods to various provinces, and one day he came to a certain kingdom and brought precious cloths to the king as a gift. The king said to him: "Why can I not find a bride for myself?" The merchant answered: "I have a beautiful daughter, and she is so clever that no matter what a man is thinking, she can guess it." The king immediately wrote a letter and called his guards. "Go to that merchant's house," he told them, "and deliver this letter to the merchant's daughter." The letter said: "Make ready to get married." The merchant's daughter took the letter, burst into tears, and prepared to go, taking also her maidservant; and no one could distinguish this maid from the merchant's daughter, they were so like each other.

They dressed in dresses that were alike and went to the king for the marriage. The maid was full of spite, and said: "Let us take a walk on the island." They went to the island; there the maidservant gave the merchant's daughter sleeping potions, cut out her eyes, and put them in her pocket. Then she came to the guards and said: "Gentlemen of the guard, my maid-servant has gone to sea." They answered: "We need only you, we have no use for that peasant girl." They went to the king; he married the maid at once, and they began to live together. The king thought to himself: "The merchant must have cheated me; she cannot be a merchant's daughter. Why is she so ignorant? She does not know how to do anything."

Meanwhile the merchant's daughter recovered from the ill-ness that her maid had brought upon her. She could not see; she could only hear and she heard an old man tending cattle. She said to him: "Where are you, grandfather?" "I live in a little hut." "Please take me into your hut." The old man took her in. She said to the old man: "Little grandfather, drive out the cattle." He heeded her and drove away the cattle. She sent the old man to a shop, saying: "Get velvet and silk on credit." The old man went; none of the wealthy merchants would give him goods on credit but a poor shopkeeper gave him some. He brought the velvet and silk to the blind maiden. She said to him: "Little grandfather, lie down to sleep. As for me, day and night are one and the same." And she began to sew a royal crown of velvet and silk; she embroidered such a beau-tiful crown that it was a pleasure to behold it. Next morning the blind maiden roused the old man and said: "Go and take this to the king, and for payment accept only an eye. And fear not, no matter what they do to you."

The old man went to the palace with the crown. Everyone admired it and wanted to buy it from him, but the old man asked for an eye in payment. Straightway the king was told that he was asking for an eye. The king came out, was delighted with the crown, and began to bargain for it, but the old man still asked for an eye. The king began to curse and threatened to put him in prison; but no matter what the king said, the old man held his ground. Then the king cried to his guards: "Go and cut out an eye from a captive soldier." Just then his wife, the queen, rushed out, took an eye from her pocket, and gave it to the king. The king was overjoyed. "Ah, you have helped me out, little queen!" he said, and gave the eye to the old man, who took it, left the palace, and returned to his hut.

The blind maiden asked him: "Did you get my eye, little grandfather?" He said: "I did." She took it from him, went outside at twilight, spat upon it, put it into its socket, and was able to see once more. Then again she sent the old man to the shops, giving him money, and asked him to pay what he owed for the silk and velvet and to bring more velvet and gold thread. He got what he needed from the poor shopkeeper and brought these things to the merchant's daughter. She sat down to sew another crown, finished it, and sent the old man to the same king. "Do not take anything," she told him, "but an eye. And if you are asked where you got this crown, answer only: 'God gave it to me.'"

The old man came to the palace. There everyone was amazed, for although the first crown was beautiful, the second was even lovelier. The king said: "I will buy it from you at any price." "Give me an eye," said the old man. The king at once ordered a guard to cut away an eye from a prisoner; but his wife again gave him an eye. The king was overjoyed and thanked her, saying: "Ah, little mother, you have been a great help to me!" The king asked the old man: "Where do you get these crowns?" He answered: "God gives them to me." And he left the palace. He came to his hut and gave the eye to the blind maiden. She again went outside at twilight, spat on the eye, put it in its socket, and could see with both eyes. She lay down to sleep in the hut, but upon awakening she suddenly found herself in a glass house and began to live in magnificent style.

The king went to see this marvel, wondering who had built such a fine house. He drove into the yard and the merchant's daughter was delighted. She received him hospitably and bade him sit down at table. He feasted there and upon leaving asked the maiden to come to see him. He returned to his palace and said to his queen: "Ah, little mother, what a house there is in such and such a place! And what a maiden there is in it! No matter what one is thinking, she knows it." The queen guessed who it was and thought to herself: "It must be the same maiden whose eyes I cut out."

The king again went to visit the maiden, and the queen was full of spite. The king came, feasted, and invited her to his palace. She began to make ready and said to the old man: "Farewell! Here is a chest of money; you will never reach its bottom, it will always be full. You will go to sleep in this glass house, but you will awaken in your old hut. Now I am going to make a visit. I shall not be alive tomorrow; I shall be killed and cut into little pieces. Arise in the morning, make a coffin, gather my remains, and bury them."

The old man wept for her. Soon the guards came, seated her in a carriage, and drove away. They brought her to the king's palace, and the queen did not even look at her; she wanted to shoot her on the spot. She went out into the courtyard and said to the guards: "When you bring this maiden home, cut her into little pieces at once, take out her heart, and bring it to me." They took the merchant's daughter home and talked to her glibly, but she knew what they wanted to do and said to them: "Cut me up quickly." They cut her in pieces, took out her heart, buried her in the ground, and returned to the palace. The queen came out to meet them, took the heart, rolled it up into an egg, and put it in her pocket.

The old man went to sleep in a glass house but awoke in a hut and burst into tears. He wept and wept, then he set about his appointed task. He made a coffin and went to seek the maiden; he found her in the earth, dug her up, gathered all the pieces, put them in the coffin, and buried them in his own land. The king did not know of all this, so he went again to visit the merchant's daughter. When he arrived at the place, there was no house, no maiden; but at the spot where she was buried a garden had grown. He returned to the palace and told the queen: "I drove and drove, but I found neither house nor maiden, only a garden." When the queen heard this she went into the courtyard and said to the guards: "Go and cut that garden down." They came to the garden and began to cut it but it turned into stone.

The king longed to see the garden again and went to that place. When he came he beheld a boy there—and what a handsome boy he was! "Surely some lord went for a drive and lost him here," he thought. He took the boy to his palace and said to his queen: "Mind you, little mother, do not maltreat him." Meanwhile the boy began to cry and there was no way of appeasing him: no matter what they gave him, he kept on crying. Then the queen took from her pocket the egg she had made from the maiden's heart and gave it to the boy; he ceased crying and began to skip around the rooms. "Ah, little mother," said the king to the queen, "you have made him happy."

The boy ran to the yard and the king ran after him; the boy ran into the street and the king ran into the street; the boy ran to the field and the king ran to the field; the boy ran to the garden and the king ran to the garden. There the king saw the maiden and was overjoyed. She said to him: "I am your bride, the merchant's daughter, and your queen is my maidservant."

They went to the palace. The queen fell at her feet. "Forgive me," she said. "You have never forgiven me," said the merchant's daughter. "Once you cut out my eyes, and then you ordered me cut in little pieces." The king said: "Guards, cut out her eyes and let her be dragged by a horse over the field." The maidservant's eyes were cut out, she was tied to a horse, and dragged to her death over the open field. And the king began to live happily with the young queen and to prosper. The king always delighted in her and dressed her in gold.

IN A CERTAIN VILLAGE a priest hired a laborer and sent him to plow a field with his dog. He gave him a whole loaf of bread and said to him: "Here, laborer, eat your fill yourself, let the dog eat his fill, and bring back the loaf whole."

The laborer took the loaf, went to the field, and began to plow. He plowed and plowed; then it seemed to him that it was time to still his hunger, for his stomach was all hollow. But how could he eat without disobeying the priest's orders? However, hunger is not to be trifled with, it teaches a man to be cunning. And so the laborer concocted a plan. He removed the upper crust of his loaf, picked out all the soft part, ate his fill and fed the dog, then put the crust back as it was before. He plowed on cheerfully until nightfall as though nothing had happened. At nightfall he went home.

The priest went out to meet him at the gate and asked: "Well, laborer, did you eat your fill?" The laborer answered: "I did." The priest asked: "And has the dog been fed?" The laborer answered: "He has." The priest asked: "Is the loaf whole?" The laborer answered: "It is whole, little father." When the priest examined it, he laughed and said: "Ah, you are a cunning fellow, I see that you will do well. I like you for your cleverness. Stay with me, I need such as you." And he kept him, adding to the wages agreed upon because he was glad to have got such a smart fellow as a laborer. And the laborer began to roll in butter and to live so well that he hoped he would never die.

THE PEASANT
AND THE CORPSE

A PEASANT WAS DRIVING a cart full of pottery. His horse got tired and stopped near a graveyard. The peasant unharnessed it, let it graze, and lay down to rest on a grave, but somehow could not fall asleep. Suddenly the grave under him began to open; feeling this, he jumped to his feet. The grave opened wide, and out of it came a corpse holding a coffin lid and dressed in a white shroud. The corpse ran to the church, put the coffin lid in the doorway, and went to the village. Our peasant was a courageous man; he took the coffin lid and stood near his cart, waiting to see what would happen next.

After a while the corpse came back and discovered that his coffin lid was gone; he began to follow the tracks, reached the peasant, and said: "Give me back my coffin lid or I will tear you to pieces." "And what is my ax for?" the peasant answered. "I will cut you to pieces myself." "Please, my good man, give it back to me," the corpse implored. "I will not give it to you," said the peasant, "unless you tell me where you have been and what you have done." "I was in the village, and I killed two young fellows there." "Now tell me how they can be brought back to life." Willy-nilly, the corpse had to comply. "Cut the left flap from my shroud," he said, "and take it with you. When you come to the house of the murdered men, fill a pot with burning coal, put the piece of shroud in it, and close the door. The smoke will bring them back to life at once." The peasant cut off the left flap of the shroud and returned the coffin lid. The corpse went back to his grave and the grave opened. He began to descend into it, when suddenly the cocks crowed, and he had no time to cover himself properly; one end of the coffin lid remained outside.

The peasant saw and took note of all this. Daybreak came; he harnessed his horse and drove to the village. He heard lamentations and cries in one house; he entered it and found that two young fellows were dead there. "Do not weep," he said, "I can bring them back to life." "Do bring them back to life," said the parents. "We will give you half of our possessions." The peasant did as the corpse had told him and the two young fellows came back to life. Their families were overjoyed but at once seized the peasant and tied him with ropes. "Now, you wise man," they said, "we shall take you to the authorities; since you knew how to bring them back to life, you surely killed them too." "Ah, ye faithful, don't ye fear God?" cried the peasant, and he told them everything that had happened to him during the night. The villagers were called together, the people went to the graveyard, found the grave from which the corpse had emerged, dug it up, and thrust a spike of aspen wood straight into his heart, so that he could no longer rise up and kill people. The peasant was richly rewarded and allowed to return home in peace.

THE ARRANT FOOL

IN A CERTAIN FAMILY there was an arrant fool. Not a day passed on which they did not receive complaints about him; every day he would either insult someone or injure someone. The fool's mother pitied him and looked after him as if he were a little child; whenever the fool made ready to go somewhere, she would explain to him for half an hour what he should do and how he should do it. One day the fool went by the threshing barn and saw the peasants threshing peas, and cried to them: "May you thresh for three days and get three peas threshed!" Because he said this the peasants belabored him with their flails. The fool came back to his mother and cried: "Mother, mother, they have beaten up a fellow!" "Was it you, my child?" "Yes." "Why?" "Because I went by Dormidoshkin's barn and his family were threshing peas there." "And then, my child?" "And I said to them: 'May you thresh for three days and get three peas threshed.' That's why they beat me up." "Oh, my child, you should have said: 'May you have to do this forever and ever.'"

The fool was overjoyed. The next day he went to walk in the village and met some people carrying a coffin with a dead man in it. Remembering his mother's words, he roared in a loud voice: "May you have to carry this forever and ever!" Again he was soundly thrashed. The fool returned to his mother and told her why he had been beaten up. "Ah, my child," she said, "you should have said: 'May he rest in peace eternal.'" These words sank deep into the fool's mind.

Next day he happened again to walk in the village and met a gay wedding procession. The fool cleared his throat and as soon as he came up to the procession, he cried: "May you rest in peace eternal!" The drunken peasants jumped down from the cart and beat him up cruelly. The fool went home and cried: "O my dear mother, they've beaten me up terribly." "What for, my child?" The fool told her. His mother said: "My child, you should have danced and played for them." "Thank you, mother," he said. He went to the village once more and took his reed pipe with him.

At the end of the village a corn loft was on fire. The fool ran there as fast as he could; he stopped in front of the corn loft and began to dance and to play on his reed pipe. Again he was thrashed. Again he came in tears to his mother and told her why he had been beaten up. His mother said: "You should have taken some water and helped them to quench the fire." Three days later, when the fool's sides were healed, he went again to walk in the village. He saw a peasant singeing a pig. The fool snatched a pail of water from a woman who was going by with her cowlstaff, ran to the peasant, and poured water over the fire. Again he was soundly thrashed. Again he returned to his mother and told her why he had been beaten up. Then his mother swore never again to let him go to the village, and until this day he has never gone farther than his own back yard.

LUTONIUSHKA

THERE WAS ONCE an old man who lived with his wife and his son named Lutonia. One day Lutonia and his father were busy in the courtyard while his mother was in the house. She wanted to remove a log from the shelf where it had been put to dry, but by accident dropped it on the hearth. She began to cry and lament in a loud voice. Her husband, hearing her cry, rushed into the house and asked her why she was weeping. The old woman said through her tears: "If our Lutoniushka were married, and if he had had a little son, and if this little son had been sitting near the hearth, I would have hit him with the log." The old man joined in her lamentations, repeating: "That is true, you would have hit him." And the old couple kept on crying and lamenting at the top of their lungs.

Lutonia came running from the yard and asked: "Why are you crying?" They told him why: "If you had been married, and if you had had a little son, and if, a few hours ago he had been sitting right here, he would have been killed by the log— it fell just on this spot, and with what a bang!" Lutonia snatched up his cap and said: "Farewell, my parents. If I find anyone more stupid than you, I shall return. If I do not find any such, do not wait for me." And he went away.

336

He walked and walked and saw several peasants dragging a cow into a house. "Why are you dragging this cow?" asked Lutonia. They said: "Don't you see how much grass has grown here?" "Ah," said Lutonia, "you arrant fools!" He went into the house, plucked out the grass, and threw it to the cow. The peasants were greatly amazed at this and began to ask Lutonia to stay with them and enlighten them. "No," said Lutonia, "there are many other such fools in the wide world." And he walked on.

In one village he saw a crowd of peasants standing around a house; they had attached a horse collar to the gate and were trying to drive a horse into the collar; they had tired the horse so that it was half dead. "What are you trying to do?" asked Lutonia. "We want to harness this horse, little father," said the peasants. "Ah, you arrant fools," said Lutonia, "let me do it for you." He removed the collar from the gate and put it on the horse. These peasants too were amazed at his feat and entreated him to stay with them for one week at least. But Lutonia refused and walked on.

He walked and walked, got tired, and stopped at an inn. The old hostess prepared a hasty pudding, put it on the table, and then over and over again went to the cellar with a spoon to get some milk. "Old woman, why do you wear out your shoes for nothing?" asked Lutonia. "What do you mean, why?" the old woman answered in a hoarse voice. "Don't you see, little father, that the hasty pudding is on the table, and the milk is in the cellar?" "You should bring the pot of milk here, old woman, then you would have a much easier time of it." "That is very true, my good man." She brought the milk to the room and invited Lutonia to sit at her table. Lutonia ate his fill, climbed upon the stove, and fell asleep. When he awakens, my tale will go on; for the time being it is over.

BARTER

WHILE CLEANING MANURE out of a shed, a peasant found some oats. He went to his wife, who was making a fire in the stove, and said: "Now wife, get busy! Rake up the fire, pour this grain into the stove; then dig it out, pound it and grind it, make a pudding, and put it into dishes; I shall go to the king, bring him a dish of pudding, and he may reward me with something."

He came to the king, bringing him a dish of pudding; the

king rewarded him with a golden heath hen. He started home-ward; passing by a field, he saw herdsmen grazing a drove of horses. The herdsmen asked him: "Little peasant, where have you been?" "I have been to see the king and I brought him a dish of pudding." "And what did the king give you?" "A golden heath hen." "Exchange your heath hen for a horse." The peasant made the exchange, mounted the horse, and rode on. He came near a herd of cows. The cowherd said: "Little peasant, where have you been?" "I have been to see the king and I brought him a dish of pudding." "And what did the king give you?" "A golden heath hen." "Where is your golden heath hen?" "I exchanged it for a horse." "Exchange your horse for a cow."

He made the exchange and led off the cow by her horns. Then he came up to a flock of sheep. The shepherd said: "Little peasant, where have you been?" "I have been to see the king and I brought him a dish of pudding." "And what did the king give you?" "A golden heath hen." "Where is your golden heath hen?" "I exchanged it for a horse." "Where is your horse?" "I exchanged it for a cow." "Exchange the cow for a sheep."

The peasant made the exchange and drove off the sheep. He came up to a herd of pigs. The swineherd said: "Little peasant, where have you been?" "I have been to see the king and I brought him a dish of pudding." "And what did the king give you?" "A golden heath hen." "Where is your golden heath hen?" "I exchanged it for a horse." "Where is your horse?" "I exchanged it for a cow." "Where is the cow?" "I exchanged it for a sheep." "Exchange the sheep for a pig."

He made the exchange and drove off the pig. Then he came up to a flock of geese. The gooseherd said: "Little peasant, where have you been?" "I have been to see the king and I brought him a dish of pudding." "And what did the king give you?" "A golden heath hen." "Where is your golden heath hen?" "I exchanged it for a horse." "Where is your horse?" "I exchanged it for a cow." "Where is the cow?" "I exchanged it for a sheep." "Where is the sheep?" "I exchanged it for a pig." "Exchange the pig for a goose."

He made the exchange and carried away the goose. Then he

came up to a flock of ducks. The shepherd asked him: "Little peasant, where have you been?" "I have been to see the king and I brought him a dish of pudding." "And what did the king give you?" "A golden heath hen." "Where is your golden heath hen?" "I exchanged it for a horse." "Where is your horse?" "I exchanged it for a cow." "Where is the cow?" "I exchanged it for a sheep." "Where is the sheep?" "I exchanged it for a pig." "Where is the pig?" "I exchanged it for a goose." "Exchange the goose for a duck."

He made the exchange and carried away the duck. Then he came up to some children playing ball with a stick. The children asked him: "Little peasant, where have you been?" "I have been to see the king and I brought him a dish of pudding." "And what did the king give you?" "A golden heath hen." "Where is your golden heath hen?" "I exchanged it for a horse." "Where is your horse?" "I exchanged it for a cow." "Where is the cow?" "I exchanged it for a sheep." "Where is the sheep?" "I exchanged it for a pig." "Where is the pig?" "I exchanged it for a goose." "Where is your goose?" "I exchanged it for a duck." "Exchange the duck for a stick."

He made the exchange and walked on; he came home, put his stick near the gate, and entered the house. His wife began to question him, and he told her everything up until the moment when he acquired the stick. "Where is the stick?" asked his wife. "Near the gate." She went out, took the stick, and began to belabor him with it, saying: "Don't exchange things! Don't exchange things, you old dotard! You should at least have brought the duck home!"

THE GRUMBLING OLD WOMAN

NIGHT AND DAY a certain old stepmother grumbled—one wondered why her tongue did not ache! She grumbled always at her stepdaughter: the girl was not clever enough and not pretty enough; no matter where she went or sat or stood, it was never right, never as it should be! And so the stepmother grumbled from dawn to dark like a gusla all wound up. She wearied her husband to death, and everyone else too felt like running away from the house. One day the husband harnessed a horse to carry millet to town, and his wife cried: "Take your daughter too, take her anywhere you want, to the dark forest, only get her out of my way!"

The old man took his daughter. It was a long and difficult road, with woods and swamps all around; where could he leave the maiden? He spied a little hut on chicken legs, supported by a cake and covered with a pancake; and the little hut turned round and round. He thought it would be best to leave his daughter in this little hut; so he put her down from his cart, gave her some millet for gruel, whipped his horse, and vanished from sight. The maiden remained alone; she pounded some millet and cooked a great deal of gruel, but there was no one to eat it. Night came, long and terrifying; she felt that to sleep would wear out her sides, to look at the dark would tire her eyes, and there was no one to exchange a word with. It was boring and fearsome. She stood on the threshold, opened the door nearest the forest, and called out: "Whoever is in the forest, in the dark night, let him come be my guest!" A wood goblin answered her call and turned into a brave youth, a Novgorod merchant; he came into the little hut and brought a present for his hostess. After that he came in for a chat quite often and sometimes he would bring her a gift; he brought her so many gifts that there was no place to put them.

Meanwhile the grumbling old woman found life empty without her stepdaughter; it was quiet in her house, she felt queasy, and her tongue was parched. "Go, husband," she said, "get my stepdaughter, raise her up from the bottom of the sea, snatch her out of the fire! I am old, I am sickly, there is no one to tend me." The husband did as she asked; the stepdaughter returned. When she opened her coffer and hung out her things on a rope that stretched from the house to the gate, the old woman, who had opened her mouth to greet her in her customary abusive way, pursed up her lips, seated the welcome guest under the icon, and said to her civilly: "What is your pleasure, madam?"

341

THE WHITE DUCK

A CERTAIN PRINCE married a beautiful princess, but before he had had time to feast his eyes upon her and listen to her sweet speech, he was compelled to separate from her, go on a far journey, and leave his wife in the hands of strangers. What was there to do? It is said that you cannot spend your life in embraces. The princess wept a great deal, and the prince comforted her a great deal, admonishing her not to leave the women's apartments, not to keep company with evil people, and not to listen to evil words. The princess promised to do all this. The prince departed; the princess locked herself in her room and did not go out.

After a long time or a short time, a woman came to her. She seemed so simple and kindly! "Why are you pining away here?" she said. "You should at least have a peep at God's world and take a walk in your garden, to dispel your grief and get a breath of fresh air." For a long time the princess refused, but in the end she thought: "Surely there is no harm in taking a walk in the garden!" And out she went. In the garden there was a spring of crystalline water. "The day is so hot," said the woman, "the sun is blazing, and the water is cool. It bubbles so invitingly; why should we not bathe in it?" "No, no," said the princess, "I do not want to!" But then she thought: "There is no harm in having a bath." She slipped off her gown and jumped into the water. No sooner had she plunged in than the woman struck her on the back, saying: "Swim now as a white duck!" And the princess turned into a white duck. The witch straightway attired herself in the princess' garment, adorned and painted herself, and sat down to await the prince. As soon as the puppy barked and the little bell rang, she ran out to meet the prince, rushed toward him, kissed him, and fondled him. He was overjoyed, stretched out his arms toward her, and did not realize that she was not his wife.

Meanwhile the white duck laid eggs and hatched its young. Two were handsome and the third a starveling. And her babies grew into little children; she brought them up and they began to swim on the little stream, to catch little goldfish, to gather little rags, to sew little coats, and to jump up on the banks and look at the meadows. "Oh, don't go there, my children," the mother said. The children disobeyed her; one day they played in the grass, the next day they ran over the meadow, ever farther and farther, until they reached the prince's courtyard. The witch recognized them by their smell and gritted her teeth; she called the children, gave them food and drink and put them to sleep, and then ordered a fire to be lighted, kettles to be hung over it, and knives to be sharpened. The two handsome brothers lay down and fell asleep. But the little starveling, whom the mother had ordered them to carry in their bosoms that he might not catch cold—the starveling did not sleep, and heard and saw everything. In the night the witch came to their door and asked: "Are you asleep, little children, or not?" The starveling answered: "We sleep and don't sleep. We think that someone wants to slaughter us all; a fire of hazel logs is being made, boiling kettles are hanging, steel knives are being sharpened." "They are not sleeping," said the witch.

She went away, walked and walked about, and again came to the door: "Are you asleep, little children, or not?" The starveling said again: "We sleep and don't sleep. We think that someone wants to slaughter us all; a fire of hazel logs is being made, boiling kettles are hanging, steel knives are being sharpened." "Why is it always the same voice?" thought the witch. She softly opened the door and saw that both the handsome brothers were sound asleep. She touched them with the hand of a corpse and they died.

Next morning the white duck called her children, but they did not come. She felt anguish in her heart, she fluttered her wings and flew to the prince's courtyard. There, as white as kerchiefs, as cold as little fish, the two brothers lay side by side. She rushed to them, spread her wings, and put them around her children, and cried with a mother's voice:

> *Quack, quack, quack, my children,*
> *Quack, quack, quack, my little doves!*
> *I nursed you with fears,*
> *I fed you with tears,*
> *I spent dark nights without sleep,*
> *And for worry over you did not eat.*

"My wife, do you hear this extraordinary thing?" said the prince. "The duck is lamenting." "You only fancy it!" said the false wife. "Have the duck driven out of the courtyard." The duck was driven out but she flew back to her children and said:

> *Quack, quack, my children,*
> *Quack, quack, my little doves!*
> *An old witch took your life,*
> *An old snake, a false wife,*
> *Because of her wicked ruse*
> *Your true father you did lose;*
> *She put us in the swift stream,*
> *Turned us into white ducks,*
> *And calls herself the queen.*

"This is strange," thought the prince, and he cried: "Catch this white duck!" Everyone rushed to catch her, but the white duck flew about and would not let herself be caught; the prince himself went out and she fell on his hands. He took her by a little wing and said: "White birch tree stand behind me, lovely maiden stand before me." A white birch stood behind him, and a lovely maiden stood before him, and in the lovely maiden the prince recognized his young wife. At once a magpie was caught, two little bladders were tied to her, and she was ordered to fill one with the water of life and the other with the water of speech. The magpie flew away and brought back the waters. The children were sprinkled with the water of life and they shuddered; they were sprinkled with the water of speech and they began to speak. And now the prince had all his family, and they began to live and prosper and forget the evil days. As for the witch, she was tied to the tail of a horse and dragged over a field; where a leg was torn off her, a fire iron stood; where an arm was torn off, a rake stood; where her head was torn off, a bush grew. Birds came swooping down and pecked up her flesh, a wind arose and scattered her bones, and not a trace or a memory was left of her.

IF YOU DON'T LIKE IT, DON'T LISTEN

THERE WERE ONCE three brothers; two were clever, and the third was a simpleton. One day they went to a wood and wanted to eat their dinner there. They filled a pot with gruel and cold water (the simpleton had told them to do this), but did not know where to get fire. Not far from them there was a beekeeper's house. The eldest brother said: "I will go to the beekeeper's house to get some fire." He went and said to the old man there: "Grandfather, give me a light." The old man said: "First sing me a song." "But I don't know any song, grandfather." "Then dance for me." "I am not quick at dancing, grandfather." "Aha, you're not quick! So you won't get any fire." And in addition the old man cut out a strip of flesh from his back. And so the eldest brother came back without a light.

The second brother began to grumble at him. "Eh, how clumsy you are, brother," he said. "You have not brought us a light. I will go myself." He came to the beekeeper's house and cried: "Grandfather, please give us a light!" "Well, my boy, sing me a song." "I don't know any." "Well, then, tell me a tale." "I don't know any tales, grandfather." The old man cut a strip of flesh from this brother's back too and sent him back without a light. Now the two clever brothers just stared at each other.

The simpleton watched them and said: "Eh you, my clever brothers, you have not yet got a light!" And he went himself to get one. He came to the house and said: "Grandfather, have you got a light?" The old man said: "First dance for me." "I do not know how, grandfather." "In that case, tell me a tale." "That I can do," said the simpleton, sitting down on a straw mat. "But mind you," he went on, "sit opposite me, listen, and do not interrupt me; if you do interrupt me, I will cut three strips of flesh from your back." The old man sat opposite him, with the bald spot on his head turned to the sun—and he had a huge bald spot. The simpleton cleared his throat and began his tale: "Now listen to me, grandfather." "I am listening, my light."

"I had a piebald horse, little grandfather. I used it to drive to the forest for wood. One day I sat on it with my ax stuck in my belt. The horse trotted—trot, trot—and the ax thumped on its back, thump, thump. It thumped and thumped and cut off the horse's rump. Now listen, grandfather," said the simpleton, giving the old man a slap on his bald spot with a mitten. "I am listening, my light."

"I rode for another three years on the remaining front part of the horse, and then I happened to see my horse's rump in a meadow: it was walking there, nibbling grass. I caught it and sewed it back to the front of my horse and rode on for another three years. Listen, grandfather!" he said, again slapping the bald spot with his mitten. "I am listening, my light!"

"I rode and I rode," the simpleton went on, "till I came to a forest. There I saw a tall oak tree; I began to climb up it and got to heaven. There I found that cattle were cheap, only mosquitoes and flies were expensive; so I climbed down to the ground, caught two bagfuls of mosquitoes and flies, slung the

bags on my back, and again climbed up to heaven. I put down my bags and began to hand out their contents to sinful mortals: I gave to each a fly and a mosquito and took a cow and a calf in exchange; I gathered up so much cattle that it could not be counted. Then I drove the cattle to the place where I had climbed up, and discovered that someone had cut down the oak. I was distressed and wondered how I could get down from heaven. Finally I made up my mind to make a rope reaching to earth; for that purpose I slaughtered all my cattle, made a long strap, and began to clamber down. I clambered and clambered and found I was short a piece of strap about as long as your cabin, grandfather, and I was afraid to jump. Listen, grandfather!" And again the simpleton slapped the bald spot with his mitten. "I am listening, my light."

"Luckily a peasant was winnowing oats; the husks flew up and I caught them and braided a rope of them. Suddenly a strong wind arose and began to shake me to and fro, now toward Moscow, now toward Petersburg; my rope of husk broke and the wind threw me into a bog. I sank into the mire up to my neck. I wanted to crawl out, but could not. A duck built a nest on my head. Then a wolf took to coming to the bog to eat eggs. I somehow managed to reach a hand out of the mire and seized the wolf's tail while he stood beside me; I seized it and cried loudly: 'Tiu-lu-lu-lu!' The wolf dragged me out of the mire. Are you listening, grandfather?" asked the simpleton, giving the old man another slap on his bald pate with the mitten. "I am listening, my light."

The simpleton saw that he was not getting anywhere; the tale was finished, and the old man had kept his word and had not interrupted him. So in order to provoke the old man, the simpleton began another tale: "My grandfather was riding on your grandfather." "No, it was my grandfather who rode horseback on yours!" the old man interrupted. The simpleton was glad; that was all he wanted. He knocked down the old man and cut three strips of flesh from his back; then he took some fire and brought it to his brothers. They made a fire, put the pot of gruel on a tripod, and began to cook. When the gruel is ready, the tale will continue; for the time being it is ended.

THE MAGIC SWAN GEESE

A N OLD MAN LIVED with his old wife; they had a daughter
and a little son. "Daughter, daughter," said the mother,
"we are going to work; we shall bring you back a bun,
sew you a dress, and buy you a kerchief. Be careful, watch
over your little brother, do not leave the house." The parents
went away and the daughter forgot what they had told her; she
put her brother on the grass beneath the window, ran out into
the street, and became absorbed in games. Some magic swan
geese came, seized the little boy, and carried him off on their
wings.

The girl came back and found her brother gone. She gasped,
and rushed to look in every corner, but could not find him. She

called him, wept, and lamented that her father and mother would scold her severely; still her little brother did not answer. She ran into the open field; the swan geese flashed in the distance and vanished behind a dark forest. The swan geese had long had a bad reputation; they had done a great deal of damage and stolen many little children. The girl guessed that they had carried off her brother, and rushed after them. She ran and ran and saw a stove. "Stove, stove, tell me, whither have the geese flown?" "If you eat my cake of rye I will tell you." "Oh, in my father's house we don't even eat cakes of wheat!" The stove did not tell her. She ran farther and saw an apple tree. "Apple tree, apple tree, tell me, whither have the geese flown?" "If you eat one of my wild apples, I will tell you." "Oh, in my father's house we don't even eat sweet apples." She ran farther and saw a river of milk with shores of pudding. "River of milk, shores of pudding, whither have the geese flown?" "If you eat of my simple pudding with milk, I will tell you." "Oh, in my father's house we don't even eat cream."

She would have run in the fields and wandered in the woods for a long time, if she had not luckily met a hedgehog. She wanted to nudge him, but was afraid that he would prick her, and she asked: "Hedgehog, hedgehog, have you not seen whither the geese have flown?" "Thither," he said, and showed her. She ran and saw a little hut that stood on chicken legs and turned round and round. In the little hut lay Baba Yaga with veined snout and clay legs, and the little brother was sitting on a bench, playing with golden apples. His sister saw him, crept near him, seized him, and carried him away. But the geese flew after her: if the robbers overtook her, where would she hide?

There flowed the river of milk with shores of pudding. "Little mother river, hide me!" she begged. "If you eat my pudding." There was nothing to be done; she ate it, and the river hid her beneath the shore, and the geese flew by. She went out, said "Thank you," and ran on, carrying her brother; and the geese turned back and flew toward her. What could she do in this trouble? There was the apple tree. "Apple tree, apple tree, little mother, hide me!" she begged. "If you eat my wild apple." She ate it quickly. The apple tree covered her with branches and leaves; the geese flew by. She went out again and ran on with her brother. The geese saw her and flew after her. They came quite close, they began to strike her with their wings; at any moment they would tear her brother from her hands. Luckily there was the stove on her path. "Madam Stove, hide me!" she begged. "If you eat my cake of rye." The girl quickly stuck the cake in her mouth, went into the stove, and sat there. The geese whirred and whirred, quacked and quacked, and finally flew away without recovering their prey. And the girl ran home, and it was a good thing that she came when she did, for soon afterward her mother and father arrived.

PRINCE DANILA GOVORILA

THERE WAS ONCE an old princess; she had a son and a daughter, both well built, both handsome. A wicked witch disliked them; she pondered and pondered as to how she could lead them into evil ways and destroy them. In the end she conceived a plan. Like a cunning fox she came to their mother and said: "My little dove, my dear friend, here is a ring for you; put it on your son's finger. With its help he will be healthy and wealthy, but he must never take it off, and he must marry only that maiden whom the ring fits." The old woman believed her and was overjoyed; before her death she enjoined upon her son that he take to wife a woman whom the ring would be found to fit.

Time went by and the little son grew up. He grew up and began to seek a bride; he would like one girl, then another, but upon trying the ring he always found it to be too big or too small; it did not fit either the one or the other. He traveled and traveled through villages and cities, tried the ring on all the lovely maidens, but could not find one whom he could take as his betrothed; he returned home and was pensive and sad. "Little brother, why are you grieving?" his sister asked him. He told her his trouble. "Why is the ring so troublesome?" said the sister. "Let me try it." She put it on her finger and the ring clasped it, and began to gleam; it fitted her as though made to her size.

"Ah, my sister," said the brother, "you have been chosen for me by fate, you shall be my wife." "What are you saying, my brother? Think of God, think of the sin; one does not marry one's own sister." But her brother did not heed her; he danced for joy and ordered that preparations be made for the wedding. The sister burst into bitter tears, went out of her room, sat on the threshold, and wept and wept. Some old women passed by; she invited them in and offered them food and drink. They asked her what her grief was, why she was sad. It was of no use to hide it; she told them everything. "Weep not, grieve not," said the old women, "but listen to us. Make four little dolls, seat them in the four corners; when your brother calls you to your wedding, go; when he asks you to come to the bridal chamber, do not hurry. Put your hope in God. Farewell!"

The old women left. The brother wed his sister, went to the room, and said: "Sister Catherine, come to the featherbed." She answered: "I will come in a minute, only let me remove my earrings." And the dolls in the four corners cried like cuckoos:

> Cuckoo, Prince Danila,
> Cuckoo, Govorila,
> Cuckoo, he takes his sister,
> Cuckoo, for a wife,
> Cuckoo, earth open wide,
> Cuckoo, sister, fall inside!

The earth began to open, the sister began to fall in. Her brother cried: "Sister Catherine, come to the featherbed!" "Just a minute, my brother, let me unclasp my girdle." The dolls cuckooed:

352

Cuckoo, Prince Danila,
Cuckoo, Govorila,
Cuckoo, he takes his sister,
Cuckoo, for a wife,
Cuckoo, earth open wide,
Cuckoo, sister, fall inside!

Only the sister's head was still above ground. The brother called her again: "Sister Catherine, come to the featherbed!" "Just a minute, my brother, I must remove my slippers." The dolls cuckooed, and she vanished into the earth.

The brother called her, he called her again in a louder voice, but she did not come. He ran to her room, banged at the door, and the door broke. He looked everywhere, but his sister was gone. Only the dolls were sitting in the corners and crying: "Earth, open wide! Sister, fall inside!" He seized an ax, cut off their heads, and threw them into the stove.

The sister walked and walked underground and saw a little hut on chicken legs, turning round and round. "Little hut, little hut," she said, "stand the old way with your back to the woods and your front to me." The little hut stood still and the door opened. Inside sat a lovely maiden embroidering a towel with silver and gold. She received her guest with kindness, then sighed and said: "My little dove, my heart is glad to see you, I will welcome you and fondle you while my mother is out. But when she comes back there will be trouble for both of us, for she is a witch." The guest was frightened by these words, but she had nowhere to go, so she sat with her hostess at the embroidery frame; they embroidered the towel and talked together.

After a long time or a short time, when the hostess knew that her mother was about to come—for she knew the time—she turned her guest into a needle, thrust the needle into a birch broom, and put the broom in a corner. She had no sooner done all this than the witch appeared at the door. "My good daughter, my comely daughter, I smell a Russian bone!" the witch said. "Madam mother, passers-by came in to drink some water." "Why did you not keep them here?" "They were old people, my mother, they would not have been to your liking."

353

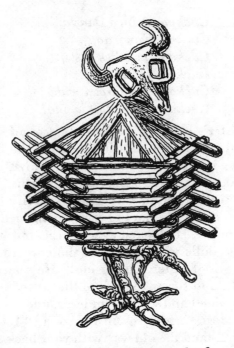

"Henceforth, mind you, invite all into the house, do not let anyone go; I will leave now to get some booty." She left; the maidens sat at the frame, embroidered the towel, talked and laughed together. The witch came flying home; she sniffed about in the house. "My good daughter, my comely daughter, I smell a Russian bone!" she said. "Some little old men stopped in to warm their hands; I tried to keep them but they did not want to stay." The witch was hungry; she chided her daughter, and flew away again. The guest had been sitting in the broom. They hastened to finish embroidering the towel; while working thus hurriedly they planned how to escape from their trouble and run away from the wicked witch.

They had hardly had time to exchange a few whispers, when the witch (talk of the devil and he will appear) stood in the doorway, catching them by surprise. "My good daughter, my comely daughter, I smell a Russian bone!" she cried. "There, my mother, a lovely maiden is awaiting you," said her daughter. The maiden looked at the witch and her heart failed her. Before her stood Baba Yaga the Bony-legged, her nose hitting

354

the ceiling. "My good daughter, my comely daughter, make a good hot fire in the stove," said the witch. They brought wood, oak and maple, and made a fire; the flame blazed forth from the stove. The witch took a broad shovel and began to urge her guest: "Now, my beauty, sit on the shovel." The beauty sat on it. The witch shoved her toward the mouth of the stove, but the maiden put one leg into the stove and the other on top of it. "You do not know how to sit, maiden. Now sit the right way," said the witch. The maiden changed her posture, sat the right way; the witch tried to shove her in, but she put one leg into the stove and the other under it.

The witch grew angry and pulled her out again. "You are playing tricks, young woman!" she said. "Sit quietly, this way —just see how I do it." She plumped herself on the shovel and stretched out her legs, and the two maidens quickly shoved her into the stove, locked her in, covered her up with logs, plastered and tarred the opening, and then ran away, taking the embroidered towel and a brush and comb with them. They ran and ran, and looking back beheld the wicked witch; she had wrenched herself free, caught sight of them, and was hissing: "Hey, hey, hey, are you there?"

What could they do? They threw down the brush and there appeared a marsh thickly overgrown with reeds. The witch could not crawl through it, but she opened her claws, plucked out a path, and again came close. Where could they go? They threw down the comb, and there appeared a dark, thick forest: not even a fly could fly through it. The witch sharpened her teeth and set to work: each time she clamped her teeth she bit off a tree by its roots. She hurled the trees to one side, cleared a path, and again came close—very close. The maidens ran and ran till they could run no longer; they had lost all their strength. They threw down the gold-embroidered towel, and there spread before them a sea, wide and deep, a sea of fire. The witch soared high; she wanted to fly across the sea, but fell into the fire and was burned.

The maidens remained alone, little doves without a home; they did not know where to go. They sat down to rest. A servant came to them and asked them who they were, then reported to his master that in his domain sat not two little birds of passage but two marvelous beauties, one exactly like the other—they had the same brows, the same eyes. "One of them," said the servant, "must be your sister, but which of the two that is, it is impossible to guess." The master went to see them and invited them to his home. He saw that his sister was there, but which of the two she was he could not guess—his servant had told the truth. She was angry and would not tell him herself. What could be done?

"This is what can be done, master," said the servant. "I will fill a sheep's bladder with blood, you will put it under your arm, and while you speak to your guests, I will come near you and strike you with a knife in your side; blood will flow and your sister will reveal herself." "Very well!" They did what they had planned; the servant struck his master in the side and blood gushed forth. The brother fell, the sister rushed to embrace him, and she cried and lamented: "My beloved, my dearest!" The brother jumped up, safe and sound, embraced his sister, and married her to a good man; and he himself married her friend, on whose finger the ring fitted, and all of them lived happily forever after.

THE WICKED SISTERS

IN A CERTAIN KINGDOM in a certain land there lived a king who had a son, Prince Ivan, so handsome, so wise, so famous that songs were sung and tales were told about him; and lovely maidens dreamed of him in their dreams. The prince felt a desire to see the wide world; he received his father's blessing, said farewell, and went forth in all four directions to see people and to show himself.

He traveled a long time, saw good and evil and things of

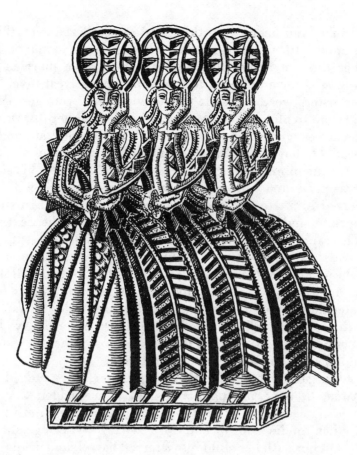

every description, and in the end came to a lofty and beautiful
palace made of stone. He beheld three beautiful sisters sitting
on the porch and speaking among themselves. The eldest said:
"If Prince Ivan married me, I would spin for him a shirt finer
and smoother than anyone else in the whole world can spin."
Prince Ivan began to listen carefully. "And if he married me,"
said the second, "I would weave for him a coat of silver and
gold, and he would shine like the Firebird." "And I," said the
youngest, "can neither spin nor weave. But if he loved me, I
would bear him sons like bright falcons, each with a sun on his
forehead, a moon on the back of his head, and stars on his
sides."

Prince Ivan heard everything and remembered everything, and upon returning to his father asked his leave to marry. The father did not refuse this request; the prince married the youngest sister and began to live with her in great love. The elder sisters were enraged; they envied their youngest sister and began to plot evil against her. They bribed her nurses and governesses, and when she bore a son to Prince Ivan, and he expected to have brought to him a child with a sun on his forehead, a moon on the back of his head, and stars on his sides, he was presented with a kitten and assured that his wife had deceived him. He was greatly distressed, was wrathful for a long time, and finally began to wait eagerly for the next son.

The same nurses and the same governesses were with the princess, and again they stole the real child with a sun on his forehead, and substituted a puppy for it. Prince Ivan fell ill of grief and sorrow; he greatly loved the princess but felt an even greater desire to see a handsome child. He began to wait for the third one. The third time he was shown an ordinary child without sun, moon, or stars. Prince Ivan lost patience, repudiated his wife, and ordered her to be tried.

Elders gathered together without number. They judged and debated, thought and pondered, and then decided that the princess' head ought to be cut off. "No," said the chief judge; "whether you heed me or not, this is what I say. Gouge out her eyes, put her with her child into a tarred barrel, and drop them both into the sea; if she is guilty she will sink, if she is innocent she will emerge." His words found favor; the princess' eyes were gouged out, she was put into a barrel with her child and thrown into the sea. As for Prince Ivan, he married her eldest sister, the same who had stolen her children and hidden them in his father's garden in the green arbor.

There the boys grew and grew, without having seen or known their own mother, who wretchedly sailed the ocean with the substitute child. And this substitute child grew not by the day but by the hour. He soon acquired sense, became reasonable, and said: "Madam my mother, by my request, by the pike's command, by God's blessing, let us reach a shore." The barrel stopped. "Madam my mother, by my request, by the pike's command, by God's blessing, let the barrel burst." He had no sooner spoken than the barrel burst asunder and he went ashore with his mother. "Madam my mother, this is an excellent, a cheerful place; it is a pity only that you cannot see the sun, nor the sky, nor the lush grass. By my request, by the pike's command, by God's blessing, let a bathhouse appear here."

That very minute a bathhouse grew as though from the earth; the door opened by itself, a fire was made in the stove, and the water began to boil. They entered; the boy took a little brush and began to wash his mother's eyes with warm water, saying: "By my request, by the pike's command, by God's blessing, let my mother see." "My little son, I see, my eyes have opened!" "By my request, by the pike's command, by God's blessing, let your husband's palace come to us with the garden and the children."

Suddenly the palace was there. In front of it a garden spread out, in the garden birds sang on branches, in the middle stood the arbor, and in it the three brothers were living. The substitute son ran to them; he entered the arbor and beheld a table all set, and three covers were on it. He quickly returned to his mother and said: "Madam my dear mother, bake me three cakes with your milk." His mother did as he told her. He took the three cakes, put them on three dishes, hid in a corner, and waited. Suddenly the room was illumined, the three brothers with the sun and the moon on their heads and the stars on their bodies came in, sat at table, tasted of the cakes, and recognized their own mother's milk. "Who has brought us these cakes?" they said. "If he would disclose himself and tell us about our dear mother, we would kiss him and love him and consider him as our own brother." The boy came out of his hiding place and led them to their mother. There they embraced and kissed and wept. They began to live well and they had enough to treat other good people too.

One day some poor monks went by; they were invited, given meat and drink, and sent away with gifts. It happened that the same old men went by Prince Ivan's palace. He stood on the porch and began to question them: "Old monks, where have you been, what have you seen?" "We have been at such and such a place and we have seen this: where formerly there was only a swamp and moss, only tree stumps, there is now a palace such as no tongue can tell of nor pen describe, and such a garden that nothing in the kingdom can match it, and people such as in the whole white world have no equals. We were there and were received by three brothers; on their foreheads was the sun, on the back of their heads the moon, on their sides many stars, and their beautiful princess mother lives with them and feasts her eyes upon them."

Prince Ivan listened to them and became thoughtful. He felt a prick in his breast, his heart began to pound; he took his faithful sword and his straight-shooting arrow, saddled his spirited steed, and without saying farewell to his wife darted off to the palace that no tale could tell of nor pen describe. He found himself there, beheld his children, beheld his wife, recognized them and was beside himself with joy; his soul was illumined.

I was there then too, I drank mead and wine and saw everything. Everyone was cheerful. Only the eldest sister came to grief, for she was tarred up in a barrel and thrown into the sea, and God did not protect her: she sank to the bottom and vanished without a trace.

THE PRINCESS
WHO NEVER SMILED

WHEN YOU COME TO THINK of it, how great is God's world! Rich people and poor people live in it, and all of them have room to live, and the Lord watches over all of them. The wealthy ones live in idleness, the wretched ones in toil. To each his lot is given.

In a royal palace, in a princely castle, in a lofty apartment, there lived the glorious Princess Who Never Smiled. What a life she had, what plenty, what luxury! She had a great deal of everything, she had everything her heart desired. Yet she never smiled and never laughed; it was as though her heart did not delight in anything.

The king was distressed when he looked at his sorrowful daughter. He opened his royal palace to all who wished to be his guests. "Let them try," he said, "to divert the Princess Who Never Smiles; he who succeeds shall take her to wife." He had no sooner said this than people began to throng the princely gate. They came from all sides—princes and dukes, boyars and noblemen, people of rank and commoners. Feasts began, mead flowed—but still the princess did not smile.

At the other end of the town, in a corner of his own, there lived an honest worker. In the morning he swept the courtyard, in the evening he grazed the cattle; he toiled incessantly. His master, a rich and righteous man, paid him proper wages. At the end of the year he put a bag of money on the table and said to the worker: "Take as much as you want." And then he went out of the room.

The worker came to the table and thought: "How shall I avoid sinning against the Lord by taking too much for my work?" He took only one coin, squeezed it in his fist, and went to drink some water at the well. He stooped over it and his coin fell out of his hand and sank to the bottom of the well.

The poor fellow was left with nothing. Another in his place would have wept, grieved, and wrung his hands in despair, but not he. "God sends us everything," he said. "The Lord knows what to give to whom: some he endows generously with money, from others he takes the last penny. I must have been careless and worked badly. Henceforth I shall be more zealous." And again he set to work, and his fingers worked more nimbly than fire itself.

Another year went by, the term came, and his master again put a bag of money on the table, telling him: "Take as much as your heart desires." And again he left the room. Again the worker did not want to displease God and take too much for his work. He took a coin, went to drink at the well, and dropped his coin; again it sank. He set to work even more zealously, hardly sleeping at night, hardly eating by day. And lo and behold, while other people's grain withered and faded, his master's throve; while other people's cattle collapsed from exhaustion, his master's capered in the street; other people's horses had to be dragged uphill, his master's could hardly be held back. The master knew to whom he owed all this, whom he had to thank. When the term was completed and the third year had passed, he put a pile of money on the table, saying: "Take, little worker, take as much as your heart desires; yours was the labor, yours is the money." And he left the room.

Again the worker took only one coin and went to the well to drink water; and lo and behold, his last coin was safe, and the two he had previously lost floated to the surface. He picked them up, guessing that God had rewarded him for his labors. He was overjoyed and thought: "It is high time for me to see the white world, to know people." He thought for a while, then went forth, he knew not whither. He walked along a field and a mouse ran by and said: "My dear comrade, give me a coin. I will be useful to you some day." He gave the mouse a coin. He walked in a wood and a beetle crawled by and said: "My dear comrade, give me a coin. I will be useful to you some day." He gave the beetle a coin. He swam across a river and met a catfish who said: "My dear comrade, give me a coin. I will be useful to you some day." He did not refuse the catfish and gave up his last coin.

He came to the city. There were many people, many doors! The worker looked and turned everywhere, but did not know whither to go. He found himself before the royal palace; at the window sat the Princess Who Never Smiled, all dressed in silver and gold, and looking straight at him. Where would he hide? His eyes grew misty, drowsiness overwhelmed him, and he fell face down in the mud. As though from nowhere came the catfish with the big whiskers, and he was followed by the old beetle and the close-cropped mouse; all of them came. They set to work: the mouse removed his coat, the beetle cleaned his boots, the catfish chased the flies away. The Princess

362

Who Never Smiled watched and watched their antics and burst out laughing.

"Who, who has cheered up my daughter?" asked the king. One said: "I!" Another said: "I!" "No," said the Princess Who Never Smiled, "it was this man." And she pointed to the worker. He was straightway taken to the palace, and there before the king stood the worker, turned into a handsome youth. The king kept his royal promise and gave him what he had said he would.

I wonder whether the worker did not dream all this. But no, I am assured that it was really so, and we must believe it.

BABA YAGA

ONCE UPON A TIME there lived an old man and his wife. When the old man became a widower, he married another wife, although he had a daughter from his first wife. The wicked stepmother disliked the girl, beat her, and pondered how she might destroy her. One day the father went away somewhere and the stepmother said to the girl: "Go to your aunt, my sister; ask her for a needle and some thread to sew a shirt for you." That aunt was Baba Yaga the Bony-legged. The girl was not stupid and she first went to her own aunt. "Good day, auntie," she said. "Good day, my beloved, what have you come for?" said her aunt. "Mother has sent me to her sister to ask for a needle and thread to sew me a shirt." The aunt told her what to do. "My little niece," she said, "when you get there, a birch will lash your eyes, but do you tie it with a ribbon. The gates will bang and creak at you, but do you pour some oil on their hinges. Dogs will want to tear you apart, but do you throw them some bread. A cat will scratch your eyes, but do you give him some ham." The girl went her way; she walked and walked and finally arrived at her other aunt's.

She saw a little hut and in it sat Baba Yaga the Bony-legged. "Good day, auntie," said the girl. "Good day, my beloved!" "Mother sent me to ask for a needle and thread to sew me a shirt." "Very well; meanwhile sit down and weave." The girl sat at the loom and Baba Yaga went out and said to her maid: "Go and heat a bath and wash my niece, but be careful; I want to eat her for breakfast." The girl sat there half dead with fright and begged the maid: "My dear, do not burn so much wood! Pour water over it and bring the water in a sieve." And she gave the maid a kerchief. Baba Yaga waited. She came to the window and asked: "Are you weaving, little niece, are you weaving, my darling?" "I am weaving, auntie, I am weaving, my dear." Baba Yaga went away from the window and the girl gave ham to the cat and asked him: "Is there no way of getting away from here?" "Here is a comb and a towel," said the cat. "Take them and run away. Baba Yaga will pursue you. But do you put your ear to the ground, and when you hear her coming close, throw the towel, and there will be a wide, wide river. And if Baba Yaga crosses that river and begins to catch up with you, put your ear to the ground again, and when you hear her coming close, throw your comb, and there will be a very thick forest—she will not be able to get through it."

The girl took the towel and the comb and ran. The dogs wanted to tear her, but she threw them some bread and they let her pass. The gates wanted to bang shut, but she poured some oil on their hinges and they let her pass. The birch wanted to lash her eyes, but she tied it with a ribbon and it let her pass. Meanwhile the cat sat at the loom and wove; he did not so much weave as tangle everything up. Baba Yaga came to the window and asked: "Are you weaving, little niece, are you weaving, my darling?" "I am weaving, auntie, I am weaving, my dear," answered the cat in a rough voice. Baba Yaga rushed into the hut, saw that the girl had gone, and took to beating the cat and scolding him for not having scratched out the girl's eyes. "I have served you so many years," said the cat, "and

364

you have not given me even a bone; but she gave me a piece of ham!"

Baba Yaga flung herself on the dogs, the gate, the birch, and the maid, and began to thrash and scold them all. The dogs said to her: "We have served you so long, and you have not even thrown us a burnt crust; but she gave us bread!" The gate said: "I have served you so long, and you have not even poured water on my hinges; but she poured oil!" The birch said: "I have served you so long, and you have not even tied me with a thread; but she tied me with a ribbon!" The maid said: "I have served you so long, and you have not given me even a rag; but she gave me a kerchief!"

Baba Yaga the Bony-legged jumped on her mortar, goaded it on with her pestle, swept away her tracks with a broom, and flew in pursuit of the girl. The girl put her ear to the ground and heard Baba Yaga coming quite close. She threw her towel—and there was a wide, wide river. Baba Yaga came to the river and gnashed her teeth with rage. She returned home, took her oxen, and drove them to the river; the oxen drank the river clean. Then she set out again in pursuit. The girl put her ear to the ground and heard Baba Yaga coming close. She threw her comb—and there grew up a deep and terrifying forest. Baba Yaga began to gnaw it, but no matter how she tried she could not gnaw through it, and she turned back.

Meanwhile the old man had come home and asked: "Where is my daughter?" "She has gone to her aunt," said the step-mother. After a while the girl also came home. "Where have you been?" her father asked her. "Ah, father," she said, "mother sent me to auntie for a needle and thread to sew me a shirt; but the aunt was Baba Yaga and she wanted to eat me." "How did you get away, my daughter?" The daughter told him how. When the old man heard all this he grew angry at his wife and shot her to death; and then he and his daughter began to live and prosper. I was there and drank mead and beer; it ran down my mustache, but it never got into my mouth.

JACK FROST

THERE WAS ONCE a stepmother who had a stepdaughter and a daughter of her own. At anything her own daughter did, the woman would pat her head and say: "Clever girl!" But no matter how hard the stepdaughter tried, she was always found in the wrong. Yet the truth of the matter was that the stepdaughter was as good as gold; in the proper hands she would have been like cheese in butter, but in her stepmother's house she bathed in tears every day. What could she do? Even an angry wind subsides at last; but when the old woman got angry she never quieted down, she would hurl one insult after another, and her mouth was so full of venom that her teeth itched.

One day the stepmother made up her mind to drive her step-daughter out of the house. She said to her husband: "Take her, take her, old man, take her wherever you wish, so that my eyes do not see her and my ears do not hear her. And don't take her to the warm house of your kin, but into the open field in the bitter frost." The old man began to grieve and lament; none the less he put his daughter on a sledge. He wanted to cover her with a horse cloth but did not dare. He took the homeless girl into the open field, set her down on a heap of snow, made the sign of the cross over her, and hastened home as fast as possible, that his eyes might not behold his daughter's death.

The poor little thing remained there shivering and softly repeating her prayers. Jack Frost came leaping and jumping and casting glances at the lovely maiden. "Maiden, maiden, I am Jack Frost the Ruby-nosed!" he said. "Welcome, Jack Frost! God must have sent you to save my sinful soul." Jack Frost was about to crack her body and freeze her to death, but he was touched by her wise words, pitied her, and tossed her a fur coat. She put it on, squatted on her heels, and sat thus. Again Jack Frost the Ruby-nosed came leaping and jumping and casting glances at the lovely maiden. "Maiden, maiden,

I am Jack Frost the Ruby-nosed!" he said. "Welcome, Jack Frost! God must have sent you to save my sinful soul." But Jack Frost had not come to save her soul at all; he brought her a coffer, deep and heavy, full of bedding and petticoats and all sorts of things for her dowry. And she sat on the coffer in her fur coat, so gay, so pretty! Again Jack Frost came leaping and jumping and casting glances at the lovely maiden. She welcomed him and he gave her a robe embroidered with silver and gold. She put it on—and how beautiful and stately she looked! She sat there happily singing songs.

Meanwhile her stepmother was preparing her funeral dinner and frying pancakes. "Go, husband," she said, "bring home your daughter, that we may bury her." The old man went. The little dog under the table said: "Bow-wow, the old man's daughter is coming home all decked in gold and silver, but no suitor wants the old woman's daughter!" "Be quiet, you fool! Here is a pancake for you, and now say that suitors will come for the old woman's daughter, but of the old man's daughter only bones will be brought home." The little dog ate the pancake and said again: "Bow-wow! The old man's daughter is coming home all decked in gold and silver, but the suitors don't want the old woman's daughter." The old woman gave the dog more pancakes and beat him, but he kept saying the same thing: "The old man's daughter is coming home decked in gold and silver, but the suitors don't want the old woman's daughter."

The gate creaked, the doors flew wide open, a coffer deep and heavy was brought in, and the stepdaughter followed, radiant, like a grand lady. The stepmother looked at her and threw up her arms. "Old man, old man," she ordered, "harness other horses, take my daughter at once, put her in the same field, in the very same place!" The old man took the girl to the same field and left her in the very same place. And Jack Frost the Ruby-nosed came, looked at his guest, leapt and jumped, but did not hear any kind words. He grew angry, seized her, and killed her. The old woman said to her husband: "Old man, go bring my daughter. Harness spirited horses—and don't overturn the sledge, don't drop the coffer!" But the little dog

368

under the table said: "Bow-wow, the suitors will take the old man's daughter, but the bones of the old woman's daughter will be brought home in a sack." "Don't lie! here is a pancake for you, and say: 'The old woman's daughter is coming home decked in gold and silver.'" The gate flew open and the old woman ran out to greet her daughter, but instead she embraced a cold corpse. She began to wail and howl, but it was too late.

HUSBAND AND WIFE

THERE WERE ONCE a husband and a wife who seemed to live well. But the wife was an ingenious woman; when the husband went away, she was merry, when he came back she fell ill; she always tried to find work for him to do, to get rid of him; one day she would send him hither, the next day thither, and while he was away she would give little parties and feasts. Her husband would return, find everything clean and in order, and his wife aching and groaning and lying on the bench. The husband believed that she was ill and for his part almost wept. One day she conceived the idea of sending him to get a medicine in Krimgrad. The husband went. On the way he met a soldier, who asked: "Whither are you going, peasant?" "To Krimgrad to get a medicine." "Who is sick?" "My wife." "Go back, go back without fail; I am an expert healer myself, I will go with you." Then he commanded: "Left, turn!" Soon they found themselves near the peasant's barn. "Have your wife sit up," said the expert. "I will find out how sick she is."

The husband entered the courtyard, put his ear to the door, and heard sounds of games, dances, and merriment. The soldier's heart boiled, he struck the door, and it opened. The wife was moving about like a swan, a young fellow capered in front of her, green wine was flowing on the table. The soldier came just in time; he drank a cup of wine and began to cut capers. The wife found him to her liking. What a soldier, what a handsome fellow—and so keen, so clever, as though he had lived there all his life! Yes, tomorrow there would be cakes to bake. "Soldier," she said, "go to the barn, bring a bundle of straw."

The soldier went, gathered the straw, wrapped the husband in it, tied it with a rope, slung it over his shoulders, and brought it to the wife. She was glad and intoned a song: "The husband went to Krimgrad, to buy healing herbs, to cure the wife's belly with plants. He will never get there, he will never come back. Hey, soldier, accompany me!" The soldier began his song: "Do you hear, straw, what's going on here?" "Oh, your song is no good, mine is better. Let us sing it together! The husband went to Krimgrad, to buy healing herbs, to cure the wife's belly with plants." She sang loudly, and the soldier sang even more loudly: "Do you hear, straw, what's going on here? The whip is hanging on the wall, and it should be on a back!" The straw heard and wriggled; the rope burst, the husband jumped out, snatched the whip, and began to belabor his wife. He cured her in no time.

LITTLE SISTER FOX
AND THE WOLF

THERE WAS ONCE an old man who lived with his wife. He said to her: "Woman, do you bake cakes, while I go fishing." He caught fish and carried home a whole cartful of them. As he drove along, he spied a fox lying wound up like a cracknel on the road. The old man got down from his cart and came close to the fox, but she did not stir; she lay like one dead. "This will be a gift for my wife," said the old man, and he took the fox, and put her in the cart, and he himself walked in front of it. The fox chose the right moment and began quietly to throw one fish after the other out of the cart. She threw out all the fish and then ran away. "Well, old woman," said the old man, "I have brought you a fine collar for your fur coat." "Where?" "There in the cart you will find both the fish and the collar." The woman went to the cart and found neither collar nor fish. She began to abuse her husband: "Ah, you old dotard, you fool! You want to cheat me!" Only then did the old man realize that the fox was not dead; he grieved and grieved, but there was nothing that he could do.

Meanwhile the fox gathered up in a pile all the fish scattered on the road, sat down, and began to eat them. A wolf came by and said: "Good day, neighbor!" "Good day, neighbor," answered the fox. "Give me some fish," said the wolf. "Catch it yourself, then you can eat." "But I don't know how." "Eh, I did it. All you have to do, neighbor, is to go to the river and drop your tail into a hole in the ice; the fish will hook themselves to your tail. But sit for a long time, else you won't catch enough." The wolf went to the river and dropped his tail into a hole in the ice, for it was wintertime. He sat and sat; he sat through the night, and his tail was frozen in; he tried to raise himself, but could not. "Eh," he thought, "so much fish has got hooked to my tail that I cannot pull it out!" Suddenly he saw women coming to fetch water. Seeing the gray wolf, they began to cry: "A wolf, a wolf! Hit him, hit him!" They ran up to him and began to belabor him, some with cowlstaffs, some with pails, others with whatever they had in hand. The wolf jumped and jumped, tore off his tail, and took to his heels without looking back. "I'll remember that, neighbor," he thought. "I'll pay you back in kind!"

Meanwhile Little Sister Fox, having eaten enough fish, decided to see whether she could not steal something else. She got into a house where women were frying pancakes, stuck her head into a tub of dough, smeared herself, and ran away. The wolf met her. "So that's the way you teach me?" he said. "I was roundly beaten for my pains." "Eh, neighbor," said Little Sister Fox, "all you have lost is some blood. But I have had my brains beaten out of me, and it was much more painful; I can hardly hobble along." "That's true," said the wolf. "How can you walk in this condition? Better sit on me, I will carry you home." The fox sat on his back and he carried her. Little Sister Fox, while sitting on the wolf's back, began to whisper: "The beaten one is carrying the unbeaten one, the beaten one is carrying the unbeaten one." "What are you saying, neighbor?" "I am saying, the beaten one is carrying the beaten one." "Very true, neighbor, very true."

"Now, neighbor, let's build huts for ourselves," said the fox.

"Let's, neighbor." "I will build myself a hut of linden bark, and you build yourself one of ice." They set to work, and built huts for themselves, one of linden bark for the fox and one of ice for the wolf, and lived in them. Spring came and the wolf's hut melted away. "Ah, neighbor," said the wolf, "you have cheated me again; for that I must eat you up." "Come, neighbor, we will make a trial to see who will eat whom." Little Sister Fox took him to a woods near a deep pit and said: "Jump! If you jump across this pit, you shall eat me; if not, I will eat you." The wolf jumped and fell into the pit. "Well," said the fox, "sit there!" And she went away.

She walked along carrying a rolling pin in her paw and asked a peasant to give her shelter in his house. "Let Little Sister Fox spend the night with you," she said. "We are crowded even without you," said the peasant. "I won't disturb you; I'll lie on the bench and put my tail under it and the rolling pin under the stove." She was allowed to come in. She lay on the bench with her tail under it and put the rolling pin under the stove. Early next morning she got up, burned her rolling pin, and then asked: "Where is my rolling pin? I would not take even a goose for it!" The peasant had no choice but to give her a goose for the lost rolling pin. The fox took the goose and walked away singing:

> *Little Sister Fox*
> *Walked on the road*
> *Carrying a rolling pin*
> *And swapped it for a goose.*

Knock, knock, knock! She knocked at another peasant's door. "Who's there?" the peasant called out. "I, Little Sister Fox. Please give me shelter for the night." "We are crowded even without you." "I won't disturb you; I'll lie on the bench and put my tail under it and the goose under the stove." She was allowed to come in. She lay on the bench with her tail under the bench and put the goose under the stove. Early next morning she got up, took her goose, plucked it and ate it, and said: "Where is my goose? I would not take even a turkey for it!" The peasant had no choice but to give her a turkey. She took it and walked away singing:

> *Little Sister Fox*
> *Walked on the road*
> *Carrying a rolling pin;*
> *She swapped it for a goose,*
> *And the goose for a turkey.*

Knock, knock, knock! She knocked at the door of a third peasant. "Who's there?" the peasant called out. "I, Little Sister Fox. Please give me shelter for the night!" "We are crowded even without you." "I won't disturb you; I'll lie on the bench and put my tail under it and the turkey under the stove." She was allowed to come in. She lay on the bench with her tail under the bench and put the turkey under the stove. Early next morning she got up, took her turkey, plucked it and ate it, and said: "Where is my turkey? I would not take even a maiden for it!" The peasant had no choice but to give her a maiden. The fox put her in a bag and walked away singing:

> *Little Sister Fox*
> *Walked on the road*
> *Carrying a rolling pin;*
> *She swapped it for a goose,*
> *The goose for a turkey,*
> *The turkey for a maiden!*

Knock, knock, knock! She knocked at the door of a fourth peasant. "Who's there?" the peasant called out. "I, Little Sister Fox. Please give me shelter for the night!" "We are crowded even without you." "I won't disturb you; I'll lie on the bench and put my tail under the bench and my bag under the stove." She was allowed to come in. She lay on the bench with her tail under it and put her bag under the stove. The peasant quietly let the maiden out of the bag and shoved in his dog in place of her. Next morning Little Sister Fox made ready to go, took her bag, walked on the road, and said: "Maiden, sing me a song!" The dog began to howl. The fox took fright, flung away the bag with the dog in it, and took to her heels.

374

The fox ran and ran till she beheld a cock perched on a gate. She said to him: "Little cock, little cock, come down, I'll hear your confession—you have seventy wives, you have always been a sinner." The cock climbed down and she snatched him and gobbled him up.

THE THREE KINGDOMS,
COPPER, SILVER. AND GOLDEN

IN A CERTAIN KINGDOM in a certain land lived a king named Byel Byelanin. He had a wife, Nastasya the Golden-tressed, and three sons, the princes Piotr, Vasily, and Ivan. One day the queen went to walk in the garden with her ladies-in-waiting and tirewomen. Suddenly a mighty whirlwind arose

375

and—God preserve us!—it seized the queen and carried her off no one knew whither.

The king was grieved and distressed and did not know what to do. When the princes grew up, he said to them: "My beloved children, which of you will set out to seek his mother?" The elder brothers made ready and set out, and then the youngest son too begged his father to let him go. "No," said the king, "go not, my little son! do not leave me a lone old man." "Give me leave, father! I greatly long to wander over the white world and find my mother." The king tried hard to dissuade him but could not. Then he said: "Well, there is nothing to be done, so go, and God be with you."

Prince Ivan saddled his good steed and set out. He rode and rode, for a long time or a short time. Speedily a tale is spun, with much less speed a deed is done. Finally he came to a forest. In that forest stood a most splendid castle. Prince Ivan drove into the wide courtyard, saw an old man, and said: "Long life to you, old man!" "You are welcome here! Who are you, brave youth?" "I am Prince Ivan, the son of King Byel Byelanin and Queen Nastasya the Golden-tressed." "Ah, my own nephew! Whither is God taking you?" "I am traveling in search of my mother," he said. "Can you not tell me, uncle, where to find her?" "No, my nephew, I know not. But I will help you if I can. Here is a ball. Throw it before you; it will roll and lead you to high, steep mountains. In those mountains is a cave; enter it, take iron claws, put them on your hands and feet, and climb up the mountain. Perhaps there you will find your mother, Nastasya the Golden-tressed."

That was good. Prince Ivan said farewell to his uncle and threw the ball before him; the ball rolled and rolled and he rode after it. After a long time or a short time, he beheld his brothers, Piotr and Vasily, encamped in an open field with a multitude of troops. His brothers met him, saying: "So it's you, Prince Ivan? Where are you going?" "Oh," he said, "I grew weary at home and decided to go in search of my mother. Send your troops home and let us travel together."

So they did; they dismissed their troops and all three of them rode after the ball. Even from a distance they beheld the mountains, so steep and high that—God preserve us!—their peaks leaned against heaven. The ball rolled straight to a cave. Prince Ivan climbed down from his horse and said to his brothers: "Here, brothers, is my good steed; I will go up the mountain to seek my mother, and you remain here. Wait for me exactly three months; if I am not back in three months, it will be of no use to wait any longer."

The brothers thought to themselves that climbing up these mountains, anyone might break his head. "Well," they said, "God speed you, we shall wait here." Prince Ivan went to the cave. He saw that the door was of iron, pushed it with all his strength, and opened it. He entered, and the iron claws slipped on his hands and feet of themselves. He began to climb the mountain; he climbed and climbed; he labored for a whole month, and with great effort reached the top. "Well," said he, "thanks be to God!" He rested for a while, then walked along the mountain peaks. He walked and walked and beheld a copper castle; at the gate terrible serpents, hundreds of them, were fastened with copper chains. Near by was a well and at the well a copper bucket hung on a copper chain. Prince Ivan drew water with the bucket and gave it to the serpents to drink. They lay down quietly and he passed into the castle.

The queen of the copper kingdom came out to him. "Who are you, brave youth?" "I am Prince Ivan." She asked: "Have you come of your own will or by compulsion, Prince Ivan?" "Of my own will; I am looking for my mother; Nastasya the Golden-tressed. A certain Whirlwind kidnaped her in the garden. Do you know where she is?" "No, I do not. But not far from here you will find my second sister, the queen of the silver kingdom; she may tell you." She gave him a copper ball and a copper ring. "The ball," she said, "will lead you to my second sister, and the whole copper kingdom is in this ring. When you defeat Whirlwind, who keeps me here and flies to me every three months, do not forget me, wretched woman that I am; rescue me from this place and take me with you back to the free world." "I will," answered Prince Ivan, and threw the copper ball. It rolled before him and the prince followed it. He came to the silver kingdom and beheld a castle even more splendid than the first. It was all silver; at the gate terrible serpents were fastened with silver chains, and near by was a well with a silver bucket. Prince Iván drew water, gave it to the serpents to drink, and they lay down quietly and let him pass into the castle.

The queen of the silver kingdom came out. "For nearly three years," she said, "mighty Whirlwind has kept me here; I have not heard a Russian voice with my ears, nor caught a glimpse of a Russian man with my eyes, and now a Russian spirit is flesh before my eyes. Who are you, brave youth?" "I am Prince Ivan." "Have you come here of your own will or by compulsion?" "Of my own will. I am looking for my mother; she was walking in the green garden when Whirlwind arose and carried her off, no one knows whither. Do you know where to find her?" "No, I do not; but near here you will find my eldest sister, the queen of the golden kingdom, Elena the Fair; she may tell you. Here is a silver ball. Roll it before you and follow it: it will lead you to the gold kingdom. But mind you, when you kill Whirlwind, do not forget me, wretched woman that I am; free me from this place and take me along with you, back to the free world. Whirlwind keeps me captive here and flies to me every two months." Then she gave him a silver ring, saying: "The whole silver kingdom is in this ring." Prince Ivan rolled the ball; where the ball went, he followed.

After a long time or a short time, he saw before him a golden castle gleaming like fire; at the gate teemed terrible serpents fastened with golden chains; near by was a well, and at the well a golden bucket hung on a golden chain. Prince Ivan drew water with the bucket and gave it to the serpents to drink; they lay down quietly. The prince entered the castle and was met by Elena the Fair. "Who are you, good youth?" "I am Prince Ivan." "How have you come here—of your own will or by compulsion?" "I have come of my own will; I am looking for my mother, Nastasya the Golden-tressed. Do you know where to find her?" "Of course I know. She lives not far from here, and Whirlwind flies to her once a week, and to me once a month. Here is a golden ball for you. Roll it before you and follow it; it will lead you where you want to go. And take

378

this golden ring too—all of the golden kingdom is in it. Now mind you, prince! When you conquer Whirlwind, do not forget me, wretched woman that I am; take me along with you back to the free world." "Yes," he said, "I will take you."

Prince Ivan rolled the ball and followed it. He walked and walked and came to such a castle that—God preserve us!—it nearly dazzled him, so brightly did it gleam with diamonds and precious stones. At the gate six-headed serpents hissed; Prince Ivan gave them water to drink and they lay down quietly and let him pass into the castle. The prince went through great chambers and in the very last one found his mother; she sat on a lofty throne, attired in royal garments and crowned with a precious crown. She looked at the visitor and cried: "Ah my God, is it you, my beloved son? How have you happened to come here?" "Thus and thus," he said. "I have come for you." "Well, little son, you will have a hard time. For in these mountains reigns the wicked, mighty Whirlwind, and all the spirits obey him; it is he who carried me off. You must fight with him. Come quickly to the cellar."

They went to the cellar; there stood two tubs of water, one on the right, the other on the left. Queen Nastasya the Golden-tressed said: "Drink some water from the right." Prince Ivan drank. "Now, how much strength is in you?" the queen asked him. "I am so strong that I could overturn this whole castle with one hand." "Now drink some more." The prince drank more. "How much strength is in you now?" "Now, if I wanted to, I could overturn the whole world." "Oh, that is a great deal of strength. Now change these tubs around; put the one on the right to the left, and the one on the left to the right." Prince Ivan took the tubs and changed them around. "You see, my beloved son," said the queen, "one tub contains the water of strength, and the other the water of weakness; he who drinks from the first will be a mighty champion, while he who drinks from the second will be quite helpless. Whirlwind always drinks the water of strength and keeps it in the tub on the right side; so we must deceive him, otherwise you will never be able to get the better of him."

They returned to the palace. "Whirlwind will come soon,"

the queen said to Prince Ivan. "Sit under my purple robe so that he will not see you. And when he comes and begins to embrace and kiss me, seize his mace. He will rise very high, he will carry you over seas and precipices; but do you be careful not to let go of the mace. Whirlwind will get tired, he will want to drink the water of strength, he will descend into the cellar, and rush to the tub on the right side; but do you drink from the tub on the left. Then he will become completely powerless and you can wrest his sword from him and with one blow cut off his head. When you cut off his head, you will hear straightway a voice behind you, saying: 'Strike again! strike again!' But do not strike, little son. Instead, answer this: 'A hero's hand does not strike twice; it fells the enemy at one blow.'"

Prince Ivan had no sooner hidden under the purple robe than the courtyard grew dark and everything shook: Whirlwind came, struck the earth, turned into a goodly youth, and entered the castle; in his hands he held a battle mace. "Fie, fie, fie!" he shouted. "Why do I smell the Russian breath in here? Did someone come to see you?" The queen answered: "I do not know why you think so." Whirlwind rushed to embrace and kiss her, and Prince Ivan at once seized his mace. "I will devour you," cried Whirlwind. "Well," replied Prince Ivan, "my old grandmother said that of two things one will happen: either you will devour me or you will not." Whirlwind dashed out through the window and soared up to the sky; and he carried Prince Ivan over mountains, on and on, saying: "I will smash you." And he soared over seas, threatening: "I will drown you." But no, the prince did not let go of the mace.

Whirlwind flew over the whole world, became tired, and began to descend. He descended straight into the cellar, rushed to the tub on the right side, and began to drink the water of weakness, while Prince Ivan rushed to the left, drank the water of strength, and became the mightiest champion in the whole world. He saw that Whirlwind had lost all his strength, wrested the sharp sword from him, and cut off his head. He heard a voice behind him crying: "Strike again, strike again, else he will come to life!" "No," answered the prince, "a hero's hand

does not strike twice, but always fells the enemy at one blow."
He made a fire at once, burned the body and the head, and
scattered the ashes to the wind.

Prince Ivan's mother was overjoyed. "Well, my beloved
son," she said, "let us make merry and eat, and then let us
hasten home, for it is wearisome here; there are no people to
talk with." "But who serves you?" "Wait and see." They had
no sooner thought of eating than the table set itself, and
various meats and wines appeared on it of themselves. The
queen and the prince dined while invisible musicians played
wonderful songs for them. They ate and drank their fill and
rested. Then Prince Ivan said: "Let us go, mother, it is time;
my brothers are waiting for me at the foot of the mountain.
And on our way we must rescue the three queens whom Whirlwind has kept here."

They took everything they needed and set out. First they
stopped for the queen of the golden kingdom, then for the
queen of the silver kingdom, and at last for the queen of the
copper kingdom. They took these queens with them and
provided themselves with linen and many other things, and in
a short time they came to the place where they had to climb
down the mountain. Prince Ivan let his mother down first on
a linen cloth, then Elena the Fair and her two sisters. The
brothers stood below waiting and thought to themselves: "We
will leave Prince Ivan up there, and will take our mother and
the queens to our father and tell him that we found them."
"I shall take Elena the Fair for myself," said Prince Piotr.
"You, Vasily, will take the queen of the silver kingdom, and
the queen of the copper kingdom we will marry to some
general."

When Prince Ivan's turn came to descend the mountain,
his older brothers seized the cloth, pulled it, and ripped it off.
Prince Ivan remained on the mountain. What could he do? He
wept bitterly and turned back; he walked and walked, over the
copper kingdom, and over the silver kingdom, and over the
golden kingdom, but not a soul did he find anywhere! He came
to the diamond kingdom, and still there was no one. What was
he to do all alone and bored to death? He beheld a reed pipe

lying on a window. He took it in his hand. "Let me play," he said, "to ease my boredom." He had no sooner put the pipe to his lips than Lame and One-eyed sprang forth. "What do you wish, Prince Ivan?" they said. "I am hungry."

Straightway as though from nowhere a table was set, and on the table were choice wines and meats. Prince Ivan ate and he thought: "Now it would not be bad to rest." He blew his reed pipe and Lame and One-eyed appeared, saying: "What do you wish, Prince Ivan?" "That a bed be made ready." He had no sooner said this than a wonderful bed was ready. He lay on it, had a good sleep, and again blew his reed pipe. "What do you wish?" Lame and One-eyed asked him. "So you can do everything?" asked Prince Ivan. "Yes, we can do everything, Prince Ivan, and we will do everything for him who blows this reed pipe. Just as we served Whirlwind before, we are now glad to serve you; only you must always keep this reed pipe with you." "Very well, then," said Prince Ivan, "I want to be in my own kingdom at once."

He had no sooner said this than he found himself in his kingdom, in the middle of the market place. He began to walk among the stalls and met a shoemaker—a merry fellow. The prince asked: "Whither are you going, little man?" "I am taking my shoes to sell, for I am a shoemaker." "Take me as your journeyman." "But do you know how to make shoes?" "I can make anything you wish; not only shoes but even clothes." "Well, come with me."

They came to the shoemaker's house. The shoemaker said: "Well, set to work! Here is material for you, the very best; let me see how well you can cobble." Prince Ivan went to his room, took out his reed pipe, and Lame and One-eyed appeared. "What do you wish, Prince Ivan?" they asked. "I want a pair of shoes ready by tomorrow." "Oh, that is a tiny service, not a task." "Here is the material." "What sort of material is that? Nothing but trash! Just good enough to throw out the window."

Next morning the prince awoke and found on the table a pair of beautiful shoes, of the very best make. The master arose too and said: "Well, my good youth, have you sewn the shoes?" "They are ready." "Show them to me." The shoemaker looked at the shoes and gasped: "What a craftsman I have found for myself!" he said. "No, not a craftsman—a real wonder." He took the shoes to sell them on the market place. At that time three weddings were being prepared for at the king's palace: Prince Piotr was making ready to marry Elena the Fair, Prince Vasily was to wed the queen of the silver kingdom, and the queen of the copper kingdom was being given to a general. They began to buy attire for these weddings, and Elena the Fair needed shoes. Our shoemaker's shoes were the best of all, and he was brought to the king's palace.

When Elena the Fair looked at the shoes, she said: "What is this? Only in the mountains can such shoes be made." She paid the shoemaker a high price and said to him: "Make me another pair of shoes without taking my measure, and let them be sewn perfectly, ornamented with precious stones, and studded with diamonds. And let them be ready by tomorrow, else you will go to the gallows."

The shoemaker took the money and the precious stones and went home a gloomy man! "Woe is me!" he said. "What am I to do now? How can I make such shoes by tomorrow, and without taking her measure into the bargain? Doubtless I shall be hanged in the morning! Let me at least drink down my misfortune with my friends for the last time." He entered an alehouse. He had many friends there and they asked him: "Brother, why are you so gloomy?" "Ah, my beloved friends, I am going to be hanged tomorrow." "But why?" The shoemaker told them of his misfortune. "It's no use trying to work; instead, let us regale ourselves together for the last time." They drank and drank and reveled and reveled till the shoemaker began to reel. "Well," he said, "I shall take a keg of wine home and go to sleep. And tomorrow, as soon as the hangman comes for me, I will drink a couple of gallons; let them hang me unconscious."

He came home. "Well, you accursed creature," he said to Prince Ivan, "do you know what your shoes have done for me?" And he told his journeyman the whole story. "Tomorrow when I am sent for," he ordered, "awaken me at once." At night Prince Ivan took out his reed pipe, blew it, and Lame and One-eyed appeared. "What do you wish, Prince Ivan?" they asked. "That such and such shoes be ready." "They will be." Prince Ivan lay down to sleep; next morning he awoke and beheld the shoes on the table, gleaming like fire. He went to rouse his master, saying: "Master, it is time to arise." "What? Have I been sent for? Give me the keg of wine at once! Here is a cup, pour the wine, let them hang me drunk." "But the shoes are ready." "What do you mean? Where are they?" The master ran to see them. "Ah," he said, "but when did we make them?" "In the night; don't you remember, master, how we cut and sewed them?" "I have been sound asleep, brother; I can barely remember anything."

The shoemaker took the shoes, wrapped them up, and ran to the palace. Elena the Fair saw the shoes and thought: "Surely, the spirits made them for Prince Ivan." Then she asked the shoemaker: "How did you make these?" "Oh," he said, "I can do everything." "If so, make me a wedding gown, and let it be embroidered with gold and studded with diamonds and precious stones. And let it be ready tomorrow morning, else your head will roll."

Again the shoemaker went home gloomy, and found that his friends had been waiting for him a long time. "Well, how was it?" they asked him. "What do you think?" he said. "Nothing but accursed trouble! The enemy of all Christian souls has come; she ordered me to make her a wedding gown with gold and precious stones for tomorrow. And am I a tailor? Surely my head will roll in the morning." "Eh, brother, the morning is wiser than the evening; let us go and revel."

They went to the alehouse and drank and reveled. Again the shoemaker got tipsy, dragged home a whole keg of wine, and said to Prince Ivan: "Well, little fellow, tomorrow when you wake me up I will swallow three gallons; let them cut off my head while I am drunk. Such a gown I could not make in a lifetime." The master lay down to sleep and soon was snoring. But Prince Ivan blew his reed pipe and Lame and One-eyed appeared. "What do you wish, prince?" they asked. "Let a gown be ready for tomorrow—exactly like the one Elena the Fair wore in Whirlwind's castle." "It will be ready."

384

At daybreak Prince Ivan awoke and the gown was lying on the table, gleaming like fire, illumining the whole room. He roused his master, who opened his sleepy eyes and said: "What is it? Have I been sent for to have my head cut off? The wine, quickly!" "But the gown is ready." "Impossible! When did we have time to sew it?" "In the night, of course; you yourself cut it." "Ah, brother, I can hardly remember it; I see it as though in a dream." The shoemaker took the gown and ran to the palace. Elena the Fair gave him much money and said: "Now see to it that by tomorrow at daybreak, seven versts out at sea, a golden palace stands, and that from it a golden bridge leads to our palace, and that the bridge is spread with precious velvet, and that at the railings on both sides marvelous trees are growing and singing birds singing in various voices. If you have not done all this by tomorrow, I shall order you to be quartered."

The shoemaker left Elena the Fair and his head hung low. His friends met him. "Well, brother?" they asked. "I am lost! Tomorrow I shall be quartered. She gave me such a task that no devil could do it." "Oh, stop worrying! The morning is wiser than the evening; let us go to the alehouse." "Yes, let us go; I should at least have a good time before I die." So they drank and drank; by night the shoemaker had drunk so much that he had to be led home. "Farewell, little fellow," he said to Prince Ivan, "tomorrow I shall be put to death." "Is there a new task to perform?" "Yes." And he told his journeyman what it was. Then the shoemaker lay down and began to snore. Prince Ivan went straight to his room, blew his reed pipe, and Lame and One-eyed appeared. "What do you wish, Prince Ivan?" they asked. "You must do this and this for me." "Yes, Prince Ivan, here at last is a real task! Well, what must be done must be done. Tomorrow everything will be ready."

Next morning at daybreak Prince Ivan woke up and looked out of the window. Heavens above! Everything was ready; the golden castle was gleaming like fire. He roused his master, who jumped up in haste. "What is it?" he said. "Have they come for me? Quick, some wine! Let me be drunk when they put me to death." "But the palace is ready." "What are you

385

saying?" The shoemaker looked out of the window and gasped in amazement. "How was it done?" "Don't you remember how we toiled together?" "Ah, I must have slept soundly; I can hardly remember." They ran to the golden palace and found in it wealth undreamed, unheard of. Prince Ivan said: "Here is a broom for you, master. Go and dust the railings of the bridge. And when anyone comes and asks you who lives in the palace, do not say anything, but give him this little note."

The shoemaker went to dust the railings of the bridge. In the morning Elena the Fair woke up, saw the golden palace, and ran straightway to the king. "Look, Your Majesty!" she said. "See what is happening here! a golden palace has been built on the sea. From the palace a bridge seven versts long reaches to here. Around the bridge there are marvelous trees, and songbirds are singing in many voices." The king at once sent men out to ask what all this meant, and whether there was not some mighty hero come to his kingdom. The messengers came to the shoemaker and began to question him. He said:

386

"I do not know the answer, but I have a letter for your king."
In this letter Prince Ivan told his father everything that had
happened: how he had rescued his mother and won Elena the
Fair, and how his older brothers had deceived him. With the
messengers Prince Ivan sent golden carriages and asked the
king and the queen, Elena the Fair, and her sisters to come to
him; and he asked that his brothers be brought behind them
in simple carts.

All of them made ready at once and set out; Prince Ivan
met them with joy. The king wanted to put his elder sons to
death for their perfidy, but Prince Ivan obtained pardon for
them from his father. Then a grand feast began: Prince Ivan
married Elena the Fair, the queen of the silver kingdom married Prince Piotr, and the queen of the copper kingdom
married Prince Vasily. The shoemaker was made a general.
I was at that feast and drank mead and wine; it ran down my
mustache but did not go into my mouth.

THE COCK AND THE HAND MILL

ONCE THERE LIVED an old man and his wife. They were
poor, very poor people. They had no bread; so they
went to the woods, gathered acorns, brought them home,
and began to eat them. They ate for a long time or a short time,
but at one point the old woman let an acorn fall and it dropped
into the cellar. The acorn struck root and in a short time grew
as high as the floor. The old woman noticed this and said:
"Old man, we must cut the floor. Let the oak grow higher; once
it has grown, we shall not have to go to the woods to pick acorns,
we shall gather them at home." The old man cut the floor; the
tree grew and grew till it reached the ceiling. The old man
hammered out the ceiling, and later removed the roof; the
tree kept on growing and growing till it reached the sky. The

old man and woman had by now eaten up their supply of acorns, so the old man took a bag and climbed up the tree.

He climbed and climbed and finally reached the sky. He walked and walked there and finally saw a little cock with a golden crest, a buttery head, and a hand mill stood near by. The old man did not think too much about it; he simply took the cock and the hand mill and climbed down to his house. When he reached the ground he said: "Now, old woman, what shall we do, what shall we eat?" "Wait," said the old woman, "let me try the hand mill." She took the hand mill and began to grind: at each turn a pancake and a pie came out, at each turn a pancake and a pie. And she fed the old man his fill.

A certain nobleman drove by and stopped at the old couple's house. "Do you have anything to eat?" he asked. The old woman said: "What shall I give you, my good man? Would you like some pancakes?" She took the hand mill and turned the handle: pancakes and pies fell out. The traveler ate them and said: "Grandmother, sell me your hand mill." "No," said the old woman, "it is not for sale." So the guest stole her hand mill. When the old man and woman discovered the theft, they began to grieve greatly. "Wait," said Little Cock Golden Crest, "I will fly after the thief and catch him." He came to the boyar's house, perched on the gate, and crowed: "Cock-a-doodle-doo! Boyar, boyar, give us back our sky blue golden hand mill! Boyar, boyar, give us back our sky blue golden hand mill!" When the boyar heard this he commanded: "Eh, little fellow, throw him into the water."

The cock was caught and thrown into the well. He began to say: "Little beak, little beak, drink the water! Little mouth, little mouth, drink the water!" And he drank all the water. Having drunk it he flew to the boyar's house, perched on the balcony, and crowed again: "Cock-a-doodle-doo! Boyar, boyar, give us back our sky blue golden hand mill! Boyar, boyar, give us back our sky blue golden hand mill!"

The boyar ordered the cook to throw him into a hot stove. The cock was caught and thrown into a hot stove, straight into the fire. And he began to say: "Little beak, little beak, pour water! Little mouth, little mouth, pour water!" and he

388

quenched all the fire in the stove. Then he took wing, flew into the boyar's room, and crowed again: "Cock-a-doodle-doo! Boyar, boyar, give us back our sky blue golden hand mill! Boyar, boyar, give us back our sky blue golden hand mill!" The guests heard him and ran away from the house; the master ran after them to bring them back; Little Cock Golden Crest snatched the hand mill and flew with it to the old man and woman.

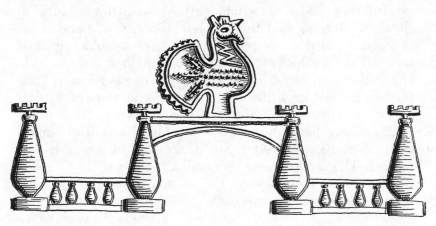

TERESHICHKA

AN OLD MAN and his wife led a miserable existence. They had lived together all of their lives, yet had no children. In their younger days they had managed somehow to struggle along; but now that they were old there was no one to give them drink, and they grieved and lamented. One day they cut a little block of wood, wrapped it in swaddling clothes, put it in a little cradle, and began to rock it and sing lullabies to it; and in place of the block of wood there began to grow in the swaddling clothes a little son, Tereshichka, a real little jewel.

The boy grew and grew and reached the age of reason. His father made him a little boat. Tereshichka went to catch fish and his mother brought him milk and curd cheese. She would go to the shore and call: "Tereshichka, my little son, sail, sail to the little shore; I, your mother, have brought you milk." Tereshichka would hear her voice from afar, sail to the shore, pour out his catch of fish, eat and drink, and go back to fish again. One day his mother told him: "My darling little son, be careful, Chuvilikha, the witch, is after you; do not fall into her clutches." Having said this she left. Chuvilikha came to the shore and called in a terrible voice: "Tereshichka, my little son, sail, sail to the little shore; I, your mother, have brought you milk." But Tereshichka was not deceived and said: "Sail farther, farther, my little boat! This is not the voice of my dear mother, but that of Chuvilikha, the wicked witch."

Chuvilikha heard him, ran away, found a skillful singing teacher, and got herself a voice like that of Tereshichka's mother. The mother came and called her son in a soft voice: "Tereshichka, my little son, sail, sail to the little shore; I, your mother, have brought you milk." Tereshichka heard her and said: "Sail closer, closer, my little boat; this is the voice of my dear mother." His mother gave him food and drink and he went again to fish. Chuvilikha, the witch, came, and chanted in the voice she had acquired, exactly like his own mother. Tereshichka was deceived and came close to shore; she snatched him, put him in a bag, and darted off. She came to a little hut on chicken legs, told her daughter to roast him, and left to get other booty. Tereshichka was not a fool; he did not let the girl hurt him. Instead, he put her to roast in the oven and climbed up a tall oak.

Chuvilikha came back, jumped into the house, ate and drank, went out into the courtyard, rolled and wallowed, and said: "I will roll and wallow, having eaten of Tereshichka's flesh." And he cried to her from the oak: "Roll, witch, wallow, witch, having eaten your own daughter's flesh!" She heard him, raised her head, looked in all directions—there was no one to be seen anywhere! Again she intoned: "I will roll and wallow, having eaten of Tereshichka's flesh." And he again answered:

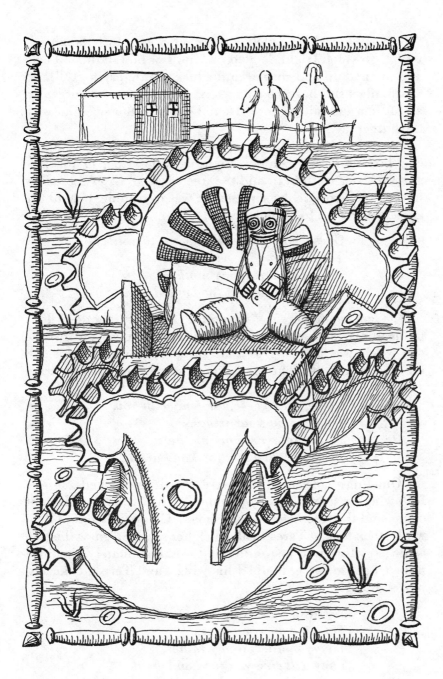

"Roll, witch, wallow, witch, having eaten your own daughter's flesh." She took fright, looked up, and saw him in the tall oak. She jumped up and rushed to the blacksmith, crying: "Blacksmith, blacksmith, forge me an ax!" The blacksmith forged an ax for her and said to her: "Do not cut with the edge but with the butt end."

She did as he had told her, knocked and knocked, cut and cut, but could not achieve anything. She clung to the tree and sank her teeth in it, and the tree cracked. Gray geese flew in the sky. Tereshichka saw that he was in trouble, beheld the geese, and began to implore them:

> *Geese, gray geese, take me with you!*
> *Take me on your wings*
> *To my father, to my mother,*
> *They will give you food and drink.*

The geese answered: "Qua-qua! There is another flock flying, hungrier than we, they will take you home!" Meanwhile the witch was gnawing so that splinters flew, and the oak cracked and shook. The second flock came. Tereshichka cried again:

> *Geese, gray geese, take me with you!*
> *Take me on your wings,*
> *To my father, to my mother,*
> *They will give you food and drink.*

"Qua-qua!" answered the geese. "A little plucked goose is following us, he will take you home!" The little goose did not come, and the tree cracked and shook. The witch would bite a while, then look at Tereshichka, lick her lips, and gnaw the tree again; any time now he would fall down. Fortunately, the little plucked goose came, flapped his wings, and Tereshichka implored him:

> *My little goose, take me with you!*
> *Take me on your wings*
> *To my mother, to my father,*
> *They will give you food and drink*
> *And wash you in clean water.*

The little plucked goose pitied him. They flew to the window of his own father's house and sat on the grass. Meanwhile the old woman had fried pancakes and had invited guests, and was serving Tereshichka's funeral repast, saying: "This pancake is for you, my little guest, and this one for you, my husband, and this one for me." Tereshichka said beneath the window: "And which one is for me?" "Look out, old man, who wants a pancake there?" the old woman asked. The old man went out, saw Tereshichka, took him in his arms, brought him to his mother—and hearty embraces were exchanged all around. As for the little plucked goose, he was given food and drink and set free. And thereafter he spread his wings wide, flew at the head of the flock, and remembered how he had rescued Tereshichka.

KING BEAR

ONCE THERE LIVED a tsar and a tsarina who had no children. One day the tsar went out to hunt fur-bearing animals and migratory birds. It was hot and he wanted to drink some water. He saw a well off to one side, approached it, bent over it, and was about to drink when King Bear seized him by the beard. "Let me go," begged the tsar. "Not unless you give me the thing in your own home that you do not know is there." "What is there in my own home that I don't know is there?" thought the tsar. "I think I know everything. I'd rather give you a herd of cows," he said. "No, I do not want even two herds." "Well, take a herd of horses." "Not even two herds; but give me the thing that you do not know is there in your own home."

The tsar agreed, released his beard, and rode home. As he entered the palace he was informed that his wife had given birth to twins, Prince Ivan and Princess Maria; they were what he had not known was in his own home. The tsar wrung his hands and wept bitterly. "Why are you so distressed?" the tsarina asked him. "How can I help weeping? I have given my own children to King Bear." "How did that happen?" "In such and such a manner," answered the tsar. "But we won't give them away!" "Oh, there is no way out of it! In the end he would destroy the whole kingdom, and take them none the less."

They thought and thought about what they should do and at last hit upon a plan. They dug a very deep ditch, furnished it, adorned it like a palace, and stored it with supplies of every sort and sufficient food and drink for a long sojourn. Then they put their children into the ditch, built a ceiling on top of it, threw earth over it, and leveled off the ground around it very smoothly.

Soon afterward the tsar and tsarina died. Their children grew bigger and bigger. Finally King Bear came for them. He looked everywhere—but no one was there! The palace was deserted. He walked and walked, went all over the house, and thought to himself: "Who will tell me where the tsar's children are?" Lo and behold, there was a chisel stuck in the wall. "Chisel, chisel," said King Bear, "tell me, where are the tsar's children?" "Take me out into the yard and cast me on the ground; where I stick, do you dig." King Bear took the chisel, went out into the yard, and cast it on the ground; the chisel turned, whirled, and stuck fast right above the place where Prince Ivan and Princess Maria were hidden. The bear dug up the earth with his paws, broke the ceiling, and said: "Ah, Prince Ivan, ah, Princess Maria. So there you are! So you were hiding from me! Your father and mother tried to cheat me, and in revenge I will eat you!" "Ah, King Bear, do not eat us! Many chickens and geese and other goods and chattels were left to us by our father; there is enough to satisfy you." "Well, so be it! Sit upon me; I will take you to be my servants."

They sat upon him, and King Bear carried them to such steep and high mountains that they seemed to be going up to the very sky; the place was utterly deserted, no one lived there. "We are hungry and thirsty," said Prince Ivan and Princess Maria. "I will run and get you something to eat and drink," answered the bear. "Meanwhile, you stay here and rest." The bear ran off to get food and the prince and princess stood there and wept. Out of nowhere, a bright falcon appeared, shook his wings, and said these words: "Ah, Prince Ivan and Princess Maria, what fate has brought you here?" They told him. "Why has the bear taken you?" "To serve him in various ways." "Do you want me to carry you away? Sit upon my wings." They seated themselves upon him; the bright falcon rose higher than standing trees, lower only than moving clouds, and set out for distant lands. At that moment King Bear came back, sighted the falcon in the skies, struck his head against the damp earth, and sent a flame straight to the falcon's wings. The falcon's wings were singed and he dropped the prince and princess on the ground. "Ah," said the bear, "so you wanted to flee from me; for that I will eat you up with all your little bones." "Do not eat us, King Bear; we shall serve you faithfully." The bear forgave them and took them to his own kingdom; there the mountains were even higher and steeper.

Some time, a short time or a long time, went by. "Ah," said Prince Ivan, "I am hungry." "I too," said Princess Maria. King Bear went off to get food and told them sternly to stay where they were. They sat on the green grass and wept bitter tears. From nowhere an eagle appeared; he dropped from behind the clouds and asked them: "Ah, Prince Ivan and Princess Maria, what fate has brought you here?" They told him. "Do you want me to carry you away?" "Impossible! The bright falcon tried to carry us away, but he could not, and you can't either!" "The falcon is a small bird; I will fly higher than he. Sit upon my wings." The prince and princess seated themselves upon him; the eagle spread his wings and soared higher than the falcon. The bear came back, sighted the eagle in the skies, struck his head against the damp earth, and singed the eagle's wings with a flame. The eagle dropped Prince Ivan and Princess Maria to the ground. "Ah, so you again tried to run away!" said the bear. "Now I will really eat you." "Do not eat us, please; the eagle lured us with false promises. We shall serve you in faith and in truth." King Bear forgave them for the last time, gave them food and drink, and took them farther away.

Some time, a short time or a long time, went by. "Ah," said Prince Ivan, "I am hungry." "I too," said Princess Maria. King Bear went off to get them some food. They sat on the green grass and wept. Out of nowhere appeared a bullock who waved his head and asked: "Prince Ivan, Princess Maria, what fate has brought you here?" They told him. "Do you want me to carry you away?" "Impossible! The falcon and the eagle tried to carry us away but could not; you can do it even less than they." And they were so drowned in tears that they could hardly speak. "The birds couldn't carry you away, but I will! Sit on my back." They mounted the bullock and he ran off at a not very fast pace. The bear saw that the prince and princess were trying to get away from him and rushed to pursue them. "Ah, bullock, bullock," cried the tsar's children, "the bear is after us." "Is he far behind us?" "No, quite close."

The bear jumped close to them and was about to seize them, but the bullock strained, and pasted the bear's eyes shut with dung. The bear rushed to the blue sea to wash his eyes, while the bullock ran on and on. After the bear had washed himself he again pursued them. "Ah, bullock, bullock! The bear is after us." "Is he far behind us?" "Oh no, quite close!" The bear jumped close to them, and again the bullock strained, and pasted the bear's eyes with dung. While the bear ran to wash them, the bullock kept on and on. He plastered the bear's eyes for the third time, and then gave Prince Ivan a comb and a towel and said: "When the bear comes close to us again, the first time cast the comb behind you and the second time wave the towel."

The bullock ran on, farther and farther. Prince Ivan looked back and saw that King Bear was pursuing them and was about to catch them! He took the comb and cast it behind him, and suddenly such a thick forest sprang up that through it bird could not fly nor beast crawl nor man walk nor horse gallop. The bear gnawed and gnawed; with great effort he gnawed out a very narrow path for himself, got through the thick forest, and rushed on in pursuit of the tsar's children; but they were far, far off! Finally the bear began to overtake them. Ivan Tsarevich looked back, waved the towel behind him, and suddenly a lake of fire spread out, immensely wide! The waves surged from one end to the other. King Bear stood some time on the shore, then turned back home. Soon the bullock and Prince Ivan and Princess Maria came to a glade.

In that glade stood a large and magnificent house. "Here is a house for you," said the bullock. "Live here without care. And now prepare a woodpile in the yard, slaughter me on it, and then burn me." "Ah," said the tsar's children, "why should we slaughter you? Rather, live with us; we will take care of you, feed you fresh grass, and bring you spring water to drink." "No, burn me and plant the ashes on three beds: from the first a horse will jump out, from the second a dog, and on the third an apple tree will grow. You, Prince Ivan, will ride on this horse, and with this dog go hunting." They did as he commanded.

One day Prince Ivan decided to go hunting; he said farewell to his sister, mounted his horse, and went to the woods. He killed a goose and a duck and caught a live wolf cub and brought it home. The young prince saw that he was lucky at hunting, so he went again, shot all kinds of game birds, and caught a live bear cub. The third time Prince Ivan went hunting, he forgot to take his dog with him. Meanwhile Princess Maria went to the lake to wash clothes. As she washed, a six-headed dragon came flying to the other shore of the lake of fire, changed into a handsome man, saw the princess, and said to her in a sweet voice: "Greetings, lovely maiden!" "Greetings, good youth!" "The old wives say that in former times this lake did not exist; if a high bridge spanned it, I would come to the other side and marry you." "Wait! A bridge will be here in a trice!" answered Princess Maria and waved her towel. In that instant the towel spread out in an arc and hung above the lake like a high and beautiful bridge. The dragon crossed it, changed into his former shape, put Prince Ivan's dog under lock and key, and cast the key into the lake; then he seized the princess and carried her off.

Prince Ivan came back from the hunt and found his sister gone, and the imprisoned dog howling; he saw the bridge across the lake and said: "A dragon must have carried Maria away!" He went to seek her. He walked and walked until, in an open field, he found a hut on chicken legs and dog's heels. "Little hut, little hut," he said, "turn your back to the woods and your front to me!" The hut turned around; Prince Ivan entered, and in it, stretched from corner to corner, lay Baba Yaga the Bony-legged, with her nose grown into the ceiling. "Fie, fie!" she said. "Hitherto one never heard a Russian breath, and now a Russian breath has come into view and thrusts itself under one's very nose! Why have you come, Prince Ivan?" "To ask your help in my misfortune." "And what is your misfortune?" The prince told her. "Well," she said, "go home. In your yard there is an apple tree. Break three green twigs from it, weave them together, and strike the lock where the dog is locked up; the lock will at once break into little pieces. Then go boldly forth to fight the dragon; he won't be able to resist you."

Prince Ivan returned home and freed his dog, who ran out in great anger. He also took the wolf cub and bear cub with him and set out against the dragon. When they found the dragon, the beasts threw themselves upon him and tore him to shreds. And Prince Ivan took Princess Maria home and they began to live happily together and to prosper.

MAGIC

ONCE THERE LIVED an old man and an old woman who had
a son. The old man was poor; he wanted to place the
boy as an apprentice, that he might rejoice his parents
in his youth, help them in their old age, and pray for their
souls after their death. But what could he do, having no wealth?
He led his son through many cities, hoping that someone would
take him as an apprentice; but no, no one wanted to take him
without being paid for it. The old man returned home, wept
and wept with his wife, grieved over his poverty, and again
led his son to the city.

They had no sooner come to the city than a man met them
and asked: "Why are you so sad, old man?" "How can I help
being sad?" said the old man. "I have been leading my son for
many months, but no one wants to teach him a trade without
being paid for it, and I have no money." "Give him to me,"
said the man. "In three years I will teach him all kinds of
crafts. And in three years, on the same day, at the same hour
as now, come for your son. But mind you: if you are not late,
if you come on time and recognize your son, you can have him
back. If you do not, he will have to remain with me." The old
man was so overjoyed that he did not ask who the man was,
where he lived, or what he would teach his son. He left his son
with him and went home. He returned joyfully and told his
wife all that had happened. But the man he had met was a
magician.

Three years went by; the old man had completely forgotten
on what day he had placed his son as an apprentice and did
not know what to do. But one day before the term was up the
son came flying to him in the shape of a little bird, struck the
mound of earth near the house, and entered as a goodly youth.
He bowed to his father and said that on the following day the
old man would have to come for him because the term of three
years would then be up; and he told his father where to come
and how to recognize him. "I am not my master's only appren-

399

tice," he said. "There are eleven others who have remained
with him forever because their parents could not recognize
them; and if you fail to recognize me, I shall be the twelfth to
remain with him forever. Tomorrow, when you come for me,
our master will set all twelve of us free in the shape of white
doves, all alike, feather for feather, tail for tail and head for
head. But do you look carefully: all of them will soar high, but
I will fly slightly higher than the others. The master will ask:
'Do you recognize your son?' Then do you point at the dove
that flies highest. Then he will lead twelve colts before you—
all of the same color, all with their manes on the same side,
and all alike. When you pass by these colts, watch carefully:
I will stamp my right foot. The master will ask again: 'Do you
recognize your son?' And do you point boldly at me. Then he
will lead twelve good youths before you, all alike, body for
body, hair for hair, voice for voice, all the same in face and
in dress. When you pass by these youths, watch carefully: a
little fly will sit on my right cheek. The master will ask you
again: 'Do you recognize your son?' And do you point at me."

He said all this, took leave of his father, and went forth from
the house, struck the mound of earth, turned into a bird, and
flew to his master. Next morning the old man arose, made
ready, and went for his son. He came to the magician. "Well,
old man," said the magician, "I have taught all kinds of crafts

400

to your son. But if you do not recognize him, he must stay with me for all eternity." Then he set free twelve white doves, all alike, feather for feather, tail for tail, head for head, and said: "Now find your son, old man!" How could he recognize his son, since the birds were all alike? He looked and looked, and when one dove soared higher than the others, he pointed at it, saying:

"I think this one is mine." "You have recognized him, old man," said the magician.

Next he led out twelve colts, all alike, with their manes on one side. The old man began to walk around the colts and to look, and the master asked him: "Well, grandfather, have you recognized your son?" "Not yet—wait a while," said the old man. But when he saw one colt stamping its right foot, he straightway pointed at it, saying: "I think this one is mine." "You have recognized him, old man." Finally, twelve good youths came forth, all alike, body for body, hair for hair, voice for voice, with faces all alike, as though they had been borne by one mother. The old man passed by the youths once and did not notice anything; he passed by a second time and still did not notice anything. But the third time he saw a fly sitting on the right cheek of one youth and said: "I think this one is mine." "You have recognized him, old man," said the master. The magician had no choice now; he gave the old man his son, and they went home together.

They walked and walked and saw a nobleman driving on the road. "Father," said the son, "I shall now turn into a dog. The nobleman will want to buy me; sell me, but do not sell my collar, for then I will not return to you." Having said this, he struck the earth and turned into a dog. The nobleman saw that the old man was leading a dog and began to bargain for it; he did not like the dog so much as he liked the collar. The nobleman offered a hundred rubles, the old man asked three hundred; they bargained and bargained, and in the end the nobleman bought the dog for two hundred rubles. When the old man began to remove the collar from the dog, the nobleman protested loudly; he insisted on having it. "I did not sell the collar," said the old man, "I sold only the dog." But the nobleman replied: "No, you are lying! He who bought the dog, bought him with his collar." The old man thought and thought that after all one cannot buy a dog without a collar, and gave it to the new owner. The nobleman put the dog in his carriage and the old man took the money and went home.

The nobleman drove and drove, when all of a sudden a hare ran across the road. "I will set the dog on the hare and see him run," thought the nobleman. He let the dog go and watched; the hare ran off on one side, the dog on the other, and both vanished into the woods. The nobleman waited and waited for the dog, then lost patience and went home with nothing, and the dog turned into a good youth. Meanwhile the old man walked and walked along the broad road thinking to himself: "How can I show myself at home, how can I tell my wife what I have done with my son?" Then his son overtook him. "Eh, father," he said, "why did you sell me with my collar? If we had not happened to meet a hare, I should never have returned, I should have been lost for nothing!"

They returned home and lived fairly comfortably. After a long time or a short time, the son said one Sunday to his father: "Father, I will turn into a bird. Do you take me to market and sell me; only do not sell my cage, for then I shall not return home." He struck the earth and turned into a bird; the old man put him in a cage and carried it to market. People thronged around the old man, vying with each other to buy the

402

bird, so greatly did he charm their souls. The magician also came, recognized the old man at once, and guessed what kind of bird was in his cage. One man offered a high price, another a still higher price, but the magician offered most of all. The old man sold him the bird but refused to give him the cage; the magician argued with him and insisted, but all to no avail. The buyer took the bird without the cage, wrapped it in a handkerchief, and took it home. "Well, little daughter," he said at home, "I have bought our rascal." "Where is he?" The magician opened his handkerchief, but the bird was gone—it had flown away.

Another Sunday came. The son said to his father: "Father, now I will turn into a horse. Mind you, sell the horse, but not the bridle; else I shall not return home." He struck the damp earth and turned into a horse; the old man led it to market. Horse dealers thronged around the old man; some offered a high price, others a still higher price, but the magician offered most of all. The old man sold him the horse but refused to give him the bridle. "How shall I lead the horse?" said the magician. "Let me bring him to my yard at least, and then you can have your bridle; I won't need it." All the horse dealers began to remonstrate with the old man, saying that this was the custom—that if he sold the horse, he also had to sell the bridle. What could he do? He gave away the bridle.

The magician brought the horse to his courtyard, put it in a stable, tethered it firmly to a ring, and stretched its head up high. The horse stood only on its hind legs; its forelegs did not touch the ground. "Well, daughter," the magician said again, "this time I have bought our rascal." "Where is he?" "In the stable." The daughter ran to see him; she took pity on the goodly youth, she wanted to loosen the reins, and began to disentangle and untie them. The horse wrested himself free and ran away. The daughter rushed to her father. "Father," she said, "forgive me! An evil thought confused me, the horse ran away."

The magician struck the damp earth, turned into a gray wolf, and ran in pursuit; he was close behind the horse now—at any moment he would overtake him. The horse came to a river, struck the ground, turned into a perch, and—plop!—into the water he jumped. But the wolf plunged after him in the shape of a pike. The perch swam and swam, came near to a jetty where lovely maidens were washing linen, turned into a golden ring, and rolled to the feet of a merchant's daughter. The merchant's daughter picked up the ring and hid it. The magician again turned into a man and said to her: "Give me back my golden ring." "Take it!" said the maiden and threw the ring on the ground. When it struck the ground, it shattered into tiny seeds of grain. The magician turned into a cock and rushed to peck the grain; while he pecked it, one seed of grain turned into a hawk. And that was too bad for the cock: the hawk tore him to pieces!

This is the end of my tale, and now I would not mind having a glass of vodka.

THE ONE-EYED EVIL

ONCE THERE WAS a blacksmith. "How is it," he said, "that I have never seen trouble? It is said that there is evil in the world; I will go and search for it." No sooner said than done; he drank heartily and went forth in search of evil. He met a tailor. "Good day," the blacksmith said. "Good day. Where are you going?" "Well, brother, everyone says that there is evil in the world; I have never seen it, so I am searching for it." "Let us go together. I too live well and have never seen evil; let us go and look for it." They walked and walked, till they came to a forest, deep and dark; they found a little path and walked along it. They walked and walked along this narrow path, and finally they beheld a big hut. It was night, they had no shelter. "Let us go into this house," they said. They entered; no one was there, it was empty and uncomfortable.

They sat down and waited. In came a tall woman, scrawny, crooked, one-eyed. "Aha," she said, "I have guests. Good evening!" "Good evening, grandmother! We have come to spend the night in your house." "That is fine; I will get something for supper." They took fright. She went out and brought in a huge load of wood; she put it in the stove and made a fire. She came to them, took one of them, the tailor, slew him, and put him to roast in the oven.

The blacksmith sat there and wondered what he could do. She ate her supper. The blacksmith looked into the stove and said: "Grandmother, I am a blacksmith." "What can you forge?" "I can forge everything." "Then forge me an eye." "I will," he said. "But do you have a piece of rope? For I must tie you, otherwise you will resist." She brought two ropes, one thick and the other thin. He tied her with the thin rope. "Now, grandmother, turn around." She turned around and broke the rope. "No," he said, "this piece is no good." He took the thick rope and fastened her tightly with it. "Turn around, grandmother!" She turned and this time did not break the rope. He took an awl, heated it, put it on her good eye, took an ax, and drove in the awl with the butt of it. She gave a turn, broke the rope, and sat on the threshold. "Ah, you scoundrel, now you won't get away from me!"

He saw that things looked bad for him and sat wondering what he could do. Later sheep came from the field; the woman drove them into her house to spend the night. The blacksmith also slept there. In the morning she began to let out the sheep. He took a sheepskin, turned the wool side out, put his arms through the sleeves, and crawled toward her like a sheep. She let out the sheep one by one, seizing them roughly by their rumps and throwing them out. Now the blacksmith came up to her; she seized him too by his rump and threw him out. When he was outside, he got up and said: "Farewell, Evil! I have suffered evil from you, but now you cannot do anything to me." She said: "Wait, you will still suffer; you have not got away yet."

The blacksmith again followed the narrow path in the forest. He saw an ax with a golden handle stuck into a tree and wanted to take it. When he seized this ax, his hand stuck to it. What could he do? There was no way of wresting his hand free. He looked back; Evil was coming up to him, crying: "There you are, you scoundrel, you have not got away!" The blacksmith took out a knife that he had in his pocket and began to saw his wrist; he cut off his hand and went away. He came back to his village and showed his stump to everybody as proof that he had seen evil. "See what it is like," he said. "It has left me without a hand and it ate up my companion altogether."

And that is the end of my tale.

SISTER ALIONUSHKA,
BROTHER IVANUSHKA

ONCE THERE LIVED a king and a queen; they had a son and a daughter, called Ivanushka and Alionushka. When their parents died the children remained alone and went wandering in the wide world. They walked and walked and walked till they saw a pond, and near the pond a herd of cows was grazing. "I am thirsty," said Ivanushka. "I want to drink." "Do not drink, little brother, or you will become a calf," said Alionushka. The brother heeded her and they went on farther; they walked and walked and saw a river, and near it a drove of horses. "Ah, little sister," Ivanushka said, "if you only knew how thirsty I am!" "Do not drink, little brother, or you will become a colt." Ivanushka heeded her, and they went on farther; they walked and walked and saw a lake, and near it a flock of sheep. "Ah, little sister, I am terribly thirsty," Ivanushka said. "Do not drink, little brother, or you will become a sheep." Ivanushka heeded her and they went on farther; they walked and walked and saw a stream, and near it pigs were feeding. "Ah, little sister, I must drink," Ivanushka said. "I am frightfully thirsty." "Do not drink, little brother, or you will become a piglet." Ivanushka heeded her again and they went on farther; they walked and walked and saw a flock of goats grazing near a well. "Ah, little sister, now I must drink," Ivanushka said. "Do not drink, little brother, or you will become a kid." But he could not restrain himself and did not heed his sister; he drank from the well, and became a kid. He leaped before Alionushka and cried: "Maa-ka-ka! maa-ka-ka!"

Alionushka tied him with a silken belt and led him on, shedding tears, bitter tears. The kid ran and ran till he ran into the garden of a certain king. The servants saw him and at once reported to the king. "Your Majesty," they said, "in our garden there is a kid; a maiden is leading him on a belt, and she is a great beauty." The king ordered them to find out who she was. The servants asked her whence she came and of what parentage she was. "There were a king and a queen and they died," said Alionushka. "We children remained—I, the princess, and my little brother, the prince. He could not restrain himself, drank water from a well, and became a kid." The servants reported all this to the king. He called Alionushka before him and questioned her about everything; she pleased him and he wanted to marry her. Soon they celebrated their wedding and began to live together, and the kid lived with them; he walked in the garden and ate and drank with the king and queen.

One day the king went hunting. While he was away a sorceress came and cast a spell on the queen; Alionushka fell ill and became thin and pale. Everything became gloomy at the king's palace; the flowers in the garden began to fade, the trees to dry, and the grass to wither. The king returned and asked the

queen: "Are you sick?" "Yes, I am sick," answered the queen.
Next day the king again went hunting. Alionushka lay ill; the
sorceress came to her and said: "Do you want me to heal you?
Go to such and such a sea at twilight and drink water there."
The queen heeded her and at twilight went to that sea. The
sorceress was waiting for her, seized her, tied a stone around
her neck, and cast her into the sea. Alionushka sank to the
bottom; the kid ran to the shore and wept bitterly. But the sorceress turned herself into the likeness of the queen and went
back to the palace.

The king came home and was overjoyed to find that the
queen was well again. They set the table and began to dine.
"But where is the kid?" asked the king. "We don't want him
with us," said the sorceress. "I gave orders that he be shut out;
he has a goatlike smell." Next day, as soon as the king went
hunting, the sorceress beat and beat the kid and threatened:
"When the king returns I will ask him to slaughter you." The
king returned and the sorceress begged him over and over again
to have the kid slaughtered. "I am annoyed with him, I am
tired of him," she said. The king pitied the kid, but there was
nothing to be done; the queen insisted and urged him so much
that in the end he consented and gave leave to have the kid
slaughtered. The kid saw that steel knives were being sharpened for him, and he wept. He ran to the king and implored
him: "King, give me leave to go to the sea, to drink water, to
rinse my insides." The king let him go. The kid ran to the sea,
stood on the shore, and cried plaintively:

> *Alionushka, my little sister,*
> *Come up, come up to the shore.*
> *Hot fires are burning,*
> *Big kettles are boiling,*
> *Steel knives are being sharpened—*
> *They want to slaughter me!*

She answered him:

> *Ivanushka, my little brother,*
> *The heavy stone is pulling me down,*
> *The cruel serpent has sucked out my heart.*

The kid wept and returned home. In the middle of the day he again asked the king: "King, give me leave to go to the sea, to drink water and rinse my insides." The king allowed him to go. The kid ran to the sea and cried plaintively:

> *Alionushka, my little sister,*
> *Come up, come up to the shore.*
> *Hot fires are burning,*
> *Big kettles are boiling,*
> *Steel knives are being sharpened—*
> *They want to slaughter me!*

She answered him:

> *Ivanushka, my little brother,*
> *The heavy stone is pulling me down,*
> *The cruel serpent has sucked out my heart.*

The kid wept and returned home. The king wondered why the kid kept running to the sea. Now the kid asked him for the third time: "King, give me leave to go to the sea, to drink water and rinse my insides." The king let him go and followed him. When he came to the sea he heard the kid calling to his sister:

> *Alionushka, my little sister,*
> *Come up, come up to the shore.*
> *Hot fires are burning,*
> *Big kettles are boiling,*
> *Steel knives are being sharpened—*
> *They want to slaughter me!*

She answered him:

> *Ivanushka, my little brother,*
> *The heavy stone is pulling me down,*
> *The cruel serpent has sucked out my heart.*

The kid again called to his sister. Alionushka swam up and came to the surface. The king snatched her, tore the stone from her neck, pulled her ashore, and asked her how all this had happened. She told him everything. The king was overjoyed and so also was the kid; he capered, and everything in the garden grew green and blossomed again. The king ordered the sorceress to be put to death; a stake of wood was set up in the courtyard and she was burned. After that the king, the queen, and the kid began to live happily and to prosper and to eat and drink together as before.

THE SEVEN SEMYONS

A WEALTHY OLD PEASANT had neither son nor daughter; he began to pray to God that he send him at least one child to rejoice him in his lifetime and succeed him after his death. One day seven sons were born to him and they were all called Semyon. God did not grant it to them to grow up under the care of their father and mother; the Semyons were left orphans. Now, it is well known what an orphan's life is: although he is little and has not yet a man's wisdom, he will follow every trail, try every task. And so it was with the Semyons. When harvest time came, people busied themselves, they mowed and reaped and brought grain to the threshing barn, and then the earth had to be plowed up and winter grain had to be sown. The Semyons thought and thought, and although they had no strength, they went with the people to the wide fields and dug there like worms. The tsar drove by and was surprised to see little children working beyond their strength. He called them to him, began to question them, and learned that they had neither father nor mother. "I will be your father," said the tsar. "Tell me, what trade you wish to practice?" The eldest Semyon answered: "Sire, I will be a smith and I will forge a pillar such as no tongue can tell of nor pen describe. It will almost reach the sky."

"And I," answered the second Semyon, "will climb that pillar and look around in all directions, and tell you what is going on in foreign lands and kingdoms." The tsar praised him. The third Semyon answered: "I will be a shipwright and

410

make a ship." "Good!" The fourth said: "I will steer the ship and be her helmsman." "Good." The fifth said: "And I, if need be, will take the ship by its prow and hide it on the bottom of the sea." The sixth said: "And if need be, I will bring it back from the bottom of the sea." "All of you want to be useful people," said the tsar. "But you," he went on, turning to the youngest, "what trade do you want to learn?" "Sire, I will be a thief." "Oh, that is an evil project! I need no thieves, I will put a thief to death." The sovereign said farewell to the children and left, having bound the Semyons as apprentices. After a long time they grew up and learned the trades they had chosen; the sovereign summoned them to him to try their skill, test their art, and examine their learning.

The blacksmith forged such a pillar that if you threw your head back to look at its top your neck hurt, for it almost reached the sky. The tsar praised him. The second brother climbed to the top of the pillar as quickly as a squirrel and looked in all directions; all the lands and kingdoms were open before him, and he began to tell what was happening in them. "And in such and such a land, in such and such a kingdom," he said, "there lives Princess Elena the Fair, of such a beauty as has never before been seen: blood red color spreads on her face, white down spreads on her breast, and one can see how her marrow flows from bone to bone." The tsar liked that best of all. The third brother hammered—bing bang!—and built a ship as beautiful as a house. The tsar was overjoyed. The fourth brother began to steer the ship; the ship ran on the sea like a live fish. The tsar was highly pleased. The fifth seized the ship in full flight, pulled it by the prow, and it went to the bottom of the sea. In one minute the sixth brother pulled it back from the bottom of the sea, like a light boat, and the ship was afloat again as though nothing had happened. The tsar liked this trick too.

But for the youngest brother, the thief, a gallows was erected and a noose was made. The tsar asked him: "Are you as skilled in your trade as your brothers are in theirs?" "I am even more skillful than they." He was about to be strung up on the gallows

412

when he cried: "Wait, Your Majesty! Perhaps I will be useful to you. Order me to steal Elena the Fair for you; but let my brothers come with me. I will sail with them in the new ship, and Princess Elena will be yours." The tsar could not get Elena the Fair out of his head, he had heard much good about her, and his heart yearned for her; but she lived far away, beyond the thrice ninth land, in the thrice tenth kingdom. The thief's project seemed good; although one could not rely on his courage, one could try him, thought the tsar. So he gave leave to the thief and his brothers to sail, and the new ship was laden with riches of every description.

Whether they sailed for a long time or a short time is not known, but they finally arrived in the kingdom where Princess Elena the Fair lived. It was not necessary to tell the thief what to say and how to go about his business. He found out everything. Having learned that there were no cats in that land, he dressed as a merchant and took a kitten with him; stroking and caressing it, he led it on a golden cord past the window of Elena the Fair. The princess saw the pretty little beast, liked it, and ordered it to be bought for her. The thief answered that he was a wealthy merchant, that he had come from the wealthiest kingdom, bringing all kinds of rarities and jewels, and that he wished to show his good will to Elena the Fair by giving her the kitten as a gift. The thief was invited to the palace; the cat performed various tricks and the princess admired them. The thief spoke so much about his extraordinary rarities, brought and spread before her such marvelous cloths, such magnificent finery, that she could not take her eyes away from them.

"But this is nothing compared to what I still have," he said. "These things I can show to anyone, whoever wants can buy them. But you, princess, would you like to see a priceless treasure that no one has seen? It is aboard my ship under heavy guard and I will show it only to you. It replaces fire by night and the sun by day, and illumines every dark spot with a marvelous light. It is a stone of extraordinary beauty; and I cannot take it out—to show it would be to doom myself, for everyone would want to possess it. I paid a high price to get it;

413

but even dearer to me is the favor of my tsar, to whom I am bringing this marvel as a gift." The princess promised to visit the ship and look at the treasure.

Next day, accompanied by nurses, governesses, and maids-in-waiting, she went from the palace to the ship. All her retinue remained on shore; only Elena was to be allowed to see the marvelous light of the incomparable stone. Everything had been prepared for her reception; the other Semyons were there to help, and as soon as she was aboard ship, the fifth brother seized the ship by the prow and brought it down to the bottom of the sea. The water seethed and swirled, and then the waves rolled as before, as though nothing had happened; only on shore the nurses and governesses and maids-in-waiting wailed and wept, and the king, Elena's father, sent men in pursuit of the princess. But they all returned empty-handed. Elena the Fair sailed far on the blue sea. The sixth brother brought the ship back to the surface; it sailed like a swan rolling on the waves, and soon came to the shores of the Semyons' native land. The tsar was overjoyed; he had not even dreamed of ever receiving Elena the Fair in his own house. He generously rewarded the Semyons, exempted them from land rent and head taxes; and he married Elena the Fair and gave a feast for all to enjoy.

I walked a thousand versts only to be there. I drank beer and mead; it ran down my mustache but did not go into my mouth. I was given a horse made of ice, a saddle of turnip, and a bridle of peas; a flowing robe was put on my back and an embroidered cap on my head. I went forth in all this attire and stopped to rest; I removed the saddle and the bridle, tied the horse to a tree, and lay down on the grass. Suddenly pigs came and ate the saddle of turnip; chickens came and pecked the bridle of peas; the sun rose and melted the horse of ice. Grieved, I continued on foot. As I walked along the road, a magpie jumped to my side and cawed: "Flowing robe, flowing robe!" I fancied that she said, "Throw the robe," so I removed it and threw it away. "And do I need the embroidered cap?" I thought. I snatched it off and threw it down, and, as you can see, was left with nothing at all.

THE MERCHANT'S DAUGHTER
AND THE SLANDERER

ONCE THERE WAS a merchant who had two children, a daughter and a son. When the merchant was on his deathbed (his wife had been taken to the graveyard before him) he said: "My children, live well with each other, in love and concord, just as I lived with your deceased mother." Then he died. He was buried and prayers were said for the repose of his soul, as is fitting. Shortly afterward, the merchant's son decided to trade beyond the sea; he rigged up three ships, loaded them with a variety of goods, and said to his sister: "Now, my beloved sister, I am going on a long voyage and leaving you at home all alone; mind you, behave properly, do not engage in evil things, and do not consort with strangers."

Then they exchanged portraits; the sister took her brother's portrait, the brother took his sister's. They wept as they took leave of each other and said farewell.

The merchant's son raised anchor, pushed off from shore, hoisted sail, and reached the open sea. He sailed for one year, he sailed for another year, and in the third year he came to a certain wealthy capital and anchored his ships in the port. As soon as he arrived he took a bowl full of precious stones and rolls of his best velvet, damask, and satin, and took them to the king of those parts as a gift. He came to the palace, gave his gift to the king, and petitioned for leave to trade in his capital. The precious gift was to the king's liking and he said to the merchant's son: "Your gift is munificent; in all my life I have never received a finer one. In return I grant you the first place on the market. Buy and sell, fear no one, and if anyone injures you, come straight to me. Tomorrow I myself will visit your ship."

Next day the king came to the merchant's son, began to walk on his ship and examine his goods, and in the master's cabin saw a portrait hanging on the wall. He asked the merchant's son: "Whose portrait is that?" "My sister's, Your Majesty." "Well, Mr. Merchant, such a beauty I have not seen in all my days. Tell me the truth: what is her character and what are her manners?" "She is quiet and chaste as a dove." "Well, if so, she will be a queen; I will take her to wife." At that time, a certain general who was spiteful and envious was with the king; at the thought that anyone else might find happiness he choked with rage.

He heard the king's words and became terribly angry. "Now," he thought, "our wives will have to bow to a woman of the merchant class!" He could not restrain himself and said to the king: "Your Majesty, do not order me to be put to death, order me to speak." "Speak." "This merchant's daughter is not a suitable match for you; I met her long ago, and more than once I lay on the bed and played amorous games with her; she is quite a dissolute girl." "How can you, foreign merchant, say that she is quiet and chaste as a dove, and that she never engages in evil things?" "Your Majesty, if the general is not lying, let him get my sister's ring from her and find out what is her secret mark." "Very well," said the king, and he gave the general a furlough. "If you fail to get the ring and tell me the secret mark by such and such a day, your head shall fall by my sword."

The general made ready and went to the town where the merchant's daughter lived; he arrived and did not know what to do. He walked back and forth in the streets, low in spirits and thoughtful. He happened to meet an old woman who begged for alms; he gave her something. She asked: "What are you thinking about?" "Why should I tell you? You cannot help me in my trouble." "Who knows? Perhaps I can help you." "Do you know where such and such a merchant's daughter lives?" "Of course I do." "If so, get me her ring and find out what is her secret mark; if you do this for me, I shall reward you with gold." The old woman hobbled to the merchant's daughter, knocked at her door, said that she was going to the Holy Land, and asked for alms. She spoke so cunningly that the lovely maiden became quite bewitched and did not realize that she had blurted out where her secret mark was; and while all this talk was going on, the old woman slipped the girl's ring from the table and hid it in her sleeve. Then she said farewell to the merchant's daughter and ran to the general. She gave him the ring and said: "Her secret mark is a golden hair under her left arm."

The general rewarded her liberally and set out on his way back. He came to his kingdom and reported to the palace; and the merchant's son was there too. "Well," asked the king, "have you got the ring?" "Here it is, Your Majesty." "And what is the merchant's daughter's secret mark?" "A golden hair under her left arm." "Is that correct?" asked the king of the merchant's son. "It is, Your Majesty." "Then how dared you lie to me? For this I will order you put to death." "Your Majesty, do not refuse me one favor. Give me leave to write a letter to my sister; let her come and say farewell to me." "Very well," said the king, "write to her, but I won't wait long." He postponed the execution and in the meantime ordered that the young man be put in chains and thrown into a dungeon.

The merchant's daughter, upon receiving her brother's letter, set out immediately. As she traveled she knitted a golden glove and wept bitterly; her tears fell as diamonds, and she gathered these diamonds and studded the glove with them. She arrived in the capital, rented an apartment in the house of a poor widow, and asked: "What is the news in your city?" "There is no news except that a foreign merchant is being made to suffer because of his sister; tomorrow he will be hanged." Next morning the merchant's daughter arose, hired a carriage, donned a rich garment, and went to the square. There the gallows was ready, troops were standing guard, and a great multitude of people had gathered; and now they led out her brother. She got out of the carriage, went straight to the king, handed him the glove that she had knitted on her way, and said: "Your Majesty, I beg of you, estimate what such a glove is worth." The king examined it. "Ah," he said, "it is priceless!" "Well, your general was in my house and stole a glove exactly like it, the other of the pair; please order that a search be made for it."

The king summoned the general, and said to him: "There is a complaint against you that you stole a precious glove." The general began to swear that he knew nothing about it. "What do you mean, you don't know?" said the merchant's daughter. "You have been in my house so many times, lain with me on the bed, played amorous games with me." "But I have never seen you before! I have never been in your house, and not for anything in the world could I say at this moment who you are or whence you have come." "If so, Your Majesty, why is my brother made to suffer?" "Which brother?" asked the king. "The one who is now being led to the gallows." Thus the truth became known. The king ordered the merchant's son to be released and the general to be hanged; and himself sat in the carriage with the lovely maiden, the merchant's daughter, and drove to the church. They married, made a great feast, began to live in happiness and prosperity, and are still living to this very day.

THE ROBBERS

ONCE THERE LIVED a priest and his wife; they had a daughter named Alionushka. One day the priest was called to a wedding; he made ready to go with his wife and left his daughter at home. "Mother, I am afraid to stay alone," said Alionushka to her mother. "Invite your friends to sit with you, then you won't be alone," said her mother. The priest and his wife left and Alionushka gathered her friends together; many came with their work—some knitted, some made lace, some brought spinning. One maiden inadvertently dropped a spindle; it rolled away and fell through a crack straight into the cellar. She went to the cellar to get her spindle, and saw a robber sitting behind a tub and threatening her with one finger. "Mind you," he said, "don't tell anyone that I am here, or you won't live much longer." She climbed out of the cellar, pale as ashes, told everything in a whisper to one friend. That friend told it to another, and this last to still another; all of them were frightened and began to make ready to go home. "Where are you going?" Alionushka asked them. "Wait, it is still early." Some said that they had to fetch water, some that they wanted to bring cloth to a neighbor, and all of them left. Alionushka remained alone.

The robber realized that everything had become quiet, came

out of the cellar, and said: "Good evening, lovely maiden, queen of cake bakers!" "Good evening," said Alionushka. The robber examined everything in the house and then went to look over the yard, and Alionushka quickly closed the door and put out the light. The robber knocked at the door. "Let me in," he called, "or I will slay you." "I won't let you in! If you wish to get in, climb through the window," she said, and armed herself with an ax. As soon as the robber put his head through the window she swung her ax and cut off his head. Then she began to wonder: soon the other robbers would come, his companions—what should she do then? She took the severed head and tied it in a bag; then she dragged in the slain robber, cut him in pieces, and put the pieces into various bags and pots.

After some time, the other robbers came and asked: "Have you done it?" They thought that their companion was alive. "I have," answered Alionushka in the robber's voice. "Here are two bagfuls of money, and here is a crock of butter, and here is a ham." And she handed to them, through the window, the bags and pots she had prepared. The robbers took them all and loaded them onto their cart. "Now let us go," they said. "Go ahead," said Alionushka. "I want to see whether there is anything else left." They went.

Daybreak came. The priest and his wife returned from the wedding. She told them everything that had happened. "So I myself overcame the robbers," she said. Meanwhile the robbers reached home, and when they opened the bags and pots they gasped. "Ah, what a woman!" they said. "Very well then, we shall destroy her." They dressed themselves in fine garments and came to the priest to woo Alionushka; they had chosen a little fool for her groom and had dressed him up too. Alionushka recognized them by their voices and said to her father: "Father, these are not matchmakers, these are the same robbers who were here before." "Why do you lie?" said the priest. "Look how well dressed they are!" He was glad that such fine people had come to woo his daughter and that they did not ask for a dowry. Alionushka wept, but to no avail. "We will drive you out of our home if you refuse to be married," said the priest and his wife. They gave her in marriage to the robber groom and celebrated the wedding. It was a most luxurious feast.

The robbers set out for their house with Alionushka and as soon as they entered the forest, they said: "Well, shall we put her to death right here?" But the little fool said: "Let her live for at least a day, so that I may look at her." "What do you want to look at her for, you fool?" "Please, brothers!" The robbers consented, drove on, and took Alionushka to their house. They drank and drank, reveled and reveled, and then said: "Well, now it is time to put her to death." But the fool said: "Let me spend at least one night with her." "No, fool, she might run away." "Please, brothers!" The robbers yielded to his entreaty and left them in a separate room.

Alionushka said to her husband: "Let me out into the yard, I want to get a breath of fresh air." "But what if my companions hear you?" "I'll be quiet; let me out by the window." "I would be glad to let you, but suppose you run away?" "Then tie me. I have a good piece of linen that my mother gave me; tie the linen around me and drop me down, and when you pull I will climb back to the window." The fool tied her with the linen. When he dropped her, she quickly untied herself and tied a she-goat to the linen in place of herself. After a while she said: "Pull me back!" And she ran away.

The fool pulled, and the goat said: "Maa-ka-ka!" Each time he pulled, the goat said: "Maa-ka-ka!" "Why do you bleat?" said the bridegroom. "My friends will hear you and destroy you at once." When he pulled the linen in, he was surprised to see a goat attached to it. The fool was frightened and did not know what to do. "Ah, the accursed woman, she has deceived me!" he said. Next morning the robbers came into his room. "Where is your bride?" they asked him. "She ran away." "Ah, you fool, you fool! We told you so in the first place."

They mounted their horses and galloped after Alionushka; they rode with hounds, cracked their whips, and whistled—it was dreadful to hear them! Alionushka heard her pursuers and climbed into the hollow trunk of a dry oak; she sat there half dead and half alive, while the hounds circled and circled around the oak. "Isn't she there?" one robber said to another.

"Thrust your knife in!" He thrust his knife into the tree hole and struck Alionushka's knee. But she was a clever girl; she seized a handkerchief and wiped off the knife. The robber looked at his knife and said: "No, there is nothing there." Again they galloped in various directions, whistling and cracking their whips.

When everything grew quiet, Alionushka climbed out of the tree trunk and ran; she ran and ran and heard her pursuers once more. On the road she saw a peasant driving, with troughs and wooden trays on his cart. "Little uncle, hide me under a trough!" she besought him. "Eh, but you're so well dressed! You'll get all dirty." "Please, hide me! Robbers are pursuing me." The peasant untied his troughs, put her under the lowest, and tied them together again. He had hardly finished when the robbers arrived. "Peasant, have you not seen such and such a woman?" "I have not, my friends." "You lie! Throw down your troughs!" He began to throw down the troughs and now only one was left, the last. "It's no use to look for her here, brothers. Let us ride on farther," said the robbers, and galloped away yelling, whistling, and cracking their whips.

When everything grew quiet, Alionushka said: "Little uncle, let me out." The peasant let her out and she ran on again; she ran and ran and again heard her pursuers. On the road she beheld a peasant driving a cart loaded with skins. "Little uncle," she implored him, "hide me under your skins. Robbers are pursuing me." "Eh, but you're so well dressed! Under the skins you'll get all dirty." "Never mind, only hide me!" The peasant untied his skins, put her under the lowest, and tied them up as before. He had hardly finished when the robbers arrived. "Peasant, have you not seen such and such a woman?" "I have not, my friends." "You lie! Throw down your skins." "Why, my friends, should I throw down my possessions?" The robbers fell to throwing down the skins themselves and threw down almost all of them; only two or three were left. "It's no use looking for her here, brothers; let us ride on farther," they said, and galloped away yelling, whistling, and cracking their whips.

When all this tumult and thunder had died away, she said:

422

"Little uncle, let me go." The peasant let her go and she ran again; she ran and ran, came home at midnight, lay in a haystack, buried herself in it completely, and fell asleep. At daybreak, the priest went to give hay to the cows, and the moment he thrust his fork into the stack, Alionushka seized it with her hands. The priest took fright, crossed himself, and said: "Good Heavens! Lord have pity on us!" Then he asked: "Who is there?" Alionushka recognized her father and crawled out of the hay. "How did you get in there?" "In such and such a manner. You married me among robbers; they wanted to kill me, but I ran away." And she told him all her adventures. After a while the robbers came to the priest, who had hidden Alionushka. He asked: "Is my daughter safe and sound?" "Thank God, she stayed at home to look after the house," said the robbers, and they seated themselves as though they were guests. Meanwhile the priest had gathered troops. He led out his daughter and said: "And who is this?" The robbers were seized, tied, and thrown into prison.

THE LAZY MAIDEN

IN A CERTAIN VILLAGE there was a maiden, a lazybones and idler who did not like to work but only to chatter and gossip. One day she decided to invite some girls to spin in her house. As is well known, in the villages lazybones always invite girls to spin in their houses, and a girl with a sweet tooth is always glad to be invited. So the Lazybones gathered spinners for a night; they spun for her and she fed and entertained them. Little by little the conversation began to turn on the subject of who of them was the boldest. Lazybones said: "I am not afraid of anything!" "If you don't fear anything," said the spinners, "go to the church, past the graveyard, take the icon from the gate, and bring it here." "I will, but in the meantime let every one of you spin a measure of yarn for me." She never missed an opportunity to do nothing herself and to let others work for her. So she went, took down the icon, and brought it back to them. Well, the other girls saw that it really was the icon from the church. Now the icon had to be taken back, and midnight was drawing near. Who would take it? The Lazybones said: "You, girls, spin; I will take it back myself, I am not afraid of anything."

She went and put the icon back in its place. As she walked back past the graveyard she beheld a corpse in a white shroud sitting on a grave. It was a moonlit night, everything was clearly visible. She came close to the corpse and dragged off his shroud; the corpse did not say anything; he was silent, apparently the time had not come for him to speak. So she took the shroud and came home. "Well," she said, "I took back the icon and put it in its place, and I also pulled a shroud off a corpse." Some of the girls were frightened, others refused to believe it and giggled. As soon as they had eaten supper and gone to bed, the corpse suddenly knocked at the window and said: "Give me back my shroud! Give me back my shroud!" The other girls were half dead with fright, but Lazybones took the shroud, went to the window, and opened it. "There it is!" she said. "Take it." "No," said the corpse, "bring it back whence you took it." Suddenly the cocks began to crow and the corpse vanished.

The next night all the spinners had gone to their homes; and at the same hour the corpse came again and knocked at the window. "Give me back my shroud," he said. Lazybones' father and mother opened the window and handed him the shroud. "No," he said, "let her bring it back whence she took it." But how could one go with a corpse to the graveyard? It was frightening! As soon as the cocks crowed the corpse vanished.

Next day the father and mother sent for the priest, told him everything, and asked him for help in their trouble. "Could you not," they said, "celebrate a mass?" The priest thought for a while and said: "That might be good! Tell her to come to mass tomorrow." Next morning Lazybones went to mass; the

424

service began, and there was a great crowd of people. The moment they began to sing the Gloria in Excelsis a terrible whirlwind arose, and everyone fell face down on the ground. The wind seized the girl and threw her down too. In a trice she disappeared completely; only her braid remained.

THE MIRACULOUS PIPE

ONCE THERE LIVED a priest and his wife; they had a son, Ivanushka, and a daughter, Alionushka. Once Alionushka said to her mother: "Mother, mother, I want to go to the woods to get berries; all my little friends have gone there." "Go, and take your brother along." "Why? He is so lazy, he won't pick any berries." "Never mind, take him! And whichever of you gathers the most berries will receive a pair of red slippers as a present." And so the brother and sister went to pick berries, and they came to the wood. Ivanushka picked and picked and put the berries in a pitcher, but Alionushka ate and ate the berries she picked; she put only two berries in her box. She still had almost nothing when Ivanushka's pitcher was full. Alionushka became envious. "Brother," she said, "let me pick the lice out of your hair." He lay on her knees and fell asleep. Alionushka took out a sharp knife and slew her brother; she dug a ditch and buried him, and took the pitcher with the berries.

She came home and gave her mother the berries. "Where is your brother, Ivanushka?" the priest's wife asked. "He straggled behind me in the woods and must have lost his way; I called and called him, sought and sought him, but could not find him anywhere." The father and mother waited for Ivanushka a very long time, but he never came back.

Meanwhile, there grew on Ivanushka's grave a clump of tall

425

and very straight reeds. Shepherds went by with their herds, saw the reeds, and said: "What excellent reeds have grown here!" One shepherd cut off a reed and made himself a pipe. "Let me try to play it," he said. He put it to his lips, and the pipe began to play a song:

> *Gently, gently, shepherd, blow,*
> *Else my heart's blood you will shed.*
> *My treacherous sister murdered me*
> *For juicy berries, slippers red.*

"Ah, what a miraculous pipe!" said the shepherd. "How clearly it speaks! This pipe is very precious." "Let me try it," said another shepherd. He took the pipe and put it to his lips, and it played the same song; a third one tried, and again it played the same song.

The shepherds came to the village and stopped near the priest's house. "Little father," they said, "give us shelter for the night." "My house is crowded," said the priest. "Let us in, we will show you a marvel." The priest let them in and asked them: "Have you not seen anywhere a boy called Ivanushka? He went to pick berries and all trace of him has been lost." "No, we have not seen him; but we cut a reed on our way, and what a marvelous pipe we made of it! It plays by itself." The shepherd took out the pipe and played, and it sang:

> *Gently, gently, shepherd, blow,*
> *Else my heart's blood you will shed.*
> *My treacherous sister murdered me*
> *For juicy berries, slippers red.*

"Let me try to play on it," said the priest. He took the pipe and it played its song:

> *Gently, gently, father, blow,*
> *Else my heart's blood you will shed.*
> *My treacherous sister murdered me*
> *For juicy berries, slippers red.*

"Was it not my Ivanushka who was murdered?" said the priest. And he called his wife: "Now you try to play on it." The priest's wife took the pipe and it played its song:

> Gently, gently, mother, blow,
> Else my heart's blood you will shed.
> My treacherous sister murdered me
> For juicy berries, slippers red.

"Where is my daughter?" asked the priest. But Alionushka had hidden herself in a dark corner. They found her. "Now, play the pipe," said her father. "I don't know how." "Never mind, play!" She tried to refuse, but her father spoke sternly to her and made her take the pipe. She had no sooner put it to her lips than the pipe began to play by itself:

> Gently, gently, sister, blow,
> Else my heart's blood you will shed.
> You treacherously murdered me
> For juicy berries, slippers red.

Then Alionushka confessed everything, and her father in his rage drove her out of the house.

THE SEA KING
AND VASILISA THE WISE

ONCE THERE LIVED a king and a queen. The king loved to go hunting and shoot game. One day he went hunting and saw a young eagle sitting on an oak; he wanted to shoot him, but the eagle begged him: "Do not shoot me, my sovereign! Instead, take me to your castle; some day I shall be useful to you." The king thought and thought and said: "What do I need you for?" And again he wanted to shoot. The eagle said again: "Do not shoot me, my sovereign! Instead, take me with you; some day I shall be useful to you." The king thought and thought and could not imagine anything that the eagle might be useful for, and quite made up his mind to shoot him. The eagle prophesied for the third time: "Do not shoot me, my sovereign! Instead, take me with you and feed me for three years; some day I shall be useful to you."

The king's heart was moved; he took the eagle to his castle and fed him for a year and a second year. The eagle ate so much that he ate up all the cattle; the king was left without a single sheep or cow. The eagle said to him: "Let me go free." The king let him go free; the eagle tried his wings—but no, he could not yet fly! And he said: "Now, my sovereign, you have fed me for two years. Feed me for a third year even if you have to borrow, feed me none the less; you will not regret it." The king did this; he borrowed cattle everywhere and fed the eagle for a whole year. Then he let the bird go free. The eagle soared high; he flew and flew, then came down to the ground, and said: "Well, my king, now sit on me; we shall fly together." The king sat on the eagle.

They flew. After some time, a long time or a short time, they came to the edge of the blue sea. Here the eagle threw the king down; he fell into the sea and got wet up to his knees. But the eagle did not let him drown, he lifted the king onto his wing and asked: "Well, my king, my sovereign, were you frightened?" "I was," said the king. "I thought that I would surely be drowned." Again they flew and flew, till they came to another sea. The eagle threw the king down in the very middle of the sea and the king got wet up to his waist. The eagle put him on his wing and asked: "Well, my king, my sovereign, were you frightened?" "I was," said the king. "But all the time I thought, if God wishes to help me, you will pull me out."

Again they flew and flew till they came to a third sea. The eagle threw the king down into deep water, so that he got wet up to his neck. And for the third time the eagle put him on his wing and asked: "Well, my king, my sovereign, were you frightened?" "I was," said the king. "But all the time I thought that perhaps you would pull me out." "Well, my king, my sovereign, now you have learned what the fear of death is. That lesson was in return for old, long-past things. Do you remember how I sat on the oak and you wanted to shoot me dead? Three times you were about to shoot me, but I besought you not to kill me and hoped that perhaps you would not, but would be moved and take me with you."

After that they flew beyond thrice nine lands; they flew for a long, long time. The eagle said: "Look, my king, see what is above us and what is beneath us." The king looked. "Above us," he said, "is the sky, and under us the earth." "Look again. See what is on the right side and what is on the left." "On the right side there is an open field, and on the left a house stands." "Let us fly there," said the eagle. "My younger sister lives in that house." They landed in the courtyard; the sister came out to meet them, welcomed her brother, seated him at an oaken table, but refused even to look at the king. She left him in the courtyard, unleashed her hounds, and set them upon him. The eagle grew very angry, jumped from behind the table, took the king, and flew on farther with him.

They flew and flew, and the eagle said to the king: "Look, what do you see behind us?" The king turned around and looked. "Behind us is a burning house." The eagle answered him: "That is my youngest sister's house, which is burning because she did not welcome you but set hounds on you." They flew and flew, and again the eagle said: "Look, my king, see what is above us and what is beneath us." "Above us is the sky and beneath us the earth." "See what is on the right side and what on the left." "On the right side is an open field, and on the left a house stands." "My second sister lives in that house; let us go to visit her." They landed in the broad courtyard; the second sister welcomed her brother, seated him at an oaken table, but she left the king in the courtyard and unleashed her hounds and set them upon him. The eagle grew angry, jumped up from the table, took the king and flew with him farther still.

They flew and flew, and the eagle said: "My king, look; what is behind us?" The king turned round. "Behind us is

429

a burning house." "It is my second sister's house that is burning," said the eagle. "And now we shall fly to the house where my mother and eldest sister live." They came to the place; the mother and eldest sister were overjoyed and received the king with honor and kindness. "Well, my king," said the eagle, "rest in our house, and then I shall give you a ship; I shall pay you back for everything I ate in your house, and God speed you home." He gave the king a ship and two coffers, one red and the other green, and said: "Mind you, do not open these coffers until you come home; open the red one in the back yard, and the green one in the front yard."

The king took the coffers, said farewell to the eagle, and sailed on the blue sea; he reached a certain island, and there his ship stopped. He went ashore, recalled his coffers, and began to wonder what could be in them and why the eagle had told him not to open them. He thought and thought and felt a great desire to know the answer; so he took the red coffer, put it on the ground, and opened it, and so much cattle of every kind came out that one could not encompass them with one's eyes, and there was hardly enough room for them on the island.

When the king saw this, he was overcome with grief. He began to weep and said: "What shall I do now? How can I gather this herd together and place it in such a small coffer?" And he beheld a man coming out of the water, who came to him and said: "King, why are you weeping so bitterly?" "How can I help weeping?" answered the king. "How can I gather together this great herd into such a small coffer?" "I can help you in your trouble; I will gather together all your herd, but on one condition. Give me that which you do not know is in your own house." The king became thoughtful. "What is there in my house that I do not know is there?" he asked. "It seems to me I know everything that is there." He thought for a while, then agreed. "Gather together my herd," he said. "I will give you that which I do not know is in my house." The man gathered all the king's cattle into the coffer; the king boarded his ship and sailed homeward.

Only upon his return home did he learn that in his absence

430

the queen had borne him a son; he began to kiss and fondle the child, shedding tears all the while. "My king," asked the queen, "tell me, why do you shed bitter tears?" "For joy," he said, fearing to tell her the truth—that he must give the prince away. Then he went out to the back yard, opened the red coffer, and out of it came oxen and cows, sheep and rams, a great number of all kinds of cattle, enough to fill all the sheds and enclosures. Then he went out to the front yard, opened the green coffer, and before him appeared a great and beautiful garden. What wonderful trees were in it! The king was so overjoyed that he forgot that he had to give up his son.

Many years went by. One day the king wished to take a walk and he went to a river. The same man as before came out of the water and said: "King, you forget quickly! Remember your debt to me." The king returned home sad and distressed and told the queen and the prince the whole truth. They all grieved and wept together and decided that there was no choice but to surrender the prince; he was taken to the seashore and left alone.

The prince looked round him, saw a path, and walked along it, trusting in God. He walked and walked and found himself in a thick forest; in this forest stood a little hut, and in the hut lived Baba Yaga. "I will go in," thought the prince, and entered the little hut. "Good day, prince," said Baba Yaga, "are you trying to do a deed, or are you shirking one?" "Eh, grandmother, give me food and drink, and question me later." She gave him food and drink, and the prince told her all about himself and whither and why he was journeying. Baba Yaga said to him: "Go to the seashore, my child; twelve spoonbills will come there, turn into lovely maidens, and bathe; do you quietly steal up to them and take the shift of the eldest maiden. When you have settled accounts with her, go to the Sea King. You will also meet Eater, Drinker, and Sharp Frost; take them all with you, they will be useful to you."

The prince said farewell to Baba Yaga, went to the place she had named, and hid behind the bushes. Twelve spoonbills came flying, struck the damp earth, turned into lovely maidens, and began to bathe. The prince stole the shift of the eldest and sat behind the bushes without stirring. The maidens bathed and came out on the shore; eleven of them took their shifts, turned into birds, and flew homeward; only the eldest one, Vasilisa the Wise, remained. She began to implore the good youth. "Give me back my shift!" she said. "When you come to my father, the Sea King, I will be useful to you." The prince gave her shift back to her, and she at once turned into a spoonbill and flew after her sisters. The prince walked on farther. On his way he met three champions, Eater, Drinker, and Sharp Frost; he took them with him and came to the Sea King.

The Sea King saw him and said: "Hail, my friend, why have you not come to see me for so long? I have become weary waiting for you. Now set to work, and here is your first task. Build a great crystal bridge in one night, see that it is ready by morning! If you do not build it, you will lose your head." The prince left the Sea King and shed tears. Vasilisa the Wise opened the window of her apartment and asked: "Why are you shedding tears, prince?" "Ah, Vasilisa the Wise, how can I help weeping? Your father has ordered me to build a crystal bridge in one night, and I do not even know how to hold an ax in my hands." "Never mind! Lie down to sleep; the morning is wiser than the evening."

She put him to sleep, but she herself went out on the porch, and called and whistled with a mighty whistle. From all sides masons came running: some cleared the place, some dragged bricks; soon they built a crystal bridge, painted it with cunning designs, and went back to their homes. Early next morning Vasilisa the Wise roused the prince. "Get up, prince, the bridge is ready, my father will soon come to see it." The prince got up, took a broom, and went to the bridge to dust and sweep. The Sea King praised him. "Thank you!" he said. "You have performed a great task. Now perform the next. By tomorrow morning have a green garden planted with tall trees and flowering branches, and let songbirds sing in the garden, and ripe apples and pears hang on the fruit trees." The prince left the Sea King's presence and shed tears. Vasilisa the Wise opened a window and asked: "Why are you weeping, prince?"

432

"How can I help weeping? Your father ordered me to plant a garden in one night." "Never mind! Lie down to sleep; the morning is wiser than the evening."

She laid him down to sleep, and she herself went out on the porch and called and whistled with a mighty whistle. From all sides gardeners came running and planted a green garden, and in the garden songbirds sang, on the trees flowers blossomed, and ripe apples and pears hung on the branches. Early next morning Vasilisa the Wise roused the prince. "Get up, prince, the garden is ready and father is coming to see it!" The prince at once took a broom and went to the garden to sweep the paths and tidy the branches. The Sea King praised him: "Thank you, prince," he said. "You have served me truly and faithfully. As your reward choose a bride for yourself from among my twelve daughters. They are all like one another, face for face, hair for hair, dress for dress; if you choose thrice one and the same, she shall be your wife; if not, I will have you put to death." Vasilisa the Wise learned of this new trial and at the first opportunity said to the prince: "The first time I will wave a handkerchief, the second time I will adjust my dress, and the third time a fly will fly over my head." Thus the prince chose Vasilisa the Wise each time. They were married, and a great feast began.

The Sea King prepared many viands of every description—not even a hundred people could eat what he spread on the oaken table—and he ordered his son-in-law to see that all of it was eaten; if anything should be left, it would go hard with him. "Father," begged the prince, "we have an old man with us, let him eat too." "He may come forward." Straightway Eater came forward. He ate everything on the table and even then he did not have enough. The Sea King served forty barrels of various kinds of drink and ordered his son-in-law to see that all of it was drunk. "Father," the prince begged again, "we have another old man with us, let him come forward to drink your health." "He may come forward." Drinker came, at once emptied all of the forty barrels, and even asked for some more to wash down what he had drunk.

The Sea King saw that nothing had been of any avail, so

434

he ordered that a cast-iron bath be heated very hot for the young couple. A cast-iron bath was heated, twenty cords of wood were burned, the stove and walls were red hot, it was impossible to come within five versts of them. "Father," said the prince, "allow our old man to steam himself, to try out the bath." "He may steam himself." Sharp Frost came to the bath: he blew into one corner, into another, and soon icicles hung there. Following him the newly wed couple went to the bath, washed and steamed themselves, and returned home. "Let us go away from my father, the Sea King," Vasilisa the Wise said to the prince. "He is very angry with you and might do us some evil." "Let us go," said the prince. Straightway they saddled horses and galloped into the open field.

They rode and rode; much time went by. "Prince," said Vasilisa the Wise, "climb down from your horse and put your ear to the damp earth. Can you hear pursuers coming after us?" The prince put his ear to the damp earth; he heard nothing. Vasilisa the Wise got down from her good steed, put her ear to the damp earth, and said: "Ah, prince, I hear strong pursuers coming after us." She turned the horses into a well, herself into a ladle, and the prince into a very old man. The pursuers came. "Eh, old man," they said, "have you not seen a good youth and a lovely maiden?" "I saw them, my friends, but a long time ago; they went by when I was still a young man." The pursuers returned to the Sea King. "No," they said, "we found neither trace nor tidings; we saw only an old man near a well, and a ladle floating on the water." "Why did you not bring them back?" cried the Sea King, and ordered his messengers to be put to a cruel death. He sent another party after the prince and Vasilisa the Wise, but meanwhile they had ridden far along.

Vasilisa the Wise heard the new party of pursuers. She turned the prince into an old priest and herself into an ancient church; its walls were crumbling, moss grew all around them. The pursuers came. "Eh, little old man," they cried, "have you not seen a good youth with a lovely maiden?" "I saw them, my friends, but very long ago; they went by when I was still young and was building this church." The second party of

435

pursuers also returned to the Sea King. "No, Your Royal Majesty," they said, "we found neither trace nor tidings; all we saw was an old priest and an ancient church." "Why did you not bring them?" the Sea King cried, even more angrily than before. He put the messengers to cruel death and himself galloped after the prince and Vasilisa the Wise. This time Vasilisa the Wise turned the horses into a river of mead, with banks made of pudding; she changed the prince into a drake and herself into a gray duck. The Sea King threw himself upon the pudding and the mead, he ate and ate, and drank and drank, until he burst and gave up the ghost.

The prince and Vasilisa rode on farther; they approached the house of the prince's father and mother. Vasilisa the Wise said: "Prince, you go first. Announce yourself to your father and mother, and I will wait for you here on the road. Only remember my words: Kiss everyone but your sister, else you will forget me completely." The prince entered his home, greeted everyone, and kissed his sister too; and no sooner had he kissed her than he forgot about his wife, as though she had never been in his thoughts.

Vasilisa the Wise waited for him three days; on the fourth day she disguised herself as a beggar woman, went to the capital, and stopped in the house of a certain old woman. Meanwhile the prince made ready to marry a rich queen; and a call was issued throughout the kingdom summoning all loyal subjects to come to congratulate the bride and groom and to bring them each a wheat cake as a gift. Vasilisa's hostess began to sift flour and prepare a cake. "Grandmother," asked Vasilisa the Wise, "for whom are you making a cake?" "Don't you know that our king is marrying his son to a rich queen? We must go to the palace and bring gifts to the young couple." "I too will bake a cake and take it to the palace; perhaps the king will reward me with something." "Certainly, go and bake." Vasilisa the Wise took some flour, mixed the dough, put some curd cheese and a pair of doves in it, and baked the cake.

At dinnertime the old woman and Vasilisa the Wise went to the palace, where the feast was in full swing. The cake made by Vasilisa the Wise was served, and as soon at it was cut in two, the pair of doves flew out of it. The she-dove snatched the piece of cheese, and the he-dove said: "My little dove, give me some cheese too!" "I will not," said the she-dove, "else you will forget me just as the prince forgot his Vasilisa the Wise." Thereupon the prince remembered his wife, jumped up from behind the table, took her by her white hands, and seated her beside him. From then on they lived together in great prosperity and happiness.

THE FOX AS MOURNER

ONCE THERE LIVED an old man and an old woman who had a daughter. One day the young girl was eating beans and dropped one bean on the ground. It grew and grew till it reached the sky. The old man climbed up the beanstalk to the sky, walked all around, and feasted his eyes upon the scene. He said to himself: "I will bring the old woman up here, she will be delighted." He climbed down to the ground, put the old woman in a bag, took the bag between his teeth, and climbed up again; he climbed and climbed, got tired, and dropped the bag. He hastened down, opened the bag, and saw the old woman lying there with bared teeth and staring eyes. He said: "Why do you grin, old woman? Why do you show your teeth?" But when he saw that she was dead, he burst into tears.

They had lived all alone in the midst of a wilderness, so there was no one to be the old woman's mourner. The old man took a bag with several pairs of white chickens and went in search of a mourner. He saw a bear go by, and said: "Bear, mourn for my wife; I will give you two white chickens." The bear roared: "Ah, my dear grandmother, how I mourn for you." "No," said the old man, "you don't know how to lament." And he went on farther. He walked and walked and met a wolf; he had the wolf lament, but the wolf did not do it well either.

437

He walked on again, met a fox, and made her lament in return for a pair of white chickens. She began to mourn: "Turu, turu, grandmother—grandfather killed you." The peasant found her song to his liking and made her sing it a second, a third, and a fourth time—then he discovered that he did not have a fourth pair of chickens. The old man said: "Fox, fox, I left the fourth pair at home; come to my house."

The fox followed him. They came to his house; the old man took a bag, put a pair of dogs in it, covered them with the fox's six chickens, and gave the bag to her. The fox took it and ran; after a while she stopped near a tree stump and said: "I will sit on the stump and eat a white chicken." She ate it and ran on; then she sat down on another stump and ate the second chicken, then the third, the fourth, the fifth, and the sixth. When she opened the bag for the seventh time, the dogs jumped out at her. The fox took to her heels, ran and ran, hid under a log, and asked: "Little ears, little ears of mine, what did you do?" "We listened and listened, lest the dogs eat the fox." "Little eyes, little eyes of mine, what did you do?" "We looked and we looked, lest the dogs eat the fox." "Little feet, little feet, what did you do?" "We ran and ran, lest the dogs eat the fox." "And you, tail, what did you do?" "I got entangled whenever we had to cross stumps, bushes, or logs, so that the dogs might catch the fox and tear her to pieces." "Ah, you wicked organ! If that is so, here, dogs! Eat my tail!" And she stuck out her tail. The dogs grabbed it, then pulled out the fox herself and tore her to pieces.

VASILISA THE BEAUTIFUL

IN A CERTAIN KINGDOM there lived a merchant. Although he had been married for twelve years, he had only one daughter, called Vasilisa the Beautiful. When the girl was eight years old, her mother died. On her deathbed the merchant's wife called her daughter, took a doll from under her coverlet, gave it to the girl, and said: "Listen, Vasilisushka. Remember and heed my last words. I am dying, and together with my maternal blessing I leave you this doll. Always keep it with you and do not show it to anyone; if you get into trouble, give the doll food, and ask its advice. When it has eaten, it will tell you what to do in your trouble." Then the mother kissed her child and died.

After his wife's death the merchant mourned as is proper, and then began to think of marrying again. He was a handsome man and had no difficulty in finding a bride, but he liked best a certain widow. Because she was elderly and had two daughters of her own, of almost the same age as Vasilisa, he thought that she was an experienced housewife and mother. So he married her, but was deceived, for she did not turn out to be a good mother for his Vasilisa. Vasilisa was the most beautiful girl in the village; her stepmother and stepsisters were jealous of her beauty and tormented her by giving her all kinds of work to do, hoping that she would grow thin from toil and tanned from exposure to the wind and sun; in truth, she had a most miserable life. But Vasilisa bore all this without complaint and became lovelier and more buxom, every day, while the stepmother and her daughters grew thin and ugly from spite, although they always sat with folded hands, like ladies.

How did all this come about? Vasilisa was helped by her doll. Without its aid the girl could never have managed all that work. In return, Vasilisa sometimes did not eat, but kept the choicest morsels for her doll. And at night, when everyone was asleep, she would lock herself in the little room in which she lived, and would give the doll a treat, saying: "Now, little doll, eat, and listen to my troubles. I live in my father's house but am deprived of all joy; a wicked stepmother is driving me from the white world. Tell me how I should live and what I should do." The doll would eat, then would give her advice and comfort her in her trouble, and in the morning, she would perform all the chores for Vasilisa, who rested in the shade and picked flowers while the flower beds were weeded, the cabbage sprayed, the water brought in, and the stove fired. The doll even showed Vasilisa an herb that would protect her from sunburn. She led an easy life, thanks to her doll.

Several years went by. Vasilisa grew up and reached the marriage age. She was wooed by all the young men in the village, but no one would even look at the stepmother's daughters. The stepmother was more spiteful than ever, and her answer to all the suitors was: "I will not give the youngest in marriage before the elder ones." And each time she sent a suitor away, she vented her anger on Vasilisa in cruel blows.

One day the merchant had to leave home for a long time in order to trade in distant lands. The stepmother moved to another house; near that house was a thick forest, and in a glade of that forest there stood a hut, and in the hut lived Baba Yaga. She never allowed anyone to come near her and ate human beings as if they were chickens. Having moved into the new house, the merchant's wife, hating Vasilisa, repeatedly sent the girl to the woods for one thing or another; but each time Vasilisa returned home safe and sound: her doll had showed her the way and kept her far from Baba Yaga's hut.

Autumn came. The stepmother gave evening work to all three maidens: the oldest had to make lace, the second had to knit stockings, and Vasilisa had to spin; and each one had to finish her task. The stepmother put out the lights all over the house, leaving only one candle in the room where the girls worked, and went to bed. The girls worked. The candle began to smoke; one of the stepsisters took up a scissors to trim it, but instead, following her mother's order, she snuffed it out, as though inadvertently. "What shall we do now?" said the girls. "There is no light in the house and our tasks are not finished.

Someone must run to Baba Yaga and get some light." "The pins on my lace give me light," said the one who was making lace. "I shall not go." "I shall not go either," said the one who was knitting stockings, "my knitting needles give me light." "Then you must go," both of them cried to their stepsister. "Go to Baba Yaga!" And they pushed Vasilisa out of the room. She went into her own little room, put the supper she had prepared before her doll, and said: "Now dolly, eat, and aid me in my need. They are sending me to Baba Yaga for a light, and she will eat me up." The doll ate the supper and its eyes gleamed like two candles. "Fear not, Vasilisushka," it said. "Go where you are sent, only keep me with you all the time. With me in your pocket you will suffer no harm from Baba Yaga." Vasilisa made ready, put her doll in her pocket, and, having made the sign of the cross, went into the deep forest.

She walked in fear and trembling. Suddenly a horseman galloped past her: his face was white, he was dressed in white, his horse was white, and his horse's trappings were white—daybreak came to the woods.

She walked on farther, and a second horseman galloped past her: he was all red, he was dressed in red, and his horse was red—the sun began to rise.

Vasilisa walked the whole night and the whole day, and only on the following evening did she come to the glade where Baba Yaga's hut stood. The fence around the hut was made of human bones, and on the spikes were human skulls with staring eyes; the doors had human legs for doorposts, human hands for bolts, and a mouth with sharp teeth in place of a lock. Vasilisa was numb with horror and stood rooted to the spot. Suddenly another horseman rode by. He was all black, he was dressed in black, and his horse was black. He galloped up to Baba Yaga's door and vanished, as though the earth had swallowed him up—night came. But the darkness did not last long. The eyes of all the skulls on the fence began to gleam and the glade was as bright as day. Vasilisa shuddered with fear, but not knowing where to run, remained on the spot.

Soon a terrible noise resounded through the woods; the trees crackled, the dry leaves rustled; from the woods Baba

Yaga drove out in a mortar, prodding it on with a pestle, and sweeping her traces with a broom. She rode up to the gate, stopped, and sniffing the air around her, cried: "Fie, fie! I smell a Russian smell! Who is here?" Vasilisa came up to the old witch and, trembling with fear, bowed low to her and said: "It is I, grandmother. My stepsisters sent me to get some light." "Very well," said Baba Yaga. "I know them, but before I give you the light you must live with me and work for me; if not, I will eat you up." Then she turned to the gate and cried: "Hey, my strong bolts, unlock! Open up, my wide gate!" The gate opened, and Baba Yaga drove in whistling. Vasilisa followed her, and then everything closed again.

Having entered the room, Baba Yaga stretched herself out in her chair and said to Vasilisa: "Serve me what is in the stove; I am hungry." Vasilisa lit a torch from the skulls on the fence and began to serve Yaga the food from the stove—and enough food had been prepared for ten people. She brought kvass, mead, beer, and wine from the cellar. The old witch ate and drank everything, leaving for Vasilisa only a little cabbage soup, a crust of bread, and a piece of pork. Then Baba Yaga made ready to go to bed and said: "Tomorrow after I go, see to it that you sweep the yard, clean the hut, cook the dinner, wash the linen, and go to the cornbin and sort out a bushel of wheat. And let everything be done, or I will eat you up!" Having given these orders, Baba Yaga began to snore. Vasilisa set the remnants of the old witch's supper before her doll, wept bitter tears, and said: "Here dolly, eat, and aid me in my need! Baba Yaga has given me a hard task to do and threatens to eat me up if I do not do it all. Help me!" The doll answered: "Fear not, Vasilisa the Beautiful! Eat your supper, say your prayers, and go to sleep; the morning is wiser than the evening."

Very early next morning Vasilisa awoke, after Baba Yaga had arisen, and looked out of the window. The eyes of the skulls were going out; then the white horseman flashed by, and it was daybreak. Baba Yaga went out into the yard, whistled, and the mortar, pestle, and broom appeared before her. The red horseman flashed by, and the sun rose. Baba Yaga sat in the mortar, prodded it on with the pestle, and swept her traces with the broom. Vasilisa remained alone, looked about Baba Yaga's hut, was amazed at the abundance of everything, and stopped wondering which work she should do first. For lo and behold, all the work was done; the doll was picking the last shreds of chaff from the wheat. "Ah my savior," said Vasilisa to her doll, "you have delivered me from death." "All you have to do," answered the doll, creeping into Vasilisa's pocket, "is to cook the dinner; cook it with the help of God and then rest, for your health's sake."

When evening came Vasilisa set the table and waited for Baba Yaga. Dusk began to fall, the black horseman flashed by the gate, and night came; only the skulls' eyes were shining. The trees crackled, the leaves rustled; Baba Yaga was coming. Vasilisa met her. "Is everything done?" asked Yaga. "Please see for yourself, grandmother," said Vasilisa. Baba Yaga looked at everything, was annoyed that there was nothing she could complain about, and said: "Very well, then." Then she cried: "My faithful servants, my dear friends, grind my wheat!" Three pairs of hands appeared, took the wheat, and carried it out of sight. Baba Yaga ate her fill, made ready to go to sleep, and again gave her orders to Vasilisa. "Tomorrow," she commanded, "do the same work you have done today, and in addition take the poppy seed from the bin and get rid of the dust, grain by grain; someone threw dust into the bins out of spite." Having said this, the old witch turned to the wall and began to snore, and Vasilisa set about feeding her doll. The doll ate, and spoke as she had spoken the day before: "Pray to God and go to sleep; the morning is wiser than the evening. Everything will be done, Vasilisushka."

Next morning Baba Yaga again left the yard in her mortar, and Vasilisa and the doll soon had all the work done. The old witch came back, looked at everything, and cried: "My faithful servants, my dear friends, press the oil out of the poppy seed!" Three pairs of hands appeared, took the poppy seed, and carried it out of sight. Baba Yaga sat down to dine; she ate, and Vasilisa stood silent. "Why do you not speak to me?" said Baba Yaga. "You stand there as though you were dumb." "I did not dare to speak," said Vasilisa, "but if you'll give me leave,

443

I'd like to ask you something." "Go ahead. But not every question has a good answer; if you know too much, you will soon grow old." "I want to ask you, grandmother, only about what I have seen. As I was on my way to you, a horseman on a white horse, all white himself and dressed in white, overtook me. Who is he?" "He is my bright day," said Baba Yaga. "Then another horseman overtook me; he had a red horse, was red himself, and was dressed in red. Who is he?" "He is my red sun." "And who is the black horseman whom I met at your very gate, grandmother?" "He is my dark night—and all of them are my faithful servants."

Vasilisa remembered the three pairs of hands, but kept silent. "Why don't you ask me more?" said Baba Yaga. "That will be enough," Vasilisa replied. "You said yourself, grandmother, that one who knows too much will grow old soon." "It is well," said Baba Yaga, "that you ask only about what you have seen outside my house, not inside my house; I do not like to have my dirty linen washed in public, and I eat the overcurious. Now I shall ask you something. How do you manage to do the work I set for you?" "I am helped by the blessing of my mother," said Vasilisa. "So that is what it is," shrieked Baba Yaga. "Get you gone, blessed daughter! I want no blessed ones in my house!" She dragged Vasilisa out of the room and pushed her outside the gate, took a skull with burning eyes from the fence, stuck it on a stick, and gave it to the girl, saying: "Here is your light for your stepsisters. Take it; that is what they sent you for."

Vasilisa ran homeward by the light of the skull, which went out only at daybreak, and by nightfall of the following day she reached the house. As she approached the gate, she was about to throw the skull away, thinking that surely they no longer needed a light in the house. But suddenly a dull voice came from the skull, saying: "Do not throw me away, take me to your stepmother." She looked at the stepmother's house and, seeing that there was no light in the windows, decided to enter with her skull. For the first time she was received kindly. Her stepmother and stepsisters told her that since she had left they had had no fire in the house; they were unable to strike a

flame themselves, and whatever light was brought by the neighbors went out the moment it was brought into the house. "Perhaps your fire will last," said the stepmother. The skull was brought into the room, and its eyes kept staring at the stepmother and her daughters, and burned them. They tried to hide, but wherever they went the eyes followed them. By morning they were all burned to ashes; only Vasilisa remained untouched by the fire.

In the morning Vasilisa buried the skull in the ground, locked up the house, and went to the town. A certain childless old woman gave her shelter, and there she lived, waiting for her father's return. One day she said to the woman: "I am weary of sitting without work, grandmother. Buy me some flax, the best you can get; at least I shall be spinning." The old woman bought good flax and Vasilisa set to work. She spun as fast as lightning and her threads were even and thin as a hair. She spun a great deal of yarn; it was time to start weaving it, but no comb fine enough for Vasilisa's yarn could be found, and no one would undertake to make one. Vasilisa asked her doll for aid. The doll said: "Bring me an old comb, an old shuttle, and a horse's mane; I will make a loom for you." Vasilisa got everything that was required and went to sleep, and during the night the doll made a wonderful loom for her.

By the end of the winter the linen was woven, and it was so fine that it could be passed through a needle like a thread. In the spring the linen was bleached, and Vasilisa said to the old woman: "Grandmother, sell this linen and keep the money for yourself." The old woman looked at the linen and gasped: "No, my child! No one can wear such linen except the tsar; I shall take it to the palace." The old woman went to the tsar's palace and walked back and forth beneath the windows. The tsar saw her and asked: "What do you want, old woman?" "Your Majesty," she answered, "I have brought rare merchandise; I do not want to show it to anyone but you." The tsar ordered her to be brought before him, and when he saw the linen he was amazed. "What do you want for it?" asked the tsar. "It has no price, little father tsar! I have brought it as a gift to you." The tsar thanked her and rewarded her with gifts.

446

The tsar ordered shirts to be made of the linen. It was cut, but nowhere could they find a seamstress who was willing to sew them. For a long time they tried to find one, but in the end the tsar summoned the old woman and said: "You have known how to spin and weave such linen, you must know how to sew shirts of it." "It was not I that spun and wove this linen, Your Majesty," said the old woman. "This is the work of a maiden to whom I give shelter." "Then let her sew the shirts," ordered the tsar.

The old woman returned home and told everything to Vasilisa. "I knew all the time," said Vasilisa to her, "that I would have to do this work." She locked herself in her room and set to work; she sewed without rest and soon a dozen shirts were ready. The old woman took them to the tsar, and Vasilisa washed herself, combed her hair, dressed in her finest clothes, and sat at the window. She sat there waiting to see what would happen. She saw a servant of the tsar entering the courtyard. The messenger came into the room and said: "The tsar wishes to see the needlewoman who made his shirts, and wishes to reward her with his own hands." Vasilisa appeared before the tsar. When the tsar saw Vasilisa the Beautiful he fell madly in love with her. "No, my beauty," he said, "I will not separate from you; you shall be my wife." He took Vasilisa by her white hands, seated her by his side, and the wedding was celebrated at once. Soon Vasilisa's father returned, was overjoyed at her good fortune, and came to live in his daughter's house. Vasilisa took the old woman into her home too, and carried her doll in her pocket till the end of her life.

THE BUN

ONCE THERE LIVED an old man and his old wife. The old man said: "Old woman, make me a bun." "Of what shall I make it? I have no flour." "Eh, eh, old woman! Scrape the bottom of the cupboard, sweep the floor of the bin, and you will have enough flour." The old woman took a duster, scraped the bottom of the cupboard, swept the floor of the bin, and gathered about two handfuls of flour. She mixed the dough with cream, fried it in butter, and put the bun on the window sill to cool. The bun lay and lay there, then suddenly rolled off—from the window sill to the bench, from the bench to the floor, and from the floor to the door. Then it bounded over the threshold to the entrance hall, from the entrance hall to the porch, from the porch to the courtyard, from the courtyard out of the gate, and on and on. The bun rolled along the road, and met a hare. "Little bun, little bun, I shall eat you up!" said the hare. "Don't eat me, slant-eyed hare, I will sing a song for you," said the bun, and sang:

> *I was scraped from the cupboard,*
> *Swept from the bin,*
> *Kneaded with cream,*
> *Fried in butter;*
> *I got away from grandpa,*
> *I got away from grandma,*
> *And I shall not find it hard*
> *To get away from you, young hare!*

And the bun rolled on farther and was gone before the hare had time to turn around. The bun rolled on, and met a wolf. "Little bun, little bun, I shall eat you up," said the wolf. "Don't eat me, gray wolf!" said the bun. "I will sing a song for you." And the bun sang:

> *I was scraped from the cupboard,*
> *Swept from the bin,*
> *Kneaded with cream,*
> *Fried in butter;*
> *I got away from grandpa,*
> *I got away from grandma,*
> *I got away from the hare,*
> *And I shall not find it hard*
> *To get away from you, gray wolf!*

And the bun rolled on farther, and was gone before the wolf had time to turn around. The bun rolled on and met a bear.

"Little bun, little bun, I shall eat you up," the bear said. "You certainly won't, Bandy Legs!" And the bun sang:

> *I was scraped from the cupboard,*
> *Swept from the bin,*
> *Kneaded with cream,*
> *Fried in butter;*
> *I got away from grandpa,*
> *I got away from grandma,*
> *I got away from the hare,*
> *I got away from the wolf,*
> *And I shall not find it hard*
> *To get away from you, big bear!*

And again the bun rolled on, and was gone before the bear had time to turn around. The bun rolled and rolled and met a fox. "Good day, little bun, how pretty you are!" said the fox. And the bun sang:

> *I was scraped from the cupboard,*
> *Swept from the bin,*
> *Kneaded with cream,*
> *Fried in butter;*
> *I got away from grandpa,*
> *I got away from grandma,*
> *I got away from the hare,*
> *I got away from the wolf,*
> *I got away from the bear,*
> *And I shall not find it hard*
> *To get away from you, old fox.*

"What a wonderful song!" said the fox. "But little bun, I am old now and hard of hearing; come sit on my snout and sing your song again, louder this time." The bun jumped on the fox's snout and sang the same song. "Thank you, little bun, that was a wonderful song. I'd like to hear it again. Now come sit on my tongue and sing it for the last time." When she had said this the fox stuck out her tongue; the bun foolishly jumped on it, and—snatch!—the fox ate up the bun.

IN A CERTAIN VILLAGE there lived a peasant who had a dog; when the dog was young, he guarded the whole house, but when wretched old age came, he ceased even to bark. His master became disgusted with him; so he made ready, took a rope, tied it around the dog's neck, and led him to the woods. He came to an aspen tree and wanted to strangle the dog, but seeing that bitter tears were rolling down the snout of the old cur, his heart was moved and he took pity on him; he tied the dog to the aspen tree and went home. The poor dog remained in the woods and began to weep and curse his lot.

Suddenly a huge wolf came from behind the bushes, saw the dog, and said: "Good day, spotted cur! I have been waiting a long time for your visit. In times past you drove me out of your house, but now you have come to me and I can do with you as I please. Now I will pay you back for everything!" "And what do you want to do with me, little gray wolf?" "Not much; —just eat you up, skin and bones." "Ah, you foolish gray wolf!" said the dog. "You are so fat that you no longer know what you are doing; after eating savory beef you wish to eat old, lean dog meat? Why should you stupidly break your old teeth on me? My flesh is now like rotten wood. I will give you a better idea: go bring me a hundred pounds or so of excellent horseflesh; let me gain a little weight, then do with me what you please."

The wolf heeded the dog, went away, and came back with half a mare. "Here is meat for you!" he said. "Now mind you, fatten yourself up!" Having said this he left. The dog set to eating the meat and ate up all of it. Two days later the gray wolf came and said to the dog: "Well, brother, have you gained weight or not?" "Just a little bit; but if you would bring me a sheep, my flesh would become much sweeter!" The wolf consented to that too, ran to the open field, lay in a hollow, and waited for the shepherd. When the shepherd came by with his flock, the wolf from behind the bush chose a big fat sheep, jumped upon her, seized her by her neck, and dragged her to the dog. "Here is a sheep for you, to help you get fat," he said. The dog set to work, ate up the sheep, and felt his strength coming back to him. The wolf came and asked: "Well, brother, how do you feel now?" "I am still a little thin. If you would bring me a boar I would get as fat as a pig." The wolf got a boar, brought it to the dog, and said: "This is my last service to you. In two days I shall come to see you." "Very well," thought the dog, "I shall be able to cope with you then."

Two days later the wolf came to the well fed dog; when the dog saw him, he began to bark. "Ah, you foul cur," said the gray wolf, "how dare you abuse me?" And he jumped on the dog to tear him to pieces. But the dog had gathered strength; he reared up on his hind legs and began to give the gray wolf such a beating that tufts of his fur flew out in all directions. The wolf wrested himself free and took to his heels; he ran some distance and wanted to stop, but when he heard the dog's bark he ran again. He came to the woods, lay under a bush, and began to lick the wounds the dog had inflicted upon him. "How this foul cur cheated me," the wolf said to himself. "The next time I get hold of anyone, I'll clamp my teeth down and he won't get away so easily."

So the wolf licked his wounds and went to look for new booty. He saw a big he-goat standing on a hill, went to him, and said: "Goat, I have come to eat you." "Ah, gray wolf," said the goat, "why should you break your old teeth on me? Rather, stand against the hill and open your jaws wide; I will take a run and jump straight into your mouth, then you can swallow me." The wolf stood against the hill and opened his jaws wide, but the goat had his own plan; he flew down the hill like an arrow and hit the wolf with such force that the wolf was knocked off his feet. Then the goat ran out of sight. After about three hours the wolf came to with a splitting headache. He began to wonder whether he had swallowed the goat or not. He thought and thought, and wondered and wondered. "If I had eaten the goat, my belly would be full; but I think the scoundrel deceived me. Well, henceforth I shall know what to do."

Having said this, the wolf ran to the village. He saw a pig

with little piglets and wanted to seize one piglet, but the pig would not let him. "Ah, you swinish snout," the wolf said to her, "how dare you be so boorish? I will tear you to pieces and swallow your young in one gulp." The pig answered: "Well, so far I have not abused you; but now I shall make bold to say that you are a great fool." "Why?" "This is why—just judge for yourself, gray one. How can you eat my piglets? They are just born. They have to be washed clean. Let us be friendly, neighbor, and baptize these little children." The wolf consented—so far so good. They came to a big water mill. The pig said to the wolf: "You, dear godfather, stand on this side of the barrier, where there is no water, and I will go to the other side, plunge the piglets in clear water, and hand them over to you one by one." The wolf was overjoyed, thinking, "Now I'll get the prize in my jaws." The gray wolf went under the bridge and the pig seized the barrier with her teeth and raised it. The water rushed through, dragging the wolf with it and whirling him around in the eddies. The pig and her piglets went their way; when the pig came home she ate her fill, fed her children, and lay down on a soft bed.

The gray wolf realized that the pig had cunningly tricked him. He managed somehow to get to the shore, and ran about the woods with an empty stomach. He starved for a long time, then could not bear it any longer, went back to the village, and saw some carrion lying near a barn. "That's fine," he thought. "When night comes I shall at least eat some carrion." For bad times had come upon the wolf; he was glad to have a meal of carrion. Even that was better than to have one's teeth chattering from hunger and to be singing wolfish songs. Night came; the wolf went to the barn and began to gobble the carrion. But a hunter had long been lying in wait for him with a couple of good bullets made ready in advance; he fired his gun and the gray wolf rolled on the ground with a smashed head. And that was the end of the gray wolf.

THE BEAR, THE DOG,
AND THE CAT

ONCE THERE WAS a peasant who had a good dog, but when the beast grew old he ceased to bark and to guard the house and barn. The peasant did not want to give him any more bread to eat and drove him away from the farm. The dog went to the woods and lay down under a tree to die. Suddenly a bear came and asked: "Why have you lain down here, dog?" "I have come here to die of hunger. For this is human justice nowadays, you see: while you have your strength, they give you food and drink, but when your strength vanishes with old age, they drive you out." "Well, dog, are you hungry?" "Very hungry." "Then come with me, I will feed you." They went off together and met a colt. "Look at me," said the bear to the dog and began to tear the ground with his paws. "Dog, dog!" The dog asked him: "What is it?" "Tell me whether my eyes are red." "They are red, bear." The bear began to tear the ground even more furiously. "Dog, dog," he said, "is my fur bristling?" "It is bristling, bear." "Dog, dog, is my tail up?" "It is up." Then the bear seized the colt by his belly; the colt dropped to the ground and the bear tore him to pieces and said: "Now, dog, eat as much as you want. And when you have finished the meat, come to see me."

The dog lived a carefree life, and when he had eaten up everything and was hungry again, he ran to the bear. "Well, brother," the bear asked, "did you eat him up?" "I did, but lately I have felt hungry again." "Why be hungry? Do you know where your women are reaping?" "I know." "Well, let us go. I will sneak up to your master's wife and steal her child from the cradle, and you run after me and rescue it. When you rescue it, take it back, and for that service she will again give you bread as of old." So far, so good; the bear sneaked up and carried off the child from the cradle. The child began to cry, the women ran after the bear; but no matter how much they ran, they could not overtake him. They turned back; the mother wept, the other women were distressed. Suddenly the dog appeared, overtook the bear, rescued the child, and brought it back. "Look," said the women, "the old dog has rescued the child!" They ran to meet him. The mother was happy, very happy. "Now," she said, "I will not give up that dog for anything." She led him home, poured milk for him, crumbled some bread into it, and gave it to him, saying: "Here, eat!" And to her husband she said: "Now, little husband, we must feed and take care of our dog. He rescued my child from the bear—and you said that he had no strength." The dog recovered his strength and grew fat. "May God," he said, "give health to the bear! He did not let me die of starvation." He became the bear's best friend.

One day the peasant had a party. At that time the bear came to visit the dog. "Good evening, dog!" he said. "How are you, do you have enough bread?" "Thank God," said the dog, "I'm living in clover. What shall I offer you? Let us go to the house; my masters are reveling and they won't see you if you enter and hide at once under the stove. Then I'll get something and give you a treat." So they stole into the house. The dog saw that the guests and the hosts were quite tipsy, and began to treat his friend. The bear drank one glass, then a second, and the liquor went to his head. The guests intoned a song, and the bear wanted to sing too. He began to sing a song of his own, but the dog begged him: "Please! Do not sing or there will be trouble." But his pleadings were of no avail—the bear refused to be silent and sang his song ever more loudly. The guests heard the howl, picked up some stakes, and began to thrash the bear; he wrested himself free and took to his heels—he barely got away with his life.

Now this peasant also had a cat; she ceased catching mice and became mischievous—wherever she went, she broke something or spilled something from the pitcher. The peasant drove the cat from his house, and the dog seeing that she was hungry, began quietly to take bread and meat to her and to feed her. The peasant's wife began to watch; when she saw what was going on she began to beat the dog; she beat and beat him,

454

repeating: "Don't take ham to the cat, don't bring her bread." After about three days the dog went out of the yard and saw that the cat was dying of hunger. "What is the matter with you?" he asked. "I am dying of hunger; I was full only so long as you fed me." "Come with me." They went off, and came up to a drove of horses. The dog began to dig the ground with his paws, and said: "Cat, cat, are my eyes red?" "They are not red a bit." "Say that they are red!" The cat said: "They are red." "Cat, cat, is my fur bristling?" "No, it is not bristling." "You fool, say that it is bristling!" "Well, then, it is bristling." "Cat, cat, is my tail up?" "Not a bit." "You fool, say that it is up." "Very well, then, it is up." The dog jumped at a mare, and the mare gave him such a kick that he gave up the ghost. And the cat said: "Now his eyes are really full of blood, his fur is bristling, and his tail is all twisted. Good-by, brother dog! I myself shall go away to die."

THE BEAR AND THE COCK

A CERTAIN OLD MAN had a foolish son. The fool asked his father to find him a wife. "And if you don't find me a wife," he said, "I will smash up the stove." "But how can I find you a wife?" the father said. "I have no money." "You have no money, but we have an ox; sell him to be slaugh-

455

tered." The ox heard this and ran away to the woods. The fool kept urging his father without respite: "Find me a wife, find me a wife!" "But I have no money, I tell you." "You have no money, but we have a cock; slay him, bake a pie, and sell it." The cock heard this and flew away to the woods. The fool again urged his father: "Find me a wife or I will smash up the stove." The father said: "I would gladly find you a wife, but I have no money." "You have no money, but you have a sheep; sell it to be slaughtered." The sheep heard this and ran away to the woods. The ox, the sheep, and the cock joined company and built themselves a hut in the woods. The bear learned about it, wanted to eat them, and came to the hut. The cock saw him and began to flutter above the roost, flapping his wings and crowing: "Where, where, where? Give him to me here! I will trample him with my feet, cut him with an ax. A knife is right here, and a nail is right there; we'll slaughter him here, and hang him up there." The bear took fright and took to his heels; he ran and ran till he dropped from fright and died. The fool went to the woods, found the bear, removed his skin, and sold it, and with that money got him a wife. Then the ox, the sheep, and the cock came back home.

DAWN, EVENING, AND MIDNIGHT

IN A CERTAIN KINGDOM there was a king who had three daughters of surpassing beauty. The king guarded them more carefully than his most precious treasure; he built underground chambers and kept his daughters there like birds in a cage, so that rough winds could not blow upon them nor the red sun scorch them with his rays. One day the princesses read in a certain book that there was a marvelous bright world, and when the king came to visit them, they straightway began to implore him with tears in their eyes, saying: "Sovereign, our father, let us out to see the bright world and walk in the green garden." The king tried to dissuade them but to no avail. They would not even listen to him; the more he refused, the more urgently they besought him. There was nothing to be done, so the king granted their insistent prayer.

And so the beautiful princesses went out to walk in the garden. They beheld the red sun, the trees, and the flowers, and were overjoyed that they had the freedom of the bright world. They ran about in the garden and enjoyed themselves —when a sudden whirlwind seized them and carried them off far and high, no one knew whither. The alarmed nurses and governesses ran to report this to the king; the king straightway sent his faithful servants in all directions, promising a great reward to him who should find traces of the princesses. The servants traveled and traveled but did not discover anything and came back no wiser than they had set out. The king called his grand council together and asked his councilors and boyars whether anyone among them would undertake to search for his daughters. To any man who might find them, he said, he would give the princess of his choice in marriage, and a rich dowry. The king asked once and the boyars were silent; he asked a second time and they still did not answer; he asked a third time and no one made a sound! The king burst into tears. "Apparently I have no friends or helpers here," he said, and ordered that a call be issued throughout the kingdom. He hoped that someone from among the common people would undertake the heavy task.

At that time there lived in one village a poor widow who had three sons; they were mighty champions. All of them were born in one night—the eldest in the evening, the second at midnight, and the youngest in the early dawn, and therefore they were called Evening, Midnight, and Dawn. When the king's call reached them, they straightway asked for their mother's blessing, made ready for their journey, and rode to the capital city. They came to the king, bowed low, and said: "Rule for many years, sovereign! We have come to you not to celebrate a feast, but to perform a task. Give us leave to go in search of your daughters." "Hail, good youths! What are your names?" "We are three brothers—Evening, Midnight, and Dawn." "What shall I give you for your voyage?" "We do not need anything, sire; only do not forget our mother, care for her in her poverty and old age." The king took the old woman into his palace, and ordered that she be given food and drink from his table and clothes and shoes from his stores.

The good youths set out on their way. They rode one month, a second, and a third; then they came to a wide desert steppe. Beyond that steppe was a thick forest, and close to the forest stood a little hut. They knocked at the window and there was no answer; they entered and no one was in the hut. "Well, brothers," said one of the three, "let us stop here for a time and rest from our travels." They undressed, prayed to God, and went to sleep. Next morning Dawn, the youngest brother, said to Evening, his eldest brother: "We two shall go hunting, and you stay at home and prepare our dinner." The eldest brother consented. Near the hut there was a shed full of sheep; without thinking much he took the best ram, slaughtered and cleaned it, and put it on to roast for dinner. He prepared everything and lay down to rest on a bench.

Suddenly there was a rumbling noise, the door opened, and there entered a little man as big as a thumb, with a beard a cubit long. He cast an angry look around and cried to Evening: "How dared you make yourself at home in my house, how dared you slaughter my ram?" Evening answered: "First grow up—otherwise you cannot be seen from the ground! I shall take a spoonful of cabbage soup and a crumb of bread and throw them in your eyes!" The old man as big as a thumb grew more furious: "I am small but strong!" He snatched up a crust of bread and began to beat Evening on the head with it; he beat him till he was half dead and threw him under the bench. Then the little old man ate the roasted ram and went into the woods. Evening tied a rag around his head and lay moaning. The brothers returned and asked him: "What is the matter with you?" "Eh, brothers, I made a fire in the stove, but because of the great heat I got a headache; I lay all day like one dazed, I could neither cook nor roast!"

Next day Dawn and Evening went hunting, and Midnight was left at home to prepare the dinner. Midnight made a fire, chose the fattest ram, slaughtered it, and put it in the oven; then he lay on the bench. Suddenly there was a rumbling noise, and the old man as big as a thumb, with a beard a cubit long, came in and began to beat and thrash him; he almost beat him to death. Then he ate the roasted ram and went into the woods. Midnight tied up his head with a handkerchief and lay under the bench and moaned. The brothers returned. "What is the matter with you?" Dawn asked him. "I have a headache from the fumes of the stove, brothers, and I have not prepared your dinner."

459

On the third day the two elder brothers went hunting and Dawn stayed at home; he chose the best ram, slaughtered and cleaned it, and put it on to roast. Then he lay on the bench. Suddenly there was a rumbling noise—and he saw the old man as big as a thumb, with a beard a cubit long, carrying a whole hayrick on his head and holding a huge cask of water in his hand. The little old man put down the cask of water, spread the hay over the yard, and began to count his sheep. He saw that another ram was missing, grew angry, ran to the house, jumped at Dawn, and hit him on the head with all his strength; Dawn jumped up, grabbed the little old man by his long beard, and began to drag him around, repeating: "Look before you leap, look before you leap!" The old man as big as a thumb, with a beard a cubit long, began to implore him: "Have pity on me, mighty champion, do not put me to death, let my soul repent!" Dawn dragged him out into the yard, led him to an oaken pillar, and fastened his beard to the pillar with a big iron spike; then he returned to the house and sat down to wait for his brothers.

The brothers came back from their hunting and were amazed to find him safe and sound. Dawn smiled and said: "Come with me, brothers, I have caught your fumes and fastened them to a pillar." They went into the yard, they looked—but the old man as big as a thumb had long since run away. But half of his beard dangled from the pillar, and blood was spattered over his tracks. Following this clue, the brothers came to a deep hole in the ground. Dawn went to the woods, gathered lime bast, wound a rope, and told his brothers to drop him underground. Evening and Midnight dropped him into the hole. He found himself in the other world, released himself from the rope, and walked straight ahead. He walked and walked, and saw a copper castle. He entered the castle, and the youngest princess, rosier than a pink rose, whiter than white snow, came out to meet him and asked him kindly: "How have you come here, good youth—of your own will or by compulsion?" "Your father has sent me in search of you, princess." She straightway seated him at the table, gave him meat and drink, and then handed him a phial with the water of strength. "Drink of this

water," she said, "and you will have added strength." Dawn drank the phial of water and felt great power in himself. "Now," he thought, "I can get the better of anyone."

At this moment a wild wind arose, and the princess was frightened. "Presently," she said, "my dragon will come." And she took Dawn by his hand and hid him in the adjoining room. A three-headed dragon came flying, struck the damp earth, turned into a youth, and cried: "Oh, there is a Russian smell in here! Who is visiting you?" "Who could be here? You have been flying over Russia and you have the Russian smell in your nostrils—that is why you fancy it is here." The dragon asked for food and drink; the princess brought him a variety of meats and drink and poured a sleeping potion into the wine. The dragon ate and drank his fill and was soon overwhelmed by drowsiness; he made the princess pick the lice from his hair, lay on her knees, and fell sound asleep. The princess called Dawn. He came forth, swung his sword, and cut off all of the dragon's three heads; then he made a bonfire, burned the foul dragon and scattered his ashes in the open field. "Now farewell, princess! I am going to seek your sisters; and when I have found them I shall come back for you," said Dawn, and set out.

He walked and walked, and came to a silver castle; in that castle lived the second princess. Dawn killed a six-headed dragon there and went on. After a long time or a short time, he reached a golden castle, and in that castle lived the eldest princess; Dawn killed a twelve-headed dragon and freed that princess from captivity. The princess was overjoyed, made ready to return home, went out into the wide courtyard, waved a red handkerchief, and the golden kingdom rolled up into an egg; she took the egg, put it in her pocket, and went with Dawn to seek her sisters. These princesses did the same thing: they rolled up their kingdoms into eggs, took them, and all of them went to the hole. Evening and Midnight pulled their brother and the three princesses out into the bright world. They all came together to their own land; the princesses rolled their eggs into the open field, and straightway three kingdoms appeared, a copper, a silver and a golden one. The king was more overjoyed than any tongue can tell; he immediately married Dawn, Evening, and Midnight to his daughters, and at his death made Dawn his heir.

TWO IVANS,
SOLDIER'S SONS

IN A CERTAIN KINGDOM in a certain land there lived a peasant. The time came for him to be taken as a soldier. His wife was pregnant, and as he bade her farewell, he said: "Mind you, wife, live decently, do not become the laughing-stock of respectable people. Do not ruin our house, but manage it wisely and await my return; with the help of God, I may be retired and return home. Here are fifty rubles for you; whether you give birth to a daughter or a son, keep the money till the child is of age. Thus you will have a dowry if you want to marry your daughter; and if God gives us a son, this money will be of no little help to him when he grows up." He said farewell to his wife and marched off to the regiment to which he was ordered.

Three months later, his wife bore twin boys and named them each Ivan. The boys began to grow; like leavened wheat dough they stood higher and higher. When they were ten years old, their mother sent them to school; soon they learned their letters and were more than a match for the boyars' and merchants' sons—no one could read or write or answer questions better than they. The boyars' and merchants' sons envied the twins and beat and pinched them every day. One of the brothers said to the other: "How long will they beat and pinch us? Our mother will never be able to make us enough clothes or buy us enough caps; whatever we put on, our comrades tear to shreds.

Let us show them what we can do." So they agreed to stand by each other. Next day the boyars' and merchants' sons began to provoke them, and they, instead of bearing it patiently, replied in kind; they smashed an eye of one, tore off a hand of another, and knocked off the head of a third. They beat them all up, to the very last one. Then guards came, shackled the two good youths, and threw them into prison. The affair was brought before the king himself, who summoned the boys, questioned them about everything, and ordered them to be released, saying: "They are not guilty. God punished those who started the fight."

When the two Ivans grew up they asked their mother: "Mother, did not our father leave us some money? If so, let us have it; we will go to town to the fair and buy us each a good horse." Their mother gave them fifty rubles, twenty-five to each, and said: "Listen to me, children! As you travel to town, bow to everyone whom you encounter." "Very well, dear mother," the two Ivans said.

The brothers went to town, came to the horse market, looked about, and saw many horses; but none was strong enough for the good youths. The one brother said to the other: "Let us go to the other end of the square; see what enormous crowds are gathered there." They made their way through the crowd and saw two colts fastened with chains to oaken posts—one with six chains, the other with twelve. The horses tugged at their chains, gnawed their bits, and pawed the ground with their hoofs. No one could go near them. "What is the price of your colts?" one of the brothers asked the owner. "Don't put your nose into this, friend," answered the owner. "These wares are not for the likes of you." "Why do you talk without knowing what you're talking about?" said one Ivan. "Perhaps I can buy them—only first I must look at their teeth." The owner smiled. "Go ahead, look—if you don't mind losing your head!" One of the brothers went up to the horse that was tied with six chains and the other to the horse that was tied with twelve chains. They tried to look at the horses' teeth, but there was no way of doing it; the colts reared up on their hind legs and snorted viciously. The brothers struck them in the breast with their knees; the chains burst asunder, the colts jumped up as high as ten yards, and fell with their legs up. "See what you boasted of!" said the brothers. "We wouldn't take such jades for a gift."

The crowd gasped with amazement at champions of such strength. The horse dealer was almost in tears: his colts had galloped beyond the town and began to run all over the open field; no one dared to come close to them and no one knew how to catch them. The two Ivans were sorry for the owner, went into the open field, called with loud shouts and mighty whistling, and the colts came back and stood as though rooted to the spot. The two good youths put the iron chains on them, led them to the oaken posts, and tethered them tightly. When they had done this they went home.

As they walked along the road, they met a gray old man, but, forgetting what their mother had told them, they passed him by without greeting him. Later one of them realized their mistake and said: "Ah, brother, what have we done? We did not bow to that old man; let us run after him and bow to him." They caught up with the old man, doffed their caps, bowed to the waist, and said: "Forgive us, grandfather, for having gone by without greeting you. Our mother enjoined upon us strictly to pay honor to everyone whom we meet." "Thanks, good youths! Whither is God taking you?" "We went to the fair and wanted to buy a horse for each of us, but we could not find suitable ones." "How is that? Shall I give you each a little horse?" "Ah, grandfather, if you do, we shall always pray to God for you." "Well, come with me." The old man led them to a big mountain, opened a cast-iron door, and brought out two mighty steeds. "Here are your horses, good youths! God speed you—keep them and enjoy them!" They thanked him, mounted the steeds, and galloped home; they reached their house, tied the steeds to a post, and entered in. Their mother asked them: "Well, my children, have you got your horses?" "We did not buy them, we received them free." "Where have you put them?" "At the side of the house." "Ah, my children, someone might take them away." "No, mother, not such horses. No one could even come near them, let alone take them away." The mother went out to the yard, looked at the horses, and burst into tears. "Ah, my dear sons," she said, "surely you are not going to be my support."

Next day the sons asked their mother's leave to go to town and buy swords for themselves. "Go, my beloved ones," she said. They made ready and went to the smithy. "Make us each a sword," they said to the master. "Why should I make them when I have them ready?" said the smith. "Take as many as you need." "No, friend, we need swords that weigh a thousand pounds each." "Eh, what kind of idea is that? Who could wield such a machine? In the whole world there is no forge big enough to forge them." The good youths hung their heads and went home; on their way they met the same old man. "Good day, young men," he said. "Good day, grandfather," they re- plied. "Where have you been?" "At the smithy in town; we wanted to buy a sword for each of us, but we could not find any suitable ones." "That's bad! Shall I give you each a sword?" "Ah, grandfather, if you do, we shall always pray to God for you." The old man led them to the big mountain, opened a cast-iron door, and brought out two mighty swords. They took the swords and thanked the old man, and their hearts were full of joy.

The two Ivans came home, and their mother asked them: "Well, my children, have you bought the swords?" "We did not buy them, we got them free." "Where have you put them?" "We have stood them up in front of the house." "Look out, someone might take them." "No, mother, no one could even lift them, let alone cart them away." The mother went out to the yard and saw two huge, heavy swords leaning against the wall, so that the little hut barely remained upright. She burst into tears and said: "Ah, my sons, surely you are not going to be my support."

Next morning the two Ivans saddled their good steeds, came into the house, prayed to God, and said farewell to their mother. "Give us your blessing, mother," they said, "for our distant journey." "Let my never ceasing maternal blessing be upon you, my children," she said. "Go with God, show your- selves, and see people; offend no one without cause, and yield

466

not to evil enemies." "Fear not, mother! We have a motto: 'When I ride I don't whistle, but when I am forced to fight, I don't yield.' " And the good youths mounted their steeds and rode off.

After they had gone a short distance or a long distance, a long time or a short time—for speedily a tale is spun, but with less speed a deed is done—they came to a crossroads where two posts stood. One post bore the inscription: 'He who goes to the right will become a king.' The other post bore the inscription: 'He who goes to the left will be slain.' The brothers stopped, read the inscriptions on the posts and wondered in which direction each should go. If both took the right, it would not do honor to their mighty strength, their youthful valor. If one went to the left—but who wants to die? But there was no choice, and so one brother said to the other: "Well, dear brother, I am stronger than you; I will go to the left and see what it is that can cause my death. But do you go to the right; perhaps God will help you and you will become king." They said farewell to each other, exchanged handkerchiefs, and solemnly agreed that each would go his way, put up posts along the road, and write about himself on these posts as a mark and guide. They pledged that every morning each of them would wipe his face with his brother's handkerchief; if one of them should see blood appearing on the handkerchief, it would mean that death had befallen his brother, and in the event of such a calamity he was to set out in search of the dead.

The good youths parted. The one who turned his steed to the right came to a glorious kingdom. In that kingdom there lived a king and queen whose daughter was Princess Nastasya the Beautiful. When the king saw Ivan, the soldier's son, he loved him for his heroic valor, and without thinking very long about it gave him his daughter to wife, called him Prince Ivan, and charged him with the rule of the whole kingdom. Prince Ivan lived happily, feasted his eyes upon his wife, gave law and order to the kingdom and amused himself by hunting animals. One day he made ready to go hunting, began to put the trappings on his horse, and found two phials sewed up in the saddle: one contained healing water and the other the water of life. He looked at these phials and put them back into the saddle. "I shall keep them for my hour of danger," he thought. "Some day they may be needed."

Meanwhile the brother who had taken the road to the left galloped night and day without rest; a month, a second month, then a third month passed, and he arrived in an unknown kingdom, in the center of its capital. There was a great sorrow in this kingdom: the houses were draped with black cloth, the people staggered about as though in sleep. He hired wretched quarters at a poor old woman's house and began to question her. "Tell me, grandmother," he said, "why are all the people in your kingdom so grieved, why are all the houses draped with black cloth?" "Ah, good youth," the old woman said, "a great misfortune has come upon us. Every day a twelve-headed dragon comes forth from the blue sea, from behind a gray stone, and devours a man; and now it is the turn of the king's family. He has three beautiful princesses; just now the oldest has been taken to the shore, to be devoured by the dragon."

Ivan, the soldier's son, mounted his horse and galloped to the blue sea, to the gray stone: on the shore stood the beautiful princess, bound by an iron chain. She saw the knight and said to him: "Go hence, good youth! Soon the twelve-headed dragon will come. I am doomed, and if you stay you will not escape death either; the cruel dragon will devour you." "Fear not, lovely maiden," he replied. "He might choke to death on me." Ivan came up to her, seized the chain with his mighty hand, and tore it into little bits as though it were a rotten rope; then he laid his head on the lovely maiden's knee and said: "Now pick in my hair for lice. But do not so much pick as watch the sea: as soon as a cloud arises, and the winds begin to roar, and the sea to surge, rouse me." The lovely maiden did as he told her; more than she picked in his hair, she watched the sea. Suddenly a cloud arose, the wind began to roar, the sea surged; a dragon emerged from the blue sea and reared up in the air. The princess roused Ivan; he rose, and had no sooner mounted his steed than the dragon flew up to him. "Why have you come here, Ivanushka?" the monster said. "This is my place. Say farewell to the white world and hasten into my throat of your own accord—it will be easier for you." "You lie, accursed dragon!" answered the champion. "You won't swallow me, you will choke on me!" He bared his sharp sword, took a swing, and cut off all the twelve heads of the dragon; he lifted the gray stone, put the heads under it, threw the trunk into the sea, returned home to the old woman, ate and drank his fill, lay down to sleep, and slept for three days.

Meanwhile the king had called his water carrier and said to him: "Go to the shore, at least gather up the princess' bones." The water carrier went to the blue sea and saw that the princess was alive and unhurt. He put her on his cart and drove into a thick forest; in the forest he began to whet his knife. "What are you going to do?" the princess asked him. "I am whetting my knife to slay you," replied the water carrier. The princess began to weep. "Do not slay me, I have not done you any harm," she begged. "Tell your father that I have rescued you from the dragon," the water carrier said. "Then I will spare you." She had no choice but to consent. They went to the palace. The king was overjoyed and made the water carrier a colonel.

When Ivan awoke he called the old woman, gave her money, and said to her: "Grandmother, go to market, buy what you need, and listen to what the people are saying among themselves. Find out what news there is." The old woman went to market, bought various provisions, listened to people's talk, returned home, and said: "This is what people are saying. There was a great dinner at the king's palace; princes and envoys and boyars and notables were sitting at his table, when an iron arrow flew through the window and fell in the middle of the chamber; to that arrow was fastened a letter from another twelve-headed dragon. The dragon wrote: 'If you do not send me your second daughter, I shall burn your kingdom with fire and scatter its ashes.' Now they are about to take the poor maiden to the blue sea, to the gray stone." Ivan straightway saddled his good steed, mounted him, and galloped to the seashore. The princess said to him: "Why have you come here, good youth? My turn has come to die and to shed my young blood; but why should you perish?" "Fear not, lovely maiden!" said Ivan. "God may save you." He had no sooner said this than the cruel dragon flew up to him, breathing flames, threatening him with death. The champion struck him with his sharp sword and cut off all of his twelve heads; he put the heads under the stone, threw the trunk into the sea, returned home, ate and drank his fill, and again lay down to sleep for three days and three nights. The water carrier went down to the shore again, saw that the princess was alive, put her in his cart, drove to the thick forest, and set about whetting his knife. The princess asked him: "Why are you whetting your knife?" "Because I am going to slay you," he said. "But if you swear to tell your father what I ask you to tell him, I will spare you." The princess swore that she would, and he brought her to the palace. The king was overjoyed and made the water carrier a general.

On the fourth day Ivan awoke and told the old woman to go to market and listen to the news. The old woman ran to the market, returned, and said: "A third dragon has appeared; he sent the king a letter demanding that the third princess be sent him to be devoured." Ivan saddled his good steed, mounted him, and galloped to the blue sea. On the shore stood the beautiful princess, bound to the stone with an iron chain. The champion seized the chain, shook it, and broke it as though it were a rotten rope; then he laid his head on the lovely maiden's knees, saying: "Pick in my hair; and do not so much pick in my hair as watch the sea—as soon as a cloud arises, and the wind begins to roar and the sea to surge, rouse me." The princess began to pick in his hair. Suddenly a cloud came up, the wind began to roar and the sea to surge, and from the blue sea a dragon emerged and reared himself up. The princess began to rouse Ivan; she nudged and nudged him, but he did not awake. She burst into tears, and burning tears dropped on his cheek. This caused the champion to wake; he ran to his steed, and the good steed had already dug up half a yard of earth with his hoofs. The twelve-headed dragon flew toward them, breathing flames. He cast a glance at the champion and cried: "You are handsome and strong, good youth, but you won't stay alive; I'll devour you down to the last bone." "You lie, accursed dragon!" Ivan answered him. "You will choke on me!"

Instantly they were locked in mortal combat. Ivan swung his sword so fast and mightily that it grew red hot, he could not hold it in his hand. He begged the princess: "Save me, lovely maiden! Take off your precious kerchief, wet it in the blue sea, and give it to me to wrap my sword in." The princess straightway wet her kerchief and gave it to the good youth. He wrapped it around his sword and fell to hacking at the dragon; he cut off all the twelve heads of the monster, put them under the stone, threw the trunk into the sea, galloped home, ate and drank his fill, and lay down to sleep for three days.

Again the king sent the water carrier to the seashore. The water carrier went there, took the princess to the thick forest, drew out his knife, and began to whet it. "What are you doing?" asked the princess. "I am whetting my knife to slay you," he answered. He terrified the lovely maiden, and she swore that she would say what he commanded. Now the youngest daughter was the king's favorite; when he saw her alive and unhurt, he was even more overjoyed than before, and to reward the water carrier wished to give him this favorite daughter to wife. The rumor of it went through the whole kingdom. Ivan the champion learned that the king was making preparations for a wedding. He went straight to the palace; there a feast was in full swing, the guests were eating and drinking, and diverting themselves with various games. The youngest princess saw Ivan, recognized her precious kerchief on his sword, jumped up, took him by his hand, and brought him to her father. "My dear father and sovereign," she said, "here is the man who saved us from the cruel dragon and from undeserved death; and all that the water carrier did was whet his knife and say: 'I am whetting my knife to slay you.'" The king was furious, ordered the water carrier to be hanged on the spot, and married the princess to Ivan, the soldier's son. There was great rejoicing. The young people began to live together happily and prosperously.

While all this was going on, this is what befell the other brother, Prince Ivan. One day he went hunting and came upon a fleet-footed stag. He spurred his horse and pursued the stag; he galloped and galloped and came to a broad meadow. Here the stag vanished. The prince looked about and wondered in what direction he should go. Then he saw a little stream flowing in the meadow, and on the water two gray ducks were swimming. He took aim with his gun, fired it, and killed the pair of ducks; then he dragged them out of the water, put them in his bag, and went on farther. He rode and rode, and he saw a white stone palace; he climbed down from his horse, tied it to a post, and went into the chambers. They were all empty, there was not a living soul anywhere. But in one room there was fire in the stove, a pan stood on the hearth, the table was set: there was a plate, a fork, and a knife. Prince Ivan took the ducks out of his bag, plucked and cleaned them, put them in the pan, and shoved the pan into the oven; when the ducks were roasted, he put them on the table and began to carve and eat them. Suddenly out of nowhere a lovely maiden appeared before him—such a beauty as neither tongue can tell of nor pen describe—and said: "Welcome, Prince Ivan." "Welcome, lovely maiden, sit down and eat with me," Ivan said. "I would sit with you, but I am afraid: you have a magic horse." "No, lovely maiden, you are mistaken; my magic horse is at home, I have come on an ordinary horse." When the lovely maiden heard this she began to swell up and turned into a terrible lioness; she opened her jaws and swallowed the prince whole. For she was not an ordinary maiden, but the sister of the three dragons that Ivan the champion had slain.

One day Ivan the champion recalled his brother, drew from his pocket the handkerchief that had been the other Ivan's, wiped himself, and lo and behold, the whole handkerchief was drenched with blood. He grieved deeply. "What does this mean?" he said. "My brother took the good road, which was to make him king, and he has met his death!" He took leave of his wife and father-in-law and went on his mighty steed to seek his brother. After he had journeyed a short distance or a long distance, for a long time or a short time, he came to the kingdom where his brother had lived. He made inquiries and learned that the prince had gone hunting and vanished without a trace.

472

Ivan the champion went hunting in the same forest and he too saw the fleet-footed stag, and started in pursuit of it. He came to the wide meadow and the stag vanished; he saw a little stream flowing through the meadow and two ducks swimming on the water. Ivan the champion shot the ducks, came to the white stone palace, and entered the chambers. It was empty everywhere, but in one room there was a fire in the stove, and a pan stood on the hearth. He roasted the ducks, took them out on the porch, sat there in the yard, and carved and ate them.

Suddenly a lovely maiden appeared before him. "Welcome, good youth!" she said. "Why are you eating in the yard?" "I don't like to eat indoors, it is more pleasant outside," replied Ivan. "Sit down with me, lovely maiden." "I would sit down gladly, but I am afraid of your magic horse." "Don't be afraid, my beauty! I have come on an ordinary horse." She foolishly believed him, and she began to swell up; she became a terrible lioness, but when she was about to swallow the good youth, his magic steed came running and took hold of her with his mighty legs. Ivan the champion bared his sharp sword and cried in a loud voice: "Wait, accursed one! You swallowed my brother, Prince Ivan! Disgorge him, or I shall cut you into little pieces!" The lioness spat out Prince Ivan; he was dead, he had begun to rot, and the flesh of his face had fallen off. Ivan the champion took the two phials with healing water and the water of life from his saddle; he sprinkled his brother with the healing water, and the flesh grew together; he sprinkled him with the water of life, and the prince stood up and said: "Ah, how long have I slept!" Ivan the champion answered: "You would have slept forever were it not for me."

Then he took his sword and wanted to cut off the lioness' head; but she turned into an exquisite maiden, such a beauty as no tale can tell of, and began to shed tears and beg for mercy. Looking on her indescribable beauty, Ivan the champion took pity on her and let her go free. The brothers went to the palace and feasted for three days. Then they parted: Prince Ivan remained in his kingdom, and Ivan the champion went to join his wife and began to live with her in love and concord.

After some time, Ivan the champion went for a walk in the open field; he met a little child, who begged him for alms. The good youth was moved, drew a golden coin from his pocket, and gave it to the boy; the boy took the alms, began to swell up, turned into a lion, and tore the champion into little bits. A few days later the same thing happened to Prince Ivan; he went to walk in his garden and met an old man, who bowed low to him and begged for alms. The prince gave him a gold piece. The old man took the coin, swelled up, and turned into a lion, seized Prince Ivan, and tore him into little bits. Thus died the two mighty champions, the soldier's sons—at the hands of the dragons' sister.

PRINCE IVAN
AND BYELY POLYANIN

IN A CERTAIN KINGDOM in a certain land there lived a king who had three daughters and one son, Prince Ivan. The king grew old and died, and Prince Ivan succeeded to the throne. Upon learning this, the neighboring kings gathered together innumerable troops and waged war against him. Prince Ivan did not know what to do. He came to his sisters and asked them: "My dear sisters, what shall I do? All the kings are waging war against me." "Ah, you brave warrior!" they said: "Why are you afraid? Think of how Byely Polyanin for thirty years has been warring against Baba Yaga the Golden-legged, without ever climbing down from his horse, without a moment's respite. And you are afraid without having seen anything!" Prince Ivan straightway saddled his good steed, donned his armor, took a steel sword, a long spear, and a silken riding crop, prayed to God, and rode forth to meet the enemy. He did not cut down as many with his sword as he trampled with his steed. He slew all the enemy troops, returned to his capital, lay down to sleep, and slept for three days without awakening.

On the fourth day he awoke, went out on the balcony, looked out on the open field, and saw that the other kings had gathered even more troops than before and were again approaching the very walls of his town. The prince was grieved and went to his sisters. "Ah, my sisters, what shall I do?" he said. "I have destroyed one army; now there is another one at the city gates, more menacing than the first." "What kind of warrior are you?" his sisters said. "You fought for a day and then slept three days without awakening. See how Byely Polyanin has been warring for thirty years against Baba Yaga the Golden-legged, without ever climbing down from his horse, without a moment's respite!" Prince Ivan ran to the white stone stable, saddled a mighty steed, donned his armor, girded on his steel sword, took a long spear in one hand and a silken riding crop in the other, prayed to God, and went forth to fight the enemy. Like a bright falcon swooping down on a flock of geese, swans, and gray ducks, Prince Ivan fell upon the enemy host; he did not slay as many himself as his steed trampled down. He defeated the great host of troops, returned home, lay down to sleep, and slept without awakening for six days.

On the seventh day he awoke, went out on the balcony, looked out on the open field, and saw that the other kings had gathered together an even greater army than before and had again surrounded the entire town. Prince Ivan went to his sisters, saying: "My dear sisters, what shall I do? I have destroyed two armies; now there's a third one before our walls, more menacing than the others." "Ah, you brave warrior!" his sisters said. "You fought for one day and slept for six days without awakening. Think of how Byely Polyanin has been warring for thirty years against Baba Yaga the Golden-legged, without ever climbing down from his horse, without a moment's respite!" The prince was stung to the quick; he ran to the white stone stable, saddled his good steed, donned his armor, girded on his steel sword, took a long spear in one hand and a silken riding crop in the other, prayed to God, and went forth to fight the enemy. As a bright falcon swoops down on a flock

476

of geese, swans, and gray ducks, so Prince Ivan fell upon the enemy troops; he did not slay as many himself as his horse trampled down. He defeated the great host of troops, returned home, lay down to sleep, and slept for ten days without awakening.

On the tenth day he awoke, summoned all his ministers and senators, and said: "My ministers and senators, I have decided to go to foreign lands, to see Byely Polyanin; I charge you to rule and govern and judge all matters in accordance with the truth." Then he took leave of his sisters, mounted his horse,

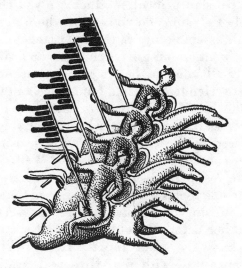

and set out on his way. After a long time or a short time, he entered a dark forest and saw a little hut in which an old man dwelt. Prince Ivan went in to see him. "Good day, grandfather," he said. "Good day, Russian prince! Whither is God taking you?" "I am seeking Byely Polyanin; do you know where he is?" "I myself do not know, but wait awhile; I shall assemble my faithful servants and ask them." The old man went out on the porch, blew on a silver trumpet, and suddenly birds began to fly toward him from all sides. A numberless host of them came, covering the whole sky like a black cloud. The old man cried in a loud voice and whistled with a mighty whistle: "My faithful servants, birds of passage, have you ever

477

seen, have you ever heard anything about Byely Polyanin?"
"No," the reply came, "we have not seen him with our eyes nor
heard of him with our ears." "Well, Prince Ivan," said the old
man, "go to my older brother, he may be able to tell you. Here
is a little ball, let it roll before you; wherever the ball rolls,
there direct your horse to go."

Prince Ivan mounted his good steed, rolled his ball, and
rode after it; and the forest grew darker and darker. The
prince rode up to a little hut and entered it; in the hut sat an
old man, hoary with age. "Good day, grandfather!" he said.
"Good day, Russian prince! Whither are you going?" "I am
seeking Byely Polyanin; do you know where he is?" "Wait a
while; I shall assemble my faithful servants and ask them."
The old man went out on the porch, blew on a silver trumpet,
and suddenly all kinds of beasts gathered around him from
every side. He cried to them in a loud voice and whistled with
a mighty whistle: "My faithful servants, my roving beasts,
have you ever seen, have you ever heard of Byely Polyanin?"
"No," answered the beasts, "we have not seen him with our
eyes nor heard about him with our ears." "Well, take a roll call
among yourselves; perhaps not all of you are here." The beasts
took count among themselves and discovered that the one-eyed
she-wolf was missing. Straightway messengers set out and soon
they brought her before the old man. "Tell me, one-eyed she-
wolf, do you know Byely Polyanin?" "How can I help knowing
him, since I am always with him? He defeats armies and I feed
on their carrion." "Where is he now?" "In the open field, on a
high mound, asleep in his tent. He battled with Baba Yaga the
Golden-legged, and after the contest he lay down to sleep for
twelve days." "Take Prince Ivan there," the old man ordered.

The she-wolf ran off and the prince galloped after her. He
came to the high mound, entered the tent, and found Byely
Polyanin sleeping soundly. He said to himself: "My sisters said
that Byely Polyanin wages war without ever resting, and here
he has lain down to sleep for twelve days. Why shouldn't I too
go to sleep for the present?" Prince Ivan thought and thought,
and then lay down beside Byely Polyanin. At that moment a
little bird came flying into the tent, circled around the head of

the bed, and said: "Arise, awake, Byely Polyanin, and make a cruel end of my brother, Prince Ivan! If you do not, he will rise up and slay you." Prince Ivan jumped up, caught the bird, tore off her right leg, threw her out of the tent, and again lay down beside Byely Polyanin. He had not yet fallen asleep when another bird flew in, circled around the head of the bed, and said: "Arise, awake, Byely Polyanin, and make a cruel end of my brother, Prince Ivan! If you do not, he will rise up and slay you." Prince Ivan jumped up, caught the bird, tore off her right wing, threw her out of the tent, and lay down in the same place. Then a third little bird flew in, circled around the head of the bed, and said: "Arise, awake, Byely Polyanin, and make a cruel end of my brother, Prince Ivan! If you do not, he will rise up and slay you." Prince Ivan jumped up, caught the bird, and tore off her beak; he threw out the bird, lay down, and fell sound asleep.

At the time he had set for himself, Byely Polyanin awoke and saw an unknown knight lying beside him; he seized his sharp sword and was about to put the knight to a cruel death, but restrained himself in time. "No," he thought, "he came here while I was asleep and did not dip his sword in my blood. It would be no honor for me to kill him; a sleeping man is like a dead man. Instead, I will awaken him." He roused Prince Ivan and asked him: "Are you a good man or a wicked man? Tell me—what is your name and why have you come here?" "My name is Prince Ivan and I have come to see you, to try your strength." "You are quite bold, prince! You entered my tent without permission, you went to sleep beside me without announcing yourself; for that I could put you to death." "Eh, Byely Polyanin, you're bragging before you have jumped the ditch! Wait, perhaps you will stumble. You have two arms, but I was not born with one arm either."

They mounted their mighty steeds, rushed at each other, and clashed so violently that their spears were shattered into smithereens and their good steeds fell to the ground. Prince Ivan unhorsed Byely Polyanin and raised his sharp sword over him. Byely Polyanin implored him: "Do not give me death, give me life! I shall call myself your younger brother, I shall honor you as a father." Prince Ivan took him by his hand, raised him from the ground, kissed him on the mouth, called him his younger brother, and said: "Brother, I have been told that for thirty years you have been warring against Baba Yaga the Golden-legged; what is the cause of your war?" "She has a beautiful daughter; I want to win her and marry her." "Well," said the prince, "since we are friends, I will help you in your trouble. Let us go to war together."

They mounted their steeds and rode into the open field; Baba Yaga the Golden-legged brought forth an innumerable host of troops. Like bright falcons swooping down on a flock of pigeons, the mighty champions fell upon the enemy army; they cut them down with their swords less than they trampled them with their horses, and indeed they cut and trampled thousands upon thousands. Baba Yaga took to her heels and Prince Ivan set out in pursuit of her. He had almost caught up with her when she ran to the edge of a sharp precipice, pulled up a cast-iron trap door, and vanished underground. Prince Ivan and Byely Polyanin bought a great multitude of oxen, slaughtered them, skinned them, and cut the skins into thongs; with these thongs they wound a cable so long that it would reach from this world to the other world. The prince said to Byely Polyanin: "Lower me into the chasm but do not pull out the cable until I give it a tug; then pull me out." Byely Polyanin lowered him into the very bottom of the chasm. Prince Ivan looked about him and went to search for Baba Yaga.

He walked and walked, and saw some tailors sitting behind a grating. "What are you doing here?" he asked. "We are sewing an army for Baba Yaga the Golden-legged." "But how do you do it?" "It is quite simple; every time we take a stitch with the needle, a Cossack with a lance mounts a horse, gets in line, and sets out to war against Byely Polyanin." "Eh, brothers, you are working quite fast, but not solidly; stand in a row, and I will show you how to sew more solidly." They stood in one row; Prince Ivan swung his sword and all their heads flew off.

Having slain the tailors, he went on farther. He walked and walked and saw some cobblers sitting behind a grating. "What

480

are you doing here?" he asked. "We are preparing an army for Baba Yaga the Golden-legged." "How do you prepare an army, brothers?" "This way," they said. "Each time we make a prick with an awl, a soldier with a gun mounts a horse, stands in line, and sets out to war against Byely Polyanin." "Eh, brothers, you are working fast, but poorly. Stand in a row, I will show you how to do it better." They stood in a row; Prince Ivan swung his sword and their heads flew off.

Having slain the cobblers, he went on farther. After a long time or a short time he reached a great and beautiful city; in that city there was a royal castle and in the castle sat a maiden of indescribable beauty. She saw the good youth through the window; she fell in love with his black curls, his falcon eyes, his sable brows, his heroic gait. She invited the prince to her room and questioned him as to whither and why he was traveling. He told her that he was looking for Baba Yaga the Golden-legged. "Ah, Prince Ivan, I am her daughter. She is now sound asleep; she lay down to rest for twelve days." The maiden led him out of the city and showed him the way; Prince Ivan went to Baba Yaga, found her asleep, struck her with his sword, and cut off her head. The head rolled and uttered these words: "Strike again, Prince Ivan!" "A hero strikes once, and that is enough," said the prince.

He returned to the castle and sat down with the lovely maiden at an oaken table with a checkered cloth. He ate and drank and asked her: "Is there anyone in the world stronger than I or more beautiful than you?" "Ah, Prince Ivan, what sort of beauty am I?" the maiden replied. "Beyond thrice nine lands, in the thrice tenth kingdom, there lives a princess in the dragon king's palace. She is really of an indescribable beauty; I am only good enough to wash myself in the water in which she has washed her feet." Prince Ivan took the lovely maiden by her white hand, led her to the place where the cable hung, and gave a sign to Byely Polyanin. The warrior pulled out the cable and with it the prince and the lovely maiden. "Hail, Byely Polyanin," said Prince Ivan, "here is your bride; live merrily, do not worry about anything. As for me, I am going to the dragon's kingdom."

He mounted his good steed, said farewell to Byely Polyanin and his bride, and galloped beyond thrice nine lands. After a long time or a short time—for speedily a tale is spun, but with much less speed a deed is done—he came to the dragon's kingdom, slew the dragon king, rescued the beautiful princess from captivity, and married her. Then he returned home and began to live with his young wife in happiness and prosperity.

THE CRYSTAL MOUNTAIN

IN A CERTAIN KINGDOM in a certain land there lived a king who had three sons. One day they said to him: "Father, our gracious sovereign, give us your blessing; we wish to go hunting." The father gave them his blessing and they set out in different directions. The youngest son rode and rode and lost his way; he came to a clearing, and there lay a dead horse, around which were gathered beasts of many kinds, birds, and reptiles. A falcon rose, flew up to the prince, perched on his shoulder, and said: "Prince Ivan, divide that horse among us; it has lain here for thirty years, and we have been quarreling ever since, unable to find a way of sharing it." The prince climbed down from his good steed and divided the carcass: he gave the bones to the beasts, the flesh to the birds, the skin to the reptiles, and the head to the ants. "Thank you, Prince Ivan," said the falcon. "For your kindness you shall be able to turn into a bright falcon or an ant whenever you wish."

Prince Ivan struck the damp earth, turned into a bright falcon, soared up into the air, and flew to the thrice tenth kingdom. More than half of that kingdom had been swallowed into a crystal mountain. The prince flew straight into the royal palace, turned into a goodly youth, and asked the palace guards: "Will your king take me into his service?" "Why should he not take such a goodly youth?" they answered. Thus he entered the service of that king and lived in his palace for one week, then a second, then a third. The king's daughter asked her father: "Father, my sovereign, give me leave to take a ride with Prince Ivan to the crystal mountain." The king gave her leave. They mounted good steeds and set out. When they approached the crystal mountain, a golden goat jumped suddenly out from nowhere. The prince chased it; he galloped and galloped, but could not catch the goat, and when he returned the princess had vanished. What was he to do? How could he dare to appear before the king?

He disguised himself as a very old man, so that he would be unrecognizable, came to the palace, and said to the king: "Your Majesty, hire me as your herdsman." "Very well," said the king, "be my herdsman. When the three-headed dragon comes to your herd, give him three cows; when the six-headed dragon comes, give him six cows; and when the twelve-headed dragon comes, count off twelve cows." Prince Ivan drove his herd over mountains and valleys. Suddenly the three-headed dragon came flying from a lake and said: "Ah, Prince Ivan, what kind of work are you engaged in? A goodly youth like you should be vying in combat, not tending cattle. Well, let me have three cows!" "Won't that be too much?" asked the prince. "I myself eat only one duck a day, and you want three cows. But you won't get any!" The dragon flew into a rage, and instead of three cows, seized six. Prince Ivan straightway turned into a bright falcon, cut off all the three heads of the dragon, and drove the cattle home. "Well, grandfather," asked the king, "has the three-headed dragon come? Did you give him three cows?" "No, Your Majesty," replied Prince Ivan, "I did not give him any."

Next day the prince drove his herd over mountains and valleys, and the six-headed dragon came from the lake and demanded six cows. "Ah, you gluttonous monster," said the prince, "I myself eat only one duck a day, and see what you demand! I won't give you any!" The dragon flew into a rage and instead of six, seized twelve cows; but the prince turned into a bright falcon, fell upon the dragon, and cut off his six heads. He drove the herd home and the king asked him: "Well, grandfather, has the six-headed dragon come? Has my herd grown much smaller?" "Come he did, but he took nothing," answered the prince.

Late at night Prince Ivan turned into an ant and crawled into the crystal mountain through a little crack. Lo and behold, the princess was in the crystal mountain. "Good evening!" said Prince Ivan. "How did you get here?" "The twelve-headed dragon carried me off," said the princess. "He lives in father's lake and has a coffer in his side. In this coffer is a hare, in this hare is a duck, in this duck is an egg, and in this egg is a seed. If you slay the dragon and get that seed, it will be possible to destroy the crystal mountain and rescue me."

Prince Ivan crawled out of the mountain, turned again into a herdsman, and drove his herd. Suddenly the twelve-headed dragon flew up to him and said: "Ah, Prince Ivan, you are not doing what you should; a goodly youth like you should be vying in combat, not tending a herd. Well, count off twelve cows for me!" "That will be too much for you!" said the prince. "I myself eat only one duck a day, and see what you demand!" They began to fight, and after a long struggle or a short struggle, Prince Ivan defeated the twelve-headed dragon, slashed open his trunk, and found the coffer in his right side. In the coffer he found a hare, in the hare a duck, in the duck an egg, in the egg a seed. He took the seed, set it alight, and brought it to the crystal mountain, which soon melted away. Prince Ivan led the princess to her father, who was overjoyed and said to the prince: "Be my son-in-law!" The wedding was held at once. I was at that wedding too. I drank beer and mead; they flowed down my beard but did not go into my mouth.

484

KOSHCHEY THE DEATHLESS

ONCE THERE WAS a king who had an only son. When the prince was small, his nurses and governesses sang lullabies to him. "Prince Ivan, when you grow up, you will find your bride," they would sing. "Beyond thrice nine lands, in the thrice tenth kingdom, Vasilisa Kirbitievna sits in a tower, and her marrow flows from bone to bone." When the prince had passed his fifteenth year, he began to ask the king's leave to set out in search of his bride. "Whither will you go?" the father asked. "You are still too young." "No, father, when I was little, my nurses and governesses sang lullabies to me and told me where my bride lives; and now I wish to go and find her." The father gave the prince his blessing and sent word to all the kingdoms that his son, Prince Ivan, was setting out to find his bride.

One day the prince came to a certain town, put up his horse to be cared for, and went to walk in the streets. He came to the square and saw that a man was being flogged with a whip. "Why do you whip him?" he asked. "Because he borrowed ten thousand rubles from a prominent merchant," they told him, "and did not pay them back at the agreed time. As for the man who redeems him, his wife will be carried off by Koshchey the Deathless." The prince thought and thought and went away. He walked through the town, then came to the square again, and saw that the man was still being flogged; Prince Ivan took pity on him and decided to redeem him. Since I have no wife, he thought, no one can be taken from me. He paid the ten thousand rubles and went home. Suddenly the man whom he had redeemed ran after him, crying: "Thank you, Prince Ivan! If you had not redeemed me, you would never have won your bride. But now I will help you. Buy me a horse and a saddle at once." The prince bought him a horse and saddle and asked: "What is your name?" "My name is Bulat the Brave," the man said.

They mounted their horses and set out. As soon as they

arrived in the thrice tenth kingdom, Bulat said: "Well, Prince Ivan, order chickens, ducks, and geese to be bought and roasted, so that there will be plenty of everything. And I will get your bride. But mind you: every time I come to you, cut off the right wing of a fowl and serve it to me on a plate." Bulat the Brave went straight to the lofty tower where Vasilisa Kirbitievna was sitting, gently threw a stone, and broke the gilded top of the tower. He ran to Prince Ivan and said: "Why are you sleeping? Give me a chicken." The prince cut off the right wing of a chicken and handed it to him on a plate. Bulat took the plate, ran to the tower, and cried: "Good day, Vasilisa Kirbitievna! Prince Ivan sends you his greetings and has asked me to give you this chicken." The maiden was frightened and sat in silence. But he answered himself in her stead: "Good day, Bulat the Brave! Is Prince Ivan well? Thank God, he is well. And why do you stand like that, Bulat the Brave? Take the key, open the cupboard, drink a glass of vodka, and God speed you."

Then Bulat ran to Prince Ivan. "Why are you sitting?" he said. "Give me a duck." The prince cut off the right wing of a duck and handed it to him on a plate. Bulat took the plate and carried it to the tower. "Good day, Vasilisa Kirbitievna! Prince Ivan sends you his greetings and has asked me to give you this duck." She sat in silence, and he answered himself in her stead: "Good day, Bulat the Brave! Is the prince well? Thank God, he is well. And why do you stand like that, Bulat the Brave? Take the key, open the cupboard, drink a glass of vodka, and God speed you." Then Bulat ran home and again said to Prince Ivan: "Why are you sitting? Give me a goose." The prince cut off the right wing of a goose and handed it to him on a plate. Bulat the Brave took it to the tower. "Good day, Vasilisa Kirbitievna! Prince Ivan sends his greetings and has asked me to give you this goose." Vasilisa Kirbitievna straightway took a key, opened a cupboard, and gave him a glass of vodka. Bulat did not take the glass, but seized the maiden by her right hand, drew her out of the tower, and seated her on Prince Ivan's horse, and the good youths galloped away at a headlong pace, taking the lovely maiden with them.

Next morning King Kirbit woke up and arose, saw that the top of the tower was broken and his daughter stolen, grew terribly angry, and ordered pursuers to set out after her in all directions. Our knights-errant rode a long time or a short time, then Bulat the Brave removed the ring from his hand, hid it, and said: "Ride on, Prince Ivan; but I will turn back and look for my ring." Vasilisa Kirbitievna began to beseech him: "Do not leave us, Bulat the Brave! If you wish, I will give you my ring." He answered: "That is impossible, Vasilisa Kirbitievna. My ring is priceless; my own mother gave it to me, and when she gave it she said: 'Wear it, lose it not, forget not your mother.'" Bulat the Brave rode back and met the pursuers on the road; he straightway slew them all, leaving only one man to bring the news to the king, and hastened to catch up with Prince Ivan. They rode for a long time or a short time, then Bulat the Brave hid his handkerchief and said: "Ah, Prince Ivan, I have lost my handkerchief; ride on, and I will catch up with you soon." He turned back, rode several versts, and met twice as many pursuers; he slew them all and returned to Prince Ivan. The prince asked: "Have you found your handkerchief?" "I have," said Bulat.

Dark night overtook them. They pitched a tent; Bulat the Brave lay down to sleep, set Prince Ivan to guarding the tent, and said to him: "If anything happens, rouse me." The prince stood and stood, then grew tired; drowsiness overcame him, he sat down at the door of the tent, and fell asleep. Suddenly Koshchey the Deathless appeared and carried off Vasilisa Kirbitievna. At daybreak Prince Ivan awoke, saw that his bride was gone, and wept bitterly. Bulat the Brave woke up too and asked him: "Why are you weeping?" "How can I help weeping? Someone has stolen Vasilisa Kirbitievna." "I told you to keep watch. This is the work of Koshchey the Deathless; let us set out to find the old rattlebones." They rode for a long, long time, then they beheld two shepherds grazing a flock. "Whose flock is this?" they asked. The shepherds answered: "It belongs to Koshchey the Deathless." Bulat the Brave and Prince Ivan questioned the herdsmen as to whether Koshchey the Deathless lived far from there, how to get to him, when they, the herdsmen, were accustomed to return home with the flock, and where it was shut up for the night. Then they climbed down from their horses, wrung the necks of the herdsmen, dressed themselves in the latters' clothes, and drove the flock home; when they came to the place they stood at the gate.

Prince Ivan had a gold ring on his hand: Vasilisa Kirbitievna had given it to him. And Vasilisa Kirbitievna had a goat: mornings and evenings she washed in the milk of that goat. A maid came with a cup, milked the goat, and turned back with the milk. Bulat took the prince's ring and threw it into the cup. "Oh, my friends," said the maid, "you are playing pranks." She came to Vasilisa Kirbitievna and complained: "The herdsmen are now making mock of us; they threw a ring into the milk." The maiden answered: "Leave the milk, I will strain it myself." She strained it, saw the ring, and ordered the herdsmen to be brought before her. The herdsmen came. "Good day, Vasilisa Kirbitievna," said Bulat the Brave. "Good day, Bulat the Brave. Good day, prince. How has God brought you here?" "We have come for you, Vasilisa Kirbitievna. Nowhere shall you hide from us; even in the depths of the sea we shall find you." She seated them at the table, gave them a variety of viands to eat and wines to drink. Bulat the Brave said to her: "When Koshchey returns from hunting, ask him where his death is. And now it would not be a bad idea for us to hide."

The guests had no sooner hidden than Koshchey the Deathless came flying back from the hunt. "Fie, fie!" he said. "Formerly there was no breath of anything Russian here, nor could a glimpse be caught of it, but now something Russian has come here in person and is offending my nose." Vasilisa Kirbitievna answered him: "You have been flying through Russia, and yourself have become full of it, and now you fancy it is here." Koshchey ate his dinner and lay down to rest. Vasilisa came to him, threw herself on his neck, and kissed him and fondled him, saying: "My beloved friend, I could hardly wait for you; I began to think that I would never again see you alive, that wild beasts had devoured you." Koshchey laughed. "You foolish woman! Your hair is long, but your wit is short. How could wild beasts devour me?" "But where is your death

then?" "My death is in that broom that stands at the threshold."
As soon as Koshchey flew away, Vasilisa Kirbitievna ran to
Prince Ivan. Bulat the Brave asked her: "Well, where is
Koshchey's death?" "In that broom that stands on the thresh-
old." "No, that is a deliberate lie; you must question him more
cunningly."

Vasilisa Kirbitievna thought up something: she took the
broom, gilded it, decorated it with many ribbons, and put it on
the table. When Koshchey the Deathless came home and saw
the gilded broom on the table, he asked her why she had
arranged it so. "I could not allow your death to stand thus
unceremoniously at the threshold," said Vasilisa Kirbitievna.
"It is better to have it on the table." "Ha, ha, ha, you foolish
woman! Your hair is long but your wit is short. Do you think
my death is here?" "Where is it then?" "My death is hidden in
the goat."

As soon as Koshchey left for the hunt, Vasilisa Kirbitievna
adorned the goat with ribbons and bells and gilded his horns.
Koshchey saw it, and he laughed again and said: "Eh, you
foolish woman, your hair is long but your wit is short. My
death is far away. In the sea there is an island, on that island
stands an oak, under the oak a coffer is buried, in the coffer is
a hare, in the hare is a duck, in the duck is an egg, and in the
egg is my death." Having said this, he flew off. Vasilisa
Kirbitievna repeated all this to Bulat the Brave and to Prince
Ivan; they took provisions and set out to find Koshchey's
death. After a long time or a short time they had used up all
their provisions and began to feel hungry. They happened to
come upon a dog with her young. "I will kill her," said Bulat
the Brave, "for we have nothing more to eat." "Do not kill
me," begged the dog. "Do not make my children orphans. I will
be useful to you." "Well," they said, "God be with you." They
walked on, and saw an eagle with her eaglets sitting on an oak.
Bulat the Brave said: "I will kill the eagle." The eagle said:
"Do not kill me, do not make my children orphans, I will be
useful to you." "So be it," they said, "live in health."

They came to the wide ocean. A lobster crawled on the shore.
Bulat the Brave said: "I will kill him." The lobster answered:

"Do not kill me, good youth! There is not much substance in me; even if you eat me, you will not be sated. The time will come when I may be useful to you." "Well, crawl on with God," said Bulat the Brave. He looked at the sea, saw a fisherman in a boat, and cried: "Come to shore!" The fisherman brought the boat; Prince Ivan and Bulat the Brave seated themselves in it and sailed for the island. They reached the island and went to the oak. Bulat grasped the oak with his mighty hands and tore it out by the roots. He got the coffer from under the oak and opened it, and from the coffer a hare jumped out and ran away as fast as it could. "Ah," said Prince Ivan, "if we had a dog here, he would catch the hare." Lo and behold, the dog was already bringing the hare. Bulat the Brave took it, tore it open, and from the hare a duck flew out and soared high into the sky. "Ah," said Prince Ivan, "if we had the eagle now, he could catch the duck." Lo and behold, the eagle was bringing the duck. Bulat the Brave tore open the duck, and an egg rolled out from it and fell into the sea. "Ah," said the prince, "if only the lobster would bring it up!" And lo and behold, the lobster was crawling toward them with the egg. They took the egg, went to Koshchey the Deathless, struck him on the forehead with the egg, and he instantly fell sprawling to the ground and died. Prince Ivan took Vasilisa Kirbitievna and they set out on their way.

They rode and rode. Dark night overtook them; they pitched a tent, and Vasilisa Kirbitievna lay down to sleep. Bulat the Brave said: "Lie down too, prince, I will keep watch." At midnight twelve doves came flying, struck wing against wing, and turned into twelve maidens. "Now, Bulat the Brave and Prince Ivan," they said, "you have killed our brother, Koshchey the Deathless, and stolen our sister-in-law, Vasilisa Kirbitievna. But you won't profit by it. When Prince Ivan comes home, he will order his favorite dog to be brought out, and she will break away from the dog keeper and tear the princess into little pieces. And he who hears this and tells it to the prince will become stone to the knees."

Next morning Bulat the Brave roused the prince and Vasilisa Kirbitievna, and they made ready and set out on their

way. A second night overtook them; they pitched their tent in the open field. Bulat the Brave said again: "Lie down to sleep, Prince Ivan, and I will keep watch." At midnight twelve doves came flying, struck wing against wing, and turned into twelve maidens. "Well, Bulat the Brave and Prince Ivan," they said, "you have killed Koshchey the Deathless, our brother, and stolen Vasilisa Kirbitievna, our sister-in-law, but you won't profit by it. When Prince Ivan comes home, he will order his favorite horse to be brought out, the horse on which he has been wont to ride since childhood; the horse will break away from the groom and kill the prince. And he who hears this and tells it to the prince will become stone to the waist." Morning came and they rode on again. A third night overtook them; they stopped to spend the night and pitched their tent in the open field. Bulat the Brave said: "Lie down to sleep, Prince Ivan, and I will keep watch." Again at midnight twelve doves came flying, struck wing against wing, and turned into twelve maidens. "Well, Bulat the Brave and Prince Ivan," they said, "you have killed Koshchey the Deathless, our brother, and stolen Vasilisa Kirbitievna, our sister-in-law, but you won't profit by it; when Prince Ivan comes home, he will order his favorite cow to be brought out, the cow whose milk has nourished him since childhood: she will wrench herself free from the cowherd and spear the prince on her horns. And he who sees and hears us and tells this to the prince, will become stone altogether." When they had said this, they turned into doves and flew off.

Next morning Prince Ivan and Vasilisa Kirbitievna awoke and set out on their way. The prince came home, married Vasilisa Kirbitievna, and after a day or two said to her: "Do you want me to show you my favorite dog? When I was little, I played with it." Bulat the Brave took his saber, whetted it— he made it very sharp—and stood near the porch. The dog was led out; it wrested itself free from the dog keeper and ran straight toward the porch, but Bulat swung his saber and cut the dog in twain. Prince Ivan was angry at him, but remembering his former services, did not say a word. The next day Ivan ordered his favorite horse to be brought out; the horse broke his halter, wrested himself free from the groom, and galloped straight at the prince. Bulat the Brave cut off the horse's head. Prince Ivan grew even angrier than before and ordered Bulat to be seized and hanged, but Vasilisa Kirbitievna obtained his pardon. "Had it not been for him," she said, "you would never have won me." On the third day Prince Ivan ordered his favorite cow to be brought out; she wrested herself free from the cowherd and ran straight toward the prince. Bulat the Brave cut off her head too.

Now Prince Ivan became so enraged that he refused to listen to anyone; he ordered the hangman to be summoned and commanded that Bulat be put to death at once. "Ah, Prince Ivan," Bulat said, "now that you have ordered your hangman to put me to death, I would rather die by my own hand. Only let me speak three speeches." Bulat told him about the first night, how twelve doves came flying, and what they had said to him—and straightway he became stone to the knees; he told about the second night, and became stone to the waist. Prince Ivan besought him not to speak to the end. Bulat the Brave answered: "Now it is all the same; I am half stone, it is not worth while living longer." He told about the third night and became stone altogether. Prince Ivan put him in a separate chamber and went there every day with Vasilisa Kirbitievna and lamented bitterly.

Many years went by. One day Prince Ivan was lamenting over Bulat when he heard a voice coming from the stone figure. "Why are you weeping?" the voice said. "I am grieved even without your weeping." "How can I help weeping? After all, it is I who destroyed you." "If you wish, you can save me. You have two children, a son and a daughter; slay them, draw their blood, and smear my stone with the blood." Prince Ivan told this to Vasilisa Kirbitievna; they grieved and lamented, but decided to slay their children. They slew them, drew their blood, and as soon as they smeared the stone with it Bulat the Brave came to life. He asked the prince and his wife: "Are you heartbroken over your children?" "We are, Bulat the Brave." "Well then, let us go to their rooms." They went, and lo and behold, the children were alive. The father and mother were overjoyed and in their joy gave a feast for all. I was at that feast too, I drank mead and wine there; it ran down my mustache but did not go into my mouth, yet my soul was drunk and sated.

THE FIREBIRD
AND PRINCESS VASILISA

IN A CERTAIN KINGDOM, beyond the thrice ninth land, in the thrice tenth realm, there lived a strong and mighty king. This king had a brave huntsman and the brave huntsman had a valiant horse. One day the huntsman went on his valiant horse to hunt in the woods. He rode and rode along the broad path, and suddenly he came upon a golden feather of the Firebird; it shone bright as a flame! The valiant horse said to him: "Take not the golden feather; if you take it, you will know trouble!" And the brave youth turned the matter over in his mind: should he pick up the feather or not? If he picked it up, he thought, and presented it to the king, he would be generously rewarded; and who does not value the king's favor?

So the huntsman did not heed his horse; he picked up the feather of the Firebird and brought it to the king as a gift. "Thank you!" said the king. "But since you have found the feather of the Firebird, get me the bird itself. If you do not, by my sword your head shall fall!" The huntsman wept bitter tears and went to his valiant horse. "Why are you weeping, master?" the good steed asked. "The king has ordered me to get him the Firebird." "Did I not warn you not to take the feather, or you would know trouble? Well, fear not, grieve not. This is not trouble yet—the real trouble lies ahead! Go to the king, ask that by tomorrow one hundred measures of corn be strewn on the open field."

494

Next day at dawn the brave huntsman rode to that field, set his horse loose, and hid behind a tree. Suddenly the woods rustled and the waves rose on the sea—the Firebird was flying. She arrived at the field, alighted, and began to peck the corn. The valiant horse approached the Firebird, stepped with his hoof on her wing, and pressed it hard to the ground; the brave huntsman jumped from behind the tree, ran to the Firebird, tied her with cords, mounted his horse, and galloped to the palace. He presented the Firebird to the king. The king gazed upon the bird with delight, thanked the huntsman for his services, promoted him to noble rank, and straightway charged him with another task. "Since you were able to get the Firebird," the king said, "you must now get me a bride. Beyond the thrice ninth land, at the very edge of the world, where the red sun rises, lives Princess Vasilisa—it is she whom I desire. If you get her, I will reward you with silver and gold; if you do not, by my sword your head shall fall!"

The huntsman shed bitter tears and went to his valiant horse. "Why are you weeping, master?" asked the horse. "The king has commanded me to get Princess Vasilisa for him." "Weep not, grieve not. This is still not trouble—the real trouble lies ahead! Go to the king, ask for a tent with a golden top and all kinds of meats and drink for the journey." The king gave him meats and drink and a tent with a golden top as well. The brave huntsman mounted his valiant horse and rode beyond the thrice ninth land. After some time, a short time or a long time, he came to the edge of the world, where the red sun rises from the blue sea. He looked out; on the blue sea Princess Vasilisa was sailing in a silver boat rowed with golden oars. The brave huntsman set his horse loose to roam in the green meadows and eat fresh grass. As for himself, he pitched his golden-topped tent, set out all sorts of food and drink, sat in the tent, and regaled himself while he waited for Princess Vasilisa.

Princess Vasilisa spied the golden top of the tent, sailed to the shore, stepped off her boat, and admired the tent. "Greetings, Princess Vasilisa!" said the huntsman. "Welcome! pray be my guest and taste my foreign wines." Princess Vasilisa entered the tent; they began to eat, drink, and enjoy themselves. The princess drank a glass of foreign wine, became drunk, and fell sound asleep. The huntsman called his valiant horse, and the horse came running; the huntsman folded his golden-topped tent, mounted the valiant horse, laid the sleeping Princess Vasilisa across his saddle, and set out on his way, as swiftly as an arrow flies from a bow.

They came to the king, who, when he beheld Princess Vasilisa, rejoiced greatly; he thanked the huntsman for his loyal service, rewarded him with an enormous treasure, and promoted him to high rank. Princess Vasilisa awoke, discovered that she was far from the blue sea, and began to weep and grieve. Her fair face was completely beclouded. No matter what the king said to comfort her, all was in vain. The king wanted to marry her, but she said: "Let him who brought me here go to the blue sea. In the middle of that sea lies a great stone, under that stone my wedding gown is hid. Without that gown I will not wed!" The king at once sent for the brave huntsman and said to him: "Hasten to the edge of the world, where the red sun rises; there in the blue sea a great stone lies, and under that stone Princess Vasilisa's wedding gown is hid. Get that gown and bring it here; it is time to celebrate my wedding! If you get it, I will reward you even more richly than before; if you do not, by my sword your head shall fall!"

The huntsman shed bitter tears and went to his valiant horse. "This time," he thought, "I surely shall not escape death!" "Why are you weeping, master?" asked the horse. "The king has commanded me to get Princess Vasilisa's wedding gown from the bottom of the sea." "Now you see! Did I not tell you not to take the golden feather, or you would know trouble? Well, fear not; this is not trouble yet—the real trouble lies ahead! Sit on me and let us go to the blue sea."

After some time, a short time or a long time, the brave huntsman came to the edge of the world and stopped at the shore of the sea. The valiant horse saw a huge crab crawling on the sand, and stepped on its neck with his heavy hoof. The crab spoke out: "Do not give me death, give me life! I will do whatever you want." The horse answered: "In the middle of the blue sea there lies a great stone, under that stone Princess Vasilisa's wedding gown is hid. Get me that gown!" The crab called in a loud voice all over the blue sea; at once the sea became agitated, and from all sides big and little crabs came crawling to the shore—a numberless multitude! The chief crab gave them a command and they jumped into the water. After an hour's time they dragged Princess Vasilisa's wedding gown from the bottom of the sea, from under the great stone.

The brave huntsman came to the king, bringing the princess' gown; but Princess Vasilisa was still obdurate. "I will not marry you," she said to the king, "unless you order the brave huntsman to bathe in boiling water." The king had an iron cauldron filled with water; he ordered that it be heated and that the huntsman be thrown in when the water came to the boiling point. Everything was ready, the water was boiling and bubbling; the unfortunate huntsman was led to the cauldron. "Now this is trouble!" he thought. "Ah, why did I ever pick up the golden feather of the Firebird? Why did I not heed my horse?" He recalled his valiant steed and said to the king: "King, my sovereign! Let me say farewell to my horse before I die." "Very well, go, say farewell to him," said the king.

The huntsman came to his valiant horse and wept bitter tears. "Why are you weeping, master?" the horse asked. "The king has commanded me to bathe in boiling water." "Fear not, weep not, you will live!" And the horse quickly charmed the huntsman, so that the boiling water would not harm his white body. The huntsman came back from the stable; servants seized him at once and threw him straight into the cauldron. He ducked his head once or twice, jumped out of the cauldron —and turned into such a handsome man as no tale can tell of nor pen describe. The king, seeing that his huntsman had become so handsome in the boiling water, wanted to bathe in it too; he foolishly plunged into the cauldron and was boiled on the spot. He was buried, and in his place the brave huntsman was enthroned; he married Princess Vasilisa, and lived long years with her in love and concord.

A PIG WAS on his way to Piter * to pray to God. He met a wolf. "Pig, pig, where are you going?" "To Piter, to pray to God." "Take me with you." "Come along, neighbor." They walked and walked and met a fox. "Pig, pig, where are you going?" "To Piter, to pray to God." "Take me with you too." "Come along, neighbor." They walked and met a hare. "Pig, pig, where are you going?" "To Piter, to pray to God." "Take me with you." "Come along, Slant Eyes!" Then a squirrel joined them and they walked and walked. At last they came to a ditch in the road, a ditch wide and deep. The pig jumped, and fell into the ditch, and after her the wolf, the fox, the hare, and the squirrel all fell in; they sat there for a long time and were very hungry, but there was nothing to eat.

Then the fox thought up a plan. "Let us," she said, "try out our own voices; whichever of us sings in the thinnest voice, him we shall eat." The wolf began in a rough voice: "O-o-o!" The pig sang in a slightly softer voice: "U-u-u!" The fox sang still more softly: "E-e-e!" And the hare and the squirrel piped in a thin voice: "I-i-i!" The bigger beasts at once tore the hare and the squirrel to pieces and gobbled them down to the last bone. The next day the fox said again: "Whoever sings in the roughest voice, him we shall eat." The wolf sang in the roughest voice—"O-o-o!"—and was eaten up. The fox ate the flesh but hid the entrails under herself. After about three days she began to eat the entrails. The pig asked her: "What are you eating, neighbor? Give me some." "Eh, pig, I am pulling out my own bowels; tear your belly open too, pull out your bowels, and eat of them." The pig did this; he tore his belly open and the fox had him for dinner. So the fox remained all alone in the ditch, and whether she finally climbed out or is still there, I really cannot say.

*Colloquialism for "St. Petersburg."

THE DOG
AND THE WOODPECKER

ONCE THERE LIVED a peasant and his wife and they did not need to work at all; they had a dog that gave them meat and drink. Then came a day when the dog grew old and could not think of feeding the peasant and his wife; in fact, he almost died of hunger himself. "Listen, old man," said the woman. "Take this dog, lead him beyond the village, and chase him away; let him go wherever he wants, we don't need him now. There was a time when he fed us; then it was worth while keeping him." The old man took the dog, led him out of the village, and chased him away. And so the dog walked in the open field and was afraid to go home lest the old man and woman beat him. The dog walked and walked, then sat on the ground and began to howl in a loud voice. A woodpecker flew by and asked: "Why do you howl?" "How can I help howling, woodpecker? When I was young I gave the old man and his wife food and drink; when I grew old, they drove me away. I don't know where to spend my last days." "Come to me, guard my children, and I will feed you," said the woodpecker. The dog consented and ran after the woodpecker.

They came to an old oak; in the oak there was a hollow, and in the hollow was the woodpecker's nest. "Sit near the oak," said the woodpecker, "do not let anyone in, and I will fly to find food." The dog sat by the oak and the woodpecker flew off. He flew and flew and saw women walking along the road carrying pots—their husbands' dinner pails. He flew back to the oak and said: "Now, dog, follow me; along the road there are women with pails, carrying dinner to their husbands in the field. You stand behind a bush, and I will plunge into water, roll in sand, and fly low before the women on the road, as though unable to fly higher. They will put their pails on the ground and run after me, trying to catch me. Then you rush to the pails and eat your fill." The dog followed the woodpecker and, just as he had been told to do, stood behind a bush, while the woodpecker rolled in sand and began to flutter before the women on the road. "Look," said the women, "the woodpecker is all wet, let us catch him." They put their pails on the ground and ran after the woodpecker, and he flew farther and farther, led them to one side, rose high, and flew away. Meanwhile the dog had run out from behind the bush, eaten up everything that was in the pots, and gone away. The women came back and found the pails empty; there was nothing they could do, so they took their pails and went home.

The woodpecker overtook the dog and asked: "Well, have you eaten your fill?" "Yes," said the dog. "Then let us go home," said the woodpecker. He flew and the dog ran after him; on the way they met a fox. "Catch the fox," said the woodpecker. The dog jumped after the fox and the fox darted off. Just then a peasant happened to drive by with a barrel of tar. The fox shot across the road, straight to the cart, and jumped through the spokes of the wheel; the dog jumped after her, but got stuck in the wheel and gave up the ghost. "Ah, peasant," said the woodpecker, "since you have run over my dog, I will cause you great trouble." He sat on the cart and began to bore a hole in the barrel, pecking at its bottom. When the peasant drove him away from the barrel, he flew to the horse, sat between his ears, and bored a hole in his head. When the peasant drove him away from the horse, he returned to the barrel, pierced a hole in it, and let out all the tar. Then he said: "That is not all!" And again he began to bore a hole in the horse's head. The peasant took a big log, sat in his cart, waited for an opportune moment, and struck with all his strength; only he did not hit the woodpecker, he hit the horse on the head and killed him. The woodpecker flew to the peasant's house and went in through the window. The peasant's wife was busy making a fire in the stove and her little child was sitting on the bench; the woodpecker sat on the child's head and began to peck at it. The woman tried to drive him away, but could not; the vicious woodpecker kept pecking and pecking. Finally the peasant woman grabbed a stick and struck: she did not hit the woodpecker, but hurt her own child.

TWO KINDS OF LUCK

THERE WAS ONCE a peasant who had two sons. After his death, the two brothers married; the older took a poor wife and the younger a rich wife. They lived together and did not divide the estate. The wives began to quarrel. One said: "My husband is the elder brother, so I should have precedence." And the other said: "No, I should have precedence, for I am wealthier than you." The brothers watched all this for a time, saw that their wives did not get along together, divided their father's estate equally, and parted. The elder brother's wife bore a child every year, and his household went from bad to worse, until he was completely ruined. While he had bread and money, his heart rejoiced over his children; but when he grew poor even his children did not make him happy. He went to his younger brother to ask for help. The brother refused bluntly, saying: "You must stand on your own feet; I have growing children of my own."

After a short time, the poor brother again came to the rich one. "Lend me some horses at least for one day," he said. "I have no beasts to do my plowing with." "Go to the field and take a horse for a day," the rich brother said, "but take care not to overwork him." The poor man came to the field and saw some men plowing the ground with his brother's horses. "Stop!" he cried. "Who are you?" "Why do you ask?" "Because these are my brother's horses." "Don't you see," said one of the plowmen, "that I am your brother's Luck? He drinks, makes merry, and does not bother about anything, while we work for him." "Then what has happened to my Luck?" "Your Luck is lying over there behind a bush, wearing a red shirt; he doesn't do anything night or day, he just sleeps all the time." "Very well," thought the peasant, "I'll take care of you."

He cut himself a thick club, sneaked up to his Luck, and hit the fellow on the side with all his strength. Luck awoke and said: "Why do you want to pick a fight with me?" "Just wait," answered the poor brother. "You'll see what a thrashing I'll give you! Look! These good people plow the ground while you sleep like a log." "Do you mean to say that you want me to plow for you? Don't expect anything like that!" "So you intend to lie here behind the bush? That way I'll starve!" "If you want me to help you, drop your farming and engage in trade. I am not used to your kind of work, but I am well versed in all kinds of business." "You want me to engage in trade? But with what? I have not even enough money to buy food, let alone for starting a business." "Well, you can take your wife's old dress and sell it; for the money buy a new one and sell it too; I will help you and won't leave you for a minute." "Very well," said the peasant.

Next morning the poor man said to his wife: "Well, wife, make ready, we're going to town." "What for?" "I want to join the merchants' guild and engage in trade." "Are you in your right mind? We have nothing to feed our children with, and now you want to go to town!" "Don't argue with me! Pack all our belongings, take the children, and let us go." They made ready, said their prayers, began to lock their little hut, and heard someone weeping bitterly in the cellar. The peasant asked: "Who is weeping there?" "It is I, Misery." "Why are you weeping?" "How can I help weeping? You're going away and leaving me here." "No, my dear, I'll take you with me, I won't desert you. Hey, wife, throw your things out of this coffer." The wife emptied the coffer. "Now, Misery, crawl into the coffer." Misery crawled in; the peasant locked it with three locks, buried the coffer in the earth, and said: "Perish, accursed Misery! Let me never in my life know you again."

The poor man came to town with his wife and children, rented a lodging, and began to trade. He took his wife's old dress, carried it to the bazaar, and sold it for a ruble; with that ruble he bought a new dress and sold it for two roubles. Through such lucky deals, getting double his cost for everything he sold, he enriched himself in a very short time and joined the merchants' guild. His younger brother heard about this, came to visit him, and asked: "Tell me, please—how have you managed to turn from a beggar into a rich man?" "That's

very simple," the merchant answered. "I locked Misery into a coffer and buried it in the earth." "Where?" "In the village, in my own old home." The younger brother was almost in tears from envy; he straightway drove to the village, dug up the coffer, and set Misery free. "Go to my brother," he said. "Ruin him to the last thread." "No," said Misery, "I'd rather stay with you. I won't go to him; you're a kind fellow, you let me go free. Your brother is an evildoer, he put me into the ground." After a short time the envious brother was ruined, and turned from a wealthy peasant into a penniless beggar.

GO I KNOW NOT WHITHER, BRING BACK I KNOW NOT WHAT

IN A CERTAIN KINGDOM there lived an unmarried king who had a whole company of archers; the archers went ahunting, shot birds of passage, and provided the sovereign's table with game. In that company there served a brave marksman by the name of Fedot. He hit the mark accurately, almost never missed, and for that reason the king loved him more than all his comrades. One day Fedot went hunting very early in the morning, at the very break of day. He entered a dark, thick forest and spied a dove perched on a tree. Fedot cocked his gun, aimed, fired, and broke one of the bird's wings; she fell from the tree to the damp earth. The archer picked her up and was about to tear off her head and put her in his bag, when the dove spoke to him and said: "Ah, brave marksman, do not tear off my rash little head, do not remove me from the bright world; rather, take me alive, carry me home, put me on the window sill, and watch—the moment that drowsiness overcomes me, strike me with the back of your right hand, and you will gain a great fortune." The archer was greatly amazed. "What is this?" he thought. "In appearance she is completely a bird, yet she speaks with a human voice! Such a thing has never happened before."

He brought the bird home, put it on the window sill, and stood waiting. A short time later, the dove put her head under her wing and fell asleep; then the archer raised his right hand, struck her lightly with the back of his hand, and the dove fell to the floor and turned into a sweet maiden more beautiful than any mind can conceive of, or tongue tell of. Such a beauty had never been seen in the whole world. She said to the good youth, the king's archer: "You have known how to win me, now learn how to live with me; you shall be my chosen husband, and I shall be your God-given wife." Fedot married her and lived on, rejoicing in his young wife without neglecting his duties; every morning as soon as day broke he took his gun, went into the forest, shot a variety of game, and carried it to the king's kitchen.

His wife saw that he was quite weary of all this hunting and said to him: "Listen, my beloved, I am worried about you: every single day you torment yourself, you wander through forests and swamps, you always return home soaked through, and we are none the better for it. What kind of trade is that? I know how to do something that will really make us rich. Get me one or two hundred rubles, and I will change our lot." Fedot made the round of his comrades, borrowing a ruble from one, two rubles from another, and thus collected two hundred rubles. He brought the money to his wife. "Now," she said, "buy me various silks for this money." The archer bought two hundred rubles' worth of silks; she took them and said: "Be of good cheer, pray to God, and lie down to sleep; the morning is wiser than the evening."

The husband fell asleep but the wife went out on the porch, and opened her magic book. Instantly two spirits appeared before her, ready to do whatever she commanded. "Take this silk," she said, "and in one single hour make me a carpet so wonderful that the world has never seen its equal. On this carpet let a view of the whole kingdom be embroidered, with towns, villages, rivers, and lakes." The spirits set to work and in less than an hour, in ten minutes, they had the carpet ready —a marvel for all to behold. They gave it to the marksman's wife and vanished in a trice, as though they had never been there. Next morning she gave the carpet to her husband, saying: "Here, take this to the bazaar and sell it to the merchants. But mind you—do not set the price yourself, take whatever they give you."

Fedot took the carpet, unrolled it, hung it on his arm, and went to the bazaar. A merchant saw it, came up to him, and said: "My good man, is this for sale?" "It is." "How much is it?" "You are a trader, so you set the price." The merchant thought and thought, but could not set a price on the carpet. Another merchant joined them, then a third and a fourth; a whole crowd of them gathered, marveled at the carpet, but could not set a price on it. At that moment the king's steward passed by, saw the crowd, and wanted to know what the merchants were discussing. He got out of his carriage, came up to them, and said: "Good day, merchants, guests from beyond the sea! What are you talking about?" "We cannot set a price on this carpet." The king's steward looked at the carpet and he too marveled at it. "Listen, marksman," he said, "tell me the real truth: where did you get such a magnificent carpet?" "My wife made it." "How much shall I give you for it?" "I don't know the price myself; my wife told me not to bargain, and to accept whatever I am given." "Well, here are ten thousand rubles for you."

The marksman took the money and gave the steward the carpet. Now this steward was always with the king, he drank and ate at the king's table. When he went to dine with the king he took along the carpet. "Would it not please Your Majesty," he said, "to see what a splendid thing I have bought today?"

The king looked and saw all of his kingdom as on the palm of his hand; he gasped in amazement. "That is a carpet!" he exclaimed. "In all my life I have not seen such skillful work. Well, steward, do what you please, but I shall not give this carpet back to you!" The king straightway gave his steward twenty-five thousand rubles and hung the carpet in his palace. "Never mind," thought the steward, "I will order a better one for myself."

Without losing a moment he galloped to the archer, found his hut, entered the woman's room, and as soon as he saw Fedot's wife forgot himself and his business. He no longer knew what he had come for: before him was such a beauty that he did not want to take his eyes off her till the end of his days—he wanted to stare and stare at her. He looked at the other man's wife and all sorts of thoughts went through his head. "Whoever heard of a simple soldier possessing such a treasure?" he said to himself. "Although I am attached to the king's person and have the rank of general, I have never seen such a beauty." At last the steward with a great effort recovered his senses and reluctantly went home. From that moment on he was not himself; awake or asleep, he thought only of the marksman's beautiful wife. He could neither eat nor drink—she was ever in his mind.

The king noticed this and asked him: "What has happened to you? Do you have some grief?" "Ah, Your Majesty," said the steward, "I have seen the wife of an archer, and there is no such beauty in the whole world; all day long I think of her, I cannot banish the thought of her by eating or drinking, nor by means of any magic potion!" The king himself desired to see this beauty; he ordered his carriage and drove to the archer's quarters. He entered the room and beheld an unimaginable beauty; she was so lovely that whoever looked at her, old or young, would fall madly in love with her. The king's heart was oppressed with a burning passion. "Why should I remain unmarried?" he thought to himself. "I should marry this beauty; she should not remain a marksman's wife—she was born to be a queen."

The king returned to his palace and said to his steward:

"Listen, you have known how to show me the archer's wife, that incomparable beauty; now learn how to destroy her husband. I want to marry her myself. And if you fail to destroy him, blame yourself, for although you are my faithful servant, you shall hang on the gallows." The steward left more grieved than before; he could not devise a way of getting rid of the archer.

He walked through waste places and back alleys and met Baba Yaga. "Halt, servant of the king," she said. "I know all your thoughts; do you want me to help you in your deep trouble?" "Help me, grandmother, I will pay you whatever you wish." "The king has ordered you to destroy Fedot the marksman. That would be an easy matter, for he is simple, but his wife is cunning. But we shall give her such a task that they will not perform it soon. Return to the king and say to him that beyond thrice nine lands, in the thrice tenth kingdom, there is an island; on that island there is a stag with golden horns. Let the king gather together fifty sailors, the worst, most inveterate drunkards, and let him order an old, rotten ship—that has been listed as out of service for thirty years—to be rigged up for the voyage; and on that ship let him send Fedot the archer to get the stag with the golden horns. To get to the island one must sail three years, not more nor less, and to return from the island one must sail another three years—six in all The ship will go out to sea, it will sail a month and then will sink; the archer and the sailors will all go to the bottom."

The steward listened to these words, thanked Baba Yaga for her advice, rewarded her with gold, and ran to the king. "Your Majesty," he said, "the marksman can be destroyed in such and such a manner." The king consented and straightway ordered his navy to prepare an old, rotten ship for the voyage, to load it with provisions for six years, and to man it with fifty sailors, the most dissolute and inveterate drunkards. Messengers ran to all the alehouses and inns, and gathered together a gang of such sailors that they were a sight to behold—some had black eyes, some had noses twisted to one side. As soon as it was reported to the king that the ship was ready, he straightway summoned the archer to his presence, and said to him: "Well, Fedot, you

508

are a brave man, the first marksman in your company; do me a service, go beyond thrice nine lands, to the thrice tenth kingdom. There you will find an island and on that island is a stag with golden horns; catch him alive and bring him here." The marksman became pensive and did not know what to say. "Like it or not," said the king. "But if you do not perform this task, by my sword your head will roll."

Fedot turned on his heel and left the palace; at night he came home sorely grieved and refusing to speak a word. His wife asked him: "Why are you sad, my beloved? Is there some trouble?" He told her everything. "So that is why you are grieved! There is little reason for it—for this is child's play, not a task. Pray to God and go to sleep. The morning is wiser than the evening; everything will be done." The marksman lay down and fell asleep, but his wife opened the magic book and suddenly two spirits appeared before her. "What do you wish? What shall we do?" they asked. "Go beyond thrice nine lands, to the thrice tenth kingdom, to the island, catch the stag with the golden horns, and bring him here." "We shall obey; everything will be done by daybreak."

Like a whirlwind they flew to that island, seized the stag with the golden horns, and brought him straight to the marksman's courtyard; one hour before dawn they had done their task and vanished as though they had never been there. The marksman's beautiful wife roused her husband at an early hour and said to him: "Go out and see—the stag with the golden horns is walking in your yard. Take him on board ship with you, sail out for five days, and on the sixth turn back." The marksman put the stag into a closed cage and carried him on board ship. "What is in there?" asked the sailors. "Various provisions and herbs," said the marksman; "the voyage will be long, we shall need all sorts of things."

On the day of the sailing a great crowd of people came to see the ship off. The king also came, said farewell to Fedot, and appointed him captain of all the sailors. For five days the ship sailed on the sea; the shores had long been lost to view. Fedot ordered a wine cask of a hundred and twenty gallons to be rolled on the deck and said to the sailors: "Drink, brothers! Do not be sparing—your wish is your measure!" They asked for nothing better, rushed to the cask, and fell to drinking. They got so drunk that they dropped right there by the cask and fell sound asleep. The marksman took the helm, turned the ship toward the shore, and sailed homeward; and to keep the sailors from being aware of anything, he poured wine into them from morning till night. As soon as they opened their eyes after one drinking bout, another cask was ready, tempting them to drink again.

On the eleventh day the ship anchored in the port, hoisted a flag, and began to fire her guns. The king heard the firing and straightway came to the port, wondering what the noise was about. He saw the archer, became angry, and fell upon him with great fury, saying: "How dare you return before time?" "Where was I to go, Your Majesty?" the archer said. "Some fool might have sailed for ten years over the seas without accomplishing anything, but we, instead of journeying six years, traveled for ten days and did the work. Would you like to see the stag with the golden horns?" Straightway the cage was brought from the ship and the stag with the golden horns was let out. The king saw that the archer was right, that he could not be charged with anything. He gave the archer leave to go home and granted the sailors who had accompanied him a six years' furlough; no one could draft them for service during those years, for they had served their time.

The next day the king summoned his steward and fell upon him with threats. "Are you playing tricks on me?" he said. "Apparently your head is not dear to you. Do it in any way you please, but find some way of putting Fedot to a cruel death." "Your Royal Majesty," the steward said, "please give me time to think, perhaps I can set things to rights." The steward went along back alleys and waste places and met Baba Yaga. "Halt, servant of the king! I know your thoughts; do you want me to help you in your trouble?" "Help me, grandmother! The archer has returned and brought the stag with the golden horns." "Oh, I have heard that! He himself is a simple man, it would be easy to destroy him—as easy as to take a pinch of snuff. But his wife is very cunning. Well, we shall charge her

510

with another task, which she will not be able to perform so quickly. Go to the king and say to him: 'Send the archer I know not whither, and let him bring back I know not what.' He won't perform that task in the time of all eternity; he will either be lost without a trace or return empty-handed."

The steward rewarded Baba Yaga with gold and ran to the king, who listened to him and ordered the archer to be summoned. "Well, Fedot, you are a brave man, the first marksman of your company. You have rendered me one service, you have brought me the stag with the golden horns. Now render me another: go I know not whither, bring me back I know not what. And mind you: if you fail to bring it to me, by my sword your head will roll!" The marksman turned on his heel and left the palace; he came home sad and thoughtful. His wife asked him: "Why are you grieving, my beloved? Do you have another trouble?" "Eh," he said, "I have just got rid of one trouble, when another one falls on my neck; the king has ordered me to go I know not whither, and ordered me to bring him I know not what. It is because of your beauty that all these misfortunes beset me." "Yes, this is no little task! To get there takes nine years, and it takes nine years to return; that makes eighteen years in all. And whether any good will come of it, God only knows." "Then what can we do?" "Pray to God and go to sleep; the morning is wiser than the evening. Tomorrow you will know all."

The archer went to sleep, but his wife waited for the night, opened her magic book, and two spirits appeared at once. "What do you wish, what is your command?" they asked. "Do you know how to go I know not whither and bring back I know not what?" "No, we do not know." She closed the book and the spirits vanished. Next morning she roused her husband. "Go to the king and ask for gold for your journey—you will have to wander for eighteen years. And when you have received the money, come to say farewell to me." The marksman went to the king, received a bagful of gold from the treasury, and came to say farewell to his wife. She gave him a handkerchief and a ball, and said: "When you are outside the town, throw this ball before you, and wherever it rolls follow it.

And here is a handkerchief I myself wrought; wherever you find yourself—when you wash, wipe your face with this handkerchief." The marksman said farewell to his wife and comrades, bowed low to all four sides, and went beyond the gates of the town. He threw the ball before him; the ball rolled and rolled, and he followed it.

A month went by. The king summoned the steward and said to him: "The archer has gone to wander about the wide world for eighteen years, and it is clear that he will not return alive—for eighteen years is not two weeks, and much can happen to him on the way. He has a great deal of money; brigands may attack him, rob him, and put him to a cruel death. I think we can set about getting his wife. Take my carriage, drive to the archer's quarters, and bring her to the palace." The steward drove to the archer's quarters, came to Fedot's beautiful wife, entered her hut, and said: "Good day, clever woman; the king has ordered me to bring you to the palace." She went to the palace; the king received her joyfully, led her to gilded chambers, and spoke to her thus: "Do you want to be queen? I will marry you." "Where has it been seen, where has it been heard of, to take a wife from her living husband?" the archer's wife said. "Although he is a simple marksman, he is my lawful husband." "If you do not yield of your own free will, I will use force." The beauty smiled, struck the floor, turned into a dove, and flew out of the window.

The archer passed through many kingdoms and lands, and the ball kept rolling. Whenever he came to a river, the ball spanned it as a bridge; whenever he wanted to rest, the ball spread out as a downy bed. After a long time or a short time—for speedily a tale is spun, with much less speed a deed is done—the archer came to a large and magnificent palace; the ball rolled up to the door and vanished. The archer thought and thought and went straight on. He walked up the stairs into the chambers and was met by three maidens of indescribable beauty, who said: "Whence and wherefore have you come, good man?" "Ah, lovely maidens," he replied, "you have not let me rest from my long journey—yet you have begun to question me. You should first give me meat and drink, put me

512

to rest, and only then ask my business." Straightway they set the table, gave him meat and drink, and put him to sleep.

The marksman had a good sleep, then rose from the soft bed; the lovely maidens brought him a washing basin and an embroidered towel. He washed himself in the spring water but refused to take the towel. "I have a handkerchief," he said, "I'll wipe my face with that." He took out his handkerchief and began to wipe himself. The lovely maidens asked him: "Good man, tell us, where did you get that handkerchief?" "My wife gave it to me." "If so, you are the husband of our own sister!" They called their old mother, and as soon as she cast a glance at the handkerchief, she recognized it. "This is the handiwork of my daughter," she said. She began to question the visitor; he told her how he had married her daughter and that the king had sent him he knew not whither, to bring him he knew not what. "Ah, my dear son-in-law, of that marvel even I have not heard!" the mother said. "But wait a minute, perhaps my servants will know of it."

The old woman went out on the porch and cried out in a loud voice. Suddenly, out of nowhere, all kinds of beasts ran up to her and all kinds of birds flew to her. "Hail, beasts of the forest, birds of the air!" she said. "You beasts run everywhere, you birds fly everywhere. Have you heard how to go I know not whither and how to bring back I know not what?" All the beasts and the birds answered in one voice: "No, we have not heard of that." The old woman sent them back to their thickets, forests, and groves; she returned to her room, got her magic book, opened it, and straightway two giants appeared before her. "What do you wish, what is your command?" they asked. "This, my faithful servants," she said. "Carry me and my son-in-law to the broad ocean and stop in the very middle of it, right above the bottomless depth."

Straightway the giants seized the archer and the old woman and carried them like impetuous winds to the broad ocean and stopped in the middle of it, right above the bottomless depth; they stood there like pillars, holding the marksman and the old woman on their hands. The old woman cried out in a loud voice, and all the sea reptiles and fishes swam up and swarmed

513

around her, in such multitudes that the blue sea could not be seen for the mass of them. "Hail, sea reptiles and fishes!" the old woman said. "You swim everywhere, you visit all the islands; have you not heard how to go I know not whither and how to bring back I know not what?" All the reptiles and fishes answered with one voice: "No, we have not heard of that." Suddenly a limping old frog, who had been living in retirement for thirty years, pushed herself forward and said: "Qua! qua! I know where such a marvel can be found." "Well, my dear, you are the one I need," said the old woman. She took the frog and ordered her giants to carry her and her son-in-law home.

In a trice they found themselves in the palace. The old woman began to question the frog: "How and by what road shall my son-in-law go?" The frog answered: "This palace is at the end of the world—far, far away. I would lead him there myself, but I am terribly old, I can hardly drag my feet; I would not get there in fifty years." The old woman took a big jar, filled it with fresh milk, put the frog in it, and gave it to her son-in-law. "Hold this jar in your hands," she said, "and let the frog show you the way." The archer took the jar with the frog, said farewell to the old woman and her daughters, and set out. He walked and the frog showed him the way.

After he had gone a short distance or a long distance, after a long time or a short time, he came to a river of fire; beyond that river was a high mountain, and in that mountain there was a door. "Qua! qua!" said the frog, "let me out of the jar; we have to cross the river." The marksman took her out of the jar and put her on the ground. "Now, good youth, sit on me, and do not spare me, you will not smother me." The archer sat on the frog and pressed her to the ground; the frog began to swell, she swelled and swelled and grew as big as a haystack. All that the marksman could think of was how to keep from falling off: "If I fall I will be smashed to death." The frog, having swelled up, took a jump; she jumped across the river of fire and made herself small again. "Now, good youth," she said, "go through that door, and I shall wait for you here. You will enter a cave, and then you must hide yourself well. After some time two old men will come there. Listen to what they say and watch

what they do; after they have left, speak and do as they did."

The archer went to the mountain and opened the door; in the cave it was pitch dark. He crawled in and groped his way about; he felt an empty cupboard, seated himself in it, and closed the door. After a short while two old men came into the cave and said: "Hey, Shmat Razum, feed us!" At once, from nowhere, chandeliers were lighted, plates and dishes clattered, wines and meats of every description appeared on the table. The old men drank and ate their fill and commanded: "Hey, Shmat Razum, remove everything!" Suddenly everything disappeared; there was neither table, nor wines, nor meats, and all the lights went out. When the archer knew that the old men were gone, he crept out of his cupboard and cried: "Hey, Shmat Razum!" "What do you wish?" "Feed me." Again the chandeliers were lighted, the table was set, and there were all kinds of meats and wines on it.

The archer sat at the table and said: "Hey, Shmat Razum! Sit down with me, brother, I don't like to eat alone." An invisible voice answered: "Ah, good man, whence has God sent you? It is nearly thirty years that I have served these two old men in truth and faith, and all that time they have not once invited me to sit with them." The archer looked and marveled: he saw nobody, but it was as though the viands had been swept from the plates with a broom, and the bottles of wine were lifted up as though by themselves, the wine poured itself into glasses—and, lo and behold, they were emptied! The archer ate and drank his fill and said: "Listen, Shmat Razum! Do you want to be my servant? Life with me will be pleasant!" "Why not? I have long been tired of living here, and I see that you are a kind man." "Well, remove everything, and come with me." The archer went out of the cave, looked back, and saw nobody. "Shmat Razum! Are you here?" he called. "Yes. Do not be afraid, I will not desert you," replied a voice. "Very well!" said the archer, and seated himself on the frog. The frog swelled up and jumped across the river of fire; the archer put her in a jar and set out on his journey homeward.

He came to his mother-in-law and made his new servant entertain the old woman and her daughters. Shmat Razum regaled them so well that the old woman almost danced with joy, and she ordered three jars of milk a day to be given to the frog for her faithful services. The archer said farewell to his mother-in-law and set out homeward. He walked and walked and got very tired; his nimble feet were worn out, his white arms drooped. "Eh," he said, "Shmat Razum, if you only knew how exhausted I am! My legs are dropping off me." "Why did you not say so long ago?" the voice said. "I would have brought you to the place in a trice." Straightway the archer was seized as by an impetuous breeze and carried in the air so fast that his cap fell off his head. "Hey, Shmat Razum, stop for a moment, my cap has fallen off!" he cried. "Too late, master, your cap is now five thousand versts behind us." Towns and villages, rivers and forests flashed before his eyes.

As the archer was flying over a deep sea, Shmat Razum said to him: "Do you want me to make a golden arbor on that sea? You will be able to rest there and acquire a fortune." "Very well, make it," said the archer, and he began to descend toward the sea. Where a moment ago only waves surged, a little island appeared, and on the island was a golden arbor. Shmat Razum said to the archer: "Sit in the arbor, take a rest, and look at the sea. Three merchant ships will sail by and moor at the island. Do you invite the merchants to sit with you, feast and regale them, and exchange me for three marvels that the merchants are carrying with them. In due time I shall return to you."

The archer looked and saw three merchant ships coming from the west. The sailors saw the island and the golden arbor. "What a marvel!" they said. "How many times have we sailed by here, and there was nothing except water—and now, lo and behold, a golden arbor is there! Let us cast anchor, brothers, and feast our eyes upon it." They stopped the ships and cast anchor; the three merchants, the masters of the ships, took a light boat and went to the island. "Good day, good man," they said to the archer. "Good day, foreign merchants! You are welcome here. Have a good time, be merry, and take a rest; this arbor was made expressly for passing guests." The merchants came into the arbor and sat on a bench. "Hey, Shmat Razum!" cried the archer, "give us food and drink." A table appeared and on the table wines and viands—whatever one's heart desired, it was all there in a trice. The merchants gasped in amazement. "Let us make an exchange," they said. "You give us your servant and take any of our marvels in exchange for him." "And what marvels do you have?" "Look and you will see."

One of the merchants drew a little box out of his pocket and opened it, and instantly a splendid garden, with flowers and paths, was spread all over the island; he closed the box, and the garden disappeared. The second merchant drew an ax from under his garment and began to strike—rap-tap!—and a ship was ready. Rap-tap, and there was another ship! He struck a hundred times, and made a hundred ships, with sails, and guns, and sailors; the ships sailed, the guns boomed, the crews asked the merchants for orders. Having shown his trick, the merchant hid his ax, and the ships disappeared as though they had never been there. The third merchant got out a horn; he blew into one end of it and an army appeared—infantry and cavalry, with muskets and cannon and flags. From all the regiments reports came to the merchant and he gave them orders: the troops marched, the music thundered, the flags waved. Having had his fun, the merchant blew into the other end of the horn, and nothing was there; the whole host had disappeared.

"Your marvels are good, but I have no use for them," said the archer. "Armies and fleets are for kings, and I am a simple soldier. If you insist on making an exchange, give me all your three marvels for my one invisible servant." "Isn't that asking too much?" "Well, as you wish; but I will not exchange otherwise." The merchants thought to themselves: "What is the use to us of this garden, this army, and these warships? It will be better to make the exchange; at least we shall live without care, sated and drunk." They gave the archer their marvels and said: "Eh, Shmat Razum, we shall take you with us; will you serve us in faith and in truth?" "Why not?" the servant's voice said. "It is all the same to me with whom I live." The merchants returned to their ships and set about treating their crews to food and drink, crying: "Hey, Shmat Razum, get busy."

All the crews got drunk and fell sound asleep. Meanwhile

the archer sat in his golden arbor, grew thoughtful, and said: "Ah, it's a pity! Where is my faithful servant, Shmat Razum?" "I am here, master!" The archer was overjoyed. He said: "Is it not time for us to go home?" He had no sooner said these words than an impetuous wind seized him and carried him through the air. The merchants awoke and wanted to drink to chase away their drunkenness. "Hey, Shmat Razum," they cried, "give us a drink!" No one answered, no one served them. No matter how they shouted and commanded, it was of no avail. "Well, gentlemen, this scoundrel has cheated us. Now the devil himself won't find him; the island has vanished and the golden arbor is gone." The merchants grieved and grieved, then hoisted their sails and went on their way.

The archer flew swiftly back to his own country and descended at a deserted place near the blue sea. "Hey, Shmat Razum, can we not build a castle here?" he said. "Why not? It will be ready at once," the servant's voice replied. In a trice there was a castle, so magnificent that it cannot be described, twice as good as the royal palace. The archer opened his box and around the castle there appeared a garden with rare trees and flowers. The archer was sitting at the open window, feasting his eyes upon his garden, when suddenly a dove flew in at the window, struck the floor, and turned into his young wife. They embraced, greeted and questioned each other, and told their tales. The archer's wife said to him: "Since you left home I have been flying in forests and groves as a blue dove."

Next morning the king went out on the balcony, looked at the blue sea, and saw a new castle on the seashore; and around the castle there was a green garden. "What insolent man has dared to build a castle on my land without my permission?" he asked. Messengers ran, made inquiries, and reported that the castle had been built by the archer, that he himself was living in it, and that his wife was with him. The king became even more enraged, ordered an army to be assembled and sent to the seashore, the garden to be cut down, the castle to be destroyed, and the archer and his wife to be put to a cruel death. The archer saw that a strong royal army was marching on him;

he quickly seized his ax, and—rap-tap!—a ship was ready. He struck a hundred times and made a hundred ships. Then he took out his horn, blew once, and infantry came out; he blew again, and cavalry galloped out. The commanders of the regiments and the captains of the ships ran up to him and took his orders. The archer bade them begin the battle. At once the music thundered, the drums beat, the regiments moved forward; the infantry broke the ranks of the royal soldiers, the cavalry gave them chase and took them captive, and the guns from the ships kept firing at the capital. The king saw that his army was fleeing; he rushed forward to stop his troops, but to no avail. Less than half an hour later he himself was slain. When the battle was over, the people assembled and asked the archer to rule the whole kingdom. He consented, became king, and his wife became the queen.

THE WISE WIFE

IN A CERTAIN KINGDOM, in a certain land, in a little village, there lived an old man and his old wife; they had three sons, two clever ones and a simple one. The time came for the old man to die, and he divided his money. He gave the eldest son a hundred rubles and the middle son a hundred rubles, but did not want to give anything to the simpleton, who, he thought, would lose the money anyhow. "But father," said the simpleton, "all the children are equal, whether they be wise or foolish; give me a share too." So the old man gave him a hundred rubles too. The father died and his sons buried him. Now the clever brothers set out to buy oxen at the market; the simpleton went there too. The clever ones bought oxen but the simpleton brought back a cat and a dog. Several days later the older brothers harnessed their oxen and made ready to take to the road; seeing them do this, the youngest brother also prepared to go. "What are you doing, simpleton?" they asked. "Why do you want to go? So that people can laugh at you?" "That's my business!" the simple brother replied. "The roads are open to the wise and they are not closed to the foolish!"

The simpleton took his dog and his cat, slung a bag over his shoulder, and left the house. He walked and walked, till he came to a big river; he had not a penny to pay at the ferry. The simpleton did not stop to think very long; he gathered dry branches, made a hut on the shore, and started to live in it. His dog began to hunt all around the neighborhood; it stole crusts of bread, took care of itself, and fed its master and the cat as well. One day a ship laden with all kinds of merchandise sailed down the river. The simpleton saw it and cried: "Hey, Mr. Shipmaster! You are sailing to trade; take my merchandise too and share half-and-half with me." And he threw his cat on board the ship. "What do we need this beast for?" said the shipworkers, laughing. "Come on, boys, let's drop it into the water." "Look here, you," said the shipmaster, "don't touch that cat! Let it hunt rats and mice aboard ship." "Why not?" said they. "It's a bargain!"

After some time, a long time or a short time, the ship came to a foreign land where no one had ever even seen cats, and there were as many rats and mice running about there as blades of grass in the fields. The shipmaster displayed his merchandise and began to sell it. A merchant became interested, bought the whole cargo, and said to the shipmaster: "Now we must wet our bargain. Come with me, I will treat you." He brought the guest to his home, got him drunk, and ordered some clerks to take him to the barn, saying: "Let the rats devour him—then we will get all his wealth for nothing." They took the shipmaster to a dark barn and threw him on the ground. But his cat had followed him all along, having become so fond of him that it would not move a step away from him. It wriggled into the barn and fell to strangling the rats. It strangled a huge number of them. Next morning the host came and saw that the shipmaster was safe and sound and that the cat was finishing the last of the rats. "Sell me your beast," he said. "Buy it!" They bargained and bargained, and finally the merchant bought the cat for six barrels of gold.

The shipmaster returned to his own country, found the simpleton, and gave him three barrels of gold. "This is a lot of gold! What shall I do with it?" wondered the simpleton, and went through towns and villages dividing it among the poor. He distributed two barrels, but with the third he bought incense, piled it up in the open field, and lighted it: the sweet smoke went up to God in heaven. Suddenly an angel appeared, saying: "The Lord has commanded me to ask you what you wish." "I do not know," answered the simpleton. "Well, go over there. Three peasants are plowing the land; ask them and they will tell you." The simpleton took his stick and went to where the plowmen were working. He approached the first. "Greetings, old man!" he said. "Greetings, good fellow!" "Tell me what I should ask of the Lord." "How should I know what you want?" The simpleton did not stop to think very long; he struck the old man with his stick, right on the head, and killed him.

He approached the second plowman and asked again: "Tell me, old man, what should I ask of the Lord?" "How should I know?" the man said. The simpleton struck him with his stick without even giving him time to gasp. He came to the third plowman and said: "Now you tell me, old man." The old man answered: "If you should get wealth, you might forget about God; so you had better ask for a wise wife." The simpleton returned to the angel, who asked: "Well, what have you been told?" "I was told to ask not for wealth, but for a wise wife." "Very well," said the angel. "Go to such and such a river, sit on the bridge, and look into the water. All kinds of fish will pass by you, big and small. Among these fish there will be a little perch with a golden ring. Snatch this fish and throw it behind you on the damp earth."

The simpleton did as he was told; he came to the river, sat on the bridge, and stared into the water. All kinds of fish swam by him, big and small, and then came the perch with a golden ring on it. He snatched it at once and threw it behind him on the damp earth, and the little fish turned into a lovely maiden. "Good day, dear friend!" she said to him. They took each other by the hand and went on their way; they walked and walked, the sun began to set, and they stopped to spend the night in the open field. The simpleton fell sound asleep, and the lovely maiden cried out in a high voice. Straightway twelve workers appeared. "Build me a rich palace with a golden roof!" the maiden ordered. In a trice the palace was ready, with mirrors and pictures and everything that could be desired. They had gone to sleep in the open field and awoke in splendid chambers. The king himself beheld the palace with the golden roof, was astonished, summoned the simpleton, and said: "Only yesterday this place was empty, and now a palace stands there! You must be a sorcerer!" "No, Your Majesty! Everything was done by God's command!" "Well, since you could build a palace in one night, you must build a bridge from your palace to my own, with one arch of silver and the other of gold—and if you have not built it by tomorrow, by my sword your head shall fall!"

The simpleton went away weeping. His wife met him at their door. "Why do you weep?" she asked. "How can I help weeping? The king has commanded me to build a bridge, with one arch of gold and the other of silver; and if it is not ready by tomorrow, he will cut off my head!" "Do not worry, my soul! Go to sleep; the morning is wiser than the evening!" The simpleton lay down and fell asleep. When he arose the next morning, everything was done; the bridge was so beautiful that you could not feast your eyes enough on it! The king summoned the simpleton and said: "You have done well! Now, in one night, make apple trees grow on both sides of the bridge, and make ripe apples hang on them, and let birds of paradise sing in them and strange kittens from foreign lands mew underneath them; and if all is not ready tomorrow, by my sword your head shall fall!"

The simpleton went away weeping; his wife met him at their door. "Why do you weep, my soul?" she asked. "How can I help weeping? The king has commanded me to make apple trees grow on both sides of the bridge, with ripe apples hanging on them, birds of paradise singing in them, and strange kittens mewing beneath them; if all this is not done by tomorrow, he will cut off my head." "Do not worry, go to sleep; the morning is wiser than the evening." Next morning, when the simpleton arose, everything was done: the apples were ripe, the birds were singing, and the kittens were mewing. The simpleton picked some of the apples and brought them to the king on a dish. The king ate one apple, then another, and said: "You deserve praise! I have never yet tasted such sweetness! Well, brother, since you are so clever, go to the other world, find my deceased father, and ask him where his money is hidden. And if you do not find him, remember this—by my sword, your head shall fall!"

Again the simpleton went away weeping. "Why do you shed tears, simpleton?" his wife asked him. "How can I help weeping? The king has bidden me go to the other world to ask his dead father where his money is hidden." "This is not yet a misfortune! Go to the king and ask him to send with you as companions the proud men who give him such evil counsel." The king named two boyars as the simpleton's companions. His wife fetched a ball of thread. "Take this," she said. "Go boldly wherever the ball rolls."

The ball rolled and rolled, straight into the sea; the sea parted and a way was opened; the simpleton took a few steps, and he and his companions found themselves in the other world. He looked around and saw that devils had harnessed a load of wood to the king's dead father and were prodding him with iron rods. "Stop!" cried the simpleton. The devils raised their horned heads and asked: "And what do you want?" "I must have a word or two with that dead man whom you have harnessed to a load of wood." "What an idea! As though there were time to talk! The fire in our hell might go out!" "Fear not, you will get there on time; take these two boyars in his place, they will move the wood even faster!" The devils quickly unharnessed the dead king, harnessed the two boyars in his place, and drove them to hell with the wood. The simpleton said to the king's father: "Your son, our sovereign, sent me to ask Your Grace where the old treasure is hidden." "The treasure lies in deep cellars behind the stone wall; but virtue is not in them. Tell my son this: if he rules the kingdom with as little truth as I did, the same thing will happen to him as happened to me! You can see for yourself how the devils have tormented me, how they have whipped my back and sides to the very bone. Take this ring and give it to my son for added proof." Just as the king said these words, the devils came back. "Ho-ho!" they said. "This is a fine pair! Let us drive them once more!" The boyars cried to the simpleton: "Have pity on us, do not give us over to the devils, take us back while we are still alive!" The devils unharnessed them and the boyars returned with the simpleton to the white world.

They came to the king. He beheld the boyars and was horrified by their appearance: their faces were hollow, their eyes were staring, and iron rods protruded from their sides. "What happened to you?" the king asked. The simpleton answered: "We were in the other world; I saw that the devils had harnessed your deceased father to a load of wood, so I stopped them and gave them these two boyars to replace him. While I spoke with your father, the devils used them to cart wood." "And what is my father's message?" "He told me to say that if Your Majesty rules the kingdom with as little truth as he did, the same thing will happen to you as happened to him. And he sent you this ring for an added proof." "This is not what I want to know! Where is the treasure hidden?" "The treasure is in deep cellars behind the stone wall." Straightway a whole company of soldiers was called and they began to break down the stone wall; they broke it, and behind the wall they found barrels of silver and gold—a treasure beyond counting! "Thank you, brother, for your service," said the king to the simpleton. "Only do not be angry with me. Since you were able to go to the other world, get for me the self-playing gusla; and if you do not get it, by my sword your head shall fall!"

The simpleton went away weeping. "Why do you weep, my soul?" his wife asked him. "How can I help weeping? No matter how much I serve, I must lose my head! The king has commanded me to get for him the self-playing gusla." "That is nothing at all; my brother makes them." She gave him a ball of thread and a towel that she herself had made, and instructed him to take with him the king's councilors, the same two boyars as before, and said: "Now you are going away for a very long time. The king may do an evil deed, he may be tempted by my beauty! Go to the garden and cut three twigs." The simpleton cut three twigs in the garden. "Now strike the palace and myself with these twigs three times each, and God speed you!" The simpleton struck; his wife turned into a stone, and the palace turned into a stone mountain. Then the simpleton took the king's two boyars and set out on his way: wherever the ball rolled, he followed.

After some time, a long time or a short time, and after he had gone some distance, a long distance or a short one, the ball rolled into a thick forest, straight to a little hut. The simpleton entered the hut and there found an old woman sitting. "Greetings, little grandmother!" he said. "Greetings, my good man! Whither is God taking you?" "Little grandmother, I seek a master who can make a self-playing gusla for me, one that plays by itself, and that plays such tunes that everyone is forced to dance to its music willy-nilly." "Ah, my own son makes such guslas! Wait a while, he will soon be home." After a little while the old woman's son came home. "Master," the simpleton said to him, "make a self-playing gusla for me." "I have a gusla all made and ready; I will give it to you as a gift, but on this condition: when I tune the gusla, no one must sleep! And if anyone falls asleep and fails to rise when I call him, he must lose his head!" "Very well, master!"

The master set to work and began to tune the self-playing gusla; one of the boyars became dreamy from the sound of the music and fell sound asleep. "Are you sleeping?" the master called to him. The boyar did not rise nor answer, and his head rolled on the floor. After two or three minutes, the other boyar fell asleep; his head also came off his shoulders. Another minute passed, and the simpleton dozed off. "Are you sleeping?" the master called. "No," said the simpleton. "I am not sleeping! Only my eyes stick together from weariness after my journey. Have you not some water? I want to wash them." The old woman brought some water. The simpleton washed himself, took his embroidered towel, and began to wipe himself. The old woman glanced at the towel, recognized her daughter's handiwork, and said: "Ah, my dear son-in-law! I did not expect to see you. Is my daughter well?" And at once they fell to kissing and embracing. For three days they rejoiced, and ate and drank and refreshed themselves. Then came the time to say farewell. The master gave his brother-in-law the self-playing gusla as a farewell gift; the simpleton took it under his arm and set out on his way home.

He walked and walked, came out of the thick forest onto the highway, and made the self-playing gusla play—if he had been listening to it for a hundred years, he would still not have heard it enough! He happened to meet a brigand. "Give me your self-playing gusla," the fellow said, "and I will give you my stick!" "And what is your stick good for?" "Oh, it is not an ordinary stick. Just say to it: 'Eh, stick, strike and hit!' and it will kill a whole army!" The simpleton exchanged the gusla for the stick, took the stick, and commanded it to kill the brigand. The stick flew at the brigand, hit him once or twice, and slew him. The simpleton took back the self-playing gusla and went on.

He came to his own country. "Why should I go to the king?"

527

he thought. "There is time for that! I would rather see my wife first." He struck the stone mountain with his three twigs, once, twice, thrice, and the marvelous palace was there; he struck the stone, and his wife stood before him. They embraced, greeted each other, exchanged two or three words; then the simpleton took the gusla—and he did not forget the stick—and went to the king. When the king saw him, he thought: "Ah, there is no way to get rid of him, he fulfills every task!" He fell upon the simpleton, cursing and shouting: "You miserable wretch! Instead of reporting to me immediately, you went first to embrace your wife!" "I beg pardon, Your Majesty!" "I cannot make a fur coat out of your contrition! Nothing you say will win my forgiveness. Hand me my steel sword!" The simpleton saw that the time had come to settle their accounts, and cried: "Eh, stick, strike and hit!" The stick flew at the king, struck him once, struck him twice, and slew him. And the simpleton became king in his stead and ruled long and mercifully.

THE GOLDFISH

NEAR THE SHORE of an island in the ocean stood a small, dilapidated hut; in this hut lived an old man and his wife. They lived in dire poverty. The old man made himself a net and began to catch fish in the sea, for that was his only means of livelihood. One day the old man cast his net and began to pull on it; it seemed to him heavier than it had ever been before—he could barely drag it out. He looked, and the net was empty; there was only one fish in it. It was not an ordinary fish, but a goldfish. The goldfish implored him in a human voice: "Do not take me, old man. Let me go back into the blue sea; I will return your kindness by doing whatever you wish." The old man thought and thought and said: "I do not want anything of you; go back to the sea!" He threw the goldfish into the water and returned home. His wife asked him: "Did you get a big catch, old man?" "Only one little goldfish," the old man replied, "and even that I threw back into the sea—it implored me so earnestly, saying, 'Let me go back into the blue sea, and I will return your kindness by doing whatever you wish.' I took pity on the little fish, I did not demand anything of it but let it go free, for nothing." "Ah, you old devil!" said his wife. "You had a great chance but did not know how to take advantage of it."

The old woman became full of spite, abused her husband from dawn to dark, and did not give him a minute's rest. "At least you should have asked for some bread! Soon we won't even have a dry crust. What will you eat then?" The old man could not bear it any longer and went to the goldfish to ask for bread. He came to the sea and cried in a loud voice: "Goldfish, goldfish, stand with your tail to the sea, and your head to me!" The goldfish came to the shore. "What do you want, old man?" he asked. "My wife is furious at me, she sent me to you to get some bread." "Go home, you will find plenty of bread." The old man returned. "Well, wife, do we have plenty of bread?" he asked her. "We have plenty of bread, but we have this trouble: our trough broke, I have nothing to do my washing in. Go to the goldfish and ask him to give us a new trough." The old man went to the sea, and said: "Goldfish, goldfish, stand with your tail to the sea, and your head to me!" The goldfish came, saying: "What do you want, old man?" "My wife sent me to ask you for a new trough." "Very well, you will have a new trough." The old man returned and as soon as he crossed the threshold his wife again beset him. "Go to the goldfish,"

she said, "ask him to build us a new house; it is impossible to live in this one—any minute, it may fall apart."

The old man went to the sea. "Goldfish, goldfish," he said, "stand with your tail to the sea, and your head to me!" The fish came, stood with his head to the old man, and his tail to the sea, and asked: "What do you want, old man?" "Build us a new house. My wife scolds me and does not give me any rest. 'I don't want to live in this old hut,' she says, 'it may fall apart any minute.' " "Grieve not, old man, go home and pray to God: everything will be done." The old man returned, and on his plot stood a new oaken house, richly carved. His wife ran out to meet him; she was even angrier than before and abused him roundly. "You old dog, you don't know how to take advantage of your luck. Just because you have got a new house, you think you have accomplished something! Now, go back to the gold-fish and say to it that I don't want to be a peasant—I want to be a governor, so that law-abiding men will obey me and bow from their waists when they meet me."

The old man went to the sea and said in a loud voice: "Goldfish, goldfish, stand with your tail to the sea, and your head to me!" The goldfish came, stood with its tail to the sea, and its head to him. "What do you want, old man?" he asked. The old man answered: "My wife gives me no peace, she has become quite foolish; she does not want to be a peasant woman, she wants to be a governor." "Very well, grieve not, go home and pray to God: everything will be done." The old man returned, and instead of a wooden house there was a stone house of three stories; servants ran about in the courtyard, cooks bustled in the kitchen, and the old woman, dressed in rich brocade, sat on a high-backed chair and gave orders. "Good day, wife," said the old man. "You boor, how dare you call me, the governor, your wife? Hey there, you servants! Take this peasant to the stable and whip him as hard as you can!"

The servants ran up, seized the old man by his collar, and dragged him to the stable, and there the stable boys began to thrash him with whips; they thrashed him so hard that he could barely stand on his feet. Then the old woman appointed the old man to be her janitor; she ordered a broom to be given him to sweep the yard, and he had to eat and drink in the kitchen. The old man led a miserable life. All day long he had to clean the yard; if any dirt was discovered, he was led to the stable. "What a witch!" thought the old man. "She has found a comfortable hole and dug herself in like a sow; she does not even consider me her husband any longer."

Some time passed; the old woman became weary of being governor, summoned the old man before her, and ordered: "Go to the goldfish, old devil, and tell him that I don't want to be a governor, I want to be a queen." The old man went to the sea and said: "Goldfish, goldfish, stand with your tail to the sea, and your head to me!" The goldfish came. "What do you want, old man?" he asked. "My wife has become even more foolish," the old man answered. "She no longer wants to be a governor, she wants to be a queen." "Grieve not, go home and pray to God: everything will be done." The old man returned, and instead of the house he found a lofty castle with a golden roof; around it sentries walked and presented arms. Behind the castle was a large garden, and in front of it was a green meadow; in the meadow troops were gathered. The old woman was dressed like a queen; she came out on the balcony with generals and boyars and began to review the troops. The drums thundered, the band played, the soldiers cried "Hurrah!"

After some time the old woman became weary of being a queen; she ordered the old man to be found and brought into her august presence. A tumult arose, the generals bustled about, the boyars ran everywhere. "What old man?" they asked. At long last he was found in the backyard and led before the queen. "Listen, you old devil," she said to him. "Go to the goldfish and say to him that I don't want to be a queen. I want to be the ruler of the sea, so that all the seas and all the fishes will obey me." The old man tried to refuse, but in vain. "If you do not go," she said, "your head will roll."

Taking his courage in his hands the old man went to the sea. When he came there he said: "Goldfish, goldfish, stand with your tail to the sea, and your head to me!" The goldfish did not come. The old man called a second time—still the goldfish did not come. He called a third time, and suddenly the sea began to roll and roar; it had been bright and clear a moment before but now it grew quite black. The fish came to the shore. "What do you want, old man?" he asked. "My wife has become even more foolish. She no longer wants to be a queen, she wants to be the ruler of the sea, to rule over all the waters and command all the fishes." The goldfish did not say anything to the old man but turned around and went down to the depths of the sea. The old man returned home, and when he looked, he could not believe his eyes. The castle was gone as though it had never been there, and in its place stood a small, dilapidated hut, and in the hut sat his wife in a ragged dress. They began to live as before. The old man again took to catching fish; but no matter how often he cast his net into the sea, he never could catch the goldfish again.

THE GOLDEN-BRISTLED PIG,
THE GOLDEN-FEATHERED DUCK,
AND THE GOLDEN-MANED MARE

ONCE UPON A TIME there was an old man who lived with his old wife and three sons; two of the boys were clever, but the third was a simpleton. The time came for the old man to die. Before his death the father said: "My beloved children! For three nights you must go and sit on my grave." They cast lots among themselves and the simpleton drew the lot for the first turn. At midnight as he sat on the grave his father came out and asked: "Who is sitting?" "I, father, the simpleton." "Sit on, my child; God be with you!" On the second night it was the eldest brother's turn to go to the grave. He said to the simpleton: "Please, simpleton, sit this night for me; take whatever you want in return." "No, you go! Ghosts come out there." "Go in my stead, I will buy you red boots." The simpleton could not persuade his brother to do his duty, so he went to sit out the second night. As he sat there, the ground suddenly opened and his father came out and asked: "Who is sitting?" "I, father, the simpleton." "Sit, my child; God be with you!"

On the third night it was the middle brother's turn to go, and he besought the simpleton: "Do me a favor, sit for me; take whatever you want in return." "No, no, you go! The first night was terrifying, and the second even more so. The ghosts yell and quarrel; I shook as if with fever!" "Please, go, I will buy you a red cap." There was no way out of it, so the simpleton went to sit out the third night. He was sitting on the grave, when suddenly the ground opened and his father came out and asked: "Who is sitting?" "I, the simpleton." "Sit, my child; God be with you! Take this great blessing from me." And he gave his son three horsehairs. The simpleton went into the forbidden meadows, singed the three hairs, and cried in a sonorous voice: "Magic steed, horse of my need, blessing of my

533

father! Stand before me as a leaf before grass!" And the magic steed ran out; from its mouth flames streamed, from its ears poured pillars of smoke. The horse stood before him as a leaf before grass. The simpleton crept into the steed's left ear and ate and drank his fill; he crept into the right ear, donned a many-colored garment, and became such a hero as no mind can imagine nor pen describe.

On the next morning the king sent forth a call: "He who will kiss my daughter, Princess Beautiful, as he gallops on his horse, while she is sitting in the third story, to him I will give her in marriage." The two elder brothers made ready to watch the spectacle and invited the simpleton to join them. "Come with us, simpleton!" they said. "No, I don't want to; I will go to the field, take a basket, and kill jackdaws—that too is feed for dogs!" He went into the open field, singed his three horse-hairs, and cried: "Magic steed, horse of my need, blessing of my father! Stand before me, as a leaf before grass!" And the magic steed ran out; from his mouth flames streamed, from his ears rose pillars of smoke. The horse stood before him as a leaf before grass. The simpleton crept into the steed's left ear and ate and drank his fill; he crept into the right ear, donned a colored garment, and became a hero such as no mind can imagine nor pen describe. He mounted the horse, waved his hand, pushed his feet down into the stirrups, and darted off. The horse galloped and the earth shook; with his tail the great beast swept hills and vales, while tree trunks and logs rolled away between his legs. The simpleton leaped his steed higher than one story, but not as high as two, and turned back.

The brothers came home and found the simpleton lying on top of the stove. They said: "Eh, you simpleton! Why didn't you come with us? There was a hero there such as no mind can conceive of nor pen describe!" "Wasn't that I, the simpleton?" "Where would you get such a horse? Wipe your nose before you speak!" The next day the older brothers made ready to go to the spectacle and invited the simpleton. "Come with us, simpleton," they said. "Yesterday a great hero came, today an even greater one will come!" "No, I don't want to; I will go to the field, take a basket, kill jackdaws, and bring them home—

that too is feed for dogs!" He went to the open field, singed the horse hairs, and called: "Magic steed, horse of my need! Stand before me as a leaf before grass!" The magic steed ran out; from his mouth flames streamed, from his ears poured pillars of smoke. The horse stood before him as a leaf before grass. The simpleton crept into the horse's left ear and ate and drank his fill; he crept into the right ear, donned a colored garment, and became a hero such as no mind can imagine nor pen describe. He mounted the horse, waved his hand, pushed his feet down into the stirrups, jumped higher than two stories but not as far as the third. He turned back, set his horse loose in the forbidden green meadows, and went home and lay on the stove.

His brothers came back. "Ah, simpleton, why did you not go with us?" they cried. "Yesterday a great hero came, and today an even greater one—and where was that magnificent horse born?" "Wasn't that I, the simpleton?" "Eh, a simpleton says foolish things! Where would you get such a beauty, where would you find such a horse? Better stay on your stove." "Well, so be it. You'll see tomorrow." On the third morning the clever brothers made ready to watch the spectacle at the palace. "Come with us, simpleton," they said. "Today he'll kiss her!" "No, I don't want to; I will go to the field, take a basket, kill jackdaws, and bring them home—that too is feed for dogs!" He went into the open field, singed the horsehairs, and cried in a loud voice: "Magic steed, horse of my need! Stand before me, as a leaf before grass!" The magic steed ran out; from his mouth flames streamed, from his ears rose pillars of smoke. The horse stood before him as a leaf before grass. The simpleton crept into the steed's left ear and ate and drank his fill; he crept into the right ear, donned a colored garment, and became such a hero as no mind can conceive of nor pen describe. He mounted his horse, waved his hand, pushed his feet into the stirrups, jumped up to the third story, and kissed the king's daughter on her mouth. She struck his forehead with her golden ring.

The simpleton returned, set his good horse loose in the forbidden meadows, went home, tied up his head with a handkerchief, and lay down on the stove. His brothers came back. "Ah, you simpleton!" they said. "The first two times great heroes came, and today an even greater one—and where was that magnificent horse born?" "Was not that I, the simpleton?" "Ah, a simpleton can say foolish things! Where would you get such a horse?" The simpleton untied his handkerchief and his radiance illumined the whole room. His brothers asked him: "Where did you get such beauty?" "One place or another, but I got it! And you never believed me. But this is your simpleton."

The next day the king made a feast for all the Christians. He gave orders that the princes and the boyars, the plain people, the rich and the poor, the old and the young, be called to the palace; then the princess would choose her destined bridegroom. The clever brothers set out to dine at the palace. The simpleton tied his head up with a rag and said to them: "This time, even if you don't invite me, I shall go." The simpleton came to the king's palace and huddled in a corner behind the stove. The princess served everybody with wine; thus she thought to choose her bridegroom among the guests. The king followed behind her. After she had served all the guests she looked behind the stove and saw the simpleton; his head was tied up with a rag and his face was dripping with spittle and sweat. Princess Beautiful led him forth, wiped his brow with a handkerchief, kissed him, and said: "King, my father, this is my betrothed!" The king saw that the bridegroom was found; true, he was a simpleton, but that mattered not, for the king's word is law! He at once gave orders that they be married. Where a king is concerned, there's no dilly-dallying—no beer to brew, no wine to press, everything is ready. In a trice the marriage was solemnized.

The king already had two sons-in-law, so the simpleton became the third. One day the king summoned his clever sons-in-law and said: "My sons-in-law, my clever ones, my wise ones! Do for me this service that I command of you. On the steppe there is a duck with golden feathers; will you get it for me?" And he ordered them to saddle good horses and set out after the duck. The simpleton heard about their quest and began to beg: "And for me, father, give me at least a mare such as is

536

used to carry water." So the king gave him a broken-down jade. He mounted her, his back to her head, his face to her back, took her tail between his teeth, and spurred her, slapping her sides with his hands. "Giddap, dog's flesh!" he shouted. He rode into the open field, seized the jade by her tail, tore off her hide, and cried: "Eh, gather around, jackdaws, crows, and magpies! Father has sent you some feed!" Jackdaws, crows, and magpies swarmed down and ate all the flesh of the jade, while the simpleton called his magic steed: "Stand before me as a leaf before grass!"

The magic steed ran out; from his mouth flames streamed, from his ears rose pillars of smoke. The simpleton crept into the steed's left ear and ate and drank his fill; he crept into the right ear, donned a colored garment, and became a hero. He caught the duck with the golden feathers, pitched his tent, sat in it, and let the duck walk around it. His clever brothers-in-law came up to his tent and asked: "Who, who can be in that tent? If it's a little old man, be our little grandfather; if it's a man of middle age, be our little uncle." The simpleton answered: "It's a man of your own age, your little brother." "Well, little brother, will you sell the duck with the golden feathers?" "No, it's not for sale, it's sacred." "And what is its sacred price?" "The little fingers of your two right hands." They cut off the little fingers of their right hands and gave them to the simpleton, who put them in his pocket. Then the clever sons-in-law went home and went to bed. The king and queen paced back and forth in the hall and listened to what their sons-in-law were saying to their daughters. One said to his wife: "Be more gentle, you're hurting my hand." The other son-in-law said: "Oh, it hurts! My hand is very sore."

Next morning the king summoned his clever sons-in-law and said to them: "My sons-in-law, my clever ones, my wise ones! Do for me this service that I command of you. On the steppe there is a pig with golden bristles, and it has twelve piglets; get them for me." He ordered them to saddle good horses, and to the simpleton he again gave a broken-down jade that usually served to carry water. The simpleton rode into the open field, seized the jade by her tail, and tore off her hide. "Eh, gather around, jackdaws, crows, and magpies!" he cried. "The king has sent you some feed." Jackdaws, crows, and magpies came swarming down and pecked up all the flesh. Then the simpleton called his magic steed, caught the golden pig with her twelve piglets, and pitched his tent; he sat in the tent and let the pig walk around it.

The clever sons-in-law came by. "Who, who can be in that tent?" they said. "If it's a little old man, be our little grandfather; if it is a man of middle age, be our little uncle." "It is a man of your own age, your little brother." "Is the pig with the golden bristles yours?" "Mine." "Sell it to us; what do you want for it?" "It's not for sale, it's sacred." "What is its sacred price?" "From each of you a toe of your foot." So each of them cut a toe off one foot and gave it to the simpleton. Then they took the pig with the golden bristles and her twelve piglets.

Next morning the king called his clever sons-in-law and said: "My sons-in-law, my clever ones, my wise ones! Do for me this service that I command of you. On the steppe there is a mare with a golden mane and she has twelve foals; can you get them for me?" "We can, father!" The king ordered them to saddle good horses, and to the simpleton he again gave a broken-down jade that usually worked at carrying water. The simpleton sat with his back to the horse's head and his front to the horse's back, took her tail in his teeth, and slapped her sides with his hands, while his clever brothers-in-law laughed at him. The simpleton rode into the open field, seized the jade by her tail, and tore off her hide. "Eh! Gather around, jackdaws, crows, and magpies! Father has sent you some feed." Jackdaws, crows, and magpies swarmed down and pecked up all the flesh. Then the simpleton cried in a loud voice: "Magic steed, horse of my need, blessing of my father! Stand before me as a leaf before grass!"

The magic steed ran out; from his mouth flames streamed, from his ears rose pillars of smoke. The simpleton crept into the horse's left ear and ate and drank his fill; he crept into the right ear, donned a colored garment, and became a hero. "We must get the mare with the golden mane and her twelve foals," he said. The steed answered him: "The first two tasks were

child's play, this one is hard! Take three copper rods, three iron rods, and three pewter rods. The mare will pursue me over hills and dales; she will get tired and fall to the ground. At that moment be on your guard, sit on her, and strike her between the ears with all nine rods. Only thus will you conquer the mare with the golden mane." No sooner said than done: the simpleton caught the golden-maned mare and her twelve foals, and pitched his tent; he tied the mare to a post and sat in the tent. The clever sons-in-law came and asked: "Who, who can be in that tent? If it's a little old man, be our little grandfather; if it's a man of middle age, be our little uncle." "It's a knight of your own age, your little brother." "Well, little brother, is the mare that is tied to that post yours?" "Mine!" "Sell her to us." "She's not for sale; she's sacred." "What is her sacred price?" "A strip of flesh apiece from your backs." The clever sons-in-law winced and hesitated, but finally agreed; the simpleton cut a strip of flesh from the back of each, put the strips in his pocket, and gave his brothers-in-law the mare with her twelve foals.

The next day the king gave a great feast, to which everyone came. The simpleton drew the cut-off fingers, the toes, and the strips of flesh from his pocket and said: "Here are the duck with the golden feathers, the pig with the golden bristles, and the golden-maned mare with her twelve foals." "What's this you're raving about, simpleton?" the king asked him, and he answered: "King, my father, order your clever sons-in-law to remove the gloves from their hands." They removed their gloves; the little fingers on their right hands were missing. "I took a little finger from each of them for the duck with the golden feathers," said the simpleton. He put the cut-off fingers in their former places and they grew back and healed. "Father, let your clever sons-in-law remove their boots," the simpleton said. They removed their boots, and a toe was missing from one foot of each. "I took the toes from them for the pig with the golden bristles," the simpleton said. He placed the cut-off toes on their feet, and in a trice they grew on and healed. "Father, let them remove their shirts," the simpleton said. They removed their shirts, and it was seen that each son-in-law had

540

had a strip of flesh cut from his back. "I took this from them for the mare with the golden mane and her twelve foals." He fitted the strips into their old places, and instantly they grew to the men's backs and healed. "Now, father," said the simpleton, "give orders that the carriage be made ready."

A carriage was harnessed and the king's family seated themselves in it and drove to the open field. The simpleton singed his three horsehairs and cried in a loud voice: "Magic steed, horse of my need, blessing of my father! Stand before me as a leaf before grass!" The horse ran out and the earth shook; from his mouth flames streamed, from his ears rose pillars of smoke. He ran, then stopped as though rooted to the spot. The simpleton crept into the steed's left ear and ate and drank his fill; he crept into the right ear, donned a colored garment, and became such a hero as no mind can conceive of and no pen describe. From that time forth he lived with his wife in kingly style, drove around in a carriage, and gave great feasts. I too was present at these feasts; I drank wine and mead, but however much I drank, only my mustache got wet!

THE DUCK
WITH GOLDEN EGGS

ONCE UPON A TIME there were two brothers, one rich and the other poor. The poor one had a wife and children but the rich one lived all alone. The poor brother went to the rich one and begged of him: "Brother, give me some food for myself and my poor children; today I have not even anything for dinner." "Today I have no time for you," said the rich brother. "Today princes and boyars are visiting me; I have no place for a poor man." The poor brother wept bitterly and went to catch fish, hoping to get at least enough fish to make a soup for his children. The moment he cast his net, he brought up an old jug. "Drag me out and break me on the shore," said a voice inside the jug, "and I will show you the way to fortune." He dragged out the jug, broke it, and a spirit came out of it and said: "On a green meadow stands a birch. Under its root is a duck. Cut the roots of the birch and take the duck home. The duck will lay eggs—on one day a golden egg, the next day a silver one." The poor brother went to the birch, got the duck, and took it home. The duck began to lay eggs—on one day a golden egg, the next day a silver one. The poor man sold the eggs to merchants and boyars and grew rich in a very short time. "My children," he said, "pray to God. The Lord has had mercy upon us."

The rich brother grew envious and spiteful. "Why has my brother grown so rich?" he wondered. "Now I have become poorer, and he wealthier. Surely he has committed some sin." He lodged a complaint in court. The matter reached the tsar, and the brother who had been poor and was now rich was summoned to the tsar's presence. What could he do with the duck? His children were small and he had to leave the duck with his wife. She began to go to the bazaar, selling the eggs for a high price. Now, she was very pretty, and she fell in love with a barin. "How have you become so rich?" the barin asked her. "It was the will of God," she replied. But he insisted, saying: "No, tell me the truth; if you do not, I won't love you, I won't come to see you any more." He stopped visiting her for a day or two. Then she called him to her house and told him. "We have a duck," she said. "Each day it lays an egg—on one day a golden egg, the next day a silver one." "Show me that duck," said the barin. "I want to see what kind of a bird it is." He examined the duck and saw an inscription in golden letters on its belly; the inscription said that whoever ate the duck's head would be a king, and whoever ate its heart would spit gold.

The prospect of such great fortune made the barin's mouth water and he began to press the woman to slaughter the duck. For some time she refused but in the end she slaughtered the duck and put it in the oven to roast. It was a holiday; she went to mass, and during that time her two sons came home. They wanted to eat something, looked into the oven, and pulled out the duck; the elder one ate its head and the younger its heart. The mother returned from church, the barin came, they sat at table; the barin saw that the duck's head and heart were missing. "Who ate them?" he asked, and finally discovered that the boys had done it. He began to press their mother: "Kill your sons, take out the brains of one and the heart of the other; if you do not kill them our friendship is ended." When he had said this he left her; she languished for a whole week, then could not stand it any longer, and sent for the barin. "Come to me," she begged. "So be it! I won't even spare my children for your sake." As she sat whetting a knife, her elder son saw her thus, began to weep bitterly, and implored her: "Dear mother, permit us to take a walk in the garden." "Well, go, but don't go far," she said. But the boys, instead of taking a walk, took to their heels.

They ran and ran, then grew tired and hungry. In an open field they saw a herdsman tending cows. "Herdsman, herdsman, give us some bread," they said. "Here is a little piece," said the herdsman. "That's all I have left. Eat, and may it serve your health." The elder brother gave the bread to the younger, saying: "Eat it; you are weaker than I, I can wait." "No, brother," the younger said, "you have led me by my hand all this time, you are more tired than I; let us divide the bread equally." They divided it equally and ate it, and both were sated.

They went on farther; they walked straight ahead along a wide road, and then the road branched into two forks. At the crossroads stood a post, and the post bore an inscription: "He who goes to the right will be a king; he who goes to the left will be wealthy." The younger brother said to the elder: "Brother, you go to the right, you know more than I do, you can understand more." The elder brother went to the right, and the younger to the left.

The elder brother walked and walked till he came to a foreign kingdom. He asked an old woman to give him shelter for the night, and in the morning he arose, washed himself, got dressed, and said his prayers. The king of that kingdom had just died and all the people assembled in the church, carrying candles; it was the law that he whose candle lighted first of itself should be the new king. "Do you too go to church, my child," said the old woman. "Perhaps your candle will light first." She gave him a candle. He went to the church and had no sooner entered than his candle lighted of itself. The princes and boyars became envious; they tried to put out the candle and drive the boy out. But the queen from high on her throne said: "Don't touch him! Whether he is good or bad, he is my fate." The boy was taken by the arm and led to the queen; she put her golden seal on his forehead, took him to her palace, led him to the throne, proclaimed him king, and married him.

They lived together for some time; then the new king said to his wife: "Give me leave to go and search for my brother." "Go, and God be with you," the queen said. He traveled for a long time through various lands, and found his younger brother living in great wealth. Great piles of gold filled his barns; whenever he spat, he spat out gold. He had nowhere to put all his wealth. "Brother," said the younger to the elder, "let us go to our father and see how he is faring." "I am ready," said the elder brother. They drove to the place where their father and mother lived and asked for shelter in their parents' house, without telling who they were. They sat at table, and the older brother began to talk about the duck that laid golden eggs and about the wicked mother. The mother constantly interrupted him and changed the subject. The father guessed the truth. "Are you my children?" he asked. "We are, dear father," they replied. There was kissing and embracing and no end of talk. The elder brother took the father to live with him in his kingdom, the younger went to find a bride for himself, and the mother was left all alone.

ELENA THE WISE

IN OLDEN TIMES in a certain kingdom, not in our land, a soldier chanced to be on guard at a stone tower; the tower was locked and sealed, and it was night. On the stroke of midnight the soldier thought he heard someone in the tower saying: "Eh, soldier!" He asked: "Who calls me?" "It is I, an evil spirit," said a voice from behind the iron bars. "I have sat here for thirty years without food or drink." "What do you want?" "Let me out of here; whenever you are in need, I will help you; just remember me, and at that very moment I shall come to your aid." The soldier straightway tore off the seal, broke the lock, and opened the door, and the evil spirit flew out of the tower, soared upward, and vanished more quickly than lightning. "Well," thought the soldier, "a fine thing I have done! All my years of service are not worth a penny now. I will be put in the guardhouse, court-martialed, and perhaps made to run the gantlet; I'd better run away while there is still time." He threw his gun and knapsack on the ground and walked away straight ahead.

He walked one day, a second day, and a third day; hunger tormented him, yet he had nothing to eat or drink. He sat on the road, wept bitter tears, and began to think: "Well, am I not a fool? I served the king for ten years, I was always sated and content; every day I received three pounds of bread. But I had to run away to die of hunger! Eh, evil spirit, it is all your fault!" Suddenly out of nowhere the evil spirit appeared before him and said: "Good day, soldier! Why are you so sad?" "How can I help being sad when I have been tormented by hunger for three days?" "Do not grieve, this can be remedied," said the evil spirit. He rushed here and there, brought all kinds of wine and provisions, fed the soldier, and invited him to his house. "In my house you will have an easy life," the evil spirit said. "You can eat, drink, and be merry as much as your heart desires. Only look after my daughters, I don't demand anything else." The soldier consented and the evil spirit seized him by the arm, raised him high, very high in the air, and carried him beyond thrice nine lands, to the thrice tenth kingdom, to a white stone palace.

The evil spirit had three daughters, who were beauties. He ordered them to obey the soldier and to give him food and drink in abundance, and himself flew away to do mischief, as is the custom of evil spirits. He never sat in one place, but kept traveling about the world, troubling people and tempting them to sin. The soldier stayed with the lovely maidens and began to have such a gay life that he did not think of dying. Only one thing worried him: every night the lovely maidens left the house and where they went he did not know. He tried to question them, but they refused to answer, denying everything. "Very well, then," he thought, "I will stand guard for a whole night and I will find out where you go." At night he lay on his bed, pretended that he was sound asleep, and waited impatiently.

When the time came, he stole quietly up to the maidens' bedroom, stood at the door, bent down, and looked through the keyhole. The lovely maidens brought in a magic carpet, spread it on the floor, struck the carpet, and turned into doves; they shook their wings and flew out of the window. "What a marvel!" thought the soldier. "I'll try it too." He jumped into the bedroom, struck the carpet, and turned into a hedge sparrow; he flew out of the window and followed the doves. They alighted on a green meadow, and the sparrow sat behind a currant bush, hiding among the leaves and peeping out from there. An immense host of doves gathered, covering the whole meadow; in the middle of the meadow stood a golden throne. After a short while, heaven and earth were illumined; a golden carriage flew in the air, drawn by six fiery dragons; in the carriage sat Princess Elena the Wise, a marvelous beauty such as no mind can imagine and no tongue can tell of. She descended from her carriage and sat on the golden throne; then she began to call each dove in turn and to teach it various cunning tricks. When she had finished teaching the doves she jumped into the carriage and drove off.

Then all the doves left the green meadow, flying each in a

different direction, and the hedge sparrow followed the three sisters and found itself together with the doves in the bedroom. The doves struck the carpet and turned into lovely maidens, and the hedge sparrow struck the carpet and turned into a soldier. "Whence do you come?" the maidens asked him. "I have been with you on the green meadow; I saw the beautiful princess on the golden throne and I heard her teach you various cunning tricks." "Well, you are lucky to have escaped! For this princess, Elena the Wise, is our powerful ruler. If she had had her magic book with her, she would have discovered your presence at once, and you would not have escaped a cruel death. Take care, soldier! Do not return to the green meadow, do not look at Elena the Wise, or you will lose your rash head." The soldier was not frightened; he let these words pass through his ears unheeded. He waited till the next night, struck the carpet, and turned into a hedge sparrow. The hedge sparrow flew to the green meadow, hid behind a currant bush, looked at Elena the Wise, feasted his eyes upon her marvelous beauty, and thought: "If I could get such a wife, I would want nothing else in the world! I will follow her and find out where she lives."

Elena the Wise came down from her golden throne, sat in her carriage, and soared in the air to her marvelous palace; the hedge sparrow flew after her. The princess came to her palace; her governesses and nurses ran out to meet her, seized her by the arms, and led her to her magnificent chambers. The hedge sparrow flew to the garden, chose a beautiful tree that stood right under the princess' bedroom, perched on a branch, and began to sing so well and so plaintively that the princess could not close her eyes all night. She listened and listened. As soon as the radiant sun arose, Elena the Wise cried in a loud voice: "Governesses and nurses, run to the garden, catch that hedge sparrow!" The governesses and nurses rushed to the garden and tried to catch the songbird, but the old women were not equal to this task. The hedge sparrow fluttered from bush to bush, never flying far, yet refusing to be caught.

The princess became impatient. She ran out into the green garden to catch the hedge sparrow herself; she came up to the bush, and the bird did not move from the branch, but sat drooping its wings, as though waiting for her. The princess was overjoyed, took the bird in her hands, carried it to the palace, put it in a golden cage, and hung the cage in her bedroom. The day went by, the sun set. Elena the Wise flew to the green meadow, returned, undressed, and lay in her bed. The hedge sparrow gazed at her white body and her wondrous beauty and trembled all over. As soon as the princess had fallen asleep, the hedge sparrow turned into a fly, flew out of the golden cage, struck the floor, and turned into a goodly youth. The goodly youth came up to the princess' bed, gazed and gazed at her beauty, could not restrain himself, and kissed her on her sweet mouth. He saw that the princess was awakening, turned quickly into a fly, flew into the cage, and became a hedge sparrow.

Elena the Wise opened her eyes; she looked around her and saw no one. "Apparently," she thought, "I dreamed all that in a dream." She turned over and fell asleep again. But the soldier could not restrain himself; he tried a second and a third time, and the princess, who was a light sleeper, awoke after each kiss. After the third time she rose from her bed and said: "Something is wrong; I must look into my magic book." She looked into it and found at once that in the golden cage there was not a simple hedge sparrow but a young soldier. "Ah, you insolent fellow," she cried, "get out of that cage! For this deception you will answer with your life."

The hedge sparrow had no choice; it flew out of the golden cage, struck the floor, and turned into a goodly youth. The soldier fell on his knees before the princess and began to beg for her pardon. "There is no pardon for you, scoundrel," said Elena the Wise, and called the executioner to cut the soldier's head off. Out of nowhere a giant appeared with an ax and a block, threw the soldier down, pressed his head to the block, and raised his ax, waiting for the princess to give the signal with her handkerchief. "Have mercy upon me!" the soldier begged with tears in his eyes. "Give me leave to sing a song before I die." "Sing, but hurry!" said Elena. The soldier intoned a song so sad, so plaintive, that Elena the Wise began to weep. She took pity on the goodly youth and said to him: "I give you ten hours; if by that time you manage to hide so cunningly that I can't find you, I shall marry you; if you do not, I shall order your head to be cut off."

The soldier went out of the palace, wandered into a thick forest, sat under a bush, and became sad and thoughtful. "Ah, evil spirit, it is all your fault!" he said. At that very moment the evil spirit appeared before him, saying: "What do you want, soldier?" "Eh," the soldier said, "my death is approaching! Where shall I hide from Elena the Wise?" The evil spirit struck the earth and turned into a blue-winged eagle. "Soldier, sit on my back," he said. "I will carry you to the skies." The soldier sat on the eagle, who soared upward and flew beyond black clouds. Five hours passed. Elena the Wise took her magic book, looked into it, and saw everything as though on the palm of her hand. She cried in a loud voice: "Enough, eagle! Stop flying in the skies. Descend! You will not hide from me." The eagle descended to the ground.

The soldier was even more grieved than before. "What shall I do now?" he asked. "Where shall I hide?" "Wait," said the evil spirit, "I will help you." He jumped to the soldier, struck him on his cheek, and turned him into a pin; then he himself turned into a mouse, seized the pin in his teeth, stole into the palace, found the magic book, and stuck the pin into it. The last five hours passed. Elena the Wise opened her magic book, looked and looked, and the book showed nothing; the princess grew very angry and flung the book into the stove. The pin fell out of the book, struck the floor, and turned into a goodly youth. Elena the Wise took his arm. "I am cunning," she said, "but you are more cunning than I." They did not stop to think too long; they wedded and began to live together happily.

IN A CERTAIN KINGDOM an old man and his old wife were living in great misery. When her time came the old woman died. Outside it was bitter, frosty winter weather. The old man went to his neighbors and friends and asked them to help him to dig a grave for his wife, but knowing his utter poverty they bluntly refused. The old man went to the priest—and the priest of his village was very greedy and unscrupulous. "Holy father," said the old man, "please bury my wife." "And have you money to pay for the burial? Pay me in advance, my friend." "There is no use hiding from you that I have not a penny in my house. But wait awhile; when I earn some money, I will pay you with interest; I swear that I will pay you."

The priest refused even to listen to the old man. "If you have no money," he said, "don't dare to come to me!" "I have no choice," thought the old man, "but to go to the graveyard, dig a grave somehow, and bury my wife myself." He took an ax and a shovel and went to the graveyard. He began to dig the grave. First he cut the frozen ground with his ax, then he took his shovel, and dug and dug; he dug up a little pot, looked into it, and found it full to the brim with gold pieces gleaming like fire. The old man was overjoyed: "Glory be to God!" he said. "Now I have enough money to give my wife a decent burial and provide a funeral dinner." He stopped digging the grave, took the pot of gold, and went home.

Money, as always, made everything go as smoothly as butter. Good people were found at once to dig the grave and make the coffin; the old man sent his daughter-in-law to buy wine and all kinds of viands, everything that is needed for a funeral feast, then took a gold piece and again went to the priest. As soon as he set foot on the doorstep, the priest fell upon him. "I told you clearly, you old dotard, not to come without money, and yet you're here again," he said. "Do not be angry, holy father," the old man begged him, "here is a gold piece. Bury my wife and I shall never forget your kindness." The priest took the money and could not find ways enough of being gracious to the old man. He begged him to sit down and spoke fawning words to him: "Well, dear old man, be of good cheer; everything will be done as it should be." The old man bowed to him and went home, and the priest and his wife began to talk about him. "The old rascal!" they said. "Everyone says he is poor, very poor, yet he came here with a gold piece. I have buried many wealthy people in my life, and never has anyone given me as much as this."

The priest gathered all his attendants and gave the old woman a decent burial. After the burial the old man invited the priest to the funeral repast. All the mourners came to his house, sat at table, and out of nowhere appeared wine and meats and plenty of everything. The priest sat there eating enough for three, and his mouth watered at the sight of another man's goods. After dinner the visitors began to go home, and the priest too rose from his chair. The old man went with him to the gate, and as soon as they were out in the yard, and the priest saw that no one could hear them, he began to question the old man. "My dear friend," he said, "confess to me, do not let a sin weigh on your soul; you may speak to me as to God himself. How have you managed to improve your fortunes so quickly? You were a poor peasant, and now all of a sudden you have everything. Confess, my friend! Whom have you killed, whom have you robbed?" "Holy father, what are you saying? I will confess the whole truth to you. I did not rob, I did not kill anyone; a treasure-trove came into my hands of itself." And he told the priest everything.

Upon hearing this, the priest began to tremble with greed. He returned home and could not attend to anything. Night and day he had only one thought: "The idea of such a wretched little peasant having so much money—how can I get my hands on his potful of gold?" He spoke about it to his wife; they put their heads together and finally thought of a plan. The priest said: "Listen, wife, we have a goat, haven't we?" "We have." "Well, that's fine. At night we shall do everything that is necessary." Late at night the priest dragged the goat to his room, slaughtered it, and removed its whole skin, with the horns and

551

the beard. Then he put the goatskin on himself and said to his wife: "Take a needle and thread and sew the skin around me so that it stays on." The priest's wife took a thick needle and coarse thread and sewed the goatskin around him.

On the stroke of midnight the priest went straight to the old man's house, came to the window, and knocked and scratched on it. The old man heard the noise, jumped up, and asked: "Who is there?" "The devil!" said the priest. "Our house is consecrated!" the peasant yelled, and began to make the sign of the cross and to chant prayers.

"Listen, old man," said the priest. "You won't get rid of me, no matter how long you pray or how many times you make the sign of the cross. You had better give me your pot of money, or I'll settle your account. I took pity on your grief—I showed you a treasure-trove, thinking that you would take just a little of it to pay for your wife's burial, but you took it all." The old man looked out of the window, saw the goat's horns and beard, and was certain that it was the devil himself. "Let him go to hell with the money," thought the old man. "I've lived without money before and I can live without it in the future." He got his pot of gold, took it out into the street, threw it on the ground, and rushed back to his house. The priest snatched up the money and ran home. Upon his return he said: "Well, now the money is ours. Here, wife, store it away in a safe place, and then take a sharp knife, cut the threads, and remove the goatskin before anyone sees me."

The priest's wife took a knife and began to cut the skin along the seam. Suddenly blood began to spurt, and the priest yelled: "Wife, it hurts! Don't cut, don't cut!" She tried to cut at another place, but the same thing happened. The goatskin had grown to the priest's body, and no matter what they did, no matter what they tried—they even took the money back to the old man—it was of no avail: the goatskin stuck to the priest. That was how the Lord punished him for his greed.

MARIA MOREVNA

IN A CERTAIN KINGDOM in a certain land lived Prince Ivan. He had three sisters—Princess Maria, Princess Olga, and Princess Anna. Their father and mother died; their parting injunction to their son was: "Whoever woos a sister of yours, give her to him; do not keep them long with you." The prince buried his parents and in his sorrow went to walk with his sisters in the green garden. Suddenly a black cloud covered the sky and a terrible storm gathered. "Let us go home, sisters," said Prince Ivan. They had no sooner entered the castle than a thunderbolt struck it. The ceiling was cut in twain and a bright falcon flew into the room; he struck the floor, turned into a brave knight, and said: "Hail, Prince Ivan! Formerly I came here as a guest, but now I have come as a suitor; I want to woo your sister, Princess Maria." "If my sister finds you to her liking I do not oppose the marriage; let her go with God." Princess Maria consented; the falcon married her and carried her off to his kingdom.

Days followed days, hours followed hours, and a whole year

went by as though it had never been. Prince Ivan went to walk in the green garden with his two sisters. Again a great cloud came with whirlwind and lightning. "Let us go home, sisters," said the prince. They had no sooner entered the castle than a thunderbolt struck it. The roof fell apart, the ceiling was cut in twain, and an eagle flew in; he struck the floor and turned into a brave knight. "Hail, Prince Ivan!" the eagle said. "Formerly I came as a guest but now I have come as a suitor." And he wooed Princess Olga. Prince Ivan answered: "If Olga finds you to her liking, let her marry you; I do not oppose her will." Princess Olga consented and married the eagle; he seized her and carried her off to his kingdom.

Another year went by. Prince Ivan said to his youngest sister: "Let us go to walk in the green garden." They walked a while; again a cloud came and a whirlwind arose and lightning flashed. "Let us return home, sister," said the prince. They returned home and before they had time to sit down a thunderbolt struck their palace. The ceiling was cut in twain and a raven flew in. He struck the floor and turned into a brave knight; the other two were handsome, but he was even handsomer. "Well, Prince Ivan," said the raven, "formerly I came as a guest, but now I have come as a suitor: give me Princess Anna in marriage." "I do not oppose my sister's will," said Ivan. "If she finds you to her liking, let her marry you." Princess Anna married the raven and he carried her off to his kingdom. Prince Ivan was left alone; for a whole year he lived alone, then he became weary. "I will go and look for my sisters," he said.

He made ready, walked and walked, and one day beheld a host of troops lying slain on the field. Prince Ivan said: "If any man is alive here, let him answer me. Who slew this great army?" One man answered him: "All this great army was slain by Maria Morevna, the beautiful queen." Prince Ivan went farther, came upon white tents, and Maria Morevna, the beautiful queen, came out to meet him. "Hail, prince," she said. "Whither is God taking you? And is it of your own will or by compulsion?" Prince Ivan answered her: "Brave knights do not travel by compulsion." "Well, if you are not in a hurry,"

said the queen, "rest in my tents." Maria Morevna found
Prince Ivan to her liking and he married her.

Maria Morevna, the beautiful queen, took Prince Ivan with
her to her kingdom. They lived together for some time, then
the queen decided to make war; she left all her household in
Prince Ivan's charge and told him: "Go everywhere, take care
of everything; only never look into this closet." But he could
not restrain himself; as soon as Maria Morevna had gone, he
rushed to the closet, opened the door, looked in. Inside the
closet Koshchey the Deathless was hanging chained with twelve
chains. Koshchey begged of Prince Ivan: "Take pity on me,
give me a drink! For ten years I have been tormented here,
without food or drink; my throat is all parched." The prince
gave him a whole keg of water; he drank it and asked for more.
"One keg will not quench my thirst," he said. "Give me another!" The prince gave him another keg of water; Koshchey
drank it and asked for a third, and after he had drunk his third
kegful he recovered his former strength, shook his chains, and
broke all twelve of them at once. "Thanks, Prince Ivan," said
Koshchey the Deathless, "now you will never see Maria
Morevna again—not any more than you will see your own
ears." And he flew out of the window in a terrible whirlwind,
overtook Maria Morevna, the beautiful queen, seized her, and
carried her off to his house.

Prince Ivan wept bitterly, made ready, and set out on his
way to seek her. "Whatever may befall me, I must find Maria
Morevna," he said. He walked one day, then a second day, and
as the third day dawned he beheld a marvelous castle; near the
castle stood an oak, and on the oak sat the bright falcon. The
falcon flew down from the oak, struck the ground, turned into
a brave knight, and exclaimed: "Ah, my dear brother-in-law!
How does the Lord favor you?" Princess Maria ran out, received Prince Ivan with joy, questioned him about his health,
and told him about her own life. The prince stayed with them
for three days and said: "I cannot stay with you a long time,
I am looking for my wife, Maria Morevna, the beautiful
queen." "It will be hard for you to find her," said the falcon.
"Leave your silver spoon here in any case; we shall look at it

and remember you." Prince Ivan left his silver spoon with the falcon and went on his way.

He walked one day, then another day, and as the third day dawned he saw a castle more magnificent than the first; near the castle stood an oak, and on the oak sat an eagle. The eagle flew down from the oak, struck the ground, turned into a brave knight, and exclaimed: "Arise, Princess Olga, our beloved brother is coming!" Princess Olga straightway ran out to receive Prince Ivan, embraced and kissed him, questioned him about his health, and told him about her own life. Prince Ivan stayed with them for three days, and said: "I have no time to visit longer; I am looking for my wife, Maria Morevna, the beautiful queen." The eagle said: "It will be hard for you to find her. Leave your silver fork with us; we shall look at it and remember you." Prince Ivan left his silver fork and went his way.

He walked one day, then another day, and, as the third day dawned he beheld a castle even more magnificent than the first two; near the castle stood an oak, and on the oak sat a raven. The raven flew down from the oak, struck the ground, turned into a brave knight, and exclaimed: "Princess Anna, come out quickly, our brother is coming!" Princess Anna ran out, received Prince Ivan with joy, embraced and kissed him, questioned him about his health, and told him about her own life. Prince Ivan stayed with them for three days and then he said: "Farewell! I must go now to look for my wife, Maria Morevna, the beautiful queen." The raven said: "It will be hard for you to find her. Leave your silver snuffbox with us; we shall look at it and remember you." The prince gave them his silver snuffbox, said farewell, and went on his way.

He walked one day, he walked another day, and on the third day came to Maria Morevna. When she saw her beloved, she threw herself on his neck, shed tears, and said: "Ah, Prince Ivan, why did you disobey me, why did you look into the closet and release Koshchey the Deathless?" "Forgive me, Maria Morevna! Do not recall the past. Instead, come with me while Koshchey is away; perhaps he will not overtake us." They made ready and left. Koshchey was out hunting; at night-

fall he returned home, and his good steed stumbled under him. "Why do you stumble, hungry jade?" he cried. "Or do you sense some mishap?" The steed answered: "Prince Ivan was here and has carried off Maria Morevna." "And can we overtake them?" "We could sow wheat, wait till it grows, reap it, thresh it, grind it into flour, bake five ovenfuls of bread, eat that bread, and after all that set out in pursuit—and even then we would overtake them."

Koshchey galloped off and overtook Prince Ivan. "Well," he said, "the first time I forgive you, because of your kindness in having given me water to drink; the second time I will forgive you too. But the third time, take care—I will cut you into little pieces." He took Maria Morevna from the prince and carried her off; and Prince Ivan sat on a stone and wept. He wept and wept, and went back again for Maria Morevna; Koshchey the Deathless happened to be away. "Let us go, Maria Morevna!" he said. "Ah, Prince Ivan, he will catch us!" "Let him catch us; we shall at least have spent an hour or two together." They made ready and left. As Koshchey the Deathless was returning home, his good steed stumbled under him. "Why do you stumble, hungry jade?" he asked. "Or do you sense a mishap?" "Prince Ivan was here and has carried off Maria Morevna." "And can we overtake them?" "We could sow barley, wait till it grows, reap and thresh it, brew beer, drink ourselves drunk, sleep our fill, and after all that set out in pursuit—and even then we could overtake them."

Koshchey galloped off and overtook Prince Ivan. "Did I not tell you," he said, "that you would not see Maria Morevna again—not any more than you can see your own ears?" And he took the queen and carried her off to his house. Prince Ivan was left alone; he wept and wept and went back again for Maria Morevna. At that time also Koshchey happened to be away. "Let us go, Maria Morevna," the prince said. "But Prince Ivan, he will catch you and cut you into little pieces!" "Let him cut me to pieces. I cannot live without you." They made ready and left. As Koshchey the Deathless was returning home, his good steed stumbled under him. "Why do you stumble?" he said. "Do you sense some mishap?" "Prince Ivan was here and has carried off Maria Morevna." Koshchey galloped off, over-took Prince Ivan, cut him into tiny pieces, and put the pieces in a tarred barrel; he took the barrel, reinforced it with iron hoops, threw it into the blue sea, and carried Maria Morevna off to his house.

At that very moment the silver blackened in the castles of Prince Ivan's brothers-in-law. "Ah," they said, "a misfortune must have happened to our brother-in-law." The eagle hurried to the blue sea, seized the barrel, and pulled it ashore, while the falcon flew for the water of life and the raven for the water of death. All three of them gathered together in one place, broke the barrel, took out the pieces of Prince Ivan, washed them, and put them together in the right order. The raven sprinkled them with the water of death, and the pieces grew together and joined; the falcon sprinkled the body with the water of life, and Prince Ivan shuddered, rose up, and said: "Ah, how long I have slept!" "You would have slept even longer had it not been for us," said the brothers-in-law. "Now come to visit us." "No, brothers! I shall go to look for Maria Morevna."

He came to the queen and said: "Find out from Koshchey the Deathless where he got himself such a good steed." Maria Morevna seized an opportune moment and began to question Koshchey. He said: "Beyond thrice nine lands, in the thrice tenth kingdom, beyond a river of fire, lives Baba Yaga; she has a mare on which she flies around the world every day. She also has many other splendid mares; I served as her herdsman for three days letting not even one mare go astray, and as a reward Baba Yaga gave me one colt." "But how did you cross the river of fire?" "I have a handkerchief of such sort that if I wave it three times to the right, a very high bridge springs up and the fire cannot reach it."

Maria Morevna listened to him, carefully repeated every-thing to Prince Ivan, stole the handkerchief, and gave it to him. Prince Ivan crossed the river of fire and went forth to find Baba Yaga. He walked for a long time without eating or drinking. He happened to come upon a bird from beyond the sea, with her young. Prince Ivan said: "I shall eat one of your little chicks." "Do not eat him, Prince Ivan," begged the bird from beyond the sea. "Some day I shall be useful to you." He went on and saw a beehive in the forest. "I shall take some honey," he said. The queen bee answered him: "Do not touch my honey, Prince Ivan; some day I shall be useful to you." He did not touch the honey and went on. He met a lioness and her whelp. "Let me at least eat this little lion, I am so hungry that I am sick," he said. "Do not touch him, Prince Ivan," the lioness begged. "Some day I shall be useful to you." "Well, so be it."

He plodded on, still hungry; he walked and walked, till he spied the house of Baba Yaga. Around the house were twelve stakes and on eleven of these stakes were human heads; only one stake was bare. "Good day, grandmother," said the prince. "Good day, Prince Ivan! Why have you come—of your own free will or from need?" "I have come to earn a mighty steed from you." "You may try, prince. One need not serve a year with me, but only three days. If you can tend my mares, I will give you a mighty steed; and if you cannot, do not hold it against me—but your head will go on the last stake." Prince Ivan consented; Baba Yaga gave him meat and drink and ordered him to set to work. He had no sooner driven the mares into the field than they raised their tails and scattered over the meadows; the prince had not even cast a glance about before they vanished from sight. He wept and was grieved, sat on a stone, and fell asleep. The sun was setting when the bird from beyond the sea flew to him and roused him. "Arise, Prince Ivan! The mares have come home." The prince arose, returned to the house, and found Baba Yaga scolding her mares and crying: "Why did you come home?" "How could we help coming home?" they replied. "Birds swarmed up from every corner of the world and almost pecked our eyes out!" "Well, tomorrow don't run in the meadows, but scatter through deep forests."

Prince Ivan slept that night. In the morning Baba Yaga said to him: "Mind you, prince, if you do not tend the mares, if you lose even one of them, your rash head will go on that stake." He drove the mares into the field; they raised their tails at once and scattered in the deep forests. Again the prince sat on a stone, wept and wept, and fell asleep. The sun was setting behind the forest when the lioness ran up to him. "Arise, Prince Ivan!" she said. "The mares are gathered together." Prince Ivan rose and returned to the house and found Baba Yaga scolding her mares even more severely than before and crying: "Why did you return home?" "How could we help going home," they replied, "when wild beasts came from every corner of the world and almost tore us to pieces!" "Well, tomorrow you are to run into the blue sea."

Prince Ivan slept again that night; in the morning Baba Yaga sent him to graze the mares. "If you do not tend them," she said to him, "your rash head will sit on that stake." He drove the mares into the field; they straightway raised their tails, vanished from sight, and ran into the blue sea; they stood in the water up to their necks. Prince Ivan sat on a stone, wept, and fell asleep. The sun was setting behind the forest when the bee flew up to him and said: "Arise, prince! All the mares are gathered together. But when you return home, do not show yourself to Baba Yaga; go to the stable and hide behind the manger. There you will find a mangy colt wallowing on a dung heap; steal him, and on the stroke of midnight leave the house." Prince Ivan arose, made his way to the stable, and hid behind the manger. Baba Yaga scolded her mares and cried: "Why did you return?" "How could we help returning?" they replied. "An innumerable host of bees came swarming from every corner of the world and fell to stinging us till the blood ran all over our sides!"

Baba Yaga fell asleep, and on the stroke of midnight Prince Ivan stole the mangy colt, saddled him, mounted him, and galloped to the river of fire. When he came to the river, he waved his handkerchief to the right three times, and suddenly, as though from nowhere, a high, magnificent bridge hung over the river. The prince went across the bridge and waved his handkerchief to the left side only twice, and there remained a thin, very thin bridge above the river.

Next morning Baba Yaga awoke and found that the mangy colt was gone. She rushed off in pursuit, galloping in an iron mortar as fast as she could, urging it on with a pestle, and sweeping her traces with a broom. She galloped to the river of fire, looked, and thought: "The bridge is good." She rode on the bridge, and as soon as she reached the middle it broke; and Baba Yaga fell into the river and died a cruel death. Prince Ivan fed his colt in the green meadows and it became a marvelous steed. The prince rode to Maria Morevna. She ran out to meet him, threw herself on his neck, and cried: "How has God brought you back to life?" "In such and such a way," he said. "Come with me." "I am afraid, Prince Ivan. If Koshchey catches you, he will again cut you to pieces." "No, he will not catch me! I now have a magnificent mighty steed that flies like a bird." They mounted the steed and rode off.

Koshchey the Deathless was returning home and his steed stumbled under him. "Why do you stumble, you hungry jade?" he cried. "Do you sense a mishap?" "Prince Ivan was here and has carried off Maria Morevna." "And can we overtake them?" "God knows! Prince Ivan now has a mighty steed better than myself." "No, I won't endure this!" said Koshchey the Deathless. "I'll pursue him!" After a long time or a short time, he caught up with Prince Ivan, jumped to the ground, and tried to cut him down with his sharp saber. At that moment Prince Ivan's steed swung a hoof with all his strength and struck Koshchey the Deathless, smashing his head, and the prince finished him off with his mace. Thereupon the prince gathered together a pile of wood, made a fire, burned Koshchey the Deathless, and scattered his ashes to the wind. Maria Morevna sat on Koshchey's steed, and Prince Ivan on his own, and they went to see first the raven, then the eagle, and last the falcon. Wherever they went, they were received with joy. "Ah, Prince Ivan," everyone said, "we had given up hope of ever seeing you again. Indeed, you have not takén all these pains for nothing; such a beauty as Maria Morevna could be sought throughout the world, but her equal could never be found!" They visited and feasted and rode back to their own kingdom; when they came there, they began to live and prosper and drink mead.

THE SOLDIER AND THE KING

IN A CERTAIN KINGDOM in a certain land there lived a peasant who had two sons. The elder son was drafted to serve as a soldier. He served his sovereign loyally and truthfully, and was so fortunate that in a few years he was promoted to the rank of general. At that time there was a new recruitment, and his younger brother was taken into service; the boy had his skull shaved, and it so happened that he was sent to the same regiment in which his brother was a general. The new recruit recognized the general, but he got nothing for his trouble; his brother said bluntly: "I don't know you, and don't you try to know me."

One day the soldier stood on guard near the general's quarters; the general was then giving a banquet, and many officers and fine gentlemen had come to attend it. The soldier saw that others were feasting and making merry while he had nothing, and began to weep bitter tears. The guests asked him: "Soldier, why are you weeping?" "How can I help weeping?" he said. "My own brother is making merry and does not remember me."

The guests told this to the general, who fell into a rage: "Don't believe him, he is lying, the fool!" He ordered his brother to be relieved of guard duty and to be punished with three hundred lashes for having dared to claim kinship with the general. The soldier felt humiliated; he put on his campaign suit and deserted from the regiment.

After a long time or a short time, he came to a thick forest that was almost never entered by anyone, and stayed there, living on berries and roots. Soon afterward the king went hunting, accompanied by a great retinue; they galloped in the open field, set their hounds loose, blew their trumpets, and began to enjoy themselves. Suddenly a beautiful stag darted past the king and jumped into a river; he swam across and vanished in the forest. The king swam across and galloped after him for a long time. He looked about him, but the stag was out of sight; the other hunters remained far behind and he was surrounded by a dark, thick forest. He did not know where to go, there was no path in sight. He wandered until sunset and grew very tired. He met the runaway soldier, who said: "Good evening, my good fellow, how have you happened to come here?" "I went out hunting and lost my way in the woods," said the king. "Lead me out to the road, brother." "But who are you?" "A servant of the king." "Well, it is dark now; let us go to spend the night in a ravine, and tomorrow morning I shall lead you out to the road."

They went to find a place to spend the night, and after some time saw a little hut. "God has been kind to us and showed us a shelter," said the soldier. "Let us go in." They entered the hut, and inside they found an old woman. "Good evening, grandmother," said the soldier. "Good evening, soldier." "Give us food and drink." "I would gladly eat myself, but I have nothing in the house." "You are lying, old hag!" said the soldier, and began to rummage in the stove and on the shelves. He discovered that the old woman was well supplied with wine and all kinds of food. They sat at table, had a good supper, and went to sleep in the attic. The soldier said to the king: "God protects him who protects himself. Let one of us rest while the other keeps watch." They cast lots, and it fell to the king to keep watch first. The soldier gave the watcher his short saber, and stationed him at the door, bidding the king not to fall asleep and to rouse him at once should something happen; then he went to sleep, wondering whether his companion would be a good guard. "Perhaps he won't be able to keep awake from lack of habit," he thought, "but I will keep an eye on him."

The king stood for some time, then he began to feel sleepy. "Why are you swaying?" the soldier called to him. "Are you sleepy?" "No," said the king. "Be careful!" said the soldier. The king stood for a quarter of an hour and again began to drowse. "Eh, friend," said the soldier, "aren't you sleeping?" "No, I have no intention of sleeping." "Well, should you fall asleep, you will have to answer for it." The king stood for another quarter of an hour; his legs gave way under him, he dropped on the ground and fell asleep. The soldier jumped up, took his saber, and began to thrash the king, repeating: "Is that the way to keep watch? I served ten years, and my superiors never forgave me a single mistake; apparently you have never been taught anything. I forgave you the first and the second time, but the third fault cannot be forgiven. Well, lie down to sleep now, I will keep watch myself."

The king lay down to sleep and the soldier stood guard. Suddenly there was a noise of stamping and whistling: robbers had come to the hut, and the old woman went out to meet them and said: "We have guests here." "That is fine, grandmother! We have been riding all night for nothing, and our luck has now come to our house. But first let us eat supper. "But our guests have eaten and drunk everything." "They must be bold fellows! Where are they?" "They went to sleep in the attic." "Well," said one of the robbers, "I'll go up and take care of them." He took a big knife and began to climb to the attic, but he had no sooner stuck his head through the door than the soldier swung his saber, and the head rolled. The soldier pulled in the body and stood waiting to see what would happen next. The robbers waited and waited, and said: "Why is he dallying there all this time?" They sent another one of their band; the soldier slew him too. Thus in a short time he slew all the robbers.

At daybreak the king awoke, saw the corpses, and asked: "Hey, soldier, what kind of place is this?" The soldier told him about everything that had happened, and then they went down from the attic. The soldier saw the old woman and cried: "Wait, you old hag! I'll settle your account. So that's what your house is—a robbers' den! Give me all your money at once!" The old woman opened a chest filled with gold; the soldier poured gold into his knapsack, stuffed all his pockets, and said to his companion: "Take some too!" The king answered: "No, brother, I don't need it; our king has plenty of money even without this, and since he has it, we too can have it." "Well, just as you like," said the soldier, and led him out of the woods. When they came to the highway, the soldier said: "Follow this road; in an hour you will be in town." "Farewell," said the king, "thanks for your kindness. Come to visit me; I'll help you make your fortune, man." "It's no use lying to you, I am a deserter and if I show myself in town, I will be caught at once." "Do not doubt my word, soldier! The king favors me very much; if I speak to him on your behalf, and tell him about your courage, he will not only forgive you but even reward you." "But where can I find you?" "Come straight to the royal palace." "Very well, then; I'll come tomorrow."

The king took leave of the soldier, went along the highway, came to his capital, and without waiting gave orders to all the guardhouses, posts, and patrols to be on the alert and as soon as a certain soldier showed himself, to give him the honors due a general. Next day, as soon as the soldier appeared at the city gate, all the guards ran out and saluted him as they would a general. The soldier wondered what that could mean, and asked: "Whom are you saluting?" they answered: "You, soldier!" He took a handful of gold out of his knapsack and gave it to the guards as a tip. He walked in the town; wherever he appeared, the guards saluted him—he hardly had time to tip them all. "What a chatterbox the king's servant is!" thought the soldier. "He has blurted out to everyone that I have plenty of money." He came to the palace, and there troops had been assembled and the king met him, dressed in the same clothes in which he had gone hunting.

566

When the soldier realized with whom he had spent the night in the'woods, he was terribly frightened. "So this is the king," he thought. "And I thrashed him with my saber as though he were a comrade." The king took him by his hand, thanked him before the assembled troops for rescuing his king, and rewarded him with the rank of general. At the same time the king demoted the elder brother and made him a simple private, to teach him not to disavow his own kin in the future.

THE SORCERESS

IN A CERTAIN KINGDOM there lived a king whose daughter was a sorceress. At the king's court there was a priest, and the priest had a ten-year-old son who every day went to a certain old woman to learn how to read. One day the boy happened to return from his lesson late at night; as he went by the king's palace he looked in at a window. At that window sat the princess, making her toilet. She took off her head, soaped it, rinsed it in clear water, combed her hair with a comb, plaited a tress, and then put her head back in its place. The boy marveled— "How cunning she is, a real magician!" He returned home and told everyone that he had seen the princess without her head. Suddenly the king's daughter fell very ill. She called her father and said to him: "If I die, make the priest's son read the psalter over me three nights in succession." The princess died, was put in a coffin, and carried to the church. The king summoned the priest and asked: "Do you have a son?" "I have, Your Majesty." "Then let him read the psalter over my daughter three nights in succession." The priest returned home and told his son to make ready.

In the morning the priest's son went to his lesson and sat listless over his book. "Why are you so sad?" the old woman asked him. "How can I help being sad when I am sure that I am to perish?" "What do you mean? Explain yourself!" "I must read the psalter over the princess, and she is a sorceress." "I knew that before you did," the old woman said. "But do not be afraid. Here is a knife for you; when you come to the church, make a circle round you, read the psalter, and do not look behind you. Whatever happens, whatever terrors beset you, keep on reading and reading. But if you look back, you will be altogether lost." At night the boy went to the church, traced a circle around himself with his knife, and began to read from the psalter. On the stroke of twelve, the lid of the coffin opened, the princess sat up, jumped out, and cried: "Aha, now I will show you what it means to look in at my window and tell people what you saw!" She tried to jump at the priest's son, but could not cross the circle. Then she began to let loose all kinds of terrors; but no matter what she did, the boy kept on reading without looking behind him. At daybreak the princess hurled herself into the coffin as fast as she could.

On the next night the same events took place; the priest's son was not frightened, read without stopping till daybreak, and in the morning went to the old woman. She asked him: "Well, did you see the terrors?" "I did, grandmother." "To-night it will be worse. Here are a hammer and four nails for you; drive the nails into the four corners of the coffin, and when you begin to read the psalter, put the hammer in front of you." At night the boy went to the church and did as the old woman had told him to do. On the stroke of twelve the coffin lid fell to the floor, and the princess rose up and began to fly in all directions and to threaten the priest's son. She let loose great terrors, then still greater ones; the boy fancied that a fire had broken out in the church, that the flames were enveloping all the walls, but he stood in his place and kept on reading without looking behind him. Before daybreak the princess hurled herself into her coffin; then the fire was gone, and the whole devilish spectacle vanished. In the morning the king came to the church; he found the coffin opened, and the princess lying in it face downward. "What is this?" he asked the boy, who then told him everything. The king ordered an aspen spike to be thrust into his daughter's chest and had her buried in the ground. And he rewarded the priest's son with money and land.

ILYA MUROMETS
AND THE DRAGON

IN A CERTAIN KINGDOM in a certain land there lived a peasant
and his wife. They lived richly, had plenty of everything,
and possessed a large fortune. One day as they sat together
the husband said: "We have plenty of everything, but we have
no children. Let us pray to God; perhaps He will bless us with
a child at least in our last years, in our old age." They prayed
to God, and the woman became pregnant; and when her time
came she gave birth to a boy. A year went by, and two years,
and three years, but the babe's legs did not move as legs move;
eighteen years went by, and still he sat as though legless.

One day the father and mother went to mow hay and the son
remained alone. An old beggar came to him asking for alms.
"Little host, give an old man alms for Christ's sake." He
answered: "Holy old man, I cannot give you alms, I am legless."
The old beggar entered the house. "Now," he said, "rise from
your bed, give me a pitcher." Ilya gave him a pitcher. "Now,"
said the old man, "bring me some water." The boy brought
water and handed it to the old man, saying: "Here, holy old
man." The old man gave it back to him, saying: "Drink all the
water in this pitcher!" Then he sent Ilya again for water,
saying: "Bring me another pitcher of water." As the boy
went to get the water, he made his way along by holding to
the trees; whenever he grasped a tree, he tore it out by the
roots. The holy old man asked him: "Do you feel strength in
yourself?" "I do, holy old man. I now have great strength: if
a ring were fastened to the world, I could turn it over." When
he brought the second pitcher of water, the old man drank half
of it and gave him the other half to drink; his strength lessened.
"The strength you have now," said the old man, "will be just
the right amount." Then the old man prayed to God and went
away, saying: "Stay here with God."

The boy grew weary of lying about, so he went to dig in the woods, to try his strength. And the people were terrified at the amount of work he did and the huge quantity of wood he piled up. The father and mother came back from hay mowing and saw that the whole forest was dug up, and they wondered who had done it. They came closer. The wife said to her husband: "Look, it is our Ilyushenka who is digging!" "You fool," he answered, "how can it be Ilyushenka? What nonsense!" They came up to the boy. "Ah my God, how did this come about?" Ilya said: "A holy old man came to me and asked for alms. I said to him: 'Holy old man, I cannot give you alms, because I have no legs.' So he entered the house and told me to rise from my bed and to give him a pitcher. I got up and gave him a pitcher. Then he told me to bring him water. I brought him water and handed it to him. He told me to drink all the water in the pitcher. I drank it, and a great strength arose in me."

The peasants gathered in the street and said among themselves: "Behold what a mighty champion he has become, how much he has dug up! We must tell people about him in the city." And so the sovereign learned about this mighty champion; he summoned Ilya to his presence, found him to his liking, and dressed him in a fitting garment. He pleased everyone and began to serve well. The sovereign said: "You are a mighty champion; could you lift up my castle?" "Yes, Your Majesty, I can even raise it on one side, just the way you want it."

The tsar had a fair daughter, so beautiful that no mind can imagine her nor pen describe her. And she was to Ilya's liking, and he wanted to marry her.

One day the tsar went to another kingdom, to another king. He came to that king, and that king too had a very handsome daughter, and a twelve-headed dragon took to flying to her and he withered her young life; she was completely worn out. The tsar said to that king: "I have a mighty champion who will kill the twelve-headed dragon." The king said: "Please send him to me." When the tsar returned he said to his tsarina: "A twelve-headed dragon took to flying to such and such a king's daughter, he sucked her young life dry, he wore her out altogether." And then he said: "Ilya Ivanovich, could you not help her, could you not slay that dragon?" "Yes, Your Majesty, I can and will slay him."

The tsar said: "You will go by stagecoach and follow such and such roads." "I will go on horseback, alone. Give me a horse." "Go to the stable," said the tsar. "Choose any horse you like." But in another room the tsar's daughter begged him: "Do not go, Ilya Ivanovich. The twelve-headed dragon will slay you, you won't be able to vanquish him." He said: "Please do not fear anything; I shall return safe and sound." He went to the stable to choose a horse. He came to the first horse, put his hands on him, and the horse stumbled. He tried all the horses in the stable; whenever he put his hand on one, it stumbled—not one could bear the weight of his hand. He came to the very last horse, which stood neglected in a corner, and struck him on the back with his hand; the horse only neighed. And Ilya said: "Here is my faithful servant; he did not stumble." He went to the tsar: "Your Majesty, I have chosen a horse, a faithful servant." He was sent off with honors and prayers were said for his safety.

He sat on his good steed and rode for a long time or a short time, till he came to a mountain; it was a very steep and very high mountain, and it was all covered with sand; he rode up it with great effort. On the mountain stood a post, and on the post three roads were indicated, and the inscription said: "If you follow the first road, you will be sated, but your steed will be hungry. If you follow the second road, your horse will be sated, but you yourself will be hungry. If you follow the third road, you will be slain." He followed the third road, although the inscription said that on this road he would be slain; for he had confidence in himself. For a long time or a short time he rode in thick forests, so thick that one could not see anything. Then a wide clearing appeared in the forest, and on the clearing stood a little hut. He rode up to the hut and said: "Little hut, little hut, turn your back to the forest, and your front to me." The hut turned around, stood with its back to the forest and its front to him. He climbed down from his good steed, and tied him to a post. Baba Yaga heard this and said: "Who is that

571

insolent fellow? My father and my grandfather never heard of a Russian breath, but now I will see a Russian being with my own eyes."

She struck the door with her wand and the door opened. She took a curved scythe, and tried to take the champion by his neck and cut off his head. "Wait, Baba Yaga," he said, "I will show you." He tore the scythe out of her hands, seized her by her hair, struck her, and said: "You should first ask me of what lineage I am, of what birth and what character, and whither I am going." So she asked him: "Of what family are you, of what birth, and whither are you going?" "My name is Ilya Ivanovich, and I am going to such and such a place." She said: "Ilya Ivanovich, please come into my room." He entered her room; she seated him at table, served him meat and drink, and sent her maid to heat a bath for him. He ate and he steamed himself, stayed two days in Baba Yaga's house, and made ready to go on his way again. Baba Yaga said: "I will give you a letter to my sister telling her not to harm you but to receive you with honor. Otherwise she will slay you as soon as she sees you." She gave him the letter and bade him farewell with fitting honors.

The champion mounted his good steed and rode through thick forests; he rode for a long time or a short time. The forest was so thick that one could not see in it. He came to a clearing, a wide clearing, and on it stood a hut. He rode up to the hut, climbed down from his good steed, and tied him to a post. Baba Yaga heard him tying his steed and cried: "What is this? My father and my grandfather never heard of a Russian breath, and now I will see a Russian being with my own eyes." She struck the door with her wand and the door opened. She swung her saber at Ilya's neck, but he said: "You cannot fight with me; here is a letter your sister gave me." She read the letter and received him honorably: "Welcome, be my guest," she said. Ilya Ivanovich came in. She seated him at table, served him meats, wines, and sweets, and sent her maid to heat a bath for him. Having eaten, he went to steam himself in the bath. He stayed with Baba Yaga for two days and took a rest; his good steed also took a rest. When he mounted his good

572

steed, she saw him off with honor. She said: "Now, Ilya Ivanovich, you will not be able to continue on your way. Solovey the Robber is lurking very near here; his nest is built on seven oaks; he will not let you come within thirty versts of him, he will deafen you with his whistling."

He rode for a long time or a short time, till he came to a place where he heard the whistle of Solovey the Robber, and when he came up halfway, his steed stumbled. He said: "My good steed, do not stumble! Serve me." He rode up to Solovey the Robber, who kept on whistling. When he came up to the robber's nest, Ilya took an arrow, drew his bow, and shot at him—and Solovey fell from his nest. When he was on the ground, Ilya struck him once, in such a way that he stunned him but did not slay him; then he put the robber in his saddle-bag and rode to the king's castle.

He was seen from the castle and there someone said: "Solovey the Robber is carrying someone in his saddlebag." The champion rode up to the castle and handed the guard a paper. His paper was given to the king, who read it and ordered him to be admitted. The king said to Ilya Ivanovich: "Order Solovey the Robber to whistle." Solovey the Robber said: "You should give food and drink to Solovey the Robber; my mouth is parched." They brought him wine and he said: "What is a quart to me? Better bring me a good-sized cask." They brought a cask of wine and poured it into a pail. Solovey drank it in one gulp and said: "If Solovey the Robber had two pails more, he would drink them too." But he was not given any more. The king said again to Ilya: "Now order him to whistle." Ilya ordered Solovey to whistle, but he took the king and all his family under his arm, saying: "I must keep you here or he would deafen you." When Solovey the Robber whistled, Ilya Ivanovich could hardly stop him; he had to strike him with his mace, or all of them would have fallen to the ground.

The king said to Ilya Ivanovich: "Will you do me the service that I ask you? There is a twelve-headed dragon that flies to my daughter; will you slay him?" Ilya said: "At your service, Your Royal Majesty! I will do whatever you ask me." "Please, Ilya Ivanovich, at such and such an hour the dragon will come

574

to see my daughter, so do your best." "At your service, Your Royal Majesty."

The princess lay in her room; on the stroke of twelve the dragon came to her. The dragon and Ilya began to fight; each time Ilya struck, one of the dragon's heads rolled—one stroke, one head off. They fought for a long time or a short time, till only one head remained. And Ilya cut off the dragon's last head: he struck it with his mace and smashed it altogether. The princess rose up joyfully, came to Ilya, and thanked him; then she told her father and mother that the dragon was dead, that Ilya had cut off all his heads. The king said: "I thank you. Won't you serve for some time in my kingdom?" "No," said Ilya, "I want to go to my own land." The king let him go, giving him great honors, and he rode back on the same road by which he had come. When he came to the first Baba Yaga to spend the night in her house, she received him with honor; when he came to the second, she too received him with all honor. He came to his own land and gave the tsar a paper from the king whom he had aided. The tsar received him with honor, and the tsar's daughter had waited for him with great impatience. "Now, father, may I become his wife?" she said. Her father did not oppose her will. "Well, if such is your desire, marry him." They wedded and are living to this day.

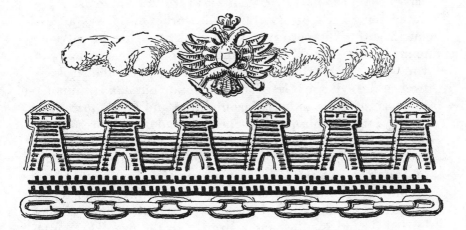

THE DEVIL
WHO WAS A POTTER

A POTTER WAS DRIVING along a road when he met a passer-by, who said: "Hire me as your worker." "But do you know how to make pots?" the potter asked him. "I do, very well indeed," the stranger said. They made a bargain, shook hands on it, and drove on together. When they came to the potter's home, the worker said: "Now master, prepare forty carts of clay; tomorrow I shall set to work." The master prepared forty carts of clay, and the worker, who was an evil spirit, said to the potter: "I shall work at night; do not come to my barn." "Why?" "Just don't. If you do come, I warn you, you will get into trouble." Dark night came. On the stroke of twelve, the evil spirit cried out in a loud voice, and a numberless host of imps gathered around him and began to fashion pottery; thunderous pounding, clatter and laughter resounded all over the yard. The master could not restrain himself and went to see what all the noise was about. He came to the barn, looked through a crack, and saw the devils squatting there and molding pots. Only one lame one was not working, but keeping watch; he caught sight of the master, seized a lump of clay, hurled it, and hit the potter straight in the eye. The master returned to his house; he had lost one eye, and in the barn there was even more uproarious laughter than before.

In the morning the worker said: "Eh, master, go and count the pots, see how many have been made in one night." The master counted: there were forty thousand. "Well," the worker said, "now prepare ten cords of wood for me; tonight I will bake the pots." Exactly at midnight the evil spirit cried out in a loud voice; imps came running to him from every corner; they smashed up all the pots, threw the shards into the oven, and began to bake them. And the master came to the barn and found a little crack and looked in. "Well, all the pots are broken," he thought. Next day the worker called him and said: "Come and see how well I have worked." The master came to look and found that all of the forty thousand pots were whole —one was better than the other. On the third night the evil spirit called the imps together, painted the pots with various colors, and put them all on one cart.

They waited till market day and carried the pots to town to sell them, and the evil spirit ordered his imps to run to all the houses, through all the streets, and invite the people to buy the pots. Crowds came to the market, thronged around the potter, and in half an hour bought all his merchandise. The peasant drove home with a bagful of money. "Now," said the evil spirit, "let us share the profits." They shared half-and-half. The devil took his lot, said farewell to the master, and vanished. A week later the peasant went to town with his pots. He stood in the market place a long time, but no one bought from him; all the people passed him by and swore at him in the most abusive language. "We know your pots, you old dotard. They look pretty, but the moment you put water into them they fall to pieces. No, brother, you won't cheat us again." They ceased buying pots from him altogether. Finally the peasant was completely ruined. Out of grief he took to drinking and began to spend all his time lying around in alehouses.

CLEVER ANSWERS

A SOLDIER HAD SERVED in his regiment for fully twenty-five years without ever having seen the tsar in person. When he returned home and was questioned about the tsar, he did not know what to say. His parents and friends began to taunt him. "You served for twenty-five years," they said, "yet you never saw the tsar." The soldier felt humiliated, so he made ready and went to have a look at the tsar. He came to the palace. The tsar asked him: "What have you come for, soldier?" "Your Majesty, I served you and God for a full twenty-five years, yet I never saw you in person; so I have come to look at you." "Well, look your fill." The soldier walked around the tsar three times examining him. The tsar said: "Am I handsome?" "Yes, Your Majesty," answered the soldier. "And now, soldier, tell me—is it far from heaven to earth?" "It is so far that when a noise is made there, we can hear it here." "And is the earth wide?" "The sun rises over there and sets over here: that's the width of the earth." "And is the earth deep?" "I had a grandfather who died about ninety years ago. He was buried in the earth and since then has never come home; so it must be deep." Then the tsar sent the soldier to prison, saying: "Keep your eyes open, soldier! I will send you thirty geese; try to pluck a feather out of each one." "Very well," the soldier said.

The tsar summoned thirty wealthy merchants and proposed the same riddles to them that he had proposed to the soldier; they racked their brains but were unable to answer the questions, and the tsar ordered them to be put in prison. The soldier asked them: "Honorable merchants, why have you been imprisoned?" "The tsar asked us how far heaven is from earth, how wide the earth is, and how deep it is; but we are uneducated people and could not find the answers." "If each one of you will give me a thousand rubles, I will tell you the answers." "Gladly, brother, only tell us."

The soldier took a thousand rubles from each and told them how to solve the tsar's riddles. Two days later the tsar summoned the merchants and the soldier before him; he proposed the same riddles to the merchants, and as soon as they answered correctly, he let them go. Then he said to the soldier: "Well, have you managed to pluck a feather from each?" "Yes, Your Majesty, and it was a golden feather, too." "And how far is it to your home?" "It cannot be seen from here, so it must be far." "Here is a thousand rubles for you; God speed you." The soldier returned home and began to live a carefree and easy life.

DIVIDING THE GOOSE

ONCE THERE WAS a poor peasant who had many children, but no possessions except one goose. He saved this goose for a long time; but hunger is nothing to be trifled with—and things had reached such a point that he had nothing to eat. So the peasant killed the goose, roasted it, and put it on the table. So far, so good; but he had no bread and not a grain of salt. He said to his wife: "How can we eat the goose without bread or salt? Perhaps I should take the goose to the barin as a gift and ask him for bread." "Well, go with God," said his wife.

The peasant came to the barin and said: "I have brought you a goose as a gift. You are welcome to all I have; do not disdain it, little father." "Thanks, peasant, thanks; now divide the goose among us, without doing wrong to anyone." Now this barin had a wife, two sons, and two daughters—all in all there were six in his family. The peasant was given a knife and he began to carve and divide the goose. He cut off the head and gave it to the barin. "You are the head of the house," he said, "so it is fitting that you should have the head." He cut off the pope's nose and gave it to the barin's wife, saying: "Your business is to sit in the house and take care of it: so here is the pope's nose for you." He cut off the legs and gave them to the sons, saying: "Here is a leg for each of you, to trample your father's paths with." And to each daughter he gave a wing. "You won't stay long with your father and mother; when you grow up, off you will fly. And I," he said, "I'm just a stupid peasant, so I'll take what is left." Thus he got most of the goose. The barin laughed, gave the peasant wine to drink, rewarded him with bread, and sent him home.

A rich peasant heard about this, envied the poor one, roasted five geese, and took them to the barin. "What do you want, peasant?" asked the barin. "I have brought Your Grace five geese as a gift." "Thanks, brother! Now apportion them among us without doing wrong to anyone." The peasant tried this and that, but saw no way of dividing the geese equally. He just stood there scratching his head. The barin sent for the poor peasant and told him to divide the geese. He took one goose, gave it to the barin and his wife, and said: "Now you are three." He gave another goose to the two sons and a third one to the two daughters, saying: "Now you also are threes." The last pair of geese he took for himself, saying: "Now I and the geese are another three." The barin said: "You are a clever fellow; you have managed to give everyone an equal share and you have not forgotten yourself either." He rewarded the poor peasant with money and drove out the rich one.

THE FEATHER OF FINIST, THE BRIGHT FALCON

ONCE THERE LIVED an old man who had three daughters: the two elder ones were fond of frills and furbelows, but the youngest was concerned only with household tasks. One day the father made ready to go to town and asked his daughters what they wanted him to buy for them. The eldest said: "Buy me cloth for a dress." The second said the same thing. "And what shall I buy for you, my beloved daughter?" the father asked the youngest. "My dear father, buy me a feather of Finist the Bright Falcon." The father said farewell to them and went to town; he bought enough cloth for dresses for his two elder daughters, but nowhere could he find a feather of Finist the Bright Falcon. He returned home, and his elder daughters were overjoyed with their new cloth. "But I could not find a feather of Finist the Bright Falcon for you," he said to the youngest. "So be it," she said, "perhaps next time you will have better luck." The elder sisters cut their cloth, made themselves dresses, and made fun of their younger sister, but she only kept silent.

The father again made ready to go to town and asked: "Well, my daughters, what shall I buy for you?" The first and the second each asked for a kerchief, but the youngest said: "Buy me a feather of Finist the Bright Falcon." The father went to town, bought two kerchiefs, but could not find the feather. He returned home and said: "Ah, my daughter, again I could not find a feather of Finist the Bright Falcon." "Never mind, father, perhaps you will have better luck next time."

The father made ready to go to town a third time and asked his daughters what he should buy for them. The elder ones said: "Buy us earrings." But the youngest again said: "Buy me a feather of Finist the Bright Falcon." The father bought two pairs of gold earrings and began to look for the feather, but no one had ever heard of that falcon; he became sad and left town. He had no sooner passed through the gate than he met an old man carrying a little box. "What are you carrying, old man?" "A feather of Finist the Bright Falcon." "What do you want for it?" "I'll take a thousand." The father paid this sum and galloped home with the little box. His daughters came out to meet him. "Well, my beloved daughter," he said to the youngest, "at last I have brought a present for you. Take it." The youngest daughter almost jumped with joy; she took the box, began to kiss and fondle it, and pressed it tightly to her bosom.

After supper all of them went to their rooms to sleep; the

youngest daughter too went to her room, and opened her box; the feather of Finist the Bright Falcon flew out at once; it struck the floor and a handsome prince appeared before the maiden. They began to speak to each other, with sweet and loving words. The elder sisters overheard them and asked: "Little sister, with whom are you talking?" "With myself," said the lovely maiden. "Well then, open the door." The prince struck the floor and turned into a feather; the maiden put the feather back in the box and opened the door. The sisters looked in all the corners but found no one. As soon as they had left the lovely maiden opened the window, took out the feather, and said: "Fly, my feather, into the open field; stay there until the right time comes." The feather turned into a bright falcon and flew into the open field.

The next night Finist the Bright Falcon came flying to his maiden; they began to talk merrily. The elder sisters overheard them and straightway ran to their father. "Father, someone comes to see our sister at night; even now he is in there talking with her." The father arose and went to his youngest daughter's room, but the prince had long since turned into the feather and lay in the box. "Ah, you malicious girls," the father scolded his elder daughters, "why do you accuse her falsely? Better mind your own business."

The next day the sisters hit upon a ruse: at nightfall, when the yard was quite dark, they took a ladder, gathered sharp knives and needles, and stuck them in the lovely maiden's window. At night Finist the Bright Falcon came flying. He struggled and struggled, but could not get into the room; he only cut his wings. "Farewell, lovely maiden," he said, "if you decide to find me, look for me beyond thrice nine lands, in the thrice tenth kingdom. But before you can find me, the goodly youth, you will wear out three pairs of iron shoes, break three cast-iron staves, and gnaw away three stone wafers." But the maiden slept on; although she heard these unkind words in her sleep, she could not waken and arise.

In the morning she woke and saw knives and needles stuck in the window, and blood trickling from them. She wrung her

582

hands. "Ah my God! My sisters must have killed my beloved!" Straightway she made ready and left home. She ran to a smithy, forged for herself three pairs of iron shoes and three cast-iron staves, provided herself with three stone wafers, and set out to seek Finist the Bright Falcon.

She walked and walked, and wore out one pair of shoes, broke one cast-iron staff, and gnawed away one stone wafer. She came to a hut and knocked at the door. "Host and hostess," she said, "shelter me from the dark night!" An old woman answered: "You are welcome, lovely maiden! Whither are you going, little dove?" "Ah, grandmother! I am going in search of Finist the Bright Falcon." "Well, lovely maiden, you have a long way to go." Next morning the old woman said: "Go now to my second sister, she will tell you what to do. And here is my gift to you—a silver spinning wheel and a golden spindle. You will spin a spindleful of flax and draw out a golden thread." Then she took a ball, rolled it out to the road, and told the maiden to follow the ball wherever it went. The maiden thanked the old woman and followed the ball.

After a long time or a short time, the second pair of shoes was worn out, the second staff was broken, and another stone wafer gnawed away; finally the ball rolled up to a little hut. The maiden knocked at the door, saying: "My good hosts, shelter a lovely maiden from the dark night!" "You are welcome," answered an old woman. "Whither are you going, lovely maiden?" "Grandmother, I am going in search of Finist the Bright Falcon." "You have a long way to go," said the old woman. Next morning, she gave the maiden a silver dish and a golden egg. "Go to my elder sister," she said. "She will know where to find Finist the Bright Falcon."

The lovely maiden said farewell to the old woman and set out on her way. She walked and walked, and the third pair of shoes was worn out, the third staff was broken, and the last wafer gnawed away, when the ball rolled up to a little hut. The traveler knocked at the door and said: "My good hosts, shelter a lovely maiden from the dark night." Again an old woman came out. "Come in, little dove, you are welcome! Whence come you and whither are you going?" "Grandmother, I go

583

in search of Finist the Bright Falcon." "Oh, it is hard, very hard to find him! He is now living in such and such a town, and is married to the wafer baker's daughter there." In the morning the old woman said to the lovely maiden: "Here is a gift for you—a golden embroidery frame and a needle; just hold the frame and the needle will embroider by itself. Now God speed you, and ask the wafer baker to hire you as her serving maid."

The lovely maiden did as she was bid. She came to the wafer baker's house and became a servant; she worked hard and quickly, heating the stove, carrying water, cooking the dinner. The wafer baker looked on and was delighted. "Thank God," she said to her daughter, "we now have a servant who is willing and intelligent; she does everything without having to be told." And the lovely maiden, having done all the housework, took her silver loom and her golden spindle and sat down to spin; she spun, drawing threads from the flax, and the threads were not ordinary ones but of pure gold. The wafer baker's daughter saw this and said: "Ah, lovely maiden, won't you sell me your wheel and spindle?" "I might." "And what is your price?" "Let me spend one night with your husband." The wafer baker's daughter consented. "There is no harm in it," she thought. "After all, I can give him a sleeping potion, and with that spindle my mother and I will enrich ourselves."

Finist the Bright Falcon was not at home; all day long he soared in the skies, returning only at nightfall. They sat down to supper; the lovely maiden served the viands and kept looking at him, but he, the goodly youth, did not recognize her. The wafer baker's daughter added a sleeping potion to his drink, put him to bed, and said to the servant: "Now go to his room and chase the flies from him." The lovely maiden chased the flies and shed bitter tears. "Awake, arise, Finist the Bright Falcon! I, the lovely maiden, have come to you; I have broken three cast-iron staves, worn out three pairs of iron shoes, and gnawed three stone wafers, and all that time I have been seeking you." But Finist slept on and did not hear anything; thus the night went by.

The next day, the maiden took her silver dish and rolled her golden egg on it; and many a golden egg did she roll out. The wafer baker's daughter saw this and said: "Sell me your plaything." "Buy it." "And what is the price?" "Let me spend another night with your husband." "Very well, I agree." And Finist the Bright Falcon again soared all day in the skies and flew back home only at nightfall. They sat down to supper; the lovely maiden served the viands and kept looking at him, but it was as though he had never known her. Again the wafer baker's daughter made him drunk with a sleeping potion, put him to bed, and sent the servant to chase the flies from him. And this time too, no matter how much the lovely maiden wept and tried to rouse him, he slept through till the morning and heard nothing.

On the third day, the lovely maiden sat holding the golden embroidery frame, and the needle embroidered by itself—and what wondrous designs it made! The wafer baker's daughter could not keep her eyes off this work and said: "Lovely maiden, sell me your plaything!" "Buy it." "And what is the price?" "Let me spend a third night with your husband." "Very well, I agree." At night Finist the Bright Falcon came home; his wife made him drunk with a sleeping potion, put him to bed, and sent the servant to chase the flies from him. The lovely maiden chased the flies while imploring him tearfully: "Arise, awake, Finist the Bright Falcon! I, the lovely maiden, have come to you; I have broken three cast-iron staves, worn out three pairs of iron shoes, and gnawed away three stone wafers, and all that time I have been seeking you, my beloved." But Finist the Bright Falcon was sound asleep and felt nothing.

The maiden wept a long time, she spoke to him a long time; suddenly one of her tears fell on his cheek·and he awoke on the instant. "Ah," he said, "something has burned me." "Finist the Bright Falcon," said the lovely maiden, "I have come to you; I have broken three cast-iron staves, worn out three pairs of iron shoes, and gnawed away three stone wafers, and all the time I have been seeking you! This is the third night that I have stood beside you while you slept and did not waken and did not answer my words." Only now did Finist the Bright Falcon recognize her, and he was overjoyed beyond all words. They formed a plan and left the wafer baker's daughter. In the morning she discovered that her husband was gone and the servant too. She complained to her mother, who ordered the horses put to and rushed after them. She drove and drove and stopped at the houses of the three old women, but did not overtake Finist the Bright Falcon; all trace of him had long since disappeared.

Finist and his destined bride found themselves near her father's house. Finist struck the damp earth and turned into a feather; the lovely maiden took it, hid it in her bosom, and went to her father. "Ah, my beloved daughter, I thought you had perished; where have you been so long?" "I went to pray to God." It was just then Holy Week. The father and the elder daughters made ready to go to matins. "Well, my dear daughter," he said to the youngest, "make ready and come with us; this is a joyful day." "Father, I have nothing to wear." "Put on our dresses," said the elder sisters. "Ah, sisters, your dresses won't fit me; I'd rather stay home."

The father with his two elder daughters went to matins, and then the lovely maiden took out her feather. It struck the floor and turned into a handsome prince. The prince whistled at the window and straightway there appeared dresses and mantles and a golden carriage. They dressed themselves, sat in the carriage, and went to church. When they entered, they stood before everyone and the people marveled to see that a prince and princess had come. When the service was over they left before everyone else; the carriage and the splendid raiments disappeared, and the prince turned into a feather. The father and the two elder daughters returned. "Oh, sister," they said, "you did not come with us, and a handsome prince and a marvelous princess were there." "Never mind, sisters! Since you have told me all about it, it is as though I had been there myself."

The next day the same thing happened again. And on the third day, when the prince and the lovely maiden rode in their carriage, the father went out of the church and with his own eyes saw the carriage drive up to his house and then vanish. The father came home and began to question his youngest

586

daughter. She said: "There is nothing to be done, I have to confess everything." She took out the feather; the feather struck the floor and turned into the prince. They were married at once, and the wedding was a magnificent one!

THE SUN, THE MOON,
AND THE RAVEN

ONCE THERE LIVED an old man and an old woman who had three daughters. The husband went to the barn to get some groats; he took them and carried them into the house, but there was a hole in the bag, and the groats poured out through it. The wife asked: "Where are the groats?" To tell the truth, the groats had all dropped out. The old man went to pick them up and said: "If the Sun would warm me, if the Moon would give me light, and if the Raven would help me to gather up the groats, I would marry my eldest daughter to the Sun, my second daughter to the Moon, and my youngest daughter to the Raven." The old man began to gather his groats, and the Sun warmed him, the Moon gave him light, and the Raven helped him to pick up the groats. The old man came home and said to his eldest daughter: "Dress yourself in your finest and go out on the porch." She dressed, went to the porch, and the Sun carried her off. He also ordered his second daughter to dress in her finest and go out on the porch. She dressed and went out, and the Moon seized her and carried her off. He also said to his youngest daughter: "Dress in your finest and go out on the porch." She dressed and went to the porch; the Raven seized her and carried her off.

The old man said: "I think that now I will pay a visit to my son-in-law." He went to the Sun. When he came the Sun said: "What shall I offer you?" "I don't want anything," said the old man. The Sun told his wife to fry some pancakes. The wife fried them. The Sun sat in the middle of the floor, the wife put the frying pan on him, and soon the pancakes were ready. The old man ate them. When he came home he asked his wife to fry pancakes; he sat on the floor and told her to put the frying pan with the pancake batter on him. "They won't fry on you," said his wife. "Don't argue," he answered, "they will fry." She put the frying pan on him; but, long as they kept the batter there, it did not fry, it only turned sour. In the end the old woman put the frying pan on the stove, the pancakes fried, and the old man ate his fill.

The next day he went to see his second son-in-law, the Moon. The Moon said: "What shall I offer you?" "I don't want anything," answered the old man. The Moon heated up a bath for him. The old man said: "It will be dark in the bathhouse." The Moon answered: "Now it will be light. Go." The old man went to the bathhouse and the Moon thrust his finger through a hole in the door; thus the bathhouse was brightly illumined. The old man steamed himself, came home, and ordered his wife to heat up a bath at night. The old woman did so; then he sent her to steam herself there. She said: "It will be too dark to steam myself." "Go, it will be light," said the old man. The old woman went, and the old man, having seen how the Moon illumined his bath, made a hole in the door of the bathhouse and thrust his finger through it. But still there was no light in the bathhouse. The old woman cried to him: "It is dark." In the end she went to get a torch and then steamed herself.

On the third day the old man went to see the Raven. "What shall I offer you?" asked the Raven. "I don't want anything," said the old man. "In that case, let us at least go to sleep in the attic." The Raven put a ladder against the attic opening and they climbed up. The Raven put his guest under his wing, and when the old man went to sleep, both of them fell down and were killed.

THE BLADDER,
THE STRAW, AND THE SHOE

A BLADDER, a blade of straw, and a shoe went to chop wood in the forest. They came to a river and did not know how to cross it. The shoe said to the bladder: "Bladder, let us swim across it on you." The bladder said: "No, shoe, let the straw blade instead stretch itself from shore to shore, and we will walk over it." The blade of straw stretched itself across the water; the shoe walked on it and the straw broke. The shoe fell into the water, and the bladder laughed and laughed until it burst.

THE THIEF

ONCE THERE LIVED an old man and his wife and they had a son called Ivan. They fed him until he grew up to be a big boy and then said: "Well, little son, we have fed you up until now, henceforth feed us till the end of our days." Ivan answered them: "Since you fed me till I grew big, now feed me till I get a mustache." They fed him till he had a mustache, and said: "Well, little son, we fed you till you had a mustache, now feed us till the end of our days." "Eh, father and mother," the son answered, "since you fed me till I have a mustache, feed me now till I have a beard." There was nothing to be done; the old parents fed him till he had a beard, and then said: "Well, little son, we fed you till you had a beard, now feed us till the end of our days." "Since you fed me till I had a beard, feed me now till the end of my days," said the son. The old man could not bear it any longer and went to the barin to complain about his son.

The lord summoned Ivan and said: "You idler, why don't you support your father and mother?" "How can I support them?" answered Ivan. "Or do you give me leave to steal? I have never learned to work, and now it is too late for me to learn." "Do as you please," said the barin; "steal if you must, but support your parents and let there be no more complaints against you!" At that moment a servant came in announcing that the barin's bath was ready, and the barin went to steam himself. It was getting dark; the barin washed himself, returned, and said: "Hey, is someone there? Give me my slippers!" Ivan, who was still there, handed him the slippers, took the barin's boots, and went home with them. "Here, father," he said, "take off your shoes of linden bark, put on the barin's boots instead."

Next morning the barin discovered that his boots were gone. He sent for Ivan and asked him: "Did you carry off my boots?" "I don't know anything, but it's my work." "Ah, you scoundrel, you cheat! How dare you steal?" "But didn't you tell me yourself that I must support my father and mother, even if I have to steal? I would not disobey your orders, master." "In that case," said the barin, "listen to this order. Steal my black ox from the plow; if you do steal him, I'll give you a hundred rubles; if you do not, I'll give you a hundred lashes with the whip." "At your orders, barin," said Ivan.

He went straightway to the village, stole a cock somewhere, plucked his feathers, and hastened to the field. He sneaked up to the edge of the furrow, lifted a clump of earth, put the cock under it, and hid behind the bushes. When the plowmen began to trace a new furrow, they caught that clump of earth and shoved it to one side; the plucked cock jumped out and rushed along the mounds and ruts. "Look at the strange beast that we dug out of the earth!" cried the plowmen, and ran after the cock. When Ivan saw that they were running like scalded creatures, he went to the plow, cut off the tail of one ox, stuck it into the mouth of the second, unharnessed the third ox, and led him home.

The plowmen chased the cock for a long time, but failed to catch him and went back. They discovered that the black ox had gone and that the speckled one had lost its tail. "Well, brothers," one of them said, "while we ran after the strange animal, one ox ate the black one whole and bit off the tail of the speckled one." They went to the barin to confess their dereliction. "Forgive us, little father, one ox ate another." "Ah, you brainless fools," the barin shouted at them, "who ever saw an ox eating another ox? Summon Ivan!" When Ivan came he asked: "Did you steal the ox?" "I did, barin." "What have you done with him?" "I have slaughtered him; sold the hide at the bazaar, and with the flesh I will feed my parents." "You're a clever fellow," said the barin. "Here is a hundred rubles for you. But now steal my favorite stallion, which stands behind three doors and six locks. If you lead him away, I'll pay you two hundred rubles; if you do not, I'll give you two hundred lashes with the whip." "Very well, barin, I'll steal him."

Late at night Ivan got into the barin's house. There was not a living soul in the entrance hall; he noticed the barin's clothes hanging on the peg, took the overcoat and cap, put them on himself, went out on the porch, and cried to the stableboys in a loud voice: "Hey, boys, saddle my favorite stallion at once and lead him up here!" The stableboys took him for the barin, ran to the stable, unlocked the six locks, opened the three doors, and in a trice the stallion was saddled and brought up to the porch. The thief mounted him, lashed him with a riding crop, and was gone.

Next day the barin asked: "Well, how is my favorite stallion?" And he learned that the horse had been stolen the night before. He again had to send for Ivan. "Did you steal the stallion?" the barin asked. "I did, barin." "Where is he?" "I've sold him to horse dealers." "You're lucky that I myself ordered you to steal him! Take your two hundred rubles. But now steal the teacher of the dissenting church." "And what, barin, do you offer me for that job?" "Will three hundred rubles be enough?" "Yes, I'll steal him for that sum." "And if you fail?" "Then, barin, do with me what you please."

The barin summoned the teacher and said to him: "Be on your guard; pray all night, do not dare to sleep! Ivan the thief has boasted that he will kidnap you." The saintly old man took fright. He did not feel like sleeping at all; he sat in his cell and chanted prayers. On the stroke of midnight Ivan the thief, carrying a burlap sack, knocked at the window. "Who are you, man?" the teacher asked. "I am an angel from heaven, sent to bring you to paradise alive; crawl into this sack." The teacher foolishly crawled into the sack; the thief tied him up, slung him over his shoulders, and carried him to the church steeple. He dragged and dragged him. "Is it still far?" asked the teacher. "Wait and see," said Ivan. "In the beginning the road is long but smooth, in the end it is short but bumpy."

Ivan dragged the sack and let it roll down the stairs; the teacher was badly bumped, he counted every step. "Oh," he said, "the angel spoke the truth: the first part of the way is long but smooth, and the last part is short but bumpy. I didn't suffer that much even on earth." "Be patient, you will be saved," answered Ivan. He lifted the sack, hung it on the fence near the gate, put two birch twigs as thick as a finger near by, and wrote on the gate: "Whoever goes by and fails to strike this bag three times, let him be cursed and anathematized." Thus everyone who went by struck the bag three times. The barin passed near the church gate and asked: "What is in that sack?" And he ordered it to be taken down and untied. The teacher of the dissenting church crawled out of it. "How did you get here?" asked the barin. "I told you to be on your guard! I am not sorry that you have been beaten with rods, but I am sorry that because of you I will lose three hundred rubles."

THE VAMPIRE

IN A CERTAIN KINGDOM in a certain land there lived an old man and his wife. They had a daughter named Marusia. In their village it was customary to celebrate the holiday of St. Andrew: the girls would assemble in one house, bake cream puffs, and make merry for a whole week or more. Upon one

such occasion the girls gathered together and baked and cooked
whatever was needed; at nightfall the young men came with
pipes and wine, and there was dancing and merriment. All the
girls danced well, but Marusia best of all. After some time a
handsome fellow entered the house, a man with a fine com-
plexion, dressed neatly and richly. "Good evening, lovely
maidens," he said. "Good evening, young man," they said.
"You're welcome to join us." Straightway he drew a purse full
of gold from his pocket, sent for wine, nuts, and gingerbread,
and began to treat all the girls and youths; he gave enough to
all. Then he danced so beautifully that it was a pleasure to
look at him. Best of all he liked Marusia, and he did not leave
her a minute.

The time came to go home. The young man said: "Marusia,
come and walk a few steps with me." So she went out and
walked with him a little. He said: "Marusia, my darling, do
you want me to marry you?" "If you want to take me as your
wife, I will marry you gladly. But whence are you?" "From
such and such a place; I am a merchant's clerk." They said
farewell, and each went his way. When Marusia came home,
her mother asked her: "Did you have a good time, little daughter?" "Very good, mother. And I want to tell you a piece of
good news: there was a fine young man there, handsome, with

594

plenty of money, who promised to take me to wife." "Listen to me, Marusia," the mother said. "Tomorrow when you go to the girls, take a ball of thread. When you say farewell to him, loop the thread around a button on his clothes and quietly loosen the ball; then you will learn from this thread where he lives."

Next day Marusia went to the party and took along a ball of thread. The young man came again. "Good evening, Marusia," he said. "Good evening," she replied. The merrymaking and dancing began; the young man clung to Marusia even more ardently than before, he did not leave her for an instant. When the time came to go home, the guest said: "Marusia, come walk a little way with me." She went out into the street, began to take farewell of him, and quietly slipped a loop of thread around a button of his clothes. He went his way and she stood there loosening the ball; when it was all unrolled, she ran to find out where her promised groom lived. At first the thread followed the road, then it stretched across fences and ditches and led Marusia straight to the main gate of the church. Marusia tried the gate, but it was closed; she went around the church, found a ladder, put it under the window, and climbed up to see what was going on inside. She peered inside: her promised groom stood near a coffin and was eating a corpse, for a dead man was then laid out in the church. She wanted to jump quietly down from the ladder, but in her fright she stumbled and made a noise. She ran home in terror, fancying that she was pursued, and when she arrived at home she was half dead.

Next morning her mother asked her: "Well, Marusia, did you see that young man?" "I did, mother," she answered, but she did not tell her mother all that she had seen. When evening came, Marusia sat thoughtful, wondering whether or not to go to the party. "Go," said her mother. "Make merry while you're young." She went to the party and the evil stranger was there. Again there were games, merriment and dancing; the girls did not suspect anything. At the end of the evening, the evil spirit said: "Marusia, will you walk a few steps with me?" She refused to go, she was afraid. All the girls pressed her: "What is the matter with you? Are you timid? Go and say farewell to the fine young man." She had no choice but to go, putting her hope in God. As soon as they were in the street, the young man asked her: "Were you in the church last night?" "No." "Did you see what I was doing there?" "No." "Well, tomorrow your father will die." Having said this, he vanished.

Marusia returned home sad and listless; next morning when she awoke, her father was dead. They wept over him and put him in a coffin; at night the mother went to the priest and Marusia remained at home. She felt frightened and decided to join her friends. When she came, she found the evil one there. "Good evening, Marusia, why are you so sad?" the girls asked her. "How can I be merry? My father has died." "Ah, poor girl!" Everyone grieved with her; so did the vampire, just as though it were not his work. The guests began to leave. The evil youth said: "Marusia, come walk a few steps with me." She refused. The other girls pressed her, saying: "What are you, a little girl or a woman? Why are you afraid? Walk with him!" She went out with him. In the street he said: "Tell me, Marusia, were you in the church?" "No." "Did you see what I was doing?" "No." "Well, tomorrow your mother will die." Having said this, he vanished.

Marusia went home even sadder than before; next morning when she awoke, her mother lay dead. All day she wept; then the sun set, it began to grow dark, and she was afraid to stay alone, so she went to join her friends. "Good evening! What is the matter with you? You look quite pale!" they said. "How can I be merry? Yesterday my father died, and today my mother," Marusia said. "Poor girl, unfortunate girl!" Everyone sympathized with her. The time came to go home. "Marusia, come walk a few steps with me," said the evil spirit. She went out with him. "Tell me," he asked, "were you in the church?" "No." "Did you see what I was doing?" "No." "Well, before tomorrow night you yourself will die." Marusia spent the night with her friends; in the morning she got up and wondered what to do. She recalled that she had a grandmother, who was very, very old and had been blind for many years. She decided to go to her grandmother and ask her advice.

She went to her grandmother. "Good day, grandmother," she said. "Good day, little granddaughter! How does God favor

596

you? How are your father and mother?" "They are dead, grandmother." And she recounted everything that had happened to her. The old woman listened to her and said: "Ah, you poor girl! Go quickly to the priest, and ask him to see that when you die a hole is dug under the door sill, and that you are carried from your house not through the door but through that hole; and also ask him to bury you at the crossroads." Marusia went to the priest and with tears in her eyes begged him to do everything that her grandmother had told her to ask for. She returned home, bought a coffin, laid herself in it, and died at once. The priest was called; he first buried Marusia's father and mother, and then buried her. She was carried out through the hole under the door and buried at a spot where two roads met.

Shortly afterward the son of a boyar happened to drive by Marusia's grave; and he beheld a wondrous little flower growing on that grave, a flower such as he had never seen. The barin said to his servant: "Go and dig up that flower with its root; we will take it home, put it in a pot, and let it blossom in our house." They dug up the flower, took it home, planted it in a glazed pot, and put it on the window sill. The flower began to grow and blossom gloriously. One night the servant somehow could not sleep. He looked out of the window and saw a miracle: the flower suddenly began to sway, fell to the ground, and turned into a lovely maiden. The flower was pretty, but the maiden still prettier. She went through the rooms, got herself food and wine, ate and drank, struck the floor, turned again into a flower, ascended to the window, and sat on the branch.

Next day the servant told the barin about the miracle that he had seen during the night. "Ah, brother, why did you not rouse me? Tonight we will both keep watch." At the stroke of twelve the flower began to stir: it flew from place to place, then it fell to the floor and a lovely maiden appeared. She got herself food and drink and sat down to sup. The barin ran to her, took her by her white hands and led her into his room; he could not feast his eyes enough upon her beauty. In the morning he said to his father and mother: "Give me leave to marry, I have found a bride for myself." The parents gave him leave. Marusia said: "I will marry you only on condition that for four years we do not go to church." "Agreed," he said.

They wedded, lived together one year, then a second, and had a son. One day visitors came to them; they made merry, drank, and began to boast of their wives. One said that his wife was good; the other said that his was better. "Well, say what you will," said the host, "my wife is better than anyone's." "She is good, but she is an infidel," answered the guests. "Why do you say so?" "She never goes to church." The husband felt insulted by these words; the following Sunday he ordered his wife to get dressed to go to mass. "Don't contradict me! Get ready without delay!" he commanded. They made ready and went to church; the husband went in and saw nothing, but she saw the vampire sitting on the window sill. "Aha, so you are here?" he said. "Do you remember what happened long ago? Were you in the church last night?" "No." "Did you see what I was doing there?" "No." "Well, tomorrow both your husband and your son will die."

Marusia rushed straight from the church to her grandmother. The old woman gave her one phial of holy water and another of the water of life, and instructed her as to what she was to do. Next day Marusia's husband and her son died. The vampire flew to her and asked: "Tell me, were you in the church?" "I was." "And did you see what I was doing?" "You were devouring a corpse." When she had said this she sprinkled him with holy water and he turned into dust. Then she sprinkled her husband and her son with the water of life and they breathed again at once. From that time on they never knew distress nor separation, and they all lived together long and happily.

THE BEGGARS' PLAN

TWO OLD BEGGARS, husband and wife, were walking along a road and approached a village. The old man said: "I will ask for some milk." His wife answered: "And I will crumb some bread into the milk." The man seized her and began to beat her, saying: "Don't crumb bread into the milk, it will get sour; don't crumb bread into the milk, it will get sour." But when they came to the village no one gave them milk.

WOMAN'S WAY

MY DEAR HUSBAND, where are you going?" "I won't tell you." "Please, my dear, where are you going?" "To town, to the fair." "My darling, take me along." "I won't." "Please, my darling, take me along." "Sit at the very edge of the cart." "What do you have in the cart, my dear?" "I won't tell." "What, my dear, is in the cart?" "Apples." "Give me an apple, my dear." "I won't give you one." "Please, my dear, give me an apple." "Take one." "Where, my dear, shall we spend the night?" "I won't tell you." "Please tell me, my dear, where shall we spend the night?" "In the big village, in the priest's hay barn."

THE FOOLISH GERMAN

ON A CERTAIN BIG ESTATE there was a German steward who did not observe the holidays of the Russian folk and forced the peasants to work all the time. One day the village elder came to him and said: "Tomorrow we have a holiday; work is forbidden." "What holiday have you thought up now?" "St. Nicholas' day, little father." "And who is he? Show him to me." The elder brought him an icon. "Oh, that is just a wooden board," said the German. "It can't do anything to me; I shall work, and so will you." So the peasants decided to play a trick on the German. Again the elder came to see him, saying: "Little father, tomorrow we have a holiday." "What holiday?" "St. Hornet's day." "Who is he? Show him to me." The elder brought him to a hollow tree, in which the hornets had a nest. "There he is," he said to the steward. The German began to peep in through the cracks and heard the hornets humming and humming. "How he sings!" said the German. "He must have drunk some vodka! Well, I am not afraid of him, and will order you to work in any case." As the German spoke, the hornets flew out and fell to stinging him. "Ai, ai!" he cried at the top of his lungs. "I swear I won't order you to work, and I won't work myself—I'll even let the peasants take a whole week's holiday!"

THE ENCHANTED PRINCESS

IN A CERTAIN KINGDOM in a certain land there lived a wealthy merchant who had a son by the name of Ivan. The merchant loaded his ships, left his house and shops in charge of his wife and son, and set out on a voyage to distant parts. He sailed the seas for one month, two months, and three months, cast anchor in foreign lands, bought their merchandise, and sold his own at a good price. During that time not a little misfortune befell Ivan, the merchant's son; for all the other merchants and burghers became angry at him, saying: "Why is he so lucky? He has robbed us of all our customers!" They put their heads together, wrote a petition stating that such and such a merchant's son was a thief and drunkard unworthy of belonging to their guild, and sentenced him to become a soldier. The poor young man had his head shaven and was sent to the regiment.

Ivan served and suffered not just one year, but ten; then he wanted to visit his native town, asked for a six months' furlough, and set out on his way. His father and mother were overjoyed at his return; he stayed with them through the appointed time, and then had to go back. His father led him to deep cellars filled with gold and silver and said to him: "My beloved son, take as much money as your heart desires." Ivan, the merchant's son, stuffed his pockets, received solemn blessings from his parents, said farewell to his family, and rode off to his regiment, for his father had bought him a magnificent horse. The separation filled the goodly youth with great sadness and sorrow. On his way he saw an alehouse, and stopped at it to drown his sorrow in wine; he drank one pint and it seemed not enough; he drank another pint, got drunk, and fell fast asleep.

Out of nowhere came dissolute drunkards, who took all his money, down to the last penny. Ivan awoke to discover that he had been robbed clean; he grieved, but continued on his way. Dark night overtook him in a deserted place; he rode and rode, till he saw an inn. Near the inn was a post, and on the post was an inscription saying that whoever should spend the night in the inn must pay a hundred rubles. What could Ivan do? After all, he did not want to die of hunger, so he knocked at the gate. A boy ran out, led him to a room, and his horse to the stable. Ivan was given everything his heart desired; he ate and drank his fill, then looked thoughtful. "Mr. Soldier," said the host, "why are you so sad? Is it because you have no money to pay me with?" "It isn't that, host! But while I am sated, my faithful

601

horse is hungry." "No, Mr. Soldier! You can see for yourself that he has plenty of hay and oats." "I know that, but our horses have this habit: if I am beside him he will eat, but without me he will not even touch his feed." The innkeeper ran to the stable, looked in, and so it was: the horse stood there, his head hanging low, and he did not even glance at the oats. "What an intelligent horse!" thought the innkeeper. "He is attached to his master." And he ordered the soldier's bed to be prepared in the stable. Ivan went to sleep there, and on the stroke of midnight, when everything was quiet in the house, he saddled his horse and galloped off.

Next day at sunset he stopped at an inn where the charge was two hundred rubles a night; here too he succeeded in cheating his host. The third day he came to an inn where lodging was even more expensive than in the two other inns; an inscription on the post stated that the charge for a night was three hundred rubles. "Well," he thought, "I'll take a chance here too." He entered the inn, ate and drank his fill, then looked thoughtful. "Mr. Soldier, why are you so sad? Is it because you have no money to pay me with?" asked the host. "No, you have guessed wrong! What I am thinking is that although I am sated, my faithful horse is hungry." "How can that be? I have given him hay and oats, and plenty of them." "But our horses have this habit: if I am beside him, he will eat, but without me he won't even touch his feed." "Well, in that case, go to sleep in the stable."

Now that innkeeper's wife was a sorceress; she consulted her magic books and learned at once that the soldier had not a penny on him. She set laborers to watch at the gate and gave them strict orders to prevent the soldier from sneaking away. On the stroke of midnight Ivan rose and made ready to take to his heels, when he saw that laborers were standing on guard. He lay down again and fell asleep. He awoke at daybreak, saddled his horse in a hurry, mounted him, and rode off. "Halt!" cried the guards. "You have not paid the host; give us the money." "What money? Get out of my way!" cried Ivan, and he tried to gallop past them; but the laborers seized him and began to belabor him. They raised such a hubbub that the

whole house was aroused. "Beat him, boys, beat him to death!" everyone shouted. "That's enough!" said the host. "Let him live, let him stay three years with us and earn three hundred rubles."

There was nothing to be done, so Ivan, the merchant's son, stayed at the inn; he lived there for one day, a second day, and a third day. The host said to him: "Mr. Soldier, I suppose you have learned how to fire a gun." "Of course I have; that's what we are taught in the regiment." "Well, then go and shoot some game; there are all kinds of beasts and birds around here." Ivan took a gun and went hunting. For a long time he wandered in the woods but did not meet any game. Only at nightfall he sighted a hare at the edge of the forest; he took aim, but the hare darted off as fast as he could. The hunter rushed after him and came to a broad green meadow. On that meadow stood a splendid castle built of pure marble and covered with a golden roof. The hare jumped into the courtyard and Ivan after him; but the hare had vanished without a trace. "Well," he thought, "at least I will have a look at the castle."

He went in and walked in the chambers. Everywhere he found such magnificence as no mind can imagine and only a tale can tell of; and in one chamber the table was set with various viands and wines and splendid covers. Ivan drank a glassful from each bottle, ate a bit from each plate, and sat there reveling to his heart's delight. Suddenly a carriage rolled up to the porch and a princess arrived. She was black, and her retinue was black, and her horses were black.

Ivan remembered his military training, jumped up, and stood at attention at the door; the princess came into the chamber and he at once saluted her smartly. "Good evening, soldier!" the princess greeted him. "How have you come here, of your own will or by compulsion? Are you shirking a deed or trying to do one? Sit by my side, let us talk peacefully." Then the princess begged him: "Could you render me a great service? If you do, you will be happy. It is said that Russian soldiers fear nothing. Now, evil spirits have taken possession of this castle of mine." "Your Highness, I shall be glad to serve you to the last drop of my blood." "Well, then, listen carefully. Until midnight, drink and make merry; but on the stroke of midnight, lie down on the bed that hangs by straps in the middle of the great chamber, and no matter what happens to you or what you fancy you see and hear, do not be afraid, but lie in silence."

Having said this, the princess took leave of him and went off. Ivan, the merchant's son, drank and made merry, and on the very stroke of midnight lay down in the appointed place. Suddenly a storm began to roar; it clattered and thundered, as though the walls might collapse at any moment and sink into the ground. The chambers were filled with devils, who yelled and shouted and began a hellish dance; and when they saw the soldier, they set themselves to frighten and torment him in every way possible. Out of nowhere Ivan's sergeant appeared and said: "Oh, Ivan, merchant's son, what have you done? You have been listed as a deserter; return to your regiment at once or you'll be sorry."

After the sergeant came the lieutenant, after the lieutenant the captain, and after the captain the colonel. "You scoundrel," said the colonel, "what are you doing here? I see that you want to run the gantlet! Hey, bring fresh sticks here!" The devils set to work and soon gathered a whole pile of fresh sticks, but Ivan lay still and did not say a word. "Ah, you rascal," said the colonel, "so you aren't afraid of sticks at all; you must have seen worse than that during your service! Send me a squadron of soldiers with loaded guns, let them shoot him!" As though out of the ground a squadron of soldiers appeared; the command rang out, the soldiers took aim, they were about to fire. But suddenly the cocks crowed, and everything vanished in a trice—gone were the soldiers, the officers, and the sticks.

Next day the princess came to the castle; she was now white from her head down to her chest, and so also were her retinue and the horses. "Thank you, soldier!" said the princess. "You have seen terrors, but you will see worse. Mind you, do not take fright, serve me two nights more, and I will make you happy." They ate and drank and made merry together; then the princess left, and Ivan, the merchant's son, lay on his bed. At midnight a storm roared, there was a clatter and a thunder, the devils came running, they shouted and yelled. "Ah, brothers, the soldier is here again!" cried a lame, one-eyed little imp. "Isn't he a nuisance! What's your plan? Are you trying to drive us from this castle? Just wait, I'll go tell our grandfather." The grandfather came himself, ordered the devils to bring a forge, and to prepare red-hot iron rods. "Strike him with these hot rods to the very bones, that will teach him to intrude in other people's houses!" The devils had no sooner prepared the forge than the cocks crowed, and everything vanished in a trice.

On the third day the princess came to the castle, and Ivan marveled when he saw that she herself, her retinue, and their horses had all become white to their knees. "Thanks, soldier, for your loyal service," she said. "How is God favoring you?" "So far I am safe and sound, Your Highness!" "Well, try to be brave this last night. Here is a sheepskin for you; put it on, or the devils will get at you with their claws. They are terribly angry now." They sat at table together, ate, drank, and made merry; then the princess said farewell and left, and Ivan donned the sheepskin, made the sign of the cross, and lay down on his bed.

On the stroke of midnight a storm roared, and the whole castle shook with the clatter and thunder; a numberless host of devils came—lame ones, one-eyed ones, and many other kinds. They fell upon Ivan, crying: "Take the scoundrel, grab him, pull him!" They set to scratching him with their claws; one seized him, another seized him, but all the claws remained stuck in the sheepskin. "No, brothers, apparently one can't get him that way," one said. "Let us then take his own father and mother and skin them alive!" That very minute they dragged in Ivan's parents and began to skin them with their claws. The father and mother cried: "Ivan, dear son, have pity on us, leave that bed! It is because of you that we are being skinned alive." But Ivan lay without stirring or saying a word. Then the cocks crowed and suddenly everything vanished, as though it had never been there.

In the morning the princess came. Her horses were white, her retinue were white, and she herself was all pure and so beautiful that one cannot imagine a more beautiful lady: one could see her marrow flowing from bone to bone. "You have seen terrors," she said to Ivan, "but there won't be any more. Thanks for your kindness; now let us hasten away from here." "No, princess," said Ivan, the merchant's son, "let us rather rest for an hour or two." "What are you saying?" she asked. "If we stay here to rest we shall perish." They left the castle and set out on their way. After they had gone some distance, the princess said: "Look back, goodly youth, and see what is happening behind you." Ivan looked back, and not a trace was left of the castle; it had fallen through the ground, and where it had stood flames were blazing.

"We would have perished in those flames if we had lingered there," said the princess, and handed him a purse. "Take it. This is not an ordinary purse; if you need money, just shake it, and at once gold pieces will pour out of it, as many as your heart desires. Go now, pay your debt to the innkeeper, and come to such and such an island; I shall wait for you near the cathedral. There we shall attend mass and be married: you shall be my husband and I will be your wife. But mind you, don't be late; if you cannot come today, come tomorrow; if you cannot come tomorrow, come the day after; but if you miss on three days, you will never see me again."

They took leave of each other; the princess went to the right and Ivan to the left. He came to the inn, shook his purse before the host, and gold poured out of it. "Well, brother," said Ivan, "you thought a soldier has no money, and so he can be taken as a bondslave for three years; but you were wrong. Take what I owe you." He paid the innkeeper three hundred rubles, mounted on his horse, and rode where he had been told to go. "What a marvel! Whence did he get this money?" thought the innkeeper's wife. She consulted her books and saw that he had rescued the enchanted princess and that the princess had given him a purse that would keep him supplied with money forever. She called a boy, sent him to graze cows in the field, and gave him a magic apple. "A soldier will approach you and ask you for water to drink," she said. "But tell him that you have no water and give him this juicy apple instead."

The boy drove the cows to the field. As soon as he was there—lo and behold—Ivan, the merchant's son, rode up to him. "Ah, brother," he said, "don't you have some water to drink? I am terribly thirsty." "No, soldier," the boy replied, "water is far from here. But I have a juicy apple; if you wish, eat it, maybe it will refresh you." Ivan took the apple, ate it, and was overwhelmed by heavy sleep; he slept for three days without awakening. The princess waited in vain for her betrothed, for three days in succession; then she decided that it was not her fate to be married to him. She sighed, seated herself in her carriage and drove off. She saw a boy grazing cows. "Little herdsman, have you not seen a goodly youth, a Russian soldier?" she asked. "He has been sleeping under this oak for three days," answered the boy.

The princess looked—and there was her soldier. She began to nudge him, in order to rouse him; but no matter how hard she tried, she could not awaken him. She took a piece of paper and a pencil and wrote this note: "Unless you go to such and such a ferry, you will not get to the thrice tenth kingdom and you will not be my husband." She put the note into Ivan's pocket, kissed him as he lay asleep, wept bitter tears, and drove far, far away.

Later at night Ivan awakened and did not know what to do. The boy said to him: "A lovely maiden has been here, and she was so well dressed! She tried to rouse you, but could not awaken you. So she wrote a note that she put in your pocket; then she got into her carriage and left." Ivan said his prayers to God, bowed low to all sides, and rode to the ferry.

After a long time or a short time he arrived there and cried to the ferrymen: "Hey, brothers, take me to the other side as fast as you can—and here is your pay in advance!" He drew out his purse, shook it, and filled their boat with gold. The ferrymen gasped. "But where are you going, soldier?" "To the thrice tenth kingdom." "Well, brother, by the roundabout way, it takes three years to get to that kingdom; by the straight way, it takes three hours. But there is no passage by the straight way." "Then what shall I do?" "Listen and we'll tell you. A griffin comes here; it is as big as a mountain, it seizes all kinds of carrion and takes it to the other shore. So do you cut open your horse's belly, and clean it and wash it, and we will sew you into it. The griffin will seize the carcass, carry it to the thrice tenth kingdom, and throw it to his young. Then do you crawl out of the horse's belly as fast as you can and go where you want to go."

Ivan cut off his horse's head, cut open his belly, cleaned it and washed it, and crawled inside; the ferrymen sewed up the horse's belly and hid themselves. Suddenly the griffin came flying, as big as a mountain; he seized the carcass, took it to the thrice tenth kingdom, threw it to his young, then flew away to look for new prey. Ivan cut open the horse's belly, crawled out, went to the king, and asked to be taken into his service. And in that thrice tenth kingdom the griffin was doing much mischief; every day they had given him a man to devour, otherwise he would have ruined the whole kingdom.

The king thought and thought, wondering what to do with Ivan, and then ordered him to be exposed to the vicious bird. The king's warriors took him, brought him to a garden, put him beside an apple tree, and said: "Guard this tree and let not a single apple disappear." Ivan stood on guard, when suddenly the griffin flew down, as big as a mountain. "Good day, brave youth," he said. "I did not know you were in the horse's belly, else I would have eaten you long ago." "God alone knows whether you would have eaten me or not," said Ivan. The monstrous bird dropped one lip to the ground and lifted the other high like a roof; he was ready to devour the goodly youth. Ivan swung his bayonet and pinned the lower lip of the griffin firmly to the damp earth; then he drew out his saber and began to lash out at the griffin. "Ah, goodly youth," said the bird, "don't cut me! I will make you a champion. Take the phial from under my left wing and drink from it, and you'll see for yourself."

Ivan took the phial, drank from it, felt great strength in himself, and attacked the bird even more fiercely than before; he just swung out and cut. "Ah, goodly youth, don't cut me!"

cried the griffin. "I will give you a second phial, from under my right wing." Ivan drank from the second phial, felt even greater strength in himself, and kept striking the griffin. "Ah, goodly youth, don't cut me!" the griffin begged. "I will guide you to your fortune. There are green meadows here; in these meadows grow three tall oaks, under those oaks are iron doors, and behind those doors are champion steeds; a time will come when they will be useful to you." Ivan listened to the bird, but kept on cutting him nonetheless; he cut the griffin into little pieces and gathered them into a huge pile.

Next morning the king summoned before him the general on duty and said: "Go and gather the bones of Ivan, the merchant's son; although he is from a foreign land, it is not fitting that human bones should lie about unburied." The general on duty rushed to the garden and saw that Ivan was alive and that the griffin was cut into shreds. He reported this to the king, who was overjoyed, praised Ivan, and gave him a letter patent written in his own hand, stating that Ivan had permission to go everywhere in the kingdom and eat and drink in all the inns and alehouses without paying.

Ivan, the merchant's son, having received his letter patent, went to the richest inn, drank ten gallons of wine, ate ten loaves of bread and half an ox, returned to the king's stable, and lay down to sleep. He lived thus in the king's stable for three full years. Then the princess appeared—she had taken the roundabout route. Her father was overjoyed and began to question her: "My beloved daughter, who rescued you from your bitter fate?" "Such and such a soldier, the son of a merchant." "He came here and did me a great service—he cut the griffin to pieces," the king said. What was there to talk about? Ivan, the merchant's son, was wedded to the princess, and a feast was given for all the people, and I was there and drank wine; it ran down my mustache but did not go into my mouth.

Shortly afterward the three-headed dragon wrote to the king: "Give me your daughter or I'll burn your whole kingdom with fire and scatter the ashes." The king was grieved, but Ivan, the merchant's son, drank ten gallons of wine, ate ten loaves of bread and half an ox, rushed to the green meadows, raised

610

an iron door, led out a champion steed, donned his steel sword and his battle mace, mounted the steed, and went forth to do battle. "Eh, goodly youth," said the dragon, "what are you trying to do? I will put you on one hand, and beat you with the other, and only a damp spot will remain where once you were." "Don't boast; say your prayers first," answered Ivan. He swung his steel sword and cut off all of the dragon's three heads at once. Then he conquered the six-headed dragon, and then the twelve-headed one, and his strength and valor became famous in all lands.

THE RAVEN
AND THE LOBSTER

A RAVEN FLEW above the sea, looked down, and saw a lobster. She grabbed him and took him to the woods, intending to perch somewhere on a branch and eat a good meal. The lobster saw that his end was coming and said to the raven: "Eh, raven, raven, I knew your father and mother, they were fine people!" "Humph!" answered the raven, without opening her mouth. "And I know your brothers and sisters, too; what fine people they are!" "Humph!" "But although they are all fine people, they are not equal to you. I think that in the whole world there is no one wiser than you." "Aha!" cawed the raven, opening her mouth wide, and dropped the lobster into the sea.

PRINCE IVAN,
THE FIREBIRD, AND THE GRAY WOLF

IN A CERTAIN LAND in a certain kingdom, there lived a king called Vyslav Andronovich. He had three sons: the first was Prince Dimitri, the second Prince Vasily, and the third Prince Ivan. King Vyslav Andronovich had a garden so rich that there was no finer one in any kingdom. In this garden there grew all kinds of precious trees, with and without fruit; one special apple tree was the king's favorite, for all the apples it bore were golden.

The firebird took to visiting King Vyslav's garden; her wings were golden and her eyes were like oriental crystals. Every night she flew into the garden, perched on King Vyslav's favorite apple tree, picked several golden apples from it, and then flew away. King Vyslav Andronovich was greatly distressed that the firebird had taken so many apples from his golden apple tree. So he summoned his three sons to him and said: "My beloved children, which of you can catch the firebird in my garden? To him who captures her alive I will give half my kingdom during my life, and all of it upon my death!" His sons, the princes, answered in one voice: "Your Majesty, gracious sovereign, little father, with great joy will we try to take the firebird alive!"

The first night Prince Dimitri went to keep watch in the garden. He sat under the apple tree from which the firebird had been picking apples, fell asleep, and did not hear her come, though she picked much golden fruit. Next morning King Vyslav Andronovich summoned his son Prince Dimitri to him and asked: "Well, my beloved son, did you see the firebird or not?" The prince answered: "No, gracious sovereign, little father! She did not come last night!"

The next night Prince Vasily went to keep watch in the garden. He sat under the same apple tree; he stayed one hour, then another hour, and finally fell so sound asleep that he did not hear the firebird come, though she picked many apples. In the morning King Vyslav summoned his son to him and asked: "Well, my beloved son, did you see the firebird or not?" "Gracious sovereign, little father, she did not come last night!"

The third night Prince Ivan went to keep watch in the garden and sat under the same apple tree; he sat one hour, a second hour, and a third—then suddenly the whole garden was illumined as if by many lights. The firebird had come; she perched on the apple tree and began to pick apples. Prince Ivan stole up to her so softly that he was able to seize her tail. But he could not hold the firebird herself; she tore herself from his grasp and flew away. In Prince Ivan's hand there remained only one feather of her tail, to which he held very fast. In the morning, as soon as King Vyslav awoke from his sleep, Prince Ivan went to him and gave him the feather of the firebird. King Vyslav was greatly pleased that his youngest son had succeeded in getting at least one feather of the firebird.

This feather was so marvelously bright that when it was placed in a dark room it made the whole room shine as if it were lit up by many candles. King Vyslav put the feather in his study as a keepsake, to be treasured forever. From that moment the firebird stopped visiting the garden.

Once again King Vyslav summoned his sons and said: "My beloved children, set out. I give you my blessing. Find the firebird and bring her to me alive; and that which I promised before will go to him who brings me the firebird." At this time Princes Dimitri and Vasily bore a grudge against their youngest brother, Ivan, because he had succeeded in tearing a feather from the firebird's tail; they accepted their father's blessing and together went forth to seek the firebird. But Prince Ivan too began to beg for his father's blessing that he might go forth. King Vyslav said to him: "My beloved son, my dear child, you are still young and unused to such long and hard journeys; why should you depart from my house? Your brothers have gone; what if you too leave me and all three of you do not return for a long time? I am old now and I walk in the shadow of the Lord; if during your absence the Lord takes my life, who will rule the kingdom in my place? A rebellion might break out, or dissension among the people, and there would be no one to pacify them; or an enemy might approach our land, and there would be no one to command our troops." But no matter how King Vyslav tried to hold Prince Ivan back, he finally had to yield to his son's insistent prayer. Prince Ivan received his father's blessing, chose a horse, and set out on his way; and he rode on and on, himself not knowing whither.

He rode near and far, high and low, along by-paths and by-ways—for speedily a tale is spun, but with less speed a deed is done—until he came to a wide, open field, a green meadow. And there in the field stood a pillar, and on the pillar these words were written: "Whosoever goes from this pillar on the road straight before him will be cold and hungry. Whosoever goes to the right side will be safe and sound, but his horse will be killed. And whosoever goes to the left side will be killed himself, but his horse will be safe and sound." Prince Ivan read this inscription and went to the right, thinking that

614

although his horse might be killed, he himself would remain alive and would in time get another horse.

He rode one day, then a second day, then a third. Suddenly an enormous gray wolf came toward him and said: "Ah, so it's you, young lad, Prince Ivan! You saw the inscription on the pillar that said that your horse would be killed if you came this way. Why then have you come hither?" When he had said these words, he tore Prince Ivan's horse in twain and ran off to one side.

Prince Ivan was sorely grieved for his horse; he shed bitter tears and then continued on foot. He walked a whole day and was utterly exhausted. He was about to sit down and rest for a while when all at once the gray wolf caught up with him and said: "I am sorry for you, Prince Ivan, because you are exhausted from walking; I am also sorry that I ate your good horse. Therefore mount me, the gray wolf, and tell me whither to carry you and for what purpose." Prince Ivan told the gray wolf what errand he had come on; and the gray wolf darted off with him more swiftly than a horse, and after some time, just at nightfall, reached a low stone wall. There he stopped and said: "Now, Prince Ivan, climb down from me, the gray wolf, and climb over that stone wall; behind the wall you will find a garden, and in the garden the firebird is sitting in a golden cage. Take the firebird, but touch not the golden cage; if you take the cage, you will not escape, you will be caught at once!"

Prince Ivan climbed over the stone wall into the garden, saw the firebird in the golden cage, and was utterly charmed by the beauty of the cage. He took the bird out and started back across the garden, but on his way he changed his mind and said to himself: "Why have I taken the firebird without her cage— where will I put her?" He returned, and the moment he took down the golden cage, a thunderous noise resounded through the whole garden, for there were strings tied to the cage. The guards woke up at once, rushed into the garden, caught Prince Ivan with the firebird, and led him before their king, whose name was Dolmat. King Dolmat was furious at Prince Ivan and cried in a loud and angry voice: "How now! Are you not ashamed to steal, young lad! Who are you, from what land do you come, what is your father's name, and what is your own name?"

Prince Ivan answered: "I am from Vyslav's kingdom. I am the son of king Vyslav Andronovich, and my name is Prince Ivan. Your Firebird took to visiting our garden night after night; she plucked golden apples from my father's favorite apple tree and spoiled almost the whole tree. For that reason my father sent me to find the firebird and bring her to him."

"Oh, young lad, Prince Ivan," said King Dolmat, "is it fitting to do what you have done? If you had come to me, I would have given you the firebird with honor. But now, will you like it if I send to all the kingdoms to proclaim how dishonorably you have acted in my kingdom? However, listen, Prince Ivan! If you will do me a service, if you go beyond thirty lands, to the thirtieth kingdom, and get for me the horse with the golden mane from the realm of King Afron, I will forgive you your offense and hand the firebird over to you with great honor. But if you do not perform this service, I shall let it be known in all the kingdoms that you are a dishonorable thief." Prince Ivan left King Dolmat in great distress, promising to get for him the horse with the golden mane.

He came to the gray wolf and told him everything that King Dolmat had said. "Oh, young lad, Prince Ivan," said the gray wolf, "why did you not heed my words, why did you take the golden cage?" "It is true, I am guilty before you," answered Prince Ivan. "Well, let it be so," said the gray wolf. "Sit on me, the gray wolf; I will carry you where you have to go."

Prince Ivan mounted to the gray wolf's back, and the wolf ran fast as an arrow. He ran till nightfall, a short distance or a long one, until he came to King Afron's kingdom. And reaching the white-walled royal stables, the gray wolf said to Prince Ivan: "Go, Prince Ivan, into those white-walled stables—all the stable boys on guard are now sleeping soundly—and take the horse with the golden mane. However, on the wall there hangs a golden bridle; do not take it, otherwise there will be trouble!"

Prince Ivan entered the white-walled stables, took the steed, and began to retrace his steps; but he noticed the golden bridle on the wall, and was so charmed with it that he removed it from its nail. And he had no sooner removed it than a thunderous clatter and noise resounded through all the stables, for there were strings tied to that bridle. The stable boys on guard woke up at once, rushed in, caught Prince Ivan, and brought him before King Afron. King Afron began to question him. "Young lad," he said, "tell me from what kingdom you are come, whose son you are, and what your name may be." Prince Ivan answered: "I am from Vyslav's kingdom. I am King Vyslav Andronovich's son, and I am called Prince Ivan."

"Oh, young lad, Prince Ivan," said King Afron, "is the deed you have done befitting an honorable knight? If you had come to me I would have given you the horse with the golden mane in all honor. But now, will you like it if I send to all the kingdoms to proclaim how dishonorably you have behaved in my kingdom? However, listen, Prince Ivan! If you do me a service, if you go beyond the thrice ninth land, to the thrice tenth kingdom, and get for me Princess Elena the Fair, with whom I have been in love, heart and soul, for long years, but whom I cannot win for my bride, I will forgive you your offense and give you the horse with the golden mane in all honor. But if you do not perform this service for me, I shall let it be known in all the kingdoms that you are a dishonorable thief, and will put down in writing how badly you have behaved in my kingdom." Then Prince Ivan promised King Afron to get Princess Elena the Fair for him and left the palace, weeping bitterly.

He came to the gray wolf and told him everything that had happened to him. "Oh, young lad, Prince Ivan," said the gray wolf, "why did you not heed my words, why did you take the golden bridle?" "It is true, I am guilty before you," answered Prince Ivan. "Well, let it be so!" said the gray wolf. "Sit on me, the gray wolf; I will carry you where you have to go."

Prince Ivan mounted to the gray wolf's back, and the wolf ran fast as an arrow; he ran as beasts run in fairy tales, so that in a very short time he arrived in the kingdom of Elena the Fair. And reaching the golden fence that surrounded the wonderful garden, the wolf said to Prince Ivan: "Now, Prince Ivan, climb down from me, the gray wolf, and go back along the same road that we took to come here, and wait for me in the open field under the green oak."

Prince Ivan went where he was bid. But the gray wolf sat near the golden fence and waited till Princess Elena the Fair should come to take her walk in the garden. Toward evening, when the sun began to set in the west, and the air became cool, Princess Elena the Fair went to walk in the garden with her governesses and ladies-in-waiting. She entered the garden, and when she came near the place where the gray wolf was sitting behind the fence, he quickly jumped across the fence into the garden, caught the princess, jumped back again, and ran with all his strength and power. He came to the green oak in the open field where Prince Ivan was waiting for him and said: "Prince Ivan, quickly seat yourself on me, the gray wolf!" Prince Ivan seated himself and the gray wolf darted off with him and the princess toward King Afron's kingdom.

The nurses and governesses and ladies-in-waiting who had been walking in the garden with the beautiful Princess Elena ran at once to the palace and sent men-at-arms to pursue the gray wolf; but no matter how fast they ran, they could not overtake him, and so they turned back.

Sitting on the gray wolf with the beautiful Princess Elena, Prince Ivan came to love her with all his heart, and she to love Prince Ivan. And when the gray wolf came to King Afron's kingdom, and Prince Ivan had to lead the beautiful princess to the palace and give her to King Afron, he grew extremely sad and began to weep bitter tears. The gray wolf asked him: "Why are you weeping, Prince Ivan?" And Prince Ivan answered: "Gray wolf, my friend, why should I not weep and grieve? I have come to love the beautiful Princess Elena with all my heart, and now I must give her to King Afron in return for the horse with the golden mane; if I do not give her to him, he will dishonor me in all the kingdoms."

"I have served you much, Prince Ivan," said the gray wolf, "and I will do you this service too. Listen to me, Prince Ivan! I will turn myself into the beautiful Princess Elena, and do you lead me to King Afron and take from him the horse with the golden mane; he will think me the real princess. And later,

618

when you have mounted the horse with the golden mane and gone far away, I shall ask King Afron to let me walk in the open field. And when he lets me go with the nurses and governesses and ladies-in-waiting, and I am with them in the open field, remember me, and once again I shall be with you." The gray wolf said these words, struck himself against the damp earth, and turned into Princess Elena the Fair, so that there was no way of knowing that he was not the princess. Prince Ivan took the gray wolf, went to King Afron's palace, and told the real Princess Elena to wait for him outside the town.

When Prince Ivan came to King Afron with the false Elena the Fair, the king was greatly rejoiced to receive the treasure that he had so long desired. He accepted the false princess and gave Prince Ivan the horse with the golden mane.

Prince Ivan mounted the horse and rode out of the town; he had seated Princess Elena the Fair behind him, and they set out in the direction of King Dolmat's kingdom. As for the gray wolf, he lived with King Afron one day, a second day, then a third, in the place of Elena the Fair; and on the fourth he went to King Afron and asked his permission to take a walk in the open field, to dispel the cruel sadness and grief that lay on him. And King Afron said to him: "Ah, my beautiful Princess Elena! For you I will do anything; I will even let you go to walk in the open field!" And at once he commanded the governesses and nurses and all the ladies-in-waiting to walk with the beautiful princess in the open field.

Meanwhile Prince Ivan rode along by-ways and by-paths with Elena the Fair, conversed with her, and forgot about the gray wolf. But then he remembered. "Ah," he said, "where is my gray wolf?" Suddenly, as though he had come from nowhere, the gray wolf stood before Prince Ivan and said: "Prince Ivan, sit on me, the gray wolf, and let the beautiful princess ride on the horse with the golden mane."

Prince Ivan sat on the gray wolf and they set out for King Dolmat's kingdom. They traveled a long time or a short time, and having come to the kingdom, stopped three versts from the town. Prince Ivan began to implore the gray wolf, saying: "Listen to me, gray wolf, my dear friend! You have done many

619

a service for me, do me this last one. Could you not turn yourself into a horse with a golden mane instead of this one? For
I long to have myself a horse with a golden mane."

Suddenly the gray wolf struck himself against the damp
earth and turned into a horse with a golden mane; Prince Ivan
left Princess Elena the Fair in the green meadow, bestrode the
gray wolf, and went to the palace of King Dolmat. And when
King Dolmat saw Prince Ivan riding on the horse with the
golden mane he was overjoyed and at once came out of his
apartment, met the prince in the great courtyard, kissed him
on his sweet lips, took him by the right hand, and led him into
the white-walled palace hall. In honor of this joyous occasion
King Dolmat gave a great feast, and the guests sat at oaken
tables with checked tablecloths; they ate, drank, laughed, and
enjoyed themselves for exactly two days. And on the third day
King Dolmat handed to Prince Ivan the firebird in the golden
cage. The prince took the firebird, went outside the town,
mounted the golden-maned horse together with Princess Elena
the Fair, and set out for his native land, the kingdom of King
Vyslav Andronovich.

As for King Dolmat, he decided on the next day to break in
his golden-maned horse in the open field; he had the horse
saddled, then mounted him and rode off; but as soon as he
began to spur the beast, it threw him, and turning back into the
gray wolf, darted off and overtook Prince Ivan. "Prince Ivan,"
said he, "mount me, the gray wolf, and let Princess Elena the
Fair ride on the horse with the golden mane."

Prince Ivan sat on the gray wolf and they continued on their
way. The moment the gray wolf brought Prince Ivan to the
place where he had torn the horse asunder, he stopped and
said: "Well, Prince Ivan, I have served you long enough in
faith and in truth. Upon this spot I tore your horse in twain,
and to this spot I have brought you back safe and sound. Climb
down from me, the gray wolf; now you have a horse with a
golden mane, mount him and go wherever you have to go; I am
no longer your servant." After he had said these words the
gray wolf ran off, and Prince Ivan wept bitterly and set out on
his way with the beautiful princess.

He rode with Princess Elena for a long time or a short time; when they were still about twenty versts from his own land, he stopped, dismounted from his horse, and lay down with the beautiful princess to rest under a tree from the heat of the sun; he tied the horse with the golden mane to the same tree, and put the cage with the firebird by his side. The two lovers lay on the soft grass, spoke amorous words to each other, and fell fast asleep.

At that very moment Prince Ivan's brothers, Prince Dimitri and Prince Vasily, having traveled through various kingdoms and having failed to find the firebird, were on their way back to their native land; they were returning empty-handed. They chanced to come upon their brother, Prince Ivan, lying asleep beside Princess Elena the Fair. Seeing the golden-maned horse on the grass and the firebird in the golden cage, they were sorely tempted, and decided to slay their brother. Prince Dimitri drew his sword from its scabbard, stabbed Prince Ivan, and cut him in little pieces; then he awakened Princess Elena the Fair and began to question her. "Lovely maiden," he said, "from what kingdom have you come? Who is your father, and what is your name?"

The beautiful Princess Elena, seeing Prince Ivan dead, was terribly frightened and began to weep bitter tears, and amid her tears she said: "I am Princess Elena the Fair; I was carried off by Prince Ivan, whom you have brought to an evil end. If you were valiant knights you would have gone with him into the open field and conquered him in fair combat; but you slew him while he was asleep, and what praise will that get you? A sleeping man is the same as a dead man!"

Then Prince Dimitri put his sword to the heart of Princess Elena and said to her: "Listen to me, Elena the Fair! You are now in our hands; we shall take you to our father, King Vyslav Andronovich, and you must tell him that we captured you as well as the firebird and the horse with the golden mane. If you do not promise to say this, I shall put you to death at once!" The beautiful Princess Elena was frightened by the threat of death; she promised them and swore by everything sacred that she would speak as they commanded. Then Prince Dimitri and

Prince Vasily cast lots to see who should get Princess Elena and who the horse with the golden mane. And it fell out that the beautiful princess went to Prince Vasily and the horse with the golden mane to Prince Dimitri. Then Prince Vasily took the beautiful Princess Elena, and seated her on his good horse, and Prince Dimitri mounted the horse with the golden mane and took the firebird to give to his father, King Vyslav Andronovich, and they all set out on their way.

Prince Ivan lay dead on that spot exactly thirty days; then the gray wolf came upon him and knew him by his odor. He wanted to help the prince, to revive him, but he did not know how to do it. At that moment the gray wolf saw a raven with two young ravens flying above the body, making ready to swoop down and eat the flesh of Prince Ivan. The gray wolf hid behind a bush; and as soon as the young ravens lighted on the ground and began to eat the body of Prince Ivan, he leaped from behind the bush, caught one young raven, and prepared to tear him in twain. Then the raven flew to the ground, sat at some distance from the gray wolf, and said to him: "Oh gray wolf, do not touch my young child; he has done nothing to you."

"Listen to me, raven," said the gray wolf. "I shall not touch your child, and will let him go, safe and sound, if you will do me a service. Fly beyond the thrice ninth land, to the thrice tenth kingdom, and bring me the water of death and the water of life." Thereupon the raven said to the gray wolf: "I will do this service for you, but touch not my son." Having said these words, the raven took wing and was soon out of sight. On the third day the raven came back carrying two phials, one containing the water of life, the other the water of death, and she gave these phials to the gray wolf.

The gray wolf took the phials, tore the young raven in twain, sprinkled him with the water of death, and the young raven's body grew together; he sprinkled him with the water of life, and the young raven shook his wings and flew away. Then the gray wolf sprinkled Prince Ivan with the water of death, and his body grew together; he sprinkled him with the water of life, and Prince Ivan stood up and said: "Ah, I have slept very long!"

The gray wolf answered him: "Yes, Prince Ivan, you would have slept forever had it not been for me: your brothers cut you in pieces and carried off the beautiful Princess Elena and the horse with the golden mane and the firebird. Now hasten as fast as you can to your native land; your brother Prince Vasily is this very day to marry your bride, Princess Elena the Fair. And in order to get there quickly, you had better sit on me, the gray wolf." Prince Ivan mounted the gray wolf; the wolf ran with him to King Vsylav Andronovich's kingdom, and after a short time or a long time reached the town.

Prince Ivan dismounted from the gray wolf, walked into the town, and having arrived at the palace, found that his brother Prince Vasily was indeed wedding the beautiful Princess Elena that very day; he had returned with her from the ceremony and was already sitting at the feast. Prince Ivan entered the palace, and no sooner did Elena the Fair see him than she sprang up from the table, began to kiss his sweet lips, and cried out: "This is my beloved bridegroom, Prince Ivan—not the evildoer who sits here at the table!"

Then King Vyslav Andronovich rose from his place and began to question Princess Elena. "What is the meaning of the words you have spoken?" he demanded. Elena the Fair told him the whole truth about what had happened—how Prince Ivan had won her, the horse with the golden mane, and the firebird, how his older brothers had killed him in his sleep, and how they had forced her under threat of death to say that they had won all this. King Vyslav grew terribly angry at Prince Dimitri and Prince Vasily and threw them into a dungeon; but Prince Ivan married Princess Elena the Fair and began to live with her in such true friendship and love that neither of them could spend a single minute without the other's company.

SHEMIAKA THE JUDGE

IN A CERTAIN VILLAGE there lived two brothers, one rich and the other poor. The poor brother came to the rich one to borrow a horse to bring wood from the forest. The rich brother gave him a horse. The poor brother also asked for a yoke; the rich one angrily refused. So the poor one tied his sledge to the horse's tail, went to the forest, cut a huge load of wood, so heavy that the horse could hardly drag it, came to his own yard, and opened the gate, but forgot to remove the board across the gate. The horse tried to push through the board and tore off its tail. The poor brother brought the now tailless horse back to the rich brother, who refused to take it back and set out to bring complaint against the poor one before Shemiaka, the judge. The poor man knew that he was in sore trouble, for he had nothing to give to the judge. Sadly he followed his brother.

The two brothers came to a rich peasant's house and asked to be allowed to spend the night. The peasant drank and made merry with the rich brother, but refused to invite the poor one to his table. The poor brother lay on the stove, looking at them; suddenly he fell from the stove and crushed to death a child lying in a cradle below. So the peasant also set out to see Shemiaka the judge, to lodge a complaint against the poor brother.

As they walked to the town (the rich brother, the peasant, and the poor brother, who walked behind them), they happened to cross a high bridge. The poor brother, thinking that he would not escape with his life from Shemiaka the judge, jumped from the bridge, hoping to kill himself. Under the bridge a man was carrying his sick father to the bathhouse; the poor brother fell onto the sledge and crushed the sick man to death. The son went to complain to Shemiaka the judge on the ground that the poor man had killed his father.

The rich brother came to Shemiaka the judge and lodged a

complaint against the poor one for having torn off the tail of his horse. In the meantime the poor brother had picked up a stone and wrapped it in a kerchief. Standing behind his brother he thought: "If the judge judges against me I will kill him with this stone." But the judge, thinking that the poor man had prepared a bribe of a hundred rubles, ordered the rich brother to give the horse to the poor one to keep until it grew another tail.

Then the rich peasant came before the judge and lodged his complaint about the death of his child. The poor man took out the same stone and showed it to the judge from where he stood behind the peasant. The judge, thinking that he was being offered another hundred rubles, for the second case, ordered the peasant to give his wife to the poor man to keep until she gave birth to another child, adding: "And then take back your wife and the child."

The third plaintiff accused the poor man of having crushed his father to death. The poor man showed the same stone to the judge. The judge, thinking that he was being offered still another hundred rubles, ordered the dead man's son to go to the bridge and said: "And you, poor man, stand under the bridge, and you, son, jump from the bridge and crush the poor man to death."

Shemiaka the judge then sent a servant to the poor man to ask for three hundred rubles. The poor man showed his stone and said: "If the judge had judged against me, I would have killed him with this stone." The servant came to the judge and said: "If you had judged against him, he would have killed you with a stone." The judge crossed himself and said: "Thank God that I judged in his favor."

The poor brother went to the rich brother to get the horse, in accordance with the verdict, until it should grow another tail. The rich brother did not want to give away his horse; instead, he gave the poor brother five hundred rubles, three measures of grain, and a milk goat, and made peace with him.

The poor man went to the peasant and, citing the verdict, asked for the peasant's wife until she should give birth to a child. Instead, the peasant gave him five hundred rubles, a cow with her calf, a mare with her colt, and four measures of grain, and made peace with him.

The poor man went to the plaintiff whose father he had killed and told him that in accordance with the judge's verdict he, the son, must stand on the bridge, and he himself, the poor man, under the bridge, and that the son must jump on him and crush him to death. The son thought: "If I jump from the bridge I shall not crush him but shall smash myself to death." He gave the poor man two hundred rubles, a horse, and five measures of grain, and made peace with him.

COMMENTARY

ON RUSSIAN FAIRY TALES

1. THEIR LIFE—THEIR STUDY

"WHEN *Juan* went his progress, many of the Commons as well as Gentry presented him with fine Presents: A good honest Bask-shoemaker, who made shoes of Bask for a *Copeak* a pair, consults with his wife what to present his Majesty; says she, a pair of fine *Lopkyes*,[1] or shoes of Bask; that is no rarity (quoth he); but we have an huge great Turnip in the Garden, we'l give him that, and a pair of *Lopkyes* also. Thus they did; and the Emperour took the present so kindly, that he made all his Nobility buy *Lopkyes* of the fellow at five shillings a pair, and he wore one pair himself. This put the man in stock, whereby he began to drive a Trade, and in time grew so considerable, that he left a great estate behind him. His family are now Gentlemen, and call'd *Lopotsky's*. There is a tree standing near his *quondam* house, upon which it is a custom to throw all their old *Lopkyes* as they pass by, in memory of this Gallant.

"A Gentleman seeing him so well paid for his Turnep, made account by the rule of proportion to get a greater Reward for a brave Horse; but the Emperour suspecting his design, gave him nothing but the great Turnep, for which he was both abash'd and laugh'd at."

This story about Ivan the Terrible is among some ten Russian folk tales recorded by an Oxford doctor of medicine, Samuel Collins (1619-1670). In the sixties he lived in Moscow as physician to the Tsar Aleksey Mikhaylovich, father of Peter the Great, and, besides a sable coat, presented to him by the sovereign, he brought back to his country curious data on the Muscovite empire. Shortly after Collins's death his notes were published under the title *The Present State of Russia* (London 1671). The tales mentioned above are entered in this booklet.

The classic, fundamental collection of Russian folk tales was gathered by the outstanding ethnographer Afanas'ev, who first brought it out in serial form from 1855 to 1864. Almost two hundred years separate this edition from the modest debut of Samuel Collins. It is worthy of remembrance that Russian folk tales were first recorded and first published, not in their homeland and not in their mother tongue, but in England, in English translation. Similarly, Russian secular folk songs first were recorded under the initiative of an Oxford bachelor, Richard James, who had been in Moscow as chaplain to an English diplomatic mission and returned to Oxford in 1620 with these invaluable texts. Not in Russia, but in England, there appeared at the end of the same century a first and, may we say, a brilliant attempt at a grammar of spoken Russian from the pen of H. W. Ludolf.

Such beginnings of active attention to oral Russian speech and poetry are, of course, characteristic of the territorial and scientific breadth of British interests in the seventeenth century. On the other hand, there arises the not unimportant question as to why, in the land of its birth, the Russian spoken language and oral tradition, and in particular the Russian folk tale, remained so long unrecorded in writing. Here we are confronted with one of the most peculiar features of Russian cultural life, which sharply distinguishes it from that of the occidental world. For many centuries Russian written literature remained almost entirely subject to the church: with all its wealth and high artistry, the Old Russian literary heritage is almost wholly concerned with the lives of saints and pious men, with devotional legends, prayers, sermons, ecclesiastical discourses, and chronicles in a monastic vein. The Old Russian laity, however, possessed a copious, original, manifold, and highly artistic fiction, but the only medium for its diffusion was oral transmission. The idea of using letters for secular poetry was thoroughly alien to the Russian tradition, and the expressive means of this poetry were inseparable from the oral legacy and oral execution.

Deviations from this dichotomic principle in the history of Old Russian literary art (ecclesiastical writings—secular oral poetry) are relatively rare. Thus, under the influence of hagiography and apocrypha, there slowly emerged new offshoots of folklore—oral legends and spiritual songs. On the other hand, in the oldest epoch of Russian history, preceding the Tatar invasion of the thirteenth century, profane elements had infiltrated from the oral tradition into the written literature, and precious fragments of ancient written epos intimately linked with the oral poetry were miraculously preserved in the Russian manuscript heritage. Moreover, echoes of this heroic epopee appeared in Russian letters also later, particularly in connection with the centuries of struggle against the Tatar yoke. But on the whole the knights' tales are drowned in the tens of thousands of old Russian religious texts, and even in the few exceptions the ecclesiastic mold obtrudes more and more dominantly.

In general, the laymen from the tsars' court and from *boyars* down to the lowest ranks, continued to seek amusement and satisfaction of their esthetic cravings, above all, in the oral tradition and in oral creations. Therefore it would be erroneous to interpret this tradition and creativeness as a specific property of the lower classes. The oral literature of Russia, in the era before Peter, was at the service of all the tiers of the social pyramid, and this multiform, interclass, national character of Old Russian folklore left its indelible stamp. In the Old Russian milieu the difference between the written and the oral literature was a matter of function and not at all of social allocation.

The manifold functions of secular fiction were performed by the folklore, and its language was close to the usual colloquial Russian. The written literature served for ecclesiastical tasks and employed Church Slavonic, a somewhat renovated and Russified version of the language in which, at the dawn of Slavic Christianity, the church books were written in Great Moravia and Bulgaria.

Unprecedented social upheavals, together with shifts and revaluations of traditional values—these are characteristic marks of the seventeenth century in Russia. The boundaries between the ecclesiastical and the secular, between letters and folklore, between the written and the spoken language, begin to be effaced: the traditional disunion is replaced by a fertile interpenetration. A laicization of the written literature begins; for the first time in the history of Muscovy written attempts at secular fiction are made. And as the only native tradition upon which these attempts could lean was the oral legacy, there appears in Russian literature of the seventeenth century a vigorous folklore influence. In its turn, the book—especially the translated book—has a much stronger effect than before on oral poetry. When Russian literature ceased to lock itself in against secular elements, translations of foreign fiction naturally became frequent. And then, in line with old habits, the oral tale, susceptible to profane elements, easily took this new material to its own. Russian literature of the seventeenth century is particularly rich in works born on the boundary between written and oral tradition; and the capricious fusion of both these elements created such peculiar, inimitable masterpieces as the tales of Woe-Misfortune (*Gore-Zlochastie*), of Savva Grudcïn, of a Lad and Lass, etc. But just such hybrid formations show with particular clarity how tenacious in the Russian consciousness was the distinction of two heterogeneous realms of literature, the written and the oral. Folklore, when fixed on paper, was radically transfigured; therefore genuine Russian folk tales and songs of the seventeenth century could not reach us except through the whim of foreign travelers such as Collins and James.

From the seventeenth century on, the development of the Russian secular book has not ceased, and the influence of the folklore forms on the literary word has continued. But the Russian eighteenth century put forward new slogans: it tended to create an aristocratic literature and to isolate and canonize the language of the select. However, the narrowing of the social base of oral production, and the transition of the folklore from the ownership of the whole people to that of the common folk, was not effected at once. Over a long period, folklore did not vanish from the household of the gentlefolk but continued to occupy its nook there, while lofty poetry on classic model held forth in the drawing room. Even so, one of the most prominent among the initiators of the new literature, Vasiliy Trediakovskiy, more than once acknowledged that even here, under the occidental, aristocratic make-up, many native folklore traits were concealed.

As early as in Russian sources of the twelfth century one may read that a rich man, suffering from sleeplessness, ordered his attendants to tickle the soles of his feet, to strum on the *gusli,* and to tell him fairy tales. Ivan the Terrible, who became one of the popular heroes of the Russian folk tale, was its most avid fancier, and three old blind men followed each other at his bedside, relating fairy tales before he slumbered. Skillful tellers of tales continued to enliven the leisure of tsar and tsarina, of princes and gentry, as late as the eighteenth century. Even at the close of that century we find in Russian newspapers advertisements of blind men applying for work in the homes of the gentry as tellers of tales. Lev Tolstoy, as a child, fell asleep to the tales of an old man who had once been bought by the count's grandfather, because of his knowledge and masterly rendition of fairy tales.

Cheap colored prints, intended for the common people, at times introduced the texts of folk tales. But in publications of a higher level the folk tale, for a long time, was inadmissible; and when, toward the end of the eighteenth century, an amateur of folklore, Chulkov, tried to regale his readers with three genuine folk tales, the critics protested "because the simplest peasant could, without any trouble, invent some ten such tales and were they all put into print, it would be a waste of paper, quills, ink, printers' type, not to mention the labor of the gentleman of letters."

Later, in the same vein, contemporary critics reacted to Pushkin's attempts at imitating the folk tale and resented the illegal intrusion of the *muzhik* into the society of nobles. If an imitation was to be sanctioned, all bluntness and vulgarity offensive to refined habits and tastes must be erased. And when the author, stylizing a folk tale, was ready and able to discolor and "prettify" it sufficiently, the critics declared with satisfaction: "Obvious it is that this tale comes not from the *muzhik's* hut but from the castle." (Pletnev, concerning the tale of Ivan-Tsarevich adapted by Zhukovskiy.)

But it was Pushkin who perceived to the full the artistic value of the folk tale. "How fascinating are these stories!" he said. "Each one is a poem." Moreover, the poet, who felt more acutely than his contemporaries the needs and aspirations of native literature, understood that the modern Russian novel was only in bud and that the oral tradition still remained for the Russian prose writer an instructive and unequaled model. "Nowhere has it been possible to endow our language with this Russian breadth as in the folk tale. But what must be done to learn to speak Russian also outside the tale!"

Pushkin could not confine himself to the remarkable achievements with which he crowned the century-old triumphal way of Russian poetry, and during the last period of his brief span (1799-1837) he tried to enrich modern Russian fiction by creating for it a foundation of indigenous prose. Precisely from this quest emerges his handling of folk tales. He knew the folk tales thoroughly and recorded them, but, strange as it may seem, his own creations in this field are based, for the most part, rather on French translations of the Arabian Nights, the Grimm brothers, or Washington Irving, than on Russian folklore. Likewise, it is curious that all of Pushkin's fairy tales are composed not in prose but in verse, and mostly in a meter foreign to the Russian tale. And, most surprising of all, he succeeded in mastering the spirit and tone of the Russian folk tale. For instance, in his famous *Tale of the Golden Cockerel* Pushkin simply retells Irving's *Legend of the Arabian Astrologer*, and he does it in trochaic tetrameters, alien to Russian folk tales; nevertheless, both Russian and American readers, willy-nilly, associate this pastiche with Russian folklore.

In the structure of the folk tales Pushkin sought the answer to the question that tormented him: What is the essence of Russian prose? From this came his attempts to invest genuine

Russian tale motifs in free narrative verse, which is used by skillful jesters and which lies on the border between prose and poetry proper.

Pushkin's experiments with Russian folk tales, and Gogol's with the Ukrainian, exemplify the formative period of modern Russian prose. Likewise, it is not by chance that the later intensive recording and impassioned study of the true folk tales, and the appearance of such vast and magnificent collections of them as the books of Afanas'ev (1855-1864),[2] Khudyakov, and others,[3] coincide with the epoch of the flowering of Russian literary prose. Great is the role of the Russian folk tale in the creative development of the classic masters of Russian prose—Tolstoy, Dostoevskiy, Leskov, Ostrovskiy. And the oral style, continuous in the Russian literature and so exemplifying it, finds its fountainhead in the folklore tradition.

Rarely are workers in the field of ethnography called upon to play such a many-sided and protracted role in the history of a national culture as was Aleksandr Nikolaevich Afanas'ev (1826-1871). Without his tales a Russian child's bookshelf is incomplete. Generations of authors have drawn and still draw upon Afanas'ev's stock. Without it and without his three-volume work on the symbolics of the tales and folk mythology,[4] there would never have been the "Snow Maiden" of Ostrovskiy and Rimskiy Korsakov; there would have been less richness of protean imagery in the poetry of Esenin, who, after long searchings in the hungry years of the civil war, procured a copy of Afanas'ev's study at the price of more than three bushels of wheat—and was jubilant over his luck.

In the quantity and diversity of its material, Afanas'ev's store of fairy tales remains unparalleled in Russian folkloristics. Collectors and investigators of folk poetry and customs have learned and still learn from it. Around this collection there began heated and fertile discussions about the methods of recording, study and classification of popular narratives.

It is characteristic that Afanas'ev came to folklore as an outsider: by education he was a lawyer. Among the more than six hundred tales that he published, only some ten were recorded personally by him. For his publication he used mostly the rich

637

stock of Vladimir Dahl, the famous collector of lexical and folkloristic materials, and the remarkable collection of folk tales assembled by the Russian Geographical Society. Unfortunately, in only two-thirds of the tales of Afanas'ev is the place of the recording noted. He paid scant attention to questions of where and from whom this and that tale were heard. Here and there the editor did not refrain from some stylistic retouching of the texts, but he did not go so far in this respect as his principal model, the Grimm brothers.

It is true that the hypothetically reconstructed archetype of a tale interested Afanas'ev perhaps more than its actual, individual variants, but he did not follow the fanatic principle that the eminent historian of literature, A. Pïpin, ascribed to him, namely, that everything expressing the arbitrary manner of the individual should be weeded out from the presentation of the tale as "twaddle that is only personal." [5] However, in sundry cases, Afanas'ev artificially constructed a single text for a tale from several variants. Further, such an approach was naturally rejected, and as early as the sixties Khudyakov put forth the thesis that "the text of folk tales must stand inviolable." At the same time P. Rïbnikov, who initiated the scientific recording of Russian epic folk songs (*bilinï*), called for the study of "all that characterizes and exemplifies the narrator—of what stamps not only the folk but also the individual." And even in the review of the first issues of Afanas'ev's tales the leading critic, N. Dobrolyubov, charged the collectors of folk poetry in the future not to confine their task to a simple textual recording of a tale or song, but to render the full social and psychological circumstances in which the song or tale has been heard—above all to note the attitude of the teller to the tale and the reaction of the audience. [6]

These principles found a still more consistent application in the works of Russian collectors and students on tales and *bilinï*. The focusing of attention on tellers and listeners became the concern of Russian folkloristics. [7] From a mere laboratory preparation the recorded text tended to become a living organism. The present day stenograph or phonogram of a folk tale with its detailed recording of background and with its careful biography of the teller, or the next forthcoming stage, the reproduction by sound film—all these are clearly brilliant technical achievements in comparison with the texts of Afanas'ev. But perhaps just the unsophisticated eclecticism of the editor of *Russian Folk Tales*, who culled his bits from all quarters, enabled him to accomplish the enormous and imperative task of displaying the repertory of tales of the Russian people in all its manifold wealth.

It is true that the further development of the Russian research on tales brought many essential correctives to the approach of Afanas'ev and was, in a certain way, an antithesis to this approach and to the romantic theories of language and lore that inspired him. But may one oppose this antithesis to the foregoing thesis, as if the former were a sober scientific conception and the latter, an antiquated fallacy? No, a creative synthesis of both is necessary.

Afanas'ev and his teachers had overestimated the genetic originality of the folklore works, and they overlooked the permanent interpenetrations between the written and the oral literature. But the later opponents of this romantic viewpoint, conversely, overestimated the significance of such genetic links and missed the functional differences between the folklore and the letters; they did not take into account the autonomous structure of both these domains. Absorbed by the problem of the individual features in the repertory of a teller, some outstanding Russian folklorists of the recent past (as for instance Boris and Yuriy Sokolov) have gone so far as to identify a tale variant with an individual literary work.[8] Meanwhile, the birth and life of a folklore work follows quite different laws than the birth and life of a literary work.[9]

A medieval author invents and writes down a tale: a literary work is born, without regard to how it will be received. Maybe it will be condemned by the community, and only one or more centuries later will descendants come across the manuscript, accept and imitate it. Or perhaps the community approves certain elements of the tale and rejects the rest. If the same author, however, invents a tale and begins to narrate it to the community, a work of oral poetry is conceived; but its entry into the folklore habit entirely depends on whether or not the community accepts it. Only a work that gains the consensus of the collective body, and of this work only that part which the collective censorship passes, becomes an actuality of folklore. A writer can create in opposition to his milieu, but in folklore such an intention is inconceivable.

And if Afanas'ev adopted from the Romanticists the thesis that the folk tale is a product of collective creation, we must now, in spite of obdurate attacks against this "superstitious revival," recognize that folklore as well as language really presupposes a collective creation. But this collective creation is not to be naively imagined as a kind of choral performance. Scientists of the Romantic school made a mistake, not in assuming that collective creation occurs, but in asserting that it gradually withers away and that the history of language and folklore is, therefore, a process of steady decadence and disintegration. In particular, the contemporary folk tale, no less than its antique archetype, represents a typically interpersonal social value.

According to the experience of modern linguistics, language patterns exhibit a consistent regularity. The languages of the whole world manifest a paucity and relative simplicity of structural types; and at the base of all these types lie universal laws. This schematic and recurrent character of linguistic patterns finds its explanation first of all in the fact that language is a typical collective property. Similar phenomena of schematism and recurrence in the structure of folk tales throughout the world have long astonished and challenged investigators.

In folklore as well as in language, only a part of the similarities can be explained on the basis of common patrimony or of diffusion (migratory plots). And, since the fortuity of the other coincidences is impossible, there arises imperatively the question of structural laws that will explain all these striking coincidences, in particular, the repetitive tale plots of independent origins.

The remarkable studies of the Soviet folklorists, V. Propp and A. Nikiforov, on the morphology of the Russian folk tale, have essentially approached the solution.[10] Both these scholars base their classification and analysis of the tale plots on the functions of the *dramatis personae*. Under the concept of function, they mean the deed defined from the viewpoint of its signification for the plot.

The investigation of fairy tales through the Afanas'ev collection brought Propp to some suggestive conclusions. What are the constant and stable elements of the tale? The functions of the *dramatis personae*. By whom and how they are performed is irrelevant. These functions build the pivotal components of the tale. The number of functions occurring in fairy tales is very limited. The mutual connections and temporal sequence of these functions are regulated and restricted by certain laws. And, finally, there is his most surprising conclusion: "All fairy tales are uniform in their structure."

The explanation that we have tried to develop in relation to corresponding linguistic phenomena suggests itself similarly for the tale patterns. The folk tale is a typically collective ownership. The socialized sections of the mental culture, as for instance language or folk tale, are subject to much stricter and more uniform laws than fields in which individual creation prevails.

Of course, in the composition of the folk tale there are, besides constants, also variables that the teller is free to alter; but these variations must not be overestimated. Afanas'ev avoided the danger of missing the tale itself behind its variants. "The reflection of the personality of the teller in the tales" is indisputably an interesting problem, but, because in the folklore hierarchy the tale comes before the teller, it is necessary here to be twice careful.

Naturally, the profession, personal interests, and inclinations of a teller find expression in the distribution of points of emphasis, in the choice of nomenclature and attributes of the *dramatis personae*—when, for instance, a teller who is a postman by trade expertly creates a twelve-headed dragon to send the king a threatening letter, first, by mail and then, by wire. But attempts at biographical interpretation, when applied to the poetics of the tales, are unconvincing. It happens that a sensitive man likes to relate a sentimental tale; but the reverse is also possible, namely, a striking anti-biographism. In the district of Vereya, in the Moscow government, I met a teller renowned throughout the region, by profession a scavenger and by nature a gutter-mouthed ruffian: his tales were by contrast always full of virginal sentimentality and high-flown expressions.

The brothers Sokolov note that among the tellers there are dreamy fantasts possessed by fairy tales, humorists addicted to tales of anecdotic tinge, and several other psychological types; and the mentality of a given teller manifests itself both in the selection of his repertory and in his manner of telling. Meanwhile, the question must be inverted. In the tale tradition there are different clear-cut genres—fairy tales, anecdotes, etc.— and a favorite manner of execution traditionally corresponds to each of these types. Among this stock and baggage the teller obviously selects those parts which most nearly correspond to his individual likes or professional interests. But we may not put aside the fact that he takes upon himself one of the roles that pre-exist in the folklore stock of roles, whereas in written literature a creative personality can shape a completely new role.

For Afanas'ev the teller did not screen the tale, and this is quite natural: the basic problem had to be and was posed before the accessory problems. The same order of tasks confronts the reader who aims to acquaint himself with the world of Russian tales. Through Afanas'ev's collection he will meet the Russian tale in its most varied and striking examples. It is from his collection that the Russian tales translated for the present anthology are derived.[11]

2. THEIR CHARACTERISTIC FEATURES

ORAL poetry, we repeat, was, during a long range of centuries, the only art of the word that satisfied the worldly demands in Old Russia. Within this age it had time to imbed its roots deeply in the Russian life. Is not this the main secret of the notable vitality of the Russian folklore and particularly of the folk tale?

Among the folklorists there reigned for a long time a romantic belief that the oral poetic tradition is richest in the remotest depths of the Russian land. This far abode focused the attention of the searchers, with the result that the Archangel taiga was better known to the ethnographer than the lore at hand in the villages close to Moscow. On the eve of the revolution, such villages were explored by a group of young researchers, and it became evident that one or two hours by rail from the city, in the immediate neighborhood of factories and mills, was ground still abounding in folklore, especially in tales.

Up to the time of the revolution the tale continued to live a robust life among the peasants, rich and poor, cowherds, hunters, fishermen, workers and artisans, soldiers and coachmen, peddlers, innkeepers, vagabonds, beggars and thieves, the haulers on the Volga, the old men, women, and children.[12] The intensive work of collecting in Soviet Russia indicates that the harvest among the Russian folk is not dwindling.[13] From a single person, the aged, illiterate, but rarely gifted peasant woman Kupriyanikha, in the Voronesh region, more than one hundred and twenty tales were recently recorded.[14] Neither in the *kolkhozes,* nor in the workers' settlements, nor in the Red Army, do the tales die out.

An expert of great authority, Yuriy Sokolov, presents a balance sheet in his textbook *Russian Folklore* (1938): "In

643

the principal printed collections of Russian tales there are more than three thousand items; there is a not lesser number of tales scattered around in various secondary publications. Almost as many, if not more, are still in unpublished manuscripts." Recordings of Ukrainian and White Russian tales in books and manuscripts hardly yield place to the Russian.

Not only the quantity but also the quality of the tales was heightened by the exclusive, privileged place that, through many centuries, oral poetry occupied among all the strata of Russian society. Students have noted striking traces of professionalism in the formal refinement of Russian tales.[15] The art of tales was cultivated and handed down from generation to generation by Russian minstrels (*skomorokhi*). Masters of the telling of tales down to the present time continue to be highly appreciated in the villages. For instance, in the Siberian associations (*artel's*) of lumberers, fishermen, and hunters there are skillful tellers especially hired to beguile the hours of work and leisure.

"The song is beautiful through its harmony, and the tale through its narrative style," a popular Russian proverb says.[16] And how beloved is this mastery, another byword testifies: "The narrative style is better than the song." [17]

The best connoisseur of the tales of the Slavic peoples and their neighbors, the famous Czech investigator J. Polívka, in his synthetic study on the Eastern Slavic folk tales, comes to the conclusion that, in the peculiarity of its ritualized form and in its wealth of narrative style, the tale of the Eastern Slavs occupies quite an exceptional place: in this regard it finds parallels among no neighbors—neither in the Western or Southern Slavic world, nor in the Germanic and Romance countries, nor in the Orient. In the Russian (Great Russian) tale these features manifest themselves, according to Polívka's observations, with a greater brightness and abundance than in the White Russian or Ukrainian tale. And on the western periphery of the Ukrainian area they disappear almost entirely.

Introductory and concluding formulas are especially cultivated in the Russian tales. The former frequently grow into complete funny preludes, designed to focus and prepare the attention of the audience. They contrast strikingly with what is to come, for "that's the flourish (*priskazka*), just for fun; the real tale (*skazka*) has not begun." The introduction of a fairy tale may carry the listener away in advance to a certain kingdom, to a certain land, "way beyond thrice nine lands." Or it may parody this well-known formula and humorously localize the fantastic action in the familiar Russian environment. "In a certain kingdom, in a certain land, namely, in the land where we are living, there lived a tsar, the Giver-of-Peace (official epithet of Alexander III), and after him, the Vendor-of-Wine (Nicholas II, who instituted the state vodka monopoly)" —so began a picaresque fairy tale as told us by a sprightly teller of the Dmitrov district, in the Moscow government, in 1916.

The conclusion, amusingly breaking into the solemn tone of the fairy tale, returns the audience to the everyday world and, in a rhymed patter, shifts attention from the tale to the teller. The epilogue of a tale recorded by the Sokolovs from one of the best tellers in the White Sea country, in the Novgorod government, goes as follows:

It's not to drink beer! It's not to brew wine!
They were wedded and whirled away to love.
Daily they lived and richer grew.
I dropped in to visit, right welcome they made me—
Wine runs on my lips, nary a drop in my mouth! [18]

In other words, the still thirsty teller awaits his refreshment. Sometimes the allusions are more transparent: "This is the end of my tale, and now I would not mind having a glass of vodka."

The traditional breaking off, in the epilogue, from the utopian happy ending of the fairy tale, may utilize also contemporary political topics. The best of the present day specialists in Russian folk tales, M. Azadovskiy, quotes the following concluding formula: "Daily they lived and richer grew, until the Soviets came into power." [19]

"The formal perfection of the Eastern Slavic (Russian, White Russian, and Ukrainian) tales is not limited to preludes and epilogues, but almost each action and each situation is conveyed by manifold, typical formulas and idioms," says Polívka. For these purposes the Russian tale efficiently draws upon other kinds of folklore, especially upon proverbs, riddles, and incantations.[20]

Sometimes the tales include ditties but it is noteworthy that the heroic epic songs (*bïlinï*) although belonging to a poetic category which is closest to the fairy tale, differ sharply from them in poetics. Where the tradition of the Russian heroic epos is still alive, this difference in types of folklore is clearly felt, and a true rhapsod of *bïlinï*, if he also tells tales, has recourse to quite other subjects and artistic devices; but where the heroic tradition ceases, many of the usual formulas and sometimes even entire plots are taken over from the epic song by the fairy tale. The favorite sovereign of the Russian heroic songs, Vladimir, the great prince who christianized Russia at the end of the tenth century, moves from the *bïlinï* to the fairy tale. In his retinue we find the leading Russian valiant knight (*bogatïr'*, from the Persian *bagadur* "athlete" borrowed through the Tatar medium), Ilya Muromec, a peasant's son, and the other popular hero, Alesha, son of a pope, whose historic prototype, Aleksandr Popovich, was mentioned in the Russian Chronicle under the year 1223 as being among the knights killed by the Tatars. The epic tradition ascribes to Alesha the victory over the dragon Tugarin, a poetic reflection of the Polovcian chief Tugor-Kan. And the fairy tale recounts this story.

If the Russian fairy tales are striking by reason of their fanciful ornamentation and ceremonious style, other narrative types—the animal tales, novelettes, anecdotes—are based preponderantly on dialogue. The precipitous dialogue of the novelettes and anecdotes is sharply opposed to the devices of retardation used in the fairy tale. In the condensed and rich dialogue, Löwis of Menar is inclined to see one of the most characteristic features of Russian narrative folklore.[21] The artistic significance of the dialogue is clearly seen by the tellers themselves. An eighty-year-old Siberian teller assured Azadovskiy that the talk in the tale is the most important and the most difficult: "If any single word is wrong here, nothing will work out right. Everything has to be done quickly here." The dialogue in the execution of the teller easily changes to scenic play. There the tale, in its techniques, borders closely on the folk drama.

Such varieties of the tale as the novelette and the anecdote show a tendency to become a part of an actual dialogue. An excellent and well-tried teller of the Vereya district, a genuine master of anecdote, was unable to commence a tale without stimulation. "But when," he said to me, "I come into an inn and people are bandying, and someone calls, 'There is a God!' and I, to him, 'You lie, son of a cur,'—then I tell him a tale to prove it, until the *muzhiks* say: 'You're right. There is no God.' But again I have to fire back: 'You brag!' And I tell them a tale about God. . . . I can tell tales only to get back at folks."

The tales of anecdotal tinge manifest a disposition to verse form, which in the fairy tales occurs only in the preludes and epilogues. This form, a spoken free verse, based on a colloquial pitch and garnished with comical, conspicuous rhymes, is related to the free meters of buffoonery and wedding orations. Expert tellers possess such an abundant hoard of rhymes and syntactical clichés that they are often able to improvise such spoken verses on any given subject, much as experienced mourners are able to improvise long dirges in recitative verse.

To what extent is the repertory of the Russian tale plots original? To this a Leningrad scholar, Andreev, tried to find the answer. He followed the system of tale cataloguing used by Antti Aarne, and completed Aarne's European tale index with an inventory of Russian plots.[22] Statistical analysis of all these data [23] indicated that the plots common to the Russian and Western European tale represent only about one-third of the united index; about one-third are specifically Russian, and do not occur in Western Europe; again, approximately one-third are present in the Western repertory and fail to appear in the Russian tales.

For all the popularity of the fairy tales in Russia, the number of their plots is relatively small. It embraces not more than one-fifth of the whole inventory of the Russian tale plots, and the set of Russian plots unknown to the Western fairy tale is very limited. The originality of the Russian fairy tale lies not in its plot, but, as has been mentioned before, in its stylistic adornments. The plots of Russian animal tales are even more scant. These include only one-tenth of the total of Russian tale plots. Most of the Western European animal tales are unknown in Russia, and the investigators link this fact to the absence of a developed animal epos in the Russian Middle Ages. The Russian animal tales are usually brief and dramatic; they are told to children and often also by children.[24]

The greatest part of the Russian inventory of tale plots (more than 60 per cent) comprises novelettes and anecdotes, and the great majority of these are unfamiliar to the Western European world. The milieu pictured in these tales is socially lower than that of the fairy tale. In the latter, a man of the people is contrasted against the court background of high titles and exalted rank; in the novelettes and anecdotes, on the contrary, the background is popular and even the speech and behavior of the crowned persons adapts itself to this environment. Azadovskiy quotes a characteristic example: "Do you know, sweetheart, what has come into my head?" the wife of the tsar said to her husband. "Why do we have to spend money in a foreign hotel? 'Twere better to open our own."

It would be an extremely tempting task to examine the plots that are current in the Russian folk tale but unknown to the Western European, and vice versa. Are there common, unifying traits in each of these two groups? In what measure would the selection of plots and motifs, and particularly the choice of favorite motifs and plots, characterize the ideology of a certain ethnic milieu?

The tale of Ivan the Terrible quoted above was set down by Collins because he was collecting historical material about the famous tsar. But can this tale be used as an historical source? The same plot is known, as Veselovskiy showed, in application to the Emperor Hadrian, Tamerlane, the Duke Othon, and Wallenstein. It occurs both in the Talmud and in the Turkish folk book *Adventures of Nasr-Eddin,* as well as in an Italian medieval collection of short novels.[25] The role of the gentleman who unsuccessfully tried to imitate the good, honest bast-

648

shoemaker is formally similar to the function of numerous fools and enviers in international folk anecdotes. Nevertheless, the application of this migratory plot to Ivan the Terrible is not accidental. It shows well how the Russian popular memory evaluated this tsar and his attitudes to the common people and to the gentlefolk. And the *lapti*, too, are characteristic of the Russian tale. They are here a symbol of poverty, and their confrontation with the person of the tsar is traditional. Compare the rhymed anecdote about Peter the Great, which I recorded several times in the Moscow government:

> Peter the First braided *lapti*
> and put a curse on them;
> "To braid *lapti*," he said,
> "is to eat once a day,
> but to mend worn *lapti*,
> is never to eat at all."
> And he cast away the awl.[26]

"The tale is an invention; the song, a truth," declares a Russian proverb.[27] Even the demonology differs sharply from the Russian folk beliefs, which have known neither Koshchey the Deathless, nor Baba Yaga, the Sea King, the Firebird, nor other fantastic figures appearing in the native fairy tale. This pantheon still presents many enigmas. Oversimplified romantic interpretation of supernatural beings in the folk tale as relics of prehistoric myths about the forces of nature was rejected by the later critics, but the question of the genesis of the Russian magic world and its original peculiar traits still awaits further delving and resolution. Among these demonic names there are both common Slavic remainders and old Turkish borrowings. Thus, for instance, Baba Yaga together with the Polish *jendza baba* and such a Czech equivalent as *jezinka*, as well as the old Church Slavonic *jendza* and an old Serbian *jeza* "illness, nightmare"—originate in the primitive Slavic form *enga*, related, for instance, to the Old English *inca* "grudge, quarrel." On the other hand the name of the chained and imprisoned demon *Koshchey* signified in Old Russian, as well as its Turkish prototype *koshchi*, simply prisoner. The intercourse and struggle of ancient Russia with the nomadic Turkish world bequeathed, in general, many names and attributes to the Russian tales.

A fairy tale performs the role of a social utopia. According to the definition of Boris Sokolov, it is a type of dream compensation. It is a dream about the conquest of nature—about a magic world where "at the pike's command, at my own request," all the pails will themselves go up the hill, the axes themselves will chop, the unharnessed sleighs will glide to the forest, and the firewood will poke itself into the stove. It is a dream about the triumph of the wretched, about the metamorphosis of a hind into a tsar. The actual technical and social reconstruction, therefore, easily gives new attributes to the tale. In the newest tale records we find an aeroplane with levers "to direct it to right and to left," instead of the wooden eagle on which the hero traveled before. And the biography of the tsar dethroned by the hero has recently been enriched with a new curious detail. The exiled monarch laments: "I was once a tsar; now I am become the lowest speculator." He is asked to present his papers, "but the tsar didn't have any sort of documents to show." [28]

It is not by chance that precisely in the epoch of the effacement of borders between utopia and reality, the question on the ideology of the folk tale began to come sharply into consciousness. The epoch of revolutionary storms incited one of the most peculiar of the Russian poets, Velimir Khlebnikov, to revise the customary images of the folk tale. The Russian fairy tale knows the magic carpet called Self-Flyer (*samolet*), and a magic tablecloth that provisions the hero and is named Self-Victualler (*samobranka*). The name Self-Flyer was borrowed by modern Russian for the aeroplane. "Self-Flyer," writes Khlebnikov in a poem, "walks through the sky. But where is Tablecloth, Self-Victualler, wife of Self-Flyer? Is she by accident delayed, or packed into prison? I believe the fairy tales beforehand: they were fairy tales, they will become truth." During the same civil war, Lenin was engrossed by the Russian folk tales and noted that, if one were to revise them from a social-political viewpoint, "he could write in this material beautiful investigations on the hopes and longings of our

650

people." At the same time, in the opposite camp, the philosopher and publicist, Evgeniy Trubetzkoy, meditating on Afanas'ev's tales, tried to define precisely these longings in a study of the "other realm" and its seekers in the Russian folk tale.[29] In a particular emphatic stress on such quests the author discerned a striking feature of the Russian fairy tale. The offended-by-fate wend their way to another realm to look for a "better place" and "easy bread." In pursuit of this aim the good fellow has to overcome a "cunning science," or, maybe, simply to "follow his eyes." And the hero declares: "I will go I know not where; I shall bring back I know not what." He believes: "It's traveling three years by a crooked way, or three hours by the straight—only there is no thoroughfare." But the dreamlike fantasy condenses the journey: "Whether his way was long or short, he got in." The tale paints this other way in extremely earthy tones. The door of Paradise opens—"And what a tidy room it is! It's large and clean. The bed is wide and the pillows are of down."

There is in the Russian tradition a particularly characteristic tale about a peasant who contrives to climb to heaven and finds there: "In the middle of a mansion, an oven; in the oven, a goose roasting, a suckling pig, and pies, pies, pies . . . ! In a word: There is all that the soul desires." It is true the peasant's expedition ends in a tumble into a bog—a pitiful return to miserable reality, as Trubetzkoy points out mockingly. But the rhymed epilogue of this tale catches far better the function of the fairy dream:

> Not that is the miracle of miracles,
> That the *muzhik* fell from heaven;
> But this is the miracle of miracles—
> How the *muzhik* did climb into heaven! [30]

ROMAN JAKOBSON

NOTES

1. *Lapti:* Russian peasant shoes woven of bast.

2. The best edition (by Azadovskiy, Andreev, and Yuriy Sokolov) is *Narodnïe russkie skazki,* I-III, Moscow-Leningrad, 1936-1940. Besides his main collection, Afanas'ev published *Russkie narodnïe legendï,* Moscow, 1860, and in the sixties, in Geneva, *Russkie zavetnïe skazki.*

3. I. Khudyakov, *Velikorusskie skazki,* I-III, St. Petersburg, 1860-1862; A. Erlenveyn, *Narodnïe skazki, sobrannïe sel'skimi uchitelyami,* Moscow, 1863; E. Chudinskiy, *Russkie narodnïe skazki, pribautki i pobasenki,* Moscow, 1864.

4. A. Afanas'ev, *Poeticheskie vozzreniya slavyan na prirodu,* I-III, Moscow, 1865-1869.

5. A. Pïpin, *Russkie narodnïe skazki,* Otechestvennïe zapiski, 1856.

6. Sovremennik, LXXI, 1858.

7. B. Sokolov, *Skaziteli,* Moscow, 1924; M. Azadovskiy, *Eine sibirische Märchenerzählerin,* Folklore Fellows Communications, No. 68, Helsinki, 1926; E. Gofman, *K voprosu ob individual'nom stile skazochnika,* "Khudozhestvennïy fol'klor," IV-V, 1929.

8. B. Sokolov, *Russkiy fol'klor,* I-II, Moscow, 1929-1930; Y. Sokolov, *Fol'kloristika i literaturovedenie,* Pamyati P. N. Sakulina, Moscow, 1931, and *Russkiy fol'klor,* Moscow, 1938 (a detailed survey of the research in Russian folklore).

9. P. Bogatyrev and R. Jakobson, *Die Folklore als besondere Form des Schaffens,* Donum natalicum Schrijnen, Utrecht, 1929.

10. A. N. Nikiforov, *K voprosu o morfologicheskom izuchenii narodňoy skazki*, Sbornik Otd. rus. yaz. i slov. Akademii nauk CI, 1928; V. Propp, *Morfologiya skazki*, Leningrad, 1928, and *Transformacii volshebnïkh skazok*, Poetika, IV, 1928.

11. An excellent anthology of Russian tales from different collections is that of M. Azadovskiy, *Russkaya skazka*, I-II, Leningrad, 1931-1932.

12. The most important collections of folk tales recorded in prerevolutionary Russia are: D. Sadovnikov, *Skazki i predaniya Samarskogo kraya*, St. Petersburg, 1884; V. Dobrovol'skiy, *Smolenskiy etnograficheskiy sbornik*, 2 vols., 1891-1903; N. Onchukov, *Severnïe skazki*, St. Petersburg, 1909; D. Zelenin, *Velikorusskie skazki Permskoy gubernii*, St. Petersburg, 1914, *Velikorusskie skazki Vyatskoy gubernii*, St. Petersburg, 1915; B. and Y. Sokolov, *Skazki i pesni Belozerskogo kraya*, Moscow, 1915; A. Smirnov, *Sbornik velikorusskikh skazok arkhiva Russkogo geograficheskogo obshchestva*, I-II, St. Petersburg, 1917. The most detailed history of collection and investigation of Russian tales up to the first world war is that of S. Savchenko, *Russkaya narodnaya skazka*, Kiev, 1914.

13. The most important collections of Russian tales made after the revolution are: M. Serova, *Novgorodskie skazki*, Leningrad, 1924; M. Azadovskiy, *Skazki iz raznïkh mest Sibiri*, Irkutsk, 1928, *Verkhnelenskie skazki*, Irkutsk, 1938, *Skazki Magaya*, Leningrad, 1940; O. Ozarovskaya, *Pyatirech'e*, Leningrad, 1931; I. Karnaukhova, *Skazki i predaniya Severnogo kraya*, Moscow, 1934; V. Sidel'nikov and V. Krupyanskaya, *Volzhskiy fol'klor*, Moscow, 1937; T. Akimova and P. Stepanov, *Skazki Saratovskoy oblasti*, Saratov, 1937; A. Nechaev, *Belomorskie skazki, rasskazannïe M. M. Korguevïm*, Leningrad, 1938; M. Krasnozhenova, *Skazki Krasnoyarskogo kraya*, Leningrad, 1938.

14. N. Grinkova, *Skazki Kupriyanikhi*, Khudozhestvennïy fol'klor, I, 1926; I. Plotnikov, *Skazki Kupriyanikhi*, Voronezh, 1937.

15. N. Brodskiy, *Sledï professional'nïkh skazochnikov v russkikh skazhakh*, Etnograficheskoe obozrenie, 1904; R. Volkov, *Skazka*, Odessa, 1924; J. Polívka, *Slovanské pohádky*, I, Prague, 1932.

16. *Krasna pesnya ladom, a skazka skladom.*

17. *Sklad luchshe pesni.*

18. *Ne pivo pit'—ne vino kurit',*
    Povenchali—i zhit' pomchali,
    Stali zhit' pozhivat'—i dobra nazhivat'.
    Ya zakhodil v gosti,—ugostili khorosho:
    Po gubam teklo,—a v rot ne popalo.

19. M. Azadovskiy, *Literatura i fol'klor,* Moscow, 1938.

20. E. Eleonskaya, *Nekotorïe zamechaniya o roli zagadki v skazke,*
    Etnograficheskoe obozrenie, 1907; *Nekotorïe zamechaniya po povodu*
    slozheniya skazok, ibid., 1912.

21. Löwis of Menar, *Russische Volksmärchen,* Jena, 1914; M. Gabel',
    Dialog v skazke, Kharkov, 1929.

22. A. Aarne and S. Thompson, *The Types of the Folk-Tale,* Folklore
    Fellows Communications, No. 74, 1928; N. Andreev, *Ukazatel'*
    skazochnïkh syuzhetov po sisteme Aarne, Leningrad, 1929.

23. N. Andreev, *K obzoru russkikh skazochnïkh syuzhetov,* Khudozhest-
    vennïy fol'klor, II-III, Moscow, 1927.

24. L. Kolmachevskiy, *Zhivotnïy epos na zapade i u slavyan,* Kazan,
    1882; V. Bobrov, *Russkie narodnïe skazki o zhivotnïkh,* Warsaw,
    1908; A. Nikiforov, *Narodnaya detskaya skazka dramaticheskogo*
    zhanra, Skazochnaya komissiya v 1927 g., Leningrad, 1928.

25. A. Veselovskiy, *Skazki ob Ivane Groznom,* Sobranie sochineniy XVI,
    Leningrad, 1938.

26. *Petr Pervïy lapti plel,*
    da ikh za eto i proklel.
    I skazal: "lapti plest'—
    odnova na den' est',
    a starïe kovïryat'—
    ni odnova ne velyat'!"
    I kochedïk zabrosil.

27. *Skazka—skladka, pesnya—bïl'.*

28. M. Schlauch, *Folklore in the Soviet Union*, Science and Society, VIII, 1944.

29. E. Trubetzkoy, *"Inoe carstvo" i ego iskateli v russkoy narodnoy skazke*, Russkaya mïsl', Prague, 1923.

30. *Ne to chudo iz chudes,*
    chto muzhik upal s nebes,
    a to chudo iz chudes,
    kak tuda on vlez.

INDEX

The figures indicate in each case the initial page of the story in which the indexed word appears.

THE AUTHOR

Aleksandr Nikolayevich Afanas'ev (1826–1871), a lawyer by education, was the Russian counterpart of the Grimm brothers. His collections of folklore, published from 1866 on, were instrumental in introducing Russian popular tales to world literature.

THE ILLUSTRATOR

Alexander Alexeieff, Russian by birth and education, has illustrated many English, French, and Dutch volumes, including *Doctor Zhivago*. He has also designed sets and costumes for various Russian theaters and was among the pioneers instrumental in developing a technique of motion picture animation. Mr. Alexeieff combines superb technical ability with an authentic knowledge of Russia and her traditions.